DENE COETZEE

Born in South Africa and educated at Grey High School, Muir College and Cedara Agricultural College, Dene Coetzee is totally committed to the success of the new democratic order in his country, fondly dubbed the rainbow nation of the world.

A successful nurseryman and farmer, he also finds time to travel and enjoy his other interests – serving his community through Lions Clubs International, family life, watching sport and game viewing.

Dene Coetzee lives with his wife and children in the beautiful Paarl Valley, blissfully surrounded by green vineyards and blue mountains.

WINDS OF CHANGE is his first novel and the fruit of eighteen months of research and writing. He is now busy on a sequel.

Winds of Change

Dene Coetzee

CORONET BOOKS
Hodder and Stoughton

Copyright © 1995 Dene Coetzee

The right of Dene Coetzee to be identified as the Author of
the Work has been asserted by him in accordance with the
Copyright, Designs and Patents Act 1988.

First published in Great Britain in 1995
by Hodder & Stoughton

First published in paperback in 1996
by Hodder & Stoughton
A division of Hodder Headline PLC

A Coronet paperback

10 9 8 7 6 5 4 3 2 1

A CIP catalogue record for this title is available from
the British Library.

ISBN 0 340 65395 7

Printed and bound in Great Britain by
Cox & Wyman Ltd, Reading, Berkshire

Hodder and Stoughton
A division of Hodder Headline PLC
338 Euston Road
London NW1 3BH

This book is dedicated to

Patty

my wife, confidante and friend
whose support, devotion, warmth and love
can never be adequately acknowledged.

'The wind of change is blowing through the African continent. Whether we like it or not, this growth of national consciousness is a political fact.'

Harold Macmillan, British Prime Minister
Cape Town, South Africa, 3 February 1960

'There is enough for all. The earth is a generous mother. She will provide in plentiful abundance food for all her children, if they will but cultivate her soil in justice and peace.'

Bourke Cockran
as quoted by Winston Churchill

Author's Note

The curtain has closed on apartheid in South Africa, with the first multi-racial elections and the installation of a government of national unity. For the first time in history each and every person can now share equal opportunities in the land of their birth. A truly wonderful scenario.

South Africa has seen magnificent co-operation, by all race groups and political groupings, in the negotiation process to democracy. To those who toiled so diligently one can be truly thankful, for their efforts have resulted in an outcast nation becoming a shining example to the rest of the world and allowing South Africa to take her place in the fellowship of nations.

Most of the characters in this novel are fictitious, but the places are real, so too the time spans of events. Although many of the people and episodes described in these pages are part and parcel of South Africa's actual history, it was never the author's intention to portray any character in a bad light. If in your opinion the author has done so, he apologises sincerely. This book remains a novel, and for the reader to construe it as anything different would be a grave error.

During the five-decade time span of the book, many facets in Southern Africa underwent change, from one order to the next. Metrication came in. A new monetary unit was introduced. Neighbouring countries changed their names. To avoid confusion all matters are referred to in modern-day terminology.

I owe thanks to a great number of people in South Africa for helping with the research for this book. Above all, to Ms Valleri Haddad of the South African Library, Cape Town, for her enthusiasm in securing the true facts in the shortest possible time.

Others who assisted greatly with research were: General Johan Coetzee of the Police Academy in Graaff-Reinet; Dr Pohl de Villiers of Paarl; Barry Feinberg of the Mayibuye Centre at the University of the Western Cape; Willie Hofmeyer of the African National Congress, Cape Town; Dr Brent Jennings of the Medical School, University of Cape Town; Donne Murray, the Public Relations Manager of the Koeberg Power Station; Colonel Patrollie Nel of the South African Police, Paarl; Liso Mgqunqwana of Umkhonto we Sizwe, Western Cape and Paul Semark the Executive Director: Corporate Affairs of ESCOM.

Thanks are also due to computer wizard Greg Fortuin, typist Stephanie Vowles, David Bolt and Tim Ross-Thompson for their editorial advice and Margaret Body, my editor at Hodder & Stoughton.

Dene Coetzee
Paarl, South Africa
March 1995

The author would like to pay homage to two great South African leaders, both men of integrity and peace, who were fittingly jointly awarded the Nobel Peace Prize for 1993.

NELSON MANDELA

Here is a man who had a dream, and for almost half a century walked an unswerving path to attain his goal. His words, uttered in the 1960s are as relevant today as they were then. During twenty-seven years in jail he stood unyielding and tall — truly the inspiration of the struggle for freedom. His election as South Africa's first fully representative State President is a fitting tribute to a great statesman.

Viva, Mandela!

FW de KLERK

Whatever your political persuasion may be, one must admire the vision and courage of FW de Klerk — the first National Party leader prepared to negotiate himself out of power for the good of the country as a whole. Without him there would certainly not have been a new South Africa.

Bakgat, de Klerk!

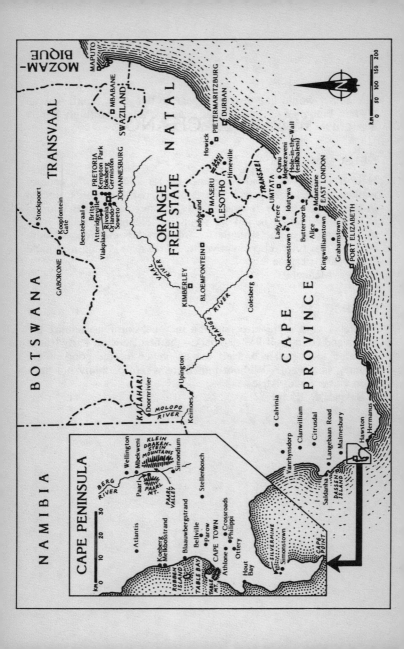

WINDS OF CHANGE

1

Fifty kilometres from the coast, in a region of majestic blue-grey mountains and deep fertile valleys, lay the town of Paarl. Dominating the rural town was the brooding presence of Paarl Mountain. Embedded in its very summit was Paarl Rock, a vast expanse of granite that glistened like a pearl in the sunlight. Between the houses were farms, with row upon neat row of grape-vines marching up the slopes. The vines were a riot of colour, resplendent in all the shades of autumn.

On a lower slope, overlooking the southern reaches of the town, stood an imposing white-gabled Cape-Dutch manor house on the farm of Hermitage. Way above the homestead, between the bushy grape-vines, sat the farmer and his son.

The boy held a vacuum flask with a map of the world pictured on it. His index finger travelled slowly down the African continent, moved to the left-hand corner and stopped. 'We're here!' Simon tapped the spot, smiling at his father. 'At the Cape of Good Hope.'

His father nodded, affectionately running his strong, calloused fingers through the youngster's mop of dark hair. 'Let's go, son.' He rose to his feet, a bull of a man, his skin burnt a deep mahogany from years of exposure to the harsh South African sun. 'While we sit and drink coffee the labourers work at half-pace.' Paulus Roux spoke in the guttural tones of Afrikaans.

It was March, the end of the long Cape summer. The months of unrelenting sun and the incessant battering of the prevailing south-easter, the summer wind, had parched everything. The picking season was over. The vines had produced another bounteous crop and the pressed berries were fermenting in the vats, slowly maturing into the famous Cape wines. On the farm it was weeding time.

Black and coloured labourers sweated in the oppressive late-afternoon heat, working faster as the boss approached. Stones and soil spattered as they levered the dried grass and withered weeds out of the hard soil. Using pitchforks they stacked the uprooted waste in heaps at the edge of the vineyard. Fourteen-year-old Simon, dressed in a khaki shirt and shorts, his feet comfortable in old, brown veldskoene, moved from heap to heap, setting the grass alight.

Thick pillars of grey smoke billowed into the torpid sky, forming erect columns, then smudging into a pall hundreds of metres above the ground. A gentle zephyr rustled in, disturbing the columns' languid ascent, and they wobbled and spiralled in the breeze.

Without warning a gust of wind burst over the peaks of the Klein Drakenstein Mountains opposite and raced across the valley, hurling itself up the slope of Paarl Mountain. The shafts of smoke disintegrated in twisted confusion. The burning heaps glowed a brighter orange as if charging themselves for the onslaught to come. Dragon tongues of flame leapt towards the edge of the vineyard where it merged with the *fynbos veld*, the indigenous plant life of the Cape.

Paulus sensed the danger and called to his son. 'Watch out, Simon. Come away from the fire.' Too late. The heat forced Simon backwards into the waist-high veld.

Fresh waves of wind buffeted in, quickly building up to gale force. Showers of sparks landed on the tinder-dry fynbos. Within minutes the mountain was ablaze.

Proteas, ericas, silver trees, pincushions and top bushes burnt like lighted beacons, the oils stored in their leaves popping and snapping as the flames engulfed them. The fine brush and grass blazed briefly, then smouldered to an ugly black stubble.

Stumbling and falling, trying to stay ahead of the wall of flame, Simon headed up Paarl Mountain, finding himself driven towards the sheer face of Paarl Rock, one and a half kilometres ahead. Creatures of the veld joined the boy in a hurried retreat. Yellow Cape cobras, mountain adders, spitting cobras and puff-adders slithered away. Buck, insects and rodents scurried from the heat. Birds flapped overhead. A sentinel barked a warning to his troop of chacma baboons and they scrambled away in the opposite direction. A leopard smelled the smoke and bounded between the rocks.

Panting heavily, Simon stopped to rest. He watched in horror

2

as the flames overtook a tortoise, its short, bandy legs unable to outrun them. The hexagonal discs on its rounded back blistered and lifted. In its last act of defence the animal withdrew into its shell – incinerated to death.

Simon sprinted forward, travelling only a dozen paces before freezing in his tracks. A huge Cape cobra blocked his path, its tail curled on the ground, its head raised to the height of his chest. The hood expanded in anger and its bright eyes glistened ominously. Simon stood motionless, not daring to breathe, mesmerised by the unblinking eyes. Only a pace separated them as the snake swayed from side to side. Slowly the cobra drew its head backwards and prepared to strike.

Salty beads of sweat rolled into Simon's eyes. He blinked, breaking their fixed stares, unwittingly saving his life. The snake flicked its eyes towards the advancing flames, then back to the boy's face. Simon blinked again and the cobra flopped to the ground and with quick undulating movements hurried away.

Simon shivered from delayed shock. He glanced around fearfully and saw that the fire was outflanking him on his right where the wind against the slope was strongest, pushing the flames ahead of the main blaze. He sprinted, arms and legs pumping furiously as he headed upwards.

A graceful russet-coloured steenbok on nimble legs outpaced Simon, then stopped and turned back towards the flames. There was terror in its large luminous eyes. Simon stopped, sharing the animal's dread. The brush was burning fiercely. On the edge of the inferno a baby buck struggled to escape from the thick bush. The mother stamped her foot in agitation, and in her anxiety to save her offspring ran right up to Simon, her maternal instincts overcoming her fear of man.

Flames engulfed the little buck and it fell to the ground, bleating desperately, a wild look in its eyes. The mother snorted in response and scrambled into the flames. Grasping the lamb with her teeth she shook her head from side to side, trying to work her offspring loose. A burning bough snapped off, forcing the ewe to her knees. She collapsed on top of her lamb, her movements becoming weaker. With a last defiant kick she succumbed and they lay with their legs entwined, their bodies pushed tightly against each other.

'No! No!' screamed Simon as he stumbled away, nauseated by what he had seen. 'It was my fault for setting fire to the heaps of

3

grass,' he sobbed as he ran. He stumbled, fell, picked himself up and sprinted further. His breath rasped in his chest. Fire surrounded him on three fronts, crackling closer and closer. The flames soared into the air, twisted and turned by the wind into dancing demons. Thick smoke blotted out the valley. Red-hot sparks surged into the heavens, chasing one another like angry fireflies.

Simon had no choice but to head towards the unburned veld. He darted up the steep slope between the large boulders that had broken off the massif of Paarl Rock and now lay scattered around its base. Running in a blind panic, his outstretched hands smashed into the base of the rock.

He looked desperately for an escape route. Further along, a copse of yellow-wood trees offered protection, but already a racing finger of fire cut off his path. Above him the smooth slab of granite rose upwards, huge and ominous, until it merged with the sky far above. With his back pressed against the rock he watched in helpless fascination as the fire bore down on him. A pincushion bush burnt like a Roman candle, leaving gnarled blackened branches glowing crimson at the tips. A sooty ash forced against the expanse of Paarl Rock rained down thickly. The smoke made Simon cough and he wrapped his shirt around his head, using the material as a filter. His eyes were red and watering. The fire crept closer.

I can run through the flames, he thought, but then he remembered the tortoise and the steenbok and quickly dismissed the idea. He looked up and his gaze followed the line of the massif. He had to get above the blaze, but how?

'Please God, help me!' he shouted. 'Don't let me die.'

A ball of fire hit the rock next to him. Simon darted away, moving his position a few paces. He felt a hollow behind his back. Turning, he saw a vertical fissure extending about six metres up the granite face. Better than nothing, he thought determinedly. Pushing his back against one side of the V-shaped crevice, he jammed his feet against the other. Alternately raising first his body then his feet he levered his way up, using his bent legs as springs to keep him in place.

His groping fingers found a horizontal ridge. He placed his hand over the edge and lifted himself up. Miraculously, there was a ledge. He pulled himself over the top, flopping gratefully on to the shelf, watching in awe as the flames surged higher than the ledge in a raging wall of fury. He backed away and saw the narrow

4

entrance to a cave in the rock face. He crawled inside, away from the intense heat.

'Thank you, God.' Simon put his palms together in deep gratitude. He lay down on a mat of rock-rabbit dung. His eyes closed and he drifted into an exhausted sleep.

Meanwhile Paulus searched desperately, dispatching labourers to look for Simon. Urged on by his distress, the men ran through the blackened remains of the once-dense veld. The fire burnt itself out against Paarl Rock but continued over the mountain. Smouldering bushes flared up, exploding into bonfires of sparks. Tendrils of smoke whirled in the turbulent air. Patches missed out in the first headlong rush caught alight, burning fiercely.

As sundown approached, Paulus became frantic, running up and down the mountain in a grid pattern, trying to cover every nook and cranny. His labourers reported on the many buck, tortoises, insects and snakes killed in the fire, but there was no sign of Simon. They shouted and called his name, but the strong south-easter whipped the words out of their mouths.

Paulus stopped near the base of Paarl Rock, catching his breath in large gulps. He looked up at the huge bulk of granite towering above him, not noticing the ledge blending perfectly into the rock façade. He searched the yellow-wood copse which nestled in a pocket at the foot of the rock. He walked carefully between the trees with hanging fungi, like old men's beards. He poked through the rotting leaf mould and undergrowth. 'Simon! Simon!' he shouted over and over in despair. Simon did not hear the calls as he slept snugly in the cave.

It was twilight when Paulus returned to the vineyard. One by one the labourers arrived.

'Did you find Simon?' Paulus asked each one in turn.

'No boss!' Each time it was the same answer.

Marie was standing in the forecourt when he came back with the men. They were never this late and the huge fire on the mountain had worried her all afternoon. One look at her husband's haggard face told her something was wrong. 'Where's Simon?' Her voice quivered with distress.

'He's missing. He ran ahead of the fire. We searched for two hours, but there's no sign of him.'

'Oh my God, let him be safe.' Marie staggered as a coldness gripped her.

Stepping forward Paulus caught her. 'I'll telephone the police and neighbours and ask them to help. We'll find him tonight. He must be alive; we didn't find any sign of . . .' His voice tailed off.

Supporting his wife, Paulus walked towards the manor house. He turned wearily to his labourers. 'Go and eat and come back at nine. We'll search until we find him.'

Paulus ate in silence while Marie worked in the kitchen, fighting back the tears. She filled Thermos flasks with sweet black coffee to sustain the men through the long night that might lie ahead.

At nine o'clock vehicles started arriving. Each man carried a powerful flashlight. They drove up the steep road through the vineyard to the large farm dam. Paulus paired the men into teams, allocating each a section of mountain to cover. One of his workers joined each team and they set off.

A red glow from the fire, which still blazed on the back slopes of the mountain, brightened the western sky. This light, coupled with the light from a waning moon, helped the searchers.

The south-easter still roared unabated. The men had to shout to each other. The landscape was bare and black, the burnt-out trees and bushes appearing stark and evil in the pale light. The men stumbled over rocks and through gullies and *kloofs*, but hours passed in fruitless search.

Around midnight Simon woke with a start. He crawled out of the cave, frightened and disorientated. Grotesque shadows cast by the moon danced and seemed to threaten him. Above him the vertical face of Paarl Rock appeared to rise upwards for ever. When he looked up he felt dizzy. He crept to the edge of the shelf and peered over the rim. Simon shied back in alarm as the wind roared in a fierce up-draught past the front of the ledge, threatening to suck him into the maelstrom.

Keeping away from the edge Simon examined the shelf. It was two paces wide and almost six long. On one side a stunted wild olive tree grew from a fissure; its twisted roots had forced their way through the cracks on the rock face, a wonder of survival. In the other corner a spring bubbled out of the rock filling a hollow on the ledge, overflowed into a crack and disappeared back into the earth. Simon was thirsty. He lay on his stomach and drank thirstily. The water was sweet, fresh and ice-cold.

Then in the distance Simon saw the beams of flashlights as they criss-crossed each other. Standing up he cupped his hands and shouted but the wind carried his voice upwards. The searchers came nearer and he tried again. He could hear their calls, but they could not hear his. They moved away and eventually the lights disappeared altogether. He felt totally forsaken.

He ventured to the edge again and looked hopefully down the V-shaped fissure. Shivering, he stepped back. It was too dangerous to attempt the descent at night. He crept back to the safety of the cave and slept.

Across the Paarl Valley the sun topped the Klein Drakenstein Mountains and the first rays of the new day streamed westwards. Sunbeams danced straight into the cave, their warmth waking Simon. He sat up quickly, confused. He glanced around and for the first time saw the Bushman drawing on the wall. The ancient San rock painting depicted three loincloth-clad hunters, bows in hand, chasing a wounded buck with arrows in its shoulder. The simplistic portrayal was so full of movement it unnerved Simon and he scurried out of the cave.

The south-easter had blown itself out during the night. Simon looked down from the edge. There was nobody to help him; he would have to make the descent on his own.

He lowered himself over the lip, his heart beating faster. It had been easy to ascend the previous day, forced upwards out of desperation. Now he had to will himself to go back down. For several minutes he remained jack-knifed in the crack, too scared to move. Eventually he forced himself down, jumping the last section to the ground.

'I made it,' he shouted jubilantly and started to run. He was hungry and growing weaker. The vineyards were still five hundred metres away when he stumbled, falling face down on the ashen soil.

'There he is, the little boss!' shouted Jafta. 'Don't worry, little boss. I will get you home.' Jafta slung Simon over his shoulder, carrying him towards the farm dam, the rendezvous for the search parties.

'What are you doing?' Simon's eyes were glassy.

'Don't worry, little boss. Jafta will look after you.'

Paulus was sitting disconsolately in his farm pick-up truck, drinking coffee. He knew he should drive down to the homestead to report to Marie, but he did not have the heart to return without news.

'Boss! Boss!'

He dropped his cup in horror as he saw Jafta stumbling towards him with a body slung over his back. He recognised Simon's shirt. Paulus jumped out of the vehicle, running towards Jafta. 'Is he all right?' he called from a distance.

'The little boss is okay.'

Jafta placed Simon tenderly in his father's arms. Paulus held his son tightly to his chest, afraid to let him go, and wept. 'My son! My son!' Paulus turned his face upwards and said a silent prayer of thanks.

Simon opened his eyes. 'Pa! Pa!' He embraced his father, feeling safe at last.

'Where have you been? Where did you get to?' Paulus choked with emotion. 'We've been worried out of our minds.'

'The fire drove me towards Paarl Rock. I found a cave and crept inside.'

'All that matters is that you're safe.' Paulus stood up with Simon in his strong arms. 'Let's go home and give your mother the good news.' He turned to Jafta. 'Recall the men. Tell them we have found my son.' His voice grew softer. 'Thank you, Jafta.'

The valley shimmered in the clear spring air, the sun brilliant and warm without the harsh bite of summer. The fresh green growth of the vines and fruit trees heralded another season of promise. The orchards were in full bloom, delicate blossoms of the plum trees ranging from snow white through ivory to dusky white, the peach blossoms a profusion of pinks. Mother Nature had contrived to make the Paarl Valley the most beautiful in all the world. The valley, as well as the slopes of Paarl Mountain, was a vibrant patchwork of different hues as each orchard and vineyard competed with the other to be the most exquisite.

Simon Roux was a mere speck as he sat on the ledge, his legs dangling in space. A kestrel circling far above the town was level with Simon as he wrote busily in his diary. He had visited the ledge many times since he had discovered it during the fire. He told no one his secret; it was his own private place. He brought wood and an iron grid and stored them in the cave for when he wanted to braai meat over the coals. He commandeered a large rectangular coffee tin from the pantry for his books, diary, pens, pencils and matches. Before he left each time he wrapped the tin carefully in a weatherproof tarpaulin to keep out the damp.

Below him the veld had recovered miraculously in the eighteen months since the fire. The old woody growth had burnt away. Many of the seeds needed heat to crack open their hard outer shells. During the first winter after the fire thousands of new seedlings had germinated in the moist conditions. The burnt skeletons of the bushes had sprouted anew and they were now short, compact shrubs. Although the blaze had been devastating at the time, fire was part of the cycle of the fynbos veld, a natural phenomenon to clear out the old and replace it with the new. The veld of Paarl Mountain was now a green mass of vigorous new growth.

Hearing a flurry of gunshots echoing off the rock, he looked down on Hermitage below him. A dot was moving in the vineyard above the manor house. Simon smiled to himself. That'll be Pa, after the guinea-fowl again. He packed away his diary and rewrapped the tin in the tarpaulin. After taking a last contented look around his special place he quickly climbed down the fissure and jogged towards home.

As Paulus Roux walked out of the wine cellar he heard the chatter of guinea-fowl coming from the vineyard above the house. His shotgun in the crook of his arm, his dogs trailing him, he set off up the slope. The dogs disappeared from view. Paulus followed, struggling to keep up, skirting around the short, stubby grape-vines.

Far ahead a flock of guinea-fowl scratched between the vines, pecking busily at morsels of food – seeds, insects and worms. They were elegant birds, over fifty centimetres tall, covered in black feathers suffused with white dots. Their necks and lower heads were an electric blue. A cap of vermilion brightened the tops of their heads, finished off with a bony casque, making them appear like ancient helmeted Roman soldiers.

The two farm dogs, South-African-bred *boerbulls*, started barking, a deep excited resonance. Instantly on guard, the birds sounded the alarm, the males calling 'ker-bek-ker-bek-ker-bek,

9

krrrrr', the females piping 't-phueet-t-phueet-t-phueet'. The panic-stricken flock scattered among the grape-vines with the baying dogs after them.

Needing a running start, the guinea-fowl headed down the slope flapping frantically, slowly gaining height, straightening their wing-tips, gliding gracefully on motionless wings.

Paulus snapped his beautifully balanced Webly and Scott 700 double-barrelled shotgun to his shoulder. He fired the left barrel, continuing the vital follow-through. The guinea-fowl's head exploded, a smear of red streaking the blue sky. The bird cartwheeled slowly to earth, its feathers ruffling and breaking its fall. Paulus shot another five birds. He walked through the vineyards picking them up. They dangled at his side, the blood smearing his twill trousers.

He made his way to the earthen dam wall and looked down on his farm and the Paarl Valley. Strongly built, Paulus was handsome in a rough sort of way, with a craggy, angular face, lined when he frowned. His shock of black hair, greying at the temples, was starting to recede from his forehead. His eyes were dark brown and his gaze direct. He was a man of the soil, a dyed-in-the-wool Afrikaner and a fervent supporter of Afrikaner aspirations. At forty-two, in the prime of his life, he was master of his realm, the fifth generation Roux to farm Hermitage which had been in the family for over two hundred years, dating back to 1750.

Since taking over from his father, Paulus had extended the vineyards, improved the wine cellar and restored the Cape-Dutch manor house. He had followed faithfully the Roux quest to make Hermitage a model wine farm.

He smiled as he saw Simon moving towards him, jogging down the slope, his stride confident and athletic. Paulus watched with delight, seeing something of himself in his son. Although only sixteen, Simon was tall and strong and well-muscled. He's a son any father would be proud of, he thought with satisfaction.

'Hullo, Pa,' gasped Simon, catching his breath. 'I see you shot some nice birds.'

Father and son stood side by side, at ease in each other's company. Paulus placed his arm over his son's shoulders, a gesture of love, as they faced the magnificent vista before them. Hermitage, up against the slope of Paarl Mountain, fell away to the Paarl Valley below. The Berg River meandered down its centre, the life-blood of

10

the farms on the river banks. From the dam wall the farm extended downwards through row upon row of vines and orchards to the Main Street of Paarl.

'One day Hermitage will be yours – sixty hectares of the best wine grapes and twenty hectares of the choicest peaches and plums in South Africa. You're a lucky young man. Other boys still have to decide what to do with their lives. You know your destiny. Soon we'll be running the country, not the English. Smuts and his United Party will fall. Our organisation, the Afrikaner Broederbond, is already planning our future. Our generations will live as God intended – in a white man's paradise, ruled by us.'

Simon looked at his father in awe. He spoke of the future with such determination. Simon felt strong and confident – his life mapped out for him. He would share fully in the wave of Afrikaner nationalism sweeping South Africa after the Second World War.

Father and son walked into the house together. Marie smiled at the two of them, so alike in ways and looks. The Roux blood is strong, she mused. One day Simon will be as tall as Paulus, but much more handsome. That part must be me, she chuckled to herself.

The crowd cheered as the rugby match finished. Walking off the field, Simon glanced up at the main school building and felt a real affinity with his school, Paarl Boys' High. It was one of the leading dual-medium schools in the country, teaching English- and Afrikaans-speaking pupils in both languages.

In the stand he spotted Helena Marais, surrounded by her friends from La Rochelle Girls' High. They had grown up together; she was the daughter of his father's best friend and neighbour, Jan Marais. He nodded to her and a smile lit up his angular face, his white teeth contrasting with his tanned olive-brown skin, as dark as a Spaniard's. Simon walked with an energetic spring in his step, light on his feet for such a big boy. When Helena smiled back at him he confidently flipped his dark hair off his forehead, watching her intently with his brown, almost black eyes.

'Hullo, Helena.'

She greeted him shyly while the girls around her giggled. He was extremely handsome and the pick of the matrics. A girl nudged Helena. 'If you don't ask him to the dance, I'm going to.'

Helena left her friends and walked over to Simon. She stood a good head shorter and had to look up at him when she spoke. She

11

was nervous and tossed her head like a skittish filly, making her pony-tail bob up and down. Sturdily built without being thick-set, she had the sort of open face one trusted implicitly.

Her friends egged her on. 'Come on, Helena, ask him.'

'Ask me what?'

She looked at him with her tawny-green eyes, and blushing deeply, fluttered her long eyelashes. 'It's our end-of-term dance on Saturday. Would you like to be my partner?'

Simon felt a strange excitement. He saw Helena in a new light. The girl he had known since childhood was no longer simply the girl-next-door but a desirable young woman. Her little-girl legs had pushed out into shapely calves and she now had curves where none had existed before.

He answered a little breathlessly, 'Thank you, Helena, I'd love to accompany you to the dance.' Whistling cheerfully he sauntered off.

She tossed her head in triumph, her auburn hair shining in the sunlight. She had her foot in the door with Simon, determined to make him hers, even if it meant breaking off with her boyfriend, Robert Morton. Simon was from the top drawer of Paarl Afrikaner society, whereas Robert was only the son of a municipal clerk.

Simon bit into his sandwich and smiled as his mind went back to the dance. It was school break on the following Monday. He glanced up in surprise as a foot prodded him.

Robert Morton glared down at Simon, jealousy in his eyes. 'Dutchman, who gave you permission to take my girlfriend to the dance?'

In a flash Simon was on his feet, belligerently returning Morton's stare. 'She's no longer your girlfriend. I'm taking her out now.'

'Bullshit!'

The atmosphere was tense. There was more to it than animosity between two boys. Everyone knew it was also an English versus Afrikaner matter, an argument with much deeper connotations, hatreds forged from centuries of distrust.

Morton swaggered forward, big and threatening. He shoved Simon in the chest and pinned him against the wall. 'Rock Spider, don't mess with me or I'll fuck you up.'

Simon felt the blood rush to his face. He glared at Morton, his fists clenched at his side. Morton was deliberately baiting him, hoping he would hit first.

'I'm not scared of you, *rooinek*.'

The other boys crowded around, egging them on. Someone shouted, 'Fight after school!'

Everyone knew what that meant – a bare-fisted fight until a knock-out or one gave up, under the supervision of a prefect.

'I challenge you, Roux.' Morton glared at Simon.

'Why must we fight?'

'Oh! so the *boertjie* is scared, is he?'

'I'm not scared of you, *soutpiel*!'

'Well, prove it, fight me,' said Morton arrogantly.

Simon's heart hammered loudly. Morton was the school heavyweight champion and had fought in Western Province trials. He didn't give a thought to the fact that such a fight would stir up the simmering Afrikaner-English hatred in the school.

'What's your decision, Roux?' Morton demanded.

'Okay Englishman, I'll fight you,' replied Simon slowly.

The fight became a matter of pride, with each language group backing its own fighter. Tension built up throughout the day as each side, in every class, insulted each other.

Simon was tense, unable to concentrate on his school work. The fight kept flashing into his mind as he pictured a sneering Morton exposing his lack of boxing skill. Instinctively he knew the afternoon could bring a turning point in his life. If he lost he could also lose Helena.

'Roux, concentrate on your work,' admonished the mathematics teacher. He was aware of the fight. All the teachers knew of the clash. They didn't approve but realised it was part and parcel of adolescence in a boys' school. They turned a blind eye as long as a prefect controlled the fight.

The bell rang to end the school day. Sarel and Kleinjan, Simon's seconds, joined him in the classroom. Sarel lectured him like a professional boxing coach. 'Keep close to him, inside his guard. Concentrate on body blows.'

As the junior, they delegated Kleinjan to bucket-and-sponge duty. He didn't mind, privileged to be part of the action. 'Simon, the Afrikaners are on your side, they want you to win,' he chattered excitedly.

13

'Time to go, it's twenty-five past two.'

The English-speaking boys commandeered the embankment behind the school. Hundreds of Afrikaners crammed the concrete standing area, leaving a square open in the middle. The crowd parted as Simon and his entourage jogged towards the centre. Morton stood in the ring of human bodies, stripped to the waist, huge, formidable.

'Take off your jacket and your shirt and tie,' the headboy instructed.

Simon struggled with the shirt buttons, watching Morton nervously out of the corner of his eye. He looked relaxed and confident, flexing his arms, punching at an imaginary opponent, ducking and weaving. There was an expectant hum from the crowd.

The headboy called the contestants together. The uproar ceased as everyone strained to hear the words. 'The rules are simple – no kicking, no biting, no gouging, no wrestling and no head-butting. You'll stop for a break when I say so and your seconds will clean you up when I feel it necessary. Do you both understand?'

They stood toe to toe, staring into each other's eyes, trying to detect a weakness. They matched each other in height and weight, but Simon was more muscular. Still the psychological warfare continued, neither wanting to show weakness by looking away. The crowd grew restless.

'Okay, let's get on with it. Go to your corners.' The headboy had to push them apart before either dropped his gaze.

The shouting grew louder. On the bank the English boys hurled their insults at the Afrikaners in dockyard language – *boertjies*, hairy backs, rock spiders, Dutchmen, trekkers, mealie munchers. The Afrikaans boys replied in kind - *rooinekke, soutpiele, bliksemse Engelse, pommies, fokken limeys*.

As the square closed in the headboy wisely changed their focus of attention. 'Fight,' he cried.

The two boys approached each other warily, circling, waiting for an opening. Morton held his fists high, ready to protect his head. Simon was not ring-wise; he held his clenched hands only half-way up, open to a punch.

Moving quickly for his size, Morton danced forward flicking out a straight left jab, hitting Simon on the mouth. Again they circled. Again the left rapped Simon on the mouth, the bare knuckles splitting open his lip. A red trickle dripped on to Simon's chest.

14

Morton had drawn first blood. Simon rushed forward. Morton stepped back expertly, the left jab doing the work. Simon seemed powerless against the sniping left which remained in his face.

'Get under his guard, get in close!' Sarel's voice sounded from a long way off.

Simon stepped forward, holding his fists high to keep out the left jab. Morton summed up the situation quickly. He swung a vicious right hook into his rib-cage. Simon grunted in pain.

One, two, three, four left jabs exploded in Simon's face, splitting his eyebrow. He lifted his hand to wipe the blood out of his eye, giving Morton the opening he wanted. He unleashed an overhand bolo, a vicious blow that caught Simon square on the side of his jaw and he crashed to the ground.

The Afrikaners grew quiet as they saw their champion felled. The English were jubilant. 'Morton! Morton! Morton! Morton!' they chanted.

Gradually Sarel's voice permeated Simon's spinning head. 'Stand up, man.' He struggled to his knees and tried to stand. A shadow blotted out the sun. Simon looked up and saw the bulk of Morton towering over him, a smile of victory on his lips.

The Afrikaners willed Simon to his feet. '*Op! Op! Op!*' Groggily Simon struggled to his feet, his knees wobbly.

The prefect stepped in. 'Are you okay, Roux? Do you want to continue?'

'*Ja.*'

'Box then.'

Morton rushed in for the kill. Two straight lefts started the bleeding again. He followed with a fast right cross to the side of Simon's head, then a left hook to the body. It took all of Simon's will-power not to cry out in pain. Simon clinched. Morton launched a blow from near his knees, which exploded under Simon's jaw. Again he was down. Sarel rolled him into a sitting position while Kleinjan sponged away the blood. The water formed a pink puddle around him.

The headboy looked carefully at Simon. 'Do you give up, Roux?'

'*Nee! Nee!*' Kleinjan shouted, the possibility of his hero losing not entering his head.

'Shut up, I'm not talking to you. I'm asking you, Roux, do you give up?' Mechanically Simon shook his head from side to side. 'Then get up and fight, man.'

Another flurry of blows struck Simon's face. His determination kept him on his feet. He felt the delicate bones of his nose break as a straight right crunched into his face. Blood flowed freely, flecking both contestants.

Queensberry Rules, rounds, ten-counts didn't come into play. It was the rule of the jungle, the fight ended when the loser succumbed. Simon didn't want to lose. His pride was at stake. He staggered around the ring, swinging like a drunkard at the elusive Morton who easily slipped the punches.

Left, right, left, right, upper cut, right cross. Not even will-power could prevent Simon's knees from buckling. His legs like rubber, he sank slowly to the ground.

Kleinjan cooled Simon's brow with the water. He could see his brain was groggy, his eyes fixed.

'Fight or give up.' The headboy looked at Simon carefully. 'You've had three knock-downs. If you go down again, I'll stop the fight and declare Morton the winner.'

'*Op! Op! Op!*'

Simon responded to the urgings of his supporters. He shook his head, trying to clear his brain. He looked across the ring and saw his unmarked opponent leering at him. Hate surged through Simon and he stepped forward, shouting in a hoarse voice, '*Kom Engelsman, kom.*'

Morton obliged by shooting out his stock-in-trade. This time Simon anticipated the left jab. He ducked under the punch and rushed his man. Simon's arms closed around Morton's waist, the force of the charge pushing Morton back into the pressing crowd. Spectators crashed in all directions. Morton's leg struck someone and he cartwheeled over backwards with Simon holding on for dear life. The two boys crashed to the ground in a tangle of bodies.

As Morton hit the concrete the full weight of Simon's shoulder slammed into his solar plexus, driving the air out of his lungs. Struggling for breath, Morton tried to sit up. Simon hit him full in the face. It had the effect of a double blow: Morton's head snapped backwards and hit the concrete. Simon hit him twice more in the face before the headboy pulled him off. 'You can't fight on the ground. I said no wrestling. Control yourself, man.'

The crowd were shouting their excitement. The fight was living up to expectations. The boxers had seen skill, the bloodthirsty gore, and the rest had witnessed courage.

'Move back!' shouted the headboy as he tried to re-form a semblance of a ring. 'Move back!' Reluctantly the crowd shuffled backwards; this was one fight they didn't want stopped. Morton recovered his breath. The prefect waved his hands. 'Fight on.'

Morton was not as confident as before. This time he waited for Simon to come to him. Simon moved forward. Morton shot out his left jab. Simon anticipated it, moved quickly to his left and the blow missed. Morton didn't have time to get in a second blow with his right hand as Simon moved inside his guard and hit him hard with an underhand right. Starting behind Simon's back, the punch whizzed forward. At the same time Simon transferred his balance to his right leg and dropped his shoulder. The blow landed with full power in the pit of Morton's stomach. Morton sank to his knees, his breath knocked out for the second time. Simon rushed in for the kill, but the headboy sprang forward, holding his arms at his side.

'You can't hit a man when he's down,' he shouted and Simon backed away reluctantly.

Morton was in difficulty. He was vomiting on the concrete and trying to catch his breath at the same time. 'Clean up the mess,' the prefect indicated to his second. They wiped him down and he stumbled to his feet looking white and far from confident.

Sarel towelled Simon down. Kleinjan had stemmed the facial bleeding. He was in better shape.

'Fight.' The headboy pushed Morton forward.

A cagey look had replaced the superior smile on Morton's face. He circled warily.

For the first time Simon felt confident. He shouted for the whole crowd to hear, '*Engelsman, nou gaan jy kak.*'

A trace of fear glimmered in Morton's eyes as he failed to hold Simon's belligerent stare. The crowd stamped their feet, clapped and screamed, enthralled by the savage contest.

Morton eyed Simon cautiously. Simon went in, bent almost double, standing up inside Morton's guard without being hit. Morton, expecting another blow to the solar plexus, instinctively covered his stomach with his left hand leaving his left side open. Simon aimed a roundhouse hay-maker at the left ear. Morton saw the blow coming and lifted his left shoulder. The blow hit the top of his arm, knocking him sideways. Using his arms to counterbalance he exposed his head again. Simon repeated the roundhouse right.

This time the blow was on target. Lights exploded in Morton's brain and he retreated desperately. Simon went on an all-out assault, hitting measured lefts and rights to Morton's head until he went down. Simon hit another blow while Morton was on his knees, rocking his head backwards.

'Cut that out, Roux,' barked the headboy. He pushed Simon towards his seconds and bent over Morton. 'Third time down, Morton. Next time you go down, Roux's the winner.'

Morton's seconds slapped his face and sponged him down, trying to revive him. He stood up swaying from side to side, glowering at Simon. Simon moved in again. He concentrated on ripping vicious body blows into his opponent's midriff. As each punch landed Morton grunted, absorbing the punishment. He was unable to retaliate, hands raised to protect his head, blows raining in on his body.

A harder blow hit him under his heart. Slowly he collapsed. A wild look shot into Simon's eyes and he aimed a kick at Morton's ribs.

'That is uncalled for,' snapped the headboy jumping forward.

Morton was past caring. 'I give up,' he mumbled.

The Afrikaners pummelled Simon on the back in congratulation. He had won the fight and the respect of the school, but the real contest had only begun. Pandemonium raged as Afrikaans and English hurled abuse at each other. A free-for-all broke out as pent-up hatreds, going back decades to the Anglo-Boer War, boiled over. The Afrikaners outnumbered the English three to one. Force of numbers pushed the English back against the embankment.

The headmaster, coming around the corner of the school building, took in the scene with rage and dismay. There were more than four hundred of his boys at each other's throats. The language was appalling. The fact that English were fighting against Afrikaners was unacceptable to him. Gawie Pretorius had tried hard to cement the relations between the two language groups. He bellowed in his deep voice, 'Stop this at once.' The noise was too great for those in the vortex to hear the first time, but those around the fringes, closest to the headmaster, froze. 'Stop this nonsense!' repeated Pretorius.

Shamefacedly the boys turned to face him.

'You're all a disgrace to the name of Paarl Boys' High.' The headmaster strode towards the boys. They moved out of his way as he walked purposefully towards the centre. He marched up to Simon, seeing Morton kneeling at his feet. Morton looked up fearfully, tears of shame on his blood-encrusted face. The headmaster took in the scene and angrily addressed the boys. 'You should all be ashamed of yourselves. You have disgraced the proud name of your school. Go home immediately. I never want a repeat of today. Roux, show your spirit,' he commanded. 'Help Morton up.'

Simon put out his hand and helped Robert to his feet. 'No hard feelings?'

Morton nodded sullenly and shuffled away.

Simon and Helena watched as teams of labourers planted new vine stock on the Marais farm, De Hoop. The dormant vines looked like rooted dead sticks but Simon knew, come spring, they would start growing into sturdy plants. After two years the vines would produce an annual harvest of grapes for the semi-sweet natural *stein* white wines for which the farm was famed.

Absorbed in the planting they didn't notice the dark, water-laden clouds sweeping in over Paarl Mountain. Without warning the rain came sheeting down, soaking the couple.

'Let's run for the house.'

Shouting in high spirits, they entered the house dripping water, stamping their soggy feet. Helena took Simon to the bathroom. He stripped off his wet jersey and shirt and she dried his hair with a towel. Her arm rubbed against his bare chest, arousing him.

Simon pulled her close. Her soft lips trembled under his. Helena allowed him to slip his hands under her jersey and caress the smooth skin of her back, but as soon as he moved one round to touch her breast she pressed herself tightly up against him, preventing him going further. Their pelvises hugging, Simon thrust against her. In panic Helena tried to pull away, a strangled sound coming from her throat. Simon's hands were on her buttocks frustrating her escape, and she felt his maleness forcing itself through the thin material of her skirt. An electric shock raced through her body and she gasped, her eyes blazing in alarm.

'No, Simon, no!'

His grip on her loosened a little. 'Why not?' His voice was husky, confused.

'You're all wet and I'm cold.' Her voice wavered in uncertainty.

'Please Helena!'

'I can't. Don't you understand?' She turned her head away trying not to show her distress.

He reluctantly let go and she twisted quickly away, her eyes downcast. Was it pain he had seen there? What did she mean? She's just keeping herself pure for me, he decided. All women have sex. After all, she had said she loved him.

Before he could say anything Helena hurried out of the bathroom, a haunted expression on her face.

Paulus lifted his glass. 'Here's to a National Party victory.'

Jan Marais leant over and clinked his glass in approval. 'Let's hope we win the 1948 election. I'm sick of United Party rule. All it's brought has been food shortages and unemployment, particularly among the Afrikaners.'

'United Party policy will lead to the ultimate downfall of the white man.' Paulus was adamant. 'Jan Smuts and his liberal policies will see blacks and coloureds introduced into parliament at an increasing rate. We can't allow that to happen.'

The National Party branch in Paarl nominated Paulus as their candidate in the coming general election. He was a good candidate. Chairman of the Paarl Farmers' Union, the Wine Makers' Association and Paarl Boys' High School committee. Nevertheless, his chances were slim against the United Party candidate, who was the sitting Member of Parliament.

With the support of his friends he canvassed actively. He spoke at meetings in Paarl, at gatherings of farmers in the district and to the white artisans and workers during lunch-time factory visits. 'A vote for me is a vote for your future,' Paulus told his audiences. 'Nothing can prevent the National Party from coming to power. The corner-stone of our policy is apartheid. Only apartheid will ensure the salvation of the white man.'

The highlight of Paulus's campaign was his final meeting in the Paarl town hall. Dr DF Malan, the leader of the National Party alliance, came to support his candidature. The hall was full. People stood in the aisles and crowded behind the pillars.

Dr Malan and Paulus received a thunderous welcome as they stepped on to the stage. Malan delivered an impassioned speech. 'If the white race wants to maintain its supremacy, and its civilisation, we as Afrikaners need to stand together. If we do not we will

20

disappear for ever, without honour, into the black sea of South Africa's non-white population.'

The white crowd rose to acclaim him. Now it was Paulus's moment to speak. 'I ask you for your vote so that we can maintain our standard of living. Vote for me and I promise you I will look after the interests of all the whites in our beautiful Paarl Valley. A vote for Jan Smuts's United Party will lead to black majority rule. Do you want kaffirs and coloureds to govern you?'

'No!' shouted the crowd in wild response. *'Donderse kaffers!'*

It was music to their ears. They stood and applauded Paulus while the English-speaking section booed him. He held up his hands for silence.

'What I also desire is a coming together of Afrikaners and English-speakers, so that we can form a combined front against the black wave which threatens to overwhelm us. It's time to stop the white-against-white fight. Together we must fight our common enemy – the black man.'

His diplomacy quietened the English-speakers and they also rose to acclaim Paulus.

The National Party alliance won the election with a majority of seven seats. Paulus Roux became the new Member of Parliament for Paarl.

Paulus and Marie hosted a victory celebration at Hermitage. They invited everyone of standing in the white community of Paarl. Food and drink flowed as the Nationalists celebrated their successes.

'I would like to thank all my friends who canvassed for me or who helped with my election campaign,' Paulus addressed the gathering. 'Our time has come, the Afrikaner is in power at last. It's our duty to rewrite the statute books to entrench white superiority. I intend to play my part fully in the exciting new order which awaits our people.'

Jan Marais proposed the toast. 'To our people and our country.'

Only Helena found herself out of step with the new politics. 'Somehow, I don't think it's right to exclude blacks and coloureds from decision making.'

Simon looked at her in surprise. 'How can you make such a statement? We are white. We must look after our own interests. The other population groups don't contribute to running the country.'

'Of course they do.' She looked at him feistily. 'The black man's

21

sweat runs the gold mines. The coloureds harvest our grapes. And if you suppress people you only make them more determined to fight back. You'll see.'

'Nonsense, Helena. Whites control South Africa.'

'I don't want to argue with you, Simon,' she replied in exasperation.

Simon started to take a serious interest in politics in his final year at Stellenbosch University. He joined the student branch of the National Party and found the debates stimulating. Although the university was predominantly Afrikaans, not all students agreed with the National Party doctrines – some vehemently opposed the changes taking place.

'Helena, what's the problem?' Simon asked her one day.

'I feel in my heart of hearts that what is happening in South Africa is morally wrong. The National Party is treating human beings like animals.'

'Animals?' Simon stopped in mid-stride. 'My Pa is a Nationalist MP. He's part of the decision-making process. Are you saying my father and his friends are not acting in our best interests?'

'They think they are, but their policies are so short-sighted. I have nothing against your father. He's a wonderful man, but they all seem blind to the realities of life.'

'One day I'll also be a Nationalist MP.' There was anger in Simon's voice. 'We talk of getting married. What happens to us then?'

'When we're married, and if you go into politics, I'll always support you as my husband. That doesn't prevent me from having my own opinion.'

The Minister of Lands, Mr JG Strijdom, was guest speaker at the branch's next meeting. As a potential future leader of the National Party he valued the opportunity to reach out to the students and gain their later support.

The town hall filled to overflowing for his visit, and Strijdom delivered a strong message demanding support for the National Party. He praised the new apartheid initiatives of the government. Most of the packed hall responded with thunderous applause; from only a minority section there were boos and catcalls. Then it was question time. The student chairman nodded to a woman in the audience. Simon, who as a committee member sat on the stage with Strijdom, reacted with growing alarm as he recognised Helena's voice. 'Mr Chairman, I would like to ask our esteemed speaker why it is necessary to pass laws alienating the black and coloured peoples from the white population. Surely apartheid is a matter of choice and does not need to be legislated for?'

Simon dropped his head in shame. Many people knew of their relationship. Surely he too would be tarred with the liberal brush? She had made a mockery of his father's position in parliament. How could she do this to him?

Strijdom enjoyed his answer. 'Madam, thank you for your question. Apartheid is a natural phenomenon, but that is not good enough for orderly government. It is our intention that the black man should occupy the land he originally came from, so that the whites in turn can control their own destinies in the land of their birthright. To do this we have to separate the various nations.'

Instead of sitting down Helena pressed home her point, to Simon's chagrin. 'Is South Africa not also the land of birth of all black people? Weren't they here first? Didn't we force them off their traditional land, claiming it as our own?'

Strijdom's face became grim. He pointed his finger straight at her. 'You talk like a communist, madam. Once all our legislation is in place we will be able to jail people for such defamatory statements. If you want to remain a free woman I suggest you change your tune, young lady.'

Simon avoided Helena after the meeting, returning directly to his residence, Wilgenhof. Half an hour later a student called him. 'Simon, a woman in the lounge to see you.'

He knew it was Helena. 'I'm busy. Tell her I'm not here.'

The next moment Helena strode angrily into his room. 'What's this nonsense, Simon?'

'But, but, you're not allowed in a man's room, it's against university rules!'

'I'm not leaving until you talk to me, Simon Roux.' Helena leant against the door, arms folded in determination.

'Okay! Wait in the lounge, I'll be there now.' He needed a few moments to gather his thoughts. His mind raced with questions and conjectures. Helena was also an Afrikaner, from the same background as his own. Why did she have so much compassion for blacks? Was it possible to love someone who differed from yourself? What was the solution, to break with Helena or accept her as she was?

He entered the lounge as Helena paced up and down restlessly. Here comes trouble, he thought.

Hearing his footsteps, she turned around, looking at him with a hurt, quizzical look. 'Simon, why did you abandon me at the hall tonight? You always walk me home.'

'You asked Strijdom those stupid questions. You embarrassed me.'

'Come and sit down and let's talk.' She patted the sofa seat alongside her. 'Let's get something straight, Simon. I'm entitled to my own opinion, too. Last time we discussed this matter I told you how I felt. Nothing has changed.'

'You can't be an Afrikaner if you're so liberal.'

'Of course I'm an Afrikaner, born and bred. You can't take that away from me.' She tossed her auburn hair, impatient at his lack of understanding.

Cornered, he tried another tack. 'Then you can't be a Nationalist.'

'What gives you that idea? Just because I don't conform to your precise interpretation of the term nationalist does not mean I cannot be every bit the patriot that you are.' Her eyes pleaded with him to understand. 'Every party has a left, a centre and a right. I'm to the left of the Nationalist spectrum. Why should it affect you so much?' She looked at him kindly. 'I love you and respect your views. Please respect mine.'

Simon's mind was a muddle of indignation and humility in the face of Helena's calm forbearance. 'Let's drop the matter,' he grumbled, preparing to leave the room.

She called him back. 'Not so fast. Aren't you going to walk me back to my hostel? We're meant to be in love, don't forget.'

Slowly they strolled down the oak-lined streets. She slipped her hand into his. 'Simon, look it's almost full moon.' She stopped suddenly, turning. He bumped into her. Then they were embracing. He backed her up against a large oak, feeling her proud breasts against his chest.

His breath quickened. 'I want you now. Let's make love. Now. Show me you love me.'

Her grip on him loosened. 'Only when the time's right, when we're married,' Helena answered slowly. Softer, she added, 'Simon,

I'll wait for you. You will be the first and only man who will ever make love to me.'

He sighed, realising nothing would change her mind, wanting nothing to change her mind.

2

A thousand kilometres to the east, in the tiny village of Qunu in the Transkei, the traditional home of the Xhosa nation, a young girl was waking to the call of her mother.

'Nomisile, your father is calling for you. Get up.' The middle-aged black woman shook her.

Nomisile sat up, rubbing the sleep out of her eyes. She wore only a loincloth around her waist, fully dressed in the Xhosa custom. She scooped a handful of water from a bucket on the earthen floor and washed her face.

'Hurry! Hurry! You know how impatient men are,' implored her mother Nosakani.

Nomisile hurried out of her hut. It was one of a cluster of many identical circular buildings – mud-brick walls plastered with a mixture of cow dung and soil and painted with white clay. A grass-thatched roof topped each hut.

Nomisile squinted in the sharp sunlight after the darkness of her hut, taking in the scene. Her father and mother, two uncles and three aunts sat in a semicircle in the shade of a sneezewood tree. In the distance other kraals, or villages, capped the summits of similar rolling, emerald hills.

'Good morning, Father.' She greeted him first out of respect and then the others.

'Good morning, my daughter. Sit down,' Morris Memani commanded. She sat down in the respectful way of Xhosa women, her legs folded under her, and faced her family.

Her father addressed her in Xhosa. 'My daughter, you have now finished school. You are sixteen years old and your breasts are starting to swell. It is time for your *ntonjaan*.'

Nomisile knew what that meant. *Ntonjaan* was the age-old tribal way of initiating a girl into womanhood, and she shivered with

27

excitement. After the rites she would no longer be a girl. She would be respected as a woman with a woman's privileges and the right to marry.

Morris continued. 'We have discussed the matter. Your initiation will start next week with four other girls of the tribe. You are fortunate to come from this family, for you are of the royal house of Thembu. Because you are of royal blood the Paramount Chief has decreed that your rites will take place in his kraal.'

'Thank you, Father. I am looking forward to being a woman at last.' He nodded and the meeting was over.

Morris Memani presented his daughter to the Paramount Chief's third wife, Gladys. She was the indindala kazi, the instructress for the two weeks' indoctrination. '*Indindala kazi*, here is Nomisile for her initiation. Teach her well in the ways of our people that she may bring honour to our tribe.'

'Come inside, my niece.' Nomisile followed Gladys into the hut where the other girls were waiting. It was dark inside. There were only two small windows, with their shutters closed. In the tradition of the initiation there was no furniture in the hut: it contained only a rolled-up woven reed mat for each girl. In the centre a sturdy pole supported the roof of rafters and thatch. A hearth of baked clay formed a circle around the centre pole. A musty smell from decades of wood fires filled the air.

Gladys presented each girl with a new red blanket. 'Go down to the river and wash yourselves. Throw away your old loincloths and return wrapped only in your new blanket,' instructed Gladys. She stood on the hill, watching that the girls did as she had told them.

When they returned they found a hollowed-out stone in the centre of the hut containing a bright-yellow liquid. 'This is your initiation clay. It comes from the banks of the Cicira River. Smear your faces and your necks and arms.'

Giggling the girls rubbed the porridge-like substance on their skins, helping each other to cover all the areas evenly.

Gladys pointed to five places against the wall, all equidistant from each other, and ordered the girls to sit down in them. She closed the door and hung a blanket over each window, turning the hut into Stygian darkness.

'Where you are sitting now is your position for the next two weeks. Do not change places, for I need to know where your spirit is to communicate with you. Lean against the wall when sitting and sleep at your post. You are not to go outside during the day, not even to do your ablutions, only at night when it is dark. Keep yourselves covered completely when you go out so that no one will recognise you. When the clay cracks off, repaint yourselves.'

The girls listened intently, noting the rules, not daring to challenge the fearful *indindala kazi*.

'You may speak to no one except each other and me. I will bring you food and water each day. During the first week you will think deeply about your life up to this point. Start with your birth and go forward year by year, memory by memory, uncovering the layers in your minds, until seven days are past, when you will have caught up with the present. That is all.'

Gladys left the hut and the girls sat in their silent tomb. They chatted amongst themselves but one by one they fell silent. The hut was dark and quiet.

Day and night became one to Nomisile as a great drowsiness settled on her. In her somnolent state flashes of light flared in the darkness, lighting up her mind. She saw the face of her mother smiling at her, talking to her. Nomisile slipped deeper into a state of torpor, into a misty haze which cleared to reveal a baby wrapped in a shawl in a woman's arms. She heard a masculine voice, wafting across time. 'My wife Nosakani, we have a beautiful girl baby. One day she will bring us lots of *lobola*, many fat cattle in return for her hand in marriage.' Nomisile concentrated on the voice until it took shape into an upstanding young man. He looked familiar, and with a start, Nomisile realised it was her father – young and noble without a grey hair on his head.

'Yes, my husband, she is a beautiful baby. We must choose a name for her that has great meaning.' Nomisile focused on the voice and her mother's features came into view, a young Nosakani, sixteen years younger.

Her father spoke. 'It is the mother's privilege to name a girl child.'

She heard her mother talking again. 'We will call her Nomisile, which means faithful and responsible.'

Their instructress brought them food twice a day, mainly mealie-meal porridge and an occasional beefy broth. They did not need much nourishment for they expended virtually no energy. Once a day – they were not sure whether it was day or night – Gladys would squat in front of each girl in turn. She talked to them in soft tones which hardly carried to the other girls so that she would not disturb their meditations.

Each in turn told the teacher about the pictures in her mind. Having known the girls and their parents all her life, Gladys could verify the authenticity of their experiences. Nomisile related her life as a bare-tailed toddler, a fat little infant with chubby cheeks and a glowing ebony skin. She told her about the scorpion which had stung her with its tail, and she felt the pain again as she had felt it then. Her hand swelled and she fell into a coma, waking only three days later, exactly as she had done the first time.

After a week she had caught up with the present and Gladys moved on to the next stage of their initiation.

'All five of you have discovered your inner selves during the past week. Your minds are cleansed of evil thoughts. Now it is time for you to learn about the life ahead of you.'

She explained to them the responsibilities associated with adulthood, the challenges which lay ahead, the changes their bodies would undergo on the journey to maturity.

Another lesson was on safe sex. No maiden was allowed intercourse with a man before the *lobola* cattle were paid and the marriage concluded. Safe sex, in Xhosa tradition, entailed the woman smearing her inner thighs with ox-fat and the man obtaining release, while her virginity stayed intact.

She told them how to guide their man's hands, fingers and lips to their own pleasure zones. She explained the physiology of a man's parts and how to pleasure him with subtle movements. They were instructed on climax and the methods to use so that both their comings could fuse into one.

Xhosa men were allowed to practise bigamy and even polygamy, depending on their status in life and how many cattle they could afford to pay for their spouses. She told them the benefits of being the principal wife, the first one. If they played their cards right their husbands would get total satisfaction from them and would not be tempted to take other wives.

She taught them about the Xhosa *lobola* system of cattle bartering for a wife. The matter was settled primarily between the bride's father, who benefited from the cattle exchanged, and the prospective bridegroom. The father, not the bride, had the final say in whom she

30

might marry. A Xhosa girl of common breeding could be bought for as little as five cattle, while a chief's daughter might cost thirty head. Daughters were valuable assets in the Transkei.

The young protégées reflected on their lessons, each intently absorbing the age-old wisdom and lore, filling herself with the communal soul of history. At the end Gladys was sure that their future would be governed by the steadfast codes of conduct of the Xhosa nation. They were ready for womanhood.

The whole tribe met at the Paramount Chief's kraal for their coming-out. Sheep provided by the girls' fathers were slaughtered and a primitive drumbeat signalled the start of the festivities.

In their hut the girls washed off the pigment they had worn for the last fourteen days and Gladys led them into the harsh glare. 'Keep your eyes closed until I tell you,' Gladys advised.

The girls were led to a grassy knoll, the music stopped and the five mothers were called forward for the painting-up ceremony.

'Wisdom,' Gladys cried, and Nosakani dipped her index finger in the yellow ochre and painted a stripe across Nomisile's forehead. The other mothers did the same.

'Truth,' she shouted and Nosakani painted a stripe below her daughter's mouth, signifying she should never lie.

'Obedience,' and a dot was dabbed on each earlobe as well as a stripe behind each ear.

'Perception.' Two circles were painted around their eyes, the eyes being the instruments of insight.

'Stand up and open your eyes,' she instructed. 'You are now *abafazi*, women, of the Thembu tribe.'

To the mothers she instructed, 'Dress them as women.'

Nosakani now carefully dressed her daughter in a new red loin-cloth which covered her from her waist to just below her knees. Around her neck she placed a broad necklace made of thousands of tiny beads. There were delicately woven bead bracelets in many colours for her wrists and copper anklets for her feet. Her head-dress was a band of woven beads around the forehead, criss-crossed over her head.

Nomisile looked breathtaking. She gave her mother a smile of thanks. Nosakani squeezed her arm in reply. 'My child, I'm proud of you.'

At Gladys's signal, the five maidens walked over to their fathers and stood in front of them with their heads bowed.

'Fathers, you gave me five Xhosa girls. I now return to your care five women, ready to take their place in our tribe.'

'Present yourselves to the Paramount Chief.' Singly the girls approached him and went on their knees at his feet. He touched them on the head with the flat metal blade of the spear. 'I welcome you as a woman to the Thembu tribe.'

Nomisile walked through East London's black township to the home of her uncle, Alfred Nkosi. The streets were potholed and filled with water from the recent rains. Weeds choked the sidewalks. Poverty showed in the dilapidated houses with their sagging fences.

The regal way she walked caused men to stop and stare. Her shoulders were square, her back straight. Her huge eyes were spaced far apart, and with her high cheek-bones, she was strikingly beautiful.

She had come to East London to look for work, for there was none in the Transkei and her family needed her help. She knocked on the door of the small municipal house.

'Come in, Nomisile, come in. It is good to see you. Come inside.' Alfred opened the door for his niece. Nomisile hugged him, her Aunt Doreen and her cousins with affection.

'My, how you've grown since I last saw you. You're almost a woman,' exclaimed Doreen. 'How old are you?'

'I'm already seventeen and I *am* now a woman.' She laughed happily. 'I have finished my initiation and I need to find a job.'

'Have you finished school already?' Alfred asked.

'Yes, Uncle. I went to Qunu Missionary School. I passed standard eight last year. I can read and write and I can talk English fluently.'

'Can you speak the oppressor's language, this Afrikaans, that the government is trying to ram down our throats?'

Nomisile shook her head. 'We never learnt that in the Transkei, only English.'

'Come, it's supper time, let's eat.' Her aunt placed a steaming bowl of crumbly maize-meal porridge on the bare wooden table. They ate with their fingers from the same bowl.

'Times are tough, we cannot afford meat and vegetables every day,' apologised her aunt.

'How is your uncle Rolihlahla?' Alfred referred to the Xhosa name of Nelson Mandela.

32

'We see him no more, he is in Johannesburg. He is a lawyer. You know he ran away, and the Paramount Chief tried to find him and bring him back to the Transkei. Now the Chief has let him be.'

'And his mother?' Alfred urged.

'Great-aunt Nosekeni is still at Mqekezweni, the Chief's great kraal.'

'What sort of work do you want?' asked her aunt.

'I would like to work in an office.' Nomisile pictured herself sitting behind a large, neat desk, with drawers on both sides, organising piles of important papers and typing on a shiny typewriter.

'No chance.' Alfred shook his head. 'The whites keep that for themselves. Perhaps they think if we work in their offices we'll get to know too much. At best you'll get kitchen work, or maybe a nanny to white children, or factory work.'

'What do they pay for a housemaid?'

'As little as they can. They know there are many of us desperate for work,' said Alfred.

'I'll start looking tomorrow. Maybe I'll get a job as a maid with good people. Where must I try?'

'Beacon Bay, first. It's a new suburb with lots of smart houses.' Alfred had jealously observed the spanking new homes continually being built for whites in the tidy white suburbs. At the same time he watched in anger and dejection the degeneration of his own people – overcrowded into black townships of squalor and waste.

Her aunt brought sweet, weak tea in chipped enamel mugs. Her uncle sat in silence.

'Why do you look so worried, Uncle?'

'There are big troubles ahead for the black people.' Alfred thought bitterly of the brutality that had stained the country since the National Party had come into power. It had to be nipped in the bud before it became a way of life for the white people and the black man lost his soul under the burden of separate development. He looked up at Nomisile. 'The government has no respect for us. Last month they killed seven of our brothers in New Brighton in Port Elizabeth. Last week it was three in Denver in the Transvaal and twelve in Kimberley.' Alfred's voice was bitter.

'But those places are far from East London.'

'Tomorrow it could be here. We have organised a march on East London to protest against the new repressive laws. We've had enough of being bullied by the police. We are going to show

33

we are a force to be reckoned with, that we must be respected. We are going to demand our rights.'

Aunt Doreen looked at the clock. 'Time for bed.'

The simple semi-detached council house had only three rooms – the living room, a tiny kitchen and one bedroom. There was a pit latrine in the back garden. Nomisile washed in the kitchen in a basin of water. She fetched her bedding roll and small suitcase containing all the clothes she possessed. She rolled out her woven reed mat on the floor, folded her only blanket double and slipped between the folds. She slept with her head resting on the crook of her arm.

Simon placed his silver knife and fork together on his plate and sat back as the maid cleared his place. She rolled across a trolley containing a selection of sweets. Simon helped himself and then turned to his father. 'Pa, I've got some things on my mind. I want to have a serious talk with you, please.'

'Problems?' Paulus raised his eyebrows.

'Not really.' Simon spread his hands on the Madeira tablecloth. 'I want to talk to you about the farm and where we're going.'

'I have a light day at parliament tomorrow, I can be home early.'

'Shall we make it at six o'clock? Then we'll have two hours before dinner?'

'Suits me fine.' Paulus nodded.

Simon knocked on the Hermitage study door. 'Come in, my boy.' Paulus rose from behind the large imbuia desk and went to sit in one of the comfortable leather armchairs next to the bookcase. He waved Simon to a chair. Simon sat opposite, placing a sheaf of papers on the coffee table. 'The floor is yours.'

'Pa, for the past eight months I've been analysing Hermitage, block by block and variety by variety. All our eggs are in one basket. Our main income is from exporting our wines and sherries to Britain. The same goes for our peaches and plums. We can't survive on the income from the local market. We depend on exports. Helena says the government's apartheid policy means we will lose friends in Europe and those nations may boycott our products one day.'

'Nonsense! Where does that girl get such stupid notions? I love her dearly, like a daughter, but that's preposterous. I'm in parliament and I'm in touch with these things, and I can tell you here and now our European trading partners are our friends. They'll never boycott us.'

Paulus poured himself a brandy from the liquor cabinet. 'For you, son?'

Simon nodded and his father splashed brandy into a snifter and handed it to him. Simon downed the neat brandy in one gulp and held up his glass. Paulus raised his eyebrows in surprise, but did not comment as he refilled the glass. Brandy drinking was a tradition amongst the wine farmers, but needed to be savoured slowly. Simon sipped the next glassful but twin patches showed on his cheeks.

'Anyway, what are you suggesting?' Paulus took a sip.

'Diversification.'

'What sort of new-fangled talk is this?' Paulus asked sharply.

'Pa, we're farming Hermitage to its optimum. We need to expand and spread our risk – another type of farm.'

'Strangely enough I was speaking yesterday to Frikkie Reitz, the MP for Gordonia. He has a farm in the Kalahari near Upington he's thinking of selling. It may suit us. And I'll be able to take my friends on hunting trips. I'll find out more details. What else do you have on your mind?'

'Helena and I want to set a wedding date. We were thinking of the end of March. We thought of holding the reception in the wine cellar here at Hermitage.'

'That sounds like a fine idea. I'm pleased about you and Helena. You make a good match. I look forward to you settling down, so your mother and I can move closer to parliament during the week. All this motoring to Cape Town and back is very tiring.'

Paulus turned on the radio for the evening news. At the end of the bulletin he switched it off in disgust. 'Damn kaffirs! Last week we had to shoot seven in New Brighton, this week it's been three in Denver and twelve in Kimberley. I wonder where the next trouble spot will be?'

Alfred Nkosi and his family were up before sunrise. They washed and dressed by candlelight. Nomisile put on her finest dress for the day. She had only two. She needed to look her best so she could get a job. They breakfasted on dry brown bread, cut in thick slabs, and sour buttermilk.

Nomisile asked her uncle, 'Can I go with you so that you can show me which bus to catch?'

'I'll take you half-way and show you the bus terminus. We're meeting at our community hall and marching to the centre of East London.'

As he spoke he reached down and picked up a panga from behind the couch. It was a crude but effective weapon made from a truck spring and set in a wooden handle, a finely honed cutting edge running its whole length.

'Why do you need such a terrible weapon when you are going on a march?'

'There may be trouble with the police.'

'The police have guns, won't they shoot you?'

'It won't come to that, I hope. We're planning a peaceful march.'

'Can't I go with you?'

'Demonstrations are men's work,' he admonished. 'You go and look for work as planned.'

As they walked the crowd swelled. Men greeted each other good-naturedly.

'Over there is the bus terminus.' Alfred pointed. 'Ask the conductor for the bus to Beacon Bay.'

A stranger told them, 'The buses have all been cancelled by the police. They think we are going to stone them.'

'Nomisile, you had better go back home.'

'Please Uncle, it's all so exciting.'

'Go straight home and that is final,' instructed Alfred in a stern voice.

Nomisile took only a few paces before deciding to risk the family wrath. She rejoined the flow of humanity. She had never seen so many people together in one place.

There are at least two thousand men, she estimated. The atmosphere was charged, men shouting to each other, some singing, while others stood around grim-faced in front of the hall.

To see the action better Nomisile stood on an old oil drum at the edge of the mêlée. From her vantage point she could see over the heads of the crowd.

They were chanting, 'We want Nkosi! We want Nkosi!'

Alfred climbed the steps of the hall to cheers. Nomisile could see why he was the leader. The gentle, fun-loving uncle she knew had turned into a natural orator.

'My friends of the Amaxhosa, we are tired of living like pigs under the white man's rule. We want justice. We demand justice. We are going to get justice. Now! We will march to the city hall to show the government we mean business.'

'What if the police stop us?' shouted someone from the crowd.

'Kill the white oppressors!' screamed another.

'Wait! Wait!' Alfred bellowed. 'Violence will get us nowhere. They have guns. They will shoot us. We will have a peaceful march. No violence.'

With Alfred in front the mob lurched forward. Nomisile jumped off the barrel and followed at a distance. What a thrilling place the city was, she thought.

Police vans blocked the road at the edge of the township. The three-quarter ton Ford pick-ups had closed-in metal rear canopies, and small iron-mesh windows, turning them into miniature prisons. The vans were parked diagonally across the road, creating a solid barrier.

Leaning against the vehicles were a score of policemen, rifles held casually over their shoulders. They sweated in their black uniforms.

A few paces in front stood an officer. He wore a black cap to distinguish himself from his men. It was a hot November day and he sweated under the impractical uniform.

A car pulled up on the East London side of the road-block and a white woman got out. 'I'm a doctor. Please move one of these vehicles so that I can get through to the township.' She spoke in crisp tones.

'You can't go in, doctor.' A policeman pointed to the township. 'There's a mob there. We think there's going to be trouble.'

'I must get to the clinic, my patients are waiting for me.'

'For your own safety you will remain where you are until this crowd has dispersed. You should go back to the city.'

'I'm staying right here.' The doctor spoke firmly. 'These are my people, they won't harm me.'

'Suit yourself.' The policeman rejoined his colleagues. Nomisile scrambled up a tree from where she had a grandstand view.

The first of the marchers were only thirty paces from him when the officer pulled out his service revolver and fired two shots in the air. 'Stop! No further. Turn around and go home.'

The men at the back of the march continued walking, forcing

those ahead of them forward. The ripple effect pushed the front of the crowd towards the police.

'Load arms,' cried the officer. The policemen all went down on one knee, their .303 short-barrelled rifles pushed into their shoulders pointing at the marchers. The sun glinted on the steel bayonets.

The march eventually halted in front of the police. Alfred confronted the officer. 'We want to go through. This is a peaceful march to the city hall.'

'One step closer and we'll shoot.' He turned to his men. 'Aim.'

Alfred and the officer stood glaring at each other. One of them would have to back down.

In the end the crowd took the decision from them. Spears, knopkieries, metal pipes, pangas, chains, knives, sticks and axes were raised. The mob pushed forward.

The police shuffled backwards until they were pressed against their patrol vans.

One step backwards by the police was one giant step forward for liberation. The crowd started agitating.

'*Uhuru*.'

'Freedom!'

'Liberation for our people!'

'Ban the pass laws!'

Fear showed in the policemen's eyes. They had never faced an incensed crowd at such close quarters. They waited for their officer's command.

A man in the front row danced forward, his axe held high in mock attack. A young policeman panicked and fired. The bullet hit him in the chest killing him instantly. More shots were fired. The front row was a seething mass of bodies as injured men fell to the ground and screamed in pain.

The sound of the shots shook the crowd. Some men ran back in panic, others forward.

'Fire!' screamed the officer and he lifted his revolver and fired into Alfred Nkosi's stomach.

Alfred felt a burning pain in his lower abdomen as the .38 hard-nosed bullet passed through his intestines, ripping and tearing. The shot hit a lower rib, shattering it, and exited through his side, spraying the comrade next to him with gore.

Instantaneously the man of peace and negotiation was turned into a dervish. He lifted the panga high and brought it down in a

38

flashing arc, striking the officer below his left ear. The blow cut clean through the neck, slicing the head off the body, and it rolled drunkenly across the road. The officer fell forward, blood pouring from his jugular vein. It ran in a rivulet to mix with the blood of the black victims. In life they were so different, but in death their blood was of the same colour and consistency.

The policemen were leaderless. They retreated, escaping between the vehicles, some dropping their rifles in their panic.

The doctor took in the scene of horror and destruction. She had ministered to these people for years. She sprang forward to help, catching Alfred Nkosi as he fell. His weight forced her to the ground where she sat cradling him in her arms. His dying words to her were, 'May God help our people.'

The Xhosas were in a frenzy. The white face of the doctor evoked hatred and they vented their rage on her, beating her mercilessly. She cried out, 'I'm your friend. I am your doctor!' Her cries were drowned in the roar of violence. She struggled to get to her feet, shouting more loudly, sensing death. 'I'm from the clinic, your clinic.' The men were past caring. Their sticks and pipes snapped her bones, their axes and pangas cut her flesh to ribbons, their spears pierced her body. She died, a battered rag doll, an innocent victim of black-white hatred.

Nomisile saw her uncle fall and raced along the fringes screaming hysterically. She forced her way to the front. She had never been so frightened, but fear kept her going.

The mob demanded action, any action. They turned to the vehicles, all that was left of the white man at the scene. They smashed the windows. They axed the tyres and the body work. A stream of fuel leaked from a ruptured tank. A man struck a match and the petrol ignited in a whoosh. Flames engulfed the vehicle.

Nomisile reached Alfred, falling to her knees at his side. 'Uncle! Uncle! Get up, get up!' she screamed, shaking his body. His eyes stared back at her. She felt a clamminess against her leg. Looking down she saw the blood from his jacket on her dress. She lifted the cloth and saw the mortal wound in his side. 'Talk to me, Uncle,' she shrieked.

'He is dead,' said a comrade closing his eyelids.

Nomisile shuddered in terror, her body racked with spasms, tears rolled uncontrollably down her cheeks and dripped on to Alfred's chest. Her flawless features were twisted in pain.

Men were running in all directions, oblivious of the dead at their feet. They wanted action, they needed revenge. They torched the remaining police vans. Nomisile felt the heat on her face. Using all her strength, she dragged Alfred away from the inferno.

Police reinforcements rushed out from East London with sirens blaring. The black men ran back into the township, leaving the dead and dying behind.

A brigadier jumped out of the lead vehicle to supervise operations. Fire extinguishers were turned on the blazing police vans. He was sickened by the tableau of destruction – the worst he had seen in his forty years of duty. The government would demand an explanation. He needed to arrest someone, anyone they could haul before the courts for this hideous crime.

He spotted Nomisile. 'Arrest that girl.'

Two policemen hauled her to her feet. She screamed in terror, twisting from their grasp, running as fast as she could.

'Shoot,' instructed the brigadier.

Nomisile tripped and fell. The bullets tore at the air over her body, some puffing up dirt around her. She jumped to her feet again, running around a corner of a house as more bullets slammed into the building, spraying her with a shower of plaster and brickwork.

Policemen chased after her. She weaved in and out through the buildings. She kicked off her shoes, giving her more speed, running like a spring hare. She reached Alfred Nkosi's house. Gasping for breath she stripped off the blood-stained blue dress and put on her other clothes. She grabbed her purse and ran out of the back door as the police burst into the front of the house. Nomisile dived behind a low bush. The policemen ran past her and stopped.

'She got away,' gasped one. 'Let's get back to the convoy.'

They turned around, running back towards her. She crept deeper under the bush, holding her breath. The policemen passed and disappeared around a corner.

She lay back panting, taking in deep breaths until her breathing returned to normal. Her mind raced, she had to get away from this place. I must go home, it is the only safe place I know, she decided.

After an hour Nomisile crept out of her hiding place behind the bush. She did not know that the police had forgotten about her and had returned to East London. She was convinced they were waiting around every corner, ready to pounce and arrest her. She avoided Alfred's house and worked her way in a wide circle to the bus terminus. There was a policeman on duty, so she crept out of sight behind a row of Kei apple trees.

Nomisile was hungry. She picked some of the ripe wild apples and ate them. They were tart. In the late afternoon, when the policeman had gone off duty, she crept cautiously out of hiding and sat huddled in the corner of the bus shelter, thinking that by making herself small she would go unnoticed. She had to wait until six o'clock before the first bus arrived. In East London she caught another bus to the Transkei. It was a single-decker with a roof carrier which was packed to overflowing with bundles wrapped in blankets, boxes, doors, window frames and even a coop of squawking chickens.

'Umtata.' Nomisile paid her fare to the driver. She went to the back. She thought that if the police stopped and searched the bus she would be discovered last.

The bus travelled on the N2 through the towns of Butterworth and Idutywa. They reached Mtento Cuttings, a place where the rock had been blasted out of the hillside to make the gradient more gradual. Above them on the left was a steep cliff face, on the other side a precipice falling away to the river.

The police had chosen that spot for their road-block – a place where escape was virtually impossible. A portable generator clattered in the still night air, illuminating three bulbs which cast a circle of light in the dark.

The bus came to a squealing halt. 'Police road-block!' shouted the driver.

Nomisile froze. They would catch her now and lock her up. They would accuse her of killing the whites. Her eyes darted around, looking for an escape route. She glanced out of the back window. A police van was parked up the road. That avenue of escape was blocked. The emergency lighting threw grotesque shadows on the cliff. As police walked past the lights their outlines were magnified tenfold against the cliff face. No escape that way either, she thought desperately. On the opposite side the slope fell into the valley, creating a lake of blackness. She shuddered.

A policeman entered the bus. 'All out,' he commanded. The people rose angrily to their feet. Nomisile cried from fear. Using the bodies in front to shield her, she dived under the back seat and waited. When the bus was empty the police made the occupants unload the roof carrier. They looked through all the contents. The blacks cursed in Xhosa.

Nomisile heard footsteps coming down the centre aisle. All she could see were black trousers and shiny black shoes approaching. A policeman was searching under the seats, the beam from his flashlight jumping from left to right.

He is looking for me, she thought desperately. He was close. She dared not breathe in case he heard her. The flashlight was almost on her. In desperation she hooked her toes and fingers into the springs under the seat and pulled herself upwards, just as the light flooded under the back seat. The policeman turned and retraced his steps.

She lowered herself, rubbing the pinched places, hoping he would not come back. The other passengers returned.

'Damn police! They do this to us every time, to humiliate us,' grumbled a passenger.

'Why were you hiding away, child?'

She looked into the face of a kindly old man. Feeling she could trust him, Nomisile told him about her experience in East London.

He looked at her seriously. 'You have had a terrible encounter today, but you need not worry. I doubt if the police will connect you to the march.'

'Thank you,' said Nomisile relaxing for the first time. At Umtata she left the bus. She walked through the night to reach Qunu.

3

'I spoke to Frikkie Reitz today about the Kalahari farm,' announced Paulus. He sat with his wife on the wide, vine-covered stoep of the farmhouse. A gentle spring breeze ruffled the new season's leaves. 'We've settled a fair price, lock stock and barrel.'

'What's this all about?' Marie asked.

'Well you see, we've decided to diversify into another type of farming, to spread our risk,' answered Paulus smugly.

'In the Kalahari?'

'You know how irritable I get in the winter when it rains for weeks. Well, now we can go off to the Kalahari, to hunt and enjoy the outdoors. There are frequently people I owe favours. They always like a hunt. Out there in the stillness of the veld there will be time to relax and talk.'

'What about the finance, Pa?'

'The Land Bank will give us a hundred per cent loan.'

'And the stock?'

'Frikkie says we can take over his stock. There are 1600 sheep, 100 gemsbok and 500 springbok on 10,000 hectares.'

Marie was swept along with their enthusiasm. 'When are we going to see it?'

'Next week. We're all going to the Kalahari.' Paulus smiled in satisfaction.

The heat of summer gave way to autumn. It was a perfect Saturday in Paarl, balmy and calm. The Marais farmhouse at De Hoop was a hive of activity all morning with well-wishers, family and friends coming and going. The men were chased out of the living area where Helena and her bridesmaids were having their hair set by local hairdressers. Wedding fever was in the air.

Helena's and Simon's wedding was the Paarl social highlight of the year, with people judging their standing in the community by the receipt of an invitation. Over four hundred guests were expected.

'Sit on this stool while I fix your headpiece.' Helena's mother Nellie placed a diamanté tiara on her head and adjusted the short front veil. She talked while she worked. 'Helena, you've been a model daughter. Today you are marrying a good man. Be a patient and forgiving wife. Never let jealousy cloud your judgement.'

'Mom, I'm dreading the sex. I'm still a virgin. I have never let Simon have sex, but tonight I can't stop him. I think I have a sexual hang-up.'

'Nonsense, darling, we all felt like that before we were married. After the first time you'll enjoy it.'

'You don't understand, Mom. I've had a problem since I was young.'

'Don't worry, it will all come right. Simon is a caring man, he'll be gentle. Remember I'm always here for you, whenever you need me.'

'But, Mom, the sex scares me.' Helena looked at her mother imploringly.

Jan Marais knocked loudly on the bedroom door. 'Come on you two. Let's get this show on the road.'

'We'll talk some other time.' Nellie kissed Helena on the cheek, careful not to smudge her make-up. 'Good luck, my darling.'

Simon stood before the pulpit looking nervously at his watch. It was past three o'clock. He cut a dashing figure in his dark morning suit.

The organ struck up the wedding march and the bridal procession entered the church. The long satin train fanned out behind Helena. Jan Marais lifted the veil slightly and kissed his daughter a symbolic farewell. Helena linked into Simon's left, with the bridesmaids, flower girls and pageboys in a long row behind her. Simon smiled at her and she squeezed his arm.

'By the powers vested in me, I declare you man and wife. You may now kiss the bride,' smiled the minister. Simon lifted the veil and folded it over Helena's head. They embraced and Simon kissed her. It was a happy moment.

As the retinue came out of the main doors, family and friends converged on the newlyweds showering them with confetti. They split up as guests lined up to shake Simon's hand, while Helena was inundated with kisses. She looked demure and radiant, smiling with pleasure at the goodwill and love she received. A man kissed her gently on the mouth.

'Robert Morton,' she cried in delight, 'I'm so pleased you're here.'

He looked at her intently. 'It may be a happy day for you, Helena, but for me it's one of the saddest days of my life. I should have been the bridegroom.'

'Robert, you're my friend, you'll always be my friend. I never kept you under any misapprehension. You knew I loved Simon.'

'True, but I never gave up hope, until today. Now it's final. I love you, Helena, and I think I always will. If ever you need my help I'll be there.'

'Thank you, Robert.' Helena was taken aback at his forthrightness. She had never realised his feelings ran so deep. 'Are you still with the police?'

'Yes, I'm doing well. I am due for promotion soon.' He moved away. 'Goodbye Helena, remember what I said.'

The manager opened the door to the honeymoon suite and a porter placed their suitcases in the dressing room. A bottle of champagne on ice waited in the lounge. He popped the cork. 'Welcome to the Mount Nelson Hotel, Mr and Mrs Roux. Congratulations on your marriage. May it be long and happy.'

'Much appreciated.' Simon escorted the manager to the door. 'Please don't disturb us tomorrow.' The manager smiled knowingly.

He strolled with Helena on to the balcony. A full moon bathed Table Mountain in a soft, eerie light. The mountain towered above them, huge and brooding, heightening Helena's uneasiness.

Simon put his arm protectively around her. 'May we have a wonderful marriage together.' He lifted his glass in a toast.

'I'll drink to that.' She clinked her glass against his, appearing much calmer than she felt.

'I want to make you a good husband,' smiled Simon. 'I love you very much, my darling.' He gathered her in his arms and carried her over the threshold of the large bedroom. The soft bedside lights were on and the bed had been turned down. Simon dumped her unceremoniously on the double bed, falling on top of her.

'Not so quick, I must go to the bathroom first.' Helena stuttered in agitation as she wriggled out from under him.

Simon let her go reluctantly and returned to the balcony. There were probably certain first-night rites to be observed and Helena surely wanted it all perfect.

Ten minutes later he heard her return to the bedroom. He went through to the bathroom and took a shower. With only a towel around his waist he entered the bedroom. Helena was sitting up in bed paging through a magazine. She had brushed her hair until it shone in the lamplight, and it hung in auburn tresses to her shoulders. Fresh lipstick highlighted her mouth. Her pink satin night-dress, low-cut with thin shoulder-straps, showed her breasts to perfection. Her skin was milky and soft. She looked utterly desirable.

'Please close the door, Simon.' Helena's voice was terse and her movements forced.

Simon slipped between the white satin sheets and removed the towel around his waist. He felt himself lying on rough material when he was expecting soft satin. He lifted the top sheet and saw a large towel. 'Whatever is this for?'

'Don't ask stupid questions Simon Roux. You know I'm a virgin.'

Simon took her into his strong arms. 'Come here, my sexy wife.'

'Simon, please be gentle with me, I'm scared. Let's turn off the lights.' Helena pressed the switch of her bedside lamp.

Simon groaned. He wanted to savour the sight of her body. The room was in darkness except for a few rays of moonlight streaming in through the chinks in the curtains. He kissed her, trying to force open her mouth with his tongue.

'Let's just kiss normally,' she implored.

The satin of her night-dress felt cool under his hand as he squeezed her breast. He lifted the front and sucked her nipples, using his tongue to make up for the French kisses he was missing. She did not respond.

Simon slipped his hand up her thighs and felt the wiry hairs of her womanhood. She stiffened beside him. He was puzzled, but pushed his fingers deeper. She was dry, secreting no love juices, and he had to push hard to get his fingers inside.

Helena sat up in bed and gasped. 'Slowly, Simon, that's very sore.' There was a tremor in her voice.

'Sorry,' he mumbled, 'but you must remember that I'm also inexperienced.'

46

He was fully erect. Animal instinct took over, he needed release. He had waited too many years, he needed to feel the ultimate joy.

He opened her legs and tried to push into her. His action was like sandpaper, rasping inside her as her soft mucous membrane lacerated. Helena screamed in agony and desperately rolled him off her.

'What's the problem now?' Simon asked gruffly.

'Oh darling! Can't we wait until tomorrow?' she sobbed.

'No. Tonight's our wedding night. I know you've never made love but it will be all right. Trust me.' This time there was more force behind his thrusts and he felt a tearing as he entered her.

Helena cried out and brought her knees up to ease the pain. Simon took this as a sign of acceptance. He was not aware of Helena's sobbing, too preoccupied with his own pleasure.

He came up on his hands, straightening his arms, arching his back and let out a bull-like bellow. His whole body shuddered spasmodically from the sensations of the after thrusts. Simon exhaled, collapsing on top of Helena, and slowly regained his breath.

Helena pushed him off her, gathering up the towel. Simon saw it was stained dark red with blood. There was a feeling on her bladder she had never felt before. She rushed to the bathroom and sat on the toilet with her elbows on her knees, her hands over her eyes, crying uncontrollably.

Simon was asleep when she returned. She slipped in next to him, her mind in turmoil. Sex had been worse, much worse, than she had imagined. How was she going to cope in the future? She lay awake, troubled and unhappy.

Simon was tucking into a hearty breakfast when Helena walked stiffly on to the balcony. She hurt and her eyes were red-rimmed. She flopped into a chair totally disillusioned. Simon looked up and smiled broadly – he was relaxed, without a care in the world.

'It was wonderful last night. Was it good for you?' There was no answer. She avoided his eyes. 'Let's go back to the bedroom for . . . you know . . .'

'Not during the day.' She was adamant, her mind revolting at the thought.

'Why not? What's wrong with sex during the day?'

'It's a long story.' Her tone was muted as she mumbled. 'Leave it for now.'

Lovemaking that night was not as rushed. Again Helena changed in the bathroom, coming to bed in her night-dress. She still insisted on turning off the lights. Simon managed to remove her clothing this time. She complied with his lovemaking, but did not initiate any actions.

When he had finished she slipped out of the bed and hurried to the bathroom. Simon lay thinking, unhappy. Was he doing something wrong? Why was she frigid? What was supposed to be a shared, fulfilling experience was turning into a one-sided, automated affair.

Helena was away so long, Simon fell into a troubled sleep. She listened at the door for his steady breathing before she re-entered the room and slipped gently between the sheets.

The next night it was the same and the next. It was time to broach the subject before it took hold and became deep resentment. 'Helena, you don't seem to enjoy our lovemaking. Tell me what's the matter.'

She looked at him for a long time before answering, 'My darling, I'm here for you. We didn't get married only for sex but because we love each other, because we wanted to make a life together and raise a family.'

'But why? Surely sex is for both of us? Shouldn't you feel more than you do? Aren't women also supposed to – you know – come?'

She realised the moment of truth had arrived, the dark secret she had held inside her for so many years would have to come into the open. 'Simon, my darling, what I am going to tell you might shock you, but you have a right to know.'

'What?'

'Uncle Andries. He was not really my uncle but a friend of my parents whom I called uncle. I had known him since I was a little girl. He gave me sweets to sit on his lap. Oh! Simon, I can't go on.'

Simon realised something was bottled up inside her, something which had to come out if they were to stand a chance of happiness together. He held her tenderly. 'Please, tell me, darling.'

Half crying, half talking, she mumbled, 'He was a bachelor who used to baby-sit us. My brother was small and went to bed early. I used to stay up to listen to the radio. He would give me sweets to sit on his lap.' She lapsed into a tormented silence.

'What happened when you sat on his lap?'

'He played with me,' she shrieked, throwing herself on to the pillow and sobbing.

'How did he play with you?' Simon was alarmed.

'He had terrible nicotine-stained fingers. He was a motor mechanic, with old oil and grease under his finger-nails. He would force those filthy fingers into me, seeing how many he could get inside.' Helena flopped on the pillow, burying her head in her hands, anguished sobs racking her body.

'Helena, look at me. Sit up.' He felt disgusted but knew he had to see the matter through to its conclusion, otherwise there would always be a cloud over their marriage. 'Is there more? Tell me,' he urged.

'He took out his . . . his . . .' unable to say the word, Helena pointed to Simon's crotch. 'He took out *that*, and made me play with it.' Her voice shook with revulsion.

Simon glared at her in horror. 'What? You mean you played with his manhood?'

Seeing his reaction the resolve left her and her face sagged. She, who had always been in control of every situation, was now a bundle of nerves, shaking in trepidation. He grabbed her roughly by the arms and shook her violently. 'Tell me in detail, Helena, tell me!'

She winced as his fingers dug into her flesh and she turned her face away in shame.

'Dammit woman, talk!' bellowed Simon.

Her voice quavered. 'Oh! God it's too terrible to tell you. I should never have started this conversation. It was better when you didn't know. You'll despise me for ever.'

'You can't stop now.' He was brutal with her. 'Get it out into the open.'

'I didn't know what it was then,' she blurted out, 'but now I know it was a condom. He would put a sweet, a nigger ball, in the little sac at the end, making me roll it down over his . . . his . . . you know what. I had to hold the sweet in my mouth, suck it, play with it using my tongue and nibbling at the sweet through the crêpe de Chine. He said it was a game and I believed him. He was an uncle, little girls believe their uncles.' Helena groaned, trying to rationalise her actions.

'Go on, I'm listening,' Simon stated coldly.

Helena looked at him closely and trembled when she saw the loathing in his eyes, but there was no turning back now. 'While I sucked and bit at the sweet, he would lie back in the chair groaning. I thought it was part of the game and would suck harder. He would groan louder, pushing *it* down my throat until I choked. He would shudder finally and I would feel a warmness spurt into the sac. Then he made me bite through the condom to get the sweet as my reward. He forced me to eat the nigger ball, watching in ecstasy as the stickiness dribbled out of my mouth.' Helena fell back exhausted, drained by the memory and stressed with pain.

Simon felt rage burst inside him. He was appalled. He sat up, knotting his fists, shouting, 'Where is that bastard now. Tell me, Helena. I'll kill him. I promise you I'll kill him.'

'He's dead,' she sobbed. 'He died a few years ago.'

Simon pushed her roughly to one side and jumped up. He kicked the door in fury. He banged his fist against the wall. 'The bastard! The bloody bastard!' he screamed in resentment as he held his injured fist in his hand, pacing up and down the room. He flung open the wardrobe and grabbed a bottle of KWV brandy. Breaking the seal he tossed the top to one side and gulped down large mouthfuls before Helena reacted. She led him to the bed, stroking him as a mother cat would her kitten.

'Okay, Simon, it's okay.' She spoke reassuringly, and slowly his chest stopped heaving as he calmed down. Gently she took the bottle away and he didn't object. Now she was in control and she held him in her arms.

He looked at her forlornly, his speech starting to slur. 'When did all this happen?'

'It started when I was about six and went on till I was about thirteen.'

'Why so long? Surely you realised what you were doing at thirteen.' His eyes flashed in anger.

'When I was small I thought it was a game, but later he threatened to tell my parents about me. He blackmailed me into believing my parents would send me to a reform school if they found out. I was gullible. I believed him. I was scared.'

'How did it stop?'

50

'I bit him. One night I bit him as hard as I could. I hurt him. He screamed in pain. I was glad. He slapped me across the face but he never tried to molest me again. He stopped baby-sitting us.'

'You never told anyone about him?' Simon searched her face.

'You are the first to know. I was too ashamed to tell my parents. I'm glad I've told you. Perhaps now you understand why I can't enjoy sex. I cannot forget that man's horrible fingers or his revolting thing. It's not your fault. It's my own private hell – something I have to live with. Please understand. The man never tried to have sex with me. I still kept myself as a virgin for you.'

'You're a liar,' shouted Simon, an ugly expression on his face. 'You always told me you were keeping yourself pure for our wedding night.' He grabbed the bottle and took another gulp. 'I believed you – now I hear you are soiled, nothing but a bloody whore.'

Helena went cold. She had hoped Simon would be sympathetic. Damn brandy! It made him aggressive. 'Please try and understand, my darling.' She looked at him imploringly, begging him to accept the situation. 'I have a problem and I need your support.' There were tears in her eyes. 'Whenever you need me, I'll be there for you. I'll be a good wife to you and mother to our children. My heart, my soul, my body is yours, but don't expect me to enjoy sex, ever.'

He seethed with anger, raising his fist to strike her, but instead grunted and turned on his side. With his back to her he was instantly asleep. Helena rolled herself into a tight little ball, alone in her misery on her side of the bed, and cried herself to sleep.

The rest of the honeymoon was strained. Neither of them referred to the matter again – it was like a ghost they had locked in the cupboard hoping that it would go away.

Simon avoided sex until the last night, when he finished the bottle of brandy and rolled her roughly on to her back, obtaining his satisfaction as soon as possible.

Simon and Helena moved into the guest house next to the manor house – a miniature Cape cottage with a steeply sloping thatched roof and Cape-style gables at each end. Rough plastered walls painted with white lime wash, and bottle-green doors and window frames finished off the building. The manor house and cottage were

51

set in the same large garden, a path winding through a shrub border separating the two dwellings.

Helena furnished it with Cape-cottage furniture, lots of floral materials and scatter cushions. The bedroom gave her the most joy. She had discovered an antique brass bed in a junk shop, and she and Simon spent nights working on it. It now took pride of place in the bedroom, restored to its former glory.

'I love my home.' Helena bubbled with enthusiasm. 'I'll have to tear myself away each day to go teaching.' She sat in front of the dressing table.

Simon watched Helena brushing her hair until it shone in the light. He looked at her closely and she smiled at him. She was most attractive when she smiled. He found the brush strokes provocative and felt a stirring in his loins. It had been three weeks and he needed release. He drew the curtains and closed the door.

'Do you want to do it tonight, darling?' Dismay flashed in her eyes and she trembled slightly. She could not help herself.

'Yes,' he replied roughly.

'I must first lubricate myself.' She hurried to the bathroom.

'Damn,' he cursed, feeling the desire draining out of him as he thought of her lying under him, mute and unresponsive. He needed a drink and walked through to the lounge. He poured half a glass from the brandy decanter and downed it in a gulp. He felt calmer. He looked up as Helena ran back to the bedroom and saw her look of fear. He poured another glass and another. He felt dizzy and put his hand to the wall for support, muttering to himself. His marriage was blissful until it came to sex. Wasn't lovemaking supposed to be a spontaneous act between husband and wife, not some pre-planned, calculated action?

Anger welled inside him as she lay submissively waiting for him. Her posture seemed one of capitulation. 'Don't look so damn scared, Helena,' he fumed as he stripped off his clothes.

'Turn out the light please, darling.'

'Not this time.' He spoke decisively, with a slight slur. 'I don't want to do it in the dark like some sort of night creature.' He stood next to the bed. 'Fondle me – make me big.'

She jerked away. 'Please, darling, we've been through this before.' Her voice was high-pitched and crackling. 'Just get on with it.'

His masculinity threatened and rejected, something inside Simon's brain snapped and he slapped her hard across the face, his features contorted in fury.

'You hit me!' she screamed incredulously, scrabbling to the furthermost corner of the bed.

He lunged at her and hit her again. She fought back in a frenzy, panting from exertion, her eyes ablaze with fury, but she was no match for Simon's superior strength. The physical grappling excited him – at last he was getting a reaction from her, something he had craved all along. She fought him, but he forced her on to her back, pinning her arms above her head and containing her struggles with his weight. Her writhing body against him brought him to full erection and he entered her, breathing excitedly. The old dread overtook Helena; she stiffened and lay compliantly, waiting for him to finish. Disappointment creased Simon's brow – the titillation was gone. There was no fervour or passion, it was only a release. As quickly as possible he finished and rolled over to his side of the bed.

Helena ran from the room, tears of humiliation running down her cheeks. She shuddered when she saw the first signs of a bruise forming under her eye. She bathed, scrubbing herself over and over again, and then made a bed for herself in the lounge. Sleep was impossible and her mind reeled as her emotions seethed and she reasoned with herself. It was all her fault, she concluded, that he must get drunk before he could make love to her. It was also her fault that he needed to hit her to get a reaction. Helena crept back to the marital bed. She snuggled up guiltily against Simon's back. He didn't notice.

'I am looking for work.' A tall, slender black girl looked pleadingly at the farm manager.

'Sir. You address me as sir or *baas* here. Do you understand?' the manager barked.

'I am looking for work, sir,' she repeated lamely.

'What sort of work do you want?'

'Any sort of work, sir, as long as I can earn some money and stay on the farm.'

'We don't allow wives or girlfriends in the black men's compound – only single males.'

'I am not a wife or a girlfriend, sir, I'm alone.'

'You're still a kaffir and black women are trouble. No, we don't have work for you.'

At that moment Simon came past. He saw the woman's shoulders droop in disappointment as she slowly turned away.

'Can I help you?' he asked in Afrikaans.

'I am sorry, sir, I only speak English.' She looked him straight in the eye.

'Okay, what's the problem?'

'The other boss says there is no work for me, because you do not have accommodation, sir.'

'Work we do have. It's our late-spring thinning and picking season and we are short of hands.' Simon's head thumped from the night before and he pressed his fingers to his temples, looking inquiringly at his manager.

'I told her we don't allow kaffir women to stay in the compound. They cause trouble.'

'My cousin works on your farm, sir.'

'Who is he?' The manager looked at her suspiciously.

'He is Jafta, my mother's brother's child.' Her voice was sweet and lyrical.

'Jafta is our best black man. He's reliable, honest and hardworking,' said Simon. 'Can't we find a place for her?'

'There is a single room free in the compound, if you really want to hire her.'

'Well, hire her then.' Simon walked away, stopping when he saw the relief on her face.

'What's your name?'

'I am Nomisile Memani, sir.'

During the early part of summer the first peaches ripened on Hermitage. The Van Riebeeck variety was picked in mid-November and the crop was good. A high percentage would be packed for export.

Simon parked his pick-up and strolled into the orchard. He watched as the labourers climbed the ladders and reached for the fruit, handling it gently to prevent bruising. He strolled further and stopped when he heard a sweet, clear voice singing in Xhosa.

'Good morning, sir.'

'Morning, Nomisile,' he replied, remembering her name.

In the warm sunshine she had stripped to her traditional way of dressing. She wore only a long skirt, the hem tucked in under the belt, showing her bare torso and long, shapely legs. She stood facing Simon, unashamed, for she was used to dressing that way in the Transkei. Simon was shocked at first for his coloured labourers never bared themselves, but he could not help admiring her figure.

Nomisile was tall for a woman but slender, holding herself with dignity. Her shoulders were straight, her back upright and proud. He glanced down at her exposed breasts. They were full and perfectly shaped – the breasts of a woman in her prime, before the ravages of suckling babies caused them to droop. Her nipples stood out like ripe black cherries. He dropped his eyes. Her narrow waist curved into shapely hips. Her long legs were beautiful and finely muscled, like those of an athlete honed from exercise. Her feet were narrow and strong with high arches and perfect toes. Her whole body glowed like polished ebony.

She was the most perfect specimen of womanhood Simon had seen. Helena hid her body from him, but here was a woman who unashamedly displayed herself. Simon could not take his eyes off her.

If her body was stunning her face was enchanting. It was oval, the most distinguishing feature being her huge almond-shaped eyes. They were alert and lively, but still soft and tender, her irises a luminous chestnut brown. Her ears were neat and compact, her lips full and slightly pouting, the nose shapely and small. Her head was framed by a halo of tight, curly black hair.

It took Simon a while to regain his composure. 'Are you enjoying your work here at Hermitage?'

'Yes, sir. The weather is hot, like the Transkei. There is food here, everybody eats well. At home there is no rain, we have a drought, sir.'

Simon was fascinated by her good English, which was without an accent. 'You speak English like a true Englishman, not like a South African. Where did you learn to speak like that?'

'I learnt English from my teacher at the mission school in Qunu, sir. She was English, the London Missionary Society sent her out, sir.'

'What standard did you pass?'

'Standard eight, sir.'

'That's very good. Why did you not go on to matric?'

'I am a woman, sir.'

'What does that matter?'

'A woman does not need an education, sir. She must become a wife and mother. Only a man needs education, to earn money for his family, sir.'

Strange, thought Simon, how white and black values differed. 'All right, Nomisile, enjoy your work.'

'Thank you, sir.'

'Why do you call me sir so often?'

'The manager said I'm a kaffir and I must address him as sir when I speak to him.'

Simon laughed aloud. 'You don't have to call me sir after every sentence. Only once, when you greet me.'

'Thank you.' Nomisile smiled, her whole face lighting up and displaying perfectly formed, brilliant white teeth.

He was captivated by her beauty and vivacity. He walked away with a twinge of uneasiness.

'The maid didn't turn up this morning,' Helena's voice was sharp with irritation. 'Your lunch isn't ready. Sorry, darling. It's really been a blue Monday.'

'Rosie was stabbed over the weekend. They had a wild party and the *vaaljapie* must have flowed very freely.'

'When will she be back at work?'

'She'll be away for a week or two. Her husband stabbed her in the chest. He has a hangover today and doesn't even know what he did.'

'Please organise another maid for us, Simon. In less than a month it will be the Christmas holidays and we'll be off to Hermanus. We must have dependable help.'

'There's a new black girl from the Transkei who started last week. She might be suitable.' Simon remembered Nomisile vividly and he felt a strange excitement as he heard his wife say, 'Well please send her to me so I can interview her.'

There was a knock at the back door. Helena opened it to a black man. 'Good evening, madam. It is Jafta. The master says you wish to speak to my cousin, Nomisile.'

'Yes, Jafta, where is she?'

'She is here, madam.' He called Nomisile, who stepped into view.

The first thing that struck Helena were her large, doe-like eyes and she took an immediate liking to her. She was open-faced, the sort of face you could rely on. Nomisile readily agreed to the terms, for her pay and work conditions would be much better than those of an ordinary farm worker. There would be more money to send home to her family.

Nomisile started work in the house the next morning. She was quick, friendly and efficient, needing only to be told once how to do something.

Helena had resumed her teaching career, so was away at school during the mornings. Nomisile made Simon his morning tea and served him his lunch. He enjoyed talking to her. She was like no other black person he had ever met. They had interesting and informative discussions.

Simon liked to make her laugh; her whole face lit up with pleasure and her eyes sparkled. He was captivated by her. He often thought of her magnificent figure but dismissed his day-dreaming guiltily, scolding himself for finding her desirable.

4

The great trek to the sea took place in the second week of December. Enough meat, groceries and clothes had to be taken for a whole month. Simon and Helena took the main bedroom: they would have the house to themselves for Christmas as Paulus and Marie were away, visiting with parliamentary colleagues.

Nomisile occupied the maid's room behind the house. She spring-cleaned the single room until it shone, even inveigling Simon to repaint the interior. Helena was so impressed she bought new linen and blankets for Nomisile, plus a wardrobe for her clothes. Nomisile's pride was infectious and Helena helped her put up pictures on the wall. She also gave Nomisile a table cloth for her bedside table and a comfortable armchair.

Because she worked quickly, Nomisile usually finished her morning duties by ten o'clock. Helena let her go off until lunch-time.

Nomisile would run down the steps to Fick's Pool. She shook her head sadly each time she saw the large sign at the tidal pool: SWIMMING RESERVED FOR EUROPEANS ONLY – BY ORDER – TOWN CLERK. So invariably she skirted the pool and would sit for hours on the surrounding rocks, fascinated by the endless movement of the sea. As she was fully clothed and not swimming she was not breaking the law, and no one bothered her.

Walking along Westcliff, Simon spotted Nomisile on the rocks. He strolled down to her. She was startled out of her reverie and looked up at him in surprise.

'Why do you spend hours watching the sea, Nomisile?'

'It reminds me of home. When I was young we used to go to a place on the Transkei coast called esiKhaleni, the Place of the Sound. The white people call it Hole-in-the-Wall.'

'I've heard of it.' Simon kept her talking as he enjoyed listening

59

to her melodious voice. Since they had been in Hermanus he had not been alone with her as was the case during the mornings at Hermitage. Now Helena was always present. He realised how much he missed their times together and wanted the moment to last. 'Tell me about Hole-in-the-Wall.'

'It is beautiful. There is a gigantic rock that juts out into the sea.' Her expressive eyes sparkled as the memories flooded back. 'Over the years the waves have made a large hole by tunnelling through its base. The waves crash through, making a great noise. That is where its name comes from. We used to swim in the sea there. Here we are not allowed to,' she said wistfully.

Simon sat down on the rock next to her. 'Sometimes the white man's laws may be strange, but it's government policy. Each race must have its own place to live and work, to play and also swim.'

She shot back at him, 'Then why can I work in a white man's area for you, and even live on the same plot in a white man's suburb?'

Simon shook his head at the anomaly. The only answer he could think of was that the white man chose to ignore apartheid when it suited him. To hide his embarrassment he said quickly, 'If you really want to swim, I'll take you to a beach where black people are allowed to bathe. There is a little coloured town near here called Hawston. It has a lovely beach, much nicer than Hermanus.'

'Oh! Yes please.' Her whole face lit up with joy. 'When can we go?'

'I can take you this afternoon.'

'I'm taking Nomisile to swim at Hawston this afternoon,' Simon announced at lunch. 'Helena, do you want to come?'

She shook her head quickly, hating the combination of sand and sun. 'I'll give it a skip as the wind is blowing, but you two go off and enjoy yourselves.'

It was well worth the drive. He parked the Mercedes-Benz in the shade of a tree and they walked down a narrow path to the sea. Once on Hawston beach Nomisile stripped to her panties and plunged into the water. Her body was magnificent, her firm breasts bouncing invitingly as she jumped to crest a wave. The beach was deserted, they could just as easily have been alone on a tropical island. He sat on the dry sand and watched her. She was so vital, so vibrant. Simon was bewitched. Nomisile came running out of the surf to him, like a nymph out of a lake. The water streaming off her body, making her skin shine like polished coal, excited him.

They drove back to Hermanus, she bubbling with enthusiasm, he quiet and pensive, scolding himself secretly. How can I have such thoughts? My father is a member of parliament and there's the Immorality Act. A black girl is taboo for a white man.

He blotted the consequences from his mind. He wanted her too strongly. He started taking Nomisile to Hawston every afternoon.

Simon came to breakfast with a huge hangover. He was still angry, casting dark looks in Helena's direction. Part of his anger stemmed from her frigidity, which caused him to drink, but there was another anger inside him. An anger at the feelings that Nomisile evoked. Was it love? He was sure it was, but love across the colour-line was illegal and contrary to his strict upbringing. What should he do? He was losing control, frustrated almost to breaking point.

Helena sported a cut lip and was fidgety, blaming herself for another night of miserable sex. She didn't speak to her husband as Nomisile served the meal in a strained silence.

Angrily pushing his plate away, Simon rose to his feet. 'I'm going back to Paarl. I need to check on Hermitage.' He needed time alone.

The house was quiet without the huge presence of Simon. Helena and Nomisile became friends during the hours of baking and sewing. Helena felt she could confide in Nomisile and discuss intimate details she could not reveal to anyone else.

'What do you do if you do not want sex and your husband forces himself on you?' Helena asked guiltily.

Nomisile was silent for a long time. She remembered her initiation, how it was the woman's task to do the bidding of her husband. Nomisile replied quietly, 'If your husband wants sex you *must* give it to him. That is the duty of a good wife.'

Helena paled, hoping for a more favourable answer from her friend, then immediately changed the subject.

One morning while they were working together in the kitchen, Helena said to her, 'You're an educated person, Nomisile – it's degrading to refer to me as madam. Please call me Helena.'

Simon took the matter up with her. 'How can you let Nomisile call you by your first name? Imagine what my father and mother and all our friends would think.'

'Simon, just because she's black doesn't mean she's not a person. I've also told her to call you Simon. Why shouldn't she, it's the name everyone else knows you by. I had long talks with her while you were away. She's not just a plain black girl, she's of royal blood. Her uncle is the Paramount Chief of the Thembu, one of the most important Xhosa tribes. That makes her a princess. We're just plain commoners, so who are we to insist she calls us madam or sir?'

Simon was secretly delighted. Helena had just solved a problem for him. The next day he spoke to Nomisile in front of Helena. 'Nomisile, you may call me Simon.' However, he could not forget his deep-rooted conservative upbringing entirely. 'Except when my father, the staff or other people are around.'

Nomisile gave him a knowing smile. 'I understand perfectly, Simon.'

'May we invite a princess to dinner tonight?' Helena looked at him sweetly. From then on Nomisile ate with them.

Simon could not wait until after lunch each day, when he took Nomisile to Hawston. Once Helena accompanied them, but soon tired of the beach and went back to the car. Thereafter she always made an excuse to stay at home. Much to Simon's disappointment, Helena purchased a bathing costume for Nomisile and talked her into wearing it. The visits to the beach became the highlight of Simon's existence.

'Why don't you swim with me?' Nomisile asked.

'Because this beach is reserved for blacks and coloureds.'

'Will you be arrested if the police catch you swimming at a blacks-only beach?'

'You see, it works like this – I can swim at a blacks-only beach but then——' His voice tailed off and he laughed at the ludicrous situation. 'But you can't swim at a whites-only beach.'

Nomisile merely smiled, unable to understand the white man's logic. Simon took off his shirt and sandals. The sun made him drowsy. He lay on his back and was soon asleep. Nomisile returned and gazed down at him. He was big and solid like a Xhosa warrior, except his chest and shoulders were more muscular than those of any man she had seen in the Transkei. His legs were also hairy, not like the smooth-legged men of her tribe. She did not find this displeasing.

Simon woke as her shadow passed over him. He rolled over to tan his back. He rubbed in sun-tan lotion, but could not reach between his shoulder-blades.

'Let me help you.' The feel of her strong fingers massaging made him want her very urgently. 'Turn over, I'll do your front.' By this time he had a full erection and was not sure what her reaction would be if she saw the bulge in his costume. 'I want to tan my back first,' he mumbled awkwardly.

My God, Simon Roux, he thought, what is happening to you? He realised there was little he could do to stop the feelings that were starting to consume him. He day-dreamed about making love to Nomisile.

'Come and swim with me please, Simon!' Nomisile cried, standing over him with an extended hand. 'Come, I'll help you up.'

What the hell, he thought, this is a deserted beach, nobody will see us. He put out his hand and Nomisile pulled him up. Knowing he was a big man she jerked extra hard. He came to his feet fast. She overbalanced backwards. Simon's natural reaction was to catch her. He stepped forward and his arms encircled her, pulling her towards him. The next thing he knew she was up against his chest, her almond eyes growing larger, her mouth open in surprise. He bent down and kissed her on the lips.

Nomisile jerked in alarm. She was playing with fire! She tried to wriggle out of Simon's embrace but he had powerful arms. Simon, exalted at the feel of her against him, squeezed her tightly. He kissed her again, more slowly. This time she did not resist.

She struggled to regain her breath. Simon relaxed his grip. She slipped out of his arms and breathlessly grabbed his hand. 'Let's swim.' The two of them ran hand in hand into the surf. Like two boisterous children they splashed each other, diving under the waves, ducking one another under the water. The sea was their camouflage, hiding their uncertainty from each other. While they frolicked in the surf they did not have to face reality. Walking back up the beach they were suddenly strangers – embarrassed and not sure what to say to each other.

I love her, thought Simon, but strangely enough I also love Helena. Could one man love two women, each in a different way? He was confused.

Nomisile was not colour conscious – she saw nothing wrong with loving a white man. There was a law against it, she knew, but it was a white man's law, made without consultation with her people. She did not feel she was betraying Helena's trust as it was Xhosa custom that men were permitted more than one woman. Her feelings churned inside her. She was utterly captivated by Simon, but she also sensed a great danger.

The sun was a golden orb in the west, and it was long after Simon and Nomisile had returned to Hermanus when the police van drove through Hawston. Near the beach they picked up a drunk coloured man lying in the bushes. Old Shadrack was well known to the police and they swore at him as they loaded him into the back of the van. '*Donnerse hotnot*, this is the third time in two weeks we've arrested you for being drunk.'

They drove him back to the police station in Hermanus. 'Book him,' the policeman instructed the duty sergeant. He left to resume his evening patrol. The charge office was deserted except for Shadrack and the sergeant.

'Sarge, be nice to me, man, let me go.'

'Let you go?' laughed the sergeant. 'I'm locking you up and you'll behave yourself in court tomorrow.'

'If I give you some important information won't you release me?' pleaded Shadrack.

'Ha! You old soak, what information could you possibly have?'

'Can a white man kiss a black woman?' Shadrack baited the policeman.

Sergeant van Blerk pricked up his ears. They had not yet had an Immorality Act case in Hermanus. If he could get a conviction the station commander would praise him and he could get promotion.

'Will you let me go if I tell you?'

'The arresting officer told me to book you. I can't let you go.'

He grabbed Shadrack by the scruff of his collar and pushed him down the passage. Van Blerk unlocked the cell door and followed him in. 'Now, tell me about the white man and the black girl.'

'Oh, it's nothing.' Shadrack hedged his bets.

'*Bliksemse hotnot*. Don't hold out on me.' Van Blerk hit him in the mouth. Shadrack fell to the floor spitting blood. The sergeant grabbed him by his shirt front and, propping him up against the wall, slapped him twice more across the face. 'Either you tell me or I'll use the hose-pipe on you. Then you'll talk for sure.' Van Blerk was perspiring freely, his fat, bloated face wet from the exertion.

'Not the hose-pipe, please, sarge. I'll tell you.'

'I'm waiting. Talk, man.'

'You see, *basie*, I live in Hawston, next to the sea. Every afternoon after we come back from the fishing trip, I buy a bottle of wine and I go and lie under the milkwood trees to drink it. Every day at three o'clock this white man comes to the beach with a black girl.'

'What do they do?' Van Blerk was impatient to get to the point.

'They lie on the sand and they swim.'

'That's not against the law, you stupid old fool. What else?'

'Today, Sarge, I see them kiss and hold each other.'

'Do they do more?'

'Like what, Sarge?'

'Do they screw?'

'I don't know,' muttered Shadrack.

The sergeant slapped him again; the force of the blow landed him in the corner. He whimpered in fear, slowly sitting up with his head buzzing. '*Ja, hulle naai*,' screamed Shadrack, cringing in anticipation of another blow.

'On the beach?'

'In the bushes. They kiss on the beach and screw in the bushes.'

'Every afternoon?'

'Yes, Sarge, yes, Sarge.'

Sergeant van Blerk returned to the charge office, a look of glee on his face. He had a suspect and he was going to make history by getting the station's first conviction under the Immorality Act.

Parking the car just off the road at Hawston, Simon touched Nomisile's hand and experienced a ripple of pleasure. She responded to his touch by turning and smiling at him. Simon bent down and kissed her on the mouth. He felt her lips respond.

'We have to be careful, Simon. What we are doing is against the law. There are people coming down the road, we mustn't be reckless.'

'You're right. Come, let's go and swim.'

A battered old coloured man sat under a tree, a bottle of wine in his hand. '*Basie, basie*, I want to talk to you.'

Simon ignored him. 'What does he want?' Nomisile asked, feeling sorry for the man.

'Oh, he's just some drunk. He probably wants a few cents for his next bottle.'

The beach stretched out before them. The afternoon was hot and cloudless. The sea was a sparkling blue to the horizon, contrasting with the lighter blue of the sky.

'There are some fishermen on those rocks over there.' Nomisile pointed to the left, her profile etched against the sky.

She's exquisite, thought Simon, his heart beating faster. The emotion he felt for Nomisile superseded anything he had felt for Helena. This was exciting, breathtaking, startling and provocative, all rolled into one. Is this what love is all about? He moved closer to her, desire making him brash.

'We must be careful.' She walked away to hide her own fervour. 'We'll get into trouble if we're careless.'

Sergeant van Blerk settled himself between the tufts of tall couch grass on the crest of a dune, commanding a panoramic view of the beach. He was sweating in the black police uniform. He looked at his watch: three o'clock. He decided to wait until four. That old drunk bastard was probably talking rubbish.

Van Blerk reflected on the story he had spun the station commander to obtain an unmarked car. The lieutenant had wanted to send a constable to accompany him, but he had persuaded him he was quite capable of looking after a 'highly sensitive' investigation himself. I want all the credit for this arrest, he thought grimly.

Through his binoculars he saw Simon and Nomisile walk on to the beach. An evil grin touched the corners of his mouth. Old Shadrack was right after all!

Big bugger, he thought, noting Simon's powerful build, as he stripped down to his costume. He looked at the black woman, noting her lithe, shapely figure. Not bad for a black. Usually they were podgy, with big backsides – built for comfort, not for speed. He licked his lips as he saw her breasts filling the front of her costume. She would make a good lay, he decided. He was not averse to taking advantage of black girls when he arrested them on some trumped-up charge. He was prepared to release them for certain favours. It did not bother him that he was prepared to ruin Simon's and Nomisile's lives when he had been guilty of the same crime.

He trained the lenses, straining to see clearly. Simon and Nomisile were next to each other in the water but Van Blerk could not make out what they were doing.

Nomisile teased Simon under water, pulling at his bathing trunks. He dived down and swam between her legs, unbalancing her, tipping her over backwards. They both came up spluttering and laughing delightedly.

They ran back up the beach and flopped on to their towels. Nomisile rubbed oil on his back. Sergeant van Blerk expelled a quiet oath. How could a white man allow a dirty kaffir's hands on his body?

They lay side by side, facing each other. Simon had his back to Van Blerk. His broad, muscular body hid Nomisile from the sergeant's view.

Were they kissing or fondling? Van Blerk asked himself.

Simon lovingly traced the profile of her face, running his finger from her forehead down to her chin, into her neck, over her adam's apple, stopping discreetly at the start of the cleft between her breasts.

She tugged at his chest hairs; Simon playfully complained. She held his hand, comparing it with hers. She had a narrow hand with long fingers, his were broad, powerful hands with strong, workman-like fingers.

Sergeant van Blerk slithered to the next dune to get a better view. '*Fokkit,*' he cursed, for now a beach bag blocked his view. I'll wait until they go into the bushes, then I'll catch them with their pants down, in the very act, he thought triumphantly.

Simon leant forward and kissed Nomisile gently. Her lips were soft and yielding. She responded by opening her mouth and flicking her tongue. He moved closer, wanting to crush her to him.

'No, Simon. Not on the beach. Anyone could see.'

'You're right.' He flopped back in frustration. 'Time to go.' They stood up and shook the sand out of their towels. Arms around each other, they walked back to the car.

'Basie,' whispered a voice alongside the path. Simon and Nomisile saw the same old coloured man squatting in the long grass, the smell of cheap wine on his breath.

'What do you want?'

'Basie, there's a policeman after you. He's lying up there on the sand dunes, watching you with binoculars.'

Nomisile froze, her worst fears realised. The police were after her again. Her panic got the better of her and she took off, bolting down the path. Simon ran after her. Suddenly she shrieked, a high-pitched scream of terror. Nomisile had collided with Van Blerk. They fell in a tangled heap. Nomisile scrambled to get away.

The sight of the black uniform, the gleaming gold buttons down the front and the pith helmet, flashed the scene of East London into her mind. Police dressed like that had fired bullets into the crowd, killing her beloved uncle. She smelt again the acrid smell of gunpowder, she again heard the sounds of pain and she acted instinctively. Nomisile struck out at right angles to the path, through the undergrowth. A thorn tore the flesh of her arm. She looked down, seeing the dripping blood, thinking a bullet had grazed her. Terrified, she ran faster.

Simon hurried after Nomisile, calling her name. He was fit and fast, but no match for her. She was running on adrenalin, dodging between the bushes.

Sergeant van Blerk regained his feet, picked up his helmet and set off in pursuit. If they are running, they have something to hide, he concluded, struggling to keep up. He followed, crashing through the foliage. He was unfit and panting from exertion.

Nomisile reached the road and ran to the Mercedes. '*Kholesa, kholesa,*' she gasped, reverting to her Xhosa tongue in panic, urging Simon to hurry. He jumped into the car, leant across and unlocked the passenger door.

She shouted, 'Drive Simon, drive, get away! We are going to die, the policeman shot me in the arm.'

He looked across, seeing the blood. Her fear was contagious. He started the engine and sped away.

Sergeant van Blerk gave chase in his Austin. Dust from the gravel roads of Hawston billowed out behind their cars.

'He's behind us, he's chasing us!' Nomisile shouted in dread. 'Faster, faster!'

Simon broadsided at a corner, sending out a shower of gravel as he turned down a side street. He ignored stop streets, intent only on getting away.

Sergeant van Blerk was the more experienced driver, used to chasing after fugitives. Van Blerk pulled his vehicle alongside Simon's car, trying to cut him off, as the two raced neck and neck down the final stretch towards the tar road. They approached the T-junction together. Logically, Simon should have turned right towards Hermanus, but his path was blocked by the overtaking Austin. On the spur of the moment, he turned left, in the direction of Cape Town. On the open road, the greater power and speed of the Mercedes-Benz gave him the advantage over the smaller car.

Simon looked in the rear-view mirror with satisfaction. He was steadily pulling away. He had time to examine Nomisile's wound. 'That's not a bullet wound. It's only a cut.' He slowed down. 'The policeman didn't shoot you, there's no need to flee.'

'Don't stop!' shouted Nomisile in alarm. 'Go faster, Simon. Get away from him.'

'Why, what can he do to us?'

'He will kill us. White policemen kill black people,' sobbed Nomisile.

'He can't kill us without reason. He can't even arrest us without a motive. We've done nothing wrong.'

'Oh! Simon, you don't realise what it's like. The police don't need a reason – they simply kill us because we're black. I've seen it with my own eyes.'

Simon held her trembling hand. 'I promise nobody will hurt you while I'm with you. I'll protect you.'

He turned on to a side road and they took a back way to Hermanus. Van Blerk had lost them. Simon drove slowly to the suburb of Eastcliff and parked the car facing the sea. Nomisile was still shaking.

Simon longed to take her into his arms, to comfort her, but there were people about. He had to be careful. He held both her hands in his, below the level of the windows, away from spying eyes, transferring his composure to her.

'Oh Simon, I was so scared today.' She told him about the march in East London and the death of her uncle. She told him every terrifying detail, omitting nothing. He listened intently, sharing her pain, squeezing her hand in understanding. She felt better, having shared it with him.

Helena bent down and kissed Simon on the cheek. He glanced up and put down the newspaper he was reading.

'I'm going to the village,' explained Helena. 'Christmas completely cleaned us out of fresh fruit and vegetables. I shouldn't be long.'

He nodded. 'Where is Nomisile?'

'She's finished in the house. I think she went down to Fick's Pool. It's her favourite spot.'

Simon's mind was in turmoil. He was under no delusion where he and Nomisile were headed. He realised it was totally against all his Afrikaner upbringing. He felt like a leaf borne along in a stream, swirled round and around, incapable of fighting the current. He wasn't even sure he wanted to. He felt a love, a tenderness for Nomisile that no other woman had evoked in him. He wanted to be with her, to protect her, to hold her, to love her.

He was deep in thought. He did not hear the cries at first. Then he sat up with a start. What was that? Then he heard it again.

'*Ncedisa*! *Ncedisa*!'

He sprang up. The cries came again from Fick's Pool. It was Nomisile.

Simon ran to the edge of Westcliff. He heard her again. '*Ncedisa*! Help!'

'There! There!' Three children were standing on the grass, pointing out to sea. He looked and suddenly saw it – a flash of yellow in the water. Then he saw her head and shoulders. A wave broke over Nomisile and she disappeared.

He sprinted down the path taking the steps three at a time. Simon threw off his shirt and sandals as he ran. He dived into the shallow water of the pool and with strong strokes swam to the wall. A wave forced him backward. On the ebb, he raised himself on to the wall and dived into the sea. He swam powerfully to the spot where he had last seen Nomisile, but she had disappeared.

In the trough between swells he could see nothing save the cliff top and the sea around him. As he rode the next swell he was able briefly to see a fair distance. He was desperate, for in those few seconds he had to spot her.

Was she further out? Was she being driven towards the rocks? The current was pulling him out and so he went with it, swimming further out to sea. Suddenly in front of him he glimpsed a flash of yellow. Urgency drove his arms in powerful strokes with his legs kicking in tandem. He reached the place but found nothing. The sea was deceiving and the distance hard to gauge.

He saw a hand disappear beneath the water. Swimming quickly

forward, he dived. In the murkiness below the surface he saw Nomisile's body entwined in sea bamboo. She looked dead.

No! No! Please no! he pleaded. He reached her and tried to force her upwards. The tendrils held her body firmly. He tore at the bamboo, ripping off her blouse as he pulled her free. He kicked towards the light. The double load made their ascent painfully slow. His lungs could hold out no longer. He felt the salty tang as sea water shot into his mouth.

They broke the surface together. Simon took in huge lungfuls of air, then retched salt water. He held her, treading water to keep them afloat. Nomisile seemed lifeless. She was not breathing. He squeezed her to his chest, his heaving stomach pushing against her diaphragm. Water gushed out of her mouth and nostrils. She gasped and took in a mouthful of air.

She's alive! he rejoiced. He forced the water out of her lungs, then allowed her to suck in another breath. Her ragged breaths became normal. She opened her eyes and looked at him. It was the most wondrous sight Simon had seen.

'Simon . . . you found me,' she gasped.

'My beauty, of course I found you. I love you.' He pulled her closer and kissed her. They spluttered and laughed together, living for the moment. Simon held her and trod water as they were pulled towards the deep sea.

She looked at him with her large, almond-shaped eyes spilling tears. 'Simon, I love you too.' The feelings which had been suppressed for so long were suddenly in the open. They gazed tenderly into each other's eyes, hanging on to each other as they tried to stay afloat in the swell.

'We're in grave danger. The current is taking us further out. We'll have to fight to get ashore.' They crested a wave and he saw how far they were from Westcliff.

Simon turned on his back, grasping Nomisile under her arms with his own folded across her chest. He kicked powerful frog strokes with his legs, forcing them to move towards the shore. Nomisile placed her hands over his.

It seemed like hours, drifting on the surface, when suddenly they heard a dull 'thud, thud, thud'. A fishing boat was approaching. He shouted at the top of his voice and waved his arms to attract the attention of the crew on deck. One of the fishermen pointed excitedly in their direction. The boat turned and headed for them.

The coloured skipper threw a rope across to Simon and pulled them against the side. Strong, rough hands manhandled them aboard. They collapsed on the deck.

'You saved our lives today.' Simon shook the skipper's hand gratefully.

'Hallo, *basie*, don't you recognise me?' One of the crew was talking to him. 'I'm old Shadrack from Hawston. Remember, I warned you about the policeman watching you?'

'I remember.' Simon looked into the weather-beaten old face.

'*Basie* and the black girl ran away so fast, you did never give me a few bob for a loaf of bread like!'

'Don't worry, Shadrack. When I get home I'll give you and the crew enough drink to have the best booze-up of your lives.'

The coloured fishermen let out a cheer. The day's catch had been poor and they had been wondering where the next bottle would come from.

Nomisile was shivering as shock set in. The skipper bundled them into his small cabin and gave them each a mouthful of brandy. Simon felt the warmth as the alcohol hit his stomach.

'You were lucky we saw you,' said the skipper. 'We had no luck off *Die Plaat* and were coming back early when you were spotted. You drifted so far out to sea that you were in the fishing boats' lanes. If you had been closer inshore, or further out, we could have missed you altogether.' Seeing the looks Simon gave Nomisile, the skipper gave a knowing wink and diplomatically left them alone.

Simon took Nomisile in his arms, kissing her warmly. She responded to his tongue, searching with hers. A tenderness he had never felt before overwhelmed him. 'My beauty, I love you deeply.'

'I adore you too,' she replied warmly. 'Why do you call me your beauty?'

'You are my black beauty – the most wondrous thing that has ever happened to me,' he answered gently.

She sighed happily as she lay against his chest with his strong arms holding her tightly.

There was a discreet knock at the door. 'We're entering harbour.'

Reluctantly Simon opened the door. 'Do you have a top for the lady?' Simon asked. 'Her blouse got torn off in the sea bamboo.'

Going to a small cupboard, the skipper took out a creased shirt. 'This should do.'

Bringing the boat around expertly, the skipper docked against the rubber tyres of the quay. He jumped to the pier to help Simon and Nomisile ashore.

The seaman smiled understandingly. 'I'm glad I could help a white man and a black girl in trouble in these times. Don't worry. Your secret is safe. As soon as we're finished I'll give you a lift back to your home.'

Simon and Nomisile watched the fishermen unloading their catch. They stood apart, to avoid the attention of hundreds of people crowding the quay, their emotions in turmoil.

When all the fish were sold the skipper divided the money between the crew. It wasn't much. They cheered up when Simon announced, 'Let's go to my house, I have wine for you all there.'

Simon slept for eight hours. It was dusk when he awoke. Ravenously hungry, he padded through to the kitchen. Helena and Nomisile were preparing supper.

'Did you sleep, Nomisile?'

'Like a log. I stirred only an hour ago.'

He opened a bottle of white Hermitage wine for their meal. The atmosphere was light-hearted, all of them rejoicing in the close escape. Simon felt Nomisile's foot reaching for his under the table and he responded.

At ten o'clock they all retired. Helena fell asleep almost immediately. Her breathing was even and regular.

Simon could not sleep. He thought of Nomisile alone in her room. After an hour he got out of bed as noiselessly as possible so as not to wake Helena. She slept on. He pulled on a pair of shorts and a shirt and padded barefooted out of the room. He gathered up a blanket and pillow from the spare room and slipped out of the back door.

Simon knocked softly on Nomisile's door.

'Who is it?'

'It's me, Simon.'

He heard the door being unlocked. Her room was in darkness.

'Come in.'

'It's a beautiful evening. Let's go for a walk.'

She slipped a loose-fitting dress over her head and quietly closed

73

her door. Silently, like two ghosts, they slipped away from the house, hand in hand.

They walked down the steps to Fick's Pool and into the shadows of a big milkwood tree. The place was deserted and quiet.

Simon and Nomisile embraced. Their lips sought each other hungrily, their tongues pushing and probing like two serpents. Helena had pushed away from him, Nomisile pulled him towards her. Simon slipped off her dress and it fell to the ground.

Her naked body was magnificent in the muted, soft moonlight filtering through the trees. He felt her breasts and gasped as her nipples came erect under his fingers.

Slowly Nomisile undid the buttons of his shirt and worked it off. She kissed his arms and chest, marvelling at his strength. Undoing the catch of his shorts, she allowed them to drop to his feet.

Together they spread the blanket. He pulled Nomisile towards him roughly, breathing hard, his movements frenzied.

'Slowly, my thandi, my sweetheart, slowly.' She remembered her *ntonjaan*. 'Play with me first.'

This was music to Simon, he thrilled as she took his hand and guided it between her legs. Her body came alive and she groaned excitedly as pleasure coursed through her. Nomisile wanted to feel the thrill of this man inside her. She was ready for him.

She pulled him upwards and in one fluid movement he entered her. She lifted, and together they tore through her virginity. She cried out at the pain, but it was a proclamation of achievement, not abhorrence. Together they rode the crest of the wave, all of their senses coming together in a mutual explosion of fervour.

In the afterglow of their intimacy they lay back regaining their equilibrium. Simon caressed her, running his fingers over her body. She sighed in contentment and nuzzled closer.

Simon's heart felt as if it would shatter from his love for her. They were hungry for each other, as if the night was their last. They made love again. Nomisile arched her back, lifting him upwards at the height of her climax. He grunted in the euphoria of release. They lay in each other's arms, falling into a contented sleep.

Simon woke with a start, as the first fingers of light rubbed the darkness from the eastern sky. He kissed Nomisile gently. 'Come my beauty, we must go.'

They dressed quickly and tiptoed past the silent houses. He kissed

Nomisile at her door and slipped into the house. He showered and felt a strange melancholy as the water washed away the musky smell of their lovemaking.

Simon slipped into bed. Helena was still sleeping peacefully. He lay back basking in the completeness of the night. How different it was, compared with his wedding night. For the first time he recognised the difference between sex and lovemaking. He was a real man, at last, able to excite and satisfy a woman. It felt very good.

5

Paarl was hot, the January mercury hovering in the high thirties, when they returned to the farm. It was not only the heat that upset Simon. He had become accustomed to having Nomisile around him all day, alone at Hawston in the afternoons and intimate under the milkwoods late at night.

Now Hermitage demanded his attention during the day and Nomisile was under the watchful eye of her cousin Jafta at night.

Simon rejoiced when school started again and Helena went back to teaching. She left just before eight o'clock, returning in the early afternoon.

Simon had Nomisile to himself every morning. Each day he made time to slip back to the house. They would draw the curtains and lock the doors – holding, touching, talking. Most mornings they made love in the brass double bed.

Weekends were the worst when Helena was at home and Nomisile was off. The lovers could not wait for school to start on Monday when they could reaffirm their feelings for each other, making love with added zest after two days of abstinence.

Simon felt ashamed that the woman he loved lived in the meagre surroundings of the black compound, but there was little he could do without drawing attention to Nomisile. To compensate he had the whole compound scraped down and repainted, the environment cleaned up and trees and shrubs planted. It made the lives of all Hermitage's black workers much more pleasant.

A standard-seven girl held up her hand. 'Miss! Miss!'

'Yes, Susan, what is it?' asked Helena.

'Miss, my mother needs the embroidery book she lent you. She needs it for tonight.'

'Sorry, Susan, I meant to bring it to school today. You know what Mondays are like! In the rush I clean forgot. I tell you what, I'll fetch the book during the break and you'll have it to take home this afternoon.'

'Thank you, miss.'

Opening the cottage door, Simon saw Nomisile busy in the kitchen. He walked up quietly behind her, capturing her in his arms. She turned to face him, putting her arms around his neck, pulling him down to her, kissing him avidly. Love glowed in her large, luminous eyes.

'My thandi, I've missed you. These days we seem to have only stolen moments together,' she breathed.

'It's only been the weekend my beauty, but it feels like weeks since I last held you.'

He opened the front of her blouse and she undid his shirt buttons. They stood, rubbing gently together. Nomisile started breathing heavily.

Her hardened nipples rubbed against his, sending undulations coursing through his body. He felt an urgency in his loins. Simon took her hand, leading Nomisile to the bedroom.

'Did you lock the front door, thandi?'

He checked. It was unlocked. He released the Yale catch. Nomisile closed the curtains, making sure that there was not even a chink of light coming through.

'I've locked the back door,' she assured him.

They entered the bedroom, closing the door behind them. Both quickly undressed. She pulled back the quilted bedspread, folded and placed it on the dresser. They lay on top of the blankets. Simon tickled her back, then her front, sensuously stroking his fingers over all her curves.

'That's wonderful, thandi, I'm ready for you,' she breathed.

Helena parked her car in the shade of the manor-house oaks. She walked quickly across the garden to the cottage. She tried the door. It was locked.

Strange, she thought, searching in her handbag for her key. She unlocked the door, glancing into the kitchen. Where was Nomisile? She should be in the house during the morning.

She passed the bedroom door on her way to the dining-room sideboard. She heard a loud cry from the bedroom.

'Oh, Simon, my thandi!'

Helena stopped. That was Nomisile's voice. She started to tremble and sat down to steady herself. In the quiet of the house, surrounded by the tranquil farm, she heard the rhythmic squeaking of the bed springs. Her mind raced. Should I rush in and catch them in the act? No, it would be degrading for all three of us. Should I wait until they come out of the bedroom and confront them? No, it would be extremely embarrassing. Should I speak to Nomisile alone? No, she would deny it. Should I discuss the matter with Simon? No, he may demand a divorce, and that's the last thing I want.

What should she do? She had suspected an affair between them. She couldn't give Simon sexual satisfaction and he was a hot-blooded male. Perhaps, she came to the incredible conclusion, it was better with Nomisile, in the confines of her home, than some other woman in Paarl.

The sounds from the bedroom decided the matter for her. Soon they would come out. Helena grabbed the book she had come for and let herself quietly out of the house. She drove back to school with tears streaming down her face.

'My dear, you're pregnant. Congratulations.' Dr VA de Villiers, the medical superintendent at Paarl hospital, smiled at Helena. As the family doctor he had known her since a toddler. She had insisted on seeing only him.

Helena started to cry, dabbing her eyes with a handkerchief. Dr de Villiers put his arm around her in a fatherly fashion. 'Don't cry now, this is a happy time for you and Simon. I know both sets of grandparents will be over the moon with delight.'

Helena dabbed her eyes, choking back the tears. 'You don't understand, Uncle VA, it's more complicated than you think.'

Diplomatically he changed the subject. 'From the dates you gave me, we can expect the infant about the third week of September.'

She thanked him and walked slowly back to her car, her mind racing. Helena knew instinctively that Simon and Nomisile were having a love affair, not just casual sex. She could tell by the way they looked at each other, the way they touched when they thought she was not looking. It's my fault, she chided herself. If only I could give Simon what he wanted in bed. If only I could put warmth and feeling and abandonment into our sex, he would not need another woman. She felt so frustrated and inadequate.

She reached a decision. As much as she liked Nomisile, there was no place for her any longer. The father of her child would have to devote himself to his family. Nomisile would have to go, but how?

'Guess what?' Helena put her arms around Simon, looking up at him. He looked at her quizzically. 'I was at the doctor's today and we're going to have a baby in September.'

Simon gave her a startled look. 'A baby?'

'Our baby. Isn't it wonderful news?'

Simon's brain whirred. Where did this leave Nomisile and himself? Now Helena was pregnant she would give up teaching and be home all day. We'll have to find another place to make love, he thought. It will be risky, we could get caught. I'll divorce Helena and marry Nomisile. But we would have to start a new life in another country. My father would disown me, we would be penniless. I would lose my wife, child, family, friends, the farms, everything. And what about my unborn child? A boy would be the logical heir to Hermitage and Doornrivier. I can't take away his heritage. No, he decided sadly, divorce is not an alternative.

Nomisile hummed to herself as she skipped to work. Her life was so complete. She loved Simon dearly and knew he shared her feelings. She watched Helena drive off to school. If she cleaned up quickly she would be finished when Simon came in for tea. She stopped in surprise as she saw Simon's frame filling the back doorway, a worried expression on his face.

'What's wrong, thandi?' She smiled at him.

'Helena's pregnant.' His voice was gruff.

She took the news in silence. Then, 'What are we going to do, Simon? Where does it leave us?'

'I don't know, I honestly don't know.'

'I feel terrible. I think I'm going to be sick.' Nomisile held her hand over her mouth and ran for the toilet. Later she sank gratefully into Simon's arms, but for the first time cried off lovemaking.

The following morning it was the same story. The colic remedy did not seem to help. Simon discussed the matter with Helena. 'I'm worried about Nomisile. Every morning she's nauseous. I think she's sick, perhaps we should take her to the doctor.'

'Does the nausea last all morning?' Helena felt her heart sink.

'No, it only seems to be early on, by mid-morning she seems fine again.'

The colour drained from her face. 'She could be pregnant. Who do you think is the father?' she asked with a tremor of uncertainty.

It was as if she had slapped him. Simon jerked backwards as the words sunk in. 'I . . . I . . . I . . . don't know,' he stammered, guilt written all over his face. He made straight for the sideboard and poured a glass of brandy, downing it neat.

His reaction gave Helena her answer – it was the first time he had taken alcohol in many weeks. Simon was the father, she was convinced of it. Savagely she repeated her question. 'Who is the father?'

'Must be a black worker down at the compound. You know how the blacks are.' He hated himself for betraying his beloved Nomisile and he needed another shot to calm his nerves. He sat down heavily and looked at his wife with loathing. She had made him lie, when he knew only he could be the father. Their relationship was too perfect, their love too true, their lovemaking too satisfying, for Nomisile ever to entertain the idea of sleeping with another man.

Helena went straight for the jugular, hoping his fuddled brain would help him tell the truth. 'Simon, are you the father of Nomisile's baby?'

He let out a bellow of rage, sprang to his feet, and in two paces reached her side. A huge hand closed around her neck and he lifted her off the ground, pulling her face towards him until their eyes were level. 'I've already told you, I don't know who she's been with.' Helena was making a liar out of him and rancour smouldered in his eyes. Simon threw her from him and she landed against the couch.

'Bastard! Woman beater!' she screamed at him in defiance.

Simon snorted, balled his hand and hit her in the face. Helena wailed as the insolence drained out of her and she lay in a foetal position, covering her stomach with her hands to protect her baby. He looked at her in contempt – a cold, sexless bitch who had him where she wanted him with a marriage certificate. He needed another drink. Helena waited until his back was turned then scrambled out of the lounge and slammed the bedroom door.

Her thoughts were jumbled, but she forced herself to concentrate. Now Nomisile was a dire threat to her and her baby's future. A plan started formulating in her mind.

* * *

81

School dragged for Helena the next day. She rushed home, bundled Nomisile into her car and took her to the non-white outpatients at Paarl hospital. They sat on a hard bench waiting for a doctor. The atmosphere was strained between the two women, their conversation stilted. Gone was their relaxed, easy-going friendship. Both were relieved when a nurse called Nomisile into an examination room.

Helena waited in trepidation. Nomisile came slowly down the passage, her eyes downcast.

'What did the doctor say?' asked Helena in a shaking voice.

'I'm pregnant, Helena. My baby's due in mid-October.'

Her worst fears had been realised. Helena had to know. 'Who is the father of your child?'

Nomisile's eyes widened in alarm. She had to protect Simon at all costs. 'Seme . . . a Pondo man.'

'Where did you meet him?' Helena's tone was brutal. 'You've only been in Paarl for four months.'

'In Mbekweni,' Nomisile blurted out nervously.

'Where is he now?' Helena's voice rasped.

'He returned to the Transkei.'

Turning on her heel, Helena marched out of the hospital. She hated herself for being brusque with Nomisile when she should have shared a moment of joy with her. Nomisile was no longer her friend, she rationalised. Helena tried one last desperate time. 'Is Simon the father of your child?'

Nomisile held on to the car for support. Why couldn't she sing out the truth from the roof-tops? Who would share her ecstasy? Everyone – black and white – would condemn her and, more importantly, castigate Simon. Was this the price she had to pay for being a black woman in a white man's world? She looked sullenly at Helena, refusing to answer.

Thwarted, Helena slammed the car door. They drove in silence. Helena dropped her off at the compound. Nomisile shut herself in her room, alone in her hour of need.

Simon was waiting impatiently for Helena when she returned home. 'Where is Nomisile?'

'I dropped her off at the compound and gave her the rest of the day off.'

'Did she see a doctor?' Simon's voice was tinged with concern.

'Yes, I took her to Paarl hospital.'

'What did the doctor say?'

'He told her she's pregnant,' she answered in barely a whisper. 'Her baby is due in mid-October.'

Simon took the news silently, her words resting heavily on his conscience. His hands started shaking and he clamped them together. Devastation etched his features. He needed the comfort of a drink. He turned on his heel and stormed towards the wine cellar. He weighed up his options. How could he admit to Helena he was the father of Nomisile's baby? The shock could make her miscarry, or she might even try to commit suicide. She would definitely demand a divorce, dragging all the sordid details through court. It would ruin his family's name. He would be branded for the rest of his life. His father's political career would be in tatters and he'd never be forgiven. He reached a conclusion – he couldn't tell Helena, he'd have to think of an alternative.

Helena watched Simon disappear into the cellar. 'That's it!' she muttered through clenched teeth. 'I am going to put my plan into action.'

The Paarl police station was busy. Helena asked to see Robert Morton and was shown to his office. She came straight to the point. 'Robert, you told me on my wedding day if ever I was in trouble I could come to you. I need you to help me now; my whole future, my very existence, is at stake.'

'Tell me your problem. I'll see if I can help.'

'Only if you promise me on the Bible the matter will stay between ourselves,' insisted Helena.

'You want me to swear on a Bible?' He sounded incredulous. 'Helena, swearing under oath is a grave matter for a policeman. You'll have to give me more details first.'

Helena started crying, sobs shaking her body. Morton quickly closed the door. He stood beside her with his arm across her shoulders. 'Talk to me, Helena.'

'I . . . can't . . . unless you are sworn to secrecy,' she sobbed.

'All right then, tell me, is what you want me to do against the law?'

Helena shook her head vigorously. 'No.'

'Could I lose my rank if I agreed to help you?'

'No, it's part of police work.'

She looked so miserable and vulnerable that reluctantly he took the Bible he used as a commissioner of oaths and did as she asked.

'Now tell me about your problem.'

Helena outlined her plan. He listened, his eyes growing larger as she spoke. 'Will you help me, Robert?'

'Yes, Helena, I'll help you,' he answered hesitantly.

Simon waited impatiently for Helena to leave the next morning to be alone with Nomisile.

'Thandi, what are we going to do?' sobbed Nomisile. 'I can't have our baby on Hermitage. People will talk. You'll get into trouble.'

'Don't talk like that, beauty. You know I'll stand by you and our child. We'll face this together.' Simon embraced her tenderly, kissing her trembling lips.

Adjutant-Officer Robert Morton peered at them from his hiding place in the shrubbery. He saw them kissing. So Helena was right, he mused.

Simon and Nomisile clung to one another, each drawing strength from the other. In their hour of trouble they turned to the physical as the logical way of expressing their feelings. There was an urgency to bury themselves in each other's bodies.

'Come, thandi.' Nomisile lead Simon to the bedroom. 'I want you to make love to me.'

The policeman crept closer, peering between the curtains. He saw Simon and Nomisile disappear. He let himself in quietly through the front door with Helena's key. Softly he walked to the bedroom door. He looked through the keyhole and saw a tangle of naked bodies on the bed.

Morton took out a police camera, attaching a flashlight. It was the latest semi-automatic model. He opened the door silently and tiptoed to the bed.

Simon and Nomisile were in a world of their own. They did not notice the policeman until the first flash. The second shot was more explicit, with their startled faces turned to the camera. Flash! Flash! Two more action photographs, before Nomisile screamed and pulled the blankets over herself. Morton clicked and wound on to the next frame. Flash! Flash! Flash! Simon was blinded as three further shots caught him in various naked poses, his face contorted in shock.

He lunged forward to grab the camera and destroy the evidence. Morton pushed his police revolver into his stomach. Simon noticed the police uniform for the first time. He covered his nakedness with his hands.

'Simon Roux, you are under arrest in terms of the Immorality Act, No. 21 of 1950.'

'Let me explain.'

'Any explaining you do, you can do in court. Put on your pants, man.' Simon hurriedly pulled on his shorts. Still pointing the revolver at Simon, he instructed, 'Turn around. Put your hands behind your back.' Simon did as he was told. The policeman slipped a handcuff over each wrist and snapped the pair shut. Simon could feel them biting into his flesh.

For Simon the end of his world had come. He sat on the edge of the bed, tears streaming down his face. He was ruined, finished. 'It's all Helena's fault!' he shouted in frustration. 'If she weren't so . . .' He let the words die unspoken but his meaning was clear.

'That's your problem, man. It's also no reason to take a kaffir. Why didn't you choose a decent white girl if you wanted someone else?'

'There's nothing wrong with Nomisile, she's as decent as any white girl.'

'Bullshit! White women don't get you into trouble with the law, only with their husbands.' Morton laughed at his own joke.

Nomisile saw Simon weeping. She put out her hand to comfort him.

Morton slapped her arm away. 'Leave your white man alone. You're in big trouble, girl. Worry about saving your own skin. Forget him. Black girls who fuck with whites go to jail for a very long time.' He held up his camera. 'You see this camera? Inside I have enough proof to keep you behind bars until you are old and ugly, so no white man will ever want you again. Get dressed, and get out of here.'

Nomisile cringed against the headrest, pulling the blankets up around her. She whimpered little sounds of terror. The policeman picked her dress up off the floor and threw it into her face. She was shaking so badly, she had difficulty in getting dressed.

'Now go,' he barked at Nomisile. 'Go to your room and wait there. Don't try to escape, or we'll catch you and shoot you. I'll come for you later.'

Looking at him with loathing, she picked up her panties and shoes, scuttled past him and ran to the compound. She slammed her door, bolting it on the inside. She fell on to the bed, great convulsions racking her body.

'Go through to the lounge, Roux.' The policeman glared at Simon. 'Sit down.'

Simon sat down heavily, his head bowed in shame. He had brought disgrace on his family. Helena would be ostracised. Their baby would be branded, even before birth.

'Do you realise that you've buggered up your life?'

Simon nodded distractedly, his stomach gnawing for a drink.

'Why did you do it, man?'

'I don't know, I really don't know.' Simon shook his head in confusion. 'It wasn't planned. It just happened slowly and naturally.' Simon lapsed into silence.

Morton removed his officer's cap and mopped his brow. Simon looked at him properly for the first time and jerked upright as he recognised his old school enemy. 'Morton,' he breathed in disgust. 'Why you of all people?'

'Because I hate your guts, Roux.'

'What have I done to you?' cried Simon in despair.

'You stole Helena from me and you humiliated me in front of the whole school.'

'Those were school days, Morton. You can't bear a grudge for so many years.'

'Oh yes, I can!' Morton cleared his throat loudly and his voice was bitter. 'You made me the laughing stock of Paarl. It took me years to live it down.'

'I'm sorry, man.'

'Too late now, Roux.'

'How do you know about the black girl and me? Did Helena tell you?'

'We have our informers, even on the farms. I haven't seen Helena for years,' he fabricated. 'I've been waiting for you to make a slip-up. At last I'm even.'

'Will I go to jail?'

'At least fifteen years.'

'That I could take. But why must my family and friends suffer as well?'

'Because it's the law, that's why.'

'Isn't there any way to prevent all this pain and agony? If not for me, for the family?'

For a moment Morton looked as if he might take pity on him. 'Perhaps. My superiors don't know what's happened here. I could destroy the film and tell them I never caught you.' He paused. 'We policemen earn paltry salaries compared with you Rouxs.'

Simon saw light. He looked intently at Morton. 'Do you want money to forget about the whole episode?' He waited. 'How much man, how much?'

'Six months' salary. Six hundred rand.'

'What about the black girl?'

'For another four hundred rand I won't lay charges against her either.'

'A thousand rand? It's a deal, but what about the negatives?'

'I keep the negatives, they're mine.'

'You could blackmail me for ever.'

'You want a deal? I'll give you a deal. For another thousand rand I'll give you the negatives, but with one proviso.'

Simon looked at him expectantly.

'That kaffir woman leaves Paarl for ever. She's never allowed to set foot in the Cape again. She stays in the Transkei, where she belongs.'

'Why are you so determined she must go?'

'Because she does not belong here. It's government policy. If she stays here you'll be tempted again. I'll catch you and, believe me, next time there'll be no deals.'

Simon pondered Morton's words despairingly. He was caught in a vice. Nomisile would go out of his life for ever. He loved her deeply, but he could not allow his love for her to destroy so many other lives. He had no option.

'I accept your terms.' It was like a death sentence.

'Good. Bring the money in cash tomorrow morning, in used banknotes.'

'What about the spool? I want the film now.'

'I'm not stupid. You get it when you've paid the money.'

Simon stood up. 'Undo these handcuffs.'

'Please, I would say.' Morton stood up to unlock the handcuffs. 'If you're not in my office by ten o'clock, I'm coming to arrest you.'

* * *

During his childhood, through his student days and even in adulthood, when Simon needed to be alone he would head up to his special place on Paarl Mountain. Just sitting there, alone with nature, he inevitably resolved his problem, returning home refreshed and determined. Never in his twenty-five years had he faced such a wretched situation as he did now.

Taking deep breaths and with a firm step in his long, powerful legs, Simon strode quickly through the vineyards behind the house. He cut up the mountain and after half an hour stood at the base of Paarl Rock regaining his breath. He made the final ascent up the fissure in the rock face. His hands closed over the ledge and he pulled himself over the top.

Simon dropped his rucksack in the cave and moved to the pool. He lay flat on his stomach, cupping his hands to his lips, feeling the coldness of the water numbing his fingers. He drank deeply, splashing the liquid on his perspiring face.

Standing on the edge, the whole Paarl Valley set out below him, he felt suspended in time and space. To his right was Hermitage, the whole place laid out in miniature. He could see every aspect of each section of the farm. It was his inheritance, which he could lose if the trade-off with Morton went wrong.

Simon knelt at the edge, his hands placed together. He prayed properly for the first time in many months. He begged for guidance, for strength and for his very life – that he might be saved from the ruin of everything he held dear. He also pleaded for Nomisile and the pain and suffering he knew lay ahead for her and their child. He prayed for Helena and the foetus she carried in her uterus. He prayed aloud, his voice echoing off the rocks. In this place he felt God could reach out and almost touch him, he felt so close to heaven. He finished, refreshed and ready to tackle his problems.

In the cave he unwrapped the old coffee tin. With his knife he prised off the lid and took out the hard-cover school exercise book that was his diary.

Sitting on the brink of the ledge, his legs dangling into space, he glanced at the other entries in the diary. All the highlights of his life came alive again on the pages: his school life, university days and his marriage to Helena.

He had not been to his private place since meeting Nomisile. He wrote now, recording their meeting, their attraction, the time at

Hermanus, the policeman Van Blerk, her pregnancy and the latest incident with Adjutant-Officer Robert Morton. He ended with a series of question marks and: 'May God grant compassion to my loved ones and me.'

There was only one course. He would have to pay the money and lose Nomisile. That made him saddest of all. He would willingly have made her his wife, in another country, and under different circumstances. He damned the Nationalists' apartheid laws. Who are they to decide whom one may love? he questioned angrily.

Simon looked down at the compound on Hermitage, tiny in the distance. He knew Nomisile was in her room. She would be suffering as much as he. Worse, she would be terrified, for she did not know of his deal with Morton. He would visit her after dark and tell her.

The shadows were lengthening when Simon stood up. He replaced his diary in the oilskin, rewrapped the canvas bundle and started for home.

It was already dark when Simon reached the compound. He nodded to the surprised black labourers, sitting around the open fire. They had never seen Simon in the compound at night before. Jafta came forward. 'Evening, boss,' he greeted. 'Can I help you?'

'I must speak to Nomisile about her work.'

'She's locked herself in her room. She's been there all afternoon. She won't open the door. I'm worried about her.'

'Okay, Jafta, leave me, I need to speak to Nomisile by herself.'

He knocked on her door.

'Go away.' He heard her muffled voice from inside the room.

Simon knocked again. 'Nomisile, this is Simon Roux. I must talk to you.' The bolts were drawn and she opened the door. Simon was shocked at what the past few hours had done to her. Her sparkling almond eyes were dull and lifeless, her once-proud posture seemed stooped and frail. She wiped her eyes. Simon's heart went out to her, he wanted to hold her and ease away her pain.

The labourers at the fire watched him intently. He couldn't comfort her in his arms, or close the door on them, without evoking their suspicions and gossip.

'Nomisile, listen to me. I've come to an agreement with the policeman. I'm going to give him money and he is not going to arrest us. We can go free.' Simon saw the relief flood into her beautiful eyes. 'But he says you must leave the Cape and never return. He says you must go back to the Transkei.'

Nomisile shuddered. 'What about my baby? It will have no father.'

'Of course it will have a father. I won't fail you. I'll send you money each month, enough for you and the baby to live on.'

'What about us? I love you, Simon. I can't just go away and forget you. I'll die without you. You're my life, my reason for living. Please don't push me away.'

The suffering on her face tore at his heart. He had thought about this moment every minute for the last few hours. He steeled himself, saying aloud the lines he had rehearsed. 'I love you, Nomisile, and I always will, but there is no place in South Africa for our love. Ours was a stolen romance, an interlude. You must go back to your people. I must go to mine, back to Helena, my family and Hermitage. Do you understand?'

Nomisile felt as if her heart was breaking and the end of her world had come. As a black person she had been born to heartache and raised on disenchantment, but how much more could one take? For Simon's sake she hid her true feelings. 'I understand.'

'Tomorrow morning I will fetch you at eleven o'clock to take you to the station. You must catch the Transkei train.'

He hardly noticed the men at the fire as he walked up the road to his cottage. A great sadness enveloped him.

6

Lightning forked across the evening sky, as bright as stainless steel against the packed, leaden clouds. Ten seconds later the clap of thunder rolled over the highveld, rattling the window panes in their frames. Nelson Mandela turned from the window, the smile on his handsome face creasing his cheeks and carrying to his eyes, causing them to half close. He looked down fondly at his friend and partner in his law firm writing busily at his desk.

Oliver Tambo glanced up, smiling his warm impish smile. He was a small man with sharp features, a scraggly goatee beard and alert, piercing brown eyes.

Nelson walked towards a chair, his movements fluid with a boxer's pent-up energy. He was tall, good-looking and powerfully built.

Painted across the outer window were the words: MANDELA AND TAMBO ATTORNEYS. The offices were on the first floor in downtown Johannesburg. The rooms were sparsely furnished with loads of papers stacked on every available surface.

Mandela cleared his throat. 'We are almost ready to call a Congress of the People. It will prove the most significant event in the annals of black nationalism.'

Oliver Tambo put down his pen, looked up and smiled, his eyes lighting up. 'When we adopt the Freedom Charter it really will be a milestone.'

'We still have to work through the thousands of suggestions sent in by ANC supporters.'

'When do you think we'll be finished?'

Mandela frowned and ran his hand over his close-cropped hair. 'Towards the end of June should give us enough time.'

'Have you decided on a venue?'

'I thought of Kliptown. It's close enough to Johannesburg to be accessible to most of our people.'

'What about a hall? Is there one big enough?'

'No hall will hold the crowd we're expecting. We'll hold the congress in an open field.'

Tambo looked worried. 'Won't the police try and disrupt the gathering?'

'I guarantee you they'll be present,' answered Nelson. 'If they attack us the delegates will have a better chance to get away if we hold the meeting in the open.'

'Good thinking. We still have lots of midnight oil to burn, altering, adding to and compiling the final draft of the Freedom Charter.'

'We'll manage,' grinned Mandela.

The Standard Bank in Main Street opened at nine o'clock. Simon pushed through the doorway. The manager came out of his office at the end of the banking hall. 'Good morning, Mr Roux. How are you? How was the grape harvest?'

Simon answered with a casualness he did not feel, obliged to make small talk for a few minutes.

'I have a fairly large cheque to cash. Wages for the seasonal workers. Will it be in order?'

The manager took the cheque, noting the amount of two thousand, six hundred rand. The Rouxs were A-grade clients. 'Of course, Mr Roux. No problem. Here, let me initial the back of the cheque for you.'

Adjutant-Officer Morton closed the door of his office firmly.

Simon counted the two thousand rand out on the desk. 'There, take your blood money.'

'Don't call it blood money, Roux,' answered the policeman with irritation. 'It's silence money and a lifeline to your future. I'm only helping you so Helena won't get hurt.'

He slipped the money into the desk drawer, removed a photographic spool and handed it to Simon.

Simon walked to the window and held the negatives to the light. There were seven exposed frames. He was shocked at the explicit scenes of Nomisile and himself. They would have been damning evidence in court. He was glad he could destroy the film for good.

'Is this mine now?'

The policeman nodded.

Simon took out a box of matches and set the spool alight. It flickered and burnt with an acrid, sulphurous smoke. He threw the burning evidence into the metal waste paper bin and watched it burn to ashes. Then he turned to the policeman. 'Are Nomisile and I safe from prosecution? Will you leave us in peace?'

Morton nodded. 'Just remember our terms – the woman returns to the Transkei immediately and never sets foot in Paarl again.'

'How can you enforce that?'

Morton held up a buff envelope. He spilt a number of enlargements on the table. Simon recoiled in shock – they were even more dramatic than the negatives.

Simon grabbed for them. 'Give them to me, they're mine, I paid you.'

Morton whipped out his police revolver. 'Not so fast, Roux. Our agreement was for the negatives. These photographs are my insurance.'

'How do I know you won't blackmail me in future?'

'You don't know,' barked the policeman, 'but I give you my solemn promise as a police officer. I will never use them in evidence against you as long as you stick to the rules we agreed. No more black girls and your kaffir whore goes back to the Transkei for good.'

'Don't call Nomisile a whore,' hissed Simon, stepping forward threateningly. Morton pushed his revolver into Simon's navel.

'Watch it, Roux. You're in no position to tell me to do anything. When is your precious Nomisile going back to the Transkei?'

'You bastard, Morton. One day I'll get you,' Simon hissed at him. 'She'll be on the eleven-o'clock train.'

'Just see she is, Roux. Now get out.'

'May I help you, sir?' The woman behind the counter at the Simondium post office, ten kilometres out of Paarl, smiled at Simon.

He looked at her intently. 'Do you know who I am?'

Taken aback, the woman shook her head. 'No sir.'

Satisfied he said, 'I'm Petrus Potgieter, from Riverside Farm. I'm new here and I'd like to rent a post box.'

'Complete this application, please.' She pushed a form across the counter.

Simon filled in the false information. He paid the annual fee and she gave him duplicate keys.

'One more thing, I want to open a post office savings book in the name of Nomisile Memani. Will she be able to draw the money in Transkei?'

'No problem, as long as she shows her pass book.'

Simon paid in two hundred rand. The clerk issued the savings book.

'Thank you.' He looked at his watch. It was past ten. He had to hurry, there was still much to do.

Nomisile was ready when Simon drove into the compound. She looked so miserable he longed to take her in his arms to console her, but he steeled himself to do what he had to.

Nomisile forced a forlorn smile. 'I'm ready to go.'

They drove in silence to Paarl station, leaving unsaid all the things they wanted to say to each other.

'One ticket to Umtata.' Simon nodded towards Nomisile.

The ticket clerk pushed a third-class ticket across the counter and they hurried on to the platform. Simon glanced at his watch. Only five minutes before the train was due. He turned to Nomisile. 'My wonderful beauty, it's tragic that what we shared has been reduced to this. Please listen carefully. If ever you are in trouble, please contact me. I've rented a post box in Simondium in the name of Petrus Potgieter. You can write to me there or send a telegram.'

He handed her a piece of paper with the name, box number and post office on it. She folded the paper and put it inside her bra for safekeeping. It was a spontaneous gesture, keeping one of his last deeds close to her heart.

Simon handed her the post office savings book. She opened it. Her eyes widened as she noted the money he had deposited.

'I'll place forty rand into your account each month. You can withdraw the money at any post office.'

'Thank you, thandi. It's more than enough to look after our child and me.' There were tears in her eyes.

Her utter dejection tugged at Simon's heartstrings. His breath caught in his throat and overcome with emotion he produced the rest of the notes and pushed them into her hands. 'Nomisile, they can stop me from giving you my name but they cannot stop me ensuring you are well cared for. Use this money for yourself and our child.'

94

Nomisile had never seen so much money. She opened her suitcase and spread the money between her clothes. 'Thank you, Simon.'

'Nomisile, you must write to me. Tell me everything. When the baby is born, go to a photographer in Umtata and send me the snapshots of the two of you. I want a photograph every few months. Please, my beauty, I must see how our child is doing.'

She nodded. 'I will do so, thandi.'

The train roared into Paarl station, belching grey clouds from its smoke stack, the metal a gleaming polished black with shining brass and copper piping down the side.

To ease his impending loss, Simon tried to be light-hearted. 'The engine looks like a policeman, all black with shiny buttons.'

Nomisile turned on him, hate burning in her eyes. 'Simon, never mention the police to me again. They have ruined my life. Three times I have come into contact with them and three times they have pointed guns, or fired, at me. I loathe the police, who uphold only the white man's law. I detest the Nationalist government for their apartheid laws. I hate the Afrikaner for his selfishness.'

Simon was taken aback at her bitterness. 'What about me?' His eyes filled with tears.

'I love you and always will, but our child will be raised to think his father is a black man, that he is illegitimate.'

'Is that best for the child?' Simon asked anxiously.

'Yes,' answered Nomisile emphatically. 'Do you accept that?' She studied his face.

He nodded sadly, forced to accept her terms.

'I will teach our child to hate the police, and to fight for human rights for all and not just the privileged few,' said Nomisile. 'Then perhaps one day in South Africa people like us can love each other freely, not hiding and running like this.'

Nomisile boarded the train. Simon passed her possessions to her as the conductor blew his whistle. He looked into the carriage and was shocked. There were only wooden bench seats, no bunks, and the compartment was crowded and dirty. The conductor waved his green flag and the train moved slowly forward.

Nomisile put the palm of her hand against Simon's face. 'Goodbye, thandi,' she whispered and the tears rolled unabashed down her cheeks.

Simon placed his hand over hers, squeezing. He swallowed at the lump in his throat.

The train moved faster. Simon ran with her to the end of the platform. When he could run alongside no more he waved until her face blurred, growing smaller and smaller until it was a speck. Simon slumped to the platform, hands covering his face, sobbing. She was gone.

'Good afternoon, Robert.' Helena walked into Adjutant-Officer Morton's office. 'How did it go?'

'Just as we planned, Helena.'

'Does Simon suspect I was involved?'

'Not at all. He paid the money. Here it is.' Morton handed her the wad of notes.

'Good gracious, I don't want the money. You keep it.'

'Look, the cash was to make it look authentic, as if I'm a crooked cop. I took no satisfaction in what I did. I hated every minute. I'm proud of being a policeman. I'm not taking any bribe.'

Helena changed the subject. 'What was Simon's reaction?'

'Of course he was deeply moved. He was so helpless in the situation. I could see he went along with it all against his better judgement. I gave him the spool, which he burnt in my bin.'

'And the prints?'

'Here in the envelope. They are the last of the evidence against him. Simon thinks I'm keeping them to make him toe the line, but I have no further need of them.'

Helena glanced at the explicit photographs, so clear in every detail. She ignored the sexuality and was saddened by the expressions of fear and hatred on Simon's and Nomisile's faces. She had deeply hurt two people whom she loved, but the preservation of the birthright of the baby growing inside her was all important. She shuddered to think of the possibility of Nomisile's baby taking away her own child's legacy. Helena had protected her child's life with the only course of action open to her.

Morton coughed lightly to bring her out of her reverie. She started. 'Do you have a match, Robert?' She burnt the photographs one by one.

She smiled for the first time that day. 'Now no evidence remains. No one can blackmail any of us. But while Simon thinks you have the photographs, Robert, he'll never see Nomisile again.'

*   *   *

Nomisile squealed in delight as she saw Jafta approaching. She jumped up and ran to meet him.

'Hullo, cousin,' he greeted warmly in Xhosa.

'When did you get back to the Transkei?' she asked, knowing he would have news of Simon.

'Two days ago, after I finished my summer contract on Hermitage.' He told her about the harvest, the farm, the other black labourers.

She was impatient. 'What about the house?'

'Rosie is back as the maid.'

'And the boss and the madam?'

'The madam is now at home every day.'

'Tell me about Simon.'

'The boss is very cross these days. He always used to smile and laugh, now his eyes are sad and he is irritable with everyone.'

Nomisile sympathised with Simon for she felt the same, as if the best part of her existence had been wrenched away. At least she had their baby in her stomach – all Simon had were his memories.

She took Jafta's arm and strolled towards her hut. 'So, now you're back, what are you going to do except watch over your father's flocks?'

'I'm going to Johannesburg.'

'Tell me more,' asked Nomisile excitedly.

'The ANC has called a Congress of the People to discuss the future of the black man in South Africa. They have asked everyone for suggestions, and after we have talked about them they will be drafted into the Freedom Charter. There will be thousands of people.'

'Johannesburg, Egoli – the city of gold,' she breathed. The words sounding intoxicating, exotic. She had never visited the north. 'How are you going?'

'By car,' smiled Jafta. 'Five of us are travelling in my friend's Ford.'

The prospect of being there excited her. 'Isn't there room for me?'

'Each one is paying his own way. You don't have enough money,' laughed Jafta.

'Oh yes I do! If I pay my share, can I go?'

He nodded slowly. 'I suppose so – I'll have to ask my friend. You know, Nelson Mandela will be there.'

'Mandela!' She breathed the word. She knew he was a cousin, born in her village, but she had never met the legendary figure. 'Will I be able to talk to him?'

'Probably – he is a very friendly man. He likes to meet people and find out what they are thinking.'

Nomisile thought of the injustices of white rule, how they kept Simon and her apart, and she determined to go. She wanted to learn more about the black struggle so she could teach her child from first-hand experience.

A week later Nomisile paid her fare and they set off. The journey took three days. The car broke down twice and they had three punctures, but late on Friday afternoon they reached Kliptown. They slept in the car surrounded by people camping out in the open veld.

The Transvaal highveld winter's morning was bitterly cold, with the grass burnt a pale brown from the nightly frosts. Little streams were iced over, willow trees on their banks dangling streamers of hoarfrost. The sun rose, its rays struggling to penetrate the grey haze hugging the ground from thousands upon thousands of open cooking fires. The only splash of natural colour was the glossy green foliage of the blue gum trees.

Kliptown was a hive of activity as people poured into the little community by car, lorry, bus, bicycle and on foot.

The mist cleared, the sun beat down warmly and Nelson Mandela's spirits rose as he saw the capacity crowd. He knew history would be made on this level stretch of veld. There were no fancy halls, not even chairs for the delegates. They sat on the ground using umbrellas to cast shade.

A makeshift wooden dais had been constructed at one end of the field. A single microphone stood on the platform. In the centre was a table, around it seven chairs to seat the leaders.

Nomisile walked between the people gawking at the colourful sights, surprised to see blacks, whites, coloureds and Indians mixing freely. She shivered as she noticed the police in the far corner, but no one else seemed bothered by their presence. Spirits were high in expectation, the hubbub ebbing and flowing as old acquaintances renewed friendships, shaking hands in the triple-grip manner of the freedom movement – first the normal handshake, then the hand moved to grip the thumb and palm together, then back to the usual grip.

At ten o'clock Nelson Mandela rose on the dais. He was greeted with an ecstatic roar as he waved to the audience. Nomisile shouted as hard as she could, swept up by the enthusiasm of the moment. Mandela bowed to the crowd's adulation, then raised his hands above his head for silence.

'My brothers and sisters in peace, we have come here today, at a Congress of the People, to discuss many issues facing us and our country. I ask for patience and cool heads, that we may debate the issues at hand and reach solutions.'

His words were greeted with rapturous applause. Mandela again held up his hands for calm. 'Let us start this historic occasion with our own anthem, the beautiful hymn, *"Nkosi sikelel 'iAfrika".*' Every delegate stood, and three thousand voices sang in unison, asking the Lord to bless Africa. The solemn, heart-rending strains filled the air.

The issues at hand, so many and so urgent, were debated by the delegates. Their common goal was to see the black man take his rightful place in the South African social and political order. The last part of the afternoon was devoted to the Freedom Charter.

Nelson explained to the delegates, 'This document has been drafted by a sub-committee of the National Action Council. You have all helped in one way or another, by giving us your views at meetings held all over the country, by memoranda from groups and letters from individuals. We have put your wishes into the document, which has been approved by the National Executive of the African National Congress. We now need the approval of this Congress of the People to make the Freedom Charter a reality.'

A delegate jumped up with a proposal. 'I request that the document be read to us, section by section. If we approve each section as we go along, by the time we are finished the whole document will have been approved.'

The delegates roared in agreement.

Mandela nodded. 'We will abide by the decision of the delegates. It is too late to deal with the matter fully today. We therefore adjourn this meeting until tomorrow morning.'

The crowd dispersed. Some lit fires where they sat to cook their evening meal. Others disappeared into the shacks and houses of

Kliptown, some to the shebeens where the illegal drinking houses did record business selling *umqombothi*, brewed in large drums from a mixture of maize meal and sorghum, which was both alcoholic and nourishing.

What fun! The younger delegates danced in the streets and Nomisile joined in vigorously. They jived to the lilting strains of the penny whistle and rawhide drums.

The atmosphere was boisterous as the happy crowd celebrated a victory for the people. Tomorrow was the big day when the Freedom Charter would be approved. It would signal the start of a new initiative against the racist policies of the white government.

Sunday, 26 June 1955 started the same as the previous day. By ten o'clock the delegates were sweltering in the hot winter sunshine and Nomisile felt uncomfortable with her swelling stomach.

'Today we take a big step forward. We approve the Freedom Charter,' announced Nelson Mandela to deafening applause. He read the preamble. The crowd sat hushed, absorbing every word. 'We, the people of South Africa, declare for all in our country and the world to know: That South Africa belongs to all who live in it, black and white, and that no government can justly claim authority unless it is based on the will of the people.' He cleared his throat and continued. 'That our people have been robbed of their birthright to land, liberty and peace by a form of government founded on injustice and inequality; That our country will never be prosperous or free until all our people live in brotherhood, enjoying equal rights and opportunities.' Mandela took a sip of water. 'That only a democratic state, based on the will of all the people, can secure to all their birthright without distinction of colour, race, sex or belief. Therefore, we the people of South Africa, black and white together – equals, countrymen and brothers – adopt this Freedom Charter and we pledge ourselves to strive together, sparing nothing of our strength and courage, until the democratic changes here set out have been won.' Mandela sat down.

The delegates with one voice chanted their approval. '*Afrika! Mayibuye!*'

Nelson read the next clause: 'The people shall govern!'

Delegates threw their hands enthusiastically into the air. 'Africa! Return!'

Clause by clause, the Congress of the People debated and approved the charter.

Nelson Mandela shouted for all to hear, 'Now, the final paragraph, and we have an unanimous agreement on the whole Freedom Charter. These freedoms we will fight for, side by side, throughout our lives, until we have won our liberty.'

The crowd, as one, rose to their feet. They waved their arms, they danced and chanted over and over again. *'Afrika! Mayibuye!'*

They surrounded the delegates on the stage. They lifted Nelson Mandela high and he waved to the wildly cheering people. Nomisile fought to get near, rewarded by being able to touch Mandela's hand.

'Madiba,' she cried in adulation.

Nelson smiled at her as they placed him on the ground. 'Are you committed to our struggle?'

'Yes, Madiba! Oh, yes! I am your cousin from Qunu in the Transkei. Morris Memani is my father.'

'I remember him well. Please send him my regards.' She nodded enthusiastically. 'What is your name?'

'Nomisile Memani.' Her eyes sparkled in fervour, but her joy was short-lived as she heard shouted orders from the police.

'Go! Go!' the officer screamed and the police swung into action. They had been watching the whole time, now the uniformed policemen ran around the perimeter of the crowd, brandishing Sten-guns.

Delegates scattered in all directions. Nomisile let out a wail and darted through the crowd not stopping until she reached the willow trees. She watched as detectives rushed the leaders, grabbing at scraps of paper and rifling through their pockets. Nelson Mandela stood tall and proud as a detective searched him. 'Now that we have adopted the Freedom Charter you will never break the will of my people,' said Mandela in a scathing tone. 'We finally have a blueprint for success.'

Jafta and his friends found Nomisile hiding in the car.

'Have the police gone?' she asked, concern filming her huge almond eyes.

'Long ago,' they laughed. 'There were too many of us for them to control.'

'I hate the police,' declared Nomisile vehemently.

On the journey home Nomisile listened intently as the men

discussed the politics of the day. Their enthusiasm rubbed off on her and she formulated her own opinions. The white Nationalist government took on the form of a multi-tentacled monster, which was responsible for keeping her and Simon apart. By the time they reached home her discontent had crystallised into full-blown hatred, which she determined to pass on to her child.

'These kaffirs are nothing but a bunch of communists, they want to undermine the stability of the people.' Paulus Roux spoke with feeling as he sat at the head of the table in the manor house.

Simon looked at his father. 'But Pa, I read the Freedom Charter, it looks a perfectly innocent document to me.'

'Innocent, my foot,' exploded Paulus. 'Do you know what they want? They want the natural wealth of our country restored to the people. What have they ever done to bring wealth to our country? If it weren't for the white man, they'd still be inventing the wheel!'

Helena spoke quietly. 'Their sweat and labour have mined the diamonds for the white man. They work deep underground in the gold mines. They farm our lands. They do the manual work no white man would do.'

'Of course they do the kaffir work, that's what they're paid for. My point is that they are not responsible for the creation of wealth; that is due to the white man's efforts alone.'

'I think you're being unrealistic, Dad.' Helena was irritated. 'You must give the black man credit too!'

'Credit be damned, all the blacks want to do is grab, grab, grab. Do you know that in that Freedom Charter of theirs they want to transfer the mineral wealth beneath the soil to all the people. They want to nationalise the banks and other industries. Well, I tell you, our government won't allow such nonsense,' stormed Paulus.

'Then the government is wrong.' Helena was becoming annoyed with her father-in-law.

Paulus jumped to his feet, banging his fist on the large stinkwood dining-room table. 'Are you mad, Helena? Let me tell you, they won't rest until they have taken it all from us and killed every white in the process. Is that what you want, girl?'

'They won't kill us. They need our expertise. They're also people with rights and dreams. South Africa is their country too.'

'Paulus, calm down, dear, you know Helena has only two

months to go before her baby is born. Don't upset her so,' pleaded Marie.

Paulus sat down, muttering under his breath.

When they retired to the lounge for coffee Helena excused herself. She went to the telephone in the hall and dialled a Johannesburg number.

'Ruth Foley, good evening.'

'Hullo, this is Helena Roux from Paarl. I would be honoured to take on the position of chairwoman of the Cape branch of the Black Sash.'

'Master! Come quick – it's Miss Helena,' cried the servant breathlessly as she found Simon in the wine cellar.

Simon looked up in alarm. 'What's wrong?'

'It's her time, master.'

He ran to the cottage. Helena was sitting in the lounge, a small suitcase at her side.

'Darling, I'm glad you've come. Our baby's due.'

Simon looked flustered. 'What must I do?'

'Telephone the hospital and our parents, but hurry.'

'Now you watch those bumpy farm roads, Simon,' admonished Dr de Villiers. 'We don't want the child born in the car.'

Simon telephoned his mother. 'Mom, I'm taking Helena to hospital. She's due.'

'Oh! How wonderful. I'll tell your father.'

'Will you please also let Helena's family know?'

'Leave it to me,' promised Marie. 'You go off now.'

As Simon drove, Helena studied his face – so strong and good-looking. He was such a good man when he was sober. She was sure he would be a doting father. Perhaps the baby would bring them closer again. Not once throughout the entire pregnancy had Simon made advances. She was not sure if this was good or bad. The thrill of the baby inside her made her life complete. She squeezed his arm as the next pain started. 'Please hurry, Simon.'

Simon parked outside the doors to the emergency section. A welcoming committee was waiting for them. Dr de Villiers shook both their hands. The sister greeted them, while an orderly rolled a hospital trolley nearer. Two nurses assisted Helena to lie down. They pushed her to the lift and the whole party travelled to the second floor. They wheeled Helena straight to the labour room.

'Out with you,' instructed the doctor. 'We don't allow nervous husbands in here.'

Simon patted her arm. 'I'll be waiting outside the door.'

Paulus and Marie Roux joined Simon in the waiting room, followed ten minutes later by Jan and Nellie Marais. It was the longest few hours Simon could remember. He paced up and down trying to will away the minutes.

'Relax,' said Jan Marais, laughing, 'we've all been through this before!'

Things happened in a rush. Nurses ran in and out carrying towels. They heard Helena groaning and the doctor urging, 'Push, push now!' Helena let out a last cry and then there was silence.

'You can come in now, Mr Roux.'

Simon walked through the door not knowing what to expect. Sitting propped up by a multitude of pillows was a very smug Helena, a tiny bundle in the crook of her arm.

'It's a boy.' Helena smiled in delight. 'I've checked all his fingers, toes and other parts – they're all there.'

Simon kissed her, turning to his son. 'Why is he so small and crinkled?'

'He's just been born, but he will grow up to be as big as his daddy.'

'He certainly has a mop of black hair.'

'There's no denying who the father is,' laughed Helena. 'We've made a wonderful baby!'

Simon took the little bundle in his arms and was smitten. A son, my very own son, he thought in wonderment. At last something positive had come out of the empty shell of his marriage. This boy will become my heir and the centre of my existence, he promised himself. He turned to Helena. 'What are we going to name him?'

'What about your great-grandfather? Let's call him Pierre.'

'Pierre.' Simon rolled the name on his tongue. 'Pierre Roux.' He smiled. 'I like the name.'

He rushed off to give the good news to the waiting parents. 'Come and see the baby.'

The labour room was filled with gaiety. Dr de Villiers intervened. 'That's enough folks – it's time for Helena to rest.'

'How long will they be in hospital?'

'The usual ten days for the mother to rest and recover her strength. We treat the mother as we would an invalid so that her body functions can return to normal in an unhurried way.'

By the end of September Dr de Villiers allowed Helena and the baby to go home. Marie organised a special 'welcome home' lunch.

Throughout the meal Paulus wore a knowing grin, waiting until the end to make his special announcement. 'Your mother and I have decided to move to Cape Town, to be nearer parliament and she has chosen a house in the Gardens. We want you to move into the manor house. Your mother and I will take over the cottage for weekends, or when parliament is in recess.'

'Thank you, Pa.' Simon hugged his father, kissing him on the forehead. 'I was wondering how we were going to manage. Won't you miss the manor house?'

Paulus shrugged. 'To be honest, I will, but in life there is a time to come and a time to go. We have happy memories of our stay, but it is not as if we are losing it. We'll visit you often. You're a worthy heir, Simon.'

'This has happened many a time between father and son at Hermitage. It's like the changing of the guard at the Tower of London,' said Marie to break the silence. 'Anyway, your father and I have chosen the cutest little Victorian cottage with lots of cast-iron lattice work and shuttered windows, which is only five minutes' walk from parliament. It will make our lives so much easier. Your father was feeling the strain of driving in and out from Paarl every day.'

Helena kissed both Paulus and Marie. 'I promise you, I will make the manor house a wonderful home for Simon and your grandchildren.'

The first thunderheads of the new summer built up in the western heavens and a torpid hush settled over the Transkei in anticipation of the storm. A heavily pregnant Nomisile perspired in the muggy heat, trying to sleep after the midday meal.

'There is an *indoda* to see you, my child,' called Nosakani Memani.

'I don't want to see a married man, I look like a fat cow.' Nomisile indicated her stomach.

'He says it's all right.'

With a sigh, Nomisile struggled to her feet and waddled out of the circular thatched hut. She greeted. 'You want to see me?'

'*Molo umfazi*, I hear your name is Nomisile?'

'That is correct, what is your name?'

'I am Wilson Longwe, from the kraal over there.' He pointed to a cluster of thatched huts in the distance, about twenty minutes' walk away.

'How can I help you?'

'I want to talk to you. Can we go and sit under the tree?' He motioned towards the sneezewood.

'All right.' Nomisile had an inkling of what was to come and looked at her prospective suitor intently.

He was small-boned and wizened with a very dark skin. He had a scraggly beard and was not even as tall as herself. He wore khaki trousers with turn-ups, home-made ox-hide boots with rubber car-tyre soles and no socks. He had on a faded khaki shirt, with a frayed collar, a green polo-neck jersey covered with another V-neck red jersey, a striped grey suit jacket over the jerseys and the traditional red blanket over his shoulder.

He must be boiling under that welter of clothes, she thought, knowing it was Xhosa custom for the men to pad themselves thickly in the belief that many clothes, like the thick wool on a sheep, kept them cool in the heat.

Nomisile's mind flashed back to Simon, who would be dressed only in shorts and a light cotton shirt in October. She felt a pang of pain shoot through her heart at the thought.

They sat under the shade of the *umtati*, Nomisile in the traditional style for a woman with her legs folded in under her. Wilson like all Xhosa men sat with his legs crossed in front of him. He gazed at Nomisile for a long time, noting her beauty. Her stomach was swollen with child but her breasts were firm and proud, her nipples enlarged and surrounded by dark-brown areolas. Pregnancy had filled out her face and she radiated serenity.

Yes, Wilson decided, she will make a fine wife. She is young, tall and strong and will be able to hoe my mealie patches in fine style.

He took off his felt hat, folding and putting it in his jacket pocket. Nomisile looked at his receding hair-line and guessed his age at about thirty-five.

Wilson was reticent, not sure how to broach the subject. To hide his discomfort he searched in his jacket pocket and took out a long-stemmed wooden pipe, the flared bowl lined with tin. From another pocket he took a yellow cotton drawstring bag of Springbok brand tobacco. He filled the bowl with the dark shag, tamping it down with his thumb. Flicking an old silver lighter, he drew deeply, puffing out grey clouds of pungent smoke.

'I have spoken to your father, Morris,' began Wilson, 'and we have reached agreement, eight head of cattle – five cows and three oxen – for you.'

Nomisile exploded. 'Do you think that I'm worth only eight scrawny cattle? You want me for a wife to slave for you in your house and on your lands, and all you offer is cattle to my father! What about me? You have not asked how I feel. You don't even know me. You don't mention love. What do you offer except cattle?'

Wilson was taken aback at the tirade and lapsed into deep thought again, sucking on his pipe. He spat out a nicotine-stained ball of saliva. It sailed through the air, striking the dry earth with a puff of dust.

Nomisile was sickened. How could one compare this simple tribal man to the strong, vital and charming Simon? Inside herself she cried for the loss of the man she loved. Oh! Simon, my love, oh! Simon, my love, she repeated over and over to herself.

Eventually Wilson cleared his throat. 'Then I am prepared to add another ox. But you must know I take you under duress, for you carry another man's child. You are second hand.'

'Second hand!' cried Nomisile vehemently. 'You still haven't got the point. Cattle are no good to me, they go to my father. What about me? What about my child?'

'No man will take you as his first wife. It is against our custom to have a woman who has had another man's child as his principal wife. I offer you the position of my third wife. I will not allow your child in my kraal.'

'You will not allow my child to live with me?'

'It is Xhosa tradition that such a child be raised by the grandparents. Morris and Nosakani have agreed to these terms.'

'I won't give up my child and I do not want to marry you.'

'You have no choice.' Wilson looked at her condescendingly. 'Your father and I have reached an agreement.'

Nomisile jumped to her feet. 'Never! Never!' She ran back to her hut and slammed the door. She wept in frustration. I'd rather be your second wife, Simon. I don't mind sharing you with Helena.

After sitting a while longer, Wilson walked across to his long-haired brown pony. He rode away, shaking his head in bewilderment.

Hours later Nosakani quietly entered the hut. 'Here, my daughter, drink this.' She handed her a calabash of *amasi*. Nomisile drank the beaten-up, soured cow's milk, the tartness easing her dry throat.

'Wilson Longwe is a good man,' began her mother.

'I don't need a husband.' Nomisile stared at her mother stubbornly. 'I can live my whole life alone with my child.'

'A husband will look after you and give you more children. A woman's lot is not to live alone.'

'It is my life, I will decide.'

'You are wrong.' Nosakani spoke seriously. 'It is for your father to decide what is best for you. We have discussed the matter and feel Wilson will make you a good husband. He is well off – he has over thirty cattle, some sixty sheep and goats and two horses.'

'If it is cattle my father wants, I have money. I can buy him cows and oxen,' declared Nomisile.

Her mother laughed. 'Where would a young girl like you get such riches?'

Nomisile was about to retort, when she felt a spasm rack her body. 'It's starting,' she gasped, holding her stomach. Nosakani jumped up to fetch help.

The contraction passed and Nomisile lay back, perspiring profusely. The pains came every ten minutes. The tribal medicine woman was summoned. The *umthiwabafaas* wiped Nomisile down to keep her cool. The hours passed.

'When will the baby come?' gasped Nomisile.

'It is your first-born, it takes longer. I think there is a great Xhosa warrior waiting to come out.' The old woman smiled a toothless smile.

Nomisile thought of Simon. This baby is his, of course it will be big and strong.

The curer of ills had a fire going in the middle of the hut, with two rectangular paraffin tins balancing on stones to one side. Nomisile could see the steam rising from the tins, mixing with the smoke from the fire. It was hot and humid in the closed hut. Outside it was dark.

'Here, drink this,' offered the medicine woman, holding an enamel cup to Nomisile's lips. She sipped the bitter concoction and coughed. 'What is it?'

'It's a herb tea, made from the *dagga* plant. The marijuana will soothe you and you will feel less pain.'

Nomisile felt the drug start to take effect. She felt drowsy and light-headed and giggled quietly to herself. Her head spun as she was transported to another world. She saw Paarl Mountain. Simon was standing before her, holding out his arms. She grabbed for his hands, sighing in satisfaction as she felt his grip, not realising that the fingers belonged to the medicine woman. Nomisile murmured contentedly as she felt hands on her body. It was Simon, stroking her with his strong hands once again. The medicine woman examined her. 'Oh! Simon, thandi,' she cried as she thrilled to his touch. The baby moved in her belly. 'I feel you inside me, thandi.'

His image faded and Nomisile shook her head in agitation. The medicine woman held the cup of medicinal tea to her lips again and she swallowed the remains in one gulp. As if by magic, Simon returned.

Nomisile sat up and shouted to him. 'I love you! I love you! You are here to see your seed germinate from my body.' The old woman fell on top of Nomisile, forcing her down, struggling to keep her still. 'Yes! Yes!' Nomisile cried in exaltation. 'I feel your weight on top of me, Simon. I love you.'

As the increased dosage of the drug coursed through her veins, Nomisile was numbed into silence, with perspiration pouring off her.

Simon moved the fish mobile out of the way and looked down at Pierre sleeping contentedly in his cot. He tenderly tucked a chubby hand under the blanket, kissed his son on the forehead and walked out of the nursery. He was tired – it had been a long and exhausting day, first transporting his parents' furniture to Cape Town and then moving their household from the cottage into the manor house.

Helena lay in the double bed; it worried her that Simon displayed absolutely no sexual interest in her. She knew that if he didn't get satisfaction he would start looking elsewhere. She smiled at him sweetly as he walked into the room. 'Close the door, my darling, turn out the light and come to bed.'

He looked at her in surprise and slowly walked towards the bed. He pulled down the sheets. She was naked. Her breasts were ugly and swollen with milk, the skin of her stomach flabby and wrinkled and stretch marks showed on her hips.

Simon shuddered. He couldn't face her sober. In the dining room he removed a bottle of KWV and a glass from the cocktail cabinet. He poured as he walked and was on his second drink by the time he reached the bedroom.

Incensed, Helena said sarcastically, 'Put that damn bottle away and just do what you are supposed to do.'

'Who said I wanted to do anything?' Simon's voice was tinged with scorn. 'With you it's like stuffing a corpse.'

'Leave it then.' Helena pulled up the sheet and turned her back on her husband.

He poured another, the alcohol unleashing his violent streak. His voice shook as he shouted at her. 'Don't you start something you can't finish.' He grabbed her by the hair and pulled her to the floor.

'Oh, God! Not this again,' she wailed and tried to dart away.

Simon was quick for a big man and caught her half-way across the room. Fury made him stronger. He hit her. Helena looked a pitiful sight, crumpled in the corner. He advanced menacingly. At the last moment he turned, walked towards the dressing table and drank straight from the bottle, wiping his mouth with the back of his hand. Helena dashed behind the *chaise longue*, keeping it between Simon and herself. He staggered towards her.

'Please, Simon, please be reasonable,' Helena cried in fear.

'Reasonable?' he asked, laughing derisively. 'I've been reasonable for over two years, always being nice to you. Well now it's your turn to be nice to me.' He undid his belt and stepped out of his pants. She tried to slip away, but he leaned over the couch and grabbed her arm, twisting and turning until he had her face downwards over the curved arm of the *chaise longue*. Helena struggled and kicked but she was no match for him. With one hand on the back of her neck he pushed her head down on to the seat, her body jack-knifed, with her legs not quite touching the floor.

Simon pushed her legs apart and entered her viciously. Helena wailed at being treated like a bitch in season. One flat hand against the back of her head silenced her. Simon closed his eyes and suddenly there was Nomisile, holding out her hands and smiling lovingly at him. She was speaking to him and he grunted in pleasure as he heard her words.

'Oh! Simon, thandi.'

He pushed in as deep as he could and he sighed as he heard her reaction.

'I feel you inside me, thandi.'

Speeding up he felt the thread coming from deep inside. 'I love you! I love you!' repeated Simon as he exploded in ecstasy.

Nomisile responded as she'd always reacted to his lovemaking and Simon saw her lips moving as she shouted at him, 'You are here to see your seed germinate from my body.'

'Yes! Yes!' he breathed as he collapsed in contentment.

Again Nomisile's voice reached him. 'I feel your weight on top of me, Simon.' Her voice was breathless and passionate and her smile was one of complete satisfaction.

Then her image faded and Simon looked around desperately. The room spun around him and he pushed himself to a standing position. The sight of Helena's white bottom made him shake his head in confusion. Where was Nomisile? Where had she gone? He forcefully turned Helena over, blanching at the sight of her face. Walking to the bed, he sat down heavily, his head in his hands.

Helena scuttled to the bathroom. She was still shaking when she returned to the room in a dressing-gown. Simon was on the bed, sobbing quietly, and her heart went out to him. It was after all her fault, she reasoned, that she had turned a once-flawless man into this Jekyll and Hyde. She timidly approached him, speaking in a deflated voice. 'I don't understand you, Simon. You batter me one moment and the next you tell me you love me.'

'When did I say I loved you?'

'You told me twice.'

'I'm confused – I don't know,' he hiccuped.

Helena helped him to his side of the bed, covering him, a forgiving look on her face. She turned out the light and crept in beside him.

The pains came one on top of another. The healer wiped her with a cloth. Nomisile felt a rush of warm liquid between her thighs. 'That is a good sign, your water has broken.' The old woman packed newspapers and magazines under Nomisile to absorb the moisture. She went to the door and called Nosakani and an aunt to help her.

It was dark in the hut except for the fire's embers. The old woman lit two candles which gave off a flickering glow. The next pain came, and the medicine woman urged Nomisile to force the foetus out.

Nothing happened. The healer could see the top of the head, but Nomisile was not dilating sufficiently. She stuck her crooked finger between the baby's head and the birth canal, circling the head and stretching the vaginal wall. At the next contraction the head emerged a little further.

Nomisile flopped back, exhausted. The contractions gave her no respite. She pushed her feet into her mother's and aunt's hips, pushing down so hard that she lifted off the ground. Nomisile felt something give.

'Good, the head is out,' cackled the old woman. 'Now for the body.' The foetus was twisted and the shoulders would not emerge. Nomisile shoved and pressed but the baby would not move. She was nearing the end of her endurance, with her thrusts becoming weaker and weaker.

Between contractions the medicine woman slipped her hands into Nomisile's womb, turning the baby, bringing out an arm and a shoulder. 'Last push, make it a big one.'

Nomisile made one last desperate effort. She felt herself tear as she rammed the baby through. A sense of emptiness followed.

The baby slid into waiting hands and the umbilical cord tumbled out. The healer placed the baby on Nomisile's stomach and with a piece of sheepskin wiped the eyes, removed the mucus from the nostrils and washed out the mouth. Nomisile lay back exhausted, gasping in great mouthfuls of air.

The medicine woman opened a small pouch, taking out thinly cut strips of lamb skin cured to a silky consistency. Three fingers from the baby's stomach she tied off the umbilical cord. Measuring two more fingers she made another knot. With a sharp knife she cut the cord between the two ties.

Picking up the baby the medicine woman put it to Nomisile's nipple and it suckled vigorously.

'Is it a boy or a girl?' she whispered to her mother.

'It's a boy, a big strong boy. His father must have been a man among men – he is a huge baby.'

'He's got a big *tonto*.' The aunt smiled shyly. 'One day he will give his wives much pleasure!'

The next morning Nomisile was up early as it was her duty to fetch the household water from the river. She washed herself and felt much better. Hefting the full paraffin tin on to her head she struggled back home.

Her baby was exquisite, she thought as she looked lovingly at the infant. She washed him, noting his light-brown skin, lighter than hers, but darker than Simon's swarthy hue. Nobody will know he is not a true Xhosa, she told herself, for many of our people, including Nelson Mandela, are lighter skinned.

She looked into his dark-brown eyes. She kissed the pink soles of his feet and the insides of his hands – much lighter than the darker upper skin. His head was covered in tight, crisp little tufts of woolly hair. His nose was not flat, but then, neither was hers nor Simon's. She saw Simon fleetingly in his face and was saddened that he could not be there to share this moment with her.

She was convinced her baby would pass as a genuine Xhosa, which was all part of her plan for him. He was of royal blood and she would guide him to play a big part in releasing her people from the white man's bondage – the apartheid laws that kept her and Simon at opposite ends of South Africa.

Nomisile pondered a name. She eventually settled on Themba, to show he was a member of the powerful Thembu tribe. She used her surname for the child. Nomisile turned to her mother. 'His name is Themba Memani.'

Her mother nodded, smiling in acceptance.

Three weeks after Themba's birth Nomisile travelled to Umtata. She had a photograph taken of the two of them, as she had promised Simon. She reread her letter to him for the tenth time.

My dearest Simon,

Our baby, Themba, was born on 20 October 1955. He is a big, strapping boy, like his father. You would be proud of him.

He is all I have of you, to remind me of our time together.

As you requested, I have enclosed a photograph of us in this letter.

I have decided my son shall grow up as a Xhosa, it will make his life less complicated. It is my wish that he must never discover a white man was his father. Please respect that desire, as you promised on Paarl station.

I am also well, but often think of Hermanus and Paarl. I blame the police and apartheid laws for us not being together.

Thank you for the money you pay into my post office book every month, it is a great help.

I miss you – all my love,

Nomisile.

Into the envelope she slipped the photograph and posted it to Petrus Potgieter, at a post office box in Simondium.

Simon's face lit up when he saw the saw the letter postmarked Umtata. He was thrilled to learn he had another son, Themba, born exactly to the day a month after Pierre.

Simon looked closely at the photograph, noting his son's features. He looks a typical Xhosa, he decided, but I can see a slight resemblance to myself in his face. He has his mother's regal way of holding his head, with the same direct gaze. Oh, my beautiful Nomisile, thought Simon, as he concentrated on her face. You look so proud of the baby, but do I detect a look of sadness in your eyes?

Simon could not bear to destroy the letter and the photograph, it was all he had to remind himself of the happiest moments in his life. Neither could he hide them in the house or anywhere on the farm for fear of discovery. That afternoon he took a new scrap book, a writing pad and a pot of glue with him and set off up Paarl Mountain to his secret place.

With only a circling kestrel for company he could think clearly. He had two sons, one would lead a life of privileged Afrikaner luxury, the other was fated to live simply, out of the mainstream of society. He determined that Themba should not suffer. He would have the best a black child could have despite the apartheid system.

He glued Nomisile's letter and the photograph on to the

first page of the scrap book, the first of many, he vowed, which would form a record of his far-away son's life – the son he could never know and whose existence he could never reveal.

7

The February south-easter ruffled the oaks as Paulus and Marie Roux walked towards parliament for the 1956 official opening ceremony. Men were dressed in their finest suits with carnation buttonholes, while the women added colour and gaiety in the latest fashions. Marie's outfit had been specially made for her by one of Cape Town's leading designers. She was in black and white from head to heel – tweed woollen suit with alternate black and white buttons, black silk blouse which spectacularly offset a large pearl brooch. Crocodile leather high-heeled shoes in black and white, white gloves, a black clutch bag and a wide-brimmed white felt hat with a black band completed her ensemble.

'You look stunning, my dear. I'm proud of you,' said Paulus.

She smiled at the compliment. 'And you look dashing, too, in your new suit.'

'Why did you choose black and white? Most of the other wives seem to have chosen pastel colours and florals. You look the most sensational, of course,' he added hurriedly.

'Well, it's a sign of the times. The colours match the future of South Africa.' She was rewarded with a sour grimace.

'Please, Mr and Mrs Roux, stand together for a photograph.' A photographer from the *Cape Times* clicked his camera, heading for the next couple. 'Watch tomorrow's paper for your photos.'

The MPs were ushered on to the broad steps of the Houses of Parliament – an impressive red brick building with huge smooth columns and topped by a classical, triangular pediment. They waited for the retinue to arrive.

It was a warm summer morning and the leafy trees rustled in the breeze. The naval band led the procession, the men resplendent in their starched white uniforms. Next came a platoon from the army, marching down Parliament Street in their khaki drill, followed

117

by a company from the air force in sky-blue uniforms. They were succeeded by a squad from the naval base at Simonstown. An open, horse-drawn carriage came next. Inside were Prime Minister Strijdom and Governor-General Jansen and their wives. Completing the procession were a hundred mounted police with long, sharp-tipped lances.

The carriage stopped opposite the entrance to the parliamentary building. A red carpet ran from the edge of the pavement to the large doorway. A footman opened the carriage door and the VIPs alighted. Everyone stood to attention while the navy band played the British anthem, 'God Save the Queen', and the South African anthem, '*Die Stem*'.

A twenty-one gun salute fired from the battery on Signal Hill, the echoes resounding in the city bowl and re-echoing off the slopes of Table Mountain.

The Prime Minister and his wife walked towards the steps. Instantly their path was barred by four women in white dresses, wearing black sashes. The Prime Minister's retinue stopped. Not a word was uttered by the women as they stood to attention, gazing levelly into Strijdom's eyes.

Seeing his carefully planned timing interrupted, the parliamentary sergeant-at-arms rushed forward. He separated the four women into two groups of two and pushed them off the red carpet.

'Damn Black Sash with their sashes and silent protests,' muttered the Prime Minister.

The women did not resist the sergeant-at-arms. They stood serenely at the edge of the carpet, looking inwards. The photographers clicked away at the unexpected action.

Paulus, standing on the steps, had a bird's-eye view of the proceedings. It was only when the women moved to the side, showing their faces, that he recognised Helena. 'What the hell is Helena doing here?' he hissed.

'Helena, where's Helena?' Marie asked, perplexed.

'Down there, damn it, wearing one of those detestable black sashes.' Paulus nodded towards the steps.

'Oh yes, I see her now.'

'How can my daughter-in-law insult me so?'

'Calm down now, she must have her reasons.'

The main procession moved forward for the official photographs to be taken. Paulus seethed with anger, but had to smile for the cameras. He wanted to go down and shake Helena, tell her how she was humiliating the Roux family name, but that would have given the English press a field day.

Every half-hour Helena and her three friends marched slowly down Parliament Street, into Government Avenue and back to their station in front of parliament. In the late afternoon they called it a day. They had made their presence felt. They retired to a cafeteria for a welcome cup of tea.

At the first opportunity Paulus went looking for Helena. She was nowhere to be seen. He clenched his fists in vexation, determined to challenge her later.

Simon put four-month-old Pierre back in his cot, nodded to Sophie the maid and went to answer the telephone.

'Hermitage, Simon Roux speaking.'

'I want to speak to Helena.' Simon recognised his father's voice and was surprised at the curt tone.

'Helena's not here, Pa. She took the train to Johannesburg this morning. She went to a Black Sash rally.'

'Damn. I hope she's not going to be part of that cavalcade to Cape Town,' growled Paulus.

'That's it; she mentioned something about a convoy to parliament. What's the problem?'

'She humiliated me at parliament yesterday. She stood with those Black Sash women. To make matters worse, there's a picture of her in the newspaper this morning. It's not good for my political career.'

'She'll be back next week.'

'Son, how can you allow your wife to campaign against us?'

'Pa, Helena has strong feelings about the government's policies, particularly the forced removal of coloureds from parliament. She wants to express her disapproval through the Black Sash in a non-violent way.'

Paulus exploded at the other end of the line. 'A woman's place is at home, caring for her husband and children. How can you let her go off alone?'

Simon could not tell his father that Helena and he had drifted apart without disclosing many sordid details. 'Sophie looks after Pierre most of the time anyway.'

119

'Humph!' growled Paulus. 'I hope this foolish act on Helena's part is not going to affect your chances of joining the Broederbond.'

Belching clouds of grey smoke, the Trans-Karoo ground to a halt at Johannesburg station. Helena and her friends, still elated from their success at the opening of parliament, stepped off the train.

Another Black Sash woman stepped forward to greet them, her eyes sparkling. 'You certainly stirred things up in Cape Town. Well done.' She showed them the front page of the *Star*, with a photograph of the four women and a full write-up of their stand.

Helena was thrown into a week of hectic activity. The mass cavalcade by motor car to Cape Town to demonstrate against the government was a milestone for the Black Sash movement. Over six hundred women drawn from all parts of the country were expected to make the journey. She made hundreds of telephone calls to help the mothers find suitable baby-sitters for their children. At last they were ready.

On the morning of departure the women fixed printed signboards to their cars, with the words: RESPECT OUR CONSTITUTION – EERBIEDIG ONS GRONDWET. Ensigns denoted their home town or city.

Leaving Johannesburg they drove slowly, stopping at towns along the way to publicise their stand. They distributed pamphlets, they talked to people, they gave public addresses explaining why the Black Sash opposed apartheid laws and how it affected the disenfranchised blacks, coloureds and Indians.

All along the route smaller groupings joined the convoy, swelling the numbers. In Bloemfontein a large contingent from Natal joined. Through the dusty Karoo they travelled, at the pace of the lead car – a green Morris Minor with a large gold book representing the constitution of the Union of South Africa fixed to the roof.

The women's spirits were high. For each the trip had become a personal crusade to register her disapproval of the practices of the Nationalist government. Singly their voices carried no weight, together they presented a unified front that would have to be noticed.

They reached Stellenbosch, where they were to spend the final evening of their journey. Helena and the executive members drove to Paarl to stay over at Hermitage.

The manor house became their headquarters. Telephone calls flew back and forth to Cape Town to organise the finale the next morning. At dawn Helena and her friends drove to Stellenbosch to meet the cars. More than a hundred and fifty vehicles set out for the Mother City and legislative capital: the little green Morris Minor headed the largest white protest in history.

Thousands of well-wishers lined the streets. People hung out of the high-rise office buildings and from balconies. Streamers of used telex paper fluttered down, giving the women a New York style ticker-tape parade.

The cavalcade parked on The Parade, the large open square opposite the city hall. The Black Sash marched the last part of the way to the Houses of Parliament. Thousands of cheering people of all races and colours fell in behind them, creating a carnival atmosphere.

Suddenly police vans blocked their path. The leaders approached the police officer in charge. 'Why are you preventing the march?' cried Helena.

'Only whites are allowed to march,' declared the officer grimly. 'If you continue we will arrest every non-white and throw them in jail.'

The Black Sash executive met hastily. Rather than force a confrontation they agreed at Helena's suggestion to proceed with a two-day vigil outside parliament.

Ninety women at a time stood silent vigil around the parliamentary complex. In white dresses, draped with their characteristic black sashes, they represented the aspirations of black people to share in the privileges afforded only to whites in South Africa.

The leaders stood vigil throughout the first night. They were relieved at dawn. 'I'm tired and absolutely famished, but it's worth it,' smiled Helena. They ate a frugal breakfast, then curled up for a few hours' sleep in the convoy cars. At nine o'clock they headed back to the Houses of Parliament, where they had secured seats in the public gallery. On the agenda was the first reading of another discriminatory piece of legislation.

Fourteen members, including Helena Roux, took their places. They looked down on the floor of the main house.

Prime Minister Strijdom rose and addressed the speaker. 'Mr Speaker, I seek your leave to introduce to this joint sitting, of this honourable House of Parliament, the terms of The Act of

121

Separate Representation of Voters, Amendment 35, for due debate, consideration and approval.'

The fourteen women donned their black sashes and stood to attention. Parliament stopped. Strijdom looked up quizzically, shocked that his beloved institution should be disrupted in this way. The opposition United Party parliamentarians rose to their feet and cheered.

Paulus stood up in disbelief as he noticed Helena standing in the gallery. He shook his fist at her.

The Speaker banged his gavel, trying to restore order. A parliamentary messenger hurried across to the women and removed the fourteen sashes. At a nod from Ruth Foley, their national president, each woman took a black silk rose from her handbag and pinned it on her dress.

Another messenger was dispatched to the gallery. 'Take off those roses, they are not allowed.'

The fourteen had made their point dramatically in front of the combined sitting, the Press and, most importantly, the foreign media. The women marched silently out of the public gallery in protest.

'Police state!' shouted opposition MPs in glee.

Helena was incensed. Turning on the sergeant-at-arms she berated him. 'Why have you confiscated our sashes?'

The confused official offered to return the sashes, as long as the women did not wear them.

'What about our roses?' asked Helena. 'Surely you can't stop a woman wearing a rose?'

The sergeant-at-arms had never had to deal with such a situation. He ruled it was in order for the women to wear the roses, but not the sashes. The women repinned the black roses to their dresses and returned to their seats in the public gallery. Opposition members greeted them with a standing ovation.

The Nationalists glowered. The women watched the rest of the morning's proceedings in dignified silence, but their presence was felt. Repeated glances from the Prime Minister testified to their success.

The showdown between Paulus and Helena took place in the study on Saturday morning.

Paulus got straight to the point. 'I would like you to resign from that Black Sash organisation of yours, Helena.'

Helena looked him in the eye. 'Why should I? I believe in the principles of the Black Sash.'

Paulus controlled his temper with difficulty, his flared nostrils and high colour the only outward sign of his rage. He stared stonily at Helena for a long time. She returned his gaze calmly.

'Simon, pour us a brandy, please.' Paulus realised he had to try another tack.

'Do you have the interests of your husband and son at heart?'

'Of course, Dad, they are the two most important people in the world to me.'

'Then this Black Sash thing must stop. It's for rich, frustrated English ladies, who pay lip-service to human rights. They sit around tea tables in high-class suburbs like Constantia and Sandown and Durban North, slandering our efforts to make South Africa a haven for white people. An Afrikaner girl doesn't belong with them. Helena, will you, for all our sakes, stop your Black Sash activities?'

'Define activities. There is our physical presence at places where cabinet ministers go, and also our background work in helping disadvantaged people affected by government policy.'

'Both,' answered Paulus abruptly.

Helena weighed up her options. Am I being a hypocrite, she wondered. I forced Nomisile to leave Paarl, compelled her to live in a homeland, used apartheid for my own ends. At the same time, through the Black Sash, I'm fighting the system. What's driving me? It's my guilty conscience, she concluded. Nevertheless she still felt a genuine desire to help the disenfranchised of South Africa.

She was realistic enough to admit her Black Sash involvement could affect Paulus in parliament, Simon in the political career that had been mapped out for him, and her child. My first loyalty is to my family, the second to my beliefs, she concluded. The study was quiet, Paulus and Simon waiting for Helena to arrive at her conclusions.

Helena cleared her throat. 'I'll agree to drop my active role in the Black Sash.'

'Very good,' started Paulus.

Helena held up her hand for silence. 'I haven't finished yet. The visible role of carrying placards and wearing sashes at conspicuous places I am prepared to stop, but not the work behind the scenes. There I can help my fellow man by giving my sympathy to those in distress and my aid to the needy.'

Paulus realised he was not going to get a better deal, that his main objective of removing her from the limelight would be achieved. The security police would still watch her and record her activities, but at least she would no longer publicly embarrass the Roux name. 'Thank you,' he said. 'I accept your terms.'

The first spring rains brought welcome relief to the Transkei. The dry, red grass came to life and the rolling hills took on an emerald-green countenance.

Every patch of cultivated land was a hive of activity from dawn to sunset. Led by young boys, teams of long-horned, hump-necked oxen toiled up and down the fields. Yokes strained at the drag of the ploughs, manned by the men, as they guided the sharp ploughshares into the earth, turning over the rich, loamy soil. Older men walked alongside, cracking long whips over the backs of the oxen to keep them moving forward.

Once Wilson had ploughed his allotted lands, he levelled them with a multi-tooth drag harrow, breaking up the clods to form a fine tilth in which to plant the mealies. Youths with sharpened sticks made holes in the soft soil. Wilson followed, accurately dropping a seed into each hole, stamping the soil and covering the seed.

The whole planting operation was completed by the end of October. Wilson could relax, for his annual task was concluded. The hoeing, reaping and milling was the women's work. 'It will be a wet year,' Wilson told his brother. 'The weeds will grow fast. I need more hands – it is time for Nomisile.'

Early the next morning he cut out five cows and four young oxen from his herd, and drove them over to Morris Memani's kraal.

Nomisile saw the procession approaching. Her heart sank – the months had passed and Themba was weaned, and her day of reckoning was at hand.

Morris turned to his daughter. 'You have to go, Nomisile.'

'I beg of you,' pleaded Nomisile, anguish on her face.

Her father shook his head. 'An agreement has been reached, you will go.'

'Give Themba to me.' Nosakani held out her arms. He went readily to her, walking on unsteady legs.

'Come and stand by my side, Nomisile.' Morris stood in front of his hut. Wilson drove the cattle past slowly so that Morris could check to see he had fulfilled his part of the bargain. Morris signalled to a young boy to open the gate of the cattle pen. Wilson chased the cattle inside, concluding his part of the barter. He addressed Morris, not even glancing at Nomisile. 'I have come for my wife.'

Morris took Nomisile's right hand, placing it in Wilson's out-stretched right palm. 'I give you my daughter in marriage.'

Wilson closed his fingers, squeezing Nomisile's hand. 'I accept your daughter in marriage.'

'Is that all,' cried Nomisile, 'no other ceremony?'

'You are my third wife.' Wilson looked at her for the first time. 'There is no ceremony.'

Nomisile darted inside, clutching Themba to her breast. 'I won't go. You can't force me.'

'You will go now!' Morris grabbed her by the arm. 'My honour is at stake.' He spoke in a gruff voice. 'Join your husband this minute.'

Wailing in despair, Nomisile handed Themba to her mother. 'Look after him well.'

Nosakani smiled in sympathy. 'Come and visit often.'

With a sense of foreboding Nomisile carried her suitcase outside. Wilson nodded to Morris, turned on his heel and walked towards his home.

'Help me with my suitcase, Wilson,' Nomisile screamed after him, stamping her foot.

He turned around and stared at her contemptuously. 'You know it is the woman's job to carry everything. I must walk in front, unhindered, to protect you.'

'You ungracious man,' she shouted. She wrapped a shawl around the top of her head to act as a cushion. Grunting, she swung up the heavy suitcase and balanced it. She started after Wilson, walking as straight as a ramrod, equalising the weight to maintain her equilibrium.

'Don't walk so fast.' She struggled to keep up. Wilson ignored her pleas. She cursed. 'Why do you treat me so badly?' Simon, she thought, would have carried her load.

When they reached his kraal Nomisile looked around at her new home. Wilson's kraal consisted of four round huts built in a circle, each one's door facing the centre.

He pointed to the largest hut. 'That is my hut. I share it with my principal wife.' Indicating two smaller huts, he explained, 'That is the hut of my second wife and that one there is shared by my mother and children. That one is yours.' He indicated a newly constructed hut.

No one welcomed Nomisile. A few pot-bellied children playing in the dirt hardly gave her a glance. Wilson disappeared into his hut for breakfast. Nomisile inspected her new home, unfurnished except for a large reed mat and a three-legged cooking pot. Inside the pot was crumbly maize meal, which she ate hungrily with her fingers.

There was a knock at the door. Nomisile opened it to Wilson, who was holding a flat weeding hoe with a long wooden handle. 'Yes?' Nomisile inquired.

'This is your *ligaba*. My other wives are already in the field, down by the river.' He pressed the implement into her hands.

'Do you expect me to hoe on my first day?' Nomisile exploded.

'It is a wife's work. You are now my wife. You must hoe.'

Nomisile ran a few paces forward and cast it from her as far as she could. It travelled in an arc, landed awkwardly on the metal tine and snapped the wooden shaft in half. Wilson turned angrily on Nomisile, but she escaped back through her doorway and locked the door. Through the ill-fitting planks she watched Wilson muttering to himself as he disappeared from view.

When the women returned from the fields in the late afternoon they called Nomisile. 'Come out, tonight we celebrate. A sheep has been slaughtered in your honour.'

Nomisile sat in front of her hut watching the preparations. A large fire was lit. When the flames had burnt down a whole sheep was spread-eagled on the coals. The smell of roasting meat pervaded the air. Fresh coals were placed inside the rib-cage and over the thicker shoulders and hindquarters. The mutton cooked in its own juices until it was tender and almost falling off the bone.

Nomisile was called over. 'I am the principal wife,' a fat, dumpy woman nodded in greeting.

'*Molo umfazi*,' acknowledged Nomisile.

The wife scowled at her. 'You are supposed to kneel in front of me.'

'Why? What makes you so important?' The wife turned around in disgust and resumed her place at the fire.

Another woman approached Nomisile. 'I am the second wife.' She smiled a welcome and squeezed Nomisile's hand.

'How do you do.' Nomisile smiled back at her gratefully. The wife resumed her seat.

Wilson stood up and cut a long strip of mutton from the shoulder.

126

He placed the meat on a wooden platter and handed it to a man at the fire.

The man came and sat cross-legged in front of Nomisile. 'I am Wilson's brother. It is my task to welcome you to our family.'

He took out a knife, cut the meat into small blocks and with a sharpened stick speared a piece, holding it to Nomisile's lips. She was hungry and took the morsel. He fed her, piece by piece, until the meat was finished.

'You have eaten of our food, now you are one of the family,' announced the brother.

The principal wife rose and cut some of the choice titbits from the sheep. She handed them to Wilson. When he had finished eating, he took out his pipe. This seemed to be a signal for the others to eat. In twenty minutes the carcass was reduced to bones.

Wilson tapped out his pipe and stood up, indicating to those present that the meal had ended. He disappeared into the largest hut. Within seconds the forecourt was devoid of people.

Nomisile was left alone. She sat for a while longer, then entered her hut. She locked the crude wooden hasp and staple by pushing a sharpened stick through the loop. She prepared to retire. She was just dozing off when she heard three distinct knocks on her door.

'Who is it?'

'Wilson.'

'Go away, I don't want you,' cried out Nomisile in defiance.

Again the evenly spaced knocks beat against the door. 'I knock three times, for you are my third wife. Let me in.'

'No,' cried Nomisile.

'I knock for the last time,' declared Wilson hammering three loud knocks.

'Good, now he will go away,' thought Nomisile, relaxing.

The next moment the wooden catch gave way as Wilson shouldered the door. It crashed open. He strode purposefully inside, kicking the door shut. He lit a sheep's-fat lamp, the small flame dimly lighting up the inside of the hut.

Wilson was dressed only in a loincloth. He looked smaller and bonier without the heavy padding of layers of clothing. Nomisile was sickened to think she was expected to make love to this little man.

He lay down beside her. He did not waste time with the finer details of kissing and foreplay. He put his hand up her crotch. Nomisile was sickened by his touch and loathed his smell. She clamped her thighs firmly together. Wilson forced her arms above her head, pinning her wrists to the floor. He straddled her, trying to enter her. She struggled free, jumping up, with Wilson following. Nomisile danced around the centre pole of the hut, dodging Wilson's lunges. He caught her arm, threw her to the ground and pounced on her.

Nomisile brought up her knee. Wilson grunted in pain and released her. Nomisile crouched in dread. 'Go away, leave me alone.'

'Stop fighting, do your duty as a wife,' he spat at her.

Nomisile quaked as she saw the murderous look in his eyes. He slapped her flat-handed across the mouth. She cried out, falling to the floor. He sat on her stomach raining blows on her face. She scratched at his eyes, feeling her nails tearing into his flesh. She fought like a cornered animal.

Wilson hit her until she lost consciousness.

She came to her senses with Wilson on top of her, raping her. Nomisile screamed and fought, trying to claw her way out from under him. He hit her until she lay still. Through a haze she felt the pain, crying quietly to herself, 'Oh! Simon, my thandi, where are you?'

Hours later, in the pitch dark, she came round. Wilson had left and she was alone. She was sore, bruised and felt degraded.

How could he rape me? she cried in anguish. She rolled herself into a tiny ball and fell into a troubled sleep. She dreamt of Simon and herself, the first time, under the milkwood tree in Hermanus. He was gentle with her, passing his strength into her with care and love.

When she awoke it was light. Her body ached. She looked into her mirror and cried out at her puffy face. I'll get back at you, Wilson, she vowed to herself.

Through the cracks in the door she saw the women leaving for the fields with their hoes balanced over their shoulders. Wilson banged the door open and stepped inside. He was brandishing the hoe fitted with a new handle.

'Here, wife, go to work,' he ordered her brusquely.

'I won't work in the fields for an ungrateful man. You demon, you raped me last night.'

'I am your husband, you will do my bidding.'

'You are wrong. I am not an animal for you to hit as you like.' Nomisile spat out the words.

'Go now, you are late.'

Nomisile walked away disdainfully. 'I refuse. I *won't* go.'

Wilson swung the hoe at her in anger, the sharp metal blade digging into her side.

'You're a fiend, a monster,' cried Nomisile, darting away.

Wilson grabbed the metal part of the hoe and beat her over her head and shoulders with the handle. She tried to fend off the blows.

Eventually she succumbed, falling to her knees, Wilson grabbing her by the shoulder. Slipping out of his grasp, she ran outside. He was nimble and fast, like a fox terrier, chasing after her, hitting the odd shot home as they dodged between the huts. Nomisile started to tire. The door to the main hut was open and Nomisile ran inside. Against the wall was a wooden club with a knobbed head.

As Wilson came forward, holding the hoe on high, she swung the club at him with all her might. The weighted end connected with his ribs. She heard bone and cartilage snap as he cried out in pain, clutching his side. 'Let that teach you, you little weasel,' cried Nomisile in triumph.

'I'll kill you. No wife of mine will better me.' He advanced more warily. Nomisile swung again. He blocked the blow with his arm but the heavy weapon ricocheted off, striking him on the side of the neck. He groaned and dropped the hoe, holding his neck, unsteady on his feet.

'You think you're a stud with three wives. Well, you're nothing but a little runt,' cried Nomisile jubilantly, and she swung the club in a high arc. The heavy end crunched into his skull. Wilson uttered a low, guttural sound as he collapsed to the floor. She waited for him to stir, but he lay motionless.

Oh, no! I've killed him, thought Nomisile in panic. She turned his limp body over, her ear pressed to his chest. She listened intently, his heartbeat was loud and regular. Relieved, she sprang up and ran to her hut. She grabbed her suitcase. She had to get away, before Wilson revived.

Nomisile was weak and she kept tripping and falling. She glanced behind her frequently, half expecting Wilson to pursue her. She reached her father's kraal and collapsed in Morris's arms.

'Members of the Paarl Broederbond cell, it gives me much pleasure to announce a new member will be sworn in tonight,' began the president in Afrikaans. 'Simon Roux has been approved by the committee and unanimously elected by the full business meeting.' The members clapped enthusiastically.

He continued. 'A prospective new brother must be proposed by a Broederbonder in good standing. Who proposes the new member, Simon Roux?'

'I do. I propose my son as a member of the Broederbond.' Paulus smiled proudly.

'Will the proposer please lead the new member forward.' Paulus took Simon by the arm and led him to the main table.

'Do you vouch for the new member's character, that he is an unblemished and upright man of good reputation, who is fit to become a member of our organisation?'

'I do.'

'Will he stand firm in his principles, and in your opinion, will he uphold the Afrikaners' proud traditions?'

'I am convinced he will.' Paulus spoke with conviction.

The president turned to Simon. 'Simon Roux, you have been chosen out of Afrikaner ranks to become a member of the Broederbond, which makes you a leader of our people. There are certain traditions that you must promise before God to uphold. Please answer the following questions with a simple yes or no.

'Will you always place the interests of the Afrikaner Nation above that of all other population groups?'

'Yes.'

'Will you pride yourself in being an Afrikaner and nurture a love for our language, religion, traditions and our people?'

'Yes.'

'Do you recognise that Afrikaners have a primary birthright to this country?'

'Yes.'

'Will you promise to further the aims and objects of the Broederbond at all times?'

'Yes.'

'Will you keep secret the nature and workings of our organisation from non-Broederbond members?'

'Yes.'

'Congratulations, Simon Roux. I declare you a member of our distinguished organisation, the Broederbond.'

The members clapped in appreciation.

'There are certain ways we distinguish each other when we meet, the main one being on greeting. We have a special handshake, used only by fellow brothers.' He showed Simon the Broederbond handshake, how to hold the three top fingers of the right hand together, dropping the little finger.

'When you shake the hand of a fellow Broeder, his little finger will slip naturally between your third and little fingers and you will know his secret. You will do the same. Practise the handshake and you will be surprised at the number of Broeders you will meet, from all walks of life, fellow Afrikaners, like yourself.'

'Here come Wilson and his brother from their kraal.' Nosakani stood at the door early the next morning.

'What are they wearing?' Morris asked. 'If they are fully clothed they will take Nomisile back with them, but if they wear skimpy loincloths it means he has disowned her.'

'They have thongs around their waists and small leather aprons,' replied Nosakani cautiously.

Morris stepped outside. He watched as the men, carrying long sticks, walked towards his cattle enclosure. His brother controlled the gate while Wilson went inside. He knew his own animals and slapped them on the rump to get them moving. By smacking their ears he manoeuvred them expertly past the other cattle in the enclosure. The brother opened the gate to allow them out one by one, until all nine were outside.

The two men drove the cattle towards Wilson's kraal. Wilson walked towards Morris and stopped in front of him. Without a word he nodded emphatically and walked away.

'What does all this mean?' Nosakani asked, concerned.

'Wilson has annulled the marriage.'

'Did you see that big bump on his forehead and the way he protected his ribs and neck while he was walking?' Nosakani pointed to the hobbling Wilson.

'That was my doing,' Nomisile shouted in triumph. 'The devil beat me up. He got his just due.'

'He has invalidated your marriage.' Morris looked at her sadly.

'Good, I'm glad. I never wanted to marry him in the first place.'

'You have brought my standing in Qunu into disrepute, daughter.'

'I will make it right for you. I will ask for permission to build my own hut,' answered Nomisile.

'The news will travel.' Morris wore a worried expression. 'Now no one will marry you. You'll stay a spinster all your life.'

'That's fine, I can devote my full attention to Themba. It's what I wanted all along.'

A week later Nomisile went to Mqekezweni, the royal kraal. She sought out Gladys, the third wife of the Paramount Chief.

'When next the Paramount Chief convenes his council, I would appreciate an interview with the council of elders.'

'It's most unusual for a woman to request an audience.'

'Please, it's important.'

Gladys studied Nomisile's face, noting her concern and determination. 'I will see what I can do,' she promised.

Weeks passed before Nomisile was granted her audience. She arrived early and was given a place with those who had requested an interview. She was the only woman among two dozen men.

The members of the council arrived for the day of indaba, where all issues affecting the well-being of the tribe were debated. The council members took their places in the circle near the royal cattle kraal. When they were seated the tribal elders moved to the head of the circle, leaving a space open. The Paramount Chief, resplendent in a leopard skin, strode from his hut and took his place. The members of his council bowed forward in reverence.

First, matters concerning the tribe were discussed and consensus reached. Thereafter they turned to individual requests. One by one they were heard. The indaba broke for lunch. All twenty-four men were called before Nomisile.

In the late afternoon one of the elders approached Nomisile. 'The elders will see you now.'

She walked into the middle of the circle of men. She fell to her knees, extending both hands to the Paramount Chief.

'You may approach closer.' He spoke in a deep voice.

Nomisile shuffled forward, her hands still extended in front of her, touching the ground. She dared not look into his face without permission. The Chief took her two hands lightly in his. 'I see you, Nomisile, daughter of Morris Memani. You may now see me.' She moved back to the centre, sitting on her knees, her hands at her side.

'You have requested an audience with this council,' said Joseph Sondika, the principal elder of the tribe, who sat to the right of the Chief. 'State your case for all to hear.'

132

'I am a woman alone, with no husband and no prospect of getting married,' said Nomisile. The headmen nodded – they were aware of her experiences with Wilson.

'All I have is my son, Themba. It is not right that I burden my father's kraal with the two of us, as I have brought disrepute to him by my actions. I request permission to obtain my own piece of land and build my own hut, so my son and I may live there.'

'Your request is unusual for a woman,' said the principal elder.

'I would be self-sufficient. To support my child and myself I would like to run my own cattle and sheep and start up a small business.'

'What sort of business?'

'I would like to begin a dressmaking business, so that I can make clothes for the royal wives and the Thembu tribe,' finished Nomisile.

'Where would that be?' asked a headman.

'It'd be best if it were here at the royal village of Mqekezweni,' answered Nomisile.

'Why Mqekezweni?' The Paramount Chief entered the discussion for the first time. 'You live in Qunu.'

'The royal wives are moving away from the old traditional way of dressing. They are starting to wear dresses, skirts and blouses. I can clothe them more cheaply than the shops. At Mqekezweni I will be close to them, making it easier for measuring and fitting.'

The Chief looked at her closely. 'And how will the men of the tribe benefit?'

Nomisile's brain raced. She should have anticipated this question. In a male-dominated society they would not agree to her request unless there was something in it for the men. 'I can also make shirts and trousers.'

'Is there another reason why you would choose Mqekezweni?' The Paramount Chief was no fool.

Throwing caution to the wind Nomisile spoke her mind. The words tumbled out. 'Themba, my son, is of royal blood.' She looked towards her father, seeking his assurance. Morris nodded to members of the council.

She continued, 'One day he will bring great honour to our tribe as a leader of our people in the freedom struggle, like his uncle Nelson Rolihlahla Mandela. It is important that he grows up in the right environment.'

'Is there anything else?'

'No, wise men of the Thembu tribe, that is all.'

'You may go then.'

Nomisile returned to Morris's kraal. He came home in the evening, but did not even mention the matter to Nomisile. She knew better than to ask – it was not a woman's place to be presumptuous.

A month dragged past before Nomisile was recalled for the verdict. Again she had to wait until all the men had spoken before she was summoned.

'We have considered your request,' began the Paramount Chief, 'and we have decided to grant the unusual request of a piece of land on which to build a hut.'

Her heart sang with joy.

'No woman may have more possessions than a man, we thus allow you to run no more than twenty cattle and forty sheep or goats. The business you propose meets the approval of my wives,' said the Chief. 'They want white men's clothes. I dare say we should move with the times.' Nomisile held her breath. 'You may start a dressmaking business.'

Three out of four, gloated Nomisile, now for the final answer.

'Your son is of royal blood from your side. We have spoken to your cousin Jafta in Paarl, but he does not know who the father of your child is.' The Paramount Chief paused.

Nomisile fought down her panic. If they knew it was a white man they would surely cancel all the concessions they had just granted. The Xhosas were a proud people and they could object to a boy of mixed blood living at the royal village.

'We assume the father is a Xhosa man,' finished the Chief.

Nomisile was shaking. She was petrified, facing the elders of the tribe alone. The Chief took her nodding to mean the affirmative.

'In that case, you may build your house at the royal kraal of Mqekezweni.' The Paramount Chief pointed to Joseph. 'He will allocate the spot. May your son Themba truly become a leader of our people. That is all.'

The principal elder set aside a plot of land one hundred paces by one hundred paces near the edge of the village. When Jafta returned from Hermitage at the end of summer she persuaded him to help her build her hut.

Making the bricks took them almost a month. They used soil from Nomisile's plot, adding clay dug from the river bank and grass clippings to bind the mixture. They carried water in paraffin tins from the river. The whole mixture was stirred by hand until the ingredients were evenly mixed into a crumbly consistency. Jafta made five moulds of planed wood to form large rectangular boxes, open top and bottom. Then the mixture was placed in the moulds and tamped down with a wooden pounder until it was a solid mass. The moulds were removed, leaving the blocks to bake hard in the sun. Re-using the moulds, the next batch was prepared. It was slow, hard, manual work. Each day they made only five batches. It seemed so little compared with the effort, but the number of blocks grew day by day until after a month they had enough.

'We are ready to build.' Jafta surveyed their handiwork with satisfaction. 'Now we must choose the most important feature of the whole house, a good centre pole,' he told Nomisile. 'This *intsika* must be strong as it carries the whole weight of the roof.'

It was five hours to the forest. Jafta and Nomisile penetrated deep to find the right sneezewood tree. They discovered a magnificent specimen, over five metres tall to the bottom of the dividing 'Y', with a straight, thick trunk. Jafta chopped down the tree. They returned to the village where they hired two strong young men. It took the four of them almost two days to reach home, carrying the large trunk balanced on their heads.

The bottom section of the trunk was placed in a fire to blacken and harden the base to prevent dry rot and attack by ants. At last the *intsika* was planted firmly in the ground, standing tall and proud in its new location. Jafta looped a thong of cowhide around the bottom of the pole. 'How big must your hut be?'

'Oh, very big, for it will be my home and business site all in one.'

Jafta measured out three paces. He attached a sharpened stick to the thong and drew a circle in the ground, giving the inside of the hut a diameter of six paces. They started packing the baked blocks on the outside of the circle line, leaving space for a single door. Three small openings were left at strategic places for the windows.

When the walls were one hand over head height they returned to the forest to cut the roof beams. These were placed at evenly spaced distances on the top of the walls, criss-crossing on the Y-apex of the main pole and secured with thick strips of cured ox-hide. Horizontal purlins were fastened to the beams and the whole roof thatched with long indigenous grass.

The rondavel was plastered inside and out with a mixture of soil and wet cattle dung. The floor received the same treatment. They fashioned the *iziko*, or hearth, with clay around the centre pole and lit a fire to bake the clay rock hard. Flanking the doorway, crude benches were fashioned out of the mud blocks and plastered with the mud and dung mixture. Jafta put up some rough shelves. All that remained was to paint the outside with white clay.

'It's magnificent,' bubbled Nomisile, hugging Jafta. 'We are so smart.'

Nomisile bought Jafta two cows for his services over the last three months. He was thrilled with the present, it was very fair compensation for his efforts.

Nomisile travelled to East London to buy a treadle Singer sewing machine from the dealers. She moved in with her aunt and took a course in dressmaking. She was a quick learner and soon mastered the techniques. She also made contact with suppliers of materials, buttons and braids.

Nomisile and Themba set up home at Mqekezweni and their hut soon became the meeting place for the Thembu women. They came from far and wide as her reputation as a seamstress of quality garments spread. She lived on the money she made and used Simon's monthly remittance to build up a small herd of cattle and a flock of sheep and goats. She was set up for life. She wrote to Simon telling him of her accomplishments, and sent him a photograph of herself and their son.

Nomisile was the finest advertisement for her business. She was the best-dressed woman at the royal kraal. She was beautiful and in the prime of her life. Many suitors called but she gave them all short shrift. She was not going to give up her new-found independence to submit to the abasement of another contrived marriage.

'I live for my son, Themba,' she told everyone. 'He is the most important person in the world to me. All my affection is reserved for my son.'

And at night, alone and lonely, she thought of Simon.

8

Athlone, on the Cape Flats, was a wind-swept township of single-storey buildings. The south-easter continually billowed across the thick groves of Port Jackson willows, eddying the white drift sand over the roads.

Noël Robb sat behind her desk at the Black Sash's Advice Office. She was a buxom woman, middle-aged with permed blonde hair. 'Since Verwoerd became Prime Minister he has intensified efforts to create separate black states. Blast the man and his fervent apartheid ideology!'

Her assistant, Helena Roux, nodded quickly in agreement. 'The government has made it very difficult with their confusing pass laws.' She angrily banged her fist on the desk. 'They are making criminals out of good law-abiding women.'

'Another problem is the government's Coloured Labour Preference Policy.' Noël's eyes blazed. 'In the Western Cape white employers get tax incentives to employ coloured workers, leading to vast black unemployment. Now the government is shipping jobless blacks back to the homelands, where there is absolutely no work for them.'

'There must be some way we can assist.'

Noël sat forward, looking intently at Helena. 'There's a black man in your area who needs help urgently.'

'Who is he?'

'Witbooi Sikade from Wellington.'

'Wellington is close to Paarl. What's happened to him?'

'He threw his passbook into a drum after Sharpeville. It took him two working days to find it, sorting through thousands of discarded books.' Noël shook her head sadly. 'When he returned to work, the Wellington municipality fired him. They employed a coloured man instead.' Noël tapped the file. 'Witbooi was arrested yesterday. Pauline, his wife, approached us for urgent help as she is unable to raise his bail money.'

'I'll see what I can do,' promised Helena.

Helena appeared at court in Wellington early the next day. She explained to the public prosecutor who she was. That she was the daughter-in-law of a member of parliament drew instant results. Witbooi's case appeared first on the role.

Witbooi was brought from the cells looking dishevelled, in a huge army greatcoat and a brown rolled-up Balaclava cap. His features were haggard and he was painfully thin.

'The state versus Witbooi Sikade,' stated the public prosecutor, 'on a charge of illegally squatting in the Western Cape. How do you plead, guilty or not guilty?'

Helena jumped up from her seat in the gallery. 'The defendant pleads not guilty.' She wore her black sash. The magistrate looked up in surprise.

'Will you be defending the accused?' the magistrate asked her.

'Yes, Your Honour.'

'Then please come into the body of the court, but take off your black sash. Our courts are impartial. I will not allow politics to affect our proceedings.'

Helena removed her sash, having made her point.

'Are you a qualified attorney, and registered as a member of the Cape Side Bar?' inquired the magistrate.

'No, Your Honour, I am a member of the Athlone Advice Office, here to see that justice is done to this poor man.'

'Then you cannot defend the accused. You may only speak in mitigation of sentence.'

'Your Honour, this man, Witbooi, has lived with his wife and two children in the squatter camp of Sakkieskamp for years. He is unaware of pass laws and Group Areas Acts. He does not understand the white man's rules – all he is trying to do is eke out an existence for his family.'

'He is a Transkei citizen and is unlawfully in the Western Cape.' The magistrate spoke firmly.

'Transkei is only recognised by our government. As far as I'm concerned it is still part of South Africa.'

'Mrs Roux, what you are doing is highly irregular. You cannot conduct an argument with this court from the public gallery. If you don't keep quiet, I will have no option but to hold you in contempt of court.'

'I have influence, Your Honour. I will see that this sham trial makes every English newspaper in South Africa, and overseas.'

'Are you threatening me, Mrs Roux?'

'No, Your Honour, I demand that justice prevails.'

The magistrate glared at her, then banged his gavel. 'Charge dismissed, next case.'

'With respect, Your Honour, it's one thing dismissing the charge, but what if he gets caught again on the same offence?'

'You Black Sash women are always trying to obstruct the course of justice. Laws are laws. They are promulgated by parliament and we merely give expression to them.'

'What if the laws are unjust and affect a person's human dignity?' Helena was angry.

'Madam, this is a white man's country and the laws are there to protect the white man's heritage in the country of his birth.' The magistrate glared at Helena. 'I'm now tired of your impertinence.'

Helena was undeterred. 'That may be so, but the arrest of the same man on the same charge is not solving the problem.'

'He and his family must return to his birthplace in Lady Frere, in the Transkei.'

'How do they do that? They have no money for train tickets, or to move their worldly goods to the Transkei.'

'I will issue him with a railway warrant.' The magistrate furiously wrote on court paper. He gave the page to the clerk of the court, who stamped it with a rubber stamp of purple ink. 'Take that to the Black Affairs Commissioner in Mbekweni and he will organise the tickets.'

Helena led Witbooi out of the courthouse. A sizeable crowd had gathered. They applauded and cheered Helena. She bundled a confused Witbooi into her car and drove to Mbekweni.

The Mbekweni offices of the Black Affairs Commissioner were situated on the outskirts of the black township, on the road to Paarl. High-security fences surrounded the complex. Inside the grounds were hundreds of black people, either standing, sitting or lounging around, all with a look of exasperation on their faces.

Helena walked into the deserted main office. She waited for ten minutes, her anger mounting as she heard laughter from a room nearby. Eventually she lost patience and stormed down the passage. The uniformed white officials were sitting in the staff room.

She cast a feisty look over them. 'Is there no service in this place?'

'It's tea-time.' An official looked Helena up and down slowly.

'There are hundreds of people out there waiting for service,' she snapped.

'The blacks can wait,' answered the official sullenly.

'The problem with you officials is you think, because your skins are white, you can play God. These poor people must waste days waiting for you to serve them, if the whim takes you.'

'So?' He shrugged nonchalantly.

'I demand service.'

One of the officials stood up, sauntering to the front office. 'How can I help you, lady?' his tone condescending.

'The magistrate in Wellington has issued a railway warrant to Witbooi and his family to travel to Lady Frere. I want the train tickets.'

The official gazed at the stamped directive from the court.

His attitude irritated her. 'Hurry up man, I haven't all day.'

He looked up superciliously. 'I must study the matter first.' After another few minutes, he cleared his throat. 'You see, lady, I cannot issue the tickets before the Black Affairs Commissioner in Lady Frere has advised us that there is place there for these kaffirs. I must first write a letter and await his reply.'

'I wish you would not refer to these people in such derogatory terms.'

'But lady, everyone calls them kaffirs, that's their name.'

'They are humans too, like you and me. They demand our respect.'

'What? Respect kaffirs? No, lady, I have more respect for my dog.'

Helena shook her head in frustration. 'How long will it take?'

'A week to attend to the documentation, two weeks for the post to reach Lady Frere, up to a month for them to react, two weeks for the return postage and two weeks for us to process the issuing of the tickets.' Counting on his fingers, he proudly announced, 'Eleven weeks. Let's add a week for delays, that makes it three months.'

'You must be mad! What's the poor man going to do? He has

140

no work. How is he going to feed his family for three months while you bungle through the motions?'

'That's his problem, not mine.' The official walked back to the staff room.

Helena marched out of the office seething. At his shelter he had great difficulty explaining to Witbooi in her limited Xhosa the ramifications of his position. It was too complicated for him to understand – he merely nodded in deference.

Three days later, whilst Helena was still in bed, Sophie knocked on the bedroom door. 'Sorry, madam, but there is a black man at the back door asking to see you.'

Still in her gown, Helena walked to the door. 'Morning, Witbooi, do you have a problem?'

Using a mixture of Xhosa, Afrikaans, English and sign language, Witbooi conveyed to Helena that his wife had been arrested.

'Give me a few minutes to get dressed.'

They drove directly to the police station in Wellington.

'You have arrested a woman called Pauline Sikade.'

The duty officer paged through his VB book. 'Yes, here it is. She was arrested for being without possession of a pass book and illegally squatting in the area. Two offences.'

'I demand she be released immediately. It's not her fault that she is here. We are waiting for a railway warrant to arrive from Lady Frere and then she will leave the area.'

'I'm sorry, I cannot release her. She has broken the law and justice must run its course. Tomorrow she will appear in court. Only the magistrate can jail, fine or release her.'

Helena felt the genuine frustration of the black people, the way they came up against red tape and how little they could actually do against it. They didn't understand the myriad apartheid laws governing their very existence. All they wanted was to survive and feed their families, not be humiliated with constant arrests. Helena realised that the Sikades were just the tip of the iceberg, only one couple amongst tens of thousands of people in a similar plight in South Africa. She felt so ineffectual. She resolved to assist them until their saga was satisfactorily concluded.

The next day Pauline appeared before the same magistrate in Wellington. Again Helena stepped into the breach, defending her from the gallery. 'Your Honour, how can you possibly charge this woman? I have spent hours at Mbekweni. There is still no reply from the Transkei, and the Mbekweni officials won't issue the railway warrant until they have the documentation.'

'She has broken two laws,' sighed the magistrate in exasperation, not relishing another confrontation with Helena.

'Unjust laws,' claimed Helena.

'That may be your opinion, madam, but I have to act within the laid-down framework.'

'I appeal to your humanity. Grant this woman clemency. Once the railway warrant is finalised, she will return to the Transkei. I give you my word.'

The magistrate shook his head. 'I cannot find her not guilty, for it will create a precedent. Thus, I find her guilty with a sentence of ten days' imprisonment on each charge.'

Helena's heart sank. She was about to retort strongly, when the magistrate added, 'Suspended for three months.'

'If she gets caught within three months, what happens then?'

The magistrate groaned in frustration, hoping it was the last time he encountered Helena Roux in his courtroom. 'She first serves the original sentence, plus any further sentences imposed by the court.'

Helena realised the futility of arguing any further and left the courthouse. She took Pauline home to her shanty made of poles and hessian bags. The shack consisted of a single room, only large enough for Witbooi, Pauline and their two children to lie down in.

Witbooi lay in the hot shack gasping for breath with a wild look in his eyes. He was perspiring freely, the sweat running in rivulets off his brow. Helena realised he was dreadfully ill. She helped him into the car and rushed off to the nearest doctor's rooms in Wellington.

'Doctor does not attend to black patients!' The white nurse looked at Helena in disgust. 'We maintain a high standard.'

'Surely a doctor's Hippocratic oath impels him to attend to this man?'

'Sorry, madam, the doctor will not see him. I suggest you try a black doctor.'

Helena drove to the surgery near the station. People were sitting on every available chair, on the floor and outside the building. They had to wait almost three hours before the doctor saw Witbooi.

Helena telephoned Hermitage to inform Simon she would not be home until mid-afternoon. It worried her that she was neglecting her family, but she could not stop now.

Helena went in with Witbooi, helping him to walk. His breath came in great rasps out of his wheezing chest. The doctor examined him. 'This man has acute asthma.'

'What can we do for him?'

'I'll give him oxygen, followed by an injection. Then he will have to take pills daily.'

'While you are about it, his children are also sick. Please give me something for their influenza.'

Three times a week Helena drove to the hut at Sakkieskamp, doctoring Witbooi for asthma, Pauline for tuberculosis and the children for the flu.

During her next visit to the Athlone office Helena told Noël about the Sikade family's plight. 'I feel so helpless. Time is of the essence before one or both are arrested again. How can we force the bureaucrats to speed matters up?'

'Let's send a reply-paid telegram to the Black Affairs Commissioner in Lady Frere,' suggested Noël.

'Good idea.'

The telegram had the desired results, for a day later telegraphic permission was granted for the family to return to the Transkei.

Noël was excited at the positive response. 'I want to accompany them to Lady Frere to see all the trials and tribulations experienced by a Xhosa family during these forced evacuations. They're becoming a daily occurrence as apartheid bites deeper. The knowledge will stand the Advice Office in good stead for the future.'

'You can't go by yourself, Noël,' Helena remonstrated. 'It's unheard of for a white woman to make such a long journey alone.'

'I'll just have to take my chances, Helena, and hope for the best.'

'That's not good enough, Noël. I'll tell you what, I'll go with you. I'm sure I can persuade my husband to let me go.'

'That would be marvellous,' breathed Noël in relief.

After insistent cajoling, and rushing between the Black Affairs Commissioner in Mbekweni and the Wellington station master,

Helena eventually secured the rail warrant. The Sikades took their departure from the area they had called home for so many years without a murmur. They could not understand why they were forced to leave a place where they could find work for a place they had not seen since their youth and where no work existed.

When Helena explained her problem to Simon he reluctantly agreed to her accompanying Noël Robb. On the day of their departure, after fetching the Sikades' paltry possessions from Sakkieskamp, he took Helena and Noël to Wellington station in the pick-up. As they drove away from the hovel the Sikades had called home they waved sadly to their friends, not knowing if they would ever see them again.

The train journey was a four-day nightmare as they chugged across the country – north, south-east, south and finally east again. Eventually, on the fourth morning, they reached Queenstown. They helped the Sikades move their possessions from the station to the bus depot. In mid-afternoon they reached Lady Frere. Leaving Pauline and the children to guard their goods, the other three hurried to the Black Affairs Commissioner's office.

The building was in a state of disrepair with holes torn in the ceiling of the main office. Four black clerks sat behind desks with identical bored expressions on their faces, while hundreds of people waited to be served. Helena waited for a desk to become clear, and then slipped in.

'We urgently want to see the Commissioner.'

Looking at his watch, the clerk shook his head. 'It's after three o'clock. The court is closed.'

Helena slipped a ten-rand bill over the desk. In a flash the clerk pocketed the money, his attitude changing instantly. He sprang to his feet, a smile on his face.

'Wait here. I'll speak to the Commissioner.'

Five minutes later he ushered them into the Commissioner's office. Lady Frere was a small town, warranting only an assistant magistrate, who doubled up as Black Affairs Commissioner.

The Commissioner was a young, cocky white man. He read the documentation, then looked up. 'I cannot help you as the man does not have property or a house in the area.'

Noël exploded, her eyes flashing in anger and her stiffly permed blonde hair bobbed up and down. 'Look at this telegram from this very office giving permission. On the strength of this telegram we

144

have travelled half-way across South Africa, by train and bus, to bring this poor, destitute family to Lady Frere. Now you have the gall to tell us they're not welcome. What must we do?'

The assistant magistrate looked at the wall-clock. 'The court has closed for the day. You'll have to come back tomorrow. I'll see what I can do for you then.' He stood up, a sign of dismissal.

It was Helena's turn to erupt. 'Where are we and the Sikade family expected to sleep tonight? Is there an hotel in town?'

'I'm afraid not.'

'Answer my question. Where must we stay?'

'I don't know. That is your problem.'

'No, Mr Assistant Magistrate, it's *your* problem. My father-in-law is Paulus Roux, the National Party MP for Paarl. If you don't help us this afternoon, I'll telephone and ask him to speak to the Minister of Justice about your apathetic attitude.'

Helena knew Paulus would never back her on the matter, but the official was not to know. She hated using her father-in-law's name, but the situation was desperate, needing a desperate solution.

He sat down abruptly, calling in the court interpreter, and issued instructions. The translator and Witbooi spoke in Xhosa for a few minutes.

'Your Honour, he says he has a stepmother who lives about thirty kilometres from Lady Frere. She is the only person he knows in the Transkei.'

'He will stay there.' The Commissioner foraged in a pigeon-hole for a form.

'How can they stay there?' cried Helena. 'Who says they are welcome? She's after all only a stepmother?'

'It's tradition in the Transkei, relatives never refuse help.' He looked up condescendingly while completing the forms. He wanted to get rid of the two women.

'How will Witbooi find work? He suffers from chronic asthma,' demanded Noël.

'Lady, I don't have all the answers! You've told me clearly I'm only an assistant magistrate in the backwater of Lady Frere. It's not my job to find Witbooi work. The mines are the only meaningful employer of Transkei labour. If he has asthma and can't work underground in the dust, they will reject him and he will have to be a burden on his stepmother for the rest of his life.'

'He is destitute, don't you understand?' Helena remonstrated sarcastically. 'He has a wife and two children to support. How can you expect a stepmother, who is not a real relative at all, to support them year in and year out?'

'I already told you! A Xhosa can't turn away people in need. It's their tradition to assist, even if they face hardship and starvation themselves.'

'Can't you organise a pension for Witbooi?'

'Definitely not. He's not old enough to qualify. Anyway the government has made no provision financially to assist the blacks they are sending back to the Transkei in terms of the homeland policy. It's going to become a grave problem. There is not an aid or a resettlement package.'

'What about a disability pension?' Helena was insistent.

'Now you're talking red tape, lady. If you're prepared to spend the next two months in Lady Frere, maybe, just maybe, you'll be able to sort out that little problem. Now it's knock-off time; I've already worked an extra half an hour to assist you.'

'You're not going home yet.' Helena glowered at him. 'There is more we want to know.'

He sat back resignedly. 'Fire away, lady.'

'I want to know about Pauline. She has TB and needs treatment twice a week. Is there a hospital near where she is going to live?'

The official burst out laughing. 'This is the Transkei. Where she's going is thirty kilometres from town and there is nothing there except mud huts – no schools, no clinics, no hospitals, no shops, no nothing! If she needs treatment she will have to walk to Lady Frere.'

Helena looked at him, aghast. She calculated the distance quickly. 'That's almost five hundred kilometres a month on foot!' The enormity of the difficulties that confronted Pauline and her family was too much for Helena. She burst out crying, collapsing on a chair, sobs of grief coursing through her body.

'Lady, I see your point, but don't worry, five hundred kilometres is nothing for a Xhosa, and anyway, she'll have lots of time. What else is there for her to do? Time is the one thing in abundance in the Transkei.'

Drying her eyes, Helena snivelled at him. 'So there's nothing further we can do for the poor Sikades? What about schools for the children?'

'The only school in the district is here in Lady Frere. If they want to go to school, they will have to walk.'

Trying to calculate the distance they would have to walk each month was too much for Helena and she started sobbing again. 'I can't bear it. How can they possibly do all those things when they are penniless, with no hope of an income?'

'Lady, in the Transkei, they can live on the smell of an oil rag! One bag of mealie meal feeds a family for a whole month!' He stood up. 'Ladies, I don't want to appear rude, but the last bus to Queenstown leaves in half an hour. If you miss that bus, you *will* be stuck in Lady Frere for the night. Do you mind if we finish off now?'

Both women stared at him in abject misery. Witbooi stood with his head bowed, accepting his fate as quietly as a man walking to the gallows.

The Commissioner stamped the form and handed it to Witbooi. Through the interpreter, he explained Witbooi's future to him. He merely nodded in mute acceptance.

'Right, ladies, the matter is settled. Witbooi understands and accepts the situation. I wish you a pleasant journey back to the Cape.' He shooed everyone out of his office, locking the door behind him.

In the dusty courtyard, Helena confronted him. 'There is one last question, and I want a truthful answer. If I hadn't threatened you with the Minister of Justice, what would have happened?'

'It would have taken at least three days to finalise the matter.'

'And if Witbooi and his family had arrived alone, what would have happened then?'

'I would have despatched them back to Wellington as they have no property in the Transkei.'

Noël and Helena gaped at the absurd merry-go-round spawned by the government's homeland policy and the system of forced removals to the Transkei. People like the Sikades, shunted back and forth – pawns in the government power game – with no thought for their basic human dignity.

They walked with Witbooi, Pauline and the children to the edge of town. Loaded with their possessions, they looked like pack mules walking into a future of uncertainty and extreme suffering.

'Goo'bye, missus,' he said simply. '*Enkosi*,' he thanked her.

The children looked back with soulful eyes, so sad and forlorn,

147

so confused and ambivalent, that Helena's heart felt as if it would shatter. She ran forward, kneeling on the ground, holding the two little mites close to her breast, crying uncontrollably. A great feeling of despair came over her in not being able to help change the system, preventing the needless suffering of the children of apartheid.

'Oh God!' she prayed. 'Bring your light to shine on these children, on all children in our troubled land. They are the innocent victims of the power struggle.'

Noël coughed gently. 'Helena, my dear, our bus leaves in five minutes.'

'Give me just one more minute, please.' She rummaged in her bag, giving each child a fifty-cent coin. Their little eyes lit up in ecstasy, and their smiles of appreciation were a great comfort to Helena.

She ran forward, catching up with Witbooi and Pauline. Opening her purse, she tipped out every note and coin into a bewildered Witbooi's cupped hands. 'Please take the money,' she beseeched him. 'I can't help every family who will be repatriated to the homelands, but I promise before God I'll help you.' Helena held Witbooi by the shoulders. 'Every month I'll send you some money – enough to feed and clothe the four of you.'

'*Enkosi*, missus.'

Overcome by grief, Helena turned and ran towards town, not having the courage to look back.

As a member of the executive of the Western Cape Agricultural Union, Simon was automatically a delegate to the 1960 national conference scheduled for East London.

He wrote to Nomisile asking her and Themba to meet him on the beach in front of the conference centre, the Kennaway Hotel, on the morning of Wednesday, 20 October 1960. It would be Themba's fifth birthday and he wanted to see his son for the first time. He promised Nomisile he would give no indication to Themba that he was his father. All he wanted to do was see him.

Nomisile received the letter, memorised the contents and then burnt it. She thought carefully about Simon's request. Merely thinking about him again excited her and she started day-dreaming about the past. Would the old love still be there? She decided the answer lay in putting it to the test. Yes, they would meet Simon.

*   *   *

The sea was greenish-blue topped with white-capped seahorses, the sun warm, shining out of a cloudless sky, when the delegates arrived in East London on the Monday afternoon for the conference. Farmers from all corners of the country were thrown together, enthusiastically renewing old friendships and telling farming stories in the crowded bar of the conference hotel. Simon found it difficult to enter into the spirit of the fun as he kept thinking of the possible visit of Nomisile and his son.

Tuesday was the first working session of the conference. His union chairman dug him in the ribs. 'Why are you day-dreaming, Simon? We are voting YES on this issue.' Simon quickly raised his voting card.

After breakfast on Wednesday Simon walked across the road to the grassy banks leading down to the sea. There she was. 'Hullo, Nomisile.' He felt awkward, not sure what to say, suddenly tongue-tied.

'Look at the sea.' She was also embarrassed. 'It reminds me of Hermanus.' Her heart lurched at the sight of him. He was still the same, except he had put on some weight and was a bit fuller in the face. He looked so dapper in his striped double-breasted suit.

It had been six years since he had last heard her lilting voice. She looked even more regal than he remembered – more beautiful and more assured.

To break the silence, Simon said, 'I like your dress, it's colourful and stylish.'

She smiled and her large almond eyes lit up. 'Thanks to you, Simon, I'm an established business woman now. This dress I designed and made myself. I'm making quite a name for myself at Mqekezweni.'

'I was hoping you'd bring Themba. I really wanted to see my son.'

'I did.' Nomisile pointed to the water's edge. 'There he is.' On the shore below a young boy was jumping gracefully from rock to rock. Simon started as he recognised his own movements in those of the boy. He was sturdy and well-built. The boy turned and waved to his mother. Something about the smile and the expression reminded him of Pierre – a vague reflection of himself, thrown back from a murky mirror. There was a likeness he could not pin-point, but it was there. Otherwise he was a typical little Xhosa boy.

'He must never know about us, Simon. You must keep your promise to me.'

'I did promise, but I want to see him close up. I want to see you too. Properly.'

'You know I cannot be with you. I'm a black woman in a white man's city. There's nowhere we can meet.'

Simon put his hand softly over Nomisile's on the rail. 'Yes, there is – my hotel room. Come tonight. It's private.'

Nomisile laughed. 'What! Walk into a hotel just like that? The hotel staff will have me arrested as I step into the front entrance.'

'I checked out the hotel, there is a way. At the back there's a metal fire escape, with emergency doors at each floor. Just before nine o'clock I will open the door. Come up to the fifth floor and slip inside. You come out next to the lifts. Just walk down the passage until you reach room 508. I'll leave my door open for you.'

'Is it worth it, Simon?' She was hesitant. 'What we had has gone. We lead different lives now. We have nothing in common.'

'Of course we do, we have a son we share. I've so much to tell you. I want to hear all your news as well.'

'I'll be there for old time's sake. Nine o'clock sharp. I'm staying with my aunt Doreen. Themba can stay with her tonight. I will come to you.'

'Thank you.' Simon sighed in relief, his heart beating faster.

'We must not stand together too long. People will be watching from the hotel. Go and sit on that bench.' Nomisile indicated a concrete bench overlooking the sea. 'I'll bring Themba, but remember, no talking.'

Nomisile fetched her son. They walked towards him, holding hands. Themba was talking excitedly in Xhosa. Simon could not understand the words, but he noted the vitality, energy and exuberance. He was a handsome boy with a clean, open face and a light toffee-brown skin. He was about the same height as Pierre, with more or less the same build. The only difference was their skin colour and their hair. Both are my very own sons, sighed Simon contentedly, his paternal instincts aroused.

Nomisile sat down at the end of the bench with Themba in the middle. He greeted Simon perfunctorily, as a stranger would greet an unknown man. Simon examined his face closely. He had the same large, luminous, brown, almond-shaped eyes as his mother, with the direct, almost contemptuous stare.

'What is your name?' Simon asked tentatively.

'Themba Memani.' He sat up proudly.

Nomisile flashed Simon a warning look, but he ignored her, the urge to hear his son speak suddenly very important.

'Where do you live?'

'I live with my mommy at—' He looked to Nomisile for help.

'Mqekezweni, in the Transkei,' finished Nomisile.

Themba cuddled up to Nomisile lovingly. 'This is my mommy.'

She looked down at him tenderly, pulling him closer and hugging him.

Simon was captivated by the obvious tenderness that existed between them. He even felt a twinge of jealousy, shut out from a relationship that by rights, in any normal society, he should have been a part of.

'Hey, you there, move along now. Can't you read? Right in front of you there's a signboard.'

The magic of the moment was broken. A cruising police van stopped opposite them. A policeman with his elbow out of the window pointed at Nomisile. She and Themba jumped up in fright. Simon turned around in anger. The policeman hurriedly added, 'Not you, sir. Sorry to disturb you, but it's those kaffirs I'm speaking to. We don't allow them at this beach, it's whites only.'

Simon cursed silently. The enchantment was destroyed, his time with his son shattered. As Nomisile and Themba walked away she nodded to Simon over her shoulder. He lingered on with his thoughts long after they had gone. He was a committed National Party supporter and a Broederbonder, supposedly accepting government policy as correct. How, he wondered, could he in all conscience continue to support a party which made it a crime for a man even to speak to his son at a public place, let alone hold him in his arms.

When Simon re-entered the hall the conference was in full swing. He apologetically weaved his way back to his seat and sat down.

'Where were you, Simon?' His chairman looked irritated.

'I wasn't feeling well, I went for a walk along the promenade for some fresh air.'

'I hope you're feeling better for the official banquet tonight.'

Simon cried off the banquet; instead he watched his friends go off boisterously to the nearby Kings Hotel for their dinner. His hotel was virtually deserted. He went up to his room and ordered a double

151

brandy from room service. While he waited for Nomisile to arrive, he sat deep in thought, his drink forgotten. Was it fair to rekindle their romance when nothing had changed in South Africa and they would still be ostracised? He thought of their times together, feeling a stirring as he remembered their intense lovemaking. He needed to show Nomisile he was still the same man, capable of taking her to the extremes of passion once again.

He looked at his watch. It was a few minutes to nine. He walked down the deserted passage and opened the emergency door.

Nomisile slipped into his room and Simon locked the door. He tried to embrace her but she slipped away from him.

'I didn't come to make love, Simon. I came for old time's sake, to talk, to catch up on events. Tell me about Hermitage and Helena and your son. You've really told me so little in your letters.'

For two hours they talked as old friends, until they had caught up to the present.

'Do you still love me?' Simon asked suddenly.

Nomisile thought for a long time before answering. 'I will always love you, for what you meant to me and because you are the father of my son. Our lives are so different now. We have grown apart.'

'I still love you.' Simon went over to her. He kissed her on the lips. Nomisile kissed him back, but the heat was gone – the urgency that had driven them towards each other before was missing. Thinking it was just restraint on her part, Simon led a protesting Nomisile over to the double bed and lay down beside her. He tried desperately to rekindle the flame. He marvelled again at her smell. She allowed him to touch her breasts and nipples but made no move towards him.

'Are we doing the right thing, Simon? I don't want a one-night stand. I'd do anything to have you as my man, but it's not possible. If tonight is not as good as it used to be it will be an anticlimax for both of us.'

'Please, Nomisile, just once more. Do it for me. I've got to know . . .' He left the words unsaid. It was a plea for his sanity. He had to know whether his drunkenness and violence, associated with sex and Helena, was a permanent blemish on his manhood. Simon looked with craving at the double brandy still standing on the table.

Nomisile felt for Simon, he looked so desperate. 'All right, Simon, let's try.'

He took her in his arms and her breathing became quicker, but it was a physical awakening not coupled to the deep emotional intensity of the past. He entered her, feeling her moistness envelop his manhood. He felt a passion and a release he had not known since they had last made love. 'Nomisile! Nomisile!' he cried out. 'Thank you! Thank you!'

Afterwards as they lay in each other's arms, satisfied but at the same time discontented. Each knew instinctively that an era had passed, that they could never recapture the wonder of former times. They had experienced sex, but not the deep wonder of lovemaking. There was consolation for Simon, however, in that he had proved to himself that he was still capable of satisfying a woman.

'Will you still write to me?' Simon asked.

'Of course I will.'

'You must still send me photographs of the two of you.'

'Do you destroy the letters and photographs, Simon?'

'No, I couldn't do that, they're too precious.'

'What do you do with them?' Nomisile sat up in fright.

Simon told her about the scrap book, how he had pasted everything into its pages since her first letter to him.

'Where do you keep the book?' asked Nomisile, alarmed. 'It could fall into the wrong hands.'

Simon explained about his hideaway, the only place in the whole world belonging entirely to him.

'What do you do with my letters?' asked Simon.

'I read them two or three times, memorise them and then I burn them.'

'Why do you burn them?' Simon looked visibly upset.

'There's no place to hide anything secret in my hut. It's too small and too sparsely furnished. I don't have a special spot like you.'

They fell silent. Nomisile knew it was time to leave. 'I must go.'

'Will you come again tonight? Please.'

He knew her answer before she replied softly, 'No, Simon. Let's hold on to our memories. I love you and I always will. Be comforted by the thought. If ever things change in our country and you still want me, I'll be waiting for you.'

'Stay a little longer. I may never see you again.'

'I must go, before I weaken. I've got to remain strong for the two of us.' She slipped off the bed and dressed. She spoke quickly to hide her grief. 'I must go and fetch Themba at my aunt's house. We'll catch the early bus to the Transkei. By tonight I'll be back at Mqekezweni, far from all temptation.'

'Let me take you back to the township.' Simon wanted to prolong their time together.

'No.' She shook her head firmly. 'The police stop all vehicles at this hour of the night. We'd be caught.' She shuddered slightly as she always did when she remembered her previous experiences with the police. 'Stay here, I'll catch a taxi back to the township.'

Simon kissed her gently at the door and she was gone.

9

The late spring night was hot and stuffy – the turgid air the forerunner of the first highveld rains. Unable to sleep, Winnie Mandela tossed and turned in bed. She sat up quickly when she heard a soft tapping on the front door and cautiously crept out of bed when it was repeated.

'Who is it?' she asked in a nervous voice. She looked through the window, making out a shadowy figure in the dark street outside her house in Orlando, a suburb of Soweto.

'Shh, it's I, it's Nelson.'

She opened the door, quickly admitting her husband. 'Didn't you take a chance, coming here tonight?'

'My darling wife, it's been five months.' Mandela embraced her tenderly. 'I watched the house for hours. I saw the security police leave – they must have thought I wouldn't come tonight.'

She kissed him tenderly. 'It's wonderful to see you again and to be in your arms.' She led him by the hand to the bedroom. Winnie curled into his arm. 'Bring me up to date. What's happening?'

'I've lived as an outlaw in my own country, avoiding the police, disguised as a chauffeur, a hobo, a beggar, even a street cleaner.' He kissed her softly. 'I visited many cities and towns. We've appointed regional commands to organise local sabotage groups. We looked at targets to attack. I have told them to act within the framework of the National High Command, to ensure no lives are endangered. Umkhonto we Sizwe members are forbidden to go armed on any sabotage operation.'

'There have been reports that Umkhonto is already active.'

'It's not true. I've heard some attacks have been ascribed to us, but it's neither the ANC nor Umkhonto. Our starting date is 16 December, 1961. The cities will erupt. That'll send the government a clear enough message. It's their precious Day of the Covenant.'

'Tell me where you have stayed. Who fed you? Who clothed you? Who looked after you? Were you treated well? I've been so worried.'

'No two days have been the same for many months now. Our people feed me, I eat when I can. As for sleep, I have slept in many houses, often just one jump ahead of the police. The clothes I needed were begged or borrowed. The police stopped me often. Luckily they don't all know my face and I could bluff my way out of trouble.'

'You know they call you the Black Pimpernel because you are so elusive.'

'I've heard so.' Nelson laughed, secretly pleased.

'How long can you stay?'

'Only until dawn. I must be gone before the security police come on duty. We have a meeting at headquarters on Lilliesleaf Farm for the Day of the Covenant offensive.'

His wife hid her disappointment. To have her husband for only one short night after five months of loneliness and longing was hard. 'Let's get some sleep. I'm so glad you came. Just to sleep in your arms again is heaven.'

Mandela rose early the next morning. He dressed quickly. He looked at Winnie sleeping. She was so beautiful, a strong-willed, vital personality who also made huge sacrifices for the freedom struggle. He suffered without a wife, but equally she suffered without a husband.

He walked softly through to the children's room where they were sleeping peacefully. He was becoming a stranger to them. He was tempted to wake them and talk to them, to see their animated faces and hear their happy voices. Reluctantly he stopped himself. It would take time, and he had to be gone before first light. He kissed the children on their foreheads, sad for a moment.

In the bedroom he softly wakened his wife. 'Goodbye my darling – it's time to go.'

She clung to him. 'When will I see you again? I miss you so when you're gone.'

'I don't know, but I'll come as often as I can. It's getting light outside. I must go now before I'm caught.'

She wouldn't let him go, crying softly. He rose, gently untangling himself from her arms, kissing her lovingly. After looking carefully through the window he slipped outside and walked quickly down the street.

'Did you hear that?' exploded Paulus, after listening to the evening news. 'The ANC has bombed government buildings in Johannesburg, Durban and Port Elizabeth. On the Day of the Covenant! Bloody kaffirs! It's not a coincidence. They chose the day deliberately to hurt us.'

'Dad, no one was hurt. Maybe it was just a warning. Don't you think maybe you should start negotiating with the ANC?' asked Helena.

He glared at her as if she were mad. 'We don't make deals with terrorists. This is the work of their new military wing, Umkhonto we Sizwe. I know all about them. The security police have briefed us.' He shot Helena a smug glance. 'When a mosquito bites you, you swat it. You don't let it bite you again. That's what we'll do to these terrorists.'

In a grey building in Durban the telephone rang at the Natal headquarters of the security police.

'I have the United States Consulate on the line. A man wishes to speak to a high-ranking officer.'

'Put him through.'

'Good morning.'

'I want to speak to the most senior officer.'

'Who are you, what do you want?' The policeman detected an American accent.

'I'm with the CIA but I don't want my identity known. I have information the security police will appreciate but I'll only speak to your highest ranking officer.'

'I can't put you through. We have many crank callers. Anyway he's out at the moment. Tell me what it's all about.'

'I know the whereabouts of Nelson Mandela.'

'What?' The officer sat bolt upright at his desk, but relaxed again as he recollected. 'Our intelligence tell us he's out of the country. You've got your facts wrong.'

'Mandela's back in South Africa and he's in Durban right now,' replied the American. 'I've told you I'm with the CIA. I wouldn't waste your time or mine with false information. I'm prepared to disclose details to your highest ranking officer. Tell him to meet me at noon on the beach opposite Natal Command. I'll have on a dark suit and a red necktie.' The telephone went dead.

He reported to his senior officer, Colonel Truter.

'Nelson Mandela, hey! Let's see if your man really is CIA.'

A few minutes before twelve Colonel Truter walked across to Battery Beach. He spotted his man, looking out to sea.

'Good afternoon, I'm Colonel Truter, of the security police. Wait a minute, I know you. You're a military advisor with the US Consulate. You're Craig Ellis.'

The American smiled. 'I know you too, Colonel Truter, from our files.'

Truter came straight to the point. 'Tell me about Nelson Mandela,' he said softly.

'He's in the Durban area visiting Umkhonto we Sizwe. He's setting up their regional command.'

'Where is he staying?'

'It's hard to tell; he moves daily to avoid detection. Sometimes he's in Isipingo, other times in KwaMashu. Yesterday he was right under your noses in central Durban.'

'We didn't know he was back in the country.'

'Nelson Mandela is a careful man,' smiled the American. 'He's been back over a month. He's returning to Johannesburg tomorrow morning by car.'

'Do you have a make or colour, or a registration number? Durban is a big place.'

The American shook his head. 'No, but you shouldn't have difficulty in trapping him. There are a limited number of highways leading to Johannesburg.'

'True. Thank you, Mr Ellis. We appreciate the tip-off. But tell me, why are you giving us this information? The American government isn't exactly our greatest supporter. You sympathise more with the black masses and their so-called freedom struggle.'

'Russia. They're supplying arms, ammunition, training and financial aid to the ANC. We don't want the cold war to spread to South Africa. We believe we must keep communism out of the Southern African arena at all costs. The ANC is their conduit. Remove Mandela from the field of play and the ANC is rudderless. That's why we're prepared to help you, Colonel Truter.'

'We are very grateful and I assure you the government will be most obliged to you and the Central Intelligence Agency, if we are successful in apprehending Mandela.'

The two men shook hands. Ellis walked south, making a long detour to his car. Truter hurried straight back to his vehicle, tingling at the thought of putting Mandela behind bars, a plan of action starting to evolve.

Truter had a busy afternoon. He called an emergency meeting of all the security police stationed in Natal at headquarters. He had the police photo-lab make twenty large black-and-white glossy prints of Nelson Mandela. He secured a large wall map of Natal. Next he telephoned the station commanders at Pietermaritzburg and Ladysmith police stations. The trap was being set.

Nelson Mandela sat in the lounge of a house in Reservoir Hills waiting for his lift back to Johannesburg. He was surrounded by members of the Natal Regional Command who had come to bid him farewell.

He turned to Bruno Mtolo. 'Keep up the good work, my friend. Your first effort on 16 December last year, when you blew up the Black Administration Building, was an excellent start.'

A double hoot sounded outside. Mandela stood up, ready to leave. 'There's Cecil Williams for me.'

'Can Williams be trusted?'

'Sure. I've known him a long time. He's a commercial traveller. He operates out of Johannesburg and travels virtually the whole country. It's an excellent cover.'

A second double hoot sounded. Mandela embraced his colleagues. They bade him farewell warmly. '*Salakakhule!*'

He walked out to the car. 'Hullo, Cecil, how are you this fine morning?'

'Couldn't be better. I think you should drive.' He gave Mandela a white dust-coat and chauffeur's cap. 'It's usual for a commercial traveller to have a chauffeur.'

'You just want to relax in the back seat like a white bourgeois gentleman, while I do all the hard work,' Mandela chuckled.

He put on the uniform. He was sweating freely in the clammy coastal humidity. 'Thank goodness we'll be in Transvaal by this afternoon. I prefer the dry highveld weather.'

The morning was already muggy in Durban. There was a murky

159

haze over the city, the subtropical humidity making it stuffy in the car. Soon they had left behind the humid cloudiness of the coastal belt. By the time they reached Hillcrest the dimness had given way to brilliant sunshine. Mandela was in good spirits. He had achieved much during his stay in Natal. The regional command was firmly in place. There were good men in control, committed to Umkhonto we Sizwe. He hummed a tune under his breath, pleased the road was not busy. 'We'll make good time to Johannesburg. We should be there by mid-afternoon.'

Through central Pietermaritzburg, up Townhill, past Queen Elizabeth Nature Reserve they travelled, climbing up the escarpment. They entered the cool pine plantations, passed the magnificent Tudor-style Hilton Hotel and dropped down to Cedara College of Agriculture.

With the town of Howick on their right, they crested a rise. The beautiful Umgeni Valley lay before them. The fields were being irrigated with rows of pulsating sprinklers sending millions of droplets sparkling into the clear air. A herd of black-and-white Friesland dairy cattle stood knee deep in the lush green grass, eating their fill, idly flicking away insects with their swishing tails.

Mandela hardly noticed two cars on either side of the road as he took in the peaceful scene. He glanced ahead and felt his throat constrict as he saw the police road-block. Police vans were parked in a zigzag formation on either side of the bridge. He slammed on the brakes.

'What's the matter?' asked Cecil quickly, jolted out of a doze.

'Police road-block ahead.' Mandela's first inclination was to turn the car around and make a dash back to Pietermaritzburg. He glanced in the rear-view mirror. Two cars were parked on the crest of the hill. 'Those are police cars,' he shouted, recognising them. 'No escape that way.'

'Stay calm, Nelson. Please stay calm. It's probably just a routine check.'

'You take the wheel so that I can slip away into the veld.' Nelson was desperate. Then he noticed further cars parked down the slope, with handlers and dogs standing next to the vehicles. 'Police dogs,' he groaned. 'I wouldn't get far.'

His mind raced. Was it just a regular police road-block? Did they know he was back in the country? Had someone betrayed him?

There were no answers. He was being sucked into a maelstrom.

There was no escape. All he could do was go forwards. 'I'll have to take my chances and bluff my way out of trouble if they question me,' he told Williams.

'Leave the talking to me.' Williams tried to appear calm. 'I'm a salesman. I can sell apartheid to the ANC! I'll talk us out of this one. It's a joke, Nelson,' he said, seeing his grim face.

The line of cars backed up in front of him forced Nelson to drive at a snail's pace. He relaxed slightly as he noted the police on the bridge were not asking the drivers for their licences. He pulled up the collar of his dust-coat, forcing the cap more firmly on his head and pulled the peak down over his face.

Cecil was leaning over the backrest of the front seat, peering ahead anxiously. 'It seems like a routine check. The police have to find something to do between riots and demonstrations. We must play it cool, Nelson.'

Slowly the line of cars became shorter as he neared the bridge. The vehicle in front of him pulled away. He drove forward, coming to a halt opposite a policeman. He looked around fearfully. He seemed to be the only agitated person in a sea of calm. Around the car and on the bridge policemen were lolling, rifles and Sten-guns held loosely in their hands.

Williams rolled down the right back window. 'Do we have a problem, officer?'

'We're looking for a fugitive, sir.'

'Good Lord. There are no renegades in this car, only my driver and I.' The policeman peered through the driver's window trying to get a better look. Cecil tried to divert the policeman's gaze. 'Officer, I'm a commercial traveller. I've just had a very successful sales trip to Natal. I'm on my way home.'

The policeman tapped on Nelson's window. 'Open up. I want to see your face.'

Cecil opened his car door, getting out, pretending to stretch his legs. 'Please, officer, we're in a hurry and Johannesburg's still a long way off. Can we go?'

'Not until I've checked out your driver.' The policeman called out to his colleagues. 'Come help me, men. There's a black driver in this car who's obstinate.'

Nelson raised his shoulders, trying to hide his face. Out of the corner of his eye he saw three policemen advancing, lifting their weapons.

He glanced about in desperation for an escape route. His options were limited. He couldn't charge the car over the bridge, he would have to swerve between police vans parked in a staggered formation. He could drive off the road into the river, but the water looked deep and the river was wide. He didn't relish a watery grave. He couldn't reverse the car. There was a whole column of vehicles backed up behind him. He could make a dash for the bushes on the river bank. He dismissed the idea. There were people in the vehicles behind him. A hail of bullets could kill innocent bystanders. Besides, I could be killed, he thought to himself. What good will I be to the freedom struggle dead?

He had no option, he had to answer the urgent tapping on the window. Fighting down his rising panic, Mandela willed himself to stay calm. He rolled down the window.

'Who are you? What's your name?'

'I'm Mr Williams's driver.'

'What's your name, dammit?'

'David.'

'David who?'

'David Motsomayi.'

'Take off your cap.'

Mandela continued to stare. The officer shoved his hand through the open window and roughly removed the chauffeur's cap. Mandela looked up, straight into the eyes of another man dressed in plain clothes. He saw him studying what looked like a glossy print, comparing features. To his horror he saw it was his own photograph.

Suddenly the man shouted. 'It's him! It's Nelson Mandela!' He was powerless to react as men on the bridge were activated. Sten-guns and rifles were trained at his head from all angles. Police vans sprang forward, blocking the bridge.

'You're wrong, I'm David Motsomayi.'

'Bullshit, you're Nelson Mandela and you're under arrest.'

Mandela's trial took place in the Old Synagogue Supreme Court in Pretoria.

'We close the prosecution's case against the accused,' stated the public prosecutor.

'Is there anything the accused wishes to add before I pass sentence?' The judge looked inquiringly at Mandela.

'Yes, Your Lordship.' Nelson Mandela spoke from the dock, his words echoing in the court. 'There comes a time when a man is prevented from living a normal life – when he can only live as an outlaw because the government has decreed to use the law to impose a state of outlawry upon him. I was driven to such a situation, but I don't regret having taken the decisions that I did take.' He paused and looked around the courtroom. 'Freedom in their own land is the pinnacle of men's ambitions, from which nothing can turn men of conviction aside. More powerful than my fear of the dreadful conditions in the prisons to which I might be subjected is my hatred for the dreadful conditions to which my people are subjected outside prison in South Africa.' Mandela looked directly at the judge. 'I have done my duty to my people and to my country. I have no doubt that history will pronounce that I was innocent and that the criminals that should have been brought before this court are the members of the Verwoerd government.'

'Will the accused please stand while I pronounce sentence,' requested the judge. 'Nelson Mandela, I sentence you to three years' imprisonment on the charge of incitement and two years for leaving the country without valid travel documents.'

Mandela was led down the stairs under armed guard to the cells below the Supreme Court. The day before, he had been a free man with a chance to lead the ANC's National High Command. Now he was condemned to spend five years of his life incarcerated, far from the mainstream of black politics.

His resolve strengthened as the sounds of chanting and singing permeated his cell. Thousands of his supporters were marching in the streets outside the Old Synagogue, singing the freedom song, *Tshotsholoza Mandela* – continue the struggle, our Mandela.'

The sun was setting below Paarl Mountain, casting lengthening shadows over Hermitage, when Jafta finished work for the day. He knocked on the back door of the manor house. Helena opened the door, surprised to see him standing there, hat in hand.

'Good evening, Jafta. How are you?'

'Good evening, madam Helena. I am well, thank you.'

'How is your cousin Nomisile?'

'She's in the Transkei, madam. She has a good business now. She makes dresses in the royal kraal. I helped her build her house.'

'Does she have children?'

'Yes, madam, a son called Themba.'

Helena nodded knowingly, quickly dismissing the thought, for she was in a hurry to get to a meeting in Mbekweni, the black township between Paarl and Wellington. The Black Sash was trying to establish an Advice Office in the township. Helena had agreed to help. She had convened a meeting with the black women of the interim committee. She looked at her watch. She had less than half an hour to bath, change and get to the meeting.

'How can I help you, Jafta?' Helena asked abruptly. 'I'm late for a meeting.'

'Madam, don't go to the meeting at Mbekweni tonight.'

'How do you know I have a meeting there?' Helena was flabbergasted that he knew.

'You're meeting with three ANC women,' said Jafta simply.

'That's right,' answered Helena incredulously, marvelling at the bush telegraph. 'What's the problem?'

'Tonight there's going to be trouble. Big trouble, madam.'

'Good Lord, I come and go in Mbekweni all the time, what sort of trouble?'

'Poqo. You know Poqo? The PAC military wing? They're marching from Mbekweni into Paarl. I'm telling you because the ANC likes you, madam, because you've been helping our people, like Witbooi Sikade.'

Helena felt flattered her Black Sash work had not gone unnoticed by the black community. 'You say Poqo are marching. Are you part of the demonstration?'

'No, madam, I'm ANC. We don't believe in killing. But the PAC, they're militant. They will kill you if you cross their path tonight, because you are a white person.'

'You are ANC?'

'Yes, madam, but please, don't tell boss Simon. He wouldn't like it.'

'All right, but what about my meeting? My friends in Mbekweni will be disappointed.'

'I'll get a message to them, madam.'

'How?'

'I know how,' answered Jafta mysteriously.

'What is the problem in Mbekweni?'

'Poqo are making ready for big trouble. While we talk here, they

164

are meeting. Some of their members were caught by the police yesterday for murder. They want to free them from jail, madam.'

'How can they possibly do that? Come now, Jafta, you're imagining things. There's no way a group of unarmed men can get prisoners out of jail.'

'Their leaders will make them. They've got spears. They've got axes, knives. They've got pangas and iron bars. Late tonight when they are worked up they will march to the police station and the jail to free their friends.'

'Thank you for warning me.'

'Good night, madam.'

'Good night, Jafta.' Helena returned to the kitchen. From what Jafta had said there could be trouble, even bloodshed. She telephoned the police station.

'Good evening, SAP Paarl.'

Helena replied in Afrikaans. 'Could you please tell me if you have any report of Poqo activity in Mbekweni tonight?'

'Who's speaking?' Helena did not want to disclose her name. She flaunted the laws often by entering Mbekweni without the required permit. She was never arrested: the police did not want to create an incident by arresting the local MP's daughter-in-law.

She fabricated. 'Paarl hospital here. Is it safe to send an ambulance into Mbekweni?'

'There's no report of any problems. Everything is quiet in the township.'

'Thank you.' She replaced the receiver, thinking perhaps Jafta has his wires crossed. I must go – the women will be very disappointed if I don't show up.

Helena walked through to the lounge. 'Darling, I have a meeting in Mbekweni tonight, will you put Pierre to bed?'

'Not again,' sighed Simon, exasperated. 'You neglect Pierre and myself – always helping the blacks. Why?'

'You wouldn't understand,' she answered curtly.

'Try me!'

She tapped her breast. 'I have an inner conviction to fight for their rights.'

'What about us?' Simon asked.

'Pierre is *your* son.'

'And me?' Simon sipped his drink.

165

She looked sarcastically from the glass of brandy to Simon's face and walked out of the room.

Helena dressed for the meeting, contemplating what she was about to do. 'The black people trust me,' she reasoned. 'They won't harm me.'

Helena drove through Paarl, then down the dusty gravel road into the township. Everything was quiet. The streets were virtually deserted. Jafta was exaggerating, she thought, I see no sign of problems.

She stopped in front of a shabby red brick building in Mbekweni and knocked on the door. There was no response. She knocked again, more loudly. Still silence. Eunice is expecting me, she thought, there must be people inside, a light is showing under the door.

'Eunice! Eunice! Open up. It's me, Helena.'

She heard a shuffling inside the house, then the door jerked open. She was pulled over the threshold. The door slammed shut behind her.

'Are you mad, coming here tonight?' screamed Eunice at Helena. 'I sent Jafta to warn you. He's just been here to tell us he alerted you and you wouldn't be coming.'

Shaken at the terror in Eunice's face, Helena replied, 'He did warn me, but there's no problem, the township is quiet.'

'Quiet?' cried Eunice. 'Tonight is the night of the long knives – tonight there's going to be bloodshed and murder.'

'Everything is quiet outside.'

'Of course everything is quiet. The people are all locked into their houses, too petrified to walk the streets.'

'What about the meeting to form the Advice Committee branch?'

'I postponed the meeting. We can have our meeting later. That's why I sent a message with Jafta. You're very lucky you managed to get here unharmed. You'd better stay here until the danger has passed.'

'When will that be?'

'Probably only tomorrow morning.'

'I can't do that. If I don't get home by about midnight Simon will come looking for me. Can't I telephone?'

'From where?' queried Eunice. 'The post office doesn't supply telephones to black people. There's only a public telephone at the general dealer's store, but most times it's out of order. No, Helena, you're cut off from your home.'

'You can't leave a Mercedes-Benz parked in front of our house,' warned Eunice's husband, 'you will get us into trouble with the PAC. Such a smart car could only be a white man's. They will burn the vehicle and attack us for harbouring you.'

Helena was appalled that an innocent gesture on her part could get her friends into trouble. 'Then I must take my chances and go home.'

'No! You cannot take the chance. Bring the car around the back of our house, we'll hide it under a sail. Don't turn on the lights.'

Helena and Eunice left the house quietly. The whole area was in darkness as the township was not equipped with electricity. They heard chanting as an angry, shouting mob ran down a side street.

'Those are Poqo, they are working themselves up. Listen to their bloodthirsty cries,' whispered Eunice. 'Look there, do you see that bright fire? It's at the poplar grove where they do their military training. It's the meeting place for those who are going to storm the Paarl police station.'

'It's a long way off, I can escape back to Paarl without passing that point.' Helena was starting to panic.

'Look on the other side.' Eunice turned around, pointing in the opposite direction. 'Do you see that bonfire? There's another group gathering who intend raiding the Paarl prison, to free their friends, and they're right next to the road back into Paarl.'

She was trapped; she had no option but to remain at Eunice's house. She started the car, careful not to rev the engine, and drove slowly to the back of the house. They pulled an old sail over the vehicle and slipped in through the back door.

They had hardly returned to the house, when there was a loud banging on the front door. Eunice extinguished the single paraffin lamp and they sat in darkness. Voices shouted in Xhosa: 'Come out, all men of honour! Tonight is the night Poqo is going to show the white man he means business! Tonight is the start of black rule!'

They moved on in a noisy surge of commotion. Helena shivered. She knew what her fate would be if she was discovered. As the clamour moved away, she asked Eunice softly, 'Won't your neighbours give me away?'

'In this section of Mbekweni we are all ANC. You are our friend, Helena.'

167

Eunice left the light off and they sat in the gloom, each with their own thoughts, too terrified really to make conversation. They dozed. Shouts woke her and she saw to her dismay it was two o'clock in the morning.

My God! she thought, Simon will be frantic. She tiptoed across the room and opened the front door. The noise was much louder, but not in the immediate vicinity. She walked outside, looking towards the two bonfires. The raging flames had burnt down to orange glows. Helena almost fainted as she felt a touch on her arm. She reacted wildly, jumping to one side, stumbling and falling to the ground.

'Shh, shh, it's me,' said a familiar voice and she realised with relief it was Eunice. She stood up, her nerves on edge, her breathing irregular.

'They're preparing to go,' said Eunice in dismay. 'They are full of liquor now and stirred up by their leaders – they are ready to march and massacre. Come inside. I'll make us some tea,' offered Eunice. 'Soon they'll be gone from Mbekweni, but God help Paarl when they unleash their anger on the town.'

'Everything is quiet, I'd rather go now. I'm so afraid Simon will run headlong into them if he comes looking for me.'

'Wait just a while longer, another twenty minutes. Let them get clear of Mbekweni, then you can go.'

A mob of over a hundred men, armed with primitive weapons, marched along the road through Noorder-Paarl heading for the police station.

The windows of cars parked in the street were smashed with axes. At Alpha Garage the mob torched two of the petrol pumps and the high-octane fuel ignited in a brilliant flame. A bus driver spotted the advancing marchers and he hurried to the police station, running into the charge office. 'There's a huge mob of angry blacks marching this way. They're armed. They're wrecking everything as they go.'

The duty officer gaped at him in horror. 'Where?'

'They're coming this way from Noorder-Paarl.'

Further down the street the throng attacked another garage, again setting the petrol pumps alight. The flames burnt fiercely above ground level, but did not ignite the huge storage tanks below the surface.

* * *

168

The second group of over a hundred and fifty Poqo men marched south down the railway line, heading for the prison. They were more orderly, causing no damage along the way. They crossed the Berg River at the concrete Market Street bridge and turned towards the jail. They surrounded the prison building and tried to batter down the front door but it was made of steel, far stronger than their weapons.

'Release our Poqo members,' demanded the gang.

The jailer shouted through the opening in the door, 'Those men are murderers, we're not holding them for political crimes!'

'Free them! Free them!'

'They will get a fair trial!' shouted the officer.

Frustrated, the men picked up stones and hurled them at the building. The solid walls thwarted their efforts. Sensing that they would not succeed in their mission, the gang milled around for a while, then at a signal from their leader they broke up in disarray, heading for home. A large contingent broke away and headed up Market Street.

'The coast is clear. I'm going now.' Helena was determined. 'I can't stay a second longer. My husband will be desperate.'

'Stay till morning,' pleaded Eunice.

'I must go. Thank you for your kindness.'

Helena threw off the sail, starting the car with trembling hands. She kept the headlights on dim and drove slowly through the deserted streets of Mbekweni and on to the tarmac towards Paarl. Everything seemed calm and peaceful and she grew in confidence. She entered Paarl through Huguenot, crossing the Berg River over Market Street bridge. Suddenly, in front of her was the mob that had stormed the prison and was now streaming back towards the bridge to return to Mbekweni. They ran straight into Helena. She screamed in fear, pumping the accelerator, turning northwards.

Simon woke with a start, feeling about in the double bed for Helena. The bed was empty. He turned on the bedside lamp. Her side had not been slept in. He looked at the alarm clock, seeing with misgiving it was after three o'clock. He jumped out of bed and threw on his clothes.

Something must have happened, he thought as he forced himself to stay calm. Maybe Helena had car problems. I'd better go and look for her. Within minutes he was driving his farm pick-up towards town.

I wonder which road she would have taken home? Opposite the park in Market Street he braked to a halt as a horde of armed black men were illuminated in his headlights. They ran forward threateningly, making for his pick-up.

'What the hell!' he cried in alarm, quickly forcing the vehicle in a tight U-turn, and sped northwards.

A crazed multitude blocked the whole width of Lady Grey Street in front of the police station. 'Get around the back of the building and attack from the rear!' shouted a Poqo leader. Groups of men slipped around each side of the building. Suddenly two .303 rifle shots rang out from the back and the screams of two dying men rent the night air, echoing and re-echoing against the high walls. The throng rushed the front entrance of the police station.

'Fire!'

A hail of bullets tore over the heads of the rioters, smashing the plate-glass windows across the street. The crowd panicked and scattered – up and down Lady Grey Street.

The mob was on the rampage, smashing the windows of shops as they ran out of control. The central business area of Paarl seethed with rioters bent on revenge. A group swarmed down Loop Street, smashing down doors and entering houses. In their bed, a couple were hacked with pangas and left for dead. A matric schoolgirl screamed in terror as her door was battered down. She forced her way past her attackers on to the pavement, a panga flashed and she was almost decapitated. A young man rushed to help and a vicious blow severed his jugular vein. The two died on the pavement. Another resident shot and killed a rioter, who was dragged away by his friends.

Helena drove ahead of the crowd. Outpacing the mob, she turned up Loop Street and was trapped between the two groups approaching from the front and behind. They rocked the Mercedes-Benz. In her terror, Helena let the car stall. The deranged crowd set about the vehicle with their weapons. Helena wailed as splintering glass cut her face. She held up her hand for protection, in a daze, as the windscreen collapsed on top of her. A panga flashed through the jagged hole, cleaving open her lower arm. Helena jumped out of the car, screaming for mercy. 'Don't kill me, please, I mean you no harm.'

Simon was confronted with rioters coming from the police station. He swerved down a side street, only to meet another band of men. He broadsided at the corner and sped away. Again his path was blocked and he hurriedly turned down Loop Street. The street was teeming with people driven mad for revenge. He ploughed into the crowd, seeing bodies disappear as he knocked them flying.

Simon watched in horror as a berserk man ran towards his pick-up, an axe held high, a scowl of hate on his face. The pick-up hit him with a sickening thud, and Simon felt the jolting, as the wheels rolled over the fallen body.

Through a gap in the crowd he saw a stationary Mercedes-Benz facing him, the headlights still burning. In a flash it struck him — it was his. The hair at the nape of his neck rose as he saw Helena stumble out of the car. The frenzied mob surrounded her. 'No! No!' he shouted.

A flying stone hit his windscreen, starring the glass, cutting off his visibility. Simon lost control of the pick-up and it ploughed into a lamp-post. He was thrown forward, hitting his head against the windscreen, knocked out cold.

Simon shook his head. His brain cleared as the horror flooded back. 'Helena! Helena!' he cried as he forced open the door. He sprang out of the pick-up, making for her. He was enveloped by the violent throng. Simon was a big man. He punched his first attacker in the face and grabbed a long-handled axe out of his hands. He swung it in a monstrous arc, cutting through flesh and bone. An assailant fell forward, his panga landing at Simon's feet. With a swoop of his left hand he scooped it up. Flashing both weapons simultaneously, he scythed a path through the line of battle. His assailants shrank from the double-handed blows. Bellowing like a bull, Simon swore as each bludgeoning blow hit home. *'Bliksems!'* *'Kaffers!'* *'Donders!'* *'Vuilgoed!'*

Helena recognised her husband's voice and turned to him. 'Simon, my darling, you're here.' A panga struck her lower back cutting through her muscles, numbing her spine as it sliced between the vertebrae. A second panga blow slashed her face from top to bottom. With a shudder she passed out. Her attacker lifted his weapon for the *coup de grâce*.

'Helena! Helena!' Simon sprang forward swinging the axe. It scythed through the air and the rioter screamed in agony as his arm

171

dangled on sinews. His fingers released their hold on the handle and the panga clattered to the tarmac. Simon shouldered him out of the way standing like a colossus over his wife's inert body, his arms windmilling destruction, and the rioters drew back in fear. Police sirens blared as patrol vans hurtled nearer.

'*Ipolisi! Ipolisi!*' The crowd fled for their lives down the street.

Simon gathered up his wife and carried her to the Mercedes-Benz, not even feeling the bleeding gash on his upper arm. He laid her gently on the back seat. The keys were still in the ignition. The engine fired and he sped to the hospital.

Casualty was humming with activity. The police had telephoned at the start of the attack and the hospital staff were geared for the emergency. As Simon stopped, two porters rushed a trolley across to the car.

'Careful, her back is injured,' Simon instructed as they lifted her out of the car. He reeled back in shock as they turned her face towards him – it was a gory mess and bleeding profusely, with flashes of white bone showing.

Dr de Villiers had come on duty as soon as he had been told of the crisis. He met Simon at the door, taking in the scene at a glance.

'Sister, we need a drip up here at once. And help me to stem the bleeding.' He grabbed some gauze dressings off a trolley, packing them tightly into the wounds. The sister slipped an oxygen mask over Helena's tattered face while the doctor searched desperately for a vein. 'We need a blood cross-match here as well. Sister, get her into surgery, stat.'

Casualty looked like a war hospital. Ambulances were pulling in with the bodies. Nurses patched up the injured, transferring them to hospital wards. They tried to treat Simon, but he was oblivious of his injury and insisted on being with Helena. Dr de Villiers gently walked him into the passage. 'Simon, her life is at stake, let me handle it. Nurse, take Mr Roux through to the dressing room and attend to his arm.'

The nurses cleaned Simon's wound, stitching and covering it with a bandage. It was getting light outside. Simon phoned the cottage at Hermitage.

'Pa, there's been a terrible accident.' He spoke to his shocked father, giving him details of the events of the night.

Paulus swore. 'Bloody kaffirs, we'll make them pay, my boy, just wait and see. Oh! How terrible! I pray Helena will be all right.'

'They're operating on her now. I'm staying until she comes out of theatre. Will you please look after Pierre – he's alone at home and is probably still sleeping, but must go to school later this morning.'

'Of course, my son. We'll be there as soon as we can. I'll let Helena's parents know.'

A sombre group sat in the waiting room. A dejected Dr de Villiers came out of the operating theatre, pulling off his gloves. He came straight to the point. 'I've bad news. The blow from the panga cut through the long muscles of Helena's back. The panga's tip entered her spine at the third lumbar vertebra and completely severed her spinal cord. There's nothing I, nor any specialist, can do to repair the damage.'

'What does that mean?' demanded Simon frantically.

'Helena is paralysed from her waist down. For the rest of her life she will be confined to a wheelchair.'

'And her face?' insisted Simon.

The doctor blanched and averted his gaze. 'It's bad Simon, very bad. I've done what I can, but Helena will be scarred for life, even with plastic surgery.'

Simon sat with his head between his hands, devastated at the news. So Helena was a cripple! He quailed when he thought of what her misshapen features might look like, and the face he would have to live with every day of his life.

'My friends,' continued Dr de Villiers, 'this is not the end of the world. Helena can still lead a full and useful life as a wife and mother. She needs your support and love right now.'

Everyone chorused agreement except Simon. The room became quiet as they turned expectantly to him. He wanted a drink to settle his nerves. Damn their anxious expressions! Why were they pressurising him? He looked from face to face, noting their questioning looks. He stood up hurriedly. 'I'll honour my obligation to Helena,' he said in clipped tones. 'She can count on my support.' He turned on his heel, quickly leaving the hospital.

'*Bliksemse kaffers,*' muttered Paulus, 'the government will see that justice is done. I'll petition the Minister of Justice. John Vorster will smoke out every Poqo in Mbekweni and make them pay for last night's atrocities.'

Simon found solace in the bottle and for a week did not leave his room. Everyone left him well alone. Marie looked after Pierre. A

173

few times she tried to speak to Simon, but the door was locked and he refused to open it. Meals were placed outside the door, but were left untouched. After the first case was finished an unkempt and bleary-eyed Simon emerged to fetch fresh supplies.

His mother slipped into the bedroom and was shocked at the mess – empty bottles littered the floor, cigarettes had burnt out on the bedside tables, the ashtrays were overflowing with butts and the air smelt musty and rancid. She opened the windows to allow fresh air into the room, and stripped the bed.

He stumbled back, carrying a fresh box of brandy, his eyes squinting in the bright light.

'Simon, what's become of you?' berated his mother. 'You look terrible – you can't go on like this. You told us at the hospital that we could rely on you. Drinking yourself into a stupor is dodging your obligations, my boy.'

He sat on the bed looking ashamedly at his mother. 'Leave me alone – it's my life.'

'No, it isn't,' she answered, her eyes flashing in anger. 'You have responsibilities to your wife, your son, your family and your farm. This drinking must stop now.' She ran the bath and bundled Simon into the water. Marie called the servants and they cleaned the bedroom. She scrubbed Simon from top to toe as she had last done when he was a little boy. He grumbled, but did not resist. After she had dried him, Marie made him shave, comb his hair, brush his teeth, and get dressed.

'It's been eight days since you last saw your wife, and that's a disgrace! They took out her stitches today and we're going to visit her now.'

Simon climbed meekly into the car. He knew he would have to face up to reality sooner or later, but he dreaded the first sight of Helena's patched face. What he needed was a drink to steady his nerves.

Holding his arm, a determined Marie propelled Simon along the hospital passage and into the private ward. Helena had her back to them, her face towards the window. When she heard them she turned and tried to smile.

'Oh, my God!' muttered Simon, his hand flying to his open mouth. He turned to run from the room but Marie held on to him; she knew her son had to overcome this crisis and come to terms with Helena's injuries.

'Hullo, my darling,' breathed Helena. 'I'm so glad you've come. I've missed you.'

Her voice seemed to calm Simon, but he averted his gaze and sat down heavily next to the bed.

'Look at me, Simon,' pleaded Helena. 'I can't change how I look and it was not your fault. You were magnificent the way you fought off my attackers. You were a real hero.'

Simon looked at her face for the first time. The straight panga cut had turned into a twisted, livid line, starting on her forehead, cutting between her eyes, slicing through her nose, splitting both lips and ending on her chin. The stitches had been removed, forming parallel rows of puce dots on either side of the cut, leaving her face mutilated far worse than he had imagined. When she tried to smile her lips were misshapen, showing her gums in a bestial, disfigured sneer. Helena placed her hand on Simon's arm. He jerked away in fright and ran sobbing from the ward.

Outside the hospital he hired a taxi and hurried home. Stuffing six bottles of brandy into a knapsack he slipped out of the back door as his mother ran into the house. He headed up Paarl Mountain to his secret place. For three days he lay in the cave, drunk, not caring. He woke on the morning of the fourth day feeling for another bottle, but all were empty. The clear water from the spring made him feel better and he sat on the ledge soaking up the early-morning sunshine. He felt remorse and prayed. Slowly his old determination returned, and by midday he was ready to return home and face up to his responsibilities.

At first light the prison came awake – iron gates clanged, the heavy boots of the warders echoed down the passages and the familiar sound of the food trolley was heard.

Nelson Mandela stretched, not looking forward to the prospect of another bleak day behind bars. He sat up quickly as heavy footfalls stopped at his gate and he heard the key grating in the lock.

'Come,' said the warder in clipped tones.

'Where are you taking me?'

'You're off to Pretoria to join the rest of your kaffir collaborators.'

'Who?' asked Mandela urgently.

'Sisulu, Mbeki and all the others caught on that Rivonia farm.

We've got the whole of your National High Command under lock and key.'

It was the first Mandela had heard of his friends' capture. Prisoners were not allowed newspapers or radios. With a heavy heart he walked between the warders. He did not allow his distress to show – he walked tall and proud as an example to the other inmates.

'Madiba! Madiba!' they whispered in awe as he marched past, and Mandela nodded in acknowledgement.

In Pretoria Local prison, Mandela was reunited with his black colleagues. They embraced sombrely, knowing that with all of them in jail the government had succeeded in damaging, if not virtually destroying, the freedom struggle inside the country.

Whispering to avoid being overheard by the security police in the bugged cell, they told Mandela of the raid on the farm and the arrests.

'Someone betrayed us to the police, but we don't know who,' said Ahmed Kathrada angrily.

'How did they implicate me?' Mandela asked.

'They found your diary of your unauthorised trip to Africa and Europe in the Lilliesleaf Farm cottage.'

Mandela nodded solemnly. 'The details of my course in military training by the Algerian Army of National Liberation will prove damning evidence.'

They lapsed into silence as they contemplated their fates.

'Where are our white colleagues?' asked Mandela.

Sisulu laughed cynically. 'Even in prison the government practises apartheid. They are being held in the white section of Pretoria Local.'

'I have appointed our friend Advocate Bram Fisher as senior counsel and leader of our defence team,' Mandela told his colleagues. 'He has briefed two Johannesburg barristers as junior counsel – our friends Arthur Chaskelson and George Bizos.' The prisoners nodded in agreement.

'Have they appointed the judge?' Kathrada asked.

'Mr Justice Quartus de Wet,' answered Mandela. 'The Judge-President of the Transvaal. He alone will decide our fate – with no assessors or jury.'

'And the State Prosecutor?' Mbeki asked.

'They have brought all the big guns to bear on us,' replied Nelson. 'The prosecutor will be the Deputy Attorney-General of the Transvaal.'

'The logical place to hold the trial will be Johannesburg,' said Sisulu. 'It's central for our defence team, the prosecutors, the witnesses and our supporters.'

Mandela shook his head sadly. 'The security police have insisted, in the interest of law and order, to have the trial moved to the Palace of Justice in Pretoria. Pretoria is the sentimental capital of Afrikanerdom and they want the Rivonia Trial to become the showpiece of government impartiality in their own capital.'

'Clever move,' stated Govan Mbeki. 'In Pretoria the local public interest will be minimal and they can prevent our supporters from attending the trial by sealing off the highways to the city.'

'This trial will create huge media interest in South Africa and overseas,' Mandela predicted.

On the stroke of nine the accused were led up the flight of stairs, straight into the body of the courtroom.

First to appear was accused No. 1: Nelson Mandela. The crowd gasped in shock. The big, powerful man had shrunk by eighteen kilograms. He looked tired and drawn. Only when he flashed his well-known confident smile, lighting up the fervour in his eyes, did the people realise the drive, motivation and dedication to the cause were still in abundance. He raised his clenched fist defiantly in salute.

'Amandla!' chorused the crowded public gallery, returning the power salute.

No. 2 accused, Walter Sisulu, appeared. 'Amandla!' screamed the people. As each of them emerged, the crown harmonised, 'Amandla!' 'Amandla!' The security police rushed around trying to silence them.

'Quiet, this is a courtroom!' shouted the police, but nothing could stop the impromptu showing of solidarity.

State Prosecutor Yutar read out the charges against the accused. 'The State versus the National High Command and others. You are accused on four charges under the security legislation: the Sabotage Act, the Suppression of Communism Act and the Criminal Law

Amendment Act. The charge sheet lists a hundred and ninety-three acts of sabotage committed between 27 June 1962 and 11 July 1963.'

The judge nodded and Yutar presented his indictment: 'The accused envisaged a military basis with hostile intent, acting in concert to conspire or commit sabotage, as members of the African National Congress or the South African Communist Party, both of which are banned organisations. They have incited, instigated, commanded, aided, advised, encouraged or procured other persons to commit the wrongful and wilful acts of sabotage, preparatory to and in facilitation of guerrilla warfare in the Republic of South Africa, coupled with an armed invasion of and violent revolution, by soliciting and receiving money and arms from inside and outside the country to further these aims.'

All applications for bail were turned down, the prosecutor claiming the accused would leave the country.

At the start of March 1964 the State formally closed its case, leaving only the cross-examination of the accused to be completed.

Each accused was cross-examined, with the exception of Nelson Mandela. Proudly he refused to plead for his freedom in an all-white court. He chose the alternative: to make a statement from the dock. Such a declaration could not be interrupted and it could be read. His refusal to be cross-examined could count against him when sentence was passed, but this did not deter him. Testimony to his leadership qualities was his desire for the true facts of the freedom struggle to be placed conclusively in the court records, for future generations to read, if he should be sentenced to death.

Mandela addressed the court. 'I choose not to give evidence in my own defence, nor to be cross-examined, but I wish to make a statement.'

'You may continue.'

Mandela rose, tall and dignified. He put on his reading glasses. Shuffling a thick wad of papers, he traced the history of the ANC and Umkhonto we Sizwe from their beginnings to the present time. He sketched his part, the roles of his fellow-accused, how they had acted in good faith in trying to obtain a just dispensation for the black nation. Violence was a last desperate step, contemplated only when all else failed.

Mandela dispelled the argument that all ANC members were

communists. 'It is true that there has often been close co-operation between the ANC and the Communist Party, but co-operation is merely proof of a common goal – in this case the removal of white supremacy – and is not proof of a complete community of interests. The history of the world is filled with similar examples. Perhaps the most striking illustration is to be found in the co-operation between Great Britain, the United States of America and the Soviet Union in the fight against Hitler. Nobody but Hitler would have dared to suggest that such collaboration turned Churchill or Roosevelt into communists or communist tools, or that Britain and America were working to bring about a communist order.'

Mandela looked up and smiled when he saw the misery on Yutar's face. He continued. 'Perhaps it is even more difficult for white South Africans, with an ingrained prejudice against communism, to understand why experienced African politicians so readily accept communists as their allies. The reason is very simple. Theoretical differences amongst those fighting against oppression are a luxury the ANC cannot afford at this stage – for many decades communists were the only political grouping in South Africa who were prepared to treat Africans as human beings and their equals – prepared to eat with us, talk with us, live with us and work with us to help us attain political rights and a stake in society. I now turn to my position. I have denied that I am a communist and regard myself as an African patriot. I must leave myself free to borrow the best from the West and from the East.'

He stopped to catch his breath, readjusting his glasses.

'Have you finished, Mr Mandela?'

'No, Your Lordship, I still have one final page.'

He read the last page slowly, placing great emphasis on the words. 'During my lifetime, I have dedicated myself to the struggle of the African people. I have fought against white domination and I have fought against black domination. I have cherished the ideal of a democratic and free society in which all persons live together in harmony and with equal opportunities. It is an ideal which I hope to live for and to achieve. But if needs be, it is an ideal for which I am prepared to die.'

Judge de Wet released Bob Hepple, Jimmy Kantor and Rusty Bernstein.

'Will the accused please rise,' instructed de Wet. The courtroom was quiet.

The judge continued, 'The other eight accused, Nelson Mandela, Walter Sisulu, Govan Mbeki, Denis Goldberg, Ahmed Kathrada, Raymond Mhlaba, Elias Motsoaledi and Andrew Mlangeni, I find you guilty.' The first four were found guilty on all four counts, the remaining four on various of the charges.

'I will pass sentence tomorrow morning at ten o'clock.'

Back in prison each accused had time to ponder his future. There was no chance of freedom – the verdict of guilty had put paid to that. Only two choices remained: if found guilty of treason, the gallows – if guilty on the other counts, a life sentence.

The prisoners climbed the stairs from the cells for the last time. At ten o'clock sharp proceedings started. 'Will the accused rise while sentence is passed.' The eight prisoners rose, feeling the sword of Damocles hanging over their heads. They were psychologically prepared for a long prison term. Death by the hangman's noose in Pretoria's Central prison was a thought too terrible to comprehend.

'All I was doing was honestly fighting for the rights of my people,' thought Elias, 'so that they could live a better life in the country of their birth. Why should I die for what I believe to be right?'

Judge de Wet spoke in his usual almost inaudible tone. 'The crime for which the eight accused have been convicted is in essence one of high treason.'

Nelson Mandela felt his hands clenching at the rail of the dock, his knees involuntarily quaking. Treason means death! he thought in despair. Am I destined to die?

'The State has decided not to charge the crime in this form. Bearing this in mind and after giving the matter my most serious consideration, I have decided not to impose the supreme penalty.' The judge looked up, seeing the eight accused shudder, relief etched on their features. He continued, 'I sentence all of the accused to life imprisonment. In the case of the accused who have been convicted on more than one count, these counts will be taken together for the purpose of sentence.'

The leader of the defence team sat down disconsolately, covering his face with his hands, sobbing quietly. At last Bram Fisher rose and walked slowly over to Mandela, shaking his head in misery. 'I have failed you, my friend.'

Nelson smiled at him, extending his hand in sympathy. 'No, you have not. Thanks to you we live to fight another day. While there's life there is hope.'

Mandela was sound asleep when his cell gate was thrown open and he was roused and marched into the yard to join his colleagues. It was dark. 'What's going on?' he asked.

He was ignored as the Rivonia trialists were bundled into the back of a police van. Racing through the deserted streets, they headed south on the Johannesburg highway to Waterkloof air force base. A Dakota was on the runway, propellers spinning. The police van reversed up to the cargo door and the prisoners were forced aboard. The aircraft rolled to the end of the runway. Slowly it gathered speed until it became airborne. As the engines settled to a cruising throb, they passed over the metropolis of Johannesburg, looking twice its size at night, with winking white and orange lights.

To many of them it was their first flight. They looked through the windows with a mixture of fear and wonder, silently thinking of their loved ones, asleep in their beds below.

'Where are we going?' Nelson ventured a second time.

'You lucky guys, you're going on an overseas journey.' The guard was enjoying himself.

Could it be? Hopes rose. Could South Africa have bowed to international pressure? Were they being transported out of the country? To where? Zambia? Botswana? Mozambique?

'Tell us where we are going.'

'I told you, overseas. You're on a one-way ticket to Robben Island.' He laughed uproariously at his own joke. The prisoners slumped back disheartened as their last hope of freedom disappeared. They were on a journey to hell for the rest of their days.

As the light strengthened, the aircraft circled the island. Looking through the window Mandela glimpsed Robben Island sparkling like a jewel in Table Bay.

Sisulu moved nearer, also looking through the window. 'Look, there is Cape Town and Table Mountain,' he said pointing towards the mainland.

The early-morning sun touched the golden beaches of Clifton and

181

Blaauwbergstrand. Dropping altitude, the pilot straightened out on his final approach.

'South Africa's own Alcatraz,' muttered Sisulu bitterly.

With a puff of smoke from its tyres the Dakota touched down on the island's airstrip. The aircraft taxied towards a huddle of vehicles and a cold reception with unsmiling prison guards brandishing automatic weapons.

'Yesterday we had the world's media focused on us,' said Mbeki as he stepped on to the tarmac. 'Today we are far removed from the limelight.'

'Into the nefarious hell called Robben Island prison,' answered Kathrada bitterly. 'For the rest of our lives.'

10

A male puff-adder, *Bitis arietans*, one of the deadly snakes of Africa, crept out of its winter lair, near the royal kraal of Mqekezweni in the Transkei. It had hibernated alone through the long winter and with the onset of spring its instinct was to seek warmth.

The male snake lay sunning itself on a rock, when the musky smell of a female in oestrus reached its nostrils. It slithered towards the smell, following the trail laid by the female, secreted from her cloaca gland. The male caught up with her on a stretch of sand next to the river. He interested her in copulation by foreplay – rubbing his body sensuously over the female, tickling her back with the bottom of his chin. The female stretched out languidly, enjoying the titillation, the muscles of her body rippling with pleasure.

After more than an hour the female had been sufficiently stimulated. Lying on her stomach, she twisted the lower half of her body around, until her smooth stomach was facing upwards. She raised her tail as high as she could force it, the muscles stretched taut, opening her vent for the male.

The vagina had one opening, but immediately split into two, each vagina leading to a uterus containing ten transparent unfertilised eggs.

The male puff-adder lay on top, curling its body around the female for purchase, its twin penises erect and throbbing. Endowed with two penises the male puff-adder is able to fornicate successfully with double pleasure. Each penis slipped into its own vagina. Clasps, or hooks, at the base of the penises, extended, locking them firmly in place. The snakes writhed backwards and forwards against each other – a mass of slippery, wriggling, viperous action. The urge to reproduce was voluptuous and compelling. Coitus was the start of a new generation, as each egg was fertilised in turn, each penis ejaculating repeatedly in its own vagina.

The soft white river sand was churned up as the snakes mated continuously for almost two hours. Nature ensured the survival of the species by the sex act lasting until sufficient semen had been ejaculated to reach the furthermost egg in each uterus. These eggs would develop the whole summer, the sacs being expelled by the female in autumn, when each young puff-adder would be born alive, breaking through the membrane and slithering away to make its own way in life.

As the male withdrew, the snakes untangled themselves, catching their breath. The male inflated his long single lung with air, forcibly expelling it through his glottis and nostrils, producing a long and pronounced hiss – making the puffing sound after which the species was named. Without a backward glance at each other they glided their separate ways.

The male was ravenous after months of hibernation. It undulated along the bank until it crossed a field rat's path in the long grass. There it lay in sinister waiting, its black unblinking eyes searching for prey.

An unsuspecting rat came down the track. The puff-adder opened its mouth wide, unsheathing its twin, hollow, curved fangs from their mucus capsule, moving them forward like a hinge.

The rat had no chance. It stopped abruptly and was frozen to the spot by fear. With a swinging side swipe of lightning-like rapidity the puff-adder drove the fangs home, injecting three drops of venom from each fang into its prey. Disengaging the fangs, the snake kept the rat in view as it ran about at random in a dazed way for almost a minute. Arching its back the rat, hind legs paralysed, fell to its side, dying with a shudder.

The puff-adder leisurely advanced on the dead rat, investigating with its sensitive forked tongue, moving around to the head. Salivating copiously to lubricate its victim, the snake swallowed the rat whole, from the nostrils down to the tail, the process taking less than half an hour.

As the sun headed towards the horizon, the satiated puff-adder slithered lazily towards its lair on the hillside for the night.

The setting sun was a huge, glowing ball. It was early spring and the heat of day was giving way to a late-afternoon chill.

Laughing happily, nine-year-old Themba chased his mother's livestock home for the night. Ahead of him the herd suddenly scattered, the cattle bellowing in fright. The sheep and goats followed, bleating in alarm.

The puff-adder moved sluggishly with its full belly. It blended perfectly with the dry grass. Themba's eyes were focused on the spooked animals, he did not see the camouflaged snake as his heel crunched down on its tail.

Instinctively the reptile swung around, unsheathing its fangs. They struck Themba's calf, but only for a fraction of a second before the momentum of Themba's forward charge dislodged the snake.

In that split second the puff-adder had time to constrict its poison glands and squirt half a droplet of venom from each fang into Themba's leg muscle.

'*Injoka! Injoka*!' Themba screamed in fright as he skidded to a halt. As he recognised the puff-adder he bellowed in fear. '*Ibululu! Ibululu!*' He looked down in horror at the twin puncture marks in his leg, oozing droplets of blood.

The villagers heard his shrill cries and came running.

'Follow that snake to his hole, but don't kill it,' instructed a wise Xhosa man. 'The witch-doctor will need it later.' A young boy followed the puff-adder at a distance, noting the hole it entered in the side of a disused antheap. He marked the spot with two stones.

The villagers carried Themba's limp body towards Nomisile's hut. 'Themba's been bitten by a snake!' they shouted. Nomisile met the crowd coming towards her and shrieked at the sight of Themba's slack body. She shouldered the people out of the way to get to him. 'Call the medicine woman!'

'Only the *igqirha* can help against *ibululu*.'

'Then call the witch-doctor, quickly.'

They laid Themba on a reed mat in Nomisile's house. She looked at the bite marks in horror. She started shaking as the surrounding muscle swelled rapidly. His skin felt cold and clammy. Desperately she opened his eyelids and saw that his pupils were hugely dilated. Themba started vomiting. Nomisile quickly turned him on his side and wiped away the retching with a cloth, tears rolling down her cheeks.

Members of the tribe gathered at Nomisile's hut. Women crowded inside to support her. They chanted and wailed in terror. The puff-adder's poison was legendary. An awed prattle greeted the appearance of the witch-doctor. He was seldom seen: most of the women and children had never laid eyes on him. He was a small, wizened old black man, with scraggly grey hair and a tatty beard. He wore a rabbit-skin cap with porcupine quills sticking out at angles from it. A dried grey mongoose tail attached to a copper necklace hung down his chest. The witch-doctor wore a waistcoat of cured antelope hide, displaying his scrawny chest and thin, muscleless arms. A skirt of patchwork skins and anklets of badger pelt completed his strange outfit.

It was the first time in years he had entered the village – mostly those needing his services had to go to his cave. He chased the women out of the hut. Nomisile protested vehemently, but he would have none of it and she was made to leave too. The witch-doctor called for an elder to assist him.

The elder came out of the house with instructions. 'The great medicine man requests you to find the snake that bit Themba and bring it to him alive.'

It was already dark. The men left, taking slow-burning torches of woven grass. Finding the stone-marked anthill, they easily dug through the hollow maze of empty ant passages. The puff-adder was engorged with the rat and tired from mating. He offered no resistance as they scooped him into a tin and carried him back to the hut.

The witch-doctor noted the suppurating fang marks. With a stabbing spear he sliced criss-cross cuts across each prick, roughing up the skin in the vicinity with a piece of broken glass. Although the glass scored the skin deeply there was no bleeding; the poison had caused the blood in the area to clot.

Out of a small skin pouch he tapped a sandy-red powder – *zibiba*, a magic snake-bite potion made from the pulverised root of the male tree-fern. The witch-doctor rubbed the powder deep into the bite marks. He cut two further criss-crosses over Themba's heart and rubbed more powder into the slits to protect the pumping organ from succumbing to the venom. He held Themba's head and opened his mouth. He dropped some of the potion on the back of the tongue. Themba swallowed involuntarily, ingesting the powder.

The witch-doctor sat cross-legged next to the hearth, chanting in a strange tongue, invoking the spirits of his forebears to help him. In a high-pitched voice he asked for the strengthening of his healing powers. He threw the bones – knuckle bones of goats and limb bones of small mammals – on the floor. He made clicking and clucking noises as he picked them up one by one, reading signs from the way they lay.

Outside a sizeable crowd had gathered, straining to hear every sound and word inside the hut. When the witch-doctor let out a final wheezing whoop the crowd fell back in terror, their worst superstitions aroused. The door flew open and the little gnome stood on the threshold, waving a carved stick aloft.

'The snake that bit the child shall decide whether he lives or dies,' he declared in a thin voice. The people stared, fascinated – all of them firm believers in his magical powers.

'Will you slaughter an ox for the people if your child lives?' the medicine man asked Nomisile.

'I would gladly butcher all my cattle for Themba's life.'

'One ox will do. Bring the snake.'

The tin was placed at his feet. He tipped out the reptile.

It was almost midnight. The night was cold, making the cold-blooded puff-adder slow and lethargic. It lay motionless in the doorway of the hut, with the healer inside and the tribe crowding around in a semicircle, all trying to get a view.

'I am going to place my stick along the serpent's back. If it shows anger or irritation, an evil spirit will enter this hut and kill the boy.' The crowd shuddered at the awful thought. 'On the other hand, if the snake shows no sign of anger or resentment the boy is assured that the spirit of a beloved dead ancestor will enter the house, to save him from death.' They gaped as the frail man bent down and straightened out the snake. He held the stick parallel over the reptile. Turning his head away, he covered his face with his hand and dropped the stick on to the whole length of the snake's back. The torpid snake lay still, as if dead. The excited chanting of the crowd gave the witch-doctor his answer.

'The child will live. Slaughter the ox.'

Nomisile and Themba looked up in surprise as the chief elder of the tribe, Joseph Sondika, presented himself at the door of their hut.

'Good morning, advisor.' Nomisile spoke respectfully. 'What brings a great man like yourself to our humble household?'

'Good morning, Nomisile. I bear a message for your son from the king, Paramount Chief Sabata Dalindyebo.'

Themba stepped forward. 'What message does the great chief send?' There was reverence in his voice.

'You are to present yourself at the council tomorrow morning.'

'The council of elders!' Themba gasped. 'Whatever for?'

'You will see tomorrow.' Joseph smiled kindly.

After he left mother and son looked at each other amazed, overwhelmed at the compliment Sabata had paid them. It was unheard of for a young boy to be granted an audience with the great man and his council.

'Let me quickly teach you our tribal traditions, how you must act in the presence of our distinguished ruler.' Nomisile proceeded to coach Themba in the decorum he was expected to uphold.

Themba was nervous as he waited his turn to be called before the council. The elders sat in a circle deliberating the problems of the tribe. He tried to catch the eye of his grandfather, Morris Memani, but he was too engrossed in the proceedings. Themba sat with several older men awaiting a hearing. He fully expected to be called last, after all he was only a boy. So there was an excited murmur when an elder walked across and announced, 'Themba Memani, it is your turn.' There was a long line of men still ahead of him.

Raising himself to his full height, head and shoulders thrown back, Themba walked with measured steps into the middle of the circle. Inside he was quaking, but determined not to show his nervousness. He performed the rites his mother had taught him, finishing off by sitting cross-legged.

The Paramount Chief whispered to his chief elder sitting to his right. Joseph stood up and took a pace forward, giving himself the floor and the right to address the gathering. All heads turned to him expectantly, knowing something unusual was about to happen. He looked at Themba with piercing eyes, using the silence to build up tension.

'Themba Memani, the Paramount Chief has been informed how you survived the bite of the deadly puff-adder. Occasionally a grown man has lived after a bite from *ibululu*, but we have never heard of a small child defeating the deadly venom. The people are saying the snake has given you mystical powers. Your knowledge of the plight of our people in our fight for freedom, to throw off the yoke the white man has placed around our necks, speaks of maturity far beyond your years.'

Themba realised his mother's teachings had reached the king's ears.

Joseph continued. 'Our people look up to you and respect your words, for you have a wisdom of the world far in advance of your age. It is said it was the puff-adder who squirted insight into your body with his fangs.'

The members of the indaba leant forward and slapped the baked ground in front of them with both their hands.

Dalindyebo held up his right hand and the sound died away. It was a signal that the Paramount Chief wished to speak. He looked at Themba. 'You have a destiny to fulfil, Themba. I will ensure you are given every opportunity to succeed.' The elders sighed in contentment, pleased to be part of an epoch in the making. 'It is my desire for you to learn all the ways and traditions of the Thembu tribe, of the Amaxhosa.' Turning to his elders, Sabata addressed them. 'Amaphakhati of the Thembu, you are to counsel this boy, to teach him all there is to learn about our history.'

'Yebo! Yebo! Yebo!'

Sabata looked directly at Joseph Sondika. 'You are my chief elder, the highest ranking iphakhati. I command you to set aside two hours every week to instruct this boy personally. Your task is to see he learns about the future. He must be instructed on the spirit of the freedom struggle; he must know about the aspirations of our people and he must grasp what must be done to keep the Xhosa nation at the forefront of South African politics. Themba's future, and ultimately our future, lies in your hands, Joseph.'

'Yebo!' Joseph threw his upper body flat on the ground, his arms extended, as a token of acceptance.

Dalindyebo turned to Themba. 'You have heard my wish. You are never to miss a lesson and must listen carefully and remember what you are taught. That is all.'

Themba could not help noticing the looks of admiration the members of the council gave him as he was led out of the circle. He ran home excitedly, bursting to tell his mother all about his audience with the leaders.

'My son, I always knew you were destined to become someone important. It's a great honour for us both. Hold your head up high, be respectful, take in what you can, like a thirsty sponge. One day you will become a leader of our people.'

It all sounded too much for a young boy to comprehend, but

189

Themba knew, deep in his heart, his life would never be the same again.

After eighteen years in parliament Paulus called it a day. He prevailed on his son to make himself available for nomination. Simon was reluctant and with good reason. He was not sure if he wanted to swop Hermitage for parliament and change his whole lifestyle. Then there were his clandestine drinking bouts that only Helena and himself really knew about, and which she covered for him when he was on the binge. Who would protect him in parliament? The aspect troubling him most was Themba. Once he was in the public eye the media would take an interest in him, and if they ever got hold of that information who knew what kind of scandal it would create. Paulus was insistent. 'It is my dream for you to follow in my footsteps. You have to honour that commitment.' Reluctantly Simon gave in.

With his father's support behind him the district council of the National Party endorsed Simon's candidature. Paulus set up a campaign and together they attended meetings throughout the area.

'What will my election message be?' asked Simon.

'Tell the people what they want to hear! Tell them you support white rule and apartheid and that you back Dr Verwoerd. Tell them the United Party's policy of federation will lead to the downfall of the white man. That will convince them.'

Election day dawned hot and sunny. Simon and Paulus visited all the polling booths, which were brightly decorated with posters, banners and placards of the two candidates. Party supporters wore large rosettes in party colours to display their affiliation.

It was a long, tiring day until the polling stations closed. Simon shuddered at the number of pancakes and cups of coffee he had consumed, not wanting to offend his supporters.

The ballot boxes were brought to the Paarl town hall where officials counted the votes. The result was expected early the next morning. Simon and Paulus went home to catch a few hours' sleep, but by one o'clock they were back at the town hall.

Supporters camped out on the broad pavement. The smoke from the portable braai fires billowed upwards, wafting the succulent smell of lamb chops and *boerewors* to the revellers.

An expectant hush fell over the crowd as the election officer appeared at the top of the steps. 'We have a result in the parliamentary election for the consistency of Paarl, for the Houses of Parliament: Mr Simon Roux, National Party 4367 votes. Mr Dawie Geldenhuys, United Party 684 votes. Spoilt papers 65. National Party majority 3683.' As in virtually every other constituency in the country, the Nationalists had gained a substantial majority.

Enthusiastic supporters carried Simon shoulder high to the top of the stairs. 'Speech, speech,' they clamoured.

Paulus turned off the radio, his face ecstatic. Lifting his glass he toasted, 'To the National Party and its increased majority in parliament.'

'I'll drink to that,' agreed Simon.

Helena rolled her wheelchair closer. 'It's a chilling majority in a whites only election.'

'Nonsense,' Simon chided her irritably, drinking his brandy. 'The National Party is riding the crest of the wave.'

'I foresee grave problems for South Africa,' she persisted.

Paulus turned to her. 'I thought those Poqo kaffirs had changed your mind, my girl!'

'A minority cannot rule over a majority without trouble erupting.' Helena's voice was scathing. 'Apartheid is doomed to failure. Only when the National Party negotiates with the black people will our country come right.'

Simon and Paulus rose in concert and left the room, shaking their heads in annoyance.

The hot summer sun beat down mercilessly out of a cloudless sky into the bowl of the lime quarry on Robben Island. By mid-afternoon it was like a cauldron in the bottom of the open pit. The men were streaked with perspiration – sweat running off their shirtless bodies and staining the tops of their khaki shorts. They shuffled around, taking small steps at a time, as leg chains restrained their movements.

'*Kap, kaffer, kap!*' Warder Suitcase van Reenen shouted at Nelson Mandela, goading him to chop faster.

Mandela looked up, wiping the sweat out of his eyes with the back of his hand. Stay calm, he told himself, lifting up the heavy, long-handled hammer above his head, letting it fall, adding strength from his biceps. The flat face of the heavy metal head shattered the limestone chunk into the tiny pieces used for paving the island's roads.

'I'm talking to you, kaffir.' As Van Reenen bumped Mandela, Walter Sisulu sprang forward. They glared at the warder, hatred in their eyes. Van Reenen shoved them both. 'You're slacking. I'm reporting you to the commandant.'

'We're not avoiding work,' Sisulu countered indignantly.

Mandela restrained him. 'Don't play their game, my friend. They are determined to break us. Remember the cause. Our followers are counting on us to hold ourselves with dignity and never to buckle under pressure.'

'Van Reenen's pushing us too far.' Sisulu bristled with anger. 'They're trying to kill us.'

'You're in big trouble already. Don't add to it,' screamed Van Reenen, walking away.

'Darn man, always carrying his small leather suitcase around with his lunch and coffee flask,' complained Mandela.

'A sign of his leanings is the nazi swastika tattooed on his forearm,' added Sisulu. 'The man is cruel and inconsistent, no wonder he's hated by the prisoners.'

A guard blew his whistle. Nelson sighed in relief. 'Another day gone, one day less to my release.'

The prisoners walked up out of the quarry, their leg chains clinking as metal hit metal. Two by two they shambled along the road towards the prison enclosure. Suitcase walked up to Nelson and butted him on the shoulder with his rifle. 'You think you're the leader, but we will break you, man.' Mandela looked straight ahead, retaining his composure.

Incensed at getting no reaction, Van Reenen baited him again. 'We'll keep you on this island so long, man, your followers will forget you ever lived.'

Mandela kept his bland expression, looking straight ahead. The next blow took him in the stomach, but boxing had taught Nelson how to flex his stomach muscles to withstand a body blow. He took the rifle butt in his solar plexus without missing a stride, not even glancing sideways at the officer.

Fuming, Van Reenen strode away. 'Just wait until I report you, man.'

The prisoners laid down their tools in a corrugated-iron shed. Their leg irons were removed at the gate of the barbed-wire perimeter security fence.

'Get to the showers,' shouted the guard. The prisoners stripped off their clothes and shoes and stood shivering as they were forced into ice-cold sea-water showers. The salt burnt their eyes. There were no towels; the men were dried by the chilly wind before dressing again in the same sweaty prison clothes.

'You two, this way.' Van Reenen pointed at Mandela and Sisulu. They were frog-marched to the commanding officer and made to stand outside the office while Suitcase made his report.

The commanding officer called them in. 'So the two of you won't work properly?'

'We are political prisoners, not ordinary criminals,' Mandela protested. 'We demand to be treated as such.'

'You demand? Who the hell do you think you are? You're here for the rest of your lives. You're political has-beens, that's what you are.'

Mandela looked him in the eye. 'Your humiliation only strengthens our defiance. We're so close to the oppressor, it keeps us united.'

'They should have hanged you, you cheeky bastard.' The commanding officer's face showed his rage. 'You'll go on to rice ration – that'll teach you to work harder and complain less.'

Nelson shook his head in amazement. Their food was bad enough as it was. As blacks they did not qualify for bread with their meals. The infamous rice ration was a thin mealie-rice gruel, with precious little nutritional value. 'How do you expect us to work harder with more inferior food?'

'Get them out of here.' The commanding officer pointed to the door.

The two returned to the isolation block. The single cells, two paces by two paces in size, contained only a thin mattress, three threadbare blankets and a chamber pot. The cell was poorly lit with a single light bulb.

Their meagre meal was insufficient for a child, let alone enough to sustain a grown man for a full day's hard manual labour. Mandela and Sisulu shivered under their blankets on the cold concrete floor that night.

The next day was Saturday. Skeleton staff were on duty, guarding only the main control points and look-outs. The rest of the staff were off, many returning to the mainland to be at home for the weekend. There was no manual labour at the lime quarry. The single-cell prisoners could meet quietly in their courtyard for half an hour each day to talk. These times became the highlight of the prisoners' lives. Mandela tended the geraniums and chrysanthemums and the grape-vines growing over the pergolas. Working with nature gave him renewed strength and the brilliant flowers added to their otherwise drab world.

'We are martyrs,' he would say, 'the last symbol of hope to all the people out there,' pointing towards Langa, Nyanga, Guguletu and the Cape Flats.

Kathrada gave him a portion of porridge he had saved. 'Here, my friend, I kept some of my food for you. I overheard the warders talking yesterday. They said Helen Suzman was coming out to the island next week.'

A cold autumn wind blew in from the sea and the commanding officer shivered as he stood on the jetty watching the prison launch approaching. Nervously he straightened his tie. General Steyn, the Commissioner of Prisons, was bad enough. Why did he have to bring along this woman? He had read about Helen Suzman in the newspapers. She was a liberal, a trouble-maker. He would have to watch his step today, otherwise she would get him into trouble. Damn, he wasn't relishing the next few hours.

The General jumped off the launch from Cape Town. He extended his hand and graciously helped the well-dressed woman on to the jetty.

'Commanding officer, let me introduce you to Mrs Helen Suzman, the Progressive Party Member of Parliament for Houghton.'

'Pleased to meet you, ma'am.'

'We are here to see conditions on the island. I want you to show Mrs Suzman whatever she wishes to see.'

'Yes, sir.' They walked towards the main administration building, beautifully built in dressed sandstone. He had organised a lavish tea. All the warders would be present. He hoped to delay her as long as possible to divert her attention from the prison section. He had decided to keep the prisoners inside their cells for the day.

'This way, ma'am.'

'Where is Mr Nelson Mandela?' Helen looked him straight in the eye. 'I want to see him.'

'After tea, ma'am.'

She shook her head. 'The Minister of Justice gave me permission to visit Mandela. That is the main reason I came to Robben Island. I demand to see him first. Tea can wait.'

The commanding officer cursed under his breath. He had planned the visit so carefully with Mandela last on the list, five minutes before the launch was due to return to the mainland. He looked at General Steyn imploringly.

'If Mrs Suzman insists on seeing Mandela first then lead the way.'

Damn, I shouldn't have put him on that rice ration, he thought, as they walked towards the isolation cell block reserved for the political leaders.

Warders unlocked gates as they approached, saluting the two senior prison officers and Helen Suzman, slamming them shut as they passed through.

Warder Suitcase van Reenen opened the gate to the isolation cells. A row of cells flanked either side of the central passage. The prisoners stood outside them. Only the previous day Nelson Mandela had been moved from No. 4 to No. 18 in the hope that Mrs Suzman would get bogged down by prisoners on the way, so that her time would be up before she reached him.

One by one the prisoners stepped backwards, allowing her to pass directly to Mandela. She extended her hand. 'I am Helen Suzman.'

'I know you from the newspapers.'

She looked him over carefully. She had heard so much about him, but it was the first time they had met. Here is a man of great dignity and undeniably a leader, she thought.

'We have no furniture,' apologised Mandela. 'Would you like to sit on my bedroll?' The commandant stood inside the doorway, with General Steyn and Warder van Reenen standing half in and half out of the tiny cell.

'How are they treating you?' Helen asked.

'They treat us terribly, like criminals. We are political prisoners,' Mandela answered bitterly.

'Anyone in particular?' queried Mrs Suzman, concerned.

Mandela pointed to Van Reenen. He related how he had butted him repeatedly with his rifle and told her about the rice gruel he was forced to eat.

The commanding officer shuffled his feet, not knowing where to look. Van Reenen blanched.

'Is this true?' snapped Helen Suzman at the commanding officer.

195

'The prisoner refuses to work properly.'

'Tomorrow morning I will take the matter up with the Minister of Justice personally. This man is the leader of his people and you treat him so badly.'

'I will do something about it.'

'Will you replace Warder van Reenen and put Mr Mandela on full rations again?'

The commanding officer nodded.

'Yes or no?' demanded Helen. 'I want a proper answer.'

'Yes, ma'am.'

'Walter Sisulu is also on the rice ration,' Mandela stated bitterly.

'Will you include Mr Sisulu as well?'

'Yes, ma'am,' replied the commanding officer.

'We are forced to work ten hours a day in rain, cold and blazing sunshine in a lime quarry, hefting heavy hammers, picking and shovelling and crushing stone – work that could easily be done by machinery.' Mandela was getting into his stride.

'That's terrible. Why?' demanded Helen Suzman.

'It is part of hard labour, ma'am.'

'Well you'd better stop, for I fully intend raising the whole matter in parliament.'

General Steyn looked on, half amused. He had to admire Helen Suzman's spirit. Mandela also earned his respect. He had the guts to speak out in front of the prison officers, who could make his life hell later.

Nomisile and Themba sat in the headmaster's office of the only white school in the Transkei – Umtata High School. 'My son has spent the last eighteen months in a black high school. I'm not happy with the standard of education. I want better for him.' She looked at the headmaster imploringly. 'Won't you take him?'

'The Cape Education Department insists we enrol only white pupils. If we take Themba, we'll lose our departmental grant. I'm sorry, Mrs Memani.'

'Is there no other white school he can go to?'

'Only a private school, but at this stage not even the church schools in Grahamstown accept black pupils.'

Nomisile's clenched fists showed her exasperation. 'I feel so helpless against this unfair system. I can afford to pay for my son to get the best education, but because of the colour of his skin he has to go to a black school that offers inferior tuition. You and I know, Mr Headmaster, that black education is not on a par with white education.'

He looked at her, understanding her distress. 'I have an excellent teacher, Mr Paul Curry, who teaches our standard nine and ten classes. He's had polio and so he's excused from taking sport in the afternoons. As a bachelor, with no family commitments, I'm sure he would tutor Themba for a bit of extra pocket money.'

'Would tutoring help, Mr Headmaster?'

'It'll raise Themba's level of knowledge tremendously, if Paul Curry will do it. He'll stay ahead of his class at the black school. It's not ideal, I know, but it's the best I can suggest under the present circumstances.'

'Where does Mr Curry live?'

The headmaster gave them the address.

The man who answered their knock had a friendly grin and a shock of unruly blond hair. Tall, thin and slightly stooped, he seemed very much the academic kind. He looked a typical bachelor with his frayed shirt collar and a hole in his sweater where the wool had unravelled.

'Mr Paul Curry?'

'That's me. Can I help?'

'I am Nomisile Memani and this is my son, Themba. We would like to discuss something with you.'

'Come in.'

'Mr Curry, we have just come from the headmaster of Umtata High School.' Nomisile told him of the conversation between herself and the headmaster. 'If Themba cannot legally get a white education I would like you to tutor him in your spare time. I'm willing to pay you.'

The teacher turned to Themba. 'How old are you, Themba? What standard are you in?'

'I'm in standard seven and I'm almost fourteen, sir.'

'And what do you want to do with your education?'

'I want to go to university to study law like my uncle Nelson Mandela. I would also like to study political science, so that I can play a part in freeing my people.'

Paul appeared impressed. 'Wait here.' He disappeared from the room. Ten minutes later he called Themba to his study. 'Themba, here are a few questions on general knowledge, science and mathematics at white standard-seven level. Sit down and complete the answers, please.'

He left Themba concentrating deeply and returned to Nomisile. 'I have set Themba a variety of questions to test his intellect. If he passes well, I may accept the challenge.' His infectious smile gave her hope.

Paul was intrigued at the possibility of taking someone like Themba up to university level. A fight against the odds. A way to hit back at the system. A challenge to his academic intellect. He liked Themba – a friendly, open-faced young boy with penetrating, bright eyes. He had a gut feeling Themba would rise to the challenge. As for his mother, she was so beautiful, so serious and so determined. How could he refuse her?

'How much will the tutoring cost?'

'Money isn't my main motivation. I feel a bit like Henry Higgins in *Pygmalion*. If Themba can succeed as Eliza Doolittle did, then the challenge will have been won.'

Themba came into the lounge and handed his completed paper to Paul Curry. Silently he marked the answers. My son's whole future rests on that piece of paper, fretted Nomisile.

Paul completed the corrections and looked up, smiling. 'Well done, Themba, you have sixty-five per cent. That's very good for a start. It would have given you at least eighty per cent at a black school. You're a bright young man.'

'Well?' Nomisile asked urgently, her liquid eyes imploring.

'I accept.' Paul saw relief mixed with gladness sweep across the faces of mother and son. It made him feel good. 'Themba, how do you get to school at present?'

'I catch the bus to Umtata every morning and out to Mqekezweni again in the afternoon.'

'Couldn't he stay in Umtata so that I can tutor him afternoons and evenings?'

Nomisile took a quick decision. 'I'll buy a house in Umtata's black township. I know a widow who might stay there and look after Themba. It will save him hours each day not having to travel to school and back. He can be here when you need him, Paul.' She thought of all the extra sewing she would have to take on to pay Paul, the house and the widow. Perhaps Simon would help? She was sure he would; he had promised.

198

'Then it'll work like this,' explained Paul. 'Themba, you'll go to Nyanga High in the mornings. Go home for lunch. Be here at three o'clock every afternoon. First, you will do your normal homework, which I will correct. Then you will tackle the standard-seven syllabus from Umtata High School. I'll get the work and books from the teacher. You'll also write all tests and examinations set for the white standard seven. That way you'll keep abreast of both schools. In eighteen months' time, when you reach standard nine, I'll teach you my own syllabus.'

'That's perfect.' Nomisile was relieved. 'What do you think, Themba?'

'I'm very grateful to you, Mr Curry. I won't let you down.'

'You'd better not.' Paul escorted them to the door. 'Together you and I are going to get you to university. See you on Monday.'

Nomisile and Themba walked to the black township on the outskirts of Umtata. She purchased a house and made a down payment on it. 'I'll pay the balance within a month,' she promised the owner.

She had a photograph taken of Themba and herself and wrote a long letter to Simon explaining the circumstances. Three weeks later she received a reply. She read Simon's letter with sadness. It seemed neither of them had found true happiness. He had an empty marriage, while she could not accept another man, not after the love they had experienced.

Included in the letter was a deposit slip made out to her, enough to cover the balance owing on the Umtata house, plus some more. She could still rely on the man she had loved so desperately. Her eyes filled with tears as all the old memories came back. She read and reread the letter, memorising the contents in her heart.

Pierre excitedly addressed his grandfather. '*Oupa*, today is the start of the Berg River canoe marathon. Won't you take us to watch?'

'Where is it?'

'At the Market Street bridge.'

'Okay, your grandma wants to go to town. We can take her first, then go to the river.'

Paulus reversed out of the garage, Marie and himself in the front of the pick-up and Pierre in a wind-cheater on the back. They dropped Marie in Lady Grey Street and drove to the river.

Vehicles were crowded around the bridge, forcing them to park a distance away. They walked the final stretch. Pierre was impatient to get to the action.

'Don't go so fast, Pierre, I can't keep up.' Paulus limped along, taking the strain off his left knee. 'I really feel my age today, these cold Cape winters bring on my rheumatism.'

Pierre ran down the bank. Lining the river on both sides, like hundreds of parallel sticks, lay the glass-fibre canoes. Competitors were making last-minute preparations.

'On your marks, get set, go.' The crack of the starter's revolver galvanised the canoeists into action. They pushed their craft out into the water, jumped in, adjusted their splash covers and set off with steady strokes of the double paddles.

After a few minutes everyone was underway, the contestants strung out in a long line. The leaders approached Lady Grey Street bridge, as the stragglers still paddled under the Market Street bridge.

'Grandpa, wasn't that good?' Pierre's face expressed his vitality.

'Looked very confusing to me,' grumbled his grandfather as he limped away.

'Grandpa, do you think Pa will buy me a canoe?' Pierre couldn't stop chattering.

'You'll have to ask him yourself. You have much too much energy,' Paulus grumbled as they walked back to the pick-up.

They fetched Marie and drove back to the farm. Pierre's thoughts were with the canoeists paddling down the mighty Berg River to Velddrif, where it entered the Atlantic Ocean.

Going down Main Street in the left lane, they had to turn right across the oncoming traffic to drive into the entrance gates of Hermitage. Standing on the back of the pick-up, Pierre was vaguely aware of the clicking sound as the right indicator flashed.

Paulus changed gear. His rheumatic left knee would not function properly and he had difficulty in depressing the clutch pedal fully. The gear lever jerked out of third gear but grated, refusing to go into second. The forward momentum was lost. Instead of shooting across the path of an approaching truck, the pick-up floundered like a wounded duck, slewing into the opposite lane.

The truck driver saw the impending danger and slammed on his brakes, but the thirty-ton load aboard kept the monstrous eighteen-wheeler rolling forward.

Pierre looked up in terror as the huge bulk bore down on their stranded vehicle. He saw the panic on the driver's face as he struggled to contain his bucking monster. Blue-grey smoke billowed around the truck as the brake pads burnt into the brake drums. Pierre screamed in panic. 'Watch out, *Oupa!*'

The next instant the huge front fender slammed into the pick-up, spinning it around like a top. The whiplash catapulted Pierre into the air. Slowly he cartwheeled in an arc, his senses blurring. With a thud he smashed, back first, into the high netting wire of the farm boundary fence. The flexible wire acted as a safety net, breaking his fall, flinging him face forward on to the pavement. He lay winded for a second with the crunching and scraping of metal on metal pervading his senses. His brain cleared and he glanced up in trepidation. He screamed as the huge bulk of the truck lifted off the ground and mounted the pick-up like some prehistoric monster scaling its mate – squeezing and pounding.

Pierre watched in helpless fascination as his grandmother covered her face with her hands, her high-pitched wail reverberating over the terrible noise of the collision. Paulus's face was contorted in fear, his heavy features showing the realisation of certain death. He held on to the steering wheel grimly, still trying to steer out of the way.

The massive truck rolled over the pick-up, crumpling it like matchwood, while the armour-plated glass splintered and shattered. The cab of the pick-up was mangled as it spun around. The load area, where only seconds before Pierre had stood, was crushed. The back tyres of the horse heaved up and over, rolling the pick-up under the body of the trailer, crushing it unrecognisably.

As the truck started to jack-knife the pick-up lodged in front of the trailer's rear wheels, acting as a screeching metal brake, and the monster shuddered to a halt. For a split second there was silence, then the air-brake pipes snapped, the pressurised air escaping in an eerie, high-pitched whine.

Cars travelling in both directions came to a halt as the drivers witnessed the terrible carnage. It happened so fast, they could not get out of the way, but at the same time so slowly that they could only stare in hideous fascination. People jumped out of their cars, horrified, rushing to the wreckage. The air was filled with the sickly smell of scraped duco and burnt rubber.

Pierre sprinted to the wreck. He darted under the trailer to the smashed cab of the pick-up. 'Grandpa! Grandma!' He screamed in horror as all he saw was crushed flesh, tattered hair and splashes of blood of the grandparents he loved. 'Talk to me,' he pleaded desperately.

A bystander pulled Pierre away. 'Son, they're dead; no one could have survived that smash.'

He ran as fast as he could to leave the horror behind. He tore headlong up the driveway of the farm, his arms and legs pumping furiously. Out of breath, he burst into the kitchen of the manor house.

Helena looked up, seeing the fear streaking his face, and quickly rolled her wheelchair closer. 'What's wrong, Pierre?' She frowned in concern, the long scar puckering up her face.

'Accident! Grandpa and Grandma.'

Helena went cold. 'Where? What happened?'

'In Main Street,' Pierre gasped between breaths. 'At the front gate.'

'Are they all right?'

'They're dead.' He was sobbing now. 'Grandpa and Grandma are both dead.'

'Good God!' Helena burst into tears. 'How awful, what a tragedy!'

The servants summed up the situation quickly and ran to find the farm manager. He had heard the crash from the vineyards. When he saw Pierre running up the driveway, he jumped into his pick-up and sped to the gate. The truck blocked the front entrance. He jumped out and had to fight his way through the curious onlookers drawn to the accident by the fascination of blood and death. He gaped at the contorted wreck. A feeling of deep despair overcame him as the accident took on a new, personal perspective. It was not some stranger who was involved but his own people, a man and woman whom he had come to respect and love. Frantically he tried to open the door but it was jammed. He looked through the shattered slit of a window and recognised what remained of Paulus's face, forced through the bars of the steering wheel. Marie was a battered pulp, her features beyond recall, only her clothing familiar to him. He turned away, deeply shocked, unable fully to comprehend the tragedy.

Police diverted the cars to the Boulevard, getting the traffic flowing again. With blaring sirens the ambulance and fire brigade arrived simultaneously.

There was nothing more the farm manager could do. He drove back to the house. He found Helena in a huddle with her son, each holding the other for strength.

'Have you let Simon know?'

Helena shook her head. 'No – I haven't.'

'Where is he today?'

'Parliament.'

The manager telephoned Simon at his private office and broke the news to him. Simon drove the sixty kilometres to Paarl at break-neck speed. He went straight to the hospital where he was met at the casualty doors by Dr de Villiers. The hospital head put his arms around him. 'I'm so sorry, Simon.'

'I want to see my parents.'

'Not now. I've already made out their death certificates, but it's better for your own good that you don't see them in the state they are.'

Simon slumped into a chair. The urgency left his body and was replaced by delayed shock and he shook uncontrollably.

'I'm going to give you a tranquillising injection, then you must go home to your family. They need you now. Tomorrow, when we have had time to patch up Paulus and Marie, you can see them, but I warn you it's not a pretty sight. These are about the worst accident victims I have ever seen in all my years as a doctor.'

Simon drove back to Hermitage with a hollow feeling, knowing that an era had passed, another generation would fill the farm's walled graveyard. Why both his father and mother at the same time? The injection helped. He felt calmer when he reached the homestead.

'What can I do, darling?' asked Helena, still ashen-faced.

'I'm going for a walk up the mountain.'

'Can I go with you?' Pierre asked.

'No, son, you stay here, I need to be alone.'

Simon walked up the slope, puffing a bit, not as fit as he used to be, eventually scaling the gully to reach his private place. He updated his diary with the day's tragic events and thought about his future. He reached a firm decision. At the end of this session, I'm finished with politics. My place is at Hermitage. I'll farm again and produce the best wines in South Africa. The responsibility shifts to me.

The sun had dipped below Paarl Rock when Simon finally

accepted the death of his parents. He returned to the homestead feeling better able to face the future.

The funeral was the largest Paarl had seen. Old colleagues from Paulus's parliamentary days were present; family, friends and associates. The service in the *Strooidak* Church was attended by so many people even chairs placed in the aisles were not enough.

Among the rows of vines stood the Roux family cemetery, a small graveyard with tall, narrow cypress trees and bounded by a whitewashed roughly plastered Cape wall. The original Roux of Hermitage was buried there, as well as every succeeding generation. Paulus and Marie were buried side by side in the newest graves in the middle of the third row.

The mourners filed past the family, nodding, taking a handful of petals from the undertakers and strewing them over the two coffins. Simon was close to tears as spadefuls of earth thudded on top of the coffins, making his parents' death so final. Helena wiped her eyes with a lace handkerchief, holding Simon's hand. Except for a stray tear, Pierre managed to hold himself in check. He would cry alone in his own room.

Tea was served in the wine cellar. Slowly the crowd dispersed until only Simon's and Helena's family remained, consoling one another in their loss.

Simon and Helena attended the reading of the last will and testament of their parents at the family attorney's. Marie's sister was the only other person present.

The executor looked around his office. 'Let's get on with it. As there are separate wills for both the late Paulus and Marie Roux, we'll read Paulus's will first.'

In his businesslike, professional manner, the attorney read from the will: 'I, Paulus Roux, do hereby bequeath my farms, Hermitage in Paarl, and Doornrivier in the Upington district, to my only son, Simon Roux, together with all movable items thereon, sheep, cattle, livestock, standing crops, vehicles and machinery. The residue of my estate I leave to my wife Marie Roux, but should she predecease me, or her death occur within thirty days after my death, the residue shall devolve upon my son, Simon Roux, or failing him, upon his lawful issue by representation.

'What this all boils down to,' explained the attorney, 'is that you,

Simon, now inherit the whole estate under your father's will as they died simultaneously. Congratulations.'

The burden of responsibility had now shifted squarely on to Simon's shoulders, giving him even more reason to give up his parliamentary career and concentrate on farming.

Clearing his throat, the attorney continued, 'We now turn to the last will and testament of Marie Roux.' He read from the will: 'I, Marie Mathilda Roux, née Smit, bequeath my assets as follows: The house registered in my name in Hof Street, Gardens, Cape Town, to my grandson, Pierre. My jewellery and personal effects to my sister. My share certificates to my daughter-in-law, Helena Roux. My investments to my son, Simon Roux. I have endeavoured to give something to all those who meant so much to me during my life.'

Helena and her aunt were reduced to tears. Simon was moved. In death, as in life, Marie had been considerate and fair.

The attorney rose and walked around the desk. 'That concludes the reading of the wills. Those were the wishes of Paulus and Marie Roux. I will attend to the details.'

Simon rose to address the district council meeting of the National Party held in the National Hall, Paarl. 'My friends, you are aware that the Prime Minister, John Vorster, has called a general election. With the breakaway of the four members of parliament to form the Herstigte Nasionale Party under Jaap Marais, the election has been brought forward a year, to capitalise on the disorganisation still within the HNP ranks. I have served the constituency of Paarl for one term in parliament, but I must now step down. You know my father died last year. I have inherited the farming ventures and must devote my time to the farms. I thank you for your co-operation and the faith you placed in me.' Simon sat down to warm applause.

The chairman thanked Simon for his commitment to the National Party and for representing Paarl as a member of parliament. 'I call for nominations for our candidate for the forthcoming elections.'

Pieter Hugo stood up. 'I would like to propose our member of the Provincial Council, Wynand Malan.'

'Seconded.' Simon put up his hand. There were no further nominations.

'*Broeder* Simon, you are due for succession as chairman of the Paarl

Chapter of the Broederbond.' The chairman looked at Simon. 'But we have a problem with your candidature.'

'Why?' Simon was surprised.

'The Broederbond supports the policy of the Nationalist Party, including its sports policy. We heard you recently went against party policy and in caucus spoke in support of black members being included in visiting sports teams.'

'That's how I felt then and how I still feel. Politics and sport are two separate issues.'

'They are not. Sport is just the tip of the iceberg. If we give way on sport, we will be forced to give way on other issues.'

A member proposed a motion. 'Mr Roux must renounce his earlier statements and sign a declaration fully supporting National Party policy on sport before he is eligible to become chairman.'

Simon was incensed. 'I'll never do that. Those are my personal views. I'm entitled to think independently.'

'Not if you want to be chairman of the Paarl Broederbond.' The chairman spoke grimly.

'If you cannot accept me as I am, I do not want the chairmanship.'

'Your continued membership of the Broederbond depends on your views,' ventured the chairman. It was not even a veiled threat.

'John Vorster also has other views.'

'Yes, but thanks to the Broederbond he changed those views and cancelled the MCC cricket tour.'

'I'm not prepared to change my opinions.' Simon rose in rage. 'You have my resignation.'

To a shocked silence, Simon stormed out of the meeting.

'My friends are meeting at the Protea Theatre. Can I go to bioscope, Mom?'

Helena glanced up from her knitting. 'As long as you're home by eleven o'clock. Don't be a minute late.'

'Okay, Mom, thanks.' He kissed her and ran off to shower. With his new bell-bottomed trousers, moccasin shoes and a bold checked shirt, he was dressed for the occasion.

At the Protea his friends stood talking to a group of girls. 'Pierre, do you know Tertia Louw?'

Pierre smiled awkwardly, glancing at Tertia. She was cute, small and fine-boned with a pixie face and a Sharon Tate hairstyle. He liked her legs, showing above calf-length leather boots. Her pleated crimplene dress showed off her ample cleavage.

With the juke-box playing she flirtatiously fluttered her eyelashes at him. 'Hallo, Pierre. Do you have a date for tonight?'

Blushing, he was at a loss for words. A friend whispered in his ear. 'Ask Tertia to sit with you. I've heard she fancies you. You'll have a great time.'

'I don't have a date,' stuttered Pierre. 'Will you sit with me?'

She answered boldly, without hesitation, 'It'll be a pleasure.' Her friends giggled in delight.

He had an expert teacher in Tertia. She led him to the back row, into the darkest corner. She sat close as they ate popcorn from the same container. His mind raced. He thought about the bragging conquests of the older boys, and the scanty conjectures of his circle of friends, but they gave him no starting point. He need not have worried. In the dark movie house, with the screen casting flickering shadows, she guided his hand. The movie ended with Pierre only vaguely recollecting small snatches.

In the café everyone ordered milkshakes. Pierre looked at his watch: he still had an hour. Their gang was in no hurry, idly chatting to each other. He longed for a car, to offer Tertia a drive up Paarl Mountain, to the popular necking spots. All he had was his bicycle.

Slowly the group broke up. In twos and threes the teenagers left the tables. Pierre and Tertia were alone for the first time.

'I must be home by eleven,' said Pierre.

'There's still time.' Tertia winked at him knowingly.

'Where would we go?'

'To the park behind the magistrates court.'

Pierre grabbed her hand. 'Let's go.'

Recognising Pierre's hesitancy, she led him to a patch of lush grass, in the shadow of tall bushes. He laid down his jacket and they sat alongside each other. Pierre became rough and bold.

'Are you crazy? You were like an express train,' Tertia complained bitterly.

With a start he looked at the luminous dial of his wrist-watch. 'Oh shit, I must go.' He sprang up, pulling up his pants, buttoning up his fly.

'Not so fast, my friend. Come and do it again, slower this time.'

'I can't. I *must* go.' Pierre headed for his bicycle. Tertia jumped to her feet, blocking his way.

'What about me?'

'Next time.'

Her mouth contorted with fury, her cute face twisted and coarse. She screamed like a fishwife, 'There won't be a next time. Pierre Roux, I never want to see you again.'

With her hair awry and her menacing expression, he wondered why he'd ever been attracted to her. Pierre shouldered her out of the way, grabbed his bicycle and pedalled furiously home.

He slipped quietly into the house. 'You're late, Pierre. Come here.' His mother's voice rang out from the lounge. She glanced up from a book she was reading, her expression furious. 'Where have you been?'

'At the café.'

'Don't fib, Pierre. Why do you have grass clippings on your jacket?'

'We went to the park.'

'Who went to the park?' Helena demanded.

'All of us.'

'You're lying, Pierre. I telephoned Jack and Albert. They were both home an hour ago.' Her scar turned purple as she glared at him and he glanced down in discomfort.

'Only some of us went,' he muttered.

'Why is one of your trouser buttons undone?' Her eyes blazed. Pierre looked down in dismay. 'You're gated for two weeks.'

'You can't do that,' answered Pierre belligerently. 'I'll tell Dad and he'll ungate me.'

'Ha, that won't help you. He's drunk again – passed out in bed.'

Pierre felt the blood rush to his face. 'Don't *you* talk about *my* father like that!' He stepped forward, clenching his fists. 'Dad *will* listen to me!'

Helena shrank back into her wheelchair. Oh! My God! He's his father's son, she thought desperately. One day the two of them will gang up against me. Bravely she held out a shaking hand in reconciliation. 'Come and kiss me good-night, Pierre.'

'Go to hell, Mom,' shouted Pierre as he stormed out of the room, tossing his head defiantly.

*   *   *

Whistling contentedly to himself, Themba walked with a light step to his mother's home. He had just learnt from his tutor that he had come first in the country in the black junior certificate examination with over ninety per cent. The December heat was warm in his face, but he didn't mind for it meant the long summer school holidays had begun.

'You are a clever young man,' congratulated Nomisile on hearing the news.

'All thanks to Paul Curry,' smiled Themba.

She looked at him in wonderment. He had grown so fast the last year he was now taller than she was. She would have to make him new shirts, his was too tight around the chest. 'I'm so proud of you.' Her eyes misted over in happiness. 'Your grandparents want to see you. Aunt Doreen is visiting with them. You have not seen her for years. I told them you would go over tomorrow morning.'

As the sun rose fiery and bright, Themba left the house, listening to the early-morning sounds. Women, walking in chattering groups towards the fields, shouted conversations to others over long distances. The men were busy at their kraals, checking their livestock, and allowing them out to graze for the day. Cattle lowed in the crisp air, while the sheep kicked their heels in delight at being allowed out of the gates. Young herd boys walked ahead of the livestock to keep them in line. Cocks chorused the new day and clucking hens scratched busily around the huts. Themba could smell the earthy scents of rural Transkei, as another tranquil and unhurried day unfolded.

He stepped into the hut and respectfully greeted his grandparents and his aunt. Themba ate breakfast with his relatives. He turned to his aunt. 'What brings you back to Qunu?'

'Longing, dear Themba. East London is all very well, but it's nice to return to your roots now and again. Since your uncle Alfred Nkozi died, I've had a hard life bringing up the children on my own.'

'I never knew Uncle Alfred. How did he die?'

'Didn't your mother tell you? He was killed in a demonstration eighteen years ago.'

'My mother never said a word to me. Does she know about his death?'

'Of course, she was there – he died in your mother's arms in one of the first actions of the apartheid struggle.'

Themba was shocked. 'She never told me.'

'She took his death badly,' answered Doreen, patting him on the arm. 'Your mother hates apartheid.'

'Apartheid is evil. One day I will fight for our freedom like Nelson Mandela.'

'First you must be educated,' answered Morris. 'In the life you want to lead there is no future for you if your heart is right but your brain power is lacking. There are already too many such men. If you really want to get to the top you need an education.'

'I'm going to university when I finish school.' Themba smiled proudly.

'Very good,' encouraged Aunt Doreen. 'Nelson is so wise because he knows the law.'

It was late afternoon when Themba returned home. 'Mother, why didn't you tell me you were involved in the demonstrations in East London in 1952, when Uncle Alfred Nkosi was killed?'

Nomisile hesitated, aware that she would have to share her experience with her son. 'It was a terrible time, which I tried to blot from my mind. Now that you are older, you will understand.' She told him about the march, her eyes glittering bitterly when she described the actions of the police. 'Learn to hate them,' she advised Themba. 'They are the ones who keep the white man in power and enforce apartheid.'

'You've always taught me to loathe apartheid.'

'It's a system that keeps our people subservient to the white man. We've discussed this many times, but I repeat it once again – you must make it your life's work to fight for the rights of our people. When the time is right, but only after your studies, you must join the ANC.'

'Why are you so bitter, Mother? Was my father in the ANC?'

'No, he was a farm worker.'

'I would like to meet my father.'

'I've lost all contact with him – for all I know he may be dead.' She justified her answer by reasoning Simon was all but dead to her, living on only in her mind.

'Where did you meet him?'

'In Paarl.'

'Paarl? What were you doing in Paarl?'

'I was on holiday visiting your Uncle Jafta. He worked on a farm there.' Nomisile was glad she did not have to lie to answer that question.

'Who was my father?' repeated Themba. 'I need to know.'

'He was a contract worker. I met him in Mbekweni, the black township.' Nomisile felt very guilty not telling her son the truth, but she was still convinced it was best for him not to know.

'From which tribe?'

'A Xhosa, from Pondoland, a long way from here.'

'What was his name?'

'Seme.'

'Seme who?'

'I only knew him as Seme.'

'Did you love my father?'

Now at last she could answer truthfully. 'Oh yes, Themba. I loved your father deeply. He was the first man I ever had and I'm convinced he'll be the last. No other man measures up to your father. I just wish you could have known him as I knew him. You'd have loved him too.'

Themba grinned with pleasure. At least now he knew.

'Hallo, Themba, how are you?' asked Hilda noting his tall, noble bearing and the way he had filled out in the six months since she had last seen him.

Themba looked at her shyly. 'I'm fine thank you.' She was the daughter of Nxele, the second eldest son of the Paramount Chief – a princess. He noticed her new red blanket and beadwork. 'You look different!' His gaze dropped – a year ago she had been flat-chested – now she displayed nubile breasts, pointing proudly upwards.

'I'm a woman now, I've been through my *ntonjaan*.' She swung her shoulders coyly, making her breasts move sensually. Themba felt himself breathing more quickly. He turned away in embarrassment. 'Where are you going, Themba?'

'I have a lesson with Joseph Sondika. He's teaching me the ways of our people.'

Admiration glinted in her eyes. 'I heard about you and the snake. The puff-adder has made you so wise, even my grandfather, the Paramount Chief, has noticed.'

'I must go. I'm late for my instruction.'

'Why don't you come back later?' She flashed him a bashful look. 'I may also have some instruction for you.'

He looked at her in confusion. He shouted over his shoulder as he hurried away, 'All right, I'll see you later, Hilda.'

At Joseph's house he told his instructor of his achievements at school and his progress with Paul. 'Paul Curry is a fine white man, who cares about my future.' Themba spoke from the heart.

Joseph nodded. 'Learn all you can from the white men, but be careful you don't fall into their ways. The Amaxhosa have many fine traditions that bind us together as a tribe. You would be wise to follow our customs.'

'I'm here to learn all I can, Joseph.'

'Good. Today I would like to tell you a great folk tale of our people. Listen well, for there is a moral to the story.'

Sitting forward, a serious expression on his face, Joseph began to speak: 'More than a hundred summers ago, lost in the mists of time, there was a young Xhosa maiden called Nongqawuse, who had a vision as she drew water from the Kei River. Reflected in the water she saw messengers from the land of the dead. They told her the Xhosa nation had to re-establish its bonds through its ancestors.

'First, all cattle had to be killed; sacrificed to the spirits. Secondly, there should be no cultivation of crops for a whole year. Thirdly, new granaries had to be built, more houses constructed and larger cattle-folds established.

'If the Xhosa nation complied, then on a certain day the sun would rise in the east. A huge whirlwind would sweep all the white people as well as all those who did not believe her into the sea, and the sun would set again in the east.

'The next day all the dead cattle would re-appear, every past generation of Xhosa would rise from the dead, filling all the new houses. The crops would be so bountiful they would fill the extended granaries to overflowing.

'Nongqawuse told her uncle, the witch-doctor Mhlakaza, of her vision. He accepted her story and spread it through the kraals. They convinced Paramount Chief Sarhili, who ordered his subordinate chiefs to begin the great cattle killing and decreed that no lands be cultivated or sowed.

'On the appointed day the Xhosa nation feasted and celebrated, but there was no whirlwind and the sun set as usual in the west. The

212

Paramount Chief turned in anger on Mhlakaza, the witch-doctor. He in turn blamed those who had refused to slaughter their cattle. Regiments of warriors were sent out: they scoured the territory, killing every last beast and razing all the crops.

'The people starved, but still Sarhili waited for the prediction to be fulfilled. Nothing happened. More than a year later the Paramount Chief renounced the belief, but the Xhosa nation had been decimated. A third of the people were lost through starvation, another third had migrated to new territories. Only a third remained alive in the Transkei.

'None of the events came to being, while those weak and starving souls who remained alive had to eke out another season before a harvest. It took decades for cattle to be re-introduced and bred again. It was truly a sombre time in the history of our proud nation.'

Themba gaped, aghast at the true folk legend. 'Who was really to blame?'

'That, Themba, is the lesson for you to learn. Belief among many Xhosa people, even today, was that the white man indoctrinated Nongqawuse with the story. They say the land-hungry colonial authorities implanted the vision into the maiden. I'm not saying it was so, but it could have been the whites who destroyed our nation over a century ago. Today the National Party is trying again, by enforcing apartheid on us and over-populating the Transkei with people forcibly moved from South Africa. Soon the crops will no longer sustain us and the cattle and sheep will overgraze the grasslands.'

'Are all white men bad?'

'No, Themba, there are many whites who are honourable. Examine a white man's heart before taking him into your trust.'

Themba took his evening meal with Hilda's family. In royal company, he was on his best behaviour, noting the traditional greetings and customs. He sat at one side talking to Hilda's father.

Nxele was impressed with the boy's intelligence, manners and general knowledge. One day he will make a fine member of our council, thought Nxele. I'll do my best to see he does.

After the meal Hilda turned coyly to Themba. 'Do you want to go for a walk?'

Themba looked towards Nxele. He nodded and the two teenagers slipped out into the moonlit landscape. The December air was

213

balmy, arousing feelings unknown to Themba. They talked as they strolled out of the village. Hilda nudged him. 'Tell me about yourself. Who is Themba Memani?'

Themba told her about his life, his schooling and his dreams. Hilda listened to his melodious voice, filled with such determination as he emphasised a point, or gentle when he spoke of his family.

They sat on the river bank, overlooking the stream, the moon a glowing, silver ball reflected in the water. Hilda cuddled closer to Themba on the pretext she was cold.

'Now you tell me more about yourself,' Themba asked awkwardly, feeling a tingling of his skin as she pressed her shoulder into his chest. Themba had never been so close to a girl before – her beautiful voice and sweet breath stirred him.

Armed with the knowledge of adulthood, Hilda was keen to practise some of the teachings she had learnt at her initiation. Themba was a very desirable young man she decided, as she snuggled closer.

11

Up long before dawn, the car packed, the Rouxs now drank a last cup of coffee in the large Hermitage kitchen.

Simon was irritated with Helena. 'We have been through this before. You can't come with – and that is final.'

'Why not?' she asked defiantly.

'You know the ten-hour car journey tires you out,' answered Simon abruptly. 'You are better off in the comforts of your own home.'

'I'll miss you both,' she said in a disappointed voice.

'We're going to rough it this trip,' Simon explained. 'The Kalahari is no place for a woman – it's a man's world!'

'I understand.' She sighed resignedly.

'Good.' Simon's face brightened as he turned to Pierre. 'I bought you a present, son.'

'A present?' Pierre breathed in excitement. 'What can it be?'

'An early birthday present.' He handed a large wrapped parcel to Pierre. 'Happy sixteenth birthday, my boy.'

Pierre tore off the wrapping of a leather gun bag. He unzipped it and let the rifle slide into his grasp. 'It's beautiful.' Pierre held a calibre .308 Sako rifle in his hands. Slapping it to his shoulder he looked through the Tasco telescope, aiming the cross-hairs at the top of the mountain peak. Stroking the glinting blue metal lovingly, he felt that it was cold to the touch. He turned to his father incredulously. 'Is it really mine?'

'Of course,' laughed Simon. 'I'll have to register it in my name until you are old enough. It is yours to keep, care for and hunt with.'

'It's a wonderful present, the best present I've ever had,' Pierre thanked his father.

'Let's get going, Pierre. The sun's up.'

They joined the N7 National Road at Malmesbury and drove over Piekenierskloof Pass to Citrusdal, leaving the verdant wheat fields behind. The road followed the Olifants River northwards past Clanwilliam.

They reached the flat Karoo-like coastal plain, the start of Namaqualand, usually dry and barren with sparse little hardy bushes. Now the good winter rains had transformed the ugliness into the most beautiful and colourful garden, as if God had sown the whole region with a rainbow of blooms.

Millions upon millions of brilliant blossoms faced the sun – wild flowers in such profusion, they took the breath away as they danced in the breeze and glittered in the sunlight. There were mesembryanthemums – indigenous vygies in sparkling mauves, pinks, reds, lilacs and whites; gazanias in shocking reds, yellows and bicolours; gorvetias in oranges and reds, with black-spotted throats; cinerarias in purple and mauves; *Venidium fastuosum* in white, yellow and orange and multi-stemmed daisies in every imaginable colour.

'I've never seen Namaqualand as magnificent as this year. It must truly be the eighth wonder of the world when the countryside turns to these hues.' Simon swept his arm in a circle to embrace the elegance as far as their eyes could see.

Up Van Rhyn's Pass – the further they travelled east the drier it became and the less the flowers were in evidence. After Calvinia they turned north, driving for hour upon hour of undeviating road through the drought-racked western Karoo. For kilometre after kilometre the landscape was the same – dried-out little stubby bushes and vast dry pans, interspersed with huge piles of rounded rocks, burnt black by the merciless sun, neatly stacked in heaps as if they were in the playing fields of some long-forgotten giants.

After nine hours the barrenness suddenly gave way to the rich Orange River Valley with its deep alluvial soils that produced the world's best lucerne, sultana grapes and cotton. The green crops, contrasting strongly with their bleak surroundings, made the valley a richly coloured patchwork quilt.

They crossed the Orange River at Keimoes and after Upington took the road heading into the Kalahari. Almost immediately they hit the dune veld. The dirt road rose and fell over the dunes like a roller-coaster. Thick red dust billowed out behind the car, penetrating into every crack of the vehicle forming a reddish-brown layer over everything.

The magnificent nests of social weaver birds surrounded the trunks of many camel-thorn trees or hung suspended from telephone poles. The birds built their huge nests from clay, saliva and grass, with hundreds of entrances, housing whole colonies of them.

As they reached the dry river bed of the Molopo River, the camel-thorn trees became more abundant and larger in size, with thick, gnarled trunks and spreading, flat, leafy tops.

The farmhouse of Doornrivier was built on the high ground on a limestone outcrop. It was a typical Kalahari-style house built to beat the searing summer temperatures – a large, square house, surrounded on all four sides by a wide covered stoep, to keep the sun off the windows. The manager came out to meet them.

'Welcome, Mr Roux, and Pierre.'

Simon greeted in return. 'Looks dry at the moment.'

'You know how deceiving the Kalahari is. Looks dry because of the winter frosts, but we had good autumn rains. There's a lot of grass and the bushes still have a lot of food left.'

Simon took in the farmyard. The walled garden consisted of a patch of kikuyu grass and two tall cypress trees. Water was scarce, not to be wasted on the luxury of extended gardens. The rest of the yard consisted of level, raked gravel. A large barn housed the implements and was converted into a shearing shed in the season. The brick-and-mortar circular reservoir was streaked, where the brack water had filtered through and seeped down the outside. Simon took a deep breath of the fresh, unpolluted air and started to unwind. 'Do you have the Land-Rover ready?'

'In the shed, tank full, ready to go. You can leave the car in the garage. Do you want to stay in the house or use the bivouac?'

'We want to rough it, thank you. We'll camp out at the *skerm*.'

He called Ben and Jan, two of the farm workers, to transfer the luggage to the Land-Rover. Direct descendants of the San, the first occupants of this huge, harsh land, these small, fine-boned men with their pale-brown skins were completely in harmony with their surroundings.

The bushmen smiled happily, knowing that with Simon and Pierre hunting a plentiful supply of meat was assured, plus the titbits the white men did not eat. These were their delicacies: livers, hearts, kidneys and brains.

The *skerm* consisted of an L-shaped screen of thorn poles, planted closely together to break the wind. It was situated under the shade of a huge camel-thorn tree. At one end a reed-covered shelter had been built on the red sand dune, doubling-up as a bedroom and provision store. Outside the skerm was a windmill and a corrugated-iron circular dam, where they drew their water for washing and drinking. The water was brackish.

Ben looked inquiringly at Simon. 'Is boss going to sleep inside or outside?'

'Outside, under the stars.'

Ben nodded knowingly, he had spent many a night himself in the open. He unrolled their bedding and mattresses and placed them inside the screen. The other goods they put into the hut. By the time he had finished, Jan had a fire going with chips and tinder. From a pile of camel-tree stumps he chose a big limb and placed it on the fire. It burnt brightly in the afterglow of the setting sun.

'Look at the sky.' Pierre looked westwards. The horizon was glowing with a bright-orange, luminous light. The sun, already set, shone through myriad dust particles, causing the beautiful radiance in the heavens, a feature of Kalahari sunsets.

The two bushmen left to return to their homes for the night. Simon disappeared into the hut and returned with a bottle of KWV and a half-full glass. He looked up as he was about to take the first sip and saw the disappointment etched on Pierre's face.

'What's wrong, son?' Simon asked softly.

'Please, Dad, don't drink tonight,' pleaded Pierre.

'Does it upset you?' asked Simon in alarm.

Pierre nodded dully, and on the spur of the moment Simon tossed the brandy into the fire and returned the bottle to the shack.

'Thank you, Dad,' whispered Pierre, a satisfied smile lighting up his face. 'I was so looking forward to you and me sharing the Kalahari to the full, together.'

With a lump in his throat Simon embraced his son. 'I didn't realise my drinking upset you so. Don't worry, I won't let brandy spoil the precious times we have together.' He squeezed harder. 'You are a wonderful son, Pierre, a son to make a father proud. Nothing will come between us, ever. I promise.'

'You are a marvellous father, Dad. Thanks for being there for me.'

Father and son sat close together and watched as the stumps burnt with a spluttering and crackling of oils trapped in the dried wood. Soon there were enough coals, Pierre working them to one side with a spade. The layer of glowing embers gave off a ruby-tangerine glow, shining brightly in the dark, almost alive as the heat trapped inside them fought to escape. Over the vibrant coals they grilled the mutton chops. Clouds of grey aromatic smoke billowed into the still air, the smell attracting the predators.

Outside the circle of firelight was a scuffling, as black-backed jackals flitted around like shadows in the dark, never still for a moment. In the motionless night air their chattering barks sounded even closer, almost as if they were in the camp.

'Nothing else has the smell of lamb braaied in the veld with camel-thorn wood,' grinned Pierre as he turned the grid, braaiing the chops quickly on the outside, sealing in the juices. The fat spluttered and dripped on the coals. They ate straight off the grid.

The meal was finished off with strong, sweet, black coffee, out of enamel mugs. Pierre sat back contentedly. 'This is the life. I could easily spend the rest of my life in the Kalahari.'

'You can if you want to, Doornrivier is waiting for you.' Simon yawned. 'Time to call it a day.'

Together they dragged a big thorn trunk on to the fire. It would burn all night, still giving coals in the morning. Crawling into their sleeping bags, they were instantly asleep.

The first slivers of dawn were just starting to push away the night when Simon awoke to sounds in the camp. He saw Ben place a coffee pot on the coals. The aromatic smell of percolating coffee twitched at his nose. 'How's the weather for hunting today, Ben?' asked Simon.

'Very good. It's a west wind, we'll find lots of buck in the lee of the dunes – to the east side. There's moisture in the air – it makes the springbok energetic.'

Pierre had been listening with interest. 'Where are the best springbok on the farm? I want a big ram with large horns.'

Ben pointed into the distance. 'In the Witgatboom camp. There are old rams that have wings on their horns.'

'Wings on their horns?' Pierre looked puzzled.

Taking a stick, Ben drew a springbok head in the sand, with the lyre-shaped horns. 'When a ram is old the tips of the horns stop growing towards each other. They start to turn backwards, making wings.' Ben expertly drew the turned-back horns in the sand, so explicitly that Pierre understood perfectly.

'Yes, I want a ram like that, Ben.'

'I'll show you one. You shoot the one I point out.'

Pierre studied Ben incredulously. 'We shoot at anything up to five hundred metres. Can you really see a tiny wing tip at that distance?'

'Oh yes, *basie*. No problem at all.'

Simon explained. 'These men have grown up in the Kalahari. Their eyesight, sense of smell and hearing are perfectly attuned to the veld. That's what makes them the world's best trackers.'

After driving for an hour over uneven roads they reached the gate of the Witgatboom camp. The manager took the wheel and Simon moved to the back. An old pick-up bench seat was welded into place. The hunter sat high up with a good view from the back of the pick-up. Ben and Jan stood behind the seat, one to each hunter, ready to point out the best buck.

The tall red Kalahari dunes ran parallel to each other for kilometre upon kilometre – sometimes only a hundred metres apart – other times up to a kilometre apart. The majestic dunes of red silica sand were topped by large tufts of tough, spiky grass. The flat areas of natural veld between the dunes were called *strate* by the locals. In the streets grew stumpy Karoo bushes, bushman grass, camel-thorn trees, boerboon trees and *swarthaak*, the black hook trees.

The manager locked the Land-Rover into four-wheel drive. He drove up the middle of a street, swinging the Land-Rover ninety degrees, heading straight for the large sand dune in front of them. The dune loomed larger and larger as they raced forward. With a bone-shattering jar the Land-Rover left the solid ground of the street, throwing itself upon the loose sand, the four-wheel drive biting in, keeping them going upwards. Dust and sand kicked out behind them. On the crest of the dune the manager brought the vehicle to a lurching stop, the nose pointing slightly downwards, cutting the engine.

'There they are!' Jan excitedly tapped Pierre on his shoulder.

'Where?' replied Pierre, seeing nothing.

'There.' Jan pointed over his shoulder. Pierre whipped the binoculars to his eyes. Even with the magnification of the Zeiss lenses, he had difficulty in locating what Jan easily saw with his naked eye. 'Third from right is a large ram.'

Simon nudged his son. 'You shoot first.'

Pierre pumped a shell into the breech, taking aim at the springbok's chest, where the light-brown hair joined the dark-brown middle stripe. He took a deep breath, pulling the trigger. Dust puffed above the buck, as the springbok scattered in all directions on their spindly legs, running flat for a few paces, then jumping into the air with long leaps. Within seconds they had dispersed.

Pierre was disappointed his first shot with his new rifle had missed. He'd wanted to impress everyone. A tap by Simon on the roof of the cab was a signal to the manager. He started the engine, roaring down the dune, the Land-Rover bucking as the tyres hit the hard surface of the next street.

They stopped on top of the next dune, but the street was clear of buck. Down again, across the street, up the next dune. Ben pointed out to the left on Simon's side.

'You can't fire across me, Pierre. I'll take this shot.'

'Fourth from left,' advised Ben.

Simon's .270 Mauser fired, the explosion and the slapping sound of the bullet hitting the buck were almost one. The springbok bounded into the air, its heart pierced. It did a death dance and then collapsed.

The herd broke to the left. 'Front one!' shouted Ben.

The springbok were running at speed. Simon followed the line, the telescopic sights crossed on its chest. He was careful not to stop the gun as he pulled the trigger. The heavy bullet struck the ram just behind the shoulder. It jumped in its stride, cart-wheeling head over heels and slammed into the ground.

They drove down to load the shot buck. Pierre looked at the dead springbok, so agile and graceful in life, so silent and still in death. He marvelled at their markings, three colours of hair on the body, almost in stripes, running along the length. Together the three shades formed a perfect natural camouflage against the semi-desert Kalahari veld.

They drove on. Just before a dune, Jan stopped the manager, explaining there was a water-hole over it and they should proceed on foot. They were panting by the time they reached the top. They fell to their stomachs and crawled to the crest.

A herd of over three hundred springbok were massing around the water-hole: rams, ewes and lambs. Ben stopped Pierre taking aim. 'Don't shoot here. We could frighten them away from their natural watering point for months, which is a bad thing.'

Simon and Pierre enjoyed watching the buck. Not hunting, they appreciated the delightful and graceful movements of the animals, undisturbed in their natural surroundings.

Young rams chased each other exuberantly, running away on stiff legs, abruptly changing their gait, taking small strides, making a series of short, sharp jumps high into the air. Holding their feet together on taut legs, they arched their backs, lowering their heads, throwing out their *pronk*, by raising the long, white, stiff hairs contained in their rump pouch, producing a tiara-like crest of white on their arched backs.

Ben pointed out a big ram with magnificent horns and a deeper colouring from the rest. 'There's a winged ram.' They watched the little group disappear over a sand dune.

Jan nodded. 'I know that ram. I've been watching him for many, many years. I know his herd's favourite grazing place, where you can find him.'

They crept off the dune back to the Land-Rover. Jan who knew every inch of the farm like the back of his hand, instructed the manager how to drive, circling the water-hole, getting into position. Approaching the third dune, Jan cautioned Pierre to get ready. The vehicle flew up the side and stopped over the crest as the engine was cut.

In front of them, not three hundred paces away, was a herd of about thirty springbok, strung out in a long line. Pierre instinctively pulled back the bolt and rammed a cartridge into position. He slapped the rifle to his shoulder, settling his cheek against the walnut stock, his elbows resting on the blanketed bar. Everyone on the vehicle froze, any movement would be transferred to the rifle.

The wily ram had not grown old and big without reason. His sixth sense warned him of impending danger and he stepped behind a large ink bush. Suddenly the ram shot forward and ran into the open. Pierre followed his movement, the cross-hairs aimed just behind the shoulder.

He felt the rifle slam into his own shoulder as he pulled the trigger, the recoil hitting hard. The 180-grain cartridge hurtled the soft-nosed bullet at a velocity of nearly eight hundred metres a second, taking less than a third of a second from barrel to buck. Instead of hitting the ram in the chest cavity the bullet smashed through the rib-cage into the abdomen. It made a tiny hole as it entered the skin, but the soft nose broke up on impact with the rib and blasted a crater of bone, blood and rumen out the far side. The force of the bullet slammed the ram to the ground, its stomach contents spewing out in a greenish mess of half-digested grass and shrub.

'You've got him,' shouted Jan as the Land-Rover sped down the dune.

They had not counted on the fighting spirit of the ram. Bleeding and mortally wounded, it forced itself to its feet and trotted off over the dune with shattered intestines hanging out of its side.

Jan jumped off when they reached the spot, reading the situation at a glance. '*Pens skoot*,' indicating to Pierre he had shot the ram in the stomach. 'We'll have to track him. This ram can still travel far.'

Ben and Jan took off in pursuit. They followed the trail through the soft sand easily. On the flat streets it was not so easy; many previous tracks criss-crossed the path. The cunning old ram kept changing direction, trying to shake off its pursuers, inborn instinct driving it on.

The bushmen were expert trackers – noting a bent grass here, a broken bush there, a tread in a soft spot, a fleck of stomach contents, or a drop of blood. Pierre followed, struggling to keep up with their pace, with the Land-Rover bringing up the rear. Over a dune, down a street, up the dune, across the next street, down the next dune, up the next street, they followed. Although terminally wounded the ram kept ahead of his pursuers for almost an hour, eventually collapsing under a camel-thorn tree. It watched balefully with large velvety-brown eyes as its persecutors approached, spent, unable to rise again.

Pierre came stumbling up, breathing hard. 'Look at those beautiful horns. Don't damage the head and neck – I want to have the head stuffed.'

Ben and Jan darted in. The magnificent ram struggled to rise but flopped down again. It bleated in fear, a guttural sound of defeat coming from its throat, as it stared death in the face. In a proud motion of defiance, it involuntarily released the *pronk* along its rump, the white hairs standing out like a cockscomb, exuding a musky smell of capitulation. Each grabbing a horn, they twisted the struggling springbok on to its back and ended its suffering.

A great sadness overcame Pierre as he looked down at the vanquished springbok. Once so proud and regal, he had caused the ram to suffer agonisingly. Racked with pain it had endured its hurt alone, away from its herd, dying in solitude.

The sombre mood passed as Simon clapped him on the shoulder in congratulation. Noticing his dejection, he bolstered Pierre. 'If you hadn't shot him, then someone else would have.'

Pierre nodded. 'I suppose so, that's the rule of nature. Kill or be killed, but nevertheless it's sad, to shoot such a dignified animal.'

They examined the ram. It was a magnificent specimen, with thick, strong horns and a wing on each tip turned back the length of the bottom joint of a man's thumb.

'Dad, can I have the head mounted, to remind me of today? Every time I think I'm hard done by, or suffering, I'll look up at the head of this ram and realise just how lucky I am to be alive.'

Simon nodded in agreement, impressed by his son's wisdom and compassion.

'On your marks, get set, go!' The starter's revolver kicked as a shot rang out. Pierre surged to the front with long, effortless strides. He held his lead and broke the tape first to set a new record for the eight hundred metres final at the Paarl Boys' High sports day.

After repeating his win at the WP Championships, Pierre was chosen to represent Western Province. Simon drove him to Cape Town station where the team had assembled to travel to the national championships in Bloemfontein – a large contingent of school athletes, boys and girls, coaches, teachers and chaperones. The station was crowded with well-wishers. Pierre made his way to the organiser. 'Pierre Roux, Paarl Boys' High, sir.'

'Welcome, Roux.' He ticked his name off, allocating him his compartment.

Father and son embraced as the team was instructed to board. 'Good luck, son, bring the SA title back to Paarl.'

'I'll try my best, Dad.'

Pierre found his compartment. 'Hullo, chaps,' he greeted with a smile.

A big, beefy boy stood up. 'I'm Helmut Schmidt from the German school in Cape Town.'

'Are you a German?'

'Of German descent,' laughed Helmut, his whole frame shaking.

'My parents were from Germany, but I was born in South Africa.'

'What event do you compete in?' said Pierre, looking him up and down.

'I'm a shot-putter,' answered Helmut proudly.

Buses transported them from Bloemfontein station to Grey College hostel. During the day they walked to the Free State Stadium where the SA Championships were held.

'Final of boys under-nineteen,' came over the loudspeaker system. Pierre made his way to the start, his heart beating faster, adrenalin pumping. He had finished second in his heat; he knew he could improve. All his training had been aimed for him to peak with this race. The honour of Paarl Boys' High and Western Province rested on his shoulders.

The starter checked the numbers against his chart. 'One minute to go.' Pierre stripped off his tracksuit and joined the finalists as they spread out across the starting line.

'On your marks . . .' He put his left foot forward, toe on the line, right leg back to give him a flying start. He rested his hand on his knee. 'Get set . . .'

He lifted his body slightly, muscles tensing. 'Go!' The shot exploded.

Pierre took off, jostling for position. A pacemaker streaked into the lead, with Pierre slipping into third spot. The athletes bumped each other trying to reach the inside lane. Pierre felt an elbow dig into his side. He held his position until the bell for the start of the second lap, keeping in touch with the leaders. With three hundred metres to go he pulled into the second lane, increased his pace and took the lead. In the same instant an athlete in the white and red of Transvaal edged past him.

Two hundred metres. Pierre mounted his challenge. Stepping up the pace, he swung out and drew level. He hit the front and started to sprint. Pierre could hear the athlete behind him breathing heavily.

One hundred metres. He concentrated on the ribbon. His lungs felt as if they were bursting; he struggled for air. He did not hear the thunderous roar of the crowd in the stands – he was in a world of his own. Out of the corner of his eye he saw the Transvaler almost at his shoulder. Pierre kicked harder and shot across the line, breaking the tape first. He fell to the track gasping for breath.

225

An official hurried across and helped him to his feet. 'Well done, son. You won.'

Pierre stepped on to the rostrum. The official walked across, shook Pierre's hand and hung the gold medal around his neck. It was all over in seconds, his moment of glory brief.

The announcement for the next race was made and the championships continued. Pierre strolled over to fetch his tracksuit. A tall girl was warming up close by. She was beautiful, with a classical face: high cheek-bones, a generous mouth and a well-shaped nose. Proud breasts pushed out her athlete's vest. Her head was crowned with a mass of blonde hair, tied in a pony-tail. He was smitten at first glance.

As she ran past she stopped in front of Pierre and looked at him with exquisite clear blue eyes. 'Congratulations, Pierre.'

Pierre saw she also wore Western Province colours. He rose to his feet, blushing. 'Thank you. You know my name, but I don't know yours.'

Her smile lit up her whole face. 'I'm Lesley Stuart. I've seen you around.'

'Where do you go to school?'

'Rustenburg Girls' High, in Rondebosch.'

'So you're English-speaking?'

'Certainly,' she answered confidently. 'Do you have anything against that?'

'No! No, I don't! But you must excuse me, my English is not so good.'

'I must get going, my number comes up next.'

'Good luck, I'll cheer for you. By the way, there's a social for all competitors tonight. Are you going?'

'Sure, I'll be there. But I do have a boyfriend at home.' She ran off on lithe legs, as light as a feather. Pierre watched her jog away – captivated by her energy and vitality.

Helmut flopped down beside him. 'What's the matter with you? You look as if you've just seen a ghost.'

'I have.' Pierre pointed towards Lesley. 'A beautiful blonde called Lesley Stuart.'

'*Mein Gott*,' nodded Helmut enthusiastically. 'She *is* sexy, my friend.'

The social at the university hall was packed. Pierre sought out

Lesley straight away. During a slow dance he tried to nuzzle into her neck, but she pulled back. 'Now! Now! Pierre Roux. I told you, I have a steady boyfriend. His name's Geoff and he's a medical student at the University of Cape Town.'

'Forget him. I'm here. Come, let's go outside for some fresh air.'

'Ha! Ha! I know your motives, *boertjie*! We'll dance and we'll talk, but no going outside.'

'Are you playing hard to get, Lesley?'

'Not hard to get. It's just that I'm wary of Afrikaners.'

'Why?' He looked at her in surprise. 'What have you got against us?'

'You lead a good life in South Africa at the expense of others. My family feel the same; we don't mix with Afrikaners.'

'Hey! That's unfair. You can't judge a person by his home language. I'll show you I'm different.'

'Easy talk in Bloemfontein,' she answered sarcastically. 'At home we have nothing to do with Afrikaners. I live in an English world.'

'Why not give me a chance?'

'You are wasting your time, *boertjie*.' She turned and left the dance floor.

Themba stopped to admire the imposing Umtata town hall and the beautiful gardens. The delightful scent of the roses wafted on the warm December breeze. He hurried to Paul Curry's house.

Paul popped open a bottle of champagne. 'Come and sit down, young man.'

'What's the occasion?'

'Your results. I've finished marking your white Department of Education papers. If you had been allowed to attend my class at Umtata High School, you would have received a first-class matriculation overall result, with an A average.'

Themba smiled happily. Paul lifted his glass, toasting Themba's achievements.

'Thank you,' Themba replied with humility. 'One day I hope the playing fields will be levelled for all races, allowing black people to compete as equals.'

'Another toast. Congratulations on being accepted at the University College of Fort Hare.' Paul lifted his glass. 'Let's go down to the coast to celebrate.'

'Can we go to esiKhaleni?'

'Only place to go. At Hole-in-the-Wall we virtually have the place to ourselves.'

'May I take Hilda this time?'

Paul's eyes widened in mock exasperation. 'Do you expect me to chaperone you the whole time?'

Themba laughed. 'She's very strict about no sex before marriage, so you don't have to worry.'

'That's the lot.' Paul attached the last of his fishing gear to the back of the Datsun pick-up that was packed to capacity.

'Can we drive past the Mtata Falls?' Themba asked eagerly. 'I hear they're full after the first summer rains.'

Paul's pick-up was specially adapted for his crippled right leg. Instead of an accelerator pushed by the right foot, speed was governed by a lever to the right of the steering wheel. They pulled away, taking ten minutes to reach the First Falls on the Umtata River. At the Second Falls they breakfasted, admiring the picturesque cascades of water, bubbling and tumbling over the rocks.

As they crested a hill, the blue sea glinted in the late-morning light, white breakers creaming towards the shore. The beach was sparkling white and unspoilt. The main feature of the bay was the gigantic rock jutting out to sea.

Paul drove along a rutted track to the base of a smooth, green, grassed hill, coming right down to the sea, to a lovely grassed glen, protected by a thicket of indigenous trees. A little river murmured through the glade. They unloaded the tents in the shade of a big tree, pitching them alongside each other. With no fences in the Transkei, cattle and sheep had free range and the grass in the glen was closely cropped, like a well-kept lawn.

'This is the fifth time Themba and I have been to esiKhaleni,' Paul told Hilda. 'Now Themba knows how to swim, fish and gather crayfish from under the rocks.'

She beamed, happy to be with Themba and the crippled white man with a heart of gold. Themba felt for her hand, giving her a squeeze of encouragement. 'Paul, I challenge you to a race at sea.'

'What sort of race did you have in mind?'

'Swimming from our bay, past esiKhaleni, around the point to the next bay and back again.'

'Wow, that's about four kilometres. We would have to swim far out to sea, to avoid the rocks at the point. Do you think you can swim so far?'

'Easily,' boasted Themba.

Themba and Paul dived in together. Themba soon left Paul far behind, forging ahead with powerful crawl strokes. Let him go, thought Paul. In a long race one has to conserve energy. I'll swim slowly but surely. By the time they had rounded the point, Themba was slowing, Paul catching up rapidly. They flopped on to the sand at the same time catching their breath.

On the return trip, Paul's sinewy frame proved decisive, and he pulled away from the heavier Themba, to win by a full two hundred metres.

'Come on, slow coach,' shouted a jubilant Paul as Themba staggered exhausted out of the water. He ignored Paul and carried on up the beach.

'What's wrong with you?' enquired Paul as he hobbled closer, grabbing Themba by the arm.

'Leave me alone!' said Themba sulkily.

'You have to learn to be gracious in defeat,' admonished Paul. 'Winning is of paramount importance.'

'Now wait here, buster.' Paul sat Themba down and looked at him sternly. 'In life you can't always come first.'

'I hate to lose,' muttered Themba.

'Come off it, Themba. A good loser is more popular than a conceited winner.'

'Who cares about popularity?' answered Themba flippantly.

'Being an only child, you've tended to become a loner, but you must learn to become a team man if you want to be successful.'

'I suppose so,' admitted Themba grudgingly.

'Of course – whatever you do give of your best, but remember the old adage – to have played the game and lost is far better than not to have played at all.'

Themba smiled suddenly, lighting up his expressive face. He extended his hand. 'You're right, as usual, Paul. Congratulations on winning our race.'

'That's more like it!' laughed Paul. 'Let's see if Hilda has finished lunch. I'm starving.'

Fort Hare University, with its many fine faculty buildings and residences, dominated the little town of Alice. From the station Themba made straight for the registrar's office and knocked loudly.

'Come in, please.'

'Good morning. My name is Themba Memani.'

'I've been looking forward to meeting you. Please sit down.'

'I've come to register for my degrees.'

'Degrees?' queried the registrar.

'I would like to take two degrees. Law and Political Science.'

'A most unusual request.' The registrar was taken aback. 'In all my twenty years at Fort Hare, no one has ever taken two degrees simultaneously.'

'I passed my matriculation well.'

'I know you did. Your average of over ninety per cent is very impressive. But why two degrees at once?'

'Time is short and I want to qualify quickly. I also want the option to be able to teach if I don't practise law.'

'You'll have to pay the fees for two courses. You must register separately for each degree, and you'll need two sets of books. Your main problem is that you write both sets of examinations at roughly the same time.' He looked at the registration form. 'I see you've registered to stay in a hostel. At least that will only be a single expense.'

'I can afford it.' Themba placed the first year's fees, in cash, on the table.

'Very well, I'll register you for both degrees. It's going to be tough, but the best of luck.'

He doesn't realise I've been doing two sets of school work for years, Themba thought. I managed just fine then, I should do the same now.

'Mr Memani, please sign here. Thank you. You've been allocated to Wesley residence.'

Themba walked through the streets of Alice. The Amatola mountain range rose majestically in the north. It was all new to him, and he stared in fascination. The whole town seemed to revolve around the university.

'You look lost.' Themba turned to see a friendly, smiling face.

'Sure am!' Themba laughed.

'I'm Ngconde Seymour. I'm at Lovedale Training College. I'm studying to be a teacher.'

230

'How do you do.' Themba extended his hand. 'I'm Themba Memani. I'm from Mqekezweni in the Transkei.'

'Let me help you with your luggage. Where to?'

'Wesley men's residence.' They walked together, chatting. Themba glanced at his new friend. 'Where are you from?'

'Alice area. I grew up here, I know my way around the town.'

Themba found his room at Wesley and met his room-mate. He didn't waste any time sounding Themba out. 'We're staging a protest tomorrow against apartheid. We're marching on the police station. All the students will be there. Will you join us?'

Themba looked at Ngconde, who answered, 'I don't mind marching, but I won't be in the front with the leaders. If I'm arrested I'll be kicked out of Lovedale.'

Themba turned to his room-mate. 'I feel the same. I've two degrees to get in the next three years and nothing must get in my way. I promised my mother.'

'Really to be part of the freedom struggle you must first see the inside of a jail,' bragged his room-mate. 'I've been locked up twice already.'

'I'll stay out of jail until I've completed my studies. Then will be the time to become involved in the freedom struggle.'

The student looked disappointed. 'Hell, it's only a march. You won't be committing any crime. Don't be a wet blanket.'

'What do you think, Ngconde?'

'Let's go, then. We can always pull out if it gets dangerous.'

'All right, we'll march.'

The next day was hectic. Themba lost his way twice as he struggled to find the right lecture rooms. He rushed from one subject to the other, doing double the work of the other students. When he joined the demonstration the crowd was already marching, singing freedom songs. '*Amandla!* Freedom!' they chanted, and they shook their arms in clenched-fist salutes.

Ngconde saw Themba and fell back to join him. 'Hullo, comrade, how are you today?'

'Fine, but rushed. What's happening up front?' Themba craned his neck to see.

'The police have cordoned off the road.'

A voice came over a loud-hailer, high-pitched and distorted. 'Stop! You are ordered to stop! We will not tolerate any demonstrations from students. Move away, please.'

231

The march continued. 'If you do not disperse we will be forced to make you do so.' The students jeered and taunted the police. 'Charge!' Policemen ran forward wielding batons and sjamboks and laid into the students. Cries filled the air as people ran in all directions.

Ngconde explained as he ran. 'We break away, then regroup further down the road and continue the march.'

Themba kept well to the pavement, avoiding the action. He was horrified at the way the police laid into the protesters; hitting them across their backs as they turned and ran. He passed the blockade and joined up with the students again further down the street.

The police vans roared around the block and drew up in front of the marchers. This time Themba and Ngconde were near the front. When the beating started they were closer to the action. As the demonstrators ran away, screaming in terror, they were next in line. Themba's eyes opened wide as a policeman bore down on him, arm raised, a hard rubber baton held high. As the weapon flashed towards his head he raised his arms and grabbed the policeman by the wrist. The policeman screamed in fury.

'I've done nothing to make you hit me,' spat Themba contemptuously.

A fellow policeman saw the scuffle and ran to his colleague's aid. Themba heard a whistling sound and a sjambok thudded against his back, causing an excruciating pain to shoot through his body. Hate flamed in Themba's eyes. He was about to retaliate when Ngconde pulled him away. Themba stumbled in a crouched half-run, his friend propelling him along.

Ngconde shouted above the noise, 'Let's get out of here!'

'Where to?'

'Back to your residence.' The two friends ran to Wesley, leaving the demonstration to the other students.

Themba's back was on fire. He felt blood dripping down the inside of his shirt where the hippo-hide sjambok had cut into his skin. He stripped off his shirt and rolled it into a bundle. 'That's one shirt written off.'

'Good God, just look at your back.'

Themba looked in the mirror. Over his upper back an ugly weal, puffy and swollen, oozed blood. 'Damn police, why did they attack me?'

'You were defying them and you're black.'

232

'Today was my first experience of police brutality.' Themba spoke with passion. 'My mother always taught me to hate the police, now I know why. What a way to rule a country!'

'Let's fix up your wound.'

In the bathroom Ngconde wiped away the blood with a wet cloth and applied antiseptic. Themba gasped as the astringent burnt his raw flesh, and gritted his teeth.

His room-mate did not come home that night. Themba asked around the residence and learnt he had been captured and would appear in court the next day. A fellow student assured him, 'It's all right, he wanted to be arrested. It makes him a martyr to the cause.'

'I can pay his fine.'

'He wouldn't like that. Leave him, let him serve his sentence. It's part of the strategy – to fill the jails to overflowing. It costs the regime money to convict, house and feed prisoners.'

Fellow students admired Themba's lash welt. 'I see they got you, too. Now you're part of the struggle.'

Themba used the three weeks his room-mate was away to work late into the night. Taking two degrees at once meant he had to miss a lecture occasionally when the two curriculums coincided. Themba discussed the matter with his professors and they kept the lecture notes for him so he did not fall behind.

Autumn was turning the grass bronze when Themba returned home after the first term. Nomisile and Hilda spoilt him. He didn't mind. He had worked hard and he felt he deserved a little pampering. He visited Joseph Sondika.

'It is time for your initiation ceremony into manhood,' declared Joseph.

'It takes almost three months. I haven't the time. Let's leave initiation until I've finished at university.'

Joseph shook his head. 'I think Paramount Chief Sabata would like to invite you to join the council of elders.'

'That would be an honour.'

'Only men are members of the council, not boys who are uncircumcised.'

'The first three months I have to spare will be during the long summer vacation – December, January and part of February.'

233

'Good. I will organise a party of eligible boys for that time. I will be your instructor.'

'I would like that, Joseph. We've come a long way together.'

Nomisile looked up from her sewing as Themba entered her hut, a smile of love touching her mouth. He had grown so tall during the past year and had filled out, he looked more like Simon each time she saw him. He had the same brisk, effortless movements and casual mannerisms, but where his father had been outgoing Themba tended to be introverted.

'Mother, at the end of the year I'm going through my initiation ceremony.'

'I'm glad, my son. It's important for you to become a man.'

'Why must I go through the ceremony? It won't make me any cleverer at university,' Themba teased her, waiting for her reaction.

'You'll be wiser in our traditions and customs. A man with a future must have a strong past. Initiation will make a man out of you, you'll see.'

Themba studied his mother. She worked so hard at her dress-making, with hardly a day's rest. She was starting to go grey at her temples, he noted lovingly – but then she was almost forty. The years were taking their toll but she was still the most beautiful woman in Mqekezweni.

'Another reason is so you can take a wife. Hilda won't wait for ever.'

'A wife! I don't need a wife. I'm a student. What must I do with a wife?'

'Another man may come along and do a deal with her father.'

'I've met a girl at university. Her name is Muriel.'

'You must marry a girl from the same background as yourself,' Nomisile lectured him sternly. 'Hilda is Thembu royalty, which is good for your future. Hilda *must* be your wife.'

The oak trees were laden with acorns and squirrels were busy gathering the harvest when Pierre arrived at Stellenbosch University to study law. He followed his father by staying at Wilgenhof residence, where Dr Danie Craven was still the resident housemaster.

'Good afternoon, Doc.'

'Simon Roux, it's good to see you again.'

'Doc, may I introduce my son Pierre?'

'Welcome to Wilgenhof, Pierre. My, a chip off the old block. Do you play rugby as well as your father used to?'

'I'm an athlete, sir. Middle distance.'

'A Roux not playing rugby? What a pity!'

Doc greeted Helena and invited them in for tea. Simon looked around the study, pleased to see it was still basically the same as twenty years previously. It even smelt the same.

'My Matie days were good days, Doc. Carefree student days, when politics didn't touch us and we lived for rugby.'

Craven agreed. 'The politics are still the same – the average white man doesn't get involved. He just flows with the current and happily lets the Nationalist government do as they like. In twenty years nothing has changed. Our coloureds and blacks are still denied the opportunity to develop their talents, they still can't be chosen for a Springbok team. I hope I'll see the day when we all play together and selection is on merit only.'

Pierre settled into his room while Helena packed his clothes away.

A young man entered and smiled at Pierre. 'So you're my room-mate? I'm Danie Conradie.' They shook hands.

Pierre introduced him to his family and they struck up an easy conversation. 'I'm from Pretoria, though my mother and father spend only six months of the year there and the other six in Cape Town.'

'What does your father do?' Simon asked.

'Private secretary to the Minister of Defence, Mr PW Botha.'

Simon nodded knowingly. 'I've heard of him. Nicolaas Conradie. It must be a trying job at present. What are you studying, Danie?'

'Political Science. I want to join the public service or the diplomatic corps. That's why I chose Stellenbosch rather than Pretoria University. I'll make friends and contacts here who will stand me in good stead in later life. After all, it's who you know that counts, not what you know.'

Coetzenburg, the university athletics stadium, had the finest facilities in the country and Pierre's athletics career flourished.

'Breathe deep, Roux, take deeper breaths,' shouted coach Bokkie Blaauw from the side of the track. 'You'll have to improve your times if you want to become a Springbok.'

Pierre finished the eight hundred metres and stood with his hands on his knees regaining his breath.

'Much better,' smiled coach Blaauw. 'You've been chosen to run for Stellenbosch at the inter-varsity in Pretoria. Well done.'

The first person Pierre met in Pretoria was his old friend, Helmut Schmidt. 'Hullo, I see you're an Ikey now.'

'*Ja! Ja!* Pierre – I'm trying to become an auditor.'

'I heard Lesley Stuart is also at UCT,' asked Pierre hopefully. 'Is she still in athletics?'

'*Himmel*, my friend! Didn't you know she's here now?'

Pierre felt his heart beat faster. 'Won't you help me meet her again? Do a favour for an old friend.'

'Why don't you ask her yourself?'

'She's got this thing about Afrikaners.'

'She has a boyfriend who is a houseman at Groote Schuur hospital. The girls look on them as prime catches. I don't think you stand a chance, Pierre.'

'Try anyway.'

'Okay, I'll see what I can do.'

Two days later Helmut walked up to Pierre, a big smile on his ample face. 'You're in luck, pal. A group of us is going to Jacqueline's tonight and we've persuaded Lesley to come along. Pop in there and look surprised to see us.'

'Helmut, I owe you.'

The night-club in downtown Pretoria was packed when Pierre arrived. He saw Helmut's muscular bulk on the dance floor, but no sign of Lesley. He peered through the smoky haze towards the tables and then he saw her. She had her back to him but there was no mistaking her blonde hair and the way she held her head. She was alone.

She didn't see him until he sat down opposite her. 'Hullo, Lesley, fancy meeting you here.'

'Hi, Pierre.' She looked around the night-club. 'Where are the rest of your team-mates?'

'I'm alone tonight.'

'Funny coincidence, don't you think? I'm inveigled into accompanying my friends and suddenly you appear out of the blue. Smacks of collusion.' She took a sip of her drink.

Pierre laughed. 'I plead guilty. I persuaded Helmut to organise things like this. It's the only way I can get close to you.'

'You're a conniving devil. Now that you have me captive, what do you plan to do with me?'

'Talk to you, dance with you, perhaps even kiss you.'

'You're very persistent, and presumptuous too. We can talk, but I don't know about your other plans, *boertjie*!'

'Can I buy you a drink?'

'Just soda water. I'm running tomorrow.'

'Tell me about your course at UCT.'

'I'm at the school for social work.' She looked at him closely. 'Are you really interested?' Pierre nodded enthusiastically and she continued. 'We do a lot of practical work at the university clinics in Guguletu and Langa. Conditions are terrible in the black townships. And there's another evil brewing, squatter camps are being established near the southern end of DF Malan airport, at a place called Crossroads. The people live there in plastic houses.'

'Plastic houses?'

'Frameworks of poles covered with plastic sheeting. There's no laid-on water, no sewerage, no refuse removals – the worst squalor imaginable. The government is more concerned with building grand edifices for their own departments than addressing black housing.'

'Aren't you afraid to go into the townships?'

'Their needs are so great I have to take the risk. The government won't do anything for them.'

'You don't like the government?'

'I detest them. Are you a Nationalist, Pierre?'

He had to be honest and nodded. 'My grandfather and father were Nationalist MPs. My room-mate at Stellenbosch is a staunch supporter – his father is PW Botha's secretary. I'm surrounded by the National Party.'

Lesley looked at him in disgust. 'I thought so! You are the enemy. You expect to dance with me, and even have the cheek to think you can kiss me! Never! We have nothing in common, *boertjie*.' She turned and faced in the opposite direction.

Pierre was desperate. 'My mother thinks differently. She's a member of the Black Sash.'

'Good. At least there's some hope for you.'

He tried to break the impasse. 'Let's dance. They're playing Liza Minelli's "Cabaret", it's one of my favourites.'

'You're a thick-skinned guy, Roux. What makes you think I want to dance with you?'

Pierre flashed her his most charming smile. 'I'm alone, you're alone, and there's beautiful music playing. Let's forget the Anglo-Boer War – at least for one dance.'

She succumbed. 'All right, *boertjie* – just one dance.' He guided her to the dance floor, achievement mirrored in his face.

He marvelled at her fluid movements, could not keep his eyes off her. The record ended and they stood waiting for the next to play. Pierre held her hand; she did not pull away. He snuggled his fingers between hers.

The next record was a slow number, the Beatles' hit 'Yesterday'. He held her in his arms and felt her breasts pushing into his chest, her stomach flat against him, her legs stepping sensually between his. She knew the words of the song and sang them softly to herself in a sweet, lilting voice. There and then, Pierre fell in love. Tightening his arms around her, he pulled her close. He kissed her neck and heard her breath quicken. Lovingly he gazed into her clear blue eyes. She looked back levelly as he bent forward and kissed her on the mouth. He felt her lips tremble as they softened under his urgency.

'Hi, partner! What are you doing here?' Helmut boomed.

'Damn,' cursed Pierre, as Lesley broke away and hurried back to the table. 'You've just spoilt the best moment of my life,' he complained.

'The night's still young, my friend. Enjoy yourself.'

Pierre hurried after her, but the moment had gone. At the table Lesley was gathering her handbag. 'Where are you going in such a hurry?'

'I told you I have to run tomorrow. I need an early night.'

'I'll take you back.'

'No need. You stay and enjoy yourself. I'll get a taxi.'

Pierre insisted on calling the taxi. They got into the back seat together and Pierre gave directions. 'Jasmine, Pretoria University women's residence.'

He tried to cuddle up to Lesley but she would have none of it. 'Forget what happened in the night-club. It won't happen again, I promise you.'

'Lesley, I love you, I want you.'

'Well, I don't love you. I love Geoff. You must leave me alone. You're an Afrikaner. I could never love an Afrikaner.'

'I can't help that.' Pierre sat back, dejected. Being an Afrikaner with National Party ties had never worried him before. Maybe she was right – he should stick to an Afrikaans-speaking girl. Then again he had never felt for any Afrikaans girl what he felt for her. He tried one last time. 'Will you go to the cinema with me tomorrow night?'

Lesley was tempted. This man from such a different background had made her feel alive and vivacious, wanted and special. Geoff could be so cold. So often he took her for granted. 'No, Pierre,' she said softly. 'Tomorrow night I'll be spending with my team.'

The taxi stopped in front of the residence. Pierre walked her to the front door and put out his hand to say goodbye. She ignored it. Instead, standing on tiptoe, she kissed him lightly on the cheek.

'Good-night and goodbye, Pierre.'

She turned and ran inside, leaving Pierre with his thoughts in a turmoil. He touched his cheek gingerly, a puzzled expression creasing his features.

12

The railway bus stopped outside the Umtata railway station. Themba jumped off, a suitcase in each hand, and hurried to Paul Curry's house. He banged on the door, not waiting for an answer before entering. He met Paul hobbling across the lounge. Paul's eyes lit up as he embraced Themba fondly.

Over a cup of tea Themba told his friend of his successful first year at Fort Hare. 'It has been a tough year, but I passed well in both degree courses.'

'How about a few days at the sea?' Paul urged.

'Sorry, but I must hurry home – I'm due to be initiated into manhood.'

'Rather you than me,' laughed Paul. 'It all sounds very barbaric.'

'All part of our traditional ritual. I must go through with it.'

Crowing cocks welcoming the new day woke Themba at Mqekezweni. He stretched and rolled off his mat. There was a knock on the door.

'I bring you an instruction from Joseph Sondika,' said the messenger. 'You are to be at his house early tomorrow morning to begin your initiation ceremony.'

'Your time has come, soon you will be a man.' Nomisile smiled at her son. 'I can hardly believe it's more than eighteen years since you were born. Time has flown.'

'For three months I'll not see a woman,' Themba joked. 'It's going to be tough.'

Soon after dawn the next morning Themba reported to Joseph's hut. 'Welcome, Themba, please sit down. The others will be here soon.'

Four other youths arrived – his cousin; a friend from Mqekezweni;

241

one from his grandfather's kraal and a much older youth who had already completed a three-year contract on the gold mines in Johannesburg.

'I will be your instructor for the next few months,' said Joseph. 'The council selected me to fulfil this function.' He pointed to a small boy standing shyly to one side. 'He will be your attendant during your initiation.' Joseph rose. 'Let's go.'

They followed the elder down to the river where they stripped and washed in the cool, clear water. 'Leave your clothes on the rock. One of your family will fetch them later. You don't need clothes for the next little while.'

Joseph handed each a hollowed-out half-gourd. Two holes drilled on either side held short leather thongs. 'Put those over your genitals.' The attendant tied the thongs at the back.

They walked up the hill to an isolated hut a distance from the village. The youths' fathers and Themba's grandfather waited for them, each holding a goat wether.

In the early afternoon the witch-doctor appeared, looking exactly the same as the last time Themba had seen him. He was ancient and wrinkled and rumoured to be over a hundred years old.

While the adults slaughtered the five goats, a fire was lit. The witch-doctor sat cross-legged in front of the fire chanting, his eyes glazed as if in a trance. Suddenly he jumped up and with unexpected energy danced before the startled youths, uttering weird cries. His animal skins flapped as he cavorted around.

'It is time.' Joseph arranged the five young men in a line.

The first youth chosen was from Morris Memani's kraal. The gourd was removed, exposing his hooded penis, flaccid and almost withdrawn into his abdomen. The witch-doctor took out a leather bag, dipped in his gnarled finger and removed a dollop of brownish paste. He forced back the youth's foreskin and smeared on the paste. It caused a burning sensation as it dissipated into his skin, and he squirmed in pain. Much to his embarrassment, his member started growing. He tried to will it down, but the medication caused a rhythmic throbbing, keeping it extended.

The witch-doctor clucked in satisfaction as he searched in his hide bag and brought out a short stabbing-spear, which he placed in the fire to sterilise it. He held up the red-hot blade and plunged it into a pot of fresh water to cool.

Dancing closer, the medicine man grabbed the upright penis. He put his thumb on the tip and pushed it towards the abdomen, at the same time pulling the foreskin over his thumb. With the sharp point of the spear he cut through the skin, slitting between the tip of the penis and the top of his thumb. The hot metal cauterised the cut, giving off a sickly smell of burnt human flesh.

The youth screamed in pain. The witch-doctor cut around the sides to the back until the foreskin hung by only a thin shred. With a last flurry he made the final cut and held the ring of skin in his hand. Nodding in satisfaction, he placed it in a leather pouch, to use later in an ointment to increase fertility in barren women.

Themba watched as the blood dripped. Joseph smeared a mixture of strongly scented herbs into the wound, causing the youth to cry out again. He packed the leaves of a wild plant around the penis.

The boy's father skinned his goat, pummelling the hide off the still warm body. He cut the goatskin into long, thin strips and handed them to the witch-doctor. Starting next to the body, working outward towards the tip, the *igqirha* bound the penis tightly with the goatskin strips.

It was Themba's turn next. The gourd was removed and the witch-doctor smeared on the paste. He felt the warmth penetrate his member. He watched in fascination as his penis flexed and grew. He waited for the next stage, fidgeting in embarrassment.

The witch-doctor reheated the spear. Themba felt the pain as the point cut through his skin. He gritted his teeth, determined not to show any sign of weakness. Finally his foreskin hung like a loose string.

Themba cried in exaltation, 'Cut it off, make me a man!' The witch-doctor smiled a toothless smile, his rheumy eyes showing admiration. With a final slashing cut he removed Themba's boyhood.

The pain was excruciating as the singed wound dripped blood; Joseph's herbs added to the agony. Themba stood to attention, not a sound escaping his lips. Morris handed the goatskin strips to the witch-doctor. He bound Themba's bloated member and tied the goatskin in place with leather thongs. Themba sat down, while his grandfather grilled rashers of goat shoulder in the fire and fed him the succulent meat.

'Eat well because this is your last meal for seven days,' Joseph advised them.

The next stage of their initiation had begun. Joseph mixed white clay and water until he had a runny paste which was smeared on Themba's face. It dried a sparkling white, contrasting starkly with the rest of his body.

'The first stage of your journey to manhood is finished.' The witch-doctor spoke in his thin, reedy voice. 'Go well, children of the Thembu, that you may complete your initiation to manhood.'

Joseph stood up. 'We go now, but first you must thank our great *igqirha*.' Each initiate in turn went and sat in front of the witch-doctor, thanking him. The elder led the way with the five youths strung out behind and the small boy brought up the rear. Walking was painful, the goatskin chafed the raw wound. A distance from the village they reached a crudely built hut. It was made of dried maize stalks stuck into the ground in a circle, bent over and tied in the middle to form an inverted bowl-shaped framework and covered with a layer of coarse veld grass. The floor was simply levelled soil. The five crept through the opening and lay exhausted on the rough earth. Soon they fell into a weary sleep. The elder walked back to the village. The small boy slept close to the opening.

'Up you get!' The five initiates woke with a start and Joseph chased them out of the hut. 'Today is day two, no food.'

'What do we do all the time we are here?'

'You avoid people – you meditate – you think. This is your transition from boyhood to manhood.'

'Who built our hut?' Themba asked.

'The women from the village.'

'Will we see them?'

'If you do, you must turn away. You may not look directly into their faces.'

'For almost three months?'

'It is the custom of *abakwetha*.'

They settled into a pattern of sleeping and lounging around their hut. From the fourth day the hunger pains started in earnest. Each one withdrew into himself as the lack of nourishment started to take its toll. Themba went into his own world, not caring about the instructor or his fellow initiates. He stumbled away and sat alone, staring into space, his hollow stomach cramping.

The fifth day was the worst. He was weak and hallucinating. He stumbled out of the camp and walked up the mountain until

244

he collapsed from exhaustion. He gazed fixedly at a tree standing tall and straight with widespread branches.

'Mother!' he whispered. In his deranged mind he saw Nomisile with her arms outstretched. As the wind played through the boughs he heard her talking to him in a whispered sigh, her voice rising and falling as the wind swirled.

'My son . . . I have raised you as best I could . . . I want the best in life for you . . . I love you . . . You are the centre of my universe . . . One day you will be a great leader of our people . . . Use your power wisely . . . Many people's lives will depend on your judgement . . .'

'I hear you, my mother.' Themba saw his mother's features vaguely in the foliage of the tree. She was smiling at him. He smiled back at her image, then lapsed into unconsciousness.

He awoke with a start. A stranger was talking to him in Afrikaans. '*Ek is jou vader, hoor my, my seun.*'

'Where! Where!' Themba cried out frantically. 'I don't understand you.'

'I am your father, hear me, my son.' The voice in his head repeated the words in English.

'I hear you, Father. Where are you?' Themba's eyes latched on to a white sandstone boulder jutting out from the hillside. Vaguely he made out the shape of a man. 'I see you, my father, talk to me, tell me who you are.' He saw the massive outline of a big man, his head a smaller bleached rock balancing on the boulder. 'You are a giant of a man.' Themba looked in awe, hardly breathing.

'*Ek pas jou op, my seun. Ek het jou nie vergeet nie. Ek sorg vir jou. Ek is trots op jou.*'

'I don't understand you.' Themba cried in despair. 'Why do you address me in Afrikaans?'

The wind blew stronger, the words floated over eternity. 'I watch over you, my son. I have not forgotten you. I take care of you. I am proud of you.'

Themba stumbled weakly to his feet, swaying dangerously. 'Come closer, Father,' he whispered through cracked lips. 'I must see your face.' The rock stood firm and unmoving. Themba collapsed.

The small boy rushed back to the village and summoned Joseph.

Softly the voice came again. '*Jy is die skakel tussen die goeie en die slegte in ons land. Ons toekoms lê in jou hande.*'

'Speak so I can understand you.'

'You are the link between good and evil in our country. Our future lies in your hands.'

'I hear your words, Father. Are you the man called Seme, who my mother says is my father?' Themba murmured weakly.

'No, my name is Simon.'

The wind died, only silence remained. Themba looked up, expecting to see his father, but all he saw were the white boulders. Through the haze of semi-consciousness it struck him. The sandstone was a whitish colour, his father was white! 'It can't be . . . '

Themba blinked as he saw a black face looking down at him. 'Now I'm confused, Father.'

'You'll catch sunstroke lying here.' Joseph Sondika helped Themba back to the shelter. 'You're delirious; tomorrow you'll feel better.' Themba felt himself supported by his father, but when he looked there were black arms around him. The memory faded from his anguished mind.

Although he had a dull headache from lack of nourishment his mind was clear when he awoke on the sixth morning. He tried to recall his dream, but his thoughts were vague and misty.

Joseph held a calabash of water to Themba's lips. He slurped thirstily, feeling the coolness of the water slipping down his throat.

They walked over to the spot where Themba had sat the previous day. The twin rocks jogged a chord in his subconscious. 'Those rocks spoke to me. They were my father.'

'You were hallucinating when I found you. What you saw was an illusion. Lack of food does that on the fifth day, before your body can adjust.'

'He spoke to me. I heard him clearly. My father is white, he's a white man.'

'What nonsense, Themba. You are a Xhosa of the royal Thembu tribe. Never talk like that again. It could affect your future.'

'I understand, Joseph.' He could not help feeling uneasy as he looked at the tree and a vague memory of seeing his mother came into his mind. 'It must have been my imagination,' Themba muttered in confusion.

The sixth and seventh days dragged by. At dawn the next day Joseph spoke to them. 'Today is the day of *jisa*: the eighth day.' He pointed to the river. Their fathers were there with the witch-doctor. Slowly, weak from lack of food, they made their way down the hill.

'You must show your will-power by spitting out the first three mouthfuls of food and drink you are offered,' explained Joseph. A sheep was roasting on the coals, its smell rich and tempting. The five initiates sat in a row. The witch-doctor chanted for almost an hour, waiting for the sheep to cook.

The witch-doctor cut off a cube of mutton, offering it to Themba on a sharpened stick. Saliva poured into his mouth as the delicious meat touched his tongue. It took all his will-power not to swallow. He spat it out with force. The others showed the same self-control.

Next he was fed roasted green maize, fresh off the cob. It tasted delectable, but once again Themba displayed his strength by spitting out the kernels.

A gourd of *umqombothi*, the maize and sorghum beer, was brought forward. Themba took a sip, and spat it out.

The old healer hopped around. 'You have all shown the will-power to become men.' He turned to the elder. 'Let the next stage begin.'

Joseph led them to the river where they were allowed to wash their bodies. Seven days' perspiration was washed off using river sand as an abrasive. They returned to the fire and their bodies were smeared with fresh white clay while they stood to attention. The witch-doctor chanted as they waited for the clay to dry.

The witch-doctor slowly unwound the goatskins from their penises, hopping on stiff legs like a pied crow, his face to their crotches. With his crinkled old nose, he sniffed the wounds, smelling for signs of sepsis. Satisfied all were healing satisfactorily, he hopped back to his place near the fire, allowing the ceremony to continue. The whole roasted sheep was removed from the fire, placed on a rock and allowed to cool off.

'You have fasted for eight days under the guidance of the elder,' chanted the witch-doctor. 'You have shown your will-power by refusing to eat meat and maize, or drink beer. Your complexion will now change from youth to manhood under the white clay. You may eat. I give you permission to partake of *jisa*.'

Like vultures the five fell on the carcass. They stuffed their mouths full. They hardly chewed, swallowing the meat whole. It tasted like manna. But their stomachs had shrunk from the week of fasting and they could eat only a little.

'Go back to your hut,' instructed the witch-doctor. 'Heed the elder. Let the next part of your initiation begin.'

They followed Joseph back to the straw hut to rest. Just before sunset they heard a shrill whistle from outside the camp. 'Don't look – for it is an *intombi*. The young girl has brought your food from the village.'

The small boy walked over to a flat rock and returned with a bowl. Every morning and evening the ritual was repeated, with the girl's whistle heralding a new bowl of food. Each meal was different. They were served mealies and pumpkin, other times soup or mealies and beans, often cooked samp and occasionally crumbly porridge.

Living on a balanced diet, the young men had more energy, making excursions into the veld to hunt birds and small game. They moved around the campsite, they talked, they exercised and, most important, they built up lifelong bonds of friendship. Themba and Tommy Bakaco, the mineworker from Johannesburg, became close. Themba was fascinated by his stories of Egoli, the city of gold – how the valuable metal was extracted out of the bowels of the earth through deep shafts extending kilometres below the earth's crust.

Joseph spent hours each day explaining to them the customs, traditions and history of the Xhosa people and of the Thembu tribe in particular. They learnt etiquette, the laws of *hlonipha*, respect, and how to honour their ancestral spirits. After each session he questioned them, reinforcing all he had taught. He told them about manhood, their obligations to themselves, their families, friends and tribe; also how to choose a suitable wife, or wives if they could afford more than one. He explained how to take care of the opposite sex, how to keep them faithful and willing.

'In the Xhosa tradition, grandparents play a key role in raising the children. While you men are away earning a living with your wives, your grandparents will stay on in Thembuland and care for your children. By the time they become old and weak you will be ready to retire to your homes. By then you will also be grandparents and you will send out your children to work in the cities while you look after your grandchildren. That is how our family system works.' Joseph spat in disgust. 'The white man washes his hands of the old people and sends them to die in old-age homes. We Xhosa have more respect for our aged.'

During the day, Joseph gave individual instruction to each youth. He enjoyed his time with Themba best; they had built up a good rapport over many years.

At intervals the initiates dressed for their *amakwetha* dances. They disguised themselves with grass masks that covered their heads completely. Around their waists they wore heavy skirts of palm leaves which rustled as they demonstrated their dancing skills.

Every day the small boy repainted their skin where the clay had rubbed off to ensure that every part of their bodies would reach manhood. Christmas and New Year came and went unnoticed as the ritual continued. One day early in February Joseph announced their time had finally come.

The next morning he torched their hut. 'This part of your initiation is over. It is tradition to burn the shelter, to obliterate everything connected with your youth. Do not look back.' He led them back to Mqekezweni where the men of the tribe had gathered to welcome the five newly qualified men into their midst. It was a time of celebration.

The older men sat drinking sorghum beer, watching the Xhosa sport of stick fighting. The young braves wrapped blankets around their left hands for protection. Sticks held high, they circled each other warily, probing for an opening. Blows were parried by stick or blanket, but many struck home, often drawing blood. The spectators cheered fancy footwork and deft strokes and acclaimed the winners.

The youths washed off the white clay and the witch-doctor sat them in a row as the men crowded around. With his spear he made a cut in each one's forehead and rubbed in a black powder. 'This is to ward off evil spirits so that they will not enter your head. The powder makes you strong, as a man should be.' He looked at Joseph and nodded.

Joseph made them stand. Dabbing his fingers into a pot of soft ox-fat he smeared it straight down their bodies and across their shoulders in the shape of a cross.

A mixture of crushed red clay was mixed with water and smeared over their bodies – red indicating maturity in the Xhosa custom. Morris presented Themba with his red blanket of manhood. Themba stood tall and proud as his grandfather draped it over his head and shoulders.

The witch-doctor began his finale. 'Members of the Thembu tribe, take note. Five boys have become five men today. Henceforth they will be known as *maqualas*. Let the feast begin.'

Great quantities of beer were consumed. Sheep, goats and oxen were cooked and the men made merry. Themba drank until he staggered around in a drunken stupor. He was expected to get drunk to show off his manhood. The next morning Joseph led the hung-over new men, wrapped in their red blankets, through the village for their final test.

'You may wash off the red clay only once an unmarried girl has spoken to you. Only then are you truly a man, and can dress in men's clothes.'

Themba held his throbbing head, groaning in pain. Young girls ran up to the men taunting and teasing them, turning away quickly when the men spoke to them, entering into the spirit of the ceremony. Try as they might, the men received only a stony but amused silence from the girls.

Themba saw Hilda. 'Hullo, Hilda.'

She smiled at him, not uttering a word. He walked up to her and whispered into her ear. 'Do you want to see my restyled *tonto*?' Laughing into her hand, she simply nodded in eager agreement.

Racking his brains to make her talk to him, he asked her a quick question. 'Will you marry me one day?'

'Oh, yes!' Hilda cried in pleasure, realising too late she had spoken.

Joseph laughed uproariously. 'Themba, you may go and wash off the red paint. You are now fully qualified for manhood.'

'Mother, I can spend only one night at home. Tomorrow I must leave for Fort Hare. I'm already two weeks behind in my second year's work.'

'I understand. Your education is important.'

'I want to know about my father.' Themba watched her reactions.

'I've already told you all I know.'

'You told me my father was a Pondo called Seme, whom you met in Paarl.'

'That's right.'

'I had a dream on the mountain while we were fasting. My father spoke to me in Afrikaans.'

Nomisile looked at him in fear: she was terrified the spirits had given away her secret.

'I saw him as an illusion. He appeared as a white man.'

'No! No! No!' Nomisile cried, her worst fears coming true. Simon's image flashed before her. 'Your vision was wrong. Don't believe ghosts – believe me, I wouldn't lie to you.' Nomisile was petrified, made more scared by her outright lie.

Themba stared at his mother. 'If it's not true, why are you so overwrought?'

Desperation gave her courage. She squared her shoulders. 'If your father were a white Afrikaner, would I demand you become involved in the freedom struggle?' She stared at him belligerently, suddenly the aggressor.

'I suppose not,' Themba muttered, not so sure of himself.

'Do you look like a half-breed, Themba?' She pressed her point home.

He shook his head. 'No, Mother.'

'I tell you here and now, you're a full-blooded Xhosa. I hear the Paramount Chief wants you to join his council. Do you think he would invite you if he thought you were not a true Thembu?'

'No, Mother.'

'Well, then, enough of this nonsense talk. Accept your father was Seme. Be grateful he made you a strong, healthy and clever man.'

The room was quiet as the two students concentrated on their studies. Pierre pushed back his chair. 'Time for a coffee break.'

Danie Conradie looked up, smiling. 'We work too hard.'

'All work and no play makes Johnny a very dull boy. Let's do something different.'

'Do you know what?' Danie looked at Pierre excitedly. 'Parliament opens tomorrow. My father can organise us places in the public gallery.'

The idea appealed to Pierre. 'I've never been to parliament, even though both my grandfather and father were members.'

'Perhaps we can also wangle an invitation to the Prime Minister's cocktail party in the evening.'

'Gets better and better,' laughed Pierre.

*   *   *

251

The sergeant-at-arms pasted blue stickers on their suit lapels, allowing them to enter parliament. Pierre watched the pomp and splendour of the opening ceremony in Parliament Street, thinking back to his grandfather Paulus and his father Simon who had actually been part of it all many times. The horse-drawn carriage stopped in front of the building and Prime Minister John Vorster and his wife Tienie, made their way to the steps of parliament. Vorster looked impassive, with his heavy jowls and large head. Over his shoulder he wore the embroidered red sash of office. Everyone stood to attention as the national anthem, '*Die Stem*', was played by the naval band.

From near the back of the crowd Pierre cast his eyes over the smartly dressed MPs and their wives. A young brunette in a red dress caught his eye. She must have felt Pierre's stare, for she looked back at him with a smile of acknowledgement.

'Who's the woman in the red dress?' Pierre asked Danie in a whisper.

'Don't know, but we can find out if you're interested.'

The parliamentarians filed into the main chamber of the House of Assembly. The sergeant-at-arms led the visitors up to the gallery and supervised the seating.

Danie turned to the official. 'The young lady in the red dress over there. My friend would like to know who she is.'

'I'll find out, sir.'

Silence settled as the Prime Minister rose to address the House, outlining his objectives for the coming parliamentary session.

Pierre, sitting near the back, hardly heard a word. His attention was on the brunette. Her face was covered by a wide-brimmed hat, but every now and again she looked around and he saw the perfection of her features. He smiled when she looked his way again. She smiled back shyly.

After the official opening the guests left by the side entrance. Danie and Pierre held back and were the last to be checked out by the sergeant-at-arms.

'Did you find out about the woman in the red dress?' Pierre asked.

'She's Rika Bosch, the daughter of the Nationalist member for Gordonia, Mr Wagner Bosch.'

Danie turned to Pierre jokingly. 'There's a good Afrikaner girl who'll make you forget your English rose.'

'Do you think she'll be at the cocktail party tonight?'

'I know her father's a widower. She'll most likely accompany him again.'

The two students drove up to the suburb of Gardens, where Danie's parents lived in a flat. 'Thanks for organising the invitations to the cocktail party, Dad. We're looking forward to mixing with the decision-makers of the day.'

'Your mother and I won't be going.' Nicolaas Conradie smiled at his son. 'Send my greetings to PW – tell him I'll see him at our meeting tomorrow morning.'

'What is PW Botha like as a man?' Pierre asked.

'Remarkable in many ways. His passion is the defence force, which he intends building into the most potent fighting force on the continent. He fervently believes that a strong, well-armed South Africa is the only answer to the ANC and their military wing, MK.'

'Is the threat real?'

'Of course, Pierre. I can't disclose military details, but the only way for the white man to survive in this country is to be well prepared – to fight fire with conflagration, guns with cannons and grenades with bombs.'

'Isn't there another way, a political solution perhaps?'

'We've given the black people their say in their own homelands, but that's not good enough for the ANC – they want the whole cake – they want to rule South Africa and force the white man into a minor role in the country of his birth. We can't allow that.'

'Which makes PW Botha an important part of our future.'

'It certainly does, and the ANC hate him.'

'Time to change.' Danie stood up. 'We don't want to keep the Prime Minister waiting!'

'We're dressed to kill, but do we have to arrive at a grand do in your battered little Volkswagen?' Pierre laughed. 'I should have asked my father to lend us his new Mercedes!'

On either side of the entrance to Groote Schuur Estate stood two guards' houses which were manned around the clock by armed police. Used to admitting VIPs in large continental saloons, the police approached the battered Volkswagen with suspicion. Danie rolled down the driver's window.

'You two wouldn't be trying to gate-crash would you? Please get out of the car so we can search you.' Danie proffered the printed cards. 'Here are our invitations.'

The officer examined them carefully. 'They seem in order. Please produce proof of your identity.' They produced their ID cards and the officer compared them with their photographs. He ticked their names off his official list. 'All right, gentlemen, enjoy the party.'

Pierre was used to the opulence of Hermitage, but Groote Schuur was so much larger, more luxuriant and lavish. The gracious Cape-Dutch home stood on the site of a grain store dating back to the 1600s, hence its name, the great barn. Sir Herbert Baker had designed the house for Cecil Rhodes; now it was the official residence of the prime ministers of South Africa. The rooms were filled with priceless antiques and paintings by famous artists.

They presented their cards and their names were read aloud.

'Mr Daniël Broodryk Conradie.'

'Mr Pierre Jan Roux.'

The guests clapped as they walked down the centre of the room. Pierre came face to face with the Prime Minister for the first time.

'Who is your father?' Vorster looked at him intently.

'Simon Roux, from Paarl.'

'This apple didn't fall far from the tree!' Vorster smiled. 'You look just like your father, my boy. He served under me in parliament, I know him well. We had our differences over sports policy, but he was right after all. As you know, our national and international events are now multiracial, exactly as Simon Roux proposed way back in 1967. Give him my regards, will you?'

'Yes, sir. I will.'

The two moved away and into the crowd. A waiter offered them champagne, another a caviar canapé. 'Everyone of importance is here tonight,' breathed Danie in wonder. 'Look, there's my father's boss, PW Botha.'

Pierre saw a tall, bald man with glasses. He also saw Rika Bosch looking demurely at him. He blushed in confusion, holding the half-eaten biscuit in one hand and the glass of champagne in the other. She came across to him and a smile played at the corner of her mouth. She held out her hand. 'Hullo, I'm Rika Bosch.'

Pierre blushed deeper, not having a free hand. Hurriedly, he popped the rest of the caviar into his mouth, grimacing at the taste. To his chagrin, it stuck in his throat and he quickly downed the champagne to wash it down. Nervously he transferred the glass to his left hand, but lost his grip. The glass fell to the marble floor and shattered. People turned to look and Pierre wished the floor would open up and swallow him. He had never been so embarrassed before. Waiters rushed across to sweep up the shards.

Danie moved away and Pierre was left alone in his discomfort. People around them saw the humour of the situation and smiled in sympathy. Pierre turned on his heel and walked quickly towards the door.

He heard light footsteps following him and felt a restraining hand on his arm. It was Rika. 'Don't go,' she urged. 'It was only a small accident.'

Pierre glanced around the room. Everyone was busy; no one was looking at him, the incident forgotten. He stopped, turning to her. 'I'm sorry,' he stammered. 'I feel like a clumsy fool.'

'Let's start again.' She extended her right hand. 'Hi! I'm Rika Bosch.'

'I know who you are. I'm Pierre Roux.' She really was attractive, he thought, looking into her face.

'How do you know who I am?'

'We asked the sergeant-at-arms at parliament this afternoon. He told us.'

'So, you've been spying on me?'

Danie came up to them, giggling. 'I've never laughed so much in all my life. You were a scream, Pierre. Much better than Laurel and Hardy!'

'Thanks. With a friend like you, who needs enemies!' Pierre relaxed for the first time. Turning to Rika, he placed the blame squarely on his friend's shoulders. 'It was his idea to ask the sergeant-at-arms to find out your name.'

'The plot thickens. You find out my name, but I don't even know yours.' She laughed, showing dazzling white, perfectly formed teeth.

'Sorry.' Pierre blushed again. 'Let me introduce you to my room-mate, Danie Conradie. We're together in Wilgenhof, at Stellenbosch University.'

She shook Danie's hand. 'Maties, hey?' She sounded impressed. 'Are you also rugger buggers?'

'I play rugby for Wilgenhof in the hostel league.' Danie was trying to impress her.

255

'What about you, Pierre?'

'No, I don't play rugby. I'm more interested in athletics.'

'I know. I read a write-up on you in the newspaper last week. I recognise you from your photograph.'

'I run the eight hundred metres.' He was on familiar terrain once again. The worst had passed.

A deep voice boomed behind them. 'Yes, my girl, and who are your two admirers?'

'Daddy, this is Pierre Roux and this is Danie, sorry Danie, what's your surname again?'

'Conradie.'

'Danie Conradie. This is my father, Wagner Bosch.'

The four stood talking while the band struck up with some soft music. People started to dance.

Danie butted in. 'May I have the pleasure of a dance, Rika?'

She looked at Pierre but he was in deep conversation with her father, and she reluctantly accepted Danie's offer. Pierre and Wagner had found something in common, a shared passion – the Kalahari. Wagner had grown up in the Upington area and he knew the Roux farm, Doornrivier.

'Your grandfather bought the farm from old Frikkie Reitz. He was my predecessor as MP for Gordonia. I knew him well, he died only last year at Hermanus.'

'My grandfather also died. Now my father Simon runs Hermitage in Paarl and Doornrivier.'

'I know your father. We were back-benchers together in Verwoerd's day. How are he and your mother?'

'My father is fine, but my mother is confined to a wheelchair. She was paralysed in the Poqo riots in Paarl in 1962.'

'I also lost my wife a few years ago. Now all I have left is my daughter. Rika is the most important person in the world to me.'

'Do you farm in Upington, sir?'

'I have a farm near Louisvale. We farm wine grapes and sultanas, but I have a very good manager who runs the farm so that I can spend six months of the year in Cape Town at parliament.'

Danie and Rika returned, but Pierre and Wagner were still so engrossed discussing a springbok hunt that they hardly noticed their arrival.

'I go with my father to the Kalahari at least once a year. We never miss the winter hunt. Being in those sand dunes and

256

the wide open spaces does something for one's soul,' enthused Pierre.

An official interrupted the conversation. 'Mr Bosch, the Prime Minister requests the company of you and your daughter.'

'Duty calls; we'll continue the conversation later.' Wagner led Rika away. She gave Pierre a forlorn look over her shoulder. Out of earshot, her father said to her, 'Rika, I've just met the first man I would consider acceptable enough to marry you.'

'Who would that be?' she asked, all innocence, but she could not help feeling excited when he put into words the nagging attraction she felt.

'Pierre Roux. His background is impeccable, he's a very presentable young man and he appreciates all the things I hold dear.'

Danie and Pierre watched the Bosches walk away. Rika's dark-brown shoulder-length hair glistened in the light. Her curvaceous body filled her long evening gown to perfection, her hips swayed voluptuously as she walked. The slit in the side of her dress opened sufficiently to display well-formed calves.

'Wow! Isn't she sexy?' breathed Danie.

Pierre looked at him sharply. 'I thought I was supposed to get keen on an Afrikaner girl.'

'Look, at least you've met a girl whom you want, even though she is English. Rika's mine; I'm bewitched. She's the woman of my dreams.'

'May the best man win,' declared Pierre.

'I'm your room-mate, you can't double-cross your best friend.' He looked at Pierre with a pleading expression.

Pierre laughed, nodded, and a truce was struck. 'Okay Danie, I'll back off. She's yours.'

'Good evening, Danie.'

PW Botha was smiling at him. 'Good evening, *oom* PW.' He used the term 'uncle' in Afrikaans as a mark of respect towards an older person.

'Enjoying yourself, my boy?'

'Very much. May I introduce you to my Matie room-mate. This is Pierre Roux.' The two shook hands. Pierre was introduced to his wife, Elize, a plump, motherly woman. Pierre was finding his rhythm in the exalted company. He was at ease talking to the Minister of Defence. They talked about his father and grandfather, who seemed to be his passport to acceptance in the parliamentary hierarchy.

'What are you studying?' Botha asked.

'Law, sir. I would like to qualify as a lawyer, then follow my grandfather's, and father's footsteps into parliament.'

'I'm glad to hear that. It's important that capable young men join our battle against the dark forces lining up against us.' Pierre nodded and moved to one side.

Danie and PW were in animated conversation, talking war strategies. Pierre stood listening. He felt a light touch on his arm. It was Rika, smiling at him. Danie noticed, too, but continued his discussion, not wanting to interrupt his father's boss.

Rika smiled coyly. 'Don't you want to ask me to dance?'

Pierre looked at Danie, who shrugged casually. 'Sure, let's dance.' A slow number was playing. Pierre held her at arm's length, playing the part of the impeccable gentleman. He felt Rika snuggle into him and smelt the musky scent of her perfume, a heady fragrance acting like an aphrodisiac. Then he remembered his promise to Danie and he moved away from her.

'Don't play hard to get,' she whispered. 'Just hold me properly.' She put her arm around his neck and pressed her body against him. He smelt the bouquet of apple shampoo as her hair brushed across his face. Lifting her head, she looked up at him with an unmistakable expression of desire. She closed her eyes. Pierre felt himself drawn irresistibly closer until their lips brushed. It was electrifying and the sensation brought him to his senses. He pushed her away brusquely. Looking guiltily over her shoulder he saw Danie watching them intently, the hurt showing on his face as he continued to talk to PW.

'What's the matter, Pierre? Don't you like me?'

'Of course, but I hardly know you. Things are moving too fast.'

They danced around the floor, gliding in sweeping circles, the band playing softly. From the other side of the hall the backdrop of voices made a humming sound. They danced in a world of their own, oblivious to their surroundings. When the music stopped Pierre and Rika separated to applaud the band.

By chance he looked towards a side entrance as an impeccably dressed black man entered. He was dressed in a dinner jacket and carried a tray of drinks. Something looked familiar about the man. Pierre concentrated on him, frowning. Suddenly recognition hit him like a hammer blow. Jafta from Hermitage? Older and greyer but definitely Jafta! What was he doing here? He was supposed to have fled the country and joined the ANC in exile.

A sickening thought struck Pierre. Umkhonto we Sizwe? Assassination? Yes! Who? The Prime Minister? He turned in horror as Jafta stopped behind PW Botha, slipped his hand into the inside of his jacket and slowly withdrew it. Pierre glanced around desperately. Only he was aware of the danger. Bodyguards stood lackadaisically against the walls.

Pierre made up his mind. He took off, sprinting as fast as he could. He was still five paces away when he saw a metallic glint inside the jacket. His loud footsteps pounding on the hard floor alerted the guests. They turned around in surprise, watching as the drama unfolded. First to react were the bodyguards. Jafta had his back to them so they did not see the weapon. Instead they concentrated on Pierre, angling to cut him off. He was still three paces away when the heavy calibre pistol come free of Jafta's jacket.

Danie saw Pierre coming and his eyes grew larger. Had Pierre gone mad? Botha, seeing Danie's startled expression, turned around and gasped as he saw a pistol aimed at his midriff. The muscles on Jafta's right index finger tightened as he pulled the trigger.

The next fraction of an instant was a blur. Pierre took off, his shoulder crashing into Jafta's upper body. Jafta yielded and a shot exploded. Pierre smelt the pungent odour of gunpowder. There was a burning pain in his shoulder. Together they crashed to the floor. A second shot went off. People screamed in panic, scurrying out of the way. Guards reached the two writhing men. Another shot went off, narrowly missing a guard. Plaster showered from the moulded ceiling. Then the guards were on him, pinning him down.

Jafta fought like one berserk, kicking and thrashing. Eventually he was overpowered and a Makarov pistol was wrenched from his grasp.

Pierre slid to one side, face down, blood running like quicksilver globules across the highly polished marble slabs. A guard turned him over; the front of his dinner jacket was soaked in blood, his white shirt streaked with red.

Botha fell to his knees next to Pierre's inert body. He grasped quickly that Pierre had taken two bullets intended for him. Deep appreciation and concern showed on his face.

A doctor rushed across and examined Pierre. 'He must get to

hospital immediately. He has two wounds, one in the left shoulder, the other in his lung.'

Guests crowded around, jostling each other to obtain a view. Rika crept along the floor. She forced her way between legs and reached Pierre. She called to him. 'Pierre! Pierre!'

Botha spoke urgently to his bodyguard. 'Take him to 2 Military hospital in Wynberg. Use my official car. I want this brave man to get the best treatment. I'll phone the hospital from here.'

Four bodyguards removed platters of food from a trestle table and used the top as a stretcher, gently placing Pierre on the table cloth. He lay unmoving as they rushed him outside and transferred him to the back of the car.

Jafta was manhandled out of the room. Waiters wiped the floor clean and within minutes all signs of an attempted assassination were obliterated. The guests huddled in small groups, chattering excitedly about the incident.

Rika stood next to Danie. 'I do hope Pierre will be all right. He looked so pale as they carried him out.'

'Pierre's a national hero; he saved PW Botha's life. Wait until you read tomorrow's newspapers.'

Botha looked at them, his face turning ashen. 'We can't allow that – our enemies will claim it as a moral victory. Imagine how the overseas newspapers will ridicule us. I must speak to Vorster.'

The Prime Minister sat at the top table, still shaky from the drama, hunched forward, his heavy features scowling darkly. Botha faced John Vorster over the table. 'Mr Prime Minister, you must make an announcement demanding everyone in this room keeps tonight's incident a secret. It comes too soon after Dr Verwoerd's assassination. It will be lauded overseas by the enemies of the State.'

Vorster nodded sagely and walked to the microphone. 'Ladies and gentlemen, we all know the forces stacked against us – the communists and the ANC. They would have a field day if they learnt of tonight's assassination attempt. It was a black man, using a Russian pistol, so we can assume the would-be killer is a trained Umkhonto we Sizwe hitman. Let us keep tonight's events between ourselves to protect the good name of our government and country.'

There was spontaneous applause. Elize took her husband's hand. 'You were lucky tonight. The gunman was at point-blank range. I very nearly lost you. Pierre Roux is a brave young man, offering his life for yours. I hope God protects him and brings him through.'

'You're right, my dear. I'm going to stay with him until he recovers consciousness.'

'Shouldn't we let Simon and Helena know?'

'Not yet. The fewer who know at this stage, the better.'

'Welcome, sir!' The officer saluted and opened the boom gate. As Botha strode through the front door, hospital staff ran forward and escorted him to the emergency section. Botha smiled in satisfaction. Military police had blocked off the passages to all unauthorised persons. He glanced through the small windows in the doors of the operating theatre.

A nurse spotted him through the glass. She nudged a surgeon who joined PW in the foyer. 'Good evening, Minister.' He pulled off rubber gloves.

'Hullo, doctor. Give me the news.'

'In a nut-shell, he's out of danger.'

Botha sighed with relief, the tension leaving his shoulders as he slumped into a chair. While they spoke, Pierre was rolled out of the operating theatre to intensive care, still anaesthetised.

'When will he come round?'

'In about an hour's time.'

'Will he have permanent damage?'

'I don't think so. He's young and strong which counts greatly in his favour. Scar tissue maybe, but no lasting damage.'

'Thank God for that,' breathed Botha.

A permanent sister was allocated to Pierre as he hovered between waking and unconsciousness. When he came around properly the next morning he was stiff and sore, unable to move. 'Water! Water!' The nurse tipped up his head and let him sip. He slept until lunch-time, dreaming of Jafta, seeing him as he remembered him – the trusty farm worker with a ready smile. He woke with a start, his dream blending with his conscious thoughts, still disorientated.

'Do my parents know?' he asked the sister.

'I don't know, it's out of our hands. You're classified top secret. You must speak to the superintendent.' Pierre nodded, but his lids drooped and he slipped away again.

Feeling a kiss on his lips, he opened his eyes. 'Rika, how did you get in?'

The sister diplomatically left the ward.

'I told them I was your fiancée. I even showed my ring to prove it.' Rika smiled at him triumphantly.

Pierre was puzzled. 'What ring?'

'This one.' She laughed, and lifting up her left hand showed him a large diamond ring on her finger. 'It was my late mother's. Dad keeps it in his wardrobe, so I borrowed it for the occasion.'

'What time is it?'

'Three o'clock in the afternoon.'

'What did the newspapers say about the incident?'

'Nothing, absolutely nothing.' She told him about the request for complete secrecy. 'There's not a word on the street. My dad tells me everyone's keeping mum. I'm afraid you're an unsung hero!'

He nodded. 'What brings you here? You're Danie's girl.'

'Nonsense.'

'Danie and I have an agreement. He wants you. I agreed to lay off.'

'So, that's why you were so cool on the dance floor. I wondered.' She tossed her head angrily. 'Well, let me tell you, I won't allow you two to make agreements about me. Danie isn't my type.'

'And me?'

'Let's say I'm intrigued at this stage.' She smiled tentatively. 'Do you have a girlfriend?'

Pierre laughed sadly. 'Sort of. I'm crazy about her, but she's got a thing about Afrikaners. If she knew I saved PW's life last night, she'd dislike me even more.'

'What sort of woman would dislike Afrikaners?'

'An English-speaking girl who believes passionately in the rights of the black man.'

'Then she's not your type, Pierre. You are an Afrikaner, whichever way you look at it, with a Nationalist background.'

The sister returned. 'I think you should go now. We don't want to tire him.'

'Won't you please just let me say goodbye to my fiancé alone?'

The sister smiled in understanding and walked out. 'Don't be long, and be gentle with him.'

'I fully intend to, sister.'

Pierre glanced at Rika. 'You're a very forward lady.'

'I know what I want from life and I intend to get it.' She kissed him on the mouth.

'Hey! Don't kiss me like that. My mouth tastes like the bottom of a parrot's cage and I don't even have a toothbrush.'

'I'll bring you one tomorrow.'

'Will you really come again tomorrow?'

'Wild horses wouldn't keep me away.'

'Why?' Pierre asked, frowning.

'Because I want to be with you, that's why. Anything wrong with that?'

'I find it very disturbing in a way.'

She gave him a lingering kiss to dispel his doubts, then left with a casual wave. 'See you tomorrow.'

On the fourth day, Botha visited Pierre. 'How are you feeling, my boy?'

'Much better, thank you, sir. The doctor says I'll be out in three days.'

'Last time I saw you, you were still confused from the anaesthetic. I want to thank you from the bottom of my heart for your brave deed. That I'm alive is due entirely to you. You have my assurance that I will always help you, in any way, in your life or career.'

'Thank you, sir, I appreciate that very much.'

'The terrorist who tried to murder me is a certain Jafta Nkosi. We made him talk. It seems he worked on your father's farm up until he left the country.'

Pierre nodded. 'I recognised him when he walked into the room. Luckily it was Jafta and not some stranger who tried to assassinate you, otherwise I wouldn't have noticed.'

'He's a top MK operative. He's had military training in Tanzania and Russia. We have still to decide what to do with him; he'll probably be tried in camera for political crimes.'

'My parents, do they know what's happened?'

'One of my confidants, an army general, went to see them. They're looking forward to having you at home for a few weeks while you recuperate fully before returning to Stellenbosch. They send their love.'

'Thank you.'

'I believe Wagner Bosch's daughter visits you every day.' Botha had a twinkle in his eye. 'She's quite resourceful. We checked, you're not engaged, but somehow she managed to twist the military police around her little finger.'

Pierre smiled. 'She's becoming very possessive, but she's the only visitor I'm allowed. They wouldn't let Danie Conradie visit me.'

'I'll arrange it with the superintendent. Danie was at the cocktail party, so he knows the circumstances. I must go; look after yourself, Roux.'

'I appreciate your visit, sir.'

'I'm glad to see you are better. Remember my promise, I'm indebted to you. By the way, Rika is a fine girl. You can't go wrong there.'

Danie winked at Pierre as he slipped a six-pack into Pierre's bedside cabinet. 'Why drink water when you can drink beer? Should help you pass a lonely evening!'

'Thanks, Danie.'

'Last time I saw you I thought you were dead – now at least you're sitting up and the colour's back in your cheeks.'

'PW Botha was here yesterday.'

'Have *you* made a good impression! PW worships the ground you walk on. He told my father he's prepared to do anything for you. You're fortunate to have such a powerful godfather.'

Rika breezed in. She embraced Pierre, ignoring Danie, and planted a kiss on his lips. 'Hullo, treasure, how are we today?'

Concern showed on Danie's face. 'So, it's treasure already? I can't see you until today, but in the meantime you two seem to have become very well acquainted.'

'It's not what you think, Danie. There's nothing between Rika and myself, we're just friends.'

'Why does she call you treasure?' Danie spoke with bitterness.

'I've no idea. Why don't you ask her?'

She turned on Danie, bright spots of indignation reddening her cheeks, making her look very alluring. 'You don't own me, Danie. I don't have to give you any explanation. You pester me day and night on the telephone, but it's Pierre I'm attracted to.'

Danie looked from Pierre to Rika, shaking his head sadly. He walked slowly from the ward, his shoulders down. Pierre felt sorry for him.

'Come back, Danie. She's talking nonsense. There's nothing between us.'

He turned in the doorway and looked intently at Rika, who burst into tears. 'Pierre, how can you say such awful things?'

'Because it's true.'

She saw his uncompromising expression. She brushed past Danie and ran sobbing from the room.

Pierre pointed down the passage. 'Go after her, Danie. If you really want her, don't let her get away.'

13

A large coral tree threw dappled shade over the lawn as a light breeze rustled the leaves. Flat on his stomach, revising his political science notes for a test, Themba lay concentrating. A shadow fell over his books. He looked up in surprise. 'Hullo, Muriel.'

'Morning, Mr High-and-Mighty bookworm, always studying,' she taunted in her arrogant voice. 'Don't you know you have to relax sometimes?'

Themba smiled at her. 'I'm catching up to you fast, Miss Tabule. In the last test I was only five per cent below you.'

He looked at her critically. She was not a classic beauty, but she had an alluring power, sometimes beautiful from one angle, then ugly from another. Her body language made her attractive. She articulated with her hands and her inner vitality showed itself in her actions – restless and quick, energetic and compelling. Her eyes were alive; she almost seemed to speak with them. She was tall for a woman, and well-proportioned. She was without a bra and her nipples showed through her thin blouse, her breasts small and firm. Themba watched her mouth as she spoke, showing her even teeth and full, sensuous lips.

He was aroused and she knew it. She strutted sexily, throwing back her shoulders to accentuate her breasts. 'What are you doing tonight, Themba?'

'Studying as usual.'

'Come to a meeting with me.'

'What sort of meeting. Where?'

'It's a secret MK meeting. I'll take you there.'

'You know I can't get involved while I'm still at university. Once I have my degrees it'll be different.'

'You're a wimp. Our people suffer every day from the cruelties of the regime and you, grand Mr Memani, think only of your own glory.'

'It's not like that!'

'Of course, it is. There are only two kinds of people – those who do something and those who do nothing.'

'What about sympathisers?'

'They sit on the fence. They don't have the courage of their convictions. Are you one of those, Themba?' Muriel examined him disdainfully, her mouth pouting in disgust, her eyes admonishing.

'I *do* care, I care very much.'

'Then you'll go tonight?'

He cursed inwardly. Muriel had a way of needling him and Themba was stung to retaliation. 'Okay, I'll go.'

'Good, I'll meet you in front of Wesley at seven o'clock.' She turned and walked away, her hips swaying in defiance, her bottom doing justice to her tight skirt.

What a woman, mused Themba. A human dynamo, pumping out power for the cause. She stayed in his thoughts the whole day. He started looking forward to the evening.

When Themba went downstairs, Muriel was already waiting. They walked in silence for a while in the gathering dusk; suddenly she grabbed his arm and yanked him sideways. 'Through here.' They scuttled up the driveway of a house, past the garage, over the back fence and through the yard of the house behind. A dog charged them, but they made it to the next street in time. They walked down the parallel street.

Themba turned to her in surprise. 'What was that all about?'

'Security police. We can't be too careful. If they tail us to the meeting they could catch our comrades.'

Three more times Muriel led Themba on a detour, each time stopping in the shadows to make sure they were not being followed. They entered the black township and made their way to a house in the side streets. Muriel knocked three times and the door opened slightly. Themba heard her whisper 'Mary Toto' and they were admitted.

The small room was filled with smoke. The men were drinking beer out of quart bottles. Muriel was the only woman among thirty men. Everyone talked in muted voices so that the noise did not carry down the street.

'Who is Mary Toto?' Themba asked in a whisper.

Muriel laughed. 'That's my MK name. Everyone here knows me as Mary Toto. We do it to hide our identities from the police. If any one of us is caught then all he or she can disclose are false names, and nobody can be arrested.'

Themba nodded at the wisdom of the system. 'Who did you say I was?'

'I said you were Philips Makeba.'

'Why such an unusual name?'

'Philips is a type of radio set which plays beautiful music. I think we're going to play beautiful music.' She rubbed against him suggestively. 'The Makeba comes from Miriam Makeba, because she sings such beautiful songs.'

Themba smiled in anticipation. 'Sounds like a whole symphony to me! When do we get to play this special music?'

'Our time will come.' Muriel fluttered her eyelashes. 'Maybe sooner than you think.' Before he could reply she slipped away maddeningly to speak to a man on the opposite side of the room.

Themba bought a quart of Lion Lager for each of them as they waited expectantly for the meeting to start. Eventually the door opened and two men darted inside. Another man slipped out to act as guard.

The MK commander rose to speak. 'Comrades, our guest tonight is a gentleman who only last year was released from Robben Island. He has travelled from the Transvaal at personal risk to himself, as he is under house arrest at present. I give you Comrade Indres Naidoo.'

A tall bearded Indian stood up. He had a sensitive mouth and soulful brown eyes. He spoke in a soothing voice. 'Comrades, I was incarcerated for ten years on Robben Island. In 1963 I was caught for blowing up a signal box next to the railway line, north of Johannesburg. The security police beat me up and tortured me mercilessly. I was shipped to the island to rot as a political prisoner.'

He paused. 'Even after ten years of hell, I would do it all over again for the ANC. Our struggle is your struggle, your struggle is the struggle of every repressed person in South Africa. We must bring the regime of the white supremacists to an end so that the majority may govern. Then, and only then, will our country experience true peace and democracy.'

He took a sip of water. 'On Robben Island we gained strength and inspiration from each other. The island has become a bastion of hope for downtrodden people all over the world.'

His voice rose. 'I call on you here in Alice tonight to be strong for our cause. Never give in. The white Nationalist government is powerful and wily. Only by supreme effort, from every one of us, will our dreams be realised. I have served my time, now it is the next generation's turn to serve the cause. Remember, to be caught and jailed is not a disgrace. It is a legitimate part of the battle against suppression. Apartheid must be crushed for ever.'

'*Amandla!*' shouted the gathering, their fervour growing.

Muriel breathed fiercely. 'I'm so fired up, I want to do something tonight.'

Themba turned to her in surprise and saw a wildness in her eyes. He spoke quietly. 'What did you have in mind, Muriel?'

'I don't know, but I'll soon find out. Get us another beer while I speak to Indres.' Muriel wormed her way to the front and Themba saw her in animated conversation with the guest speaker. He sipped his beer, starting to feel light-headed.

Muriel returned, bubbling with enthusiasm. 'I'm going to devote my life to the struggle.'

Themba was feeling decidedly drunk. 'Let's go. It's almost eleven o'clock.'

'Just give me a minute.' Muriel disappeared into the crowd and returned a few minutes later. 'All set, let's go.'

Together they walked, arms about each other for support. They left the township and headed for the university. She stopped him. 'This way,' and turned in the opposite direction.

'Where are we going?'

'To the railway line to blow up a signal box.'

Themba's brain was fuzzy. 'Blow up a signal box? Ha! Ha! With what?' He laughed uproariously.

'Shh! Be quiet. With this.' She took a stick of dynamite from her blouse. Themba examined the waxy brown tube.

'Dynamite!' He whistled in surprise. 'Where did this come from?'

'A friend gave it to me,' she said proudly. 'We attach the dynamite below the signal box with the tape.'

Themba saw she was deadly serious. Something told him they were being foolhardy, but the beer turned him into a daredevil. 'Okay, let's do it.'

Hand in hand they ran to the deserted railway station. They walked along the platform looking for a likely target. Down the track they saw a signal box. 'This is just perfect.' Muriel breathed excitedly, her warm breath coming in little gasps. 'Help me, Themba.'

They strapped the stick of dynamite to the bottom of the box with insulation tape, allowing the fuse to hang down. Muriel struck a match, but the flame was blown out by the wind. She tried again.

'You have to cup your hands to protect the flame.'

'You do it then.'

They were so engrossed they did not hear the patrol van approaching. Themba struck the match, shielding the flame. With a splutter the fuse ignited, giving off an acrid smoke. 'Run, get out of here!'

As they turned to run along the track, headlights swept across the veld towards them. Themba saw the blue light on top of the cab. 'Police, the police are here!' He pulled Muriel down, not ten paces from the burning fuse. The spluttering flame burnt brightly, giving off a cloud of sulphurous smoke. He watched the flame devouring the unburned section like a voracious animal. The arc of headlights was almost upon them.

The headlights fell full square on the spot where they lay. The police would surely see the swirling smoke and the two of them lying next to the track. Themba held his breath. They swept on past them, heading further along the track. Themba let out a moan of relief. He looked at the fuse. The coiled parts had burnt away. It was on the final stretch to detonation.

He pulled Muriel to her feet. Both sides of the track were lined with high-security fencing. Further down the track was the police vehicle. Themba's mind was clear; he had sobered up quickly. The only escape route left to them was back past the spluttering fuse, towards the station. Steeling his nerves he pulled her past the signal box. He dared not look. They stumbled and fell over the raised railway sleepers. The coarse gravel twisted at their ankles. Muriel fell, but Themba grasped her hand harder, dragging her along until she regained her feet.

She cursed, 'For chrissake, man . . .'

A whoosh of air flung them to the ground as the dynamite exploded. The signal box shattered, blasting shrapnel in all directions. The noise of the discharge hammered at Themba's eardrums.

271

He shook his head to clear his brain, holding his nose and blowing to free his ears.

Themba looked back dazedly. The signal box had disappeared. Ruptured electric cables stuck out of the ground, sparking wildly. He saw the police van roaring back towards them, lights flashing, siren wailing.

'Quick, we must get away from here!' Themba jerked Muriel to her feet. They scrambled on to the platform as the police van pulled to a screeching halt outside the station, its headlights shining through the open entrance arch. He heard the vehicle door slam and footsteps running up the outer steps.

Themba was panic-stricken. He tried a toilet door. To his relief it opened and they slipped inside. He closed the door quietly as a policeman drew level. They heard the snatch of a conversation.

'Did you get them on the radio?'

'Back-up's on its way.'

Within minutes there was the sound of more sirens and vehicles converging on the station. Heavy boots clattered down the platform.

Themba and Muriel crept into the end toilet cubicle in the semi-dark and closed the door. The half walls were level with the top of the doors, the cubicles open on top. At the bottom there was a gap below the door.

How did I get into this? Themba wondered. I promised my mother and Paul I would let nothing jeopardise my education.

Muriel was pushing up against Themba. She pulled his head down, kissing him, her tongue seeking his, highly aroused by the fear of discovery and unworried by their precarious position. A true revolutionary on a high from the danger.

Themba was in a cold sweat. He listened to the footfalls rushing backwards and forwards along the platform. Voices shouted instructions. Chaos reigned outside and there were only two flimsy doors between them, arrest, torture and incarceration. Their hiding place was so obvious – it was a wonder the toilets had not yet been searched.

'They must have got away,' a man outside the toilet shouted.

Another voice interrupted. 'We've checked up the line for almost a kilometre, there's no sign of anyone.'

'They're not down the line either.'

'Check all the station buildings, just in case.'

Themba went cold. Discovery was imminent. There was no place to hide. They were trapped in their cell. He stood on the toilet seat and crouched down. He pulled Muriel on to his lap. He felt her respond to his touch, breathing hard. The front door crashed open, torchlight spraying weird patterns against the walls. 'This is a whites' toilet; they won't be here.'

'Don't count on it; today's damn kaffirs think they are white.'

Themba froze as the door of the first cubicle was flung open. 'Nothing here.' The second door crashed open. Holding his hand over Muriel's face, he pulled tight to stop her loud breathing. A pool of light played around the floor as a policeman bent down and shone his torch under the doors.

'I see nothing here; the place is deserted.'

'Let's just make sure.' The third toilet door banged open. They were next. Themba was numb with fear. He had to fight Muriel as she wriggled against his hand, struggling for breath. Steps approached their door. Should he run? He answered the question himself. There are too many of them – they'll shoot me down like a rabid dog.

'Sergeant,' a voice called from the platform.

'I'm in here, in the women's toilets.'

Themba heard a hand on the handle. It started to turn, the door opened slowly. Themba watched stupefied, unable to move. He held his breath.

'Sergeant, we've found a man in the baggage room.'

'Good, I'm coming.' The door handle was released. It turned and clicked back into place.

Themba released his hand over Muriel's mouth. She gulped air into her burning lungs, turning frenzied eyes on him. Their miraculous escape fanned her desires. She pushed forwards, forcing her breasts against his hands, almost savagely encouraging him to squeeze harder and harder. He covered her mouth to silence her groaning. She raised herself and undid the buttons of his trousers.

He lay half backwards as she stood over him, legs apart, moving up and down. He could feel himself deep inside her. She stiffened as she came, oblivious to the policemen on the platform – totally consumed by her passion and fired by the excitement of the night. As she opened her mouth to scream, Themba stifled her with his hand, letting go only when he was satisfied her rapture had passed.

Muriel was insatiable, her appetite for sex ferocious and nymphomanic. Themba could hold out no longer. He felt himself expand, setting her off again as he exploded in his own coming. To prevent them both crying out he covered her mouth with his, each one's throat absorbing the other's fervour as a rush of air escaped through their nostrils.

Outside the station grew quiet. The long night dragged on until at last dawn lit the room. They were intimate again, this time slowly and more deliberately. Muriel, considerate and gentle, awakened love in Themba. He could hardly believe it was the same woman as before. As he climaxed, he whispered to her, 'I love you, Muriel.'

The next morning a train puffed into the station and squealed to a halt. Themba moved to the main door and peeped out. The platform was full of people moving to and from the train. He called to Muriel, 'Now is our chance.' As the crowd surged past the door they slipped out and mingled with them unnoticed. Themba glanced down the track to where the signal box had been. The area was cordoned off and workmen were busy with repairs. He fought down rising panic as two policemen blocked the station entrance – checking the commuters' bags and parcels. He wanted to turn and run, but thought of his initiation days when his will-power had been tested three times. He squeezed Muriel's hand to reassure her. 'They don't suspect us,' he whispered. 'Just keep walking.'

The police waved them through. 'So far so good,' Muriel spoke offhandedly. 'Those white pigs are either very stupid or very inefficient, letting us walk away from under their noses.'

'We were lucky.' Themba could hardly believe they were free. He walked Muriel to her hostel. 'Will I see you tonight?'

'What for?'

'So we can continue where we left off.'

'Forget it. When I need you again, I'll contact you.'

'Didn't last night mean anything to you? You were so warm and loving.'

'Danger arouses me, otherwise I don't have a need for men. All they do is complicate my life. I'm going to sleep. I'm bushed.' She walked casually into her residence with not a backward glance. Themba shook his head – she was once again the taunting, blasé Muriel he had known before.

He crept up to his room and flopped on to his bed, fully clothed, and was instantly asleep. Ngconde Seymour woke him in the late afternoon. 'Themba, wake up. Have you heard Umkhonto we Sizwe blew up a signal box near the station last night?'

Themba wiped the sleep from his eyes, pretending to be surprised. 'Who did it?'

'They say it was a professional job by guerrillas – comrades who trained overseas and infiltrated back into the country.'

Blowing in short bursts, the south-easter eddied in the Green Point Stadium making record times impossible at the Inter-Varsity Dalrymple Championships. Still not fully recovered from his injuries, Pierre was a spectator in the stands with Helmut Schmidt. Helmut pointed to the inside of the track. 'Look, there's your old flame, Lesley Stuart, warming up for her heat.'

They walked across the track to the grassed centre and stood watching as she did her stretching exercises. 'My, my! Hullo *boertjie*, I haven't seen you for a whole year.'

'How are you, Lesley, I've missed you.'

'I'm engaged now.' She flashed a sparkling diamond ring.

'Engaged? Really?' He did not want to believe it.

'Yes. To Geoff. Come along to the athletics party tonight and you'll meet him.'

'I'll be there,' he said flatly. 'Good luck with the heats.'

Helmut shook his head as they walked away. 'Pierre, there are literally hundreds of girls free tonight, what's the big attraction in Lesley?'

'I don't know, I really don't know. She's crawled right under my skin. I can't forget her.'

'I have a piece of information that might interest you – tomorrow the Ikey Mountain and Ski Club has a climb up Table Mountain. I'm the secretary, so I know who's put their names down to go. Lesley's going – without the boyfriend.'

'I'd be welcome?'

'As my guest, no problem. It's not all necking and holding hands though. It's a tough walk to the top, and the descent is even more difficult.'

The social was in full swing when Pierre arrived. He looked around for Lesley. Her blonde hair caught his attention and he walked across. 'Good evening, Lesley. Enjoying the party?'

She introduced him to Geoff, who looked at Pierre jealously.

He was not anything like Pierre had imagined. He had thinning, rust-coloured hair, a freckled skin and a ruddy complexion. His face was beefy and he had fleshy lips. When he stood up he was short and plump. Pierre had expected a tall, blond Adonis – only the perfect male – to attract her.

He was heartened enough to ask, 'May I have a dance, Lesley?'

She looked at Geoff, who grunted a reply, 'Lesley is with me tonight and I was about to dance with her. Sorry, old chap.'

Boiling inside, Pierre returned to the Matie contingent where he knew he was welcome.

'Hullo, Pierre, we missed you this year. The team's not the same without you.'

He looked at a pretty girl athlete. 'How did you do in the hurdles?'

'Came first, seven points for Maties.'

'Hey, well done. Won't you dance with me?'

They laughed and joked as they danced and Pierre wondered why he had such a fixation about Lesley when he could pick and choose the girls in his life. Helmut was right. After four beers, Pierre was decidedly merry and entering into the spirit of the party. He was laughing at a tale of a student prank when he heard an English voice. He looked up and Lesley was standing in front of him.

'You asked me to dance. I'd like to now.'

Leading her away, he looked at her scathingly. 'What's suddenly changed? Has Geoffrey given you permission?'

'Geoff was called back to work. He's a registrar now and Groote Schuur hospital is incredibly busy on Saturday night. Duty called.'

'Let me get this straight. While dear Geoffrey is present, you're not allowed to dance with me. Once he's gone, then the *boertjie* is all right. I don't like playing second fiddle, you know.'

'Stop fighting and dance – it's what you wanted to do.'

As he held her in his arms his anger evaporated and he pulled her close. She did not resist. She fitted snugly against him. She had a mesmerising effect on him, all else was blotted out except the two of them, dancing slowly to the music. He continued where he had left off a year previously in Pretoria. He kissed her on the neck and she sighed contentedly. The music stopped but Pierre did not notice, he danced on.

My God, she's beautiful, he thought as he looked into her face which lit up when she smiled, her blue eyes sparkling. They danced until the music finished at midnight.

'May I drive you home?'

'I'm staying in residence for the weekend.'

'May I walk you there?'

'That would be nice, thank you.'

They walked slowly. Pierre wanted the magic to last for ever. He held her hand and pulled her close, feeling very protective. He waited until they were in the shadows, then stopped and wrapped his arms around her. He kissed her; she tasted sweet and delicious.

Suddenly Lesley pulled away. 'No, Pierre, we mustn't. I'm engaged to another man.'

'When you're with me, you're happy and carefree. I saw you with Geoff. You weren't natural – you were guarded and pensive. Give us a chance.'

'I can't, Geoff's already set the wedding date.'

'When?' Pierre demanded savagely.

'At the end of next year, once I've graduated. I'm sorry. Now I must go.'

Pierre watched sadly as she ran across to the door and disappeared into the building. Damn that Geoff, he cursed. Well, at least I'll see her the whole day tomorrow.

The first Sunday church bells were ringing in the city when Pierre pulled into the cable station car-park at the foot of Table Mountain. He looked around for the climbing party and saw Helmut's huge frame sitting hunched on a rock, head in his hands.

'What's the problem Helmut, hangover?'

'*Ach grosser Himmel*,' groaned Helmut. 'The party lasted till four o'clock. I had only three hours' sleep, but the mountain will soon sober me up.'

'Pierre, what are you doing here?'

He looked up, smiling at Lesley. 'I'm an invited guest.' He went up to her and whispered, 'After last night I've decided to take my chances with you. Geoff versus me, and may the best man win!'

'You're not playing fair! Geoff's not here to compete.'

'Hullo, folks, please gather around. I'd like to introduce myself to those who don't know me. I'm Brent, your group leader for today. Our plan is to ascend the mountain via Platteklip Gorge. We'll go on to Maclear's Beacon, which is the highest point. On the plateau everyone can do their own thing, then we meet at the upper cable station for our descent via the India-Venster route. Any questions? Right, let's climb.'

Brent took the lead, climbing with long flowing paces until the contour path. Pierre found it pleasant to have Lesley in front of him. He admired her shapely legs, her dainty backside and swaying hips, and her blonde hair streaming out in the breeze. They stopped at a deep gorge stretching all the way up to the summit, the most noticeable gorge on the face of central Table Mountain.

'This is Platteklip Gorge,' explained Brent. 'From here the going gets tougher. Helmut, how are you feeling? I see you're sweating a bit.'

'*Ach Scheisse*, my friend. It's only last night's Castle Lager escaping. I'm getting my second wind now.'

'Let's go then.'

They tackled the gorge, a stony path rising in a series of natural rock steps, getting steeper the higher they ascended. Pierre was in line behind Lesley, hoping all the time she'd stumble and give him the opportunity to catch her. She was a seasoned climber, as nimble as the tahrs, the Himalayan mountain goats with curved horns which stood on the high rocks watching them. Pierre was breathing hard and he felt his muscles straining. He was athletics fit, but the climbing made the muscles work in different ways. His lungs were pumping freely, with no after-effects from the bullet.

They reached the top of Platteklip Gorge and came to the cross-roads between the western and central tables of the mountain. From the table proper they looked down on Cape Town. They could see Table Bay, the skyscrapers on the reclaimed foreshore and the cluster of tall buildings of the city centre, as well as a number of prominent landmarks such as the City Hall, Grand Parade, the Gardens and the Castle.

Two kilometres' level walking brought them to Maclear's Beacon. They were on top of the world. Looking south, Pierre could see the peninsula down to Cape Point. He took off his rucksack and sat down next to Lesley. They were comfortable in each other's company. Pierre was pleased. She seemed to have lost her aggression towards him.

'Okay, each one can do his own thing for a few hours, but try not to wander off alone. Don't forget, we meet at exactly two o'clock at the upper cable station.' Brent and some friends walked towards

Waaikoppie and Junction Peak. Others went to Orion's Cave and the Woodhead and Hely-Hutchinson Reservoirs. Pierre and Lesley found themselves alone.

'You conniving fox.' Lesley looked at him sternly. 'How did you manage to wangle things so we'd be alone?'

'Don't blame me,' laughed Pierre. 'You had your opportunity to go with one of the other groups.' He saw the smile playing around the corners of her mouth. He grinned back happily.

'At least I'm safe with you in the daylight. If you try anything untoward, I can scream and someone will be sure to hear me!'

'Let me take you to lunch. The restaurant serves a nice meal.'

'That sounds a good idea.'

They strolled back to the cross-roads. Lesley stopped to admire the stunning view and moved nearer the precipice. Pierre put his arms around her from behind to hold her back. She turned around, searching his face, looking very vulnerable. With one hand Pierre brushed her silky hair out of her face, tracing her features with his finger. She was so pure and flawless. As he outlined her lips she kissed his finger, a small gesture saying more than a thousand words. Pulling her closer he kissed her. This time she did not resist, opening her mouth, her tongue hesitantly seeking out his.

Pierre looked into her eyes intently. 'I love you, Lesley.'

'I'm bewildered, I don't know what to think any more,' she said breathlessly. 'But I do feel something, too.'

'Hey! You two. Are you crazy? Come away from the edge or you'll fall over.' The moment was broken, they looked up to see Helmut glaring at them.

'I thought you were my friend,' Pierre cried in mock desperation. 'Every time I make it with Lesley, you come along and spoil the moment.'

'I came back to look for you. After all, I invited you along. I didn't know you were shaping, otherwise I wouldn't have interrupted you two lovebirds.'

'You're not very tactful, Helmut, are you?' Lesley stared at him, irritated.

Helmut blundered on. 'So, where do we go from here?'

'Lesley and I are going to have lunch at the restaurant.'

'Sounds a good idea. I'll join you.'

Pierre looked at Lesley in exasperation. 'We don't have much of a choice,' he whispered.

'We mustn't eat too much.' Helmut led the way babbling on. 'We've a tough descent ahead of us.'

They found a table next to the window. Helmut plonked himself down while Pierre guided Lesley to the opposite side, sitting next to her. He placed his hand on her thigh. She responded by entwining her fingers with his and shooting him a coy glance. Pierre sat back contentedly.

'We must order, otherwise we'll be late.' Helmut looked at the menu. 'Steak and chips. Steak for protein and chips for carbohydrates. Ask a shot-putter, he knows all about diets and maximum power.'

Even Lesley was frustrated, kicking Helmut under the table. 'You stupid Kraut. Don't you stop talking for a minute?' Pierre smiled. Lesley wasn't afraid to speak her mind. He loved her spirit.

'Helmut, you finish your coffee in peace,' said Pierre when their meal was over. 'Lesley and I are going to look around. We only have twenty minutes before we assemble.' A quick wink conveyed the message.

'No problem. Enjoy yourselves.'

Pierre wanted Lesley to himself every precious second. They moved to the most westerly vantage point. A sheer precipice fell away many hundreds of metres before it merged with the steep mountain slope.

'Do you see those two rocks showing on Paarl Mountain?' Pierre pointed them out to Lesley. She nodded. 'On the other side, below the rocks, is our family farm Hermitage. One day it could be your home, too.'

'I don't know, Pierre.' Lesley pointed out into Table Bay. 'There's Robben Island, where the Nationalist government has incarcerated the true leaders of our country. Men like Nelson Mandela, Walter Sisulu and Govan Mbeki, living under the most appalling conditions as political prisoners. What have they done wrong? Nothing! All they wanted was justice, equality and peace. While we whites lead prosperous lives, they suffer for their people. I'm English-speaking, you're an Afrikaner, we're poles apart. I don't think we really have a future together.'

'That's where you're wrong, my sunshine. Love will find a way. We were meant for each other. Just wait and see.'

She put her hand on his arm. 'Pierre Roux, you've really

complicated my life. Up until last night my whole future was clearly mapped out.'

He pulled her to his chest and kissed her, not caring about anything except the moment. She felt wonderful in his arms and a flame was kindled deep inside Pierre, a glow he knew would burn for ever.

They only became aware of Helmut on his third call.

'Hey, you two.'

Pierre looked at his watch. They were five minutes late. He stared at Helmut. 'You're making a habit of this, you know.'

'Sorry, friend, but Brent is waiting.' Reluctantly they followed Helmut to the cable station.

'Come on, slow coaches,' scolded Brent. 'The best is yet to come. Follow the same order as this morning.'

There was so much Pierre wanted to tell Lesley but there was no time to talk, he had to concentrate on his climbing. A few hundred metres below the plateau they took a level path skirting around the end of the mountain until they were directly above Cape Town. They headed down towards India ravine, reaching the most tricky section of the descent. Below them was a difficult Grade C rock pitch, a very steep section, the rock smooth in places with only small hand- and foot-holds for purchase.

Brent went down like a spider, sure-footed and confident, feet first, his chest against the rock. 'Okay, come down slowly now, be careful. Make sure one foot is taking your full weight before you move.'

One by one the climbers descended, then it was Lesley's turn. Without a qualm she took off. When she was half-way down, the climber above Pierre nudged him. 'Right, it's your turn to go.'

Pierre swung out and down, flattening himself against the rock. He felt for the next foothold with his toe, pushing his boot into the small hole, testing his weight before finally committing himself. He looked down and his stomach churned as he saw the drop. He froze, experiencing the same feeling of doom he had felt as a child when he had climbed through the Devil's Chimney in the Cango Caves near Oudtshoorn.

The climber above shouted to Pierre, 'Get moving mate, we haven't got all day!' He looked up and saw the massif towering menacingly above him. A cable car approaching the upper cable station seemed to be dangling in space. Feeling dizzy, he diverted his gaze to the rock in front of his face. His heart beat in his throat, his breathing grew ragged. He was starting to panic, his hands and feet were growing tired. Pierre knew he could not hold out much longer, his legs were starting to spasm. He looked at Lesley, hoping his love for her would give him strength. Blotting out everything else he concentrated on her movements, watching her descend one step at a time.

Without warning her foot slipped and she was left hanging by her fingers, her legs swaying in the air. Pierre watched her fingers turn white as the blood drained away. She was slipping, her legs kicking wildly as she tried desperately to find a foothold. She looked up at Pierre pleadingly. 'Help me, Pierre. Please help me.' Her fingers scrabbled, then she pitched into space.

Pierre stared in horror as her body tumbled slowly backwards and landed with a sickening jar on a ledge ten metres below. Seeing Lesley's crumpled form drove all fear from him. 'My sunshine, I'm coming.' He climbed down the rest of the rock face quickly until he reached the ledge, his only concern for Lesley's safety.

'Don't move her!' Brent shouted up in alarm. 'She may have serious injuries. Is she alive?'

Could she be dead? thought Pierre in panic. Please God, now that I've found her please don't let me lose her. He forced himself to stay calm, feeling for a pulse on her outstretched arm. He felt a regular throb under his fingertips. He cried out triumphantly, 'She's alive!'

Brent, as the group leader, took charge of the situation. 'You guys at the top,' he shouted up. 'Get to the upper cable station as fast as possible. Ask them to telephone the police and the Mountain Club. Take the cable car down.' He turned to the group with him. 'Who has first-aid experience?' A girl called Jill nodded. 'You help me with Lesley. Helmut and Will, take the shortest route to the lower cable station and sound the alarm. Contact Groote Schuur hospital, too. Ask them to have the heli-pad and an emergency room ready.'

Helmut and Will took off down the mountain, moving as fast as they could. Every minute saved could mean the difference between life and death.

'Pierre, come down here. That ledge is not big enough for four people!' shouted Brent.

'I'm not moving, I'm staying right here with Lesley!' Pierre hollered back mutinously.

'Damn, we're not going to budge that guy. Jill, make your way up there. I'll wait here.' The girl nodded and started climbing.

Lesley lay face down on the rock, unmoving. Pierre blanched as blood seeped out from under her head and ran down a fissure in the rock. 'Hurry up, she's bleeding badly!'

'I'll be there now.' Jill heaved herself over the ledge. After checking her breathing and pulse she untangled Lesley's legs, feeling carefully. 'Left leg's broken below the knee. Right arm is okay.'

Working in tandem they moved Lesley into the recovery position, partially on her side, releasing her left arm from under her. 'She's also fractured her left upper arm.'

Pierre looked aghast at the cut on Lesley's face. There was a gash right down to her cheek-bone, the skin lacerated and bruised. Her soft blonde hair was matted with blood. Pierre groaned in grief. 'Oh! Lesley, my golden girl, what's happened to you? You're all battered and broken, my sunshine.'

Jill watched him with compassion as they worked to stop the bleeding. 'Don't worry, Pierre, the face, arm and leg they can fix with pins and plastic surgery. It's the internal, head, back and neck injuries we must worry about. You love her very much, don't you?'

He nodded numbly, the severity of her words sinking in. He had often wondered what his father saw in a wheelchaired, paraplegic wife – now he understood. He would marry and take care of Lesley for the rest of her life, even if she was an invalid. His love would transcend all barriers.

Jill was worried. 'We must stanch the bleeding. We need absorbent cloth.' Pierre took off his shirt and tore it into strips. She applied them to the jagged wound, stemming the flow of blood.

'When will they come? It's been hours already.'

Jill looked at her watch. 'It's only been half an hour since she fell, the messengers wouldn't have reached the cable station yet. Stay calm, Pierre. I know you're worried, but there's nothing we can do until help arrives.'

The minutes seemed to drag into hours. Pierre became more frantic as Lesley appeared to grow weaker. Her breathing seemed shallower, more laboured; her cheeks paler.

He kissed her on the temple and leant closer until he was talking into her ear. 'Sunshine, listen to me, I love you. Stay strong, for us, for our future. The will-power you know you have on the athletics track, you must use now. This is the most important race you'll ever run. I'm with you and I love you.' Lesley stirred slightly, groaning.

'She heard you, Pierre,' said Jill excitedly. 'Now you have blood all over the side of your face. Here let me wipe it off.'

Pierre drew back hurriedly. 'It's her blood, leave it there!'

'Lesley's engaged to Geoff. Where do you fit in?'

'Lesley is mine, not his.' Pierre spoke loudly. 'I'll show that stuffy, jealous lout.'

'You're batting in the big league, Pierre. Geoff's father is the famous Professor Summers at UCT Medical School. Geoff's following in daddy's footsteps – the crown prince of Groote Schuur hospital.'

'That doesn't worry me. He's a cold fish – he's egocentric and selfish. He can't give Lesley what she really wants – proper love and respect.'

Helmut slipped on a patch of loose stones and tumbled forward, grazing his arm badly. He bounced up like a rubber ball, impervious to the pain. He used his great strength to forge ahead. Pierre was his friend; he had to make a supreme effort. He took chances, jumping down the rocks oblivious to the danger. He left Will far behind.

With a sprint he reached the lower cable station. The official took one glance at Helmut's face and stained clothing and knew instantly there was a crisis on the mountain. 'Where was the accident?'

'On the C-grade rock pitch above India ravine.'

'How many?'

'One, a woman. She fell ten metres.'

'Is she conscious?'

'No.'

He swung into action, telephoning the police, the mountain club and Ysterplaat air force base. 'Everything is organised, the rescue will soon be under way.'

Will reached the office, staggering against the door in exhaustion. 'What about Lesley's fiancé? We must let Geoff know. He'll insist on meeting the helicopter when it lands at Groote Schuur.'

Helmut was alarmed, he knew Pierre would be on the chopper. 'Leave it, he'll hear soon enough.'

Undeterred, Will confronted the cable car official. 'The girl on the mountain is Lesley Stuart. She's engaged to Geoff Summers. His father is Professor Summers, the famous surgeon at Groote Schuur. They must be told, otherwise there'll be big trouble.'

'I'll phone the hospital.' The official dialled the number and was put straight through to Geoff.

'Oh, my God!' responded Geoff to the news. 'She may need an orthopaedic surgeon. I'll tell my father to come in. I'll also let Lesley's parents know. Don't worry, everything will be ready when she arrives.'

The distant beat of rotor blades made Pierre look up. He saw a speck in the sky coming from the direction of Ysterplaat. He shouted excitedly, 'Here comes the chopper, it's heading straight for us!'

The dot in the sky grew larger until an air force Alouette hovered over them, like a huge dragon-fly blotting out the sun. From the open door calm faces summed up the situation. A uniformed paramedic waved his arm, indicating to Pierre and Jill that they should leave the ledge to give them space.

Jill had to shout to make herself heard above the noise. 'Come on, Pierre, we must go down.'

'Never, my place is with Lesley. I'm staying.'

Seeing she could not budge a determined Pierre, she slipped over the edge and climbed down to Brent.

The paramedic stood in the open doorway. He motioned to Pierre with urgent movements to get off the ledge. His voice wafted down. 'Hey you! Get the hell off that ledge!' Pierre shook his head, he was not moving under any circumstances.

'That fool refuses to move. We'll have to go in, anyway.' A paramedic in a harness was winched down, the pilot expertly correcting the chopper to allow him to land. After a quick examination the paramedic reached the same diagnosis as Jill. Standing up, he outlined a rectangle with his hands. The man at the open door nodded. He attached a stretcher to the cable and lowered it carefully. The medic below caught the stretcher and placed it flat against the rock face.

He shouted to Pierre, 'Hold it in position, don't let it fall!' A second paramedic was lowered, all of them crowding on the narrow ledge. The pilot gave a thumbs-up signal and took the helicopter up, looking for a suitable spot to touch down. He landed at a point above the rock pitch, half resting on the rock, engine running.

The medic turned to Pierre. 'You're really in the way. Don't you want to get off the ledge?'

'My place is with Lesley. I'm staying.'

'Okay, buddy, but then move right out of our way. Don't hamper our work. Go over there.' Pierre shuffled across to the furthest corner until the points of his boots were sticking over the edge. His back was pressed against the rock face. He looked down fearfully and saw the mountain fall away beneath him. The chasm seemed to be drawing him forward. It took all his will-power to stay upright, balanced on his heels, like a fly high up on a wall. Waves of nausea swept over him. His stomach lurched and he could not control himself – he threw up, the vomit ran in streaks down his chest, soaking into his trousers.

He forced his gaze away from the abyss and watched in dazed fascination as the medics expertly slipped the stretcher under Lesley, hardly moving her as they did so. They secured her neck and covered her with a blanket, strapping her firmly in place. One of the paramedics gave a thumbs-up signal and a mountaineer's rope tumbled over the rock from above.

He glanced at Pierre. 'Up you go. Get up there and help the medics haul the stretcher up.'

'You won't leave me alone up here?' Pierre was suddenly afraid.

'You'll go with the chopper.' Reassured, Pierre shuffled back to the main part of the ledge. Grasping the rope tightly he was pulled upwards, his feet scrabbling against the rock face as he half walked up the steep slope. Hands gripped his arm, pulling him to safety. He looked around. They were on top of the rock, back in the veld with vegetation growing around them. He sighed in relief, the worst was past.

'Help us, man. Don't just stand there.' Pierre hurried over and grasped the rope. Two sharp tugs came. 'The casualty is secure, help guide her up.' Together they strained, hand over hand, pulling in the rope. Pierre held the top of the sturdy stretcher and pulled it over the rim of the rock. They undid the clasp, allowing the rope to fall. Within minutes both paramedics joined them at the top. They carried Lesley to the helicopter and manoeuvred the stretcher inside.

The pilot revved the engine. The blades spun faster and faster. On maximum revolutions the helicopter drew away from the mountain. The pilot adjusted the trim and they moved forward, gathering speed. They skirted Devil's Peak, flying towards the hospital. Pierre sat next to Lesley, stroking her undamaged cheek gently.

One of the paramedics looked at Pierre. 'You're a real mess, fellow, and you smell like a polecat.'

Pierre gave him a sidelong glance. 'A good shower will sort me out. Lesley is my most important consideration at this moment.'

They hovered over the heli-pad on the lawn in front of the trauma unit. A sea of faces looked up at them, moving outwards to allow the helicopter to land. The wheels had barely touched the grass when Geoff jumped aboard. He saw Pierre holding Lesley's hand.

He shouted in anger. 'What the hell are you doing here? Get away from my fiancée.'

'My place is with Lesley.'

'Like hell it is, she's my fiancée. Move!'

Two hospital orderlies helped slide out the stretcher and placed it on a trolley. Pierre jumped out, not wanting to let her out of his sight. The pilot waved as the helicopter revved up; it gained height and clattered away. The trolley was surrounded by people. Geoff examined the gash on Lesley's face, still oozing blood.

He turned to a worried-looking couple. 'Don't worry, we'll give her the best medical attention possible, Mr and Mrs Stuart, I promise you.' Pierre looked at her parents holding each other, the kindly woman sobbing bitterly, the man standing tall and solemn.

The orderlies pushed the trolley towards the hospital. Pierre sprang forward and held Lesley's hand.

'I told you to clear off.' Geoff pushed Pierre violently away. 'Look at you, you dirty Afrikaner. You're half-dressed, you're covered in blood and vomit, your hair is a tangled mess and you're filthy. Lesley is my fiancée! I warn you to keep away.'

People sniggered and Pierre saw red. He grabbed Geoff by the tie and twisted, pushing him backwards.

'Stop that madman!' a voice with authority shouted.

'Yes, Professor Summers.' The two orderlies left the trolley to restrain Pierre. He fought like a demon, but could not break their grasp.

'I don't know who you are and I don't know what you want.' The professor confronted Pierre. 'This is a family affair and you're not welcome.'

'I'm Pierre Roux, and I love Lesley.'

'It's his fault, all his fault, that Lesley fell and injured herself!'

Geoff screamed. 'Dad, call the hospital security to remove this piece of filth.'

'Right, my boy. Roux, do you leave of your own accord, or do we forcibly remove you?'

'I'm not leaving, I'm staying with Lesley.'

The sobbing woman stepped forward, wiping away the tears with the back of her hand, suddenly calm and composed. 'Pierre, while you're fighting, Lesley's life is in danger. If you love her, as you say you do, you'll do the best by her. Let us get her into hospital.'

Pierre nodded, the fight going out of him. He walked away and sat down on the embankment. Geoff glared at him, abruptly turning around to follow the trolley.

Dejected, Pierre sat with his head in his hands. In a moment everything had gone wrong. On the mountain and in the helicopter he'd been with Lesley, gaining comfort for himself by being at her side. Now he was alone in his misery and Geoff was in control.

'*Ja, mein Freund*, look at you. It seems as if you have been in World War Two! *Ach du Schande*, you sit all alone and look so sad.'

Pierre looked up at the concerned expression on Helmut's face. He told him of the events at the heli-pad in a bitter voice.

'You are a *verrückter Kerl*, a *malkop*, a silly person. Professor Summers is a big wheel here at Groote Schuur.'

'How am I going to get to Lesley? I must be near her when she comes out of the operating theatre.'

'I don't know, but we'll think of something. First, we must get you cleaned up. Come with me to my residence, we'll make a plan.'

While Pierre showered he considered his options, realising he had been outflanked. Helmut borrowed clothes from a student who was the same size as Pierre.

'My car's still in the parking lot at the lower cable station. Won't you drop me off there, so I can collect it?'

'Sure, then we'll come back here and I'll get one of the medical students to telephone the hospital to get us an update on Lesley.'

'The news isn't good, I'm afraid. She's out of theatre. Her leg has a multiple fracture with splintering. Lesley is now in the ward, but it seems the head injuries are more serious than was thought.'

'I must be with her. Did they say which ward she's in?'

'She's in E2.'

Taking the stairs two at a time to the fifth floor, Pierre hurried into the single ward. Lesley's leg was in traction, suspended above the bed, her left arm in a plaster cast and her head heavily bandaged. Pierre looked down at her pasty-white face. He touched her cheek gently.

'You cheeky bugger, you're back again.'

Pierre looked Geoff in the eye. 'You may be engaged to her, but you don't own her. She loves me, not you.'

Professor Summers stepped forward. 'Calm down Geoff, don't let him get to you.'

'I want him out of here, out of Lesley's life. We've got to protect Lesley from this oaf, Dad. If you won't call security, I will.'

'Leave it to me, son.' Professor Summers went to the sister's office. 'Security is on its way,' he announced on his return.

The security guards, well trained, half-dragged, half-carried Pierre to the door.

'I'll be back,' he hissed in a sharp whisper. 'You can't keep me away. My place is with Lesley.'

'I want a guard on duty outside this ward, twenty-four hours of the day. Do you understand?'

'Yes, Professor Summers.'

Lesley's mother blocked their path. 'I'll tell Lesley you were here, when she comes round.'

'Thank you, Mrs Stuart.'

He was escorted to the car-park. The guard looked at him. 'Buddy, for your own good, stay away for a while. If you tangle with the professor, you're sure to come off second best.' They watched him carefully as he slammed the car door and drove away.

Pierre stood outside the swing doors leading to E2, looking through the small windows. It was Tuesday lunch-time. He watched the security guard sitting outside Lesley's door. The guard looked at his watch. One o'clock. He stretched lazily and sauntered towards the swing doors. Pierre sprinted around the corner. He watched as the guard pushed the lift button. The doors opened and the guard stepped inside.

Quickly Pierre moved through the swing doors. Lesley's door was open, her mother was dozing in a chair. He tiptoed to the bed. Lesley was sleeping, breathing evenly. Pierre bent over, holding her shoulders, hugging her gently, then kissed her on the lips, nose and forehead. He took her hand and kissed each finger. Her long shapely nails, which had been torn in the fall, had been neatly clipped.

'You really do love her, don't you?' a voice said softly. Pierre recoiled with shock and looked up, straight into her mother's eyes. She was gazing at him levelly, a smile playing at the corners of her mouth.

'I love Lesley deeply, Mrs Stuart. Please don't call security. All I want to do is be with her.'

The older woman nodded and came to stand next to Pierre. He spoke in a whisper. 'She's beautiful, like a porcelain doll sleeping.'

'It's serious, Pierre. Lesley is comatose from very bad concussion. She hasn't yet regained consciousness. We are praying for her, and either my husband or myself keeps constant vigil. One of us will be here when she comes round.'

'How long will it take?'

'The doctors don't know. It could be days. She's in the hands of our Lord.'

They both turned to look as the door opened. The security guard's eyes popped when he saw Pierre. He slammed the door and ran down the passage. 'Get Professor Summers and Dr Summers here immediately. That man is in Miss Stuart's ward again. Call for extra security, too.'

Five minutes later Pierre was bundled out of the room again. Geoff shouted, 'How many times must we warn you, Roux? Get the hell out of here for the last time!' His face flushed with anger.

Pierre waited until the weekend before trying again, hoping everyone would have relaxed their guard. On Sunday afternoon he slipped into the hospital. The chair and the guard were gone. Both Lesley's parents were at her bedside. They turned to look at him, her mother with a welcoming smile but her father with hostility. 'What are you doing here again, Roux?' demanded Mr Stuart.

'I've come to visit Lesley.'

'I'm going to inform Geoff Summers.' Mr Stuart strode towards the door. Pierre winced as he pictured his fate – security guards, removal, humiliation – he knew it all so well by now.

'Dad, I *want* to see Pierre. I've something to tell him,' said Lesley softly.

Her father ignored her plea, striding purposefully from the ward.

His heart sang as he heard Lesley's voice. He bounded to the bed. 'Lesley, my sunshine, you're conscious, how wonderful!' He kissed her. She looked at him sadly.

'You're looking much better. The colour's returned to your cheeks. When did you come round?' Pierre bubbled on.

Lesley's shoulders drooped as dejection flitted across her features. 'Pierre . . . Pierre . . . sorry . . .'

He grinned from ear to ear. 'I've been so worried about you. Seeing you awake and talking again, it's wonderful. What do the doctors say?'

'Oh Pierre . . . please . . . understand!' There was sadness in her voice.

In his excitement, Pierre put his arm around Mrs Stuart. 'I'm so happy, today is a wonderful day.' She smiled at him fondly – he was so spontaneous and warm.

Mr Stuart was waiting for Geoff in the passage and they burst into the ward together. Pierre held up his hands in surrender. 'All right, I'm going, but the drive from Stellenbosch was worth it just to see my sunshine awake and recovering.'

Geoff smiled triumphantly as he walked across to Lesley. He held up her left hand. 'Do you see this ring?' Pierre looked at the solid gold band next to her engagement ring. A desperate sadness washed over him. He nodded mechanically. 'Lesley and I were married yesterday. We decided not to wait. We had the ceremony here in the ward.'

Pierre looked at Lesley, a pained expression on his face. 'Is it true?'

She nodded slowly, a tear rolling down her cheek. 'Yes . . . Pierre . . . it's true. I'm so sorry . . .'

'You can't be serious! You don't love Geoff Summers, you love me. You've just come out of a coma, how could you decide on such a drastic step? Summers forced you into marriage because he was jealous.'

'Exactly what I said,' exclaimed Mrs Stuart. 'They should have waited, at least until Lesley came out of hospital. But Geoff insisted.'

Furious, Pierre turned to Geoff. 'You bastard, you took advantage of the situation when Lesley was weak and confused.' A thought came to him. He looked at Geoff in elation. 'A marriage only becomes official once it's been consummated.' He looked at Lesley beseechingly. 'Lesley, annul this marriage, it's a sham.'

Geoff held Lesley protectively. 'Tell him darling – tell him the truth.'

She burst out sobbing. 'Oh! God! I feel so cheap and ashamed to admit it in front of everyone.' Her voice dropped to a mere whisper and she looked devastated. 'The marriage . . . was consummated . . . last night . . .' She turned her head away in shame and buried her face in the pillow.

Pierre's shoulders drooped, forced to accept the inevitable. He walked slowly out of the ward, shaking his head in disbelief. Geoff followed him to the lift, enjoying his triumph. 'She's my wife now. Don't try any more funny tricks. Just keep well away from us.'

Themba turned around as he heard footsteps behind him. 'Muriel, I haven't seen you for weeks. How are you?'

'I've been occupied with the ANC Youth League. We've been summoned to a special meeting tonight,' she said breathlessly.

'I'm studying, I have a political science test tomorrow. I can't go.'

'You have to. We've been instructed to be there by the commander of Umkhonto we Sizwe in the Border region. When he speaks, you jump.'

Themba sighed. 'Why is it so important?'

'They must have something special in mind for us. We cannot refuse.'

'It seems I have no option. Where do we meet?'

'I'll call for you at Wesley at seven o'clock.'

Walking through the darkened streets, Muriel again led Themba on a devious route, cutting back, double crossing, checking carefully at each intersection. They entered the black township and Muriel became more wary as they neared their destination. 'Can't be too careful; there are eyes at every turn.'

They slipped into the back yard of a run-down unplastered brick house. They froze in fright when the cooped chickens squawked. Once the fowls had quietened down they made for the back door. Muriel knocked twice, quick hard knocks. The door opened and they crept inside, their eyes adjusting to the light from a single paraffin lamp. The man who had opened the door disappeared

292

through a doorway leading to the front of the house. A big man sat at the table, the lamplight shining off his smooth and polished head. His back was to the light, making his features indistinct.

'Please sit.' He spoke in a deep voice. Themba and Muriel pulled chairs closer to the table. 'You must be Mary Toto, and you Philips Makeba?' Both nodded. 'I was informed about your sabotage of the signal box at Alice station last year. You were reckless and lucky not to be caught, but you showed guts. MK has another mission for you. Are you prepared to help?'

'Yes, of course,' Muriel breathed excitedly.

Themba took his time. 'Depends on what's involved. At the moment, my studies are of paramount importance. I would like to know more before I commit myself.'

'Caution is not a bad quality, Philips. What I can tell you is that it concerns reconnaissance of a target identified by MK. During your July vacation we want you to watch an installation day and night. You must keep notes and make sketches so MK will know how to attack, where to plant explosives and how best to enter and leave the premises.'

'Come on, Philips, it sounds intoxicating. And we'll be together for a whole month.' Muriel was sitting on the edge of her chair with excitement.

The prospect of spending a month with her appealed to Themba. 'Will we only do surveillance, no bombing or things like that?'

'Correct. You merely pin-point the aspects I mentioned and leave a later attack to the professionals.'

Muriel held his hand under the table, squeezing urgently. 'I promise you we'll have a good time.'

He looked at her and saw the pleading in her eyes shadowing the lust. 'I accept the assignment.'

'Good, I'm pleased. You two are bright students, you will do a thorough job and supply us with valuable information. Now your mission. South of King William's Town, at Zwelitsha, there is a huge textile mill called Good Hope Textiles. They make camouflage cloth for army uniforms. MK wants to destroy this mill.'

Themba felt Muriel's foot rubbing his leg under the table. Her eyes sparkled in delight. 'What is expected of us?'

'The mill has its own housing estate for its workers. We will arrange for you to stay with a sympathiser. You must watch all aspects. Guards – how many, when they change, how they patrol.

Employees – shifts, numbers and when the factory is clear of workers. Management – layout of offices and mill, and how they come and go.

'One of you must get a temporary job so that you can identify the key spots that would put the factory out of commission for at least a year, if destroyed by explosives.'

'Phew! Sounds a tall order, but I think Mary and I can manage.'

'Of course we will.' Muriel was ecstatic. 'We'll give you the most complete set of facts and figures possible.'

The commander smiled for the first time. 'We're counting on you.' He gave them details of their contact in Zwelitsha and then dismissed them.

The reconnaissance project had seemed so exciting when outlined by the MK commander. In practice it was a hard and mainly boring slog. In the sympathiser's house they had to share a bedroom with four children, but most times Themba and Muriel lived as opposites. He slept while she kept watch for twelve hours, then they swopped around for the next shift.

They established hides from where they could keep the mill under surveillance without being seen. Each shift they changed their vantage point so that they did not alert the security guards.

They kept notes of all movements to and from the factory. Themba walked around the perimeter fence, pacing off the distances. He drew a sketch and filled in the details: roads, doorways, windows.

After the first two weeks a pattern emerged. They knew the movements and registration numbers of the vehicles of the mill management and could describe the drivers in detail. The mill worked two nine-hour shifts, but between eleven at night and five in the morning the place was deserted except for two security guards. This, they noted, was the ideal time for an MK strike, as no lives would be in danger.

Another important finding was that early each morning a municipal refuse truck entered the premises. It was such a regular occurrence that the guards did not even bother to look into the enclosed back, neither on entry nor exit from the factory.

During the third week Themba applied for work at the textile mill and was given a position on the late shift. He registered under the name of Philips Makeba.

Themba was assigned to the opening room where the bales of raw cotton were stored, laid out and blended. It was back-breaking work handling the bulky bales. During the Tuesday shift he crept away to the toilet and made a detailed drawing of the opening room.

The foreman was in a foul mood when he returned. 'Listen, you little shit, if you aren't prepared to work get the hell out of here – there are thousands of other starving kaffirs who will take your place.'

Themba found he had to stay at his post except for their meal break, when he took a quick walk through the maze of buildings to get an idea of the interior layout.

'What are you doing here?' shouted the dye-house foreman. 'You're supposed to be in the canteen eating your meal.'

'Sorry, sir. I was looking for my sister, but she's not here.'

'Try the canteen, or the women's toilets.'

After his shift he discussed the problem with Muriel. 'I'm never going to see the whole mill during my shifts. The foremen are alert, they don't allow you to leave their sections.'

'Why don't you slip in with the workers of the first shift. Posing as a cleaner, you'll surely be able to move from section to section?'

'Of course it'll work,' exclaimed Themba in admiration. 'Now, why didn't I think of that!'

'I'm tuned in to the struggle, that's why. Come and warm me up, Themba, it's cold tonight.'

Themba mingled with the workers for the early shift. Fortunately both shifts were issued with the same green identification cards. Themba showed his card and strolled casually past the security guards.

Once inside the grounds he made his way to the cleaning room. Rows of blue dust-coats hung against the walls. Themba slipped one on, grabbed a large broom and dustpan and entered the mill. It was much easier than he had imagined. He was able to pace out the buildings, memorising the distances until he could reach the toilet and then sketch them into a notebook.

He followed the milling process through the spinning room and pretended to be sweeping in the grey cloth store. Next he wandered into the dye house and on to the finish-cloth store.

By the end of the shift Themba had sketched the entire layout, identifying and describing five key areas where explosions would cause maximum damage. He had to leave with the outgoing workers, then turn back in the mêlée of bodies outside the gate and enter the factory again with his own shift. He held his hand to his face to hide his features, hoping the guard would not recognise him. He looked only at the cards and Themba walked through unchallenged.

When the hooter went for the end of the shift he stumbled out of the gates thankfully. He found Muriel at the hide on the river bank. He handed her the notebook. 'In the finish-cloth store there are thousands of rolls of camouflage cloth which could be very useful to MK.'

Muriel immediately grasped his meaning. 'We could make uniforms similar to the SADF. Imagine how that would blow their minds if we wore them in our raids.' She was excited. 'How could we get the material out of the mill?'

'If I hide among the cotton bales after my shift I can break into the store-room and remove the rolls. I could get the material to the door near the waste area. When the municipal refuse truck comes in, we could smuggle them out. We know the security guards never inspect the loads.'

'You sleep; I'll take the plans to the MK commander.'

Themba woke half-way through the morning. The house was quiet. He rose, dressed and made himself breakfast, waiting for Muriel to return. At midday she arrived with the MK commander. They sat at the kitchen table.

'You have done well, Philips, both you and Mary.' He smiled, his ample face crinkling. 'I've examined your schedules, they're very complete. Your drawings of the inside of the mill are excellent. Even more important is your plan for securing the camouflage material.' The commander outlined his strategy.

Themba reported for duty on the late Thursday shift, again working hard, not wanting to draw attention to himself. He managed to manoeuvre the heavy cotton bales so that he left a space big enough to hide in.

He made sure he was working near the bales at the end of the shift. When the hooter sounded, and in the confusion of downing tools and clearing up, Themba slipped unseen up the tunnel and into his hideaway.

The mill grew quiet as the workers left. He heard the heavy steps of the foreman checking, then the lights went off and the footsteps receded. Themba waited for the guards to make their last round. He heard their footfalls enter the opening room and then leave.

Themba hurried to the finish-cloth store. A trolley stood inside the doorway and Themba pushed it to where the camouflage material was stored. The rolls were big and unwieldy and he had difficulty lifting them on to the trolley. He managed to load four rolls, then pushed them slowly to the side door of the mill. He returned with a second trolley.

Muriel staggered into the road, her blouse torn to shreds, her breasts exposed, blood staining her shoulder.

The truck driver saw her in his headlights. Braking hard as she collapsed on the road, he stopped metres from her prostrate body. He and the other refuse workers jumped down to investigate.

'No! No! No!' Muriel screamed as they approached her. 'Leave me alone, you've already raped me.'

'It wasn't us, we want to help you!' cried the driver in alarm. 'Come on, men, help me.' He bent down to assist Muriel.

Their attentions were centred on Muriel. They did not hear the MK cadres as they burst from the bushes and surrounded them, AK47s at the ready.

'Don't try anything stupid.' The commander waved his weapon in the driver's face. 'We'll shoot to kill.'

Slowly the municipal workers stood up, raising their hands in the air. To their amazement Muriel jumped up and sauntered across.

'Sorry, men, it was a trap. I'm not hurt.'

'What about the blood?'

'Tomato sauce,' she laughed, pulling on a jacket.

The commander had chosen the ambush spot well – a quiet stretch of road between King William's Town and Zwelitsha. He pointed to the driver. 'Get back into the truck.'

His assistants were led into a clearing behind the bushes. The commander jumped into the cab while Muriel hid in the enclosed back, armed with an AK47.

'Driver, make as if this is your normal visit to Zwelitsha.' The commander dug a gun barrel into his ribs. 'What's your usual round?'

'We go to the mill first to collect waste, then pick up refuse at

297

various places in the township.' The driver looked fearfully at the weapon. 'Please don't shoot. I have a wife and children at home.'

'Do as I say and you won't get hurt.'

The truck slowed at the entrance gates. The driver rolled down the window, waving casually. The security guard threw open the gates. They drove inside and around the building to the waste area.

Muriel jumped off the truck and ran to the corner of the building. She smiled in satisfaction as she saw the security guards safely ensconced in their office. 'All clear.' She knocked on the metal door. 'Philips, are you there?'

'Yes. Just give me a chance to break open the lock.' He pushed a crowbar between the door and the jamb, putting his weight against the metal bar. With a clatter the lock shattered and the door swung open. Muriel signalled to the commander.

Themba ran across. 'I've twelve rolls ready for loading, but I'll need help.'

The commander barked an order to Muriel. 'Cover the driver while we load. If he tries to escape, let him have it.'

Quickly they loaded the heavy rolls, pushing them to the front, covering them with cotton waste. Within five minutes the task was completed. It had all been so easy. The commander waved Muriel into the back of the truck. She covered herself with the waste. The commander and Themba leapt into the cab. The driver started the engine and they drove around the corner towards the gates. The gates were closed.

'That's funny,' said Themba in alarm. 'They usually leave the gate open and the truck just drives through. Something's wrong.'

The driver muttered. 'One of my assistants is a brother of one of the guards. He usually brings freshly baked bread from town for him. He may be suspicious.'

'You'd better tell him a convincing story, otherwise you get the first bullet,' warned the commander menacingly.

The two security guards walked towards the truck. The driver rolled down his window. 'Morning men.'

'Where's my brother today?'

'He's been put on another round, I've got new assistants.'

Suspicious, the guard climbed on the step and peered into the cab. 'Why did they change mid-week? I've never seen these men before.'

The second guard walked around the truck and hopped on to the step to look into the back. Muriel tried frantically to hide herself completely under the waste, but the guard saw her. He pulled out his pistol. 'Come out where I can see you, and no funny tricks.'

In one flowing movement she threw off the waste, came to her feet in a crouch, aimed and fired a salvo of shots. At such close range she could not miss. The guard screamed as the bullets hit his chest, the force throwing his hands into the air. He tumbled off the tailgate, dead before he hit the ground.

The first security man looked up in alarm. He backed off, firing into the cab. A shot hit the driver in the side of the head. He collapsed across the steering wheel. A second shot slammed into him. The commander ducked behind the driver. Muriel jumped off the back and ran around the truck. Crouched in the assault position, she fired a burst. Bullets kicked up dust around the guard as he turned towards his office. She lifted the weapon and fired another torrent. Solid slugs hit him in the back, twisting him around grotesquely and he fell to the ground.

Muriel stood over him, AK47 aimed at his head. He tried to scrabble away, screaming. 'Don't kill me, please don't kill me.'

Muriel's eyes glinted as she followed the guard's crab-like movements. He left a trail of blood across the tar.

Themba was horrified. He jumped out of the cab. 'Muriel, stop, you don't have to kill the man.' He ran forward to restrain her, but was too late. Muriel screamed in triumph and pulled the trigger. She emptied the whole magazine into the guard, blowing the entire top of his head away.

Themba turned away in disgust, sickened at what he had seen. 'You bitch – you bloodthirsty bitch!'

She turned on him in cold fury. 'He was going to push the alarm. What option did I have?'

The commander opened the driver's door and pushed the dead driver out, taking the wheel. 'Open the gates, Philips.' The commander's voice was gruff. 'Let's get the hell out of here.'

Themba ran to the gates. 'They're locked. The key must be on one of the guards.'

'No time. Mary, shoot the lock away.'

Muriel ran to the gate. She clicked in a fresh clip of bullets and fired at the lock. It shattered. The truck roared through the gates, slowing down just enough for Themba to jump on the tailgate. He held out his hand and grabbed Muriel's outstretched arm, swinging her on board as the truck gathered momentum. Together they tumbled on to the rolls of fabric. Muriel was hyped up. She had made her first two killings for the cause and was totally aroused.

'Come on, Themba, I want you now.' She rolled on to Themba. He pushed her away forcibly. 'Not now, dammit woman. You make me sick.'

Anger welled up in her. 'You'll still come crawling to me, just wait and see.'

The commander pulled the truck into the clearing. Quickly the camouflage cloth was transferred to the back of a waiting panel van. The trussed-up municipal workers were locked into the cab of the refuse truck.

'Philips, Mary, you've done very well.' The commander nodded approvingly. 'We must hurry before the police react. One of my MK cadres has a car waiting to take you back to Alice. Lie low for a while and don't talk to anyone.'

Themba was outraged. 'The killing was unnecessary. The ANC is supposed to avoid taking innocent lives.'

The commander's cold stare bored into Themba. 'Mary Toto did what she had to. Terrorism is not a picnic, my friend.'

14

'Dad, may I speak to you? I want your advice,' Pierre asked.

Simon saw the serious expression on Pierre's face. 'Sure, son, let's go to my study where we'll be private.' They sat in the comfortable leather armchairs. 'Fire away.'

'I'm in a rut, I want a change.'

'What's the problem?'

'Rika Bosch – she's too possessive and she's smothering me. I turned to her on the rebound, after Lesley got married.' Simon nodded knowingly. Pierre continued: 'I like Rika, but I don't love her. Every weekend and vacation she wants to be alone with me. She insists on being at all my athletic meetings – wherever I turn, she's there.'

'She adores you – you're lucky to have a woman who cherishes you and who puts you first.' Simon thought wistfully of his own hollow sex life with Helena. He was no fool, he had seen Pierre and Rika disappear together. When they returned she had the serene expression of a woman satisfied, and she cuddled up lovingly to Pierre. Life had strange twists and turns, he thought. Pierre had it all, but he was dissatisfied. Perhaps it was the impetuosity of youth that thought the grass was always greener on the other side of the fence.

'Dad, I need space. I must get away for a while to some place where I can be alone, can find myself again. Somewhere Rika can't follow.'

'What did you have in mind?'

'At the end of the year I finish my BA. I have to do one year of military duty. I thought I'd join the South African Police; the authorities accept it as the equivalent of a year of service. I'd have a break from studies, complete my military commitment and avoid Rika.'

'Three birds with one stone.' Simon smiled. 'Tell me why you prefer the police to the army.'

'It's a six months' basic course at the Police College in Pretoria, then six months' active police work. I'll be with Major John Short; he's the best athletics coach in South Africa. The year's break will do me good, then I'll resume my studies and finish off my LL B.'

'What's happened to Danie Conradie?' Simon asked astutely.

'He's very sour with me because I stole Rika from him. He moved to another room at Wilgenhof. I still see him occasionally, but the friendship is strained. I think he's still very much in love with her.'

'I understand how you feel. I think a year in the police is just what you need. Why not do it?'

The members of the council gathered sombrely at the royal kraal, Mqekezweni. Everyone took their places in the traditional circle. Paramount Chief Sabata Dalindyebo arrived. All rose, as a mark of respect. Themba, as the junior member, sat at the bottom of the circle. The closer they sat to the chief, the more senior the men. Flanking the great man were his closest advisors, the *amaphakathi*.

Themba greeted his grandfather, who was half-way around the circle. Morris Memani was proud of his grandson, pleased at the rapid progress he had made into the inner circle of the Thembu tribe. His future was assured.

To the right of Sabata was Themba's mentor, Joseph Sondika, the principal elder.

Joseph addressed the gathering. 'We are here today for a special meeting to discuss only one thing – the independence of the Transkei, scheduled for next year. You know at present the Transkei is run by Chief Kaiser Matanzima – a minor Thembu chief – as a limited self-governing territory but controlled by Pretoria?' The members growled their disapproval.

'You're also aware that Pretoria has appointed all sixty members to the regional authority!' Again they groaned in frustration. 'Now Matanzima has fallen for Pretoria's bait and is opting for full independence for the Transkei. As a token gesture forty-five extra seats will be created and these members can be elected by the people.'

Joseph stabbed his finger in the air. 'Between Matanzima and the South African government they have ensured that the sixty appointed members have the majority.'

Morris Memani jumped angrily to his feet. 'We cannot allow that to happen.'

'Hear! Hear!'

Joseph continued. 'Matanzima, the conniving devil, has formed TNIP, the Transkei National Independence Party, to contest the remaining forty-five seats. The question today is, are we for independence, or against it? If against, what is our plan of action?'

For over two hours, the councillors discussed the matter backwards and forwards, achieving no consensus. Themba followed the debate keenly. He had just completed his BA Law and had three years of legal study behind him. In class they had practised with mock trials – today there were real issues at stake. He held his counsel, aware of the Xhosa tradition of not usurping the place of the older men. Eventually the Paramount Chief held up his hand for silence. 'We're going around in circles, we must reach consensus.'

Themba saw Joseph Sondika lean across and whisper in Sabata's ear. The chief nodded and Joseph stood up. 'We would like to ask the opinion of our newest member, Themba Memani.'

A hush settled on the indaba as they all turned to look at Themba. It was an unprecedented move to ask the most junior for his views.

He quickly gathered his thoughts. 'Independence for the Transkei is a ploy by the South African government. They want to isolate the Xhosa people into a small tract of the total South Africa and force apartheid on us. We must resist.'

A roar of approval greeted his words. 'Well spoken,' encouraged his grandfather.

Themba waited respectfully for silence. 'Paramount Chief Sabata Dalindyebo is the traditional leader of the Xhosa nation, not Kaiser Matanzima, who is a puppet of Pretoria.'

Clapping and cheering followed. Sabata smiled broadly, his esteem greatly enhanced.

'Enter the circle.' Dalindyebo waved him forward. 'You have identified the core of the problem, how do you suggest we solve it?'

Themba looked around from one man to the next, making eye

contact, stamping his authority on the gathering. 'The time for action has come. We must answer Matanzima and his TNIP with fire. This council must change from its traditional form, sorting out problems of the tribe, to a council that assists the Xhosa nation. We must become a political party with Paramount Chief Sabata Dalindyebo as our leader. We must contest and take all forty-five elected seats in the Transkei government. We will be the true representatives of the people, not the TNIP. The people will support our party.'

Themba was cheered loudly. He was expressing their thoughts.

'What should we call our party?' asked Joseph Sondika.

Themba stood deep in thought for a few minutes, then he spoke. 'Our party would be a democratic party, truly accountable to the people. It would also be something new, displaying the progress our people are making. We could name our party the Democratic Progressive Party.'

While the men thumped the ground in approval, Sabata turned to Joseph. 'He has wisdom and maturity far exceeding his years. He has a way of cutting through the fat to the lean meat, and he takes the people with him – he's a natural leader.'

Joseph nodded, standing up. 'By the will of the people, DPP it shall be.'

'We have not yet finished,' said Themba. The members settled down again. 'We know the constituent assembly has forty-five ordinary seats and sixty seats for the chiefs appointed by Pretoria. That is a total of one hundred and five delegates. To obtain a majority we need fifty-three seats. If the new DPP takes the forty-five ordinary votes, we are still eight short. We must find a minimum of eight chiefs who share our views and persuade them to throw their weight in behind the DPP.'

'The chiefs of western Thembuland can be persuaded.' Joseph was enthusiastic. 'Will we be able to prevent independence?'

Themba shook his head. 'Sadly, independence will be agreed to by the present Transkei government, but we must be ready by the next election. Once we achieve majority in the Transkei government, we can reverse the position.'

Clapping and cheering greeted the proposal. Within ten minutes Themba had turned confusion and uncertainty into clarity and a plan of action. He took his place again at the bottom of the circle.

Paramount Chief Sabata rose. He stepped a pace to his right and placed his hand between Joseph Sondika and the next elder, motioning the whole circle to move down. The men shuffled to their right, leaving a gap. A murmur rose. All sensed something historic was about to happen. Sabata held up his hand, cutting conversation. 'Themba Memani, please rise.'

Themba stood up, shaking involuntarily. 'Your insight and sound judgement are respected by the council. I invite you to join the ranks of the *amaphakathi* of the Thembu tribe.'

His heart beating with pride, Themba crossed the circle. Morris could not contain his excitement. He rushed across and embraced his grandson. 'I always knew you had potential. Today you realised that capability.'

Themba sat down two places away from the great Paramount Chief – the crowning achievement of his life. The men looked at him with respect, awed that so young a man had advanced so quickly.

'Mother, I must go to East London to find a law firm where I can do my articles.'

'Why East London? What's wrong with Umtata?'

'Umtata is a small town, I must go where there's lots of litigation. Also, Muriel is there.'

'What about Hilda? I thought Hilda was your woman!'

'Mother, Hilda is a simple tribal girl. Muriel is a woman of the world – she's vivacious and exciting.'

'Listen carefully, my son. You don't marry that sort of woman. They're trouble in later life. When you choose a wife you go back to your roots. You look for a woman from your own background, someone who has the same traditions as yourself, who will raise your children in the way of the Thembu. Hilda is such a woman.'

'I'm not talking of marriage, only a girlfriend.'

'I don't care. Hilda is the right woman for you. Her father is the Paramount Chief's son. She is of royal blood. You will marry Hilda and no more arguments.'

Early the next morning Themba caught the bus to Umtata. Paul was still in his dressing-gown when he answered the door to Themba's knocking. They breakfasted together.

'I created history at Fort Hare, Paul, by passing two degrees in only three years. It was all thanks to you.'

'Nonsense. I started you on the way, but you did it. Besides, it was a pleasure for me. What now, Themba? What's your next move?'

'I'm off to East London, to find a law firm to accept me as an articled clerk. I want to practise as an attorney. That's my aim.'

'I know a law firm. Evans, Roberts and Simons. They're our family's attorneys. I can give you an introduction. How are you travelling to East London?'

'By bus. It leaves from the station at ten.'

'No way! I'm on holiday, I'll take you down. Let me get dressed and packed, then we'll leave.'

'Let's try the Kings Hotel. It overlooks the sea.' They parked in front of the hotel and walked in with their suitcases. 'Two single rooms, please.'

The receptionist looked at Paul. 'I'm sorry, sir. We can book you in, but your friend is not permitted to stay here.'

'I thought things had changed,' remarked Paul bitterly.

'Only certain five-star hotels have international status. We're registered as a four-star hotel by the Hotel Board and could lose our grading if we broke the law and admitted blacks.'

'What a crazy set-up. This man has higher qualifications than you or I will ever have. He has two university degrees and on top of it all he's from the Thembu royal family.'

'Sorry, sir. Rules are rules. I'm only obeying orders.'

'I demand to see the manager.'

'I can call him, but it won't help. He can't accept your friend as a hotel guest.'

'Which hotel in East London will admit him?'

'None, sir. We're all governed by the same regulations and there is no five-star hotel in East London. White hotels are reserved for white guests only.'

Themba intervened. 'Paul, it's all right. I can stay with my Aunt Doreen in the township.'

'That's not the point, Themba.' Paul was angry as they walked back to their vehicle. 'The point is we came down together, to stay together and visit the law firms together.'

'Would you like to stay with my aunt? I'm sure it will be all right with her.'

'If it's okay with her, then at least we'll be together.'

At the entrance of the black township they were flagged down by a white official in khaki uniform, standing next to a Black Affairs Administration Board vehicle. A uniformed black

306

official stood to one side, an uninterested expression on his face.

'Do you have a permit?'

'A permit for what?' Paul demanded.

'You need a permit to enter a black area.'

Paul exploded. 'Good God, what on earth for?'

'Look, all I do is follow the rules, and the rules say you need a permit.'

'Rules! Dammit man, in South Africa it's all rules, rules and more rules. What about freedom? Do we have no freedom of choice where we go, what we do and whom we see?'

The officer grew impatient. 'Man, it's government policy. You must move your vehicle, you're blocking the road.'

'Paul, it's no use arguing with minor officials. They're like clockwork soldiers, they only do what they're programmed to do. Let me walk to my aunt's house and stay the night.'

'Okay,' said Paul dejectedly. 'I'll set up the appointment with the attorneys and meet you here at nine o'clock.'

Paul was excited when he collected Themba the next morning. 'Your appointment is with Mr Evans himself, the senior partner. They're a very reputable firm of attorneys.'

'I'll do my best at the interview.'

'Mr Evans will see you now.' The receptionist smiled a plastic smile.

'Paul, how nice to see you. Won't you please sit down. How is your father?'

They made small talk for a few minutes. Paul turned to Themba. 'Mr Evans, this is Mr Themba Memani, my friend. He has just completed a law degree at the University College of Fort Hare and needs to do his articles. Our family has always done business with Evans, Roberts and Simons, so I brought him here first.'

Evans appeared decidedly uncomfortable as he looked at Themba. 'Paul, may I speak to you alone?'

'Mr Evans, whatever you have to say to me you can say in front of Themba. You told me you had a vacancy for an articled clerk when we spoke on the telephone.'

The attorney fidgeted with his collar. 'You didn't tell me he was a black man, old chap.'

'No, I didn't. What difference does it make?'

307

'You see, most of our clients are white. They expect to be defended by white men. Even our black clients like to be represented by a white attorney.'

'That's apartheid,' said Paul firmly. 'Themba received a first class in his finals. He has perception, polish and maturity. He would be an asset to your firm.'

'No doubt, my boy, no doubt. By Jove, the decision isn't really mine. I'm only one of the partners. We do have a policy, of course.'

'Then you must change your policy. How are black men going to get ahead in South Africa, if the bastions of the legal profession are not prepared to give them a chance?'

'I'm sorry, Paul, but those are our rules.'

'Rules! There's that word again. Ever since we reached East London, that's all we've heard. Rules at the white hotels, rules at the black townships and now rules preventing a potential top attorney from doing his articles. Next I suppose you'll tell me it's government policy?'

'Good Lord no, heaven forbid. We just don't have a vacancy for Mr Memani.'

Themba stood up, patting Paul on the shoulder. 'Don't take it personally, Paul. There are many law firms in East London. I'm sure we'll find one. Besides, I wouldn't be happy working here.' He turned around and walked with dignity out of the office – shoulders proud, his back straight.

Evans looked apologetic. 'Sorry again, old chap.'

Paul stormed out of the room, slamming the door behind him. 'Paul, don't get so upset, it's not your problem,' urged Themba.

'Your welfare is my problem, Themba. I want the best for you in life. You deserve the best. Let's try the other law firms, one by one.'

Six attorneys later, they had six refusals. Both of them were downcast.

'Where to from here?' Themba looked at Paul despondently.

'Themba, you just keep plugging away. Somewhere in East London there must be a firm who will accept you. If not, we'll try King William's Town, then Grahamstown and finally Port Elizabeth.'

'I need some fun to restore my self-confidence. I think a visit to Muriel will be the right medicine. She lives in Mdantsane township.

I'll catch a bus to save you the ignominy of having to apply for a permit. Meet you here at nine tomorrow morning.'

Themba jumped off the bus at the Mdantsane terminus. He asked directions to Muriel's street and, finding the right address, knocked on the door. He heard a scuffling sound inside, then the door opened. Muriel closed it quickly behind her. She wore only a night-gown and looked dishevelled.

She was agitated. 'What do you want?'

'I came to visit you. I thought you'd be glad to see me. We are lovers you know.'

'That was at university.'

'We had good times together. You once said you loved me.'

'Don't be naive, Themba. It was puppy love.'

The door opened and a huge brute of a man in shorts stepped out. His left eye was swollen and puffy, he had a plaster over a broken nose and there were dark bruises on his chest and shoulders. He looked at Themba disdainfully.

'Good evening, I'm Themba Memani.' Themba extended his hand.

He crushed Themba's hand in a vice-like grip. 'Terror Ngceke.'

'Terror is a boxer.' Muriel put her arm around the man, breaking the strained atmosphere. 'He won the Cape heavyweight title last night. He knocked out his opponent in the tenth round. It was so bloodthirsty and exciting. I love boxing.'

'Who are you?' Terror looked at Themba suspiciously.

'A friend of Muriel's from university.'

'Nice meeting you.' The boxer scowled at Themba and went back into the house. 'Come on, Muriel, get back inside. We were having a good time until this guy disturbed us.'

Muriel looked at Themba apologetically. 'I must go, Themba. Terror is jealous and possessive. He'd beat me up if he knew about us.'

'Beat you up? He'd hit a woman? What do you do about it?'

'I hit him back. I fight like an alley cat, kicking and scratching, but eventually he crushes me. Then we make up with explosive sex.'

'What about us, Muriel, we also had a good thing going?' Themba looked at her sadly. 'Have you forgotten our night at Alice station, or our times together in the hides while watching the cotton mill?'

'Themba, you are so innocent. I'm his girl now. You must forget me. I must go before Terror gets violent.' She hurried inside, slamming the door in his face.

Themba walked slowly back to the bus terminus. His mother was right after all. Girls like Muriel were fine for a good time, but not for marrying.

The next day Themba took a bus to East London's city centre to meet Paul Curry. 'Let's go home, Paul.'

'Why the sudden change of plan? I thought you were looking for a position with a law firm?'

Themba told Paul about his visit to Muriel. 'All I want to do at this moment is get out of the city, back to the serenity of home. We can come back after Christmas to look for my job.' They drove back to Umtata.

'Mother, I have decided to marry Hilda.'

Nomisile sighed with relief. 'You won't be sorry. She'll make you a good wife.'

The next day Themba went to Qunu to see Morris Memani. 'Grandfather, I would like to marry Hilda. Will you please make the arrangements with her father?'

He flashed Themba a smile. 'A very good choice, Themba. You will be cementing the hierarchy of the Thembu tribe with the marriage. I'll ask my brother to accompany me tomorrow morning. Do you have a present for your prospective father-in-law?'

Themba handed him the cash equivalent of one beast, the accepted opening gambit in the marriage proposal.

Soon after sunrise Morris and his brother walked to Mqekezweni. They sat next to the cattle enclosure in front of Nxele's house, their actions indicating they wished to speak to the head of the household. After a while Nxele walked over, greeted his visitors and sat down. They talked of rain, the harvest, cattle, and finally got down to the point of the visit.

'How can I help you, Morris?'

'My brother and I represent Themba Memani as he has no father to speak for him.'

'I understand.'

'We are here to arrange a marriage between Themba and your daughter Hilda.'

Nxele looked pensive. He gave no outward show of his emotions; to do so would weaken his bargaining power. Secretly he was overjoyed at the news as he had a high regard for Themba. He was the rising star of the tribe, a very eligible bachelor and the ideal husband for his daughter.

'Do you bring me a gift, a token of your good intent?'

'I do.' Morris handed over the money.

Nxele counted it slowly. 'Hilda will command many cattle as *lobola*.'

Parrying in the battle of wits to bring the bride price down, Morris sang Themba's praises. 'Themba is the youngest elder of the tribe. There are many maidens who would swoon at the chance to marry him.'

'Twenty head of cattle will be the price.'

'With respect, that's an unheard of amount. No maiden is so important as to warrant twenty head of cattle.' Morris rose to his feet, a strategic move.

'Sit down, please.' Nxele waved Morris down.

Morris had scored a point. The price would no longer be twenty head.

Nxele altered the stakes. 'Fifteen head, but all heifers, in calf for the first time.'

'Fifteen head, ten heifers and five oxen,' countered Morris.

'Twelve heifers and three oxen, that is my final offer.'

'Done.' Morris shook Nxele's hand, cementing the deal.

'When will the exchange take place?'

'Tomorrow morning.'

'I will tell Hilda to get ready.'

Morris reported to Themba and Nomisile. 'I don't have so many cattle, grandfather.'

Nomisile sat forward. 'I will lend you the balance. You can pay me back out of your earnings once you are working.' Nomisile was keen for the matter to be finalised as soon as possible.

'Thank you, Mother. Don't you think things are going along too fast? Shouldn't we wait until I have found work?'

'No, Themba, tomorrow is the day. You may meet another one of those city girls and change your mind.'

He walked with his grandfather to Nomisile's kraal and they cut out twelve pregnant heifers, swopping them around until they were satisfied that they had not given their best breeding stock. The quality would be good enough not to offend Nxele. The oxen were easier and they soon selected three with long, straight horns. Themba memorised the markings of the white and red cattle so they could separate them easily from the herd the next morning.

Themba and Morris opened the gate of Nxele's kraal and chased the fifteen cattle through. They sat cross-legged outside the enclosure, waiting for the next move in the time-honoured ritual.

Nxele cast an expert eye over the cattle, noting each addition to his herd, satisfied that the new cattle were adequate for his daughter's hand in marriage. He sat down opposite them.

A sheep had been slaughtered, the rib sections were roasting on the coals. Morris and Themba ate their fill of mutton and were served traditional beer to drink. After the meal, Themba was presented with a whole hindquarter from the sheep, which he was expected to take home and cook that evening.

They stood up and walked to Nxele's hut. Hilda was standing inside, ready, a small suitcase packed. She greeted her parents and followed Morris and Themba as they walked in single file towards Nomisile's hut.

Once out of sight Themba fell back to walk with Hilda, breaking with tradition. He wanted to treat her as an equal, as the women at university had been.

'We're married, I'm very happy,' smiled Themba, squeezing her arm affectionately.

'So am I. If I'd had any choice in the matter, which a Xhosa girl doesn't, I would have chosen you, Themba. I'm glad you chose me. Everything has worked out perfectly. My father says the ceremony will be next Saturday.'

She laughed as she saw his frown and guessed his thoughts. 'It's all right, you can make love to me. You've paid your cattle; I'm legally yours now.'

Nomisile's hut was deserted. The sewing machines had been packed away, the material neatly stacked in a heap. A fire was burning in the hearth, a pot simmered at the side. Themba's reed mat was unrolled, neatly covered with a blanket. 'Where are my mother and her two assistants?'

'They are away for the day.' Morris laughed, acknowledging his daughter's diplomacy. 'Nomisile will be back at nightfall. You two have the whole day to yourselves.'

He turned and walked home. Hilda shut the door, bolting it from the inside. She washed herself all over with soap and warm water and then did the same for Themba.

He held her in his arms. 'Welcome to my home.' He looked into her tearful eyes, her serene face.

'I love you, my husband. I have loved you for many years.'

Themba gently laid her down, kissing her, feeling all the familiar places, also exploring where he had not been before. Hilda did not resist, she encouraged him. This time there was no ox-fat. She lay back, her eyes closed, surrendering completely. Slowly it built up inside them, until with a celebration of feeling they let themselves go, then moaning in the afterglow.

He rolled over on to his back, cradling Hilda in his arm. With Muriel it had been exciting and intense, but somehow cheap. Hilda was fulfilling and satisfying, and for life.

Hilda had a woman's inborn intuition that Themba was vastly more experienced than she had suspected, but she held her counsel. What happened before their marriage was not her place to ask.

'You two look radiant.' Nomisile smiled when she returned at nightfall. The way they touched secretly and the loving glances and smiles reminded her of how it had been after her first time with Simon under the milkwood tree. Their reactions had been the same when they, too, could not get enough of each other. Oh Simon, she thought, if only you could see your son today, you would be so proud.

'You rascal, why didn't you tell me you were getting married?' exploded Paul.

'It all happened so quickly after our return from East London. I would like you to be my best man.'

'What an honour.'

When he returned to Mqekezweni there was a letter waiting for Themba. 'It's from my friend Ngconde Seymour, whom I knew when I was at Fort Hare. He finished a year before me and went to teach in Johannesburg.'

'What does the letter say?' Hilda asked excitedly.

'Ngconde is leaving Dobsonville Secondary School in Soweto. He has accepted another teaching post in Carltonville. He says jobs are hard to come by. If I haven't yet found work, he has recommended me for his old post as English teacher.'

'Johannesburg?' Nomisile's heart sank. 'That's so far away. You can't accept.'

'What about me?' Hilda suddenly worried.

'Ngconde writes I can hire his house, so you can go with me.'

Hilda smiled with relief. She didn't want to be parted from her husband, or let him travel to the city of gold alone, with all the temptations she had heard about.

'What about your articles? You wanted to become an attorney?'

'True, but I can always finish later. Now the most important thing is to find work – I'm a married man with responsibilities. I can't sit around here, looking after cattle and tilling the soil. I'm too highly qualified.'

Nomisile looked annoyed. 'There's nothing wrong with that, my son. Being an elder is an honourable profession. The Paramount Chief is relying on you to help him establish the Democratic Progressive Party. Please stay, Themba.'

'No, mother. I've always wanted to see Egoli. Now's my chance. I'm going to write to the principal and apply for the post.'

Mqekezweni was a hive of activity the Saturday of the wedding ceremony. Nomisile donated three sheep, Nxele, as the father-in-law, six sheep and two head of cattle. Even Sabata Dalindyebo gave two sheep to his newest elder.

Twenty huge cast-iron pots were to be used. Each could hold a whole sheep or a quarter beast. The pots were arranged in a semi-circle with coals raked underneath, keeping them bubbling away.

Large quantities of thick sorghum beer were brewed for the hundreds of thirsty throats. Enamel and aluminium plates and drinking mugs were borrowed to cater for the guests.

They arrived from many outlying kraals. Everyone was in tribal dress – over eight hundred people in all – gathered in the village assembly place.

At the head sat the Paramount Chief, his wives and children. To his left his immediate family. On his right were Nomisile, Themba, Morris and Nosakani Memani and Paul Curry. Paul was the only white face in the whole crowd. The guests sat in a big oval around them, the children in front, then the women, with the men at the back.

The ceremony began. Paramount Chief Sabata stood up and a hush settled on the assembled guests. It was a mark of Themba's importance and Hilda's lineage that Dalindyebo was to conduct the ceremony.

Themba was barefoot. He wore only a loincloth with a red blanket over his shoulder. Paul sweated in his best Sunday suit.

Hilda had on a red blanket skirt. She wore colourful bracelets of beads around her ankles and wrists, copper bangles above her calves and elbows and a wide, beaded necklace. On her forehead was a bead headband, criss-crossed over the top of her head. She was bare chested, her ample breasts standing out proudly.

Themba walked forward with Paul at his side. Hilda was accompanied by her father. A pace away from Sabata, they knelt in the dust.

Dalindyebo looked at Paul, speaking in English. 'Will your friend Themba accord his wife the status of a principal wife in his household?'

'Yes, he will.'

Sabata then spoke to Nxele. 'Has the *lobola* been paid to your satisfaction?'

'As agreed, in full.'

The Paramount Chief took both their right hands, enclosing them in his palms. He raised his voice, for all to hear. 'I declare Themba and Hilda duly wed. You may rise. Let the wedding feast begin.'

Family and friends surrounded the newly-weds, bringing all manner of presents. His grandfather and Sabata presented Themba with heifer calves. Others gave him young ewes led forward on leather thongs. Some presented chickens, their legs tied together, flapping and squawking as they were laid on the ground. Most gave cash, the amount depending on their station – from a few coins, to paper money of all denominations.

Steaming bowls of stewed meat from the pots were dished up. The first food, the beef, was served to Sabata and his royal family, next Themba and Hilda, then their wedding parties. Eventually the remaining beef, then the mutton, was shared out to the guests, starting with the council members.

People laughed and shouted in delight, enjoying the good food and beer, happy to be sharing a good party with the newly-weds. It was the biggest wedding at Mqekezweni in years. The meat was finished in half an hour. Those still hungry settled for boiled whole mealies. Then it was time for the dancing. The plentiful supply of beer cast away all inhibitions. First the men danced a tribal dance to the steady beat of rawhide drums. They danced in perfect time, lifting their right knees high, then crashing their feet to the ground as the drum beat grew louder. Sweat poured off their bare torsos as they danced in line, turning and spinning in harmony. One by one the older men fell out, leaving the young, fit warriors to continue. The audience spurred them on, clapping in time as the beat grew faster and faster and the steps became more and more intricate.

Paul, fired by the beer, joined in, much to the delight of the crowd. He hopped around like a stricken heron on his good leg, his shrivelled polio leg flapping around. He stripped off his jacket, shirt, shoes and socks and rolled up his trousers, joining in the merriment. He did not last long before he collapsed next to Themba – the *kwenkwe-njani* dance proving too much.

At last the men gave up and retired to replenish their beer, content to watch as the women took over. They danced smaller, more intricate steps to a slower beat, their bare breasts bouncing up and down in time with the drums, their ample buttocks swaying from side to side in fluid movement. They danced all their favourites – *lelebani*, *chi-ki-cha*, *sebetu*, *lamlani* and *pozana*, while the spectators encouraged them. They danced in rows, then alternated to circles – light on their feet and agile in their movements.

Themba and Hilda rose to leave. They bowed to the royal party and waved to the guests who formed two long rows for them to walk through.

The newly-weds made love to the distant beat of the cowhide drums, eventually falling asleep in each other's arms as the revellers made merry far into the night.

Themba asked the next council meeting for permission to build his own house. He was offered land of his own, but chose to share Nomisile's allocation. He wanted to build next to his mother's hut. Sabata instructed a team of men to help and within a week a large, round, thatched hut was completed. Themba painted it with white clay to match Nomisile's.

Hilda was overjoyed to have her own home and Nomisile was pleased to have her son living next door to her. 'My life is now complete,' she told her son.

Her happiness was soon shattered. A week later, Themba received a letter from the principal of Dobsonville Secondary School offering him the English teaching post.

'What about the council? You have an obligation to the Paramount Chief. You cannot leave, he will stop you.' Nomisile was frantic.

'Nelson Mandela also left to go to Johannesburg against the royal wishes.'

'The Chief sent representatives to track him down and bring him back, to fulfil his tribal duties. The same will happen to you. Why don't you settle down here at Mqekezweni and devote your life to your people?'

'I'm young. I want to see new places, do new things. I really want to go to Johannesburg. I will speak to Sabata first and get his permission.'

'I'll lose you for ever. You'll never come back. Please stay, my son, you are so precious.'

'Transkei and Mqekezweni will always be my home. I have my new house as my base. I'll be back.'

Dalindyebo was not pleased to hear the news at a private audience. 'You are my up and coming councillor, Themba, the one man with the foresight and determination to play a major part in the Democratic Progressive Party. We have an uphill fight against Kaiser Matanzima. I need you.'

'Let me go for a trial period . . . just one year,' Themba pleaded.

'Once you get used to the big city with all its distractions, you won't want to come back to Mqekezweni and its simple life.'

'After the year, if you demand it, I will return to play my part in the DPP.'

Sabata sat for a long time in contemplation. He could not really stop him. Themba had set his heart on going. Reluctantly he gave his consent. 'For one year only,' he stressed. 'Then you must return to your tribal duties.'

'I hear you, great Paramount Chief.'

Belching steam and with a squealing of wheels the Trans-Karoo shuddered to a halt at Pretoria station. Pierre grabbed his duffel-bag and jumped to the platform, along with a coach load of Cape recruits.

'Line up! Line up!' shouted a police sergeant, forming them into a squad. He checked their names against a list and they filed on to waiting buses. A five-kilometre drive followed to the Police College in Pretoria West.

At six the next morning the bell woke Pierre from a deep sleep. Two seconds later the sergeant burst into their barracks. 'Wake up, let's go!' He rapped his cane against the metal beds.

They dressed in their civilian clothes and stood at the ends of their beds. 'Good morning, gentlemen, I am Sergeant Patrollie Retief, your platoon sergeant. For the next six months I will be your father, mother, brother and sister. You either listen to me and we get on well, or you don't – in which case, I promise, you'll shit. The choice is yours.' He walked up to a boyish-looking recruit. 'What do you say, sonny?'

The youngster recoiled in fright. '*Ja, oom.*'

'I'm not your uncle, dammit. Call me sergeant.'

He stopped opposite Pierre. 'What do you say, tough guy?'

Pierre looked at him levelly, holding his gaze, neither belligerent nor frightened. 'Yes, Sergeant.'

'That's better. Now move your arses and get down to the dining room for breakfast.'

At seven o'clock the twelve hundred recruits presented themselves on the parade ground. The police chaplain started proceedings with a prayer, then it was time for the morning parade.

They visited the quartermaster where they were kitted out with uniforms, blue overalls and bedding. They had to run everywhere, chased by the superbly fit platoon sergeant.

On the second day Patrollie announced they were going on a bus tour of the whole college. They looked around in vain for the bus. He laughed at their discomfiture. The bus tour, he told them, consisted of a quick jog from facility to facility. He led them on a tour, at the double, of the whole academy.

They soon fell into the routine – up at six o'clock, then breakfast, prayers and morning parade, followed by classes until four in the afternoon. They rotated through the various sections – physical training, drill, musketry and law.

15

A highveld thunderstorm was brewing, the cumulus clouds packed and threatening, as the East London train steamed into Johannesburg station.

Themba helped Hilda off-load their suitcase and a roll of blankets tied with leather thongs. They walked out of the station building, down Eloff Street.

'Look at all the people.' Hilda gazed in amazement. 'I've never seen so many people at the same time – they look like ants scurrying around.'

Themba pointed upwards. 'Wow – just look at those buildings with row upon row of windows high into the sky.'

'I don't see even a blade of grass or the leaf of a tree in this concrete jungle.'

He looked at his watch. 'We must go to Soweto. We can return another time.' Themba asked directions but the black man had difficulty understanding his pure Xhosa. 'Man, here we talk fanagalo. It's a mixture of Zulu, Xhosa, Tswana, English and Afrikaans.' He pointed them to the Putco bus terminus, where they boarded a single-decker bus.

'What are those yellow hills?' Themba asked a fellow passenger.

'You must be new here, man. Those are mine dumps from the gold mines. They're coloured yellow by the cyanide used to extract the gold.'

At their stop they jumped off the bus and walked to Dobsonville Secondary School. The principal was in his office. 'Welcome, Mr and Mrs Memani. Themba, I hope you enjoy our school and will be happy in Soweto.'

'Thank you, Mr Keke. I'm sure we will. This is a big school compared to our Transkei schools.'

'We have two sessions, mornings and afternoons, to accommodate all the pupils. You'll have to do a double shift each day. You'll be teaching English to the senior pupils – the standard nines and tens.' The principal showed Themba and Hilda around the school and then offered to drive them to their new home. He dropped them off in front of the house. 'See you next week when school opens.'

Themba and Hilda stood in the dusty road, completely disorientated. Kilometre upon kilometre, row upon row, up hill and down dale, stood identical matchbox houses, each denominated by a large number painted on the front. Open spaces were littered with loose piles of used cartons, bottles, tins, bags and plastic. Tattered plastic bags, caught in the fences, fluttered in the wind.

'Why is Soweto so untidy?' Hilda asked her neighbour when she fetched the house key.

'We all hire the houses from the council. Who wants to improve the government's property? If we owned our own places we'd look after them better.'

They unlocked the door. Outside it was unkempt: an unplastered brick house with a corrugated asbestos roof. Inside, the Seymours had left the place immaculate. 'That's more like it.' Hilda was relieved. She walked through the small house. 'Two rooms and a kitchen.'

'The toilet is at the back.' Themba unlocked the back door and walked to the pit-latrine, a small building standing against the back boundary fence.

Hilda stared at the garden. 'This is no good. Surely we can take a pride in our surroundings. We must clean up the yard and grow flowers and vegetables.'

Themba walked disconsolately through the echoing rooms. 'We didn't need furniture in the Transkei. Now we need a lot of new things.'

'We'll manage,' smiled Hilda. 'You have some money and my father gave me a bit of cash.'

That night they slept in their bedroll on the cement floor. The next day they went shopping for the bare necessities.

Hilda arranged her new house proudly. 'I'm so happy, Themba. Our home looks lovely – all we need now is a child to make our lives complete.'

'All in good time.'

*   *   *

320

The heat of summer faded, bringing the autumn winds that dried out the highveld and turned the green swaths of grass to russet shades. On a cloudless April day Themba was summoned to the principal's office. He hummed a catchy tune as he strolled down the passage, happy to have settled so quickly into his new surroundings.

'You wished to see me, Mr Keke?' Themba's voice was warm and friendly.

'Please sit down, Mr Memani,' said Keke with a frown, knowing the next few minutes would not be easy. 'We are most satisfied with your teaching ability and your pupils think highly of you, but I have to clarify a point. Do you speak Afrikaans?'

Themba shook his head. 'At both school and university I received instruction only in English. Why do you ask?'

'You have probably heard the government is pressing for Afrikaans to replace English as the medium of instruction in our schools.'

'That's been going on since Verwoerd's time. What's changed?'

'In the 1950s there were no black teachers proficient in Afrikaans, or any textbooks in the Afrikaans language. The policy was difficult to implement. Now, twenty years later, there are trained teachers and enough textbooks, and they are making it compulsory.'

'Where does that leave me, Mr Keke?' The first signs of anxiety showed on Themba's face.

'I'm afraid that unless you're prepared to change to teaching in Afrikaans I may have to replace you, Themba.'

He looked at the principal in horror. 'Afrikaans is the language of the oppressor. I won't learn or teach Afrikaans.'

'Very well. I'll bear it in mind. I hope you don't regret your decision later.'

In May the first frosts of winter burnt the amber grass a bleached white, turning the landscape into a vista of austere bleakness. Themba stamped his feet as he walked to work. Somehow he knew that the day would present problems; he had a further meeting with the principal.

He knocked and walked in. Mr Keke was not alone – two white officials from the Black Education Department were also present. He sat down, expecting the worst.

The principal cleared his throat. 'Mr Memani, you remember we discussed the matter of giving tuition in Afrikaans?'

Themba nodded. 'I remember.'

'What we talked about has now come to pass. These two inspectors are here to see that the government's wishes are carried out. We have been instructed to implement the Afrikaans directive.'

One of the white inspectors rose and looked at Themba antagonistically. 'Mr Memani, we understand you are a trouble-maker, that you refuse to heed this instruction. Do you know we are sacking teachers for refusing to use Afrikaans in schools?'

Themba looked intently at the two white officials. 'You may be able to convince the teachers, but your main problem lies with the students. They won't accept your ruling. Only last week there was a class boycott at Orlando West Junior Secondary.'

The taller inspector thumped angrily on the desk. 'Who do you think pays for black education? The white Nationalist government. Don't you think we have a right to insist on our language being used?'

He was supported by his colleague. 'Mr Memani, it begins with the teachers. If you would start teaching in Afrikaans, the students would adapt. They would have no option.'

Themba sat back, spreading his hands in an act of reconciliation. 'Gentlemen, please. Don't you realise we're all sitting on a powder keg? Over the years the government has systematically crushed black opposition by throwing the leaders of any organised protest into prison. This time around it's going to be too big to contain. It will start at grass roots. The pupils will hit back at the system through a new ideology – black power. Have you gentlemen heard of the Black Consciousness Movement?'

'Of course, but it's a fad that will blow over.'

Themba shook his head. 'You are wrong. The discontent is growing. I predict that within a month there will be unrest on a scale never seen before – class boycotts, marches, demonstrations. The pupils will not be forced into accepting Afrikaans as their first language – they will revolt rather than capitulate.'

The shorter inspector bridled with anger. 'We'll crush any dissidents. We'll cut our subsidies to boycotting schools and withhold teachers' salaries until they toe the line.'

Themba looked at the principal. 'Mr Keke, don't let Dobsonville Secondary School bow to the bullying of the government. Sooner or later they must realise negotiation will achieve more than trying to force a hard-line stance.'

The principal looked sad. 'If we take a stand the children will suffer, which will only make matters worse, Themba. I've only five years left before I go on pension. All my life I've lived under the white man's laws. I can't start changing now, it's too late for me. Sorry.'

'Where does that leave me, gentlemen?'

'Simple – teach in Afrikaans or you're fired.'

'I'm a qualified English teacher. I have never learnt, nor do I desire to learn, the damnable Afrikaans language of the Boers. I refuse on principle to give instruction in Afrikaans.' Themba slapped his hand against his leg to emphasise his determination.

The inspector was adamant. 'Then you finish at the end of the term. There's no place for revolutionaries in the Black Education Department.'

Keke looked despondent. 'Themba, I feel for you, but there's nothing I can do.'

'Then I have nothing to lose.' Themba reached a decision. 'I'll side with the students in their struggle for justice. I can help them organise themselves in their fight against the system.'

'Then you'll be arrested and thrown into jail.' The inspector waved his finger under Themba's nose. 'And be warned, the police don't play around with trouble-makers.'

'What will be, must be!' Themba stormed out of the office.

'Class, I have an announcement to make.' The pupils looked at Themba expectantly. 'It grieves me, for I have enjoyed every moment of teaching you, but I have been fired from my post because I will not teach in Afrikaans. I leave at the end of the term.'

The matriculation class broke into uproar. 'We must fight the system,' a front-row pupil shouted.

'You must stay on as our teacher. We demand you stay!'

'Calm down, class.' Themba held out his arms for silence. 'My predicament should not stop you learning and getting your matric at the end of the year. Let's continue the lesson.'

At the end of the period the students filed out for break. Two of the older boys stayed behind, waiting until the classroom was empty before approaching Themba. He was aware they were members of the Soweto Students' Representative Council. 'May we speak with you, Mr Memani?'

'Of course.'

'The SSRC is selecting delegates from each secondary school to be represented on an action committee. We know we can trust you to represent Dobsonville Secondary. We would like you to represent us.'

'I've been fired anyway.' Themba shrugged. 'I'll certainly be of assistance if I can. I'll be proud to represent the school.'

'The first meeting is tomorrow afternoon at Orlando West Secondary.'

'I'll be there.'

That evening Themba broke the news to Hilda. She was shattered. They had settled down to life in Soweto, having made their little house into a home with furniture they had added every month from Themba's salary. 'What is our future, my husband?'

'I don't fancy working in the mines, it's dirty, soul-destroying work. I'm too well trained to be a labourer. I can't work in an office because those jobs are reserved for whites only.'

'You are a tribal elder, your work at Mqekezweni is fitting for a man of the royal line.' She moved closer and looked imploringly into Themba's eyes. 'Can't our baby be born in the Transkei? Soweto is no place to raise a child.'

'You're right. We've still got our home there and my mother will be pleased. I can again become involved in the Democratic Progressive Party.'

Themba walked the few blocks to Orlando West Secondary where he joined the representatives from the other high schools. The classroom was packed for the meeting.

'Who are you?' a student called Dan asked suspiciously.'

'I'm a teacher from Dobsonville Secondary School, but I've been sacked because I refuse to teach in Afrikaans. I'll help where I can, for I believe strongly in your cause.'

His *bona fides* accepted, the meeting continued. It was chaotic, with the chairman, Tebello, struggling to maintain order. The mood of the students was rebellious and some of their violent demands made Themba feel very uncomfortable.

Themba stood up to be heard. Holding up his hand he quietened the crowd. Slowly the interjections ceased as they looked up at the tall, dignified man. He waited for complete silence before speaking. 'Comrades, violence is out.' Themba's authoritative voice filled the room. 'We'll achieve nothing by violence. Our cause will only be advanced if we can speak to the authorities and get them to abandon their demand for Afrikaans instruction.'

'What do you suggest,' asked Tebello.

'A peaceful protest march,' answered Themba firmly.

The children clapped spontaneously. With their new-found direction the details were discussed. Eventually they decided a protest march would be held through the streets of Soweto on Wednesday, 16 June 1976. Schools would be visited on the way to swell the numbers. The march would end at Orlando Football Stadium, where they would present a list of their grievances to a government delegation.

'Soweto is crawling with *impimpi*. How do we stop these informers from telling the police?'

Themba nodded in agreement. 'Secrecy is vital. If the police know beforehand, they'll break up the march and the protest will lose its impact.'

An individual promise of silence was elicited from everyone at the meeting. The logistics of the march were gone over in minute detail. Fourteen assembly points were identified, giving an even spread throughout the townships. Routes to the stadium were worked out so that they would pass all the schools and so swell the numbers.

Dan spoke. 'How are we going to get the information through to the pupils without alerting the police?' It was decided each committee member should visit a few schools and pass on the message to their leaders, stressing the need for silence.

It was still dark on the cold highveld winter's morning when the pupils started gathering at the assembly points. They stamped their feet and clapped their hands to keep warm. Spirits were high as they laughed and talked excitely to each other, their hot breaths making white puffs in the freezing air. Hundreds of thousands of children had maintained virtually total secrecy, for not a policeman or army vehicle was in sight. The students had the dawn to themselves.

Elsewhere in Soweto workers streamed to the stations to catch the trains taking them into Johannesburg for another day's work. Parents, unaware of the intended march, thought their children were off to school.

Themba noted with satisfaction the large crowds already gathered at the assembly point near his home. At school he headed for his classroom, ready for the day ahead.

Committee members had worked wonders as thousands of students congregated at each point. At seven o'clock, on schedule, the marchers set off, chanting and waving hand-made slogans on flattened cardboard boxes.

Near White City a police van came around the corner. The police stopped in surprise when they saw the horde of marchers on the move. After firing shots over their heads they raced away to raise the alarm.

A watery sun had just cleared the smoke haze when one group reached Dobsonville Secondary School, streaming through the gates into the classrooms to urge the scholars to join them. Themba watched as first his class, then the whole school, staged a mass exodus. The principal and teachers stood at the gates watching the mob growing by the minute, powerless to do anything.

Mr Keke confronted Themba. 'Where are you going, Mr Memani?'

'To join the demonstrators.' Themba flashed a clenched-fist salute.

'It's their fight against the system. Let them be. Come back.'

Themba laughed in derision. 'What have I to lose? I'll support the students and have a clear conscience, thank you.'

The phalanx of bodies grew as more and more pupils joined in, sub-groups meeting sub-groups, meshing into long, milling columns as wide as the road permitted. Themba made his way through the surge of relaxed and enthusiastic children. They laughed and joked, enjoying the fun as if it were a public holiday and they were missing a day's schooling. There was no aggression; Themba prayed the police would react in similar fashion.

Themba reached the front of the marchers as they got to Orlando West Junior Secondary just on nine o'clock. Within minutes the school had emptied and the pupils joined the march.

The principal came running to the gate as a police helicopter clattered overhead, the downward draught of the spinning rotors kicking up dust and scattering the refuse. He addressed the marchers. 'The police have just telephoned to say they are on their way. It's best if you all disperse.'

Themba climbed up the inside of the high wire-mesh fence

surrounding the school, standing with his feet in the loops of wire, balancing his knees against the top strand of the fence. He was above the crowd, waving them to silence. 'Brothers and sisters, I appeal to you to keep calm and act responsibly. We have just heard the police are on their way. Don't taunt them, don't do anything to antagonise them. Stay calm and cool. We are not fighting, we are demonstrating. There must be no violence.'

Minutes later they heard the sirens as police vehicles raced towards them, screaming to a halt in front of the crowd. Fifty policemen jumped out, rifles and sub-machine-guns at the ready.

'Disperse! I order you to disperse!' a policeman shouted over the loudspeaker system. The children answered by calmly singing '*Morena Boloka Sechaba sa heso* – God save our nation'.

'Ours is a peaceful protest,' cried Themba from his elevated position. 'We have grievances and we are marching to Orlando Stadium to meet with the authorities to discuss the situation.'

'Get off that fence before we shoot you down.' A policeman slapped a shotgun to his shoulder and aimed it at Themba.

'We only want to negotiate,' called Themba urgently. 'We don't want violence.'

'I'm warning you for the last time.'

'Don't you understand?' protested Themba indignantly. 'We want to talk, not fight.'

'Fire!'

A shotgun exploded. Themba cried out in pain. He lost his footing and crashed to the ground. Holding his side, he watched in horror as the blood oozed between his fingers. He had to try one more time. Desperately he pulled himself upright against the fence, his face contorted in agony. 'Stop! Stop!' Themba screamed at the top of his voice.

The officer turned away, his lips a hard line of contempt. He signalled to one of his policemen. A tear-gas cylinder curled in a lazy arc, turning end upon end, falling into the crowd as they jumped out of the way. The gas billowed out, blinding the pupils and stinging their eyes. They ran, pushing outwards towards the police, leaving an empty crater in the middle.

'Fire!'

Rifles barked. 'No!' bellowed Themba as he saw Hector Peterson, a thirteen-year-old schoolboy, slump to the ground, blood streaming from a bullet wound.

327

Terrified children ran helter-skelter to escape the carnage, leaving Hector lying in the dust.

'Help him, Mbuyisa,' shouted Themba. To his relief Mbuyisa Makhuba turned around to help his friend. He gathered Hector in his arms and stumbled away, his face twisted in anguish. Antoinette, Hector's elder sister ran alongside, her right hand thrown up in torment, a look of total heartbreak on her face.

'Hector is dead,' sobbed Antoinette.

Themba sagged to the ground in distress, a great sadness enveloping him. Hector was the demonstration's first victim. The peaceful march was no more.

Under a barrage of stones the police retreated towards Orlando East. Themba hobbled across and found another dead child. There were twelve injured pupils also, whom they carried into the school building.

A teacher cut Themba's clothes away from the wound. 'You're very lucky they used bird shot and not heavy buckshot pellets. Your jacket absorbed most of the impact.' Using forceps from the school's first-aid box, she removed the small lead pellets one by one from under Themba's skin.

'That's the last one.' The teacher dabbed antiseptic on the pock-marks. He thanked her and walked out of the school.

The street was deserted, the pupils well on their way to Orlando Stadium. In the distance Themba heard sirens as the police rushed in reinforcements. There was the sporadic sound of gunfire, always followed by the screaming of children, their high-pitched young voices carrying far in the still air.

Themba went home to change into fresh clothing. Hilda cried out when she saw the pink, puffy marks from the bird shot.

'Where are you going now?'

'Back to the students, to see what's happening.'

'Stay with me,' she pleaded. 'Let them fight if they want to, but you keep away, you've already been injured.'

'Their fight is our fight, Hilda. If I stay home I'm a coward to the cause. I must go.'

'Please be careful. You've had one lucky escape, next time could be fatal.'

Themba hurried back to the action. The police had broken up the peaceful protest march to Orlando Stadium. The protesters had scattered into smaller groups. Stung to retaliation the pupils

328

barricaded the streets, using any objects at hand. The mood became violent, turning the whole of the sprawling township into a battleground. Themba tried desperately to persuade the pupils to return peacefully to their homes, but by now they were resentful and past caring.

At noon a dark column of smoke rose into the air. Themba raced across the township, skirting around the fortifications. He found the West Rand Administration Board offices on fire. The flames forced the government officials out of the building. They were attacked by angry crowds and two of the officials were killed. The angry pupils also torched the Board's vehicles. There was no stopping them – they were blood-crazed and intent on vengeance.

Themba stared in disbelief as the police spread out and simply fired into the mob instead of practising proper riot control. His heart bled as children were hit by the bullets.

'You stupid police,' he shouted, sickened by the carnage. 'Can't you show some compassion?' He shook his fist angrily. 'Shooting and killing isn't the answer. Why don't you negotiate?'

He ducked as a bullet ricocheted alongside his head, and he dived behind a car chassis.

Palls of smoke hung over Soweto as more and more government buildings were fired: clinics, schools, beer halls, bottle stores and the Black Education offices. The streets were congested with barriers, preventing police reinforcements going in. He saw the mayhem the pent-up anger of the black pupils had created in one day. Themba realised that for ever afterwards, 16 June would be known as the day on which it was irrevocably proved that the combined masses wielded more power than the government forces.

Themba had never witnessed wanton destruction on the scale he had seen that day. He returned home late in the evening, sickened, but realising it had been a turning point in the struggle.

Pierre and his fellow students at the Police College heard the news of the Soweto riots over the radio. It seemed there were too few police to control the situation.

At six o'clock on the morning of Thursday, 17 June, Sergeant Patrollie Retief stormed into the dormitory. 'Up, cadets! Get up quickly! You joined the police to see active service – now you're going to see it sooner than you thought. Get your police uniforms on.'

The barracks buzzed with urgent talk. 'They're going to send us to Soweto.'

'There are twelve hundred of us, we'll sort out those bloody kaffirs.'

They assembled on the parade ground. The police chaplain started with his usual prayer but added a rider: he asked God to bless and guide them in their first confrontation. Sergeant Retief checked his platoon were all present. He stood in front of his charges.

Head of the college, Captain Bothma, addressed them. 'Men, there has been an eruption of violence in Soweto, which is spreading to other areas. It has been decided to interrupt your training so that you may help the police maintain law and order. Once the situation is under control, you will return to college to complete your course.

'Most will be used to guard strategic installations such as petrol storage facilities, filling stations and government buildings. Some of you will be sent to active trouble spots where the police strength is not sufficient to cope with the situation. Remember your training and uphold the proud name of the Police College.

'You will proceed to the armoury, company by company, to draw weapons and ammunition. Good luck.'

There was a hushed silence as the officer's words sunk in. Pierre wrestled with his emotions – would he cope with the situation if the occasion demanded it?

They walked through the armoury in single file, each receiving an R1 semi-automatic rifle and three packs of 7.62 mm cartridges.

Patrollie Retief led his men to one of twenty buses brought in to transport them and they clambered aboard. Once out of the college gates the buses split up, going in various directions.

'Where are we going, Sarge?'

'We've been ordered right into the heart of Soweto. I hear things are bad there. It's our job to assist those police.'

The bus took them south, skirting Johannesburg. At the entrance to Soweto a Caspir armoured vehicle met them and escorted them into the township. Burnt-out wrecks of vehicles lay alongside the road; the smouldering shells of gutted buildings gave testimony to the previous day's anger. Rocks, stones, tins, poles, pipes, crates, boxes and all manner of objects littered the roads, forcing the bus to swing this way and that to find a passage through.

Chanting masses of youths sporadically blocked their path. They

330

hurled stones at the Caspir and were answered by weapon fire from inside. Pierre watched them scatter in confusion while their companions pulled the injured away from the scene.

The Caspir turned a corner straight into an ambush. A blazing car blocked the road. Instantly the vehicle was surrounded by a mass of youths. They placed logs behind the wheels and hacked the tyres with pangas, immobilising the vehicle. The police fired out of the slits in the side but the youths hugged the vehicle, out of the line of the bullets. Screaming triumphantly, they clambered on to the roof and beat the high-tensile metal with rocks, making the vehicle reverberate like a kettle drum. The policemen inside screamed in fear, their cries reaching the cadets in the bus.

Petrol bombs – bottles filled with petrol and containing a long cloth wick – were set alight and thrown through the ventilation slits. The bottles shattered and the liquid flooded the floor, creating a blazing inferno inside the vehicle. Flames licked through the firing slits, billowing into black smoke. Ammunition in the Caspir popped in the intense heat and ricocheted inside the confined interior.

The stench of burning flesh permeated the air, sickly-sweet and cloying. The Caspir and its crew were destroyed. Heat from the glowing vehicle drove the youths back as they stood and watched their handiwork in shocked fascination. Paint blistered off as the Caspir bent and buckled in its final throes.

The nightmare passed in minutes and the black students turned away, noticing the bus for the first time. They ran forwards with bloodshed mirrored in their eyes.

Throwing the vehicle into reverse, the driver pushed his foot full on the throttle. The bus shot backwards, swaying drunkenly from side to side as he tried to avoid the obstacles in the road. The youths gave chase, howling in derision as they closed the distance.

The trainees, trying desperately to hold on to their weapons, were tossed around inside and thrown into the aisle. Sergeant Retief knew instinctively that serious trouble lay ahead which would test his greenhorn charges to the maximum.

Stones rained on the front window, starring the safety glass. Youths sprang on to the front bumper, smashing the windscreen with metal pipes. Now the driver was exposed to their full fury. As a vicious blow struck him on the head he lost control and the bus slewed sideways, slowly falling on its side. The cadets were dumped in a tangled mass of bodies.

With the weight off the tyres, the diesel engine screamed at full revolutions. The bus was still in gear and the double back wheels revolved furiously, like the death spasms of a dying dinosaur. The reek of diesel filled the air.

Patrollie Retief screamed furiously, 'Get up, men, get up!' Pierre disentangled himself from the human mêlée, pulling his rifle out from under a body. He tried to scramble to his feet, but stepped on bodies underneath him. Men groaned in pain at the bottom of the pile. Pierre looked around, completely disorientated. A few seconds previously he had been sitting in the familiar layout of a bus, now the seats were against the sides, the roof was a row of windows and underfoot was crunching glass.

Black students jumped on top of the bus and Pierre could see their wild faces peering down through the panes. They started smashing the windows, spraying the police trainees with showers of glass.

One by one the trainees disentangled themselves. They stood between the lopsided seats, looking up fearfully as rocks hurtled down on the windows.

A blue-shirted black man heard the gunfire and hurried closer. As he turned the corner he came upon the wrecked bus. To his horror he saw students leaping on to it and heard the cries from inside.

'Stop, there's been enough killing already,' he shouted, as he pulled himself on to the bus. 'Stop! Stop!' He grabbed at a student's iron bar.

'Leave me,' screamed the boy in indignation, grappling for his weapon.

They wrestled for the crowbar. The man stepped on to the glass pane, his foot taking his full weight. The rubber window-housing gave way and the pane of plate glass was wrenched loose. The man hurtled through the opening, hitting his head on the metal part of a seat, and was knocked unconscious.

Over the din came the barking voice of Patrollie. 'Load your rifles. Fire!'

A black youth clutched at his stomach, screaming, blood spraying down on the upturned faces. He teetered, then plunged head first on top of the policemen. The trainees dodged to avoid the falling bodies, then fired more salvos upwards.

Stones were no match for 7.62 mm slugs and the youths jumped from the bus on to the road. Sergeant Retief rallied his men. 'Help each other, climb through the windows and secure the bus.'

Arms pushed Pierre upwards and he hoisted himself through the window opening. The overturned bus was surrounded by a vicious stone-throwing mob. A stone caught him in the back, knocking him flat. His rifle was handed up to him. He turned and fired a sharp burst at the crowd. His first reaction was to aim for their chests, to kill as many as possible, but he allowed his blind fury to be replaced by reason. He dropped the barrel and fired the burst at their feet. The youths fell back as the bullets kicked up grit. During the brief respite the trainees clambered out of the windows.

Patrollie Retief supervised the trainees inside and helped the wounded. When all had been safely passed upwards, he pulled himself through a window. On his instructions the policemen crouched back to back, facing outwards, rifles at the ready.

The ruptured fuel tank had emptied, forming a long slick of diesel fuel across the road. One of the youths bent down and struck a match. A sliver of flame ran up the gutter, approaching the bus in a wall of fire. Within seconds the back of the bus was ablaze, with the policemen trapped on top. Now wound up, the black youths chanted in unison and hurled stones at the cornered cadets.

'Fire over the crowd,' instructed the sergeant. A withering hail of metal spun out from the axis on top of the bus, knifing through the air above the mob. Their bravado was crushed. They turned and ran, glancing back with fearful expressions.

Tongues of flame were lapping over the bus as Retief issued the evacuation order. Cadets jumped to the ground and the injured policemen were passed down. The platoon sergeant did a quick head count, satisfying himself that all his charges were accounted for.

'Form up in ranks, we are marching to Dobsonville police station. Those in the middle take turns to carry the injured, those on the outsides hold your rifles at the ready. Forward march!'

Pierre heard a groaning sound coming from inside the bus and he stopped in his tracks. 'Sergeant Retief,' he shouted, 'there's someone still alive inside. We must save him.'

'How? Just look at the bus.'

The rear of the vehicle was a sheet of flame and the fire was spreading rapidly. Pierre passed his rifle to the man next to him and ran back to the bus. He clambered up the chassis.

'Come back,' screamed a fellow cadet. 'You'll get yourself

killed for someone who tried to kill us all! Leave the kaffir, let him die.'

Others echoed his words.

'I'm going in.' Pierre disappeared through a window. The heat was searing, it singed his eyebrows and scorched his uniform. He struggled between the tilted seats, searching for the sound. He found a youth and turned him over, but he was already dead. Pierre struggled on, finding two more bodies, getting desperate. At last he reached a figure trying feebly to sit up. It was a man wearing a blue shirt.

'Don't worry, I've come to get you.' Pierre turned the man on to his back.

'Thank you, white man.'

With his arms around the man, he forced him to his feet. Pierre found himself panting from exertion, his lungs burning as he gasped for breath. He jammed his shoulder under the man's armpit, struggling away from the heat.

With a great whooshing sound the diesel tank exploded sending out an advance wave of air. It knocked them off their feet and they lodged behind a seat. An orb of flame and metal debris engulfed the bus.

Outside, the startled policemen jumped back in fear as the rear end of the bus disintegrated in the explosion. 'Dammit,' cursed Patrollie sadly. 'Roux can't possibly have survived that blast.'

Again they struggled to their feet, stumbling over the rubble, wheezing as the fumes threatened to overpower them. At last they reached the partition between the driver's cab and the passenger section. Pierre kicked at the hardboard. It splintered and gave way. He crawled through the hole, over the driver's dead body. He pulled the man through and together they wormed out of the front window, falling in a heap on the road.

The cadets cheered in admiration. Patrollie Retief darted forward and pulled the two men away from the flames. They lay in the road gulping for air.

Pierre looked up in surprise as he heard the cheering of hundreds of black youths. He stood up, and taking the black man in his arms walked slowly towards the crowd.

'Cover him with your rifles,' barked Retief, a lump forming in his throat. The black youths threw down their weapons and applauded the man who had risked his life to save one of their own.

Pierre walked to the edge of the crowd. He held out his arms and passed the man over to willing hands. The crowd swirled around, slapping him good-naturedly on the back.

'You're very brave, white man. What's your name?' gasped the injured man.

'Pierre Roux, and yours?'

He looked at Pierre grudgingly, slowly acknowledging that there could be a decent policeman. 'Themba,' he muttered, 'Themba Memani.' He grasped Pierre's arm. 'I owe my life to you – if every white man were like you, South Africa would be a wonderful land. Go in peace.'

'You too, Themba. Get your head wound attended to. I must go.'

The youths lifted Pierre shoulder high and carried him back to his platoon. The cadets stared in surprise as they set him down gently, then formed into a friendly row and saluted him, '*Mayibuye*, Pierre Roux.' All animosity had evaporated as they waved at the policemen and danced away from the scene.

Patrollie Retief had witnessed an act of humanity he had never experienced in all his years on the force. He clasped Pierre by the shoulder. 'Well done, Roux. Out of the despair and misery of Soweto you've restored hope.' He turned to the cadets. 'Okay, men, let's go, it's still two kilometres to Dobsonville police station.'

Africa's grape-vine was at work: silent messages, inaudibly transferred over vast distances with no apparent effort on the part of the originators, told what had happened. As the platoon made its way through the litter-strewn streets of the township, youths performed the unthinkable. They lined the streets, chanting 'Pierre Roux! Pierre Roux! Pierre Roux!' Most of the way the platoon marched unhindered with not one act of aggression.

16

Themba walked slowly past Dobsonville Secondary – only a smouldering ruin was left. The roof was gone, the asbestos sheets were scattered in fragments around the buildings. The glass in the windows had melted in the heat, forming stalactites hanging from the window-sills. Some of the walls had crumbled in the inferno, others still stood, blackened mementoes of the students' rage.

Principal Keke was poking forlornly around in the ruins, looking for items to save. 'You were right after all, Themba. Now we're all out of work. Why didn't the government leave things as they were?'

With a wistful smile, Themba turned for home. Students still ran around in groups but not with the same intensity as the previous day. Tebello came running across. 'The police are after the leaders of the riots – especially the committee members of the Soweto Students' Representative Council. You must watch out.' Themba hurried home to be with Hilda and to keep out of sight. They ate supper and went to bed early. Hilda was fast asleep when she was woken by an urgent hammering on the front door. She nudged Themba. He lit a lamp. Opening the door, he found an agitated Tebello outside.

'The police are after two of my friends. Can you hide them in your house?'

'Who are they?'

Tebello pushed two youths forward, introducing them as Solomon and Khotso.

'Please take care of them.' Then he was gone, melting into the night.

Themba welcomed them to his home. 'When last did you eat?'

'Yesterday,' said Solomon. 'We've been on the run ever since. We are hungry. We would appreciate food.'

Hilda prepared a meal of bread and coffee for the guests. She gave them blankets and they settled down for the night. Themba and Hilda went back to bed.

The next day they stayed indoors. The authorities had managed to regain control of the streets. Barricades were cleared. Empty police vans roared into the township and drove out, filled with prisoners.

After breakfast there was nothing to do, so they sat around chatting. Hilda plied them with numerous cups of tea and it was not long before the guests had to relieve themselves.

'Go cautiously over the open space between the house and the toilet,' warned Themba. 'We don't know where the police are. We don't want them to see you.'

The next-door neighbour, looking out of her kitchen window, saw the furtive movements of the two strangers and wondered idly who they were.

During lunch they listened to the news. The riots had spread to all the major cities of South Africa – Durban, Port Elizabeth and Cape Town.

'Did you hear that?' asked Solomon excitedly. 'South African gold shares crashed on the London Stock Exchange today. De Beers fell fifty cents. Our efforts were not in vain.'

'Yes,' agreed Khotso. 'When the Afrikaners' standard of living drops, then the government will be forced to make reforms.'

'I need to piss again, it's all Hilda's tea.'

'Again?' queried Themba. 'Just be careful.'

The woman next door again saw Solomon and Khotso slink to the toilet and back to the house before the penny dropped. Of course, she thought, they are hiding from the police. If I report them, I'll collect a reward. She put on her coat and walked to the police station. The desk officer listened to her intently. 'Strangers you say. And they're being hidden by a teacher from Dobsonville Secondary School?'

'Yes, sir.'

A police van stopped outside the police station. Adjutant Koos Koekemoer and a student constable rushed inside. The duty officer called them. 'Come and listen to this.' The black woman repeated her story.

'What's the address?'

She told him.

'How many in the house?' queried Koekemoer.

'The teacher and his wife, plus two strangers.'

'Okay, we'll take a look, but we must have back-up – at least two policemen for the front and three around the back.'

The duty officer radioed for another patrol van and more policemen to come in to the station.

'What about my reward?' wailed the woman.

Koekemoer turned around. 'Sort that out with the duty officer.'

'How much do I get?' she demanded.

'This is what you get.' The duty officer leant over the counter and gave her a flat-handed blow across the face. 'Now fuck off, kaffir, before I arrest you.'

The woman staggered out of the police station, muttering to herself. The police vans roared off in clouds of dust. The informer was angry and remorseful, but there was nothing she could do. The police vans would reach Themba's house before she could walk one block. She headed home, cursing the police.

A block away Koekemoer gave final instructions. With engines barely idling they advanced from opposite sides, free-wheeling the last part.

Three ran silently to the back on rubber-soled boots. Two stationed themselves at the back corners of the erf while the third guarded the back door.

The student constable stood on the pavement covering the front door while the adjutant walked forward. The officer aimed a high kick at the door. The lock shattered and the door flew open. With one bound Koekemoer landed in the front room, his R1 rifle cocked, ready to fire.

Themba reacted instinctively. He dived forward, his arms closing around the policeman's legs. As he toppled over, Koekemoer tightened his finger on the automatic trigger. The R1 jerked upwards, spewing out a continuous dose of lethal lead into the ceiling. Solomon fled towards the back door, with Khotso following.

The policeman fell to the floor with Themba on top of him. As he tried to bring his weapon around, it was strength versus strength. With a supreme effort Themba pushed the weapon away, twisting it out of the policeman's grasp and tossing it into the far corner. He straddled Koekemoer, sitting on his chest, pinning his arms to his side.

The policeman at the back heard the front door breaking, followed by a round of automatic fire. He kicked at the back door, but it remained shut. He aimed a second kick, much higher, still off balance when Solomon and Khotso burst through. They knocked him sprawling as they ran towards the back fence. The men at the corners opened fire. Bullets whined through the air as the students swerved across the yard.

Khotso jumped the fence in one fluid movement, but a bullet tore into Solomon's leg. His momentum kept him going and he tumbled over the wire fence. In the heat of the moment, Solomon felt no pain, only a burning sensation as he staggered across the next plot. Dust flew around his feet as the bullets kicked up soil. Solomon and Khotso split up, running in different directions. The police gave chase, but soon lost their quarry amongst the fowl runs and tin lean-tos of the back yards.

Themba saw a shadow cross the threshold and looked up straight into the barrel of an R1, the ominous small circle just waiting to spatter his brains against the wall.

'Get up slowly, very slowly, and no tricks.' It was only when Themba was standing and the two were face to face that they recognised each other. 'Themba Memani,' breathed Pierre.

'We meet again,' grimaced Themba with a crooked smile.

The policeman at the back door came running into the house. He raised the butt of his weapon and smashed it down on Themba's shoulder. Themba crashed to his knees, crying out in pain, holding his injured shoulder.

Getting to his feet, Koekemoer cried in triumph, 'Fucking kaffir, I'm going to teach you a lesson!' Flexing his fingers into a tight ball, he hit Themba square in the face. Themba reeled over backwards, his nose broken and streaming blood. Koekemoer jumped forward. Using all his force, he kicked Themba in the stomach with the heel of his boot. Themba doubled up and fell on his side. Koekemoer stepped forward and trampled his face, the treads of his boots tearing Themba's lips.

Hilda wailed like an animal in pain. She covered her face with her arms, trying to blot out the horror. She shook uncontrollably as she pushed herself up against the wall, trying to get as far away as possible.

Reason took hold of Pierre. As Koekemoer raised his leg to stomp on Themba's face again, Pierre stepped forward. 'That's enough, Adjutant. Let's handcuff him and go.'

'The man attacked me.' Koekemoer looked at Pierre uncomprehendingly. 'I have the right to beat him up.'

'No, you don't.'

'You cadets from the Police College are taught new-fangled ideas. I've been a policeman for fifteen years and I tell you there's only one language a kaffir understands – beat the shit out of him and then he respects you.'

Pierre looked at his superior belligerently. 'I say no, Adjutant Koekemoer.'

'Hah, still wet behind the ears! You'll learn. The longer you stay in the police force, the more you learn to hate kaffirs. They're the cause of all our problems. We should shoot them all, clear the country of the scum and make it a safe place for the white man.'

'I don't want to argue with you, Adjutant Koekemoer. You are my superior officer, but we will achieve nothing by beating up this man.'

'Yes, I am your superior and it'll do you good to remember that in future, student constable.' He turned away in disgust.

Pierre helped Themba to his feet and the two half-brothers stared at each other, ignorant of their blood bond.

They were so similar, yet so different. Both were the same height and similarly built – lithe, powerful and well-muscled. The way they held themselves, the way they moved, were the same. Their eyes were dark-brown, clear, steady and perceptive. The faces were similar in shape, with identical cheek-bones and high foreheads.

There were contradictions, too. Pierre had an aquiline nose with a well-shaped mouth and lips, while Themba had inherited his mother's flatter, broader nose with a bigger mouth and fuller lips.

Glaring at each other, the half-brothers from opposite ends of the political spectrum acknowledged the pride and power in each other.

'My hands are handcuffed behind my back. Won't you please wipe the blood off my face?'

Without hesitation, Pierre produced his handkerchief, carefully cleaned Themba's face, stopping the flow of blood from his nose.

'What are you doing now?' The adjutant stared aghast at Pierre. 'You've ruined your hanky for a fucking kaffir!'

Pierre stared at him contemptuously.

Koekemoer shook his head in outrage, about to take umbrage, when the two policemen burst into the house. 'They got away, Adjutant – they ran like hares.'

'I got one, I shot him in the leg. We'll pick him up when he goes to a clinic or hospital for treatment.'

Koekemoer turned to Themba. 'Who are you?'

'I am Themba Memani, I'm a teacher from Dobsonville Secondary School.'

'I recognise his name from the confidential lists,' said a policeman. 'Themba Memani was a founder member of the Soweto Students' Representative Council. He's one of the ringleaders.'

'Is that so?' demanded Koekemoer.

'It's true, I was on the executive of the SSRC,' Themba answered. 'I fought for peaceful protest, I did not want violence. The police turned a peaceful mass rally into a blood-bath.'

Koekemoer stepped forward. 'So you're a bloody commie, and you were harbouring terrorists in this house. Who were those two men who escaped?'

'Just friends,' answered Themba.

'What are their names?' demanded Koekemoer.

There was no answer.

'Talk, or I'll beat it out of you.' Koekemoer raised his fist, his eyes filled with hate.

At that moment Hilda crawled out from under the table, screaming in fear. 'Leave my husband alone – don't beat him up.' She rushed forward, clinging to Themba.

Before Pierre could stop him, Koekemoer punched Hilda, spinning her around towards the next constable. He swung the rifle butt at her, catching her on the arm. There was a loud crack as her arm broke. Koekemoer booted her in her swollen stomach as she fell to the floor.

Themba tried to go to her help but he was forcibly restrained by two policemen holding his arms. In frustration and helplessness he cried out, 'Bastards, look what you've done to my wife. She's pregnant!'

Malice gleamed in Koekemoer's eyes as he booted her a second time, a full-blooded kick, landing squarely on her extended abdomen. 'That's the end of another kaffir child then. One less to worry about.'

Themba's cry roused Pierre. He stepped between Hilda and

342

Koekemoer. 'Stop! Stop it!' He bent down to look at Hilda. Her left arm flopped uselessly. She groaned in agony, holding her stomach with her good hand.

Pierre cradled Hilda in his arms. She was in a cold sweat, large drops forming on her forehead. 'Bring water and a cloth,' Pierre barked at a constable.

The policeman looked questioningly at Koekemoer. He nodded coldly and the constable went through to the kitchen, returning with a bowl of water and a towel.

Pierre bathed her face and neck with the cool liquid, softly comforting her. 'Don't worry, I won't let them harm you again.'

Hilda was in great pain, but looked gratefully at Pierre. She cried out as her stomach contracted tightly. Waves of agony washed over her. She passed out as her water broke and amniotic fluid puddled the floor.

'Adjutant, I'm going to report you for your cruelty.' Pierre was furious.

'Do that – nothing will come of it. She's only a kaffir. The brigadier will laugh at you, man.'

Furious, Pierre stood up, taking control. 'Constable, go out to the police van and radio headquarters. Ask them to send an ambulance urgently.'

Themba slumped to the floor in grief, his mind tortured at Hilda's pain, his heart breaking at the loss of his child. He prayed silently: God, give me strength to survive this day. Look after my wife and I promise I will devote the rest of my life to the struggle, to fight for justice to end the evil of apartheid.

The policeman came back. He had been in contact with the police station. 'We must go. People are gathering in the street. There could be trouble.'

'We'll wait until the ambulance arrives,' Pierre declared firmly.

The ambulance screamed up the road, sirens wailing and red lights flashing. Orderlies straightened Hilda's arm, temporarily binding it with wooden splints, then lifted her gently on to a stretcher.

'May I say goodbye to my wife?' Themba looked at Pierre.

'No, you can't.' Koekemoer stared at him belligerently.

'Of course you may.' Pierre overrode his superior. Koekemoer stared sullenly but did not contradict him.

The orderlies stopped in the doorway. Themba went across and kissed Hilda on the mouth, tears running down his cheeks. Pierre unlocked one handcuff. Themba nodded gratefully and held his wife in his arms. 'Goodbye, my darling wife, take care.' He turned to Pierre. 'Can I count on you to see she gets proper treatment? A miscarriage can lead to complications.'

Pierre nodded. 'She's going to hospital. They'll treat her well.'

Themba turned to the adjutant-officer, a murderous expression in his eyes. 'Koekemoer, I will remember your name and face for the rest of my life.' There was cold hatred in his voice. 'If ever we meet again, I promise you I'll kill you, like you killed my unborn child.'

'Stupid kaffir,' screamed Koekemoer and shoved Themba in the chest.

He stumbled towards the door landing on all fours. Raising his head he saw the crowd of curious onlookers in front of the house. In a flash Themba was on his feet and running. He dodged between the people and sprinted across the road.

'After him!' roared Koekemoer.

The policemen poured out of the house. They raised their weapons but could not fire because of the crowd. The onlookers grasped the situation instantly and bunched together, giving Themba a few extra seconds. He darted between the houses and soon shook off his pursuers.

Koekemoer was furious. He turned on Pierre. 'You stupid bugger, you unlocked the handcuffs. Now we'll see who has to explain to the brigadier.'

Pierre nodded dully, a loathing for Themba growing as his fellow policemen derided him. He kept his mouth shut, but inwardly seethed with uncurbed pique. Ungrateful bastard, I saved his life and this is how he repays me! Wait until next time, he promised himself.

Buttoning up her raincoat and snapping open her umbrella, Lesley Summers stepped out into the teeming rain. She glanced towards Table Mountain but it was lost in the swirling mists of the cold front. Coming towards her was a huge man with blond hair, looking even bigger in a bulky coat. Around his neck was a red scarf. She recognised him immediately and stopped.

'Helmut Schmidt! How are you?'

She lifted her umbrella and he recognised her. '*Mein Gott*, but it's Lesley Stuart.'

'Summers,' she corrected him, with a look of indifference.

'*Himmel*, woman, it's cold and wet. Let's go for a cup of coffee.'

They ran to a coffee shop in Greenmarket Square. Now she would be able to ask after Pierre. She removed her coat and beret and shook her head to fluff out her hair.

She certainly is a beautiful woman, thought Helmut. 'Filter coffee for two,' he boomed, 'and add two slices of Black Forest cake.'

'Helmut,' began Lesley tentatively, 'when did you last see Pierre?'

'Ah-ha! I thought you were glad to see me! Now I see it's information on Pierre Roux you're after, you devious vixen!'

Lesley had the grace to blush. 'I miss him terribly, I really do.'

'Why don't you leave him be, woman? Don't you think he's been through enough already?'

'I suppose so.' She nodded sadly. 'Then just tell me about him. Is he well? Is he happy?'

'*Ja! Ja!*' Helmut studied her face intently, aware of her trembling as his words sunk in. He told her all he knew – university, Police College and athletics. Helmut concluded: 'He has a sexy girlfriend who really loves him. Her name is Rika Bosch.'

'Does he love her?' Lesley asked in a strained voice.

He nodded. 'I think so. She's good for him, from the same background – both Afrikaners.' Tact was not one of Helmut's better traits. 'Anyway, you always made him feel second rate with your anti-government views and your disdain for his Afrikaner upbringing.'

Lesley shifted uncomfortably in her seat. 'I realise now I made a mistake.'

'Too late for tears,' Helmut hooted. 'Anyway you're happily married now to that podgy little doctor of yours.'

'That's where you're wrong. I'm terribly unhappy.'

'My advice to you is leave Pierre alone.' He ate a mouthful of cake and sighed as he licked his lips. 'Don't you go and muddle his brain again by trying to have an affair or something like that. Do you understand?' He pointed the fork towards her to emphasise his point.

'You're right.' She dabbed her lips with her napkin and stood

345

up. 'I mustn't be selfish.' She pulled on her raincoat. 'Don't you tell him I asked after him.'

'*Ja! Ja*! That is better,' smiled Helmut.

'Thanks for the coffee.' She waved and walked away. He could see by the set of her shoulders she had lost the great zest for life she'd once possessed.

Lesley let herself into the house. She cursed when she saw Geoff's raincoat had dripped a large wet patch on the new worsted carpet. His muddied shoes lay half-way across the hall where he had kicked them off.

'Is that you, Lesley?' called Geoff from the study. 'Come here this minute.'

She stood in the doorway looking at him. 'You're home early.'

'Where have you been?' Irritation flashed in his eyes. 'I had to make my own darned tea.'

'Out.' She shrugged nonchalantly.

'You haven't answered my question, woman.' His ruddy face flushed a deeper shade.

'Since when do I have to report all my movements to you, husband dear?'

'I have a right to know, now tell me.' His voice rose a few octaves.

'I went into Cape Town. So what?'

'You didn't ask my permission,' he declared, glaring at her, his mouth curled.

'I'm sick and tired of your insane jealousy.'

'So that's it!' He rose and walked around the desk. 'It's that bloody Pierre Roux again.' He grabbed her by the shoulders and shook her. 'Can't you keep out of his pants?'

Lesley slapped him as hard as she could. 'I hate you. Oh, how I hate you, Geoff Summers.'

'You're an ungrateful, double-crossing slut!' He rubbed his cheek slowly.

'Don't talk to me like that.' She pushed him away, disgust showing in her eyes.

'I'm your husband and you'll do my bidding.' He walked back around the desk. 'Now, get my slippers.'

She ran from the room and was back seconds later, a slipper in each hand. She aimed the first one at his head. He ducked but it still caught him on his forehead. 'You horrible man,' she cried. Turning, she saw a framed family photograph on the wall. She unleashed the second slipper. The picture crashed to the floor, the glass shattering. 'That's what I think of you and your family.'

He grabbed her neck with both hands. 'You ungrateful little bitch. You don't deserve my family.' He tightened his grasp. 'My mother told me I was marrying below my station when I took you. I didn't listen then, but now I know.'

Lesley fought like a hellcat, hitting out with tightly knotted fists. She broke his grasp and ran to the bedroom. From the top cupboard she pulled down three suitcases. Sweeping handfuls of her clothes out of the wardrobe, she stuffed the suitcases full. One by one she dragged them to the front door while Geoff stood watching.

'Where do you think you're going, Lesley?'

'I'm leaving you. I've had enough.'

'You can't do that.'

'I don't love you – not even so much.' She clicked her fingers in disdain. 'Enough is enough. I want a divorce.'

He grabbed her left arm and held up her hand in triumph. 'Those rings prove I own you. I won't allow you to leave.'

'Oh, yeah!' She slipped the rings off her fingers and shoved them into his hand. 'Now you don't own me any more, Mister.'

He watched while she loaded the suitcases into her car, then slammed the front door and returned to his study, muttering loudly.

Mrs Stuart met Lesley in the driveway, took one look at her daughter's distraught face and the suitcases on the back seat, and knew there were problems.

'I've left Geoff, Mom. May I stay with you and Daddy for a while?'

'As long as you like, dear. Is it serious?'

Lesley nodded. 'I can't, and won't, take any more. I'll file for divorce as soon as possible.'

'I'm surprised it lasted so long. The marriage was ill-conceived from the start, what with all that drama in the hospital.' Mrs Stuart put her arms around her daughter. 'Now that you've made your decision, I must tell you I never liked that pompous Geoff Summers.' She kissed Lesley on the forehead. 'Pity about that nice young man, Pierre Roux.'

Lesley's face crumpled. Her mother had put her finger squarely on the cause of her failed marriage. She wiped away a tear and whispered, 'My life's a mess, and I've lost Pierre for ever.'

Patting her on the back sympathetically, Mrs Stuart led her daughter into the house.

Simon Roux sat in the stands, along with thousands of other parents and relatives, watching the Police College passing-out parade. It was a warm morning with a slight breeze flapping the flags – a South African and a yellow-and-blue police flag.

Brigadier van Zyl took the salute in the march past, and in his speech proclaimed all cadets who had completed the course as qualified police constables. Various awards were presented to students who had excelled in different aspects of the training.

The most prestigious award, the General Mike Geldenhuys floating trophy was awarded last – the highlight of the ceremony.

'The award is presented to the best all-round student,' said the brigadier, 'to the cadet with the finest combination of academic results, good conduct, leadership and outstanding achievement. The 1976 award is presented to Constable Pierre Roux.'

Pierre marched proudly forward and came to attention in front of the dais. He saluted the Commissioner of Police, who shook his hand and presented the large cup.

After the ceremony guests milled around congratulating their sons on their achievements. Simon and Pierre stood together chatting comfortably. 'How is Mom?'

'She's fine and sends her love. She apologises for not being here today. She finds it increasingly difficult to move. It's easier for her to stay at home where the servants can help her.'

'I understand, Dad. It can't be easy for you.'

Simon searched his son's face. 'I'm an affluent farmer, with a high standing in the community, but actually my life is an empty shell.'

Pierre felt his father's loneliness. He put his arm around Simon's shoulders, feeling great compassion for his father. 'Don't worry, Dad, you still have me.'

'I don't think you realise how important you are to me, son.' Simon's eyes misted over. 'You're the light of my very existence.' He again longed to tell Pierre about Themba, but being a policeman,

Pierre would surely not understand. He abruptly changed the subject.

'By the way, Pierre, Rika contacted me last week. She wanted to know your movements. I think she loves you very much.'

'She probably does, but I don't want a long-term commitment. I'm not even sure she's the right woman for me.'

'Pity, she'd make you a good wife. Your backgrounds are so similar, and I like her and Wagner Bosch.'

'Let's change the subject, please, Dad.'

'Are you ready to resume your studies next year?'

Pierre shook his head. 'I've decided to stay on with the police. They have offered me a post with the flying squad in Pretoria. Another year away from Rika will do no harm.'

Pierre was shown into the station commander's office. 'You wished to see me, sir?'

'Constable Roux, you may sit. Congratulations – you are turning into a fine policeman. I've received good reports on your work.'

'Thank you, sir. I'm trying my best.'

'Roux, we are overstaffed in Pretoria at present. You come from the Cape so I'm offering you a transfer to Cape Town. A new trouble spot has developed at a place called Crossroads, a shanty town of makeshift houses occupied by blacks from the Transkei.'

'I've heard of Crossroads, sir.'

'The area is served by the Philippi police station. They've called for extra constables. If you're interested, we could arrange a transfer for you.'

'Sir, if I can serve the police better at Philippi, I'd be glad to accept a transfer.'

'Thank you, constable, I appreciate your co-operation. I'll arrange the necessary paperwork and transport.'

The Trans-Karoo pulled into Cape Town station. Pierre jumped off nonchalantly and walked towards the entrance.

'Pierre! Pierre!'

He turned in surprise, not expecting a welcome. The next minute Rika was in his arms, kissing him passionately.

'How did you know I was arriving? I told no one.'

'I spoke to your station commander in Pretoria when I couldn't raise you at the barracks.' She smiled slyly. 'He gave me all the details.'

'You're very resourceful, I must say. I have to get to Philippi police station to report for duty.'

'I've sorted that out too. I spoke to your new station commander – Lieutenant Fullard. You don't have to book in until tomorrow morning. I've got you to myself for a whole day and night.'

'You seem to be organising my life for me.' There was a hint of irritation in his voice. 'Who says I don't have other plans?'

'Don't be cross, darling. I only wanted to be with you. Remember, I've been longing for this day for almost a year and a half.'

'What did you have planned?'

'I've a picnic basket in my car. I pictured us spending the day at Clifton. I thought you might like to spend time on the beach after being inland so long.'

'Sounds good.' Rika linked arms with him, leading him to the car-park on the station roof. Pierre stopped in surprise when she opened the door of a Mercedes-Benz sports coupé. 'Is this your car?'

She tossed her head casually. 'A birthday present from Daddy.'

She drove like the wind, carefree and a little reckless. Her dark hair streamed out behind her in the slipstream. She's very beautiful, he thought, feeling the first pangs of desire, aware his resolve was weakening and he would eventually capitulate to her charms.

They drove to Clifton's Fourth Beach. Pierre changed into his bathing costume in the car. Rika simply removed her dress, she was already in a bikini. They walked down the steps winding between the houses to the beach. Passing men stared in open admiration at Rika.

She had a magnificent body, full and voluptuous. When Rika rubbed against him, playfully kissing him, he threw his inhibitions aside, took her in his arms and kissed her roughly.

'Slowly, Pierre,' she gasped. 'Don't be in a hurry, we have lots of time.'

They chose a sunny, sheltered spot between the big round boulders to suntan. Rika undid her bikini top. As he looked at her firm breasts Pierre felt an insistent stirring.

'Lunch-time.' Rika unpacked the basket of cold roast chicken, potato salad, tossed salad and buttered rolls. Pierre munched contentedly, enjoying the home-cooked taste after months of barracks food. She poured a dry Riesling into two fluted wine glasses, still cold from the coolbag.

'Cheers.' Pierre clinked glasses in a toast. 'To sun, and sea, and home-cooked food.'

'I'll drink to us,' Rika answered seriously. 'To our future together.'

In the late afternoon they returned to Rika's flat in the city. 'Why don't you have a shower, darling, while I pop the pizza into the oven?'

'Good idea.' It was the first time he had visited Rika's new flat and he looked around at the modern decorated interior with interest. Rika had contemporary tastes, with lots of glass and chrome. The main feature of the bedroom was the bed, not an ordinary double bed but a king-sized version dominating the room. A white towelling bathrobe was laid out on the counterpane. The red embroidered letters on the pocket caught his attention. He looked at them closely, surprised to see a neat PR in an italic design. Pierre Roux, he thought, why do you get the idea Rika is trying to control your life?

In the shower he washed off Clifton's salt and sand, closing his eyes tightly as he shampooed his hair. The shower door opened and he felt Rika pressing against him. She had a cake of soap in her hands and started to soap his chest, his arms, then slipped lower. She kneeled and engulfed him. Her warm mouth and probing tongue drove him wild. He pulled her up and kissed her, forcing her against the wall and making love to her at the same time. Squealing in delight, she held him around the neck, lifting herself, wrapping her legs around his waist.

With water spraying and gurgling over them, they were transported to another world. Like surfers riding the crest of the wave they rode the aphrodisiac wave of passion, breaching the fine line between sex and rapture. She hung limply against him, uttering little animal noises of contentment, untangling her legs.

'I love you, Pierre, I *really* love you.' She hugged him. 'Do you know how much I love you?'

'I love you too.' Such compatible sex must be love, he thought.

Once out of the shower they dried one another, thrilling to each other's bodies. Pierre picked her up and carried her through to the bedroom. Rika slipped out of his embrace, and with a naughty chuckle ran out of the room. She returned with a pot of honey.

Turning Pierre on his back, she allowed the honey to drip on to his masculinity. She licked him clean. He was ready for her, but she wagged her finger at him, smiling impishly.

'My turn,' she cooed, turning on her back. 'Take it slow, my hunk.'

He dipped the honey spoon into the jar, and starting at her breasts, allowed the liquid to drip in a ribbon across her stomach, into her navel and between her legs. Beginning with her nipples he licked the trail he had laid. Rika murmured in pleasure, changing to a groan, then a vociferous shriek as she stiffened, and a husky whimper as she relaxed.

They were ready for each other again. She cried out in ecstasy and lifted off the bed, her back arched, her toes tautening, scratching Pierre's back with her long fingernails.

Pierre, energised, thrust faster while Rika lay with attentive, loving eyes, revelling in the satisfaction of her body giving him enjoyment. She felt his muscles tensing and rose to meet him. He bellowed in triumph. As the heat of passion left him, Pierre collapsed on top of her, whispering endearments in her ear, nibbling her neck.

After the businesslike operations at Pretoria, Pierre found it hard to settle down to the disorderly procedures of a small station. The police buildings were dilapidated, the surroundings decrepit and the community poor and starving.

The squatter camp of Crossroads, just three kilometres east of Philippi police station on the Cape Flats, was squalor at its worst. There was no formal planning, no orderly streets, no laid-on water or sewage disposal. The settlement had sprung up among the sand dunes and Port Jackson willows, each family erecting their structures where they pleased. The result was a higgledy-piggledy jumble of confusion and disorder. Many shacks butted on to existing hovels, creating a honeycomb effect. Narrow pathways wound between the shanties making it impossible for the police vehicles to patrol through the area.

An assortment of building materials had been used, all makeshift – old roofing sheets, asbestos, metal, plastic, sacking, planking, malthoid – anything the inhabitants could lay their hands on cheaply. In many cases a small tree formed the framework, with plastic sheeting tied down over it to form a tent. The hovels were like ovens in the summer, freezing cold and leaky in the winter. During the rainy season the high water-table resulted in the low-lying hollows becoming flooded, creating a muddy, messy quagmire. Refuse removals were not performed by the authorities, consequently rubble piled up against the huts creating an unhygienic, stinking wretchedness.

During the day the men, mainly Xhosas from the Transkei, left Crossroads to work in the nearby factory areas. The women scoured the surrounding bush collecting firewood to cook the evening meal. Unkempt, bare-bottomed children played among the decay. There were no parks or schools.

Placed in charge of a murder investigation, Pierre entered Crossroads on various occasions. Each time the suspect slipped through the net.

'You have no option but to go in at night,' said Lieutenant Fullard. 'Catch the man while he's sleeping.'

'I'll need assistance.' Pierre did not relish the task one little bit.

'You can take two patrol vans and three constables. Do it tonight, around midnight.'

The police vehicles left the road, then drove as far as they could between the dunes. The four policemen alighted quietly. 'One of us must stay to guard the vehicles. We can't leave them unattended, otherwise they'll be minus tyres or smashed up when we come back.'

'I'll stay,' offered a constable.

'We shouldn't be long.' Pierre led the other two policemen to the edge of the squatter camp. 'We must split up and approach the suspect from different angles, otherwise he'll simply escape like a ghost through the plastic.'

It was dark and Pierre was forced to use his torch. This alerted the township mongrels. The dogs attacked him, growling fiercely, snapping at his legs. He swung his baton and struck a hound which ran off yelping. People started waking up and lighting lamps.

Pierre came face to face with a black man. He took one look at Pierre and ran away yelling, 'Police! Police!' at the top of his voice. A hum of angry voices built up as men came out to investigate.

'Stay there, policeman!' shouted a man. He pointed a spear at Pierre's stomach. Within seconds he was surrounded by angry men brandishing home-made weapons. A blow hit him on the head, but his police cap took the force out of the strike. He pushed the spear to one side and ran further up the alleyway, hotly pursued. As he reached the suspect's shelter he saw his two colleagues pulling a man, kicking and struggling, from the hut.

The mob came running up, the firebrands in their hands casting flickering pools of light over the shacks. Their ugly mood was heightened when they saw the two policemen holding one of their fellow squatters.

'*Bulala ipolisa*!' they shouted. 'Kill the policemen!' The spear carrier drew his arm back. The spear flew through the air, striking one policeman in the chest. The force of the throw sent the spear through his body and it protruded out of his back. Slowly he toppled over and fell face first into the debris.

Pierre grabbed the prisoner, and using him as a human shield retreated until his back was against a solid asbestos wall. He took out his pistol, ready to fire.

Instinctively the other policeman pulled out his service pistol and shot into the crowd. A man screamed, throwing up his hands, releasing a burning torch which fell against a shack. The plastic immediately caught alight. The fire burnt fiercely, spreading to the adjacent hovels.

The crowd were incensed. 'Necklace him!' screamed someone. Others took up the chant. 'Necklace *ipolisi*!' A man ran up and put down an old motor-car tyre. Another produced a bottle of paraffin.

Pierre watched in horror as the surging mob tied the policeman's arms to his side and slipped the tyre over his neck. Then they splashed paraffin into the cavity and set it alight. The constable trumpeted like an animal as first his moustache and hair were singed off, then as the tyre burnt more fiercely his nose, ears and lips burnt away. The stench was appalling – a mixture of acrid rubber and charred human flesh.

Bile shot into Pierre's throat as he stared in morbid fascination. The policeman stumbled around inside the circle of squatters. There was no escape, they kept shoving him towards the centre. The skin of his face peeled off leaving a hideous bony skull. Splotches of molten rubber dripped off the tyre, setting his uniform alight. He burnt in an orb of flame from the waist up, a human Roman candle.

The policeman fell to his knees, but still he lived, even though he was reduced to an incoherent, blubbering zombie. Slowly he toppled over, collapsing in a flaming heap. The burning body was no longer recognisable as a man – it was reduced to a carcass of bone and flesh. The legs kicked spasmodically, then stiffened, and the body was still.

Pierre pulled the prisoner closer, holding his pistol to the man's temple. 'Make one move and I'll shoot you.'

'The policeman is dead,' shouted a squatter poking the lifeless body.

A man pointed to Pierre. 'There's another.' They turned and surged towards him.

Pierre tightened his arm around the prisoner's neck. His instinct told him to fire into the advancing mob, but logic told him he had only eight shots in his magazine, which was useless against the large crowd.

Men tackled him with sticks, hitting around the prisoner. They knocked off his cap and his dark hair glinted in the firelight. Another blow numbed his arm. Pierre's heart thumped in his throat. He was petrified, more terrified than at any other time in his life. His end was near. He was going to die!

'Stop! I demand you stop!' A voice of authority rang out. Surprised, the attackers turned. When they saw who it was they cleared a path to allow the man to step forward.

The man walked up to Pierre and he shifted the prisoner slightly to block the new threat. The man's back was to the fire – all Pierre could see was his silhouette, but not his features.

Flickering flames lit up Pierre's face. The man looked at him intently. 'I thought so, you're Pierre Roux.'

'Yes . . . yes . . . I am,' stuttered an astonished Pierre.

The man turned to the pressing crowd and held up his arms in reconciliation. 'We will not kill this policeman; he once saved my life.' The mob held back, grudgingly respecting the man's wishes.

'Who . . . are . . . you?' gasped Pierre.

He turned to allow Pierre to see his face. 'I am Themba Memani. You saved me in the blazing bus.'

Contempt replaced raw fear as Pierre remembered the incident. 'Memani, you double-crossed me in Soweto. I unfettered you to greet your wife and you took unfair advantage of me by escaping.'

'So, you should be thankful,' growled Themba. 'If I were in jail,' he indicated the squatters, 'you would be dead now.'

'You betrayed my trust – I'll never forgive you for that.' Pierre was highly indignant.

'You saved my life, now I've saved yours – we are even.' With that Themba twisted the pistol out of Pierre's grasp. The prisoner burst free.

Themba and Pierre stood glaring at each other. Pierre broke the silence, his voice dripping with scorn. 'Now you've saved my life, what are you going to do with me?'

'Release you,' barked Themba. 'If it were Koekemoer, I'd have killed him here and now with my bare hands.' Bitterness tinged his voice. 'I'd kill him like he killed my child.'

'I don't owe you any favours, Memani. You belong in jail. We'll still catch you.'

'Better men than you have not succeeded,' retorted Themba acidly. 'Go, before I change my mind.'

'What about my prisoner? He's a suspect in a murder investigation.' Pierre was breathing more easily.

Themba turned to the squatters. 'Did this man commit a murder?'

The crowd nodded assent, one man piping up, 'He killed one of our comrades during a fight at a shebeen. They were both drunk.'

'He will get a fair trial,' shouted Pierre. 'If he is found guilty of the murder, he will be fairly sentenced. Let the law run its course.'

'Take the prisoner,' instructed Themba. The men pushed him forward. Pierre snapped handcuffs on his wrists. He picked up his cap, dusted it off and replaced it on his head.

Themba issued a command and the men reacted quickly. The burning tyre was pulled off the dead policeman and the smouldering corpse was wrapped in a blanket. Someone pulled the assegai out of the other body and Pierre winced as it came away with a sucking sound.

'Escort them out of Crossroads,' instructed Themba.

'Thank you, Memani, but I'll get you yet.'

Themba smiled wryly and turned away.

Pierre was guided to the police vans. The constable on guard watched wide-eyed as the bodies of the policemen were placed in the back of a van. Pierre locked the prisoner in the other vehicle and the squatters melted back into the night.

The considerable might of the police force was brought to bear after Pierre returned to Philippi police station and the horror unfolded. Lieutenant Fullard was hastily summoned. He radioed for immediate reinforcements. Police reservists were called up and every police station in the Cape Peninsula rushed over policemen and vans. The killing of a policeman was never taken lightly.

As dawn approached, the long convoy headed towards Cross-roads. Vehicles fanned out and by the time the sun rose the squatter camp was surrounded by a human chain of law enforcers.

The community were forced out of their shacks, until every inhabitant – man, woman and child – was driven into a milling group, away from the hovels.

'Identify the man who placed the tyre around the constable's neck,' shouted Fullard angrily.

'That's him,' pointed Pierre.

He was handcuffed and pulled to one side.

'Now the paraffin thrower and igniter.'

Again Pierre pointed, and two men were manhandled towards the police vans.

'Where is the spear thrower?'

'It was dark, I couldn't see properly.'

'Nonsense! You have to point out someone. We can't allow such a hideous crime to go unpunished.'

'Well it could be him . . . or him,' indicated Pierre.

'Arrest them both,' commanded Fullard.

'There is another man in the crowd that I'm looking for,' said Pierre.

'Who's that?'

'A certain Themba Memani, who escaped from custody during the Soweto student riots.'

'A ringleader, hey?' scowled Fullard. 'He's probably one of the trouble-makers who spread the rioting to the Cape. Find him, Roux.'

Like sheep being forced through a crush, the squatters were made to walk between a line of policemen, one by one. Pierre stood at the end searching for Themba to come through. Released squatters dodged away towards the dunes, running as fast as they could.

A man wrapped in a blanket, with a thick scarf covering his lower face and a hat pulled down over his forehead, appeared between the policemen. The way he walked, light on his feet, with a spring in his step, alerted Pierre.

He pointed. 'Remove that blanket.'

Ready hands pulled the blanket off the man. Pierre noted the tall, lithe figure.

'Pull off the scarf.'

The strong jaw line, generous mouth and muscular neck looked familiar. 'Take off his hat.' The high forehead and piercing brown eyes set well apart completed the picture. With a shaking hand Pierre shouted: 'That's him, that's Themba Memani.'

Themba had no chance to escape as he was grabbed by half a dozen policemen. He held himself regally, allowing himself to be handcuffed. He walked with a powerful, measured step and stopped level with Pierre. 'Are you satisfied now, Roux?'

'You belong in jail, you cheeky bastard,' retorted Pierre, much to the delight of the other policemen.

A sneer touched the corner of Themba's mouth. 'You have betrayed me, Roux.'

'You betrayed me first,' snorted Pierre.

'In Soweto I felt an affinity towards you, but now I hate your guts!'

'Again, we're even, because I loathe you too.' Pierre turned to the policemen. 'Take him away.'

From Philippi, Themba was transferred to Jeppe police station in outlying Johannesburg. He was held in a single cell; the only person he saw was a warder, three times a day at mealtimes. Days and nights rolled into one, his life outside the cell became a distant memory.

He pleaded with the warder to convey a message to Hilda and find out how she was. The warder was willing to take the risk, but at a price. Themba had no money; his watch had been confiscated, he had nothing left to use as payment. The warder laughed at him. 'You gotta pay if you want results.'

Two weeks later, without any explanation, he was handcuffed and marched outside. Two policemen lifted him up and threw him face down on to the hard metal floor of a police van. They drove through the streets of Johannesburg. Themba felt alone in his suffering as he saw how life went on as usual on the outside – blacks and whites mingling, mothers pushing babies in prams, businessmen walking around in smart suits. Johannesburg was bustling and busy, far removed from the chaos and murders of Soweto or Crossroads.

The police drove through heavy steel gates, stopping in a courtyard. 'Welcome to No. 4, I hope you enjoy your stay!' the policeman joked as he pulled Themba out. He pushed him towards a wall, undoing his handcuffs.

Themba rubbed his wrists while he glanced around. He was in a prison with high walls, built into a hill. He was alone but there was no escape – armed guards looked down at him from raised towers. Nobody seemed to be concerned about him, so he sat with his back to the wall, enjoying the warmth of the sun.

At intervals throughout the morning more prisoners were brought in and dumped in the courtyard. They followed his example and sat in a row against the wall. He learnt they had all been rounded up after the Soweto uprising, kept in various small prisons in and around Johannesburg and now brought to The Fort.

'What is this place, No. 4?' Themba asked.

'It's the Johannesburg Fort, built by the British to hold Boers during their war. Now it's a jail for prisoners awaiting trial, or for newly sentenced convicts before they are sent off to other prisons to serve their sentences.'

The Fort consisted of a number of individual buildings and Themba could see it was never designed as a jail.

Ten white warders converged on them. 'Stand up, you kaffirs,' shouted one in Afrikaans. Those not rising quickly enough were hit with batons.

'Strip.'

Themba took off his clothes and folded them neatly into a pile. He stood naked, covering his private parts with his hands. They were forced into a row, their backs against the wall, with the warders parading back and forth in front of them.

'Come on, kaffir, let me see your prick.' A warder smacked Themba's hands away with his baton. His eyes bulged as he saw Themba's member and he called his colleagues across to look.

'What a weapon,' he teased, lifting up Themba's penis with his baton.

The other warders laughed derisively.

Themba stood powerless. Their clothes were carried away. Themba protested and was hit a stinging blow. 'Shut up.'

The white warders left and were replaced by black officials, wielding sjamboks. 'Run, prisoners, run.'

Themba and his fellow inmates were chased back and forth

across the courtyard, the sjamboks slashing across their backs and buttocks if they did not run as fast as the warders wanted. They ran and ran, hour after hour. Feeling degraded and disheartened, they realised their hell had only just begun. One by one the prisoners fell exhausted. They were sjamboked to their feet and stumbled forward until not even the lashings could move them. Themba was the last to succumb to the senseless beatings, invented by some maniacal jailer to break black prisoners' spirits at the start of their odyssey behind bars.

Water jets were turned on them, the force so strong it burnt their skins and stung the lash cuts. Their battered bodies were covered with raised welts. Each prisoner tried not to show his agony, aware that any display of weakness would prolong the atrocious beatings.

The black warders are more cruel than the whites, thought Themba, if that's possible. They have no compassion for a fellow black man.

'Now who's the boss?' the black warders shouted gleefully.

The prisoners were forced to shout at the top of their lungs until they chanted in unison: 'You are! You are!'

'Get dressed.'

From a pile each prisoner gathered a pair of khaki shorts, the size unimportant. Themba's shorts were too small and he had to leave the top button undone. Each grabbed a striped red-and-white skipper, which was a thick, short-sleeved T-shirt. The one Themba secured was much too big, almost reaching his knees. There were no shoes or socks. Finally the prisoners were escorted by the guards into one of the buildings to a large cell. The gate clanged shut behind them.

In the middle of the cell was a large pile of mats and blankets. Some fifteen prisoners lounged on the blankets, smoking cigarettes. These were the prison mafia of the communal cell. Another hundred prisoners sat against the walls, at the beck and call of the fat cats.

Around the centre pile the floor was spotless, it gleamed from repeated rubbings. As Themba stood, adjusting his eyes to the gloom, he noticed a prisoner dart forward from the wall and crush a fat and bloated body louse. It had tried to cross the spotless circle. The prisoner cleaned the smatter of blood off with his skipper, then returned obediently to the wall.

Themba looked around. The cell was large, like a medieval castle dungeon, with a flagstone floor and lofty, crumbling walls. High up, just below roof level, were small barred windows, covered with mesh grilles, that let in pale streaks of light.

The new prisoners were careful not to step on the cleaned area. The fat cats appraised them, looking them slowly up and down as a man might assess a shapely woman.

Someone shouted from the back of the cell. 'Themba!'

Themba looked closely as a familiar figure walked towards him. 'Ngconde Seymour! What are you doing here?' Themba was overjoyed at finding a friend.

'I was arrested in Carltonville. The police thought I was hiding students, but I wasn't.' Ngconde smiled at Themba.

'I was caught for concealing two youths, but I escaped to the Cape. They arrested me there and brought me back here to stand trial. They know I was one of the leaders of the Soweto Students' Representative Council.'

'Then you're in big trouble, my friend. Under Section 29 of the Internal Security Act you'll get a jail sentence of between five and seven years.'

Themba thought of Hilda alone in their Soweto house. He told Ngconde about the events surrounding his arrest.

'You can get a message to Hilda and she can visit you.'

Themba looked at him in disbelief. 'How can I do that?'

'You see that man on the very top of the pile of blankets?' Ngconde pointed. 'That's Sly, the ringleader; he controls the whole cell. The warders are in his pocket; he trades freely in cigarettes, dagga, soap, food and liquor. He even gets two newspapers a day, morning and evening. He can't read or write, his lackeys read to him.'

'Can I ask him to help?'

'Wait a day or two. Settle down before you ask. He's a dangerous man to cross; he metes out punishment in this cell worse than any court, from lashings to the death penalty.'

Themba scratched the insect bites on his body. He looked closely at the filthy blankets against the wall, horrified to see they were crawling with bedbugs and lice. He tried to wipe the insects off his skin.

'You're wasting your time,' laughed Ngconde. 'Leave the bugs, you'll get used to them after a while.'

'Why must we suffer while those in the middle have it good?' Themba demanded.

'They're called the scooters, the privileged few led by Sly. They aren't political prisoners like us. They're hardened jailbirds whose lives revolve around prison. If they're ever released they immediately commit another crime to return here. This is their home, their life. They're actually happy to stay inside this hell-hole.'

'Why are they called scooters?'

'You'll see at counting time. They scoot us into line for the warders. They scoot us to the bathrooms. They scoot us to meals.'

'Hullo, Themba,' greeted a pupil from Orlando West Junior Secondary, one of the members of the SRCC.

'So they arrested you, too,' said Themba.

'They found my hiding place. By the way, Solomon and Khotso are still free. I heard you hid them in your house?'

Themba nodded. 'According to the police, one of them was shot in the leg.'

'That was Solomon. Luckily it was only a flesh wound. He'll be okay.'

'I'm glad.' Themba was relieved.

'No doubt they'll try and leave the country.' The student went back to his section of the cell.

There was a rattle of the gate and a newspaper was thrown in. One of the prisoners picked it up and carried it to the edge of the cleaned circle. He handed it to one of the scooters.

A paraffin lamp was lit and by lamplight the *Star* was read to Sly. Themba heard snatches of the commentary. He was convinced he heard his name read out but Ngconde could not confirm this.

In the distance a bell rang. 'Scoot! Scoot!' Sly yelled from the centre.

The prisoners lined up in single file to collect their food. Each was handed an aluminium plate with two scoops of soft maize porridge. They had only three minutes to eat the mushy food with their fingers. It was Themba's first food since breakfast. He ate every scrap but still felt hungry. They were shepherded back to their cell by the guards.

The scooters had not moved. They did not bother with prison food. They ate their own meal, brought straight to them from the kitchens – chunks of meat, potatoes and bread. I'm sure that's meant for all the prisoners, Themba thought, and he was tempted to go across and demand some for himself. He held back. It was only his first day and he wanted to sum up the situation first.

362

A second bell rang. 'Scoot! Scoot!' The prisoners shuffled into line, five deep, while the scooters continued to lounge on their blankets. Themba followed the example of the others. The door was flung open and armed guards entered the cell. Only then did the scooters take their places in the front of the rows. A warder counted them: 'Five, ten, fifteen, twenty, twenty-five, thirty,' until he reached the total.

'All correct and accounted for.' The mafia returned to their positions on the pile. Prisoners from against the walls, chosen by the scooters as the day's task force, rushed forward and repolished the circle with their skippers. As the light faded the electric lights came on, a few weak bulbs, high up in the roof, covered with dust. It was almost as dark as during the day.

'Lights out in half an hour,' said Ngconde.

'Blanket time,' called one of the scooters.

'Do we also get those,' Themba pointed to the pile, 'or must we be satisfied with these pest-ridden excuses for blankets?'

'You have to qualify for the good blankets by doing tasks for the scooters. You must get into their good books first.'

Themba stood up purposefully. 'Damned if I'm going to use these stinking blankets without a mat. It's going to be freezing tonight on the stone floor.' Before Ngconde could stop him Themba walked to the centre.

'I'd like a mat and blankets for Ngconde and myself.'

'You'd like! Who do you think you are?' screamed a scooter at him.

'My name is Themba Memani.'

'Themba Memani,' said Sly carefully. 'Sounds familiar.' He called to his commentator, asking him to read again from the newspaper.

He read slowly. 'The police have confirmed that most of the student leaders from the Soweto riots have now been arrested, including one of the ringleaders, Themba Memani, who was a teacher at Dobsonville Secondary School. They will be brought to trial under the Riotous Assemblies Act and the Internal Security Act during the next few weeks. A police spokesman stated he was confident all black leaders would be in custody by the end of the week.'

'Is that you?' Sly asked.

Themba nodded. 'Yes, I was involved.'

'What did you hope to gain by fighting the system, Memani?'

'Self-respect for the black man. We started a peaceful rally. The police caused the violence.'

'It has spread to every city in South Africa, according to the newspapers we read,' said Sly. 'Over five hundred black people have been killed countrywide, and you actually started it all?'

'The schools were like a time bomb, ready to explode anyway over the forced use of Afrikaans. I never started it. I was merely on the SRCC.'

'Are you ANC?'

'I'm a member of the ANC.'

'Memani, where do you come from?'

'I'm a Xhosa from the royal kraal of Mqekezweni in Thembuland.'

'Do you know Paramount Chief Sabata Dalindyebo?'

'Of course I know him. I'm an elder of his council, an *iphakathi*. I'm married to Hilda, whose father Nxele is Sabata's son.'

Sly was impressed and it showed. He invited Themba to sit on the pile. 'Do you know Nelson Mandela?'

'I have never had the privilege of meeting him, but he is my uncle. I am related to him through his mother's line. She was Nosekeni and was a cousin of my grandfather, Morris Memani.'

'In that case you may have a mat and three blankets.' Sly declared.

'Thank you, but what about my friend, Ngconde? He's also part of the freedom struggle.'

'Don't chance your arm too far, Memani.' Sly stared at Themba, waiting for him to back off as every other prisoner did. When Themba continued to hold his gaze, Sly became uncomfortable. 'Okay, Memani, two sets of bedding for you.'

'Here's a bonus,' said one of the scooters, handing Themba two hard-boiled eggs and four cigarettes.

Themba gave an egg to Ngconde and kept the other for himself. He had never appreciated a lowly hen's egg as much as this one. He peeled it slowly, careful not to waste a scrap and popped the whole egg into his mouth.

The prisoners around him stared jealously. Themba felt wicked, not having shared his treat with them, but he reasoned it was impossible to share out an egg without a knife. He gave them the cigarettes which they distributed around, puff for puff.

It's the law of the jungle inside prison, he thought, the survival of the fittest.

'For the first time since I've been in prison, I'm going to sleep warm tonight. You have guts, Themba,' Ngconde praised.

'Nothing ventured, nothing gained. Tomorrow I'm going to ask them to help me find out about Hilda.'

Another bell rang and three minutes later the lights went out, giving the two friends just enough time to roll their blankets into cocoons, into which they slipped. For safety, the two stuck together.

Much later, Themba heard a scuffle where a young teenager who had been part of their intake during the day was sleeping.

The youngster screamed, 'Leave me! Please leave me alone!'

Themba sat up. He felt Ngconde's restraining hand on his arm. 'Leave him, let him be. Don't get involved.'

'What's happening?' Themba demanded.

'The scooters have fetched him.'

'What do they want him for?'

'He's young and attractive, like a virgin girl. First Sly, then the other scooters will rape him tonight. They don't have women, so they use young boys.'

'That's terrible, we must save him. He's so young and innocent.'

'Don't try and be a hero, Themba, you'll end up a dead hero.'

Themba lay back, sickened by the sounds coming from the centre of the cell. The youngster was screaming in pain, his voice echoing and re-echoing off the walls. The scooters held him face down on the blankets they had packed under his stomach to raise his backside. Themba pictured the terrible sodomy taking place by the scooters in turn. The teenager's cries became weaker until he was babbling disjointedly. Hours later he was returned to his spot where he lay retching and muttering incoherently.

It was still dark the next morning when the lights went on. The prisoners queued up at the five open lavatories for their early morning ablutions. The sixth toilet at the end was reserved exclusively for Sly and the scooters.

The prisoners used the pans faster than the cisterns filled up. By the time a toilet could be flushed it contained the excrement of over half a dozen men, and then did not flush fully. Themba felt ill from the stench. There was no paper except at the scooter's toilet, and no one was prepared to risk stealing one of their rolls. To make matters worse, the drinking taps were against the wall behind the toilets. Themba tried to drink from the tap, but the foul odour when he stretched over a toilet took away his thirst and he walked away in disgust.

The young rape victim was too weak to get up. Themba tried to help him sit up, but he screamed in agony when pressure was put on his anus. His shorts were caked with dried blood. Themba laid him down again gently and covered him with blankets.

The bells rang. They filed out down a passage. They stripped off their clothes, their skippers going on one heap, their shorts on another. They were chased like cattle through a spray-race down a long cement walkway containing a dozen cold-water shower-heads. Without any soap, they had to wash as best they could within fifteen paces. They could not stop, the guards kept the line moving by sjamboking the bare bottoms of the men at the back so that those behind pushed them forwards. It was a case of one pace for each body part – hair, face, ears, left arm, right arm, left armpit, right armpit, back, chest, stomach, crotch, penis, backside, left leg, right leg, and out the other side.

They had no towels. They ran back to the heaps and grabbed the first skipper and pair of shorts that came to hand. This time Themba's skipper was far too small and his shorts much too big. From the awful smell, Themba doubted if the clothing was ever washed.

Still in line, they received their plates of porridge, and three minutes later they were chased back to the cell.

Again a bell rang. It was time for the morning head count. The second day at The Fort started as the first had ended – a never-ending scenario of misery and degradation.

Midway through the morning Themba was summoned by Sly. He was given a cup of tea sweetened with condensed milk. He was offered a cream doughnut, and Themba wondered how he managed to obtain such luxuries.

'Tell me about yourself and the ANC,' Sly demanded.

For over an hour Themba related his own experiences as well as the aims and objectives of the ANC. He told him as much as he could about the Soweto disturbances.'

'I'm impressed.' Sly smiled at him expansively. 'You are welcome to join me in the middle permanently, as part of my team.'

'I'll join you on four conditions.'

'You've got a damn cheek, Memani. Any other prisoner would be only too pleased to get an invitation, without laying down conditions. Not you, you don't have one condition, but four!' Sly looked visibly upset. 'Let me hear your conditions, but I reserve judgement on my offer.'

'One. Ngconde must join me in the middle.'

'Why?'

'Ngconde has been a close friend since our student days in Alice. He also secured me my teaching post in Soweto and organised a house for me to live in.'

Sly nodded in acceptance.

'Two. The young boy you raped must be hospitalised immediately. Have you no compassion?'

Coughing in embarrassment, Sly nodded again.

Themba held up three fingers. 'I want you to get a message to my wife. I'm worried about her and she must be frantic about me.'

'No problem.' Sly smiled.

'Four.' Themba thrust home his last request in a voice loud enough to carry to the inmates around the walls. 'I demand you treat the other prisoners better; like people, not slaves.'

Sly glared at Themba and the other scooters waited for him to explode – they had never heard such impertinence before. Themba held his gaze and suddenly Sly threw back his head and laughed, a deep-throated chortle. 'You're a sassy one, Memani. You talk like a lawyer.'

'I was trained as a lawyer at Fort Hare.'

'Why should I grant you four wishes, when I could just as well wash my hands of you?'

'One day, when the ANC comes to power, we will seek you out and make you pay, Sly.'

'Ha! Ha! Ha! That will be years from now.'

'Well then, how about this? The ANC trains comrades abroad as terrorists. We'll infiltrate a professional killer into The Fort to eliminate you.'

'You'd do that?' Sly suddenly looked agitated. 'You'd really try and eliminate old Sly?'

'Not if you help me make things better for everyone in the cell.'

'I agree to your first three requests, but not the last.'

'All or nothing.' Themba was adamant.

'You're undermining my authority in the cell.'

Themba's eyes bored into him. Sly shuffled nervously, not used to being challenged. The whole cell held its breath.

'All right, I agree.' He glared around the cell. 'Don't get too happy – it won't be for long. We'll soon be back to our old ways, once Memani is tried and transferred. Anyone stepping out of line now will shit then, I promise you.'

At Sly's instruction the young boy was taken to the cell gate, which was rattled until a warder appeared. He was carried off to the prison sick bay.

Ngconde joined the scooters on the pile. Sly made use of his contacts and money to smuggle bread into the cells to supplement the prisoners' diets. Mats and blankets were distributed more fairly.

Themba spent the days lecturing the prisoners on the origins and objectives of the ANC. Because of his legal and teaching training, he was able to put his points across with meaning. The whole cell brightened up, the men now had a purpose. The cleanliness of the cell and toilets improved. Sly even persuaded the prison authorities to wash all the clothes and blankets and to have the cell disinfected.

The cell became a model, much to the amazement of The Fort's superintendent. Each prisoner was given soap and toilet paper and they were allowed to walk slowly through the showers without the sjamboks. Only the food from the kitchen did not improve.

Themba received word that Hilda was well and back home in Soweto. It was a joyous day when he was called to the reception office and Hilda was standing there. They embraced tenderly for many long minutes, Hilda's tears soaking into his skipper. He held her at arm's length, looking intently at her. She looked wan and worried.

'How are you, my darling?'

'I'm fine thank you, Themba, but you've lost weight. Oh! I love you and miss you so much. I hope this will soon be over and you can come home.'

'What happened to the baby?'

'We lost our child. Luckily I'm all right, there's no permanent damage. We can try again. We can have many children.'

'Do you have money to live?'

'Your last salary cheque came through. I deposited it in the savings account. I have enough for about four months. Do you need money?'

'You can give me some, but not too much. I may need it later.'

'Time up, back to your cell.'

'I'll come again next week,' she promised.

'Please do. It's wonderful to see you. I love you.'

'I love you too.'

Lieutenant Fullard took the matter of the murdered policemen to the commissioner of police, who in turn consulted the Minister of Justice. A meeting was set up with all concerned parties.

'We would remove a festering sore if we wiped out Crossroads,' offered Lieutenant Fullard. 'The crime rate in the squatter camp is appalling, the Philippi police find it almost impossible to maintain law and order. Two fine policemen were killed last week and the other two were lucky to escape with their lives. It won't get better, gentlemen.'

'Your point is taken, Lieutenant. In addition to law and order, we also have to consider our policy of separate development,' said the Minister. 'Crossroads meets neither criteria – it should disappear from the map.'

'I concede we must eliminate Crossroads,' said the Minister of Black Administration, 'but how?'

'The Administration Board has heavy-duty equipment, bull-dozers and front-end loaders?' The Minister left the idea hanging in the air.

So it was decided – Crossroads would disappear once and for all.

Pierre was on morning patrol duty at the bottom end of Lansdowne Road, near Crossroads, when he heard the throaty roar of bulldozers and the clanking of their chained tracks. Puzzled, he left the road and drove between the sand dunes to investigate.

He turned to his assistant. 'Wait in the van. I want to climb up that dune to see what's happening.' From the top he gazed down at the edge of the shanty town, staring in disbelief at the scene below him.

Three huge D6 Caterpillar bulldozers and three front-end loaders were advancing in a row upon the shacks, their blades raised high in the air.

A hundred metres in front of the machines a row of women, arms linked, stood defiantly protecting their homes. Meanwhile the machines advanced on them.

In between the black faces a flash of blonde hair caught Pierre's attention. He recognised her familiar proud stance. He looked again. Yes. It was Lesley, without a doubt. He started running down the hill just as the khaki-clad administration board official gave the signal to the drivers. They lowered their blades, skimming off a layer of soil in whorls, like shavings from a woodworker's plane.

Pierre reached the level ground running as fast as he could. The line of women wavered, then broke in panic as the huge earth-moving machines reached them. Lesley stood firm. She tossed her head in contempt and braced her body, waiting for the inevitable contact.

She was forced off her feet into the maelstrom of sand, vegetation and stones. She screamed in disdain. 'To hell with you bastards, you bloody bastards!'

Pierre waved desperately at the machine operator. The driver saw the police uniform and slammed his foot on the brake. Pierre bent over her. There was a bump on her forehead where a stone had caught her. She was unconscious.

All six machines stopped, their engines idling. The administration board official was screaming, 'Forward! Forward!' He gesticulated with his arms, furious at his orders being disobeyed.

Pierre carried Lesley to the line of women and handed her over to ready arms. He walked boldly towards the bulldozers, his arm raised above his head, palm forward, indicating to the drivers to stay where they were. He was vaguely aware that what he was doing was contrary to government policy and police rules, but suddenly he did not care any more. He had found Lesley again and he was not going to allow a few bulldozers to push her out of his life.

He turned around for assurance and saw the anxiety on the squatters' faces. For the first time he felt an empathy with black people.

Pierre jumped on to the first bulldozer and turned off the ignition. He pocketed the key. He went from machine to machine until the last engine had died. The howling of their exhausts was replaced by the cheering of the women.

The official hurried across. 'What are you doing, constable? I have my orders to destroy the shacks. Give me those keys.'

'Chase him away!' thundered Pierre.

The women turned on the man. He ran as fast as he could to his pick-up and roared off in a cloud of dust.

Pierre laughed out loud, light-headed at his brazenness. He turned to the operators. 'Get off your machines. Go home. We have enough trouble in South Africa without destroying people's homes.'

Women ran alongside Pierre as he hurried down an alleyway looking for Lesley. They showed him to a squatter shack, and he entered one for the first time. He looked around in admiration at the neat interior, everything fastidiously arranged. He was in a home lovingly tended by a proud housewife. Lesley lay unconscious on a bed. Her encounter with the bulldozer had left her grimy, her blonde hair matted with pieces of grass. Pierre felt the same protectiveness towards her that he had felt on Table Mountain.

He washed the grime off her face and dabbed cold water on the bump on her temple. He held her in his arms, feeling her against his chest, her heart beating in time to his. This time he would not allow Geoff Summers to keep them apart. She stirred, then opened her large blue eyes.

'Lesley, it's me, Pierre.'

She smiled wanly. She was disorientated. 'Pierre, what are you doing here?'

He told her about the bulldozers, how he had stopped them from destroying Crossroads.

'Thank God for that.' She fell back on to the bed in relief, admiration in her eyes as she looked at him.

'Now I've found you again I'm not going to give you up.' He spoke determinedly. 'I love you, Lesley.'

'You needn't worry about Geoff any more – we're getting a divorce.'

'Why?' Pierre's heart soared.

'The marriage was a disaster from the start. Geoff wasn't looking for a wife – he wanted a nursemaid.'

Pierre smiled in satisfaction. 'I told you so.'

'I moved back to my parents' house a month ago. I've started divorce proceedings.'

His voice quavered with emotion. 'I don't think I ever stopped loving you, Lesley. I promise I always will.' He kissed her softly on the mouth. 'Why didn't you contact me, when your marriage was a failure? You knew I loved you.'

'I did try. I spoke to Helmut and he told me about Rika Bosch. He said you were happy together. I didn't want to spoil your future with my failure.'

'Rika and I only got together after your marriage, when I thought I had lost you for good. It was a romance on the rebound.'

Lesley sat up quickly, a frown on her face. 'Do you love her?'

'I like her, but I don't love her.'

'Are you sure? I don't want to hurt anyone.' There was genuine concern in Lesley's voice.

'I'm certain. This time, nothing will come between us.'

'We can talk later, Pierre. Let's go before I become too stiff.'

Together they walked out of the shelter, Lesley leaning against him for support. The squatters waved to them as they passed between the shacks, clapping and toyi-toyiing in appreciation.

'Doctor, I want you to do a pregnancy test on me.'

The doctor examined Rika, he asked questions and compared dates. 'My dear, you're six weeks pregnant. Congratulations.'

Rika was overjoyed at the prospect of a baby, it was the culmination of her and Pierre's love. She left the surgery with a spring in her step and returned to her flat. She would have exciting news for Pierre when he visited that evening. Impatience got the better of her and she telephoned the Philippi police station.

'Constable Roux has just left,' Lieutenant Fullard told her. 'There was trouble at Crossroads this morning and he asked for the rest of his shift off. I gave him permission to go off duty.'

'Is he all right?' Rika asked anxiously.

'He looked in good health to me.'

'Did he say where he was going?'

'He mentioned going back to his flat in Ottery.'

'Thank you, Lieutenant.'

'You're welcome.'

Pierre ran a hot bath, steaming and full. He lent Lesley a bulky jersey and a pair of athletics shorts. She went into the bathroom and closed the door. Pierre heard groans of delight as the hot water loosened her muscles.

Twenty minutes later she came out. She dried her hair until it shone and was loose and fluffy.

372

'You are beautiful, you're absolutely stunning,' Pierre breathed in admiration.

'It's nice to be beautiful for you. What are you grinning at, Pierre Roux?'

'My clothes on you,' he laughed. 'You look so comical in my jersey down to your knees!'

'You promised me a massage.'

'So I did. Lie on the bed, I'll get some skin lotion.'

Lesley lay face down. She had taken off the jersey, exposing her back. Pierre squirted the lotion between her shoulder-blades and she giggled at the coldness. He spread the lotion and slowly kneaded her muscles, while she murmured in enjoyment. He rubbed with long sensual strokes from her shoulders to her waist.

'You've missed your vocation,' she said. 'You should have been a professional masseur.'

He patted her bottom. 'Turn over, now for your front.'

Lesley turned over and covered her breasts with her arm, blushing.

Pierre mockingly admonished her. 'How can I massage you properly like that?'

Lesley sat up. 'Pierre, we're both responsible adults.' She spoke frankly. 'I think we both know where we're headed, but I don't want to appear cheap, or give you the impression this is – how did you put it? – a romance on the rebound, for me.'

'I love you, Lesley. Nothing else matters.'

'I love you, too.' She put her arms around his neck and they kissed. 'Come now,' she eventually murmured, 'you haven't finished the massage.' This time she lay with her arms spread out.

Pierre looked at her breasts, feeling the passion rising inside him. To prolong the enjoyment he started at the opposite end. He massaged her feet and her toes, even finding them a turn-on. He nibbled the tips of her toes while she squealed in delight.

At last he concentrated on her torso. Lesley closed her eyes, sighing in pleasure. She put her arms behind her neck, tautening her breasts to heighten the feeling. To Pierre's surprise her body stiffened, and she uttered little subdued murmurs as her nipples quivered in excitement.

He fell on top of her and they kissed passionately. They were both breathing hard. Like two madmen they ripped off each other's clothes, and then they were making love. Together they rode on the fringes of sanity. At the height of their passion their cries mingled. Afterwards, with gentleness, they touched and felt each other, kissing tenderly, slowly letting the spiral wind down.

'Pierre! Pierre, my darling. I love you.'

'Lesley, will you marry me?'

She pushed him aside to sit up. She searched his face. 'Do you really mean that? Are you serious?'

'Never been more serious in all my life. Of course I mean it. I want you to be my wife.'

'Pierre, oh darling, I'm so happy. Of course I'll marry you. It'll make all my dreams come true.'

The wonderment of love overwhelmed them. They lay in each other's arms, planning their future, their prospects stretching out before them.

'I must go back to Stellenbosch University next year to complete my LL B, before I can start my articles. I'll ask my father to help us financially.'

'Don't do that. I'll get a job as a social worker in Stellenbosch. We'll manage somehow.'

He kissed her, and the ardour returned. This time they made slow, deliberate love, trying different ploys to please each other. They did not hear the key turn in the front door, as Rika let herself in.

'Pierre, I've wonderful news,' she cried as she walked into the bedroom.

Each became aware of Rika in the same split-second. They rolled over, frantically trying to cover their nakedness. Rika stared aghast. She threw up her hands to cover her face. Pierre scrambled off the far side of the bed and found the shorts discarded by Lesley. He led a devastated Rika to a chair.

'What's going on, Pierre?' She was totally confused.

'Rika, this is Lesley Stuart, I mean Summers. We love each other and are going to be married.'

'Married?' Rika exclaimed in a terrified voice. 'I thought you and I were going to get married, Pierre?'

'I'm sorry Rika, but I don't love you,' Pierre answered honestly. 'I love Lesley.'

Eyes blazing, she turned to Lesley. 'You're a married woman, how can you marry Pierre?'

'I'm getting a divorce, I'll marry him the day it's finalised.'

'Do you love him?' Rika searched Lesley's face.

'With all my heart.'

'Oh my God! Only this morning my world was so perfect, now everything is shattered.' Rika sobbed quietly.

Pierre sat on the bed, holding Lesley around the shoulders. 'I'm sorry, Rika, but life can sometimes be cruel. You must accept our relationship is finished. Lesley is the woman of my dreams. She will be my wife and is my future.'

Each word was like a hammer blow. Rika grimaced, in agony. 'Just answer one question before I go, Pierre. How long have you been double-crossing me?'

'If you really want to know, we met again only today.'

'*Today*, and you're already in bed, fucking like two rabbits.' Her voice cracked bitterly.

Lesley felt the other woman's pain. 'Rika, I'm sorry. I would never want to hurt you, but you did burst in without warning.'

'Shut up, you bitch.' Rika's eyes flashed dangerously. 'You take my man and you still have the gall to say you're sorry. Well, you can have him, I don't want him now.' She threw the flat keys at Pierre and stormed from the room, crying hysterically.

Pierre ran after her. 'Please try and understand, Rika.'

She looked at him contemptuously. 'Fuck off, Pierre Roux. Just piss off.' She slapped a stinging blow across his face. 'I never want to see you again.' The door slammed. Rubbing his cheek ruefully, Pierre watched through the window as she ran to her car and out of his life.

Lieutenant Fullard was in a foul mood when Pierre reported for duty the next morning. 'The decision to destroy the squatter camp was taken at Cabinet level. Then you come along and have the cheek summarily to stop proceedings.'

'I did what I thought was right in the name of justice.'

'What do you know about justice?' Fullard asked angrily. 'The law says illegal blacks must be repatriated to their homelands and squatter camps destroyed.'

'With respect, sir, the law is wrong if it excludes basic human rights from people.'

'The blacks have no rights in South Africa. Policemen have to accept government policy if they want to make a success of their careers.'

'I don't intend to make a career in the SAP, sir. I'll buy

my discharge at the end of December to go back to university.'

'I should give you a dishonourable discharge from the force for your conduct, Roux, but it will appear on your record.'

'Please don't do that, sir.'

Fullard saw in Pierre's face the genuine concern of an upright man. He thought carefully. 'All right, Roux. I'll tell you what I'll do with you. You have only a few weeks to go before completing your term. As punishment, you'll be confined to desk duty.'

Pierre breathed a sigh of relief. 'Thank you, sir.'

'By the way, constable, your squatter friends at Crossroads have done great damage to the six earth-moving machines. They poured sand into the diesel tanks and sumps, they undid every nut and bolt they could lay their hands on. The Administration Board is screaming blue murder; it will take them weeks to get the machines serviceable again. You have stayed Crossroads's execution by at least a month.'

Sparrows in the eaves started twittering as the light grew stronger. Heavy footsteps sounded in the passage of the Johannesburg Fort, coming to a halt at the cell gate. Two warders entered. 'Themba Memani,' barked an autocratic voice.

Surprised, Themba looked at Sly. 'What now?'

'You're probably wanted for questioning,' Sly answered. 'I hope they don't take you to The Grays.'

'Themba Memani?' shouted the guard louder.

'You'd better go,' advised Sly. 'There's nothing I can do if the security police are involved.'

With a weapon jammed into his back Themba walked along the twisted alleyways. Two plain-clothes policemen met him, bundled him into a car and handcuffed him to the back door.

'Who are you?' Themba asked nervously.

'Security police.'

'Where are you taking me?'

'The Grays, security police headquarters in Johannesburg.'

'Why?'

'Wait and see. You ask too many questions.'

They parked the car in an enclosed parking lot near the entrance to a lift. They got out at the seventh floor. A heavy gate clanged shut behind them and Themba was pushed down a passage into a sparsely furnished office.

'Good morning, Mr Memani. How are you? I am Lieutenant van Rensburg of the security police.'

He seems friendly enough, thought Themba.

'Memani, look here. This is your file.' Themba saw a buff manila file, half full of papers. They seemed to have a lot of information on him. He sensed the friendliness was just an opening ploy. 'Memani, either you play ball and talk, or we play ball on you and you talk anyway. Take your pick.'

Themba kept quiet, looking intently at the policeman as he opened the file and rattled off details of Themba's life. He told him about his mother, his schooling, his university career, his in-laws, the school he had taught at, about his wife and his arrest at Crossroads.

'You know a lot about me. There is nothing more to tell.'

'Oh yes, there is! You were sheltering two student agitators in your house in Soweto. I want to know about them and all the other leaders of the SSRC.'

'I knew them only as Joe and John.'

'Don't lie to me. I want the names and details of all the members of the Soweto Students' Representative Council and where to find them. Also your contacts in Cape Town.'

'I'm sorry, I can't remember.'

'All right, Memani, you've had your chance. You want to play difficult, we'll see how difficult.'

The lieutenant dialled a number. 'Swiegers.' Within moments two burly men appeared. They dragged Themba out of the office to a room at the end of the passage, The Gray's torture chamber. On one side was a room with one-way glass where the officers could sit sipping coffee as they watched the side-show in the torture room, out of sight of the prisoner.

The inside of the room was like a huge shower, the walls and floor tiled in gleaming white. The floor sloped towards a drainage hole; Themba wondered how much blood had flowed down it over the years. A tap with a thick green garden hose attached to it protruded from the wall. Against the wall was a single wooden chair. The only light on in the room, a spotlight, was focused on the chair. There was a government-issue table near the door, with three wooden chairs facing the prisoner.

'Sit, Memani.' Themba sat on the chair, blinded by the strong spotlight. He heard the voices of the two men at the table, but could not see their faces in the darkness.

'Talk, Memani. Tell us about Soweto.'

'I have nothing to say.'

'You hard-arsed kaffir! You will sing like a canary when we've finished with you,' thundered Swiegers.

They moved forward purposefully. Themba was yanked to his feet. Swiegers kicked the chair out of the way. The first punch caught Themba in the stomach. He doubled over in pain, his wrists straining at the handcuffs behind his back. Punches rained on him from all angles, until mercifully he blacked out. Vaguely he felt water splashing over him. He came round shaking his head. Again he was forced to his feet and beaten – again he passed out.

'Are you ready to talk, Memani?' He shook his head.

They propped him up against the wall while they cut off his skipper and short pants. They set about his torso, buttocks and legs with lengths of rubber hose-pipe. The pain was terrible, coming in excruciating waves of agony. The hose-pipes raised thick, dark welts on his skin. They beat him until his legs gave way. Themba was conscious, but a haze clouded his mind, like fluffs of cotton wool on a misty Transkei morning. He cried out for them to stop.

'We'll stop, if you talk.' Swiegers's ruddy face was flushed from exertion.

Themba kept quiet. They put the chair back in position and sat him roughly on the seat, his handcuffed arms over the backrest so that he was powerless to move. They brought forward a small bench, lifted his legs and placed his calves on the bench, so that he sat with his legs straight out in front of him.

The policemen hit the soles of his feet with the hose-pipes, sending more shock waves, worse than before, coursing through his battered body. The torture made him urinate, the liquid spurted out involuntarily and dripped off the chair.

'He's pissing, we have him!'

Swiegers shook his head. 'Not until he shits – hit!'

Themba hung limply in the chair, past caring, having broken through the pain barrier – a whooshing of air in a kaleidoscope of rainbow colours. He wavered between reality and fantasy as the hours slipped past.

They continued beating the soles of his feet, the agony relaxing the muscles in his anus. His faeces flowed over the chair, degrading and inhuman. Themba was unaware of the humiliation, he was past caring.

'*Sis*, he's shit himself!'

'Wash away the mess.'

They turned the hose on full blast, the force so strong it knocked the chair over backwards, Themba crashed to the ground. Cold water swirled around him, washing his blood, urine and faeces mixed together down the drain.

The policemen left him while they went off to the canteen for their lunch break.

Lieutenant van Rensburg came out of the observation room. 'Is Memani ready to talk?'

'Don't know. He's a tough nut, that one. I think he's had enough for one day. If we continue any longer we may kill him.'

'We can't return him to No. 4 in his condition. Put him in the special cell until tomorrow.'

When Themba regained consciousness many hours later, he lay shivering in a tiny cell. The only light came from the grille in the door. He heard people talking in the passage, but he was too weak to call out. He slipped into unconsciousness again and it was quiet in the building when he re-awoke. He ached all over and was icy cold. He was lying on a thin sponge mattress with a pile of blankets in the corner. He pulled two blankets over his naked body and after a while his teeth stopped chattering. In another corner he saw two slices of dry brown bread and a mug of water, but his battered stomach could not face the prospect of eating. He dozed again.

Themba was awakened by a boot kick in his side. He sat up stiffly, his heart sinking as he saw Swiegers bending over him. 'Get up, kaffir, you're going back to the circus. Today we'll break you for sure.'

They hauled Themba to his feet and he stumbled ahead of them down the passage, his eyes squinting in the bright morning light. Swiegers kicked him on the backside. As he sprawled face downwards the guards laughed in derision. He was too weak to stand again – he crawled on hands and knees through the torture-room door. He made for the arc of light, scrabbling on the highly polished tile surface.

The hell started again, hose-pipes thudding into his body, until the relief of unconsciousness swept over him. They revived him with cold water and set about him again.

Lieutenant van Rensburg left the observation room and walked into the torture chamber. 'All right men, try the bag, then go on to the electric-shock machine.'

'If those don't work, Lieutenant?'

Van Rensburg shrugged casually. 'Then I'll arrange for a doctor to issue a death certificate.'

A canvas bag was slipped over Themba's head and the draw-string pulled tight around his neck. Inside it was pitch dark and stank of previous users' vomit. Themba tried desperately to suck in a mouthful of air, but the bag lodged against his mouth, suffocating him. He tried to pull the bag off with his hands, but his torturers held his arms at his side, laughing as he struggled against the canvas.

Themba almost lost his mind. Madness was replaced by reason as he forced himself to stay calm and took in short, little breaths. It was a solution, but only a short-term respite. He used up all the oxygen in the bag and eventually he was breathing in his own carbon dioxide. He blacked out. The policemen took off the bag and thumped his chest to revive him. Twice more they used the bag and twice more he passed out.

His torturers dumped him back in the small cell, where he clung desperately to life.

'He's a determined one, Lieutenant. Tomorrow we'll give him the shock treatment. He'll either talk or die.'

Themba woke during the night. He attempted to force down some bread to build up his strength, but vomited it straight out again. He tried to remember his tormentors' faces. He focused on Swiegers, known as the red Russian. He burnt minute details of Swiegers's features into his subconscious to give him something abhorrent on which to concentrate at the height of torture.

They tied Themba to the chair so tightly he could not move. He watched in morbid fascination as they bound his penis and testicles with thin copper wire. The other end was attached to an ordinary bicycle dynamo, which ran off the outer rim of a workshop grinder – a home-made contraption of torture.

Swiegers turned the handle and Themba spasmed to the worst pain ever inflicted on him. His arms and legs jerked involuntarily as electric shocks coursed through his body. His sex organs felt as if they were on fire. Again Swiegers cranked the handle. The shock waves cramped his muscles, causing Themba to shudder and convulse in agony.

'Stop! Please stop!'

'Will you talk?'

Themba shook his head. He closed his eyes and saw the red face of Swiegers in his mind. 'I won't.'

Swiegers smiled with relish. 'You think that was bad, Memani? Now I'll give you the worst pain on earth.'

He attached a thinner wire to the main wire. Opening the vent on the tip of Themba's penis, he pushed the end a match-stick length down his urinary tube. He cranked the handle vigorously. Themba spasmed so forcefully the chair crashed over. He lay on his side, his penis muscles twitching uncontrollably, the pin-point of pain making him scream at the unendurable agony — an intense and piercing suffering not even the face of Swiegers could blot out. 'No! No! No!'

Slackening slightly, Swiegers shouted, 'Will you talk?'

Themba could not face another split-second. 'Yes!'

They turned on the hose-pipe and washed the perspiration off him. They untied him and placed the chair under the spotlight. He held his penis in both hands, squeezing hard, trying to force away the pain.

Van Rensburg strolled in. Swiegers had softened Themba up, now it was his turn for the final interrogation. Blinded by the spotlight, Themba answered as best he could. He gasped out answers between spasms of pain. He told them of Solomon Mahlangu and Khotso Seathlolo, about the members of the action committee, about his role in the Soweto riots and Cape Town. The grilling went on for hours. Van Rensburg asked the same questions from different angles, trying to trip him up. When he fainted from exhaustion they gave him sweet, warm tea to revive him.

At last Van Rensburg was satisfied. 'We'll type out a statement for you to sign.'

Themba was too exhausted to read the statement. He merely put pen to paper, unaware he had signed away his freedom.

That evening he was returned to the Johannesburg Fort. Even the scooters were appalled. Sly made Themba comfortable in the centre of the cell, he bribed a warder to supply antiseptic and ointment to treat his wounds. Themba slept the sleep of the dead for the next forty-eight hours.

He awoke still feeling stiff and sore, but his body was starting to heal. He looked around. 'Where is Ngconde?' Themba asked worriedly.

'They sentenced him this afternoon. Prisoners who came back from court said he was given three years. He's been transferred to Leeuwkop. They'll probably send him to Robben Island.'

'I miss him already,' said Themba. 'I'm sure our paths will cross again.'

Sly handed Themba a folded page of paper. 'He gave me a message for you.'

Themba unfolded the paper and read the words: *'Hope lies in those who dare to dream dreams, and are committed to pay the price to make those dreams come true.'*

17

'Philippi police station, Constable Roux speaking. May I help you?'

'Pierre, it's Danie Conradie. I've wonderful news. Rika and I are getting married. I want you to be my best man.'

'Congratulations, Danie, I'm genuinely happy for you.'

'It's like a dream come true. I have to pinch myself to believe it. The wedding is the Saturday after next, in Upington.'

'Next week! Why the rush?'

'I don't know, but Rika insists we get married as soon as possible. She has some crazy idea of wanting to spend Christmas in the Seychelles. Her father's paying for the trip, a wedding present to us. It will be our honeymoon.'

'Is Rika happy with my being best man?' Pierre asked cautiously.

'She did jib at first, but when I insisted she seemed to accept it. Why?'

'We had a rather nasty break-up. I'm glad she turned to you. You'll be good for her. By the way, you remember my old flame, Lesley Stuart? We're together now.'

'I heard. There's one small problem though, Pierre. Rika refuses to have Lesley at the wedding.'

'I understand and I think Lesley will understand too. When do you want me in Upington?'

'Friday afternoon will be fine. We'll have a few drinks together. I'm staying at the Gordonia Hotel.'

'I'll see you there. And Danie, I'm looking forward to being your best man.'

In Upington the east wind was blowing, kicking up clouds of Kalahari red dust which billowed over the town, cutting down the visibility. The Dutch Reformed church filled up. Pierre and Danie stood together in front of the pulpit. Danie was fidgeting, looking at his watch. 'The bride is five minutes late, what if she's changed her mind?'

'Relax, Danie, brides are always late. It's their way of showing the bridegroom who's boss!' Pierre cast an eye over the congregation. The church was almost full, an indication of the importance of Wagner Bosch in the community.

The organ struck up 'Here comes the bride', and the congregation rose. Rika walked down the aisle on her father's arm, her face veiled.

'Who gives this woman to be married?'

'I do.' Wagner lifted the veil and took his place in the front pew.

Rika looked at Pierre sadly, tears brimming in her eyes as she took her place beside Danie. Pierre was confused, he was convinced she hated him.

'You may kiss the bride.'

Danie kissed Rika tenderly, glowing with happiness. As Rika walked out of the church she looked miserably at Pierre. She made a brave effort to smile. She knew she had married the wrong man, but she had been determined her baby would have a father.

The reception was held in the Upington Hotel. The speeches seemed to go on for ever. Pierre listened impatiently. The band played the first waltz. A beaming Danie led his bride on to the dance floor. The crowd cheered as they swept around.

'Aren't you going to ask me to dance?'

Pierre looked questioningly at Rika. 'I didn't ask you because I thought you were still upset with me.'

'Nonsense, it's the best man's duty to dance with the bride.' She sloshed some of her champagne on the table. Pierre realised she was slightly tipsy.

He looked at Danie, who was studying them intently. 'Do you mind if I dance with your beautiful bride?'

'Go ahead, old friend.' His smile signalled Pierre would never be a threat again. 'Enjoy yourselves, I'm going to chat to my father-in-law.'

A slow foxtrot was playing when they reached the floor. Rika put her head on Pierre's chest and sighed contentedly. As she stumbled Pierre caught her.

'You've had too much champagne, Rika.'

'I don't care, I think I'll get drunk tonight.'

'It's not done for a girl to get drunk on her wedding night.' Pierre was shocked. 'Anyway, Danie will be expecting fireworks from you later.'

'Ha . . . ha . . . ha!' Rika threw back her head in laughter. 'Fireworks you should have given me, Pierre Roux.'

'Sh! People will hear you.' He looked at her sharply. 'Rika, what we had is in the past. You're married to Danie now.'

'That's where the problem lies.' She walked to the main table and poured a glass of champagne. She downed it in a gulp.

Pierre stopped her pouring another glass. 'Go slow, Rika.'

'I want to talk to you in private,' she slurred. 'Come outside with me.'

'We can't go outside, what will Danie and the guests think?'

'Bugger them all.' She marched to the door. Pierre ran after her. Once out of the hotel, she lifted her skirts and ran to the bank of the river.

'Rika, what on earth are you doing?' Her mood had changed completely. Where she had been sad and composed before, she was suddenly bitter and brazen. She turned on Pierre, hands on her hips. 'Pierre, I hate you. I hate you for what you have done to me and I hate your new woman too. You can have her, but you'll never have our baby. It's mine, mine alone.'

'Baby, what baby, Rika?'

'I'm two and a half months pregnant, from you.'

'Why didn't you tell me?'

'I came to tell you, but found you in bed with that married whore. I want you to suffer, Pierre Roux, as you made me suffer. I want you to know about your child, but never have the pleasure of holding or cherishing it. There's nothing you can do about it without devastating your best friend. I've outwitted you, Pierre.'

Pierre's shoulders slumped. His child would become Danie's child. Danie was so gullible, so much in love, he would accept any explanation from Rika.

'What's going on here, angel?' Danie came running up to them.

'I had too much champagne, sweetheart. I came out for some fresh air. I'm fine now, we can go back to the reception.'

Danie glanced at Pierre inquiringly. 'Why are you here?'

'I followed her to see if she was all right.'

Danie put his arm protectively around his wife. As they walked to the hotel together, Rika glanced back over her shoulder. It was a look of victory.

As the first light of day forced its way through the tiny windows, feebly lighting up the cell, the gate rattled and various prisoners were summoned. Themba and twenty other prisoners were loaded into a police truck and transported to the cells below the Johannesburg Supreme Court.

'T Memani, T Memani,' his name echoed down from above. He was led up a flight of stairs into the body of the court, shuffling along in leg-irons and handcuffs.

Hilda was in court. She smiled to encourage him. Themba felt more confident. The charges were read out.

'How do you plead?' barked the public prosecutor.

'Not guilty, Your Lordship.'

'Do you have legal representation?'

'I am not guilty, I don't need an attorney.'

'I represent Mr Memani,' said an attorney, stepping forward.

Themba was surprised, unaware that Nomisile had transferred money for his defence.

The court case lasted two days. Themba's signed statement to the security police proved damning evidence. The report was read out and filed. Themba had admitted to being a member of the action committee and the SSRC, helping to organise the Soweto riots and concealing suspects wanted by the state and inciting violence in Cape Town.

'Themba Memani, I find you guilty as charged under Section 29 of the Internal Security Act. You are hereby sentenced to five years' incarceration on Robben Island, with hard labour, as a political prisoner of the state.'

Hilda was shattered. She had been so sure their attorney's arguments had persuaded the court of Themba's innocence. Now her husband would be totally removed from her life for five years. 'Can't we appeal?' Hilda pleaded with the attorney.

'It would be a waste of money. The Appeal Court would probably uphold the supreme court's verdict. I'm sorry.'

Hilda slumped in her seat, resigning herself to loneliness for a considerable time. As they led Themba away she pushed past the duty policeman and caught up with Themba at the head of the stairs. She embraced him. 'I'll miss you, my darling husband.'

'It will be hard for me, too, but we must be positive and look at it as an honour to be a political prisoner. Hilda, move from Soweto, go back to the Transkei. Return to our home next to my mother – at least you'll be safe among family and friends.'

The court policeman separated them forcibly. He pulled Hilda away and pushed Themba down the stairs. The last glance Themba had of her was her devastated, tear-stained face.

Back at The Fort he spent his final night in familiar surroundings. Sly laid on a special treat – beers and meat pies – as a last supper. Themba knew he would miss Sly and the scooters. Although hardened criminals, they had their humane side as well. The next day he was taken to Leeuwkop, a marshalling prison for those on their way to Robben Island.

The entrance gates were guarded by stone lions in repose, one on either side of the gateway. The prison consisted of two parts – a farm for rehabilitating prisoners and a maximum-security section for hardened criminals and political transferees.

Themba was driven past the farm to the maximum-security area. In the courtyard he was made to strip. He was becoming accustomed to it by now. A warder shaved his head with an electric hair clipper and he was chased into a cold shower. He was given a pair of shorts and a khaki shirt, again regardless of size. Finally a warder with a stick chased him down a passage into an isolation cell.

'Run. Run.' It seemed everything in prison was done at the double. Themba's section consisted of row upon row of small iron-barred cages running the length of the building, with passages in between. Above the cells were long walkways, patrolled by warders. They marched up and down, keeping talk to a minimum.

'Exercise time,' shouted Warder Magalies, earning his nickname from the rolled tobacco he chewed incessantly. It grew in the Magaliesberg region of the Transvaal. Every now and then he would spit out a long streak of brown, tobacco-tainted spittle.

Magalies had a metal-tipped cane, which he swung lustily, keeping the naked prisoners on the run. He chortled in delight each time the steel tip cut into a prisoner's flesh. Any man displaying weakness was targeted, often rendering them hospital cases. Themba kept out of his way, always a pace ahead, and avoided being branded by the cane.

After half an hour they trooped back to their cells, collecting a coir mat and two filthy blankets along the way. A trolley with supper was pushed up and down the passages. In front of each gate, warders placed an aluminium plate with a chunk of overcooked meat and a small loaf of undercooked prison bread. Two cups were set down, one containing a watery soup, the other a brown chicory extract, serving as coffee. There were no eating utensils.

Themba thought back fondly on all the little luxuries Sly and his friends had managed to secure. Ten minutes later the empty utensils were collected and the lights turned off. Except for a toilet bucket and a plastic bottle of water the cells were bare.

Themba spent almost a month at Leeuwkop. He learnt to hate all warders, but not to let his feelings show. He discovered the trick of getting lost in the crowd, doing nothing to attract attention to himself.

One cold morning Themba was escorted into the courtyard. Three large trucks stood inside the gates. They had high sides covered with tarpaulins. The prisoners were lined up into three groups of thirty each. Themba realised the long journey to Robben Island was about to start.

Leg irons were snapped to their ankles, a chain on each leg attached to the man alongside. They formed a thirty-man human snake. Each man was handcuffed to the prisoner on either side, making individual escape impossible.

They shuffled towards the waiting trucks, each one matching his movements to the prisoner's directly behind and in front of him, otherwise they tripped each other up. Climbing on to the truck was the most difficult, they got no help from the warders – only curses and blows. Once inside they were forced to sit on the bare metal floor.

Themba felt debased and angered by a system which had reduced him to his present station. He was a man of refinement – educated and proud. He silently cursed his persecutors – the Nationalist government, the apartheid structure and even the whole white race. He knew he was wrong when he thought of Paul Curry, but blaspheming helped nevertheless.

The trucks left in convoy and travelled south over the Vaal River. They drove five hundred kilometres across the Orange Free State, crossing into the Cape Province. The convoy rarely stopped. Equipped with long-range diesel tanks, they kept going hour after hour. When they did halt for the warders to stretch their legs, or relieve themselves, the prisoners were not allowed out.

It grew stuffy in the back, with thirty jolting bodies sweating under the canvas. Prisoners tried to reach the back of the truck to urinate over the tailgate, but it was a complicated manoeuvre. The men and leg irons became so entangled that they had to urinate where they sat. Sharp, acrid liquid eventually swilled around the back of the truck, soaking everyone's clothes, adding to the stench.

In the late afternoon the trucks pulled into the yard of Colesberg prison. Magalies made them all climb down. They frequently tripped and fell, and were rewarded with a lash of the iron-tipped cane.

Nobody had bothered to let the Colesberg station commander know three truckloads of prisoners were arriving, and no food was prepared. He sent out for eighteen loaves of brown bread. Each prisoner received a fifth of a dry loaf and a mug of brackish water.

The prison cells at the small Karoo town were not designed to hold ninety inmates. Even though they protested, Magalies would not let them be unchained. He forced them into two cells – a group of thirty in one cell intended for only five prisoners, the other sixty into another planned to house a maximum of twelve. There was not enough room to lie down. Some slept sitting upright while others had to stand. Every two hours they rotated.

During the night, two Bedford trucks arrived from Cape Town and reversed into the yard. By six o'clock the next morning the bakery had not finished baking bread, so the prisoners went without breakfast.

Magalies insisted on counting the men. He made the Cape crew sign for the human cargo. As there were now only two trucks, one team was split in half and chained to the other two teams, resulting in even more of a crush.

'Goodbye, boys,' said Magalies sarcastically. 'Enjoy your journey to the island.' Magalies and his three trucks headed back to Leeuwkop, while the two Bedfords continued south.

The whole day they motored through the hot, dry Karoo, not once being allowed off the trucks. Urine flowed again. After two days the men could no longer contain their bowel movements and they defecated in their trousers, making conditions in the back of the trucks unbearable.

The night was spent in the police cells at Parow, a northern suburb of Cape Town. Once again they were forced to sleep shackled to one another. Supper was a bowl of half-raw mealie-meal porridge. Themba ate every morsel.

Early the next morning they were driven to Cape Town docks, to No. 5 quay in the Victoria Basin.

A light drizzle was falling which, combined with a strong wind, gave a wind-chill factor around freezing. The prisoners shivered in their skimpy wet clothes as they lined up on the quayside.

Robben Island's commuter launch was too small to carry ninety passengers, forcing the prison services to use their converted fishing boat *Blouberg* to make the crossing.

They stood in a circle around the edge of the deck with Themba facing the bows.

Battling into the teeth of the wind, the trawler headed for the island. Themba had known cold, but nothing ever like this island crossing. He felt as if his blood had frozen in his veins and his circulation would never return. The salt sea spray splashed over them as the bows crashed through the waves, driving the temperature down into minus figures.

Themba looked at the welcoming committee as they docked against the pier: there were scores of warders, some holding fierce German shepherds straining at their leashes. Hundreds of seagulls circled the blue-painted trawler, screeching their piercing cries, seemingly mocking the new arrivals.

Once they had disembarked they were again counted. Themba's teeth were chattering from the cold and he was pleased when they moved towards the prison. He could not help noticing the anomaly on the concrete arch that formed the entrance. Across the top was emblazoned ROBBENEILAND, while down the left-hand pillar stood the incongruous word WELCOME, and down the pillar on the right the same word in Afrikaans, WELKOM.

'Welcome to hell, no doubt,' Themba shouted defiantly.

Up the road they shuffled. At strategic places along the fences were stone guard towers occupied by armed warders. The security fence was V-shaped at the top and had twin coils of barbed razor wire. The older prison buildings were made of rock walls created by master masons.

Inside the prison their handcuffs and leg chains were removed. It felt strange to be free of the weight, to move unrestricted once again. Themba swung his arms.

'Move it,' shouted a warder, leading the way. They were expected to run, but after the degradation they had suffered they could manage no more than a slow walk. They were taken to A section, the observation section for all new arrivals to the island.

'You smell terrible,' cried a short, stocky warder. Of course we do, thought Themba, after all we've been through! 'Into the showers with you.'

Even the cold sea-water showers were warm after the freezing journey, and there was the luxury of carbolic soap. They formed up naked. 'It's time for you to do the thausa for us. We want to see you've brought nothing to Robben Island hidden up your arse-holes,' shouted the guard gleefully.

One by one, the new inmates performed the degrading thausa in front of the warders. They had to jump high into the air, spin around and land with their backs facing the warder, opening their legs wide, arms above their heads. On landing they bent forward to expose their open rectums fleetingly to the man.

'Okay, you can dress now. Form up in line.' Walking forward in single file, they grabbed a pair of khaki shorts from one pile, a khaki linen jacket from another, a floppy hat, a right shoe and a left shoe, each on separate heaps. Again the clothes were either too big or too small, or the shoes were different sizes. Often the shoes were muddled up and a prisoner got two left or two right shoes, but he knew better than to complain. It was only for a day, tomorrow he might be luckier! The jacket was warmer than the skipper, the shoes kept out the cold from the ground and Themba felt reasonably comfortable for the first time in weeks.

'Line up for registration,' barked the warder. Again they stood in a queue, waiting for hours to be attended to by a solitary official.

'Next.'

Themba walked into the office. A warrant officer sat behind a table. '*Naam?*'

'I only speak English.'

'Damn you, kaffir. If you want to survive here, you'd better learn Afrikaans, and fast. We don't speak English to kaffirs. *Naam?*'

'Themba Memani.'

The officer searched through the heap of files until he pulled out the right one. 'I see you got five years in Johannesburg Supreme Court. You were a leader in the Soweto students' uprising. You caused the police a lot of grief, didn't you? I'm classifying you as One Notch. No privileges. You're a trouble-maker. Any sicknesses or abnormalities?'

'None, that I know of.'

'Don't get smart with me, kaffir. Just answer yes or no. And you call me *baas*.'

'No, *baas*.'

'Good. I'm allocating you to D General Section. Memani, you are now officially prisoner number 287/76. Here is your card. Don't lose it, it's your passport on the island. You no longer have a name, only a number. Do you understand?'

Themba nodded. '*Ja, baas*.'

'Next!' shouted the registration officer loudly.

Themba walked out into the sunshine. Through the fences he could see the work teams returning from the lime quarry. They marched in sections, four deep. Last came the small group from the isolation cells.

A prisoner shouted excitedly, 'There's Nelson Mandela!'

It was Themba's first glimpse of the legendary leader, a tall man with a fine posture, walking regally. He was thinner than in the photographs Themba had seen of him, but those had been taken before his imprisonment. Nelson turned his head briefly to look at the new intakes. He flashed them a smile of encouragement.

Supper was cold mealie-meal porridge. Dished up hours beforehand, a hard skin had formed on the top. It was tasteless, without salt, but Themba ate every scrap. He drank the mug of *puzamandla*, a powdered vegetable extract to which water was added to make a thin gruel. The coffee tasted awful, black and bitter. After the meal Themba still felt hungry, but he would have to get used to his ration – here there was no Sly to supplement his diet.

Three weeks later Themba passed his medical examination; he was declared fit for manual labour. He knew this meant the dreaded lime quarry. He remained classified at One Notch, with no special privileges.

Month followed dreary month on Robben Island. Themba worked in the lime quarry by day and rested his weary body at night. He had just recovered his strength after a night's sleep when the whole routine started over like a wheel turning, turning on a long journey to nowhere.

Themba became an adroit prisoner. He was smart enough to realise he had to work within the system, so he found out all the tricks of the trade, all the nuances for foiling the warders.

When he first reached D Section, he had been a celebrity; he had to tell, many times over, the events of the Soweto students' riots. One day had been a highlight. He had been shuffled around, swopped from team to team in the quarry right under the watchful eyes of the warders, until suddenly he was in the midst of the great men.

'Mr Mandela, I am Themba Memani, from Mqekezweni. It is an honour to meet you.'

'How do you do, Themba. I did receive your note about my family at the royal kraal. I'm pleased to hear everyone is well, and I'm very glad to meet a nephew.'

'Psst,' Walter Sisulu warned, 'the guard is looking this way. Keep your heads down and make as if you're working.' Themba bent over his spade, the floppy hat hiding his face from the warders.

'Tell me about the events at Soweto.'

When Themba had finished the story, including the trial and his sentence, Nelson congratulated him. 'You have struck a blow at the regime. I and the struggle are proud of you.' He introduced Themba to two other ANC leaders, Sisulu and Govan Mbeki.

All too soon his time was up. The reverse swops were carried out and Themba found himself back in his section. A few days later he swopped into a team off-loading supplies from the barge *Diaz*, and he spent the day with his old friend Ngconde Seymour. The work was back-breaking, but they finished unloading before lunch. It was too late to send them to the quarry team, and the two old friends had the whole afternoon sitting in the sun, renewing their friendship and recounting experiences.

'Ngconde, I'm determined to escape from this island. The mainland looks so close, I'm sure I could swim across.'

'The shortest distance is towards Blaauwbergstrand,' said Ngconde, pointing due east. 'They say it's eight kilometres.'

'I swam four kilometres with Paul Curry at esiKhaleni.'

393

'That was in the warm Indian Ocean. Here you have to contend with the Atlantic. There's a vast difference.'

'I agree, but one would attempt it in late summer, when the water is at its warmest.'

'Rather you than me, Themba, but I know you. Once you get an idea into your head, nobody can change your mind.'

The letter Simon read from Nomisile was upsetting.

> Dear Simon,
>
> I have very bad news. Themba was sentenced to five years' imprisonment on Robben Island for his part in the Soweto uprising.
>
> His wife Hilda and I badly want to visit him, but the Prison Department won't allow us. They say he does not qualify for visits.
>
> It has already been one year and we are anxious to see him. We also get no letters, so I don't know if he is fine. We are at out wits' end. I appeal to you to help us in our efforts to visit him.
>
> We count on you. I know you will help your son, as in the past. Please try your very best. Thank you Simon.
>
> Yours,
>
> Nomisile.
>
> PS I send you a photo of Hilda and me.

During the afternoon, Simon climbed Paarl Mountain. He racked his brains for a plausible plan. Sitting on the ledge, alone with nature, he could think clearly. At last he knew what to do. He pasted the letter and photograph in his scrap book. He looked with longing at Nomisile's photograph. Neither of them had found true happiness – both lived empty lives and gained their greatest comfort from their sons.

The second session of parliament was in progress, which suited Simon as the man he had to see was in Cape Town. He telephoned the private secretary of the Minister of Justice, Police and Prisons, and requested a meeting. Being a past Nationalist member of parliament was sufficient for him to be scheduled an appointment for the next week.

*   *   *

'How can I help you, Mr Roux? I'm afraid I can give you only fifteen minutes, as I have a meeting with the Prime Minister at midday. You know how it goes!'

'Let me get straight to the point, Minister. Many years ago we had a very faithful black maid who worked for us in the kitchen on our farm in Paarl. She had an illegitimate child and left the farm to raise him in the Transkei. Over the years I have supported the boy financially, I've even helped with his university education.'

'Very commendable, Mr Roux.'

'Last year he was arrested, tried and sentenced to jail.'

'I see. Why?'

'He was part of the 16 June Soweto riots. He was sentenced to five years on Robben Island.'

'Then I can't help you, Mr Roux. You know, of course, Robben Island houses only political prisoners. It contains men who have tried to subvert justice, have committed acts of terrorism and want to overthrow the government. I have no sympathy whatsoever with them. There is no way I would even consider releasing him or lessening his sentence. I'm sorry, Mr Roux.'

'I'm not asking you to do that, Minister.'

'What is it then?'

'His mother is sick and his wife pregnant. All I ask is for you to allow them one visit to him on the island.'

'It depends on his classification, Mr Roux. All prisoners are classified according to their behaviour. If he behaves himself, in due course he will qualify for visits.'

'By that time his mother may be dead and his wife's baby born, which would prevent her travelling. They would like to see him as soon as possible.'

'Why should I grant your request, Mr Roux?'

'Because I'm a member of the National Party and a former MP. A faithful member who makes a large contribution to the party coffers every year!' Simon shouted in anger, banging his fist on the desk.

'Calm down, I'll grant your request.' He called in his private secretary. 'I want you to draft a letter to the Commissioner of Prisons instructing him to move a prisoner on Robben Island to a Four Notch classification, with immediate effect, and to sanction combined visits from his mother and wife every six months.'

The secretary smiled. 'Could you give me the details, Mr Roux?'

'The prisoner's name is Themba Memani. His mother is Nomisile Memani and his wife is Hilda.' Simon gave the secretary the postal address in the Transkei.

'I'll have the letter ready for signing on your desk tomorrow morning, Minister. Anything else?'

'No.' He dismissed him. 'Well, Mr Roux, I trust you are satisfied?'

'Yes, I thank you.'

'I really must run. Doesn't pay to keep John Vorster waiting!'

Themba knocked on the door of the censor's office. 'I've been on the island for more than a year, but I've never received a letter.'

'Name and number, and don't forget to call me *baas* otherwise you'll get nothing out of me.'

'Themba Memani, 287/76, *baas*.'

The warder looked into a cubby-hole marked M and took out a handful of letters tied together with an elastic band. 'There are fourteen letters for you Memani, but you are still classified One Notch; you have no privileges.'

Themba lost control, he grabbed the bundle out of the officer's hand, instinctively holding them to his chest. 'These are mine. I'm entitled to them. I want them!' he cried in despair. 'It's been fourteen months, *baas*.'

He looked up into the barrel of a service revolver. 'Give those letters back to me, kaffir, otherwise I'll shoot you.'

Themba was shaking with frustration. News of his loved ones was so near, yet so far. In his hand he held fourteen jewels, more important to him at that moment than fourteen diamonds or fourteen bars of gold.

'I'm counting to three.'

Themba let the bundle fall to the floor. Apologising profusely, he bent to retrieve them. The table was between Themba and the guard. In one fluid movement he slipped a letter out from the middle, pushed his foot forward, lifted his heel in the ill-fitting shoe and hid the letter under his foot, then stood upright again. 'Sorry *baas*, very sorry.'

The warder grabbed the bundle from Themba's outstretched hands and shoved them roughly back into the pigeon-hole. 'You were nearly dead then, kaffir.'

Themba was shaking from his audacious deed, the warder thought he was quaking because he was scared of the gun. 'Scared hey, kaffir?'

'Yes, *baas*, thank you *baas*.' Themba bowed his head.

A look of superiority flashed across the warder's face. It made him feel important when the prisoners grovelled. He returned his gun to its leather holster. 'Bugger off, before I change my mind.'

'*Ja, baas*.' Themba walked away, flexing his toes to prevent his shoe flapping. His heart soared. He had a letter to read. Once out of sight he transferred the letter to his pocket. He was tempted to read it straight away, but it was not post day. The guards would be suspicious. All he saw was the postmark, 'Umtata'.

He was so excited, he never thought so simple an item as a letter could change his whole disposition. He sang as he worked in the quarry, willing lunch-time to arrive. It was the longest morning he could remember.

At last lunch break came. For once Themba was not hungry, impatient for the guards to go. He took out his envelope. The letter was from Hilda. A few sentences were blacked out, in one case a whole paragraph. He cursed the censor, but there was enough to make him cry great sobs of joy, mixed with pain and longing. He read and reread every word. The longing for his wife, her smile, her smell, her body, was overwhelming.

'Oh God, how I miss you!' he cried aloud. The other prisoners smiled in compassion. They had been through the same experience – the loneliness, the longing, followed by the utter joy of knowing you were not forgotten. You were not left rotting on an island, but loved, missed and cared for. A letter restored confidence to a flagging spirit and gave a reason for living.

The last page was from Nomisile. A tear fell on the page, smudging the ink. Themba dabbed the letter dry. Even one word was too precious to be lost. His loved ones were safe and they missed him. Men of history might have written magnificent speeches or brilliant prose and poetry, but all these paled into insignificance, compared with the three pages he pressed to his chest.

'I must go home,' he told his friends. 'I must escape.'

Perspiration poured off Pierre as he dug over the flower bed. He wiped his brow with the sleeve of his T-shirt. Popping petunia plants out of their cell-packs he planted them into the composted and fertilised soil. Pierre stood up and stretched. He looked towards the cottage, smiling proudly. Their very own house, and bond-free, a wedding present to them from his parents. A glow of well-being enveloped him.

His eyes travelled upwards to the wooded slopes of Papegaaiberg outside Stellenbosch. He thought of the many hours of training he had put in up and down the slopes, until he knew every pathway in his sleep. Lesley was the best athletics coach he had ever had, driving him constantly to improve his times. She was good for him – even his studies had improved.

'Darling, telephone for you. It's a Mr Conradie, private secretary of the Minister of Defence.'

Pierre looked startled. Was something wrong? Rika's baby would have been born by now. Could there be a problem? He hurried inside and picked up the receiver.

'Hullo, Mr Conradie, Pierre Roux here.'

'Good afternoon, Pierre. How are you?'

'I'm fine. Is there a problem with Rika or Danie?'

'Good Lord no. They're as fit as fiddles. Did you hear they had a son, born at the beginning of July?'

Pierre's heart beat faster. A son, his son! 'No, I didn't know. What is his name?'

Mr Conradie answered proudly, 'They named him after me. His name is Nicolaas.'

Nick Roux. Pierre rolled the name silently around his tongue. Not Roux, Nick Conradie. I must forget about my son.

'Pierre, that is not why I telephoned. The Minister of Defence wants a meeting with you urgently.'

'With me? Whatever for?'

'He'll tell you himself, but it's something important he wants you to do for him and for the future of the country.'

'I'm in the middle of my legal studies. Surely there are many other competent men?'

'He trusts you, Pierre. Don't forget you once saved his life. He's never forgotten. Please just come and hear what he has to say.'

Flipping through his diary, Pierre noted he had no lectures the next afternoon. 'I can make it to Cape Town by three o'clock tomorrow.'

'Done.' Nicolaas Conradie gave him directions to the office.

Pierre replaced the receiver slowly, a frown on his face. Lesley was leaning casually against the kitchen doorway, looking at him with raised eyebrows. 'You look worried, darling.'

He told her about the conversation, omitting the part about Rika's baby. Lesley was too astute, she'd work out the dates in a flash.

'You never told me about saving PW Botha's life.'

'It was kept away from the media. Miraculously, not a word ever reached the press.' He told her the full story.

'So, I've got an unsung hero who kept alive one of the principal perpetrators of apartheid?'

'It was a reflex action, sunshine. You can't hold that against me.'

Lesley laughed. 'I don't. Well, you'd better go and see what PW wants.'

Pierre walked up Parliament Street and disappeared into the enormous Hendrik Verwoerd Building, where the ministers had their offices. He was met by Nicolaas Conradie, who ushered him into a huge room. PW Botha, neat in a dark suit, white shirt and striped tie, stood up and walked around the big desk, hand extended.

'Pierre Roux. How nice to see you. Please be seated.'

Conradie quietly went out, leaving Botha and Pierre looking at each other over the desk. The Minister smiled, putting Pierre at ease. 'Tell me about yourself.'

Pierre told him all his news. His marriage, his police days and his resumed studies. Botha nodded and Pierre had the distinct feeling he was divulging facts already known to him. He would have had me checked out, thought Pierre to himself. I wonder what he wants?

A silver tray with china cups was brought in and tea poured for each man.

'Why are we meeting today, Mr Botha?'

'Pierre, I need someone whom I can trust implicitly. No doubt you've heard of Eschel Rhoodie, the Secretary of the Department of Information, of Dr Connie Mulder, the Minister of Information, and of General Hendrik van den Bergh, head of BOSS, the Bureau for State Security?'

Pierre nodded.

Botha sat forward looking intently at Pierre. 'I suspect them of orchestrating dirty tricks with State money. To start with, the Department of Information was funded by contributions from a special account in the Prime Minister's office. Rhoodie and Mulder soon used up these funds with grandiose schemes. Then they started demanding ever increasing sums of money.

'In the past few years the money has come out of my Special Defence Fund, intended for procuring overseas weapons. The money goes straight to BOSS, who then distributes it to the Department of Information. As Minister of Defence, I'm being asked to give away a large slice of my budget, but I have no knowledge of what the money is used for.'

Pierre looked puzzled. 'Is expenditure not controlled by the Auditor-General?'

'That's the rub, Pierre. Secret funds, because of their sensitive nature owing to the arms embargo, are not subject to audit. I resent giving up the taxpayer's money for hair-brained schemes concocted by Rhoodie.'

'Why don't you speak to the Prime Minister?'

'I've spoken to Vorster on five separate occasions. I think he knows all about Information's tricks, but Van den Bergh has him firmly in his pocket and all Vorster does is shrug apologetically.'

'Surely the Department of Information is using the money for legitimate propaganda purposes?'

Botha's face flushed and he slapped his hand on the desk. 'So far they've drained sixty-five million rand from Defence's Special Fund. One hears via the grape-vine they are funding a magazine, *To the Point*, and only yesterday I was told Rhoodie had used the funds to start *The Citizen* newspaper.'

'Where do I fit in, Mr Botha?'

'I need someone I can trust inside the Department of Information who will report to me and keep me abreast of developments.'

'You're looking for a spy?' Pierre asked incredulously.

Botha shook his head. 'Not a spy, Pierre, but someone with brains who will stop the rot and save South Africa from the consequences of this troika.'

'You know I'm not strictly National Party orientated, but you still ask me?'

'I know about your police career and the Crossroads incident. I also know you married Lesley, who is not a supporter of the government.'

'And you still want me for the job?'

'What Rhoodie and company are up to affects us all – Nationalists

400

and all the other political parties; whites, blacks, coloureds and Indians. I'm asking you to help me, and by so doing to help your country.'

'You said you wanted me inside the Department of Information?'

'Information recently opened an office in Cape Town and are recruiting staff. I want you to apply for a position.'

'Would I be appointed?' asked Pierre.

'I have a supporter with good contacts who would recommend you for a post. The troika won't connect him to me.'

Pierre nodded. 'I know what you want me to do, but I must still make the decision. Lesley would have very definite feelings; I'd have to consider them.'

'Let me put it to you this way, Pierre. You take the position and find out all you can. If you think what the Department of Information is doing is above board and in South Africa's interests, you tell me so. Then at least I'll have peace of mind.'

Botha stabbed his right index finger into the air. 'On the other hand, if you do find discrepancies and irregularities, I want you to inform me, so we can stop them.'

'What about university?'

'This is more important, Pierre. The country's future is at stake. You can resume your studies later.'

'And my athletics?'

'You are so close to Springbok selection, I would hate to prejudice your chances. Continue with your sports career, it will be a good diversion from the rigours of the office.'

'Can I have a few days to think it over? I'll have to discuss it with Lesley.'

'Of course.'

'Pierre Roux, you must be bananas, even contemplating getting mixed up in a National Party internal struggle!' Lesley studied her husband's face. 'If you want to get involved in politics, choose the ANC.'

'Sadly, they're banned.'

'Then choose the Opposition. Join the Progressive Federal Party, but why help the hated Nationalists?'

'Look at it this way, Lesley. If there is corruption, it should be weeded out. It affects us all.'

'I suppose you're right. It looks as if you've made up your mind?'

'Not at all. I won't accept unless you're behind me. It must be a joint decision.'

'We're so nicely settled at the moment. You're doing well at university. I'm earning a salary. Your athletics is flourishing. I'd be loath to change all that. With you away in Cape Town during the day, our time together will be limited. Life just wouldn't be the same any more.'

Pierre held her close. 'I could give it a trial period. If all looks kosher in the Department of Information I'll resign and return to Stellenbosch, catch up with my studies and complete my degree.'

Lesley held his face in her hands. 'Promise me you won't do anything that will hurt our black brothers and sisters and I'll give you my blessing, Pierre.'

'Mr Botha, my wife and I have talked the matter over. My political views differ from yours and you must accept that. I won't do anything to do a disservice to the black people of our country.'

'I understand, Pierre.'

'If you accept my viewpoint, I will accept the post. Part of my reason for wanting to be a lawyer is to be able to fight for the truth. If there is corruption in high places, I will find it.'

Themba was called into the chief warder's office one day in early December and told his classification had been raised from One Notch to Four Notches. From no privileges to maximum benefits in one fell swoop was unheard of on the island. He could not believe his luck.

'How come?' Themba asked suspiciously.

'I don't know. The directive came from the big boss, the Commissioner of Prisons himself. You must have influence in high places.'

Themba shook his head in amazement, racking his brains to think of someone who could have helped achieve such a miracle. The only person he could think of was Paramount Chief Sabata Dalindyebo, but he did not have such clout. Sabata had never been able to help Mandela. It remained a mystery.

'If I'm officially classified as Four Notches, I'm entitled to receive one letter a month. I've been here sixteen months, so I'm due sixteen letters. The warrant officer at the censorship office is holding a whole batch of letters addressed to me. I'd like them, please.'

'I'll see you get your letters.'

True to his word, he gave Themba the letters on the next post day. Themba's hands trembled with excitement, he did not know which one to open first. Eventually he worked from the date stamps on the envelopes, reading from the oldest to the most recent. Themba cried unashamedly as he read Hilda's and his mother's letters. His fellow inmates looked on sympathetically, they knew a letter was an umbilical cord between a loved one and a prisoner. He counted his blessings and gazed longingly eastwards towards the Transkei.

Themba's high spirits affected the whole section as he sang in the quarry while he picked, shovelled and hammered the limestone.

Walter Sisulu looked up from his work. 'That's Memani working with such vigour.'

'I think he's a born leader. Men seem to look up to him and follow him with confidence.' Nelson Mandela smiled knowingly. 'The ANC and Umkhonto we Sizwe can use a man like him. His sentence finishes in just over three years' time. We must advise Oliver Tambo to use him wisely.'

'He talks about escaping from the island at the end of the summer.'

'That's never been done before.' Mandela frowned in concern. 'We can't lose a good man on some foolhardy escape stunt.'

'I'll speak to him.'

Sunday was a rest day but Themba felt elated. He walked around energetically, chatting and laughing with his fellow prisoners.

To the east, way over the Karoo, big cumulus clouds were forming in the early afternoon; they turned into thunderheads, spitting lightning. Looking at the far-off storm made Themba even more restless. He paced up and down. Something invigorating was in the air, he could feel it in his bones.

'Prisoner 287/76.'

'That's me.' He walked forward, showing his card.

'Come with me.' The warder walked a step behind Themba, his rifle half slung, instructing him where to go.

'Where are you taking me?'

'You'll see.' Guards opened gates to sections Themba had never been allowed into before. They stopped in a grassed courtyard. Standing there were Hilda and Nomisile. Themba froze in shock, thinking it was a dream. It could not be true! Hilda was the first to react, she ran forward with a shout of glee and embraced Themba. He put his arms around her. He felt the familiar shapes and curves, but was he dreaming? Then he smelt her special smell and knew she was real.

'Hilda, my darling wife!' He kissed and kissed her, crushing her to his chest.

Nomisile held back, the wise and considerate mother. She looked with love at her only child. He was thinner, but in fine physical shape. Tears of joy ran down Hilda's cheeks. Themba's eyes were also wet as he turned to Nomisile. 'My darling mother.'

She flew into his arms, hugging him with all her might, afraid he might disappear again. She, too, started crying. Even the warder turned away at the spontaneous show of love, his hardened mind touched by the scene in front of him.

'You can sit on the grass.' The warder pointed out a spot.

'Would you leave us alone, please, out of earshot?'

He walked off and positioned himself a respectful distance away. Themba looked around. All over the courtyard were other prisoners with visitors, each party with its own armed guard.

He shut out the outside world and concentrated on the two women, remembering their features so he would not forget them in the lonely months ahead. They all talked excitedly at once.

'How did you get here?' Themba asked.

'We came from Umtata by bus, then the prison boat brought us to the island.'

'I got seasick on the boat,' giggled Hilda.

'Tell me about Mqekezweni.'

The women spoke about home, the animals, the mealie crop, the council. Themba moved into another world as they talked. He pictured the people they spoke of, experienced the landscape, saw the markings on the bull, the twist of the ram's horns and the beard of the billy-goat. He forgot his prison clothes and his awful surroundings, soaring in the clouds of his imagination. His happiness was rudely interrupted.

'Five more minutes, finish off now.'

They looked at one another in distress, realising the next five minutes would have to last the next six months. They lapsed into silence, keenly aware of their imminent separation. The seconds ticked away.

'How is Paul Curry? You didn't tell me about him.'

'Paul is fine. He has written you many letters, but every one has been returned to him as he is not family.' Hilda leant forward. She slipped a few objects out of her bra, down the front of Themba's shirt. 'Those are for you, from Paul.'

'Please thank him warmly.' He turned to Nomisile. 'Mother, how is Sabata Dalindyebo? Did he organise for my classification to be changed?'

'The Paramount Chief is fine, opposing Kaiser Matanzima as usual.' Nomisile coughed nervously, hiding her discomfort. 'I don't know who changed your classification.' She diverted his attention by holding his hand.

'Time up.'

'Warder, these women have travelled for two days to see me. With the return journey, it will be ninety-six hours for only half an hour's visit.'

'It's not my fault you're in prison.'

Nomisile walked across to the warder. Themba could not hear their conversation, but he saw her slip a roll of money into his palm.

The warder grinned in satisfaction. 'Okay, you can stay until the last group has finished.'

They gained fifteen precious extra minutes, hugging, squeezing, touching. The last of the visitors left the courtyard.

'Now you must go, otherwise I'll get into trouble.' The warder stepped forward.

The parting was tearful and passionate. They had to will themselves apart as the warder approached threateningly.

'Goodbye, my darling wife and mother. Thank you for coming. You've made my life worth living again.'

The women were too emotional to say their farewells. They ran hand in hand out of the courtyard. Just before they were out of sight they turned and waved forlornly together. They held each other in their grief, tears streaming down their faces.

Themba was alone, terribly alone.

'Let's go.' The warder prodded him in the back.

Themba walked slowly back to D Section. He felt Paul's letter in the front of his shirt, but there was something else as well. He

405

went straight into the bungalow, ignoring the eager questions from his section companions. Out came Paul's letter, a bar of chocolate, another letter and paper money. He broke off a piece of the chocolate and let it dissolve in his mouth. It was very sweet to a palate no longer used to sugar.

The rest of the afternoon he spent reading the two letters. Post-visitation depression common to all prisoners was kept in abeyance as Themba first read Paul's letter. It was intellectual, as was Paul's way, newsy and flippant, designed to raise Themba's spirits. It had the desired effect. The best news was that Paul had secretly joined the ANC branch in Umtata.

Good for you, thought Themba, our organisation needs white men like you. You are truly my best friend.

The other letter was a combined one from Hilda and Nomisile. It was wonderful to read an uncensored letter, where true feelings could be expressed without lines and paragraphs blotted out.

His cell mates crowded around. He told them about the visit, he read them the letters, he gave them half the slab of chocolate. They listened enraptured, for such was their utter isolation on the island that they shared, like close family, the correspondence and visits of a fellow prisoner. There was no hint of jealousy that Themba had been fortunate, while they had nothing. In their mind's eye he was talking about *their* wives, *their* mothers and *their* best friends. They sighed in contentment. It was a good day for them all.

'The letter from Paul would be dynamite if the warders got hold of it. It could incriminate him,' advised a prisoner.

'Also the letter from Hilda and Nomisile is uncensored. The authorities would spot it immediately. You can't keep the money in the cell, either. If they find it you'll be for the high jump.'

'What must I do?' Themba cried. 'I refuse to destroy them.'

'Use our DLB.'

'That's a good idea,' enthused Themba. They trooped out to the soccer field to dig up the dead letter box. The prisoners stood or sat around a bare patch of ground, shielding the digger from the sight of the guards in the towers while they uncovered the wooden box. Themba brushed the soil off the lid and lifted it carefully. Inside was a sealed plastic bag – to keep the contents dry and intact – containing documents, letters, old newspapers and even books.

Themba placed the money and the letters into Paul's envelope. His name appeared on the front; it would be safe. Ten minutes later the soil was level, tramped down by many feet, completely obliterating any signs of disturbance.

The next day Themba *had* to see Ngconde to share his good news. During the morning assembly he slipped between the rows to Ngconde's section while another prisoner shuffled across to take his place. It was a well-practised routine.

While Themba's squad marched off to the lime quarry, Ngconde's section climbed aboard a flat-nosed Bedford truck and were transported to the eastern shore. Guards stood high on the beachhead, armed with rifles, but they knew the prisoners were contained on the beach and left them to work at their own pace.

Themba, Ngconde and other prisoners waded out into the sea. Their job was to bring the long strands of seaweed to the shore. Other prisoners dragged the kelp above the high-water mark and spread it to dry in the sun.

'I see what you mean, Ngconde. The Atlantic water is cold.'

'Your idea of escaping is madness. You won't last long in this water. You'll freeze to death.'

'Not if you keep moving, keeping the circulation going.' Themba pointed across the sea. 'Look how close Blaauwbergstrand is! I should be able to swim that distance.'

'Why don't you make yourself a raft, then you could rest when you're tired?'

Themba looked at him with respect. 'Excellent idea, but I need material.'

'Yesterday when we were working on the other side of those rocks,' Ngconde pointed southwards, 'I saw three big beams of wood.'

'Where? Show me.'

They walked a hundred metres down the beach. There were three solid beams. 'Just what I need.' A plan was forming in Themba's mind. 'We must drag them above the high-water mark, and bury them until I need them. We'll need help.'

'We have many willing hands.' Ngconde warmed to the idea. The beams were refloated and pushed around the rocks to the section where the prisoners were working. They covered the wood with seaweed and dragged the beams up the beach. Under the beachhead, just below a gnarled lone tree, the prisoners dug a large trench with their hands. They rolled the square beams into the hole and covered them with sand.

They returned to their tasks. The tide was going out, exposing thousands of black mussels on the rocks. The prisoners twisted off handfuls and placed them in their floppy hats.

'What are you going to do with so many?' Themba asked.

'We cook them at lunch-time, in sea water.'

'You need a big pot to cook them all.'

'We use the big metal container they send out with our mealies.'

Just before lunch, the outgoing tide exposed many gullies and channels usually covered by the sea. Hiding in the crevices were crayfish. Themba had helped Paul take them from the water at esiKhaleni. Holding his breath, he dived. Under the rock a wily crayfish backed away, looking at him with black eyes out on stalks. Themba's hand closed over the crayfish's thorax, scooping it out from under the rock and above his head in one fluid movement. The crustacean kicked out, legs, pincers and feelers gyrating in the air.

'Take it, Ngconde. I'm going down for more!'

'No, man, I'm not holding that thing! It'll bite me.'

'Nonsense, just hold it by its shell.' Themba could not persuade Ngconde, so he found a shallow rock pool for the crayfish. He dived down again and caught another, only this time he was not so quick. The crustacean nipped his finger and he cut his hand on its sharp body protuberances. After ten he called a halt, his hand and fingers bleeding from the brown-shelled creatures.

Lunch-time proved to be the biggest feast of the year. They cooked the mussels and crayfish together in the canister. When the black mussels popped open, they were done. The prisoners tipped out the hot water, allowing the seafood to cool. Then, scooping out handfuls of mussels, they sucked out the scrumptious flesh. Themba and Ngconde each had a crayfish while the other prisoners divided the rest among themselves.

'Fall in! Fall in!' shouted the warder.

Themba burped with satisfaction, rubbing his stomach in pleasure, as they returned to collecting kelp. 'The last few days have certainly been memorable. I hope my luck holds.'

'Luck comes in threes,' answered Ngconde.

'If that's the case my quota is up. First, it was the changed classification. Yesterday it was the wonderful visit, and today was the third piece of luck - the start of my escape bid.'

At the end of the day the warder blew his whistle. 'Fall in!'

The section formed up and a warder counted them. 'All here.'

'Jump, you kaffirs.' They clambered on the truck. With two warders sitting on the tailgate they headed back to the prison. The other sections were also arriving, some from the brick works, others with the cleaning squad, the rest from the lime quarry.

'Cheers, Ngconde, see you again.'

Themba darted between the men forming up, heading for D Section. He felt a heavy hand grasp his shoulder. Looking up, he stared into the unsmiling face of Colonel Badenhorst. 'Where are you headed?'

'My hat blew away. I ran after my hat.'

'Don't lie. I've just seen you jump off the seaweed truck.'

'You're wrong, *baas*. It must be a mistake.'

'Are you calling me a liar? Show me your card. Number 287/76, D Section. Just as I thought, you're in the wrong section.' Badenhorst turned to a warder. 'Officer, take this prisoner to Detention. I'll attend to him later.'

In the confusion the man who had swopped with Themba managed to slip back to his section unobserved.

Damn them all, thought Themba as he was escorted away. At the top of the stairs he raised his clenched right hand and shouted in defiance, '*Amandla*! Power!'

The men below answered, '*Ngawethu*! To the people!'

The warder hit Themba in the small of his back with his rifle. As Themba collapsed, the mass of prisoners spontaneously started singing the freedom hymn, '*Senzenina*? – What have we done?' The warders shouted at them, trying to regain order.

Themba hobbled to the Detention Section. He was made to sit on the floor. Badenhorst marched in, his face contorted with rage, but refusing to look Themba in the eye.

'Stand up, kaffir.' Themba received a stinging flat hander across his face, spinning him around. 'That's for you and your black-power salute.' He hit him again. 'That's for the freedom song.'

Oh God, it's starting all over again! Themba thought.

'Talk, kaffir, tell me the truth.'

Yes, my luck certainly has turned, thought Themba. 'I slipped into the seaweed team.'

'*Baas*, what about, *baas*?'

'*Baas*.'

'Why?' Badenhorst barked out the word.

'I wanted to walk on the beach, to see the sea.'

'Wanted to walk, hey? All right, kaffir, I'll let you walk. You're going to walk down a long passage. Wanted to see, hey? I'll let you see the inside of a single cell. Lieutenant, take this prisoner to Isolation. Book him for two months.'

Two warders force-marched Themba to the Isolation Section. The gate was unlocked. Themba walked down the passage. The gate to number seventeen was open. He was shoved inside and the metal gate clanged shut behind him. Themba looked across the passage at number eighteen. There stood Nelson Mandela.

'Good evening, *Madiba*,' Themba greeted in respect.

'Hullo, Themba. Welcome to B Section. Why are you here?'

'They caught me skipping section. I've been sentenced to two months in Isolation.'

'Good,' said Mandela. 'I will have time to talk to you. There is much for us to discuss.'

'Quiet down there!' shouted a guard.

In the silence Themba reflected on Mandela's words. His luck had not changed after all; he had beaten the odds. Now he was with the cream of the ANC leadership. He would be able to talk with them and learn from them. Instead of punishing him, they were actually doing him a favour. In D Section he would never have had the opportunity of mixing with the legends. Now Themba relished the next two months.

The time Themba spent in Isolation Section was one of the most rewarding of his life. It was a period of growth for him as a person, making him even more determined to devote his life to the freedom struggle. Themba had to laugh at the folly of the Nationalist government's policy in grouping well over one thousand political prisoners on Robben Island. Under the direction of their leaders they formed a strong core of resistance, allowing the ideals of the struggle to be concentrated in one place. If they had been scattered in various prisons throughout the country the strength of the resistance would have been largely dissipated. On the island, schools of instruction passed on the complete history of the ANC to new arrivals. Those leaving were armed with an iron resolve to continue the fight and passed the latest ideology to ANC members on the outside.

From Monday to Friday it was work as usual in the lime quarry.

In the evenings they were locked in their individual cells in the Isolation Section.

The weekends were the best. So, too, was the ten-day Christmas break, with only a skeleton staff of warders on duty. The cell doors were left open and prisoners could move about freely between their cells and the enclosed courtyard. Themba had time to become acquainted with them all. His times with Mandela were unforgettable. Themba absorbed every word he uttered.

After New Year it was back to the lime quarry. Every weekday without fail, rain or sun, hot or cold, they walked the one and a half kilometres to the quarry. Bordering the road were high-security fences. The prisoners marched inside the wire, the warders and dogs kept pace on either side. Once they reached the quarry the sections spread out, each to its own area.

News from the outside world came in to the communal cell sections in various ways – through new inmates, newspapers stolen from the warders or retrieved from the rubbish dump, amateur radios and crystal sets and letters and documents smuggled in by visiting relatives.

By swopping around in the quarry a messenger would convey news to the Isolation Section, then return to his place. The leadership discussed the merits of each item, deciding what to do, then passed back their comments. Themba enjoyed their probing debates. Often they found novel solutions to seemingly insurmountable problems. Themba contributed; he was able to argue logically, sometimes summing up the discussion with a practical answer. Slowly he gained the respect of the leadership.

'Themba, when you're released you must further your law studies.' Mandela looked at him keenly. 'We need men like you in Lusaka, at ANC world headquarters.'

'I'm not waiting until I'm released. I'm going to escape.'

Mandela smiled at his enthusiasm. 'Funny, I was looking at a photograph in the library last week. It is of a white woman called Florrie Berndt. She swam from Robben Island to the mainland. It looks as if she smeared her whole body with grease.'

Themba nodded. 'That would be to keep out the cold and to glide more easily through the water. It can be done, Madiba. I'm determined to go through with it. I've already got three beams buried on the east beach. If I tie them together as a raft I can float behind them. I'll only need to kick – then I can save my strength.'

'Interesting. We'll talk some more.'

During the weekend they discussed the possibilities of an escape. It intrigued the leadership, as it had never been accomplished before.

'That's because it wasn't planned properly.' Themba bubbled with determination.

'One would need purlins and nails to hammer the beams together.'

'There are pallets at the brickyards. One could use those planks and nails.'

'We'd need a hammer.'

'No one would miss a four-pound hammer from the quarry.'

'What about grease?'

'There are tins of grease in the shed at the harbour. Also rope to bind the raft.'

'Themba would have to swim naked. He would need proper clothes once he landed on the mainland.'

'Could be organised. One of the men who cleans the warder's quarters could surely steal a pair of pants, a shirt and some shoes.'

'The clothes would get wet in the sea.'

'There are lots of thick plastic bags in the kitchen.'

'Themba cannot just be left to his own devices once he lands.' Walter Sisulu was practical. 'He'll be missed and the police will search for him.'

'Not insurmountable. The escape could be organised after a prison visit. We could smuggle a letter out to our contact in Langa. He would be waiting for Themba on the beach.'

The think-tank was working. As the men concentrated on the problem, the answers to the questions unfolded, making the whole escape plan seem possible. Mandela had kept quiet up to that point. The men now turned to him for his opinion.

'You all know about my court case against the authorities?'

Themba looked puzzled. 'I don't know about the case. Please tell me, Madiba.'

'It's a long story.' Nelson looked at Themba. 'It started when a Lieutenant Prins turned down a visit by my wife Winnie, on the grounds that I didn't wish to see her. Can you imagine such a preposterous suggestion? Me not wanting to see my wife, when we live for our visits!

'When I confronted Prins he claimed Winnie was only seeking publicity. I stopped just short of physically attacking him. I swore at him and shook my fist in his face. I stormed out of his office. I slammed the door in rage.' Mandela scowled at the memory.

'The authorities indicted me for misconduct. With the help of my attorney we prepared our case. We went further, attacking the whole system. They planted a listening device in the room where we held our consultations. We found the bug, but they knew our whole defence strategy. Then they blocked my lawyer from coming to see me by continually deferring visits.' Mandela sighed in frustration.

'I'd spent months preparing our case. I had details from all the sections on Robben Island – our rations, the cruelty of the warders, the maladministration, even the names of the warders. I tied in my whole defence with the apartheid system, how cruel and unjust it was. Eventually I had a thick file of evidence.' Mandela stopped to catch his breath.

'What happened then, Madiba?'

'In a surprise move they set a date for the trial. I was thrilled. Once my evidence was heard, my documents would form part of the court record. My lawyer could legally release them for the world to know of our suffering. Then they cunningly informed my lawyer that the case had been dropped, he no longer needed to come to the island.

'As my file no longer constituted evidence, the prison authorities applied the right of access to prisoners' property. I had no alternative but to hand it over.'

Walter Sisulu spoke. 'The prison authorities are real bastards. Tell Themba how it took you months of arguing to get it back.'

'I fought with them to hand the file to my lawyer. They refused, as they did not want it made public. I then instituted a counter-action against them. Only last week I received my file back. They think it is safe with me, for who can read all the damning evidence while the file gathers dust in my cell? The lawyer is searched every time he comes and goes.'

'I'll take the file with me when I escape,' said Themba earnestly.

Mandela smiled. 'That would be very good, but the file must go straight to Oliver Tambo in Lusaka.'

'I promise I will deliver the file personally to Tambo.' Themba's eyes gleamed. 'May I make my escape bid, Madiba?'

413

Nelson looked around at the expectant faces waiting for his answer. He smiled. 'Yes, Themba, you can attempt to escape.'

During the next few weeks the plan was carefully executed. A hammer disappeared from the quarry and was smuggled to the beach by the kelp team. Crate slats from the brick fields were hidden under clothes, taken back to the prison at night, then out with the seaweed teams the next morning. Plastic bags, grease, rope, clothes, shoes and nails were put into place under the sand.

Themba was transferred from B Isolation Section back to D General Section. His cell mates were aware of the escape plan, it had gripped the imaginations of all the prisoners on the island. No one doubted Themba would launch the raft and drift out to sea, but few gave him any chance of making Blaauwbergstrand alive.

18

Pierre sat at his desk in the new suite of offices in the Groote Kerk Building. He was pleased with the progress he had made in the five weeks since he'd started. The Cape Town office of the Department of Information was fully functional, with Pierre as senior assistant.

Twice Eschel Rhoodie had visited the Cape Town office. Rhoodie was suave and always impeccably dressed. Dark-haired and deeply tanned, he was charismatic and outgoing, an egotist with supreme confidence in his own ability. Pierre quickly learnt that the way to impress Rhoodie was by flattery, and he laid it on thick. Rhoodie responded; he took a liking to Pierre and accepted the idea of the Cape Town office, which was close to parliament and convenient to many of the foreign embassies.

Rhoodie started passing specific projects on to Pierre to handle, but nothing secret or irregular. Pierre felt there was more to Rhoodie, but it would take time to break through his defences. He shied from Pierre's suggestion that he visit the Pretoria headquarters of the department. What was he trying to hide? wondered Pierre.

He had also met General Hendrik van den Bergh, but from the outset there was mutual dislike. They were like two fighting cocks, squaring up to each other. When Van den Bergh looked at Pierre with his piercing blue eyes, Pierre felt himself being analysed and evaluated. The general had a reputation for perceptiveness and Pierre sensed Van den Bergh did not trust him.

After the start of the parliamentary session, Dr Connie Mulder, the Minister of Information, became a regular visitor to the offices. A man with a ready smile, he was like a big teddy bear, warm and outgoing. Pierre was conscious that Mulder seemed genuinely interested in his portfolio, condoning all actions of the Department of Information as vitally important to the total onslaught waged on

South Africa. Pierre was convinced Rhoodie could twist Mulder around his little finger.

Pierre looked up at the knock on his open door. 'Good morning, Minister. Please come in.' He ordered coffee for them both.

Mulder was in an expansive mood. 'Well, Pierre, tell me about Eschel's visit.'

Pierre decided to take the bull by the horns and test Mulder. 'I have a problem, Dr Mulder. Eschel Rhoodie feeds me certain information, but withholds the main functions of the Department. How am I expected to do my work if I don't know what's going on?'

'I take your point, Pierre. What did you want to know?'

'For a start, *The Citizen* newspaper. I had an irate reporter in my office yesterday, claiming the newspaper was covertly funded by the Department of Information. What reply can I give the man if I'm in the dark myself?'

Mulder sighed. 'Project Annemarie is a project of our Department.'

'Why on earth would we want to own a newspaper?'

'The English press is anti-government, Pierre. We tried to buy out an existing group, South African Associated Newspapers, but our bid was unsuccessful. So we started our own. We need an English-language newspaper in South Africa which is objective and pro-National Party. You know how the English press always criticise everything we do?'

Pierre felt the excitement build inside him. He had made his first breakthrough.

He pushed his luck. 'How did you finance the deal?'

Looking uncomfortable, Mulder realised he was in so deep he might as well brief Pierre fully. 'We have certain ways of procuring secret funds. We put up thirty-one million rand, but used front men to do the deal. The Department of Information was kept out of the arrangement.'

'Whom did you use, Dr Mulder?'

He hesitated before committing himself. 'Louis Luyt, the fertiliser millionaire.'

Pierre looked at Mulder intently. 'Is *The Citizen* operating at a profit?'

Mulder shook his head. 'It's a big mess. We're running at a loss of four hundred thousand rand a month. But help is at hand, I'm pleased to say.'

'In what way?'

'We're negotiating for someone to take over the newspaper. The deal is due to be finalised in February.'

'Is there more I should know?'

Sighing in exasperation, Mulder looked forlornly at Pierre. 'There's more, much more. I sometimes feel I'm losing control of my own Department. I'll speak to Eschel Rhoodie and ask him to put you in the picture on all the schemes.'

'Dr Mulder, I get the impression from our conversation you don't altogether condone Rhoodie's projects and methods. I wonder if I shouldn't visit Pretoria.'

The Minister stood up slowly and gave a wry smile. 'I'll ask Dr Rhoodie to organise it.'

The temperature in the bowl of the lime quarry was in the thirties. Themba wiped his brow and looked into the cloudless sky.

A prisoner nudged him. 'Nelson Mandela wants to see you.'

For almost an hour Themba wormed his way from one work team to the next, until eventually he was in the midst of the leaders.

'Madiba, you wished to speak with me.'

Mandela nodded, bending double so the warders would not notice him talking. 'It's all arranged for tomorrow night. Listen carefully and memorise what I tell you.'

'I'm listening, Madiba.'

'Tomorrow at lunch-time stay in the shed when your section returns to work. We have arranged for jute bags to be nailed over some of the rafters. Climb up and hide above the beams. Stay there until well after we have returned to the prison for the night. We will cover for you in the lines and in your barracks. Just before dark make for the eastern beach.'

'Stop loafing, you two,' shouted a warder.

They worked until the warder moved away, then Mandela continued. 'Buried under a cairn of stones, you will find the beams, planks, nails, hammer and rope. Make your raft. Close by, you will find a flat stone with a smaller one balancing on top. Dig down and you will discover three plastic bags.'

'What's in the bags?'

'The soft bag contains clothes for you to use on the other side. The heavy flat bag holds my file with the important documents and a letter to Oliver Tambo. The manuscripts have been sealed in three

417

plastic bags so the paper will not get wet. The third bag contains a tin of grease, extra rope to lash yourself and the bags to the raft, and a tin.'

'A tin?' queried Themba.

Nelson nodded. 'Inside the tin you'll find a waterproof watch and rations. There are biscuits, chocolate and sugar to give you energy. Tonight, take your money from the DLB so you will have cash on the mainland.'

Mandela stopped, pretending to work as a guard neared. Themba lowered his head in case he was recognised. The warder passed on and Nelson continued.

'As we worked out, you will land somewhere near Blaauwberg-strand. Get dressed and make for the rendezvous as unobtrusively as possible. Two points have been established. The first is at nine o'clock in the morning, behind the Blaauwberg Hotel on Marine Circle. Look for a man with a red shirt. He will have the hood of his car open and will be tinkering with the engine. His name is James Libode.'

'James Libode.' Themba repeated the name slowly. 'Is he a big or a small man?'

'I think he's big and fat,' laughed Mandela. 'If for some reason you are late, a second rendezvous is scheduled for four in the afternoon, behind the Killarney Hotel in Koeberg Road. James will wait until five o'clock.'

'What if I don't make contact?' asked Themba.

'Head for the men's hostels in Langa. They are brown build-ings. You will find James in number five. Do you understand, Themba?'

'I understand, Madiba.'

'Repeat the details, word for word.'

The next day Themba's section covered for him in the lime quarry. He faked work, saving his strength for the night. Friends shared their food, building up his reserves. The morning passed and they trooped into the corrugated-iron hut for their lunch. Themba noticed the bagged-off section in the rafters.

'Fall in!'

Ready hands helped him aloft and he grabbed on to the trusses. He shuffled along a beam until he was above the hessian. The hours passed slowly and Themba baked under the tin roof. The hot air from the shed collected in the ridge, creating a stifling, sultry heat.

'Fall in! Fall in!'

Outside, the warders were counting the prisoners. In Themba's section a spot was left open in the middle of the formation. The guard counted from left to right. Once counted, a prisoner crouched down and moved quickly between the rows, then rose casually in Themba's empty spot. The whole section fidgeted to distract the guard.

'All accounted for!'

They marched back to prison. As the sounds receded, everything became quiet in the quarry. Themba jumped down from his perch. He was used to the continuous ringing of metal on stone, the voices, the sounds of people all around him. Now the quarry was silent and eerie. As the sun sank low in the western sky, Themba carefully climbed to the rim of the quarry, looking over the edge. All was still. Running double, he headed for the first clump of bushes.

He froze as he heard a startled movement, his heart hammering in his throat. Squawking guinea-fowl scattered, the covey flapping into the air in fright. They landed a distance away, twittering for a time, then silence returned.

Themba cautiously moved on, heading eastwards. He heard a twig snap ahead of him and fell to the ground, hiding between the spiky grass. A herd of graceful springbok moved past, unaware of Themba. He didn't want to spook them, so he lay quietly until they gradually moved on.

As the sun tipped the horizon Themba reached the gnarled tree. He jumped off the headland, landing in the soft sand. He immediately found the cairn of stones, digging out the three beams, placing them alongside each other. The beams were very heavy. Themba decided to drag them individually to the water's edge and construct the raft there, rather than try and drag the finished raft down to the sea.

He found the flat stone and the three plastic bags, exactly as Mandela had described. Themba put on the watch and ate some of the biscuits and chocolate. It was just after sunset when he had all the components at the water's edge. He nailed the planks at right angles across the beams. Then he lifted the raft on to its side, flipped it over and nailed four planks to the reverse side.

At each hammer blow he looked up in fear, fully expecting

419

someone to hear and investigate. The sound was loud in his ears, but was actually muffled by the noise of the surf. Themba placed the two plastic bags with the clothes and Mandela's documentation in the middle of the raft. He twined the rope across the bags and knocked nails through the strands to attach them firmly to the woodwork. He looped the rest of the rope around the edges of the raft as handholds for himself.

The tide was coming in, lapping at the raft. It was almost dark. Themba looked across the bay. The lights of Blaauwbergstrand winked at him, giving him a beacon towards which he could head. He ate the remainder of the biscuits and half the sugar, keeping the rest for later. Themba covered himself from top to toe with a thick layer of grease. The incoming tide was lifting the front of the raft. He was ready.

When a big wave came Themba pushed the raft forward and it shot along in the backwash, following the swell into the sea. The next wave threatened to beach it again. Themba wasted a lot of energy in the first few minutes until he had the raft floating. He pushed and pushed until only the tips of his toes still touched the bottom. Now he could kick behind the raft. He battled the incoming tide as the waves broke over him. At times he felt he was not moving forward, that he was see-sawing on the spot, one metre forward, one metre back. At last he was behind the breakers, the open sea beckoning.

Near the shore the water was relatively warm, but the further he travelled the colder it became. Now he was exposed to the chilly wrath of the Atlantic Ocean and the icy Benguella current.

In his planning Themba had not taken the Benguella into account, a steady stream that would force him northwards, making it impossible to head straight across the bay to Blaauwbergstrand.

Darkness surrounded him. He kicked steadily, keeping the raft pointed towards the lights of Blaauwbergstrand. Behind him were the yellow and white lights of Robben Island. He estimated he was a kilometre out to sea. Seven to go.

Themba lost track of time as he travelled. He kicked for about ten minutes, then forced himself to rest for five. Rather than use up energy treading water, he flopped on to the raft. The raft was difficult to force through the water, but it did allow him his rest periods. At one stage he considered jettisoning it as he would make better time swimming freely, but when he thought of the two important plastic bags he dropped the idea.

Kick, kick, kick. Rest. Kick, kick, kick. Rest. The hours dragged past. The cold affected him, chilling his flesh to the bone. He kept moving.

The longer he swam, the slower and more deliberate his movements became. His brain became hazy, too tired to co-ordinate his movements. He flopped on to the raft and fell fast asleep.

Thud! Thud! Thud! Thud! Whoosh! Whoosh! Thud! Thud! Thud! Thud! Themba woke with a start. What was that noise? He saw nothing. Thud! Thud! Thud! Thud! Whoosh! Whoosh! Closer, it was closer!

Suddenly the stars were blotted out by a dark shadow. He came fully awake. He stood on the raft balancing precariously, horrified to see a white wave creaming towards him. Then he saw the lights, a red light and a green light, high above him. With a start Themba realised it was a huge ship heading straight for him. He jumped into the water and kicked desperately, trying to get out of the way. His efforts were futile. He watched helplessly as the huge bows bore down on him until they seemed to fill his entire vision.

'Help! Help! Help!' he screamed at the top of his lungs, but he might as well have saved his breath. No one could hear his faint cries.

Thud! Thud! Thud! Thud! The diesel engines beat monotonously, louder and louder. Whoosh! Whoosh! The twin propellers spun, forcing the ship forward. The sharp bow was heading straight for him. Themba closed his eyes, praying fervently.

The mighty bow-wave caught the raft, tossing it into the air like a cork from a champagne bottle. Miraculously it did not overturn. It plopped back into the water, right side up, and sank below the surface. Themba held on for dear life, holding his breath.

The raft resurfaced and he gulped in air gratefully. It bobbed away from the ship, down its slipstream. The forces created by the bow-wave pushed it towards the coast, doing more in five minutes than two hours of Themba's kicking would have achieved. The wake from the churning propellers further aided his progress, thrusting the raft shorewards.

As the early hours of the morning passed, Themba's kicking became more feeble. Exhaustion overcame him as he alternated between awareness and oblivion. A pale moon rose, glinting ghostly lights off the swells and troughs of the restless sea. He slept.

A rumbling noise penetrated Themba's subconscious. He shook himself awake and looked ahead, seeing white caps in the moonlight. The sound was the thunder of the surf. He was approaching shore. Like some helping hand from above, the waves quickened his pace, breaking over the raft, driving him forwards. As the first feelers of dawn lit the eastern sky he clearly saw the beach and a row of houses. He was moving much faster, almost planing on the waves.

He felt sand under his feet. With the last of his energy he pushed the raft on to the beach and collapsed on top of it. He fell into an exhausted sleep. The ebb tide receded, leaving the raft high and dry.

A voice entered the innermost recesses of his mind. It can't be, Themba reasoned abstractly. I'm dreaming. A hand on his shoulder shook him. With a start he sat up, looking into the concerned face of a white man. Like a leper he cowered away in fright, staring dumbly.

Dressed in jogging gear, the man looked at Themba intently. 'Who are you? Where have you come from?'

Themba ignored the questions, his mind racing. He was on the mainland, he had made the crossing! He glanced down, realising he was naked. He covered himself with his hands.

'Answer my questions.' The man was insistent.

'I jumped ship.'

'Nonsense. Look at your home-made raft. A sailor would have used a life jacket.' A thought struck the jogger as he looked out to sea. 'You're a convict, aren't you? You've escaped from Robben Island.'

Alarm flashing in Themba's eyes gave him away. The man stepped backwards, suddenly wary. He stood a few paces from Themba, out of danger from sudden attack. 'I was right. You are an escaped prisoner.'

On the spur of the moment Themba decided to tell the truth. Honesty and sympathy were the only courses open to him. He nodded. 'I am from Robben Island, but you have nothing to fear, sir. I'm a political prisoner, not a criminal. I won't harm you in any way. Will you help me, sir?'

422

'A convict is a convict. The police will search for you. I don't want to be implicated.'

Themba looked around at the neat houses lining the beach. He was confused. This place was much smaller than Blaauwbergstrand. 'Where am I, sir?'

'You're in Melkbosstrand.'

Picturing the coastline in his mind, Themba realised he was eight kilometres north of where he should have landed. He looked at his watch, it was seven o'clock. Two hours to reach his first rendezvous. He would never make it.

'Please help me, sir. Give me a lift.'

'Good heavens, no.' He started jogging on the spot. 'Where are you headed?'

Themba knew he had to lie in case the man alerted the police. He must give himself a head start. 'Atlantis.'

A triumphant look came into the jogger's eyes. 'I must go. I have to get to work.' He headed for the row of houses.

He's going to telephone the police, thought Themba. I must hurry. He ran into the surf and scrubbed the last of the grease off his body. He tore open the clothing bag and dressed in a blue-and-white checked shirt, grey trousers with a brown belt, socks and shoes. All were a perfect fit. He gobbled down the last of the sugar, instinctively knowing he would need his strength in the hours ahead.

Themba looked around the deserted beach. His first inclination was to head south along the coast, straight for Blaauwbergstrand. His better judgement prevailed. At this moment the man was probably speaking to the police. He would tell them he was headed north for Atlantis. Themba had to make it look genuine. He pulled at the ropes, freeing Mandela's bundle of documents, then headed north up the beach. Once past the houses he cut inland, disappearing among the groves of Port Jackson willows.

The jogger ran straight home, determined to do his duty as a good South African citizen. He dialled 600, connecting with the Melkbosstrand police station. At first the duty officer thought he was a practical joker, but when he heard the caller was a doctor he took notice. 'The station commander should be in any minute now. I'll report straight to him.'

Each minute wasted was a hundred metres gained by Themba.

423

His rubber-soled shoes were comfortable and he made good time.

Five minutes after the station commander reported for duty he raised Robben Island on the telephone and passed on the information. The warder was sceptical. No prisoner had ever escaped from Robben Island before. With a laugh in his voice he reported the matter to Colonel Badenhorst.

Badenhorst choked on his early-morning coffee and ordered a Red Alert. Alarm bells rang and warders scurried to action stations. They chased the prisoners out of their dormitories and a head count began. The prisoners tried to confuse the issue by shuffling around, changing position and swopping ID cards. Badenhorst was frantic, he instructed the warders to lay into the prisoners with their batons. But time had been gained, and an hour later Badenhorst pronounced prisoner 287/76, Themba Memani, officially missing.

The prisoners, convinced Themba had succeeded, raised their clenched fists in triumph. '*Amandla! Amandla! Mayibuye! Viva Themba!*' Badenhorst chased them back to their sections, pronouncing there would be no work parties for the day.

The prisoners in the isolation cells were not allowed out. They were counted and all gates firmly locked. They heard the prisoners chanting outside and knew something strange was afoot.

'Why are we staying in our cells today?' Mandela demanded.

'Most of the guards have been rushed to the mainland,' shouted back a warder.

'Why?'

'A convict has escaped.'

The prisoners broke into a spontaneous cheer.

Badenhorst raised Cape Town docks and the island's motor launch tore towards Robben Island. It didn't even dock. Only a skeleton staff was left on the island as all spare warders and dogs jumped aboard and the launch headed back to Cape Town. It was nine o'clock and the search was underway.

Colonel Badenhorst cursed as he looked down at the raft on Melkbosstrand beach. 'Examine it for clues.'

'The eyewitness says the prisoner was naked when he saw him, but this broken plastic bag could have contained clothes.'

'Where would he have obtained clothes on Robben Island?' Badenhorst was pacing up and down.

'Two weeks ago various warders reported missing items of clothing, sir. They could have been stolen for the escape.'

A warder pointed to where the bag with the file had been attached. 'What could have been transported in this small rectangle?'

Badenhorst kicked up the sand in frustration. 'He could not have operated alone. There must have been collusion between the prisoners on the island. I see Mandela's hand in all this.'

'Mandela, sir? Mandela is in Isolation.'

The blood drained from Badenhorst's face as a thought struck him. 'Memani was also in Isolation. I only recently gave Mandela back his file of evidence.' He looked at the spot on the raft with growing alarm. 'If that documentation ever reaches the outside world, it could mean a lot of trouble for all of us. Get them to check Mandela's cell for the file.'

'I must get to a telephone, sir.'

The station commander from Melkbosstrand police station offered his facilities. 'You may telephone from the police station. Use it as a temporary headquarters.'

'Yes, sir.' The warder ran off.

A warder pointed to Themba's footprints. 'Looks like he ran north, Colonel.'

The Melkbosstrand station commander suddenly remembered. 'Our eyewitness said the convict told him he wanted to get to Atlantis.'

Badenhorst's eyes glittered. He sent six warders and three dogs on Themba's spoor. 'You have portable radios. Keep in touch. The rest of you scour the bush and roads between here and Atlantis. Call in the help of the Atlantis police and search every house in town. Whatever you do, find Memani. If you need me I'll be at Melkbosstrand police station.'

A warder hurried to Mandela's cell. 'Where are the documents Colonel Badenhorst gave back to you a little while ago?'

'What documents?'

'The file from the court case against you that was withdrawn.'

Mandela shrugged. 'In my cell somewhere.'

'Give me the file please.'

Mandela riffled through his papers, ostensibly searching, playing for time. The file had been green. He withdrew a similar file. With his back to the warder he added documents at random, a few old

425

hand-written pages, some notes from his correspondence studies, until the file was about the same thickness as the original one.

'What's taking you so long, Mandela?'

'I am looking for it.' Mandela marked the tab on the file to correspond with the original. 'Ah! Here it is.' He pushed the file through the bars of his cell door.

The guard grabbed it and hurried back to the office. He telephoned through to Melkbosstrand. Badenhorst came on the line. 'We have the Mandela file, Colonel.'

Badenhorst breathed a sigh of relief. 'Tell me what it looks like.'

'Green, Colonel. About sixty centimetres thick and marked: MANDELA VERSUS ROBBEN ISLAND PRISON AUTHORITIES.'

Taking out a pack of Texan, Badenhorst drew deeply, letting the smoke curl out of his nose. Finding the file placed a whole new perspective on the chase. He could now treat Memani as he would any other escaped convict. State security was no longer threatened. He needn't inform the Commissioner yet. Rather wait until he had apprehended Memani, then he could report on a successful mission.

He called in: 'Pass the message out to the squads. Tell them to bring Memani in, dead or alive – I'm not fussy.'

'Colonel, I spoke to the island a few minutes ago. Esterhuysen reported a blue-and-white checked shirt missing, and a pair of grey flannels from Heunis.'

'Good, put out the description on the radio. Get hold of the air force base at Ysterplaat and ask them to send an Alouette helicopter to assist in the search. Tell them to concentrate on the area between Melkbosstrand and Atlantis.'

Themba reached the West-Coast road, the main highway between Blaauwbergstrand and Saldanha. He decided to go south, parallel to the road. He dared not chance running alongside the road so he kept to the bush. It was heavy going in the sand dunes. Mandela's bundle was awkward to carry and he moved it continually from arm to arm.

He stumbled up the side of a sand dune and stopped at the top to catch his breath. He heard the baying of hounds on his spoor. He looked south and saw kilometre upon kilometre of undulating sand dunes covered with stunted bushes. He would weaken quickly in the loose sand. He looked east across the highway. The sand dunes quickly petered out, leaving a flat area with tall Port Jackson willows. The trees would offer him good protection and he would make better time on flat ground. He decided to cross the West-Coast highway and loop around to the south.

He slid down the dune and stood in the bushes alongside the road. He watched the vehicles passing, tempted to stop one and hitch a lift. He dismissed the thought as too risky. The plastic bag with the file, covered in perspiration, slipped from under his arm.

Damn file, he cursed. It's holding me up. I can run much faster without it. He saw a milestone with 20km engraved on the side about half a kilometre down the road. I'll bury the plastic bag near the milestone and come back for it later. Nothing can happen to it.

Passing motorists idly looked at him, but none slowed down or stopped. He walked back to the road, wiping away his prints, then headed south again. He could hear the dogs; they were closer. Themba struck out eastwards, at right angles to the highway.

At the police station the radio crackled. Badenhorst sat forward. 'Colonel, we've tracked him to the West-Coast road but we've lost his trail. The traffic seems to have blotted out his spoor. The dogs are confused.'

Badenhorst lit a cigarette. 'In which direction is he headed?'

'South, Colonel.'

'South? I thought he was headed for Atlantis?'

'Colonel, he's travelling towards Blaauwbergstrand and Table View.'

'Damn. I've got the search concentrated towards the north.'

'What must we do, Colonel?'

'Cross the highway and see if you can pick up his spoor on the other side.' The radio went dead.

Themba made much better time east of the West-Coast road. Instead of loose sand there was soil. He dodged through the Port Jackson willows, avoiding the densely growing thickets. The years of under-nourishment in prison were starting to tell and he felt his energy sapping. He forced himself to continue at a stumbling run. His foot caught in the loop of a tree root and he crashed forwards, his head hitting the trunk. Stars exploded in his head as he lost consciousness.

*   *   *

The handlers and dogs crossed the West-Coast road. As they headed south the dogs picked up Themba's scent. They bayed excitedly, straining at their leashes. At the 20km milestone two dogs ran straight ahead. One dog branched off towards the buried documents. His handler looked at the other two dogs wagging their tails, noses to the ground, heading south. He pulled on the leash and turned the dog around. At the fence alongside the highway they found Themba's shoe prints in the soft sand.

'Come in, Colonel Badenhorst,' the warder called excitedly on the radio.

'Badenhorst here.'

'Colonel, we're hot on the spoor. We found the place where Memani climbed through the fence. He's headed east towards the N7 National Road.'

'Good! Good! Keep after him. I'll recall the teams from Atlantis and have them patrol the N7.' He looked at a map on the wall. 'I see the West-Coast road and the N7 run almost parallel, ten kilometres apart. I'll have the teams in place before he reaches the N7. I think we've got him.'

'Roger, Colonel. Over and out.'

Badenhorst sat back in satisfaction. He telephoned Ysterplaat air force base, requesting them to direct the helicopter southwards, to the new search area. He pictured Memani in his mind's eye, beaten until he collapsed, with six months in solitary confinement on rice gruel. He would come out looking like a Belsen inmate.

Pierre fastened his seat belt as the Boeing 727 touched down at Jan Smuts Airport. He looked at his watch: eleven o'clock. He thought ahead to his meeting in Pretoria with Eschel Rhoodie at the Department of Information offices. Dr Connie Mulder had intervened in the deadlock between the two men. He had received a copy of Mulder's letter to Rhoodie. One phrase stuck in Pierre's mind. 'Bring Mr Roux up to date on all projects of the Department.' He was looking forward to the two-day meeting.

He crossed the apron and entered the arrivals hall. A pretty redhead held up a sign: PIERRE ROUX, DOI.

'I'm Pierre Roux.' He smiled at the woman.

She extended her hand. 'How do you do, Pierre. Welcome to Johannesburg. I'm Molly Benade.' Her grip was firm, her smile expansive and her eyes inviting. 'I have instructions from Dr

Rhoodie to look after you for the next two days, to make your stay as memorable as possible.'

'What exactly do you mean?' he asked sharply.

Molly had the grace to blush, but looked him straight in the eye. 'Whatever you want, Pierre.'

'I'm a married man,' he said firmly.

With a coy smile she linked her arm in his and led him towards the luggage-collection area. Her voice was husky. 'I've yet to come across a married man who refused a nibble offered to him on a plate.'

Pierre stopped, looking at her calculatingly. So that is Rhoodie's game, he thought. Side-track me with a beautiful woman to keep my nose out of his affairs. Very convenient, but it won't work, Rhoodie.

'What position do you hold in the Pretoria office?'

'I don't work in the office, Pierre.' She talked flippantly, tossing her head, making her hair bounce provocatively. 'My job is to entertain visiting VIPs.' Again the not-so-veiled hint in her voice. 'I have a car to take you to Pretoria.'

She unlocked the trunk of the Mercedes and he placed his suitcase inside. Opening the passenger door, Pierre was aware of the way she rubbed her bosom suggestively against his arm and of the alluring scent of her expensive perfume. Pierre wondered at Rhoodie's methods as he climbed into the car. Was sexual exploitation part of Information's way of obtaining the support of foreign dignitaries? Was there a dirty-tricks scam after all, possibly involving high-class call girls?

They drove to Pretoria, Pierre deep in thought. 'Sorry, what did you ask?'

'I asked if I must book for dinner tonight, for the two of us?'

'Where will I be staying?'

'In the VIP guest lodge. It has its own staff to pamper important visitors.'

Pierre looked at her in surprise. She spoke as if she knew the place intimately, but then she probably did. What other surprises would pop out of the hat? Money was no problem – it seemed it flowed like water in Pretoria.

Molly parked in the basement of the Ad Astra Building. Pierre noticed her car's registration number was affixed to a small plaque on the wall in front of the parking bay. Was she so important to

Information as to have her own reserved parking place?

'Would you like me to accompany you to the office, Pierre? What about the dinner booking? I know a very cosy restaurant in Sunnyside.'

'Forget dinner. I'll eat on the run. As for your services, I really won't be needing them, thank you.'

Rhoodie's sixth-floor office was certainly the most magnificent he had ever seen. One whole wall was solid glass with a view all the way to the Union Buildings straddling a distant ridge. The carpet was deep pile and luxurious. The desk was solid imbuia, the size of a snooker table. The office was so large it housed a matching ten-seater boardroom table and a bar, stocked with every type of liquor from all over the world.

Rhoodie stood up, flashing his handsome, flamboyant smile, and extended his hand. 'Welcome to headquarters, Pierre.'

He shook Rhoodie's hand and flopped into a sumptuous chair facing the desk. 'Let's get straight to the point of my visit, Dr Rhoodie. I'm here to find out everything there is to know about the Department of Information. It's time to get behind the smoke and mirrors.'

The smile faded from Rhoodie's face and his eyes glinted menacingly. 'Whatever we do, we do for the benefit of the country.'

'How do high-class hookers help the country?'

Rhoodie regained his composure, smiling expansively. 'Oh! You mean Molly Benade? It's accepted practice in every world capital. Some visiting VIPs actually expect a woman to be laid on. It's part and parcel of the diplomatic scene.'

'Dr Rhoodie, I should like to get to work straight away.'

Rhoodie looked at his watch. 'I have a meeting in twenty minutes. I'm afraid I must leave you, but I have arranged for one of my assistants to help you.'

Pierre erupted. 'I made this appointment a week ago and you guaranteed me two days of your time. I don't want to be fobbed off on some assistant.'

'Something unexpected has come up, Pierre.' Rhoodie looked apologetic. 'Matters of State cannot be controlled. An emergency has arisen. I must shoot.'

'I'll go with you.' Pierre rose, walking determinedly to the door.

'I'm sorry, Pierre. It's a highly secret meeting. You can't come with me.' He pressed the buzzer on his desk and a middle-aged man entered the office. He introduced Eric Loots. Rhoodie grabbed his briefcase. 'Eric, please take care of Mr Roux until I get back.' Then he was gone.

'What instructions did Dr Rhoodie leave for you, Mr Loots?'

'Nothing specific. He asked me to introduce you to the staff and take you out to lunch.'

'Damn!' Pierre cursed loudly. He knew he was being given the run-around and Rhoodie was deliberately avoiding him. Matters are serious in the Department of Information, Pierre decided.

Themba rubbed a bump on his head, still dizzy from the blow. Then he heard the dogs giving tongue. They sounded close, very close. He stood up shakily and ran on for a few hundred metres until the throbbing pain in his head forced him to slow down.

Think, Themba, think, he admonished himself. You can't beat them without a trick or two. He started doubling back on his tracks, then branching out at a tangent, smiling in satisfaction as he heard the dogs' confused barking. It was not for long, then they were back on his spoor.

Ahead he saw a grove of large Port Jackson willows. He ran under the outer tree and continued on for twenty paces. He carefully retraced his steps, stepping in his own footprints in the sand. Then he grabbed hold of a branch and swung himself off the ground, clambering from tree to tree like a monkey. At the sixth tree he jumped to the ground, headed north, doubled back, struck out east, then looped around and travelled south.

Dogs and handlers followed his trail to the tree. There the trail suddenly petered out. The hounds ran in circles, obliterating Themba's tracks. The German shepherds sat whining mournfully, looking perplexed. The warders ran about in a frenzy. They wasted ten minutes before they finally figured out Themba's ploy. They circled the copse and picked up the trail again.

The warders pointed out the staggered footprints. 'Memani is tiring. Why don't we release the dogs and let them run free? They'll catch up to him much quicker.'

Two warders disagreed. 'Badenhorst will blow a fuse if something goes wrong.'

'Release one dog and keep the other two on the leash.' It sounded like a good idea and a German shepherd was let free. It bounded ahead and was soon lost between the trees.

Themba heard the heavy panting behind him. Horrified, he saw the dog gaining on him, its pink tongue lolling out, its brown eyes fixed intently on him. He looked around hurriedly. He could not make it in time to the nearest tree. He could not outrun the dog. There were no stones close to hand. Three paces from Themba the German shepherd launched itself into the air. Its fangs closed around his upper arm, tearing his flesh, knocking him sprawling.

In a cloud of dust the dog battled for supremacy, shaking its head, strengthening its grip. They rolled over, the dog on top. It released its hold on his arm, going for his jugular. Themba quickly brought up his knees and knocked the dog away. He scrambled on to all fours and faced the animal. The dog circled, looking for an opening. Themba followed. Its lips curled over its dangerous fangs as it snapped and snarled, darting in and out.

Precious minutes were ticking past. The hound lunged forward. Themba threw himself to one side. He managed to force his arm under its neck. They rolled over and over. He forced his other arm around the animal's neck and pulled the back of the dog to his chest. The dog was thrashing around, trying to move its head to bite into Themba's arm. He wrapped his legs around the dog's midriff and squeezed with all his might. The dog's struggles grew weaker, it started making little whimperings of submission.

Themba held on, squeezing its breath from its body. It quivered, then went limp. He continued the pressure for a few moments, then threw the dog from him.

He scrambled to his feet, scratched, sore and bleeding, and floundered on.

The warders burst from between the trees and saw the German shepherd lying in the clearing. 'He's killed the dog! Now there's going to be hell to pay.' The other two dogs sniffed at their dead companion and yowled.

'It was your idea, Andries.' The dog handler turned angrily on his colleague. 'It was a lousy idea. Now my dog is dead and I have to explain to Badenhorst.'

The two tore into each other. The third warder interceded, moving between the combatants. 'Stop! Stop! Save your energy. We must catch the convict, not fight among ourselves.'

Sheepishly they separated, dusting themselves off. 'Damn Memani!

That kaffir is keeping ahead of us and we don't seem to get any closer.'

Chop! Chop! Chop! Chop! The warders looked up in astonishment as an Alouette helicopter appeared over the trees. The pilot saw the warders below him as he hovered overhead.

'Now we'll catch Memani.' They pointed in the direction Themba had taken. The chopper pilot gave the thumbs-up and skimmed away over the trees.

Themba was leaning against a tree catching his breath when he heard the whistling of rotor blades passing directly above him. The dappled shade camouflaged him perfectly and the helicopter continued south. He struck out east, running flat out for five minutes. The helicopter returned, working on a grid pattern. Themba dived into the shade and lay there until it passed. He looked back at Table Mountain, trying to get his bearings. He turned south towards it, hiding at the next passing of the chopper. Then he struck out eastwards again. The helicopter was driving him towards the N7 National Road.

Abruptly the trees ended and he was at the edge of a large wheat field. The wheat had been harvested in spring, now the field was a brown stubble patch. Four hundred metres in front of him the sun reflected off a wide stretch of water, running roughly north to south.

He considered his options. He couldn't turn back into the jaws of the approaching dogs. If he ran forward his tree cover would be gone. The dogs decided matters for him. He heard their baying close behind. He waited for the helicopter to pass, then ran into the open, heading for the water.

The pilot saw Themba when he was half-way across and swooped low to cut him off. The down-draft of the rotors flung him to the ground. He struggled to his feet and ran on, bent forward. The pilot tried to butt him with the nose-cone but Themba dodged in time. The pilot harassed him, chasing him in all directions as he darted to avoid the aircraft.

Handlers and dogs burst from the trees. 'Unleash the dogs!'

Concentrating on Themba, the pilot did not see the dogs. He set the helicopter down, jumped out and aimed his service revolver at Themba's back. 'Stop, or I'll shoot!'

Themba froze. He turned slowly, accepting the inevitable. His escape bid had failed. Then he saw the dogs running over the open field.

'Watch out! Here come the dogs.'

The pilot glanced over his shoulder. The dogs were frothing at the mouth. His eyes widened in fear. They were headed straight for him. He quickly jumped into the chopper and slammed the door.

Themba turned and ran full tilt for the water. Yelping with excitement the dogs gained on him. He looked over his shoulder – they were two paces behind. Desperation spurred him on. Their lathering jaws snapped at his heels. Themba reached the bank and dived into the Riet River. The dogs stopped in confusion, circling, uncertain what to do.

As he dived, Themba saw houses in the far distance to his right, towards the south. He hit the water and disappeared beneath the surface. He turned south, making for a clump of fluitjiesriet, whistling reeds. Hiding behind the reeds, not twenty paces from the warders, Themba clearly heard their conversation.

'What must we do now?'

'Get Badenhorst on the radio and ask for instructions.'

Themba heard the radio crackle and Badenhorst's irritated voice squawked out. 'Send the chopper to fetch me. I'll supervise the next stage.'

Themba was almost half a kilometre downstream when he heard the helicopter returning.

Colonel Badenhorst jumped down followed by his men. 'Where the hell is Memani?'

'Don't know, Colonel. We think he's either drowned or hiding in the reeds.'

North and south of where Badenhorst stood were two large clumps. His eyes glinted maliciously. 'We'll burn him out. Set fire to the reeds.'

At the end of summer the reeds were tinder dry, with large tasselled heads. The fires spread quickly to the whole clump, creating two orange fireballs belching grey smoke. The heat was so intense the men had to retreat far from the bank.

Themba crept up the bank and saw the flames shooting into the air. The warders were hidden in a depression. He could travel much faster on land than in the water. He ran along the bank making good time. The houses of Table View were closer, he could make out windows and see trees growing in the gardens.

As the fire abated the warders ran forward, earnestly scanning the river. The reeds had burned away leaving blackened smouldering stalks showing above the water. There was no sign of Themba.

Badenhorst cursed. He gave instructions to the warders to torch the reeds up and down the river. They looked up in surprise as a vehicle approached. Badenhorst held up his hand to stop his men, expecting trouble.

The vehicle slammed to a halt and a well-built, tanned man jumped out. 'What the hell do you think you're doing on my land?'

Badenhorst stepped forward. 'A prisoner escaped from Robben Island. We chased him to the river and now we're trying to burn him out.'

'You bloody fools,' cursed the irate farmer. 'In February nobody lights a fire. If it spreads to my stubble lands it could burn all the way to Malmesbury and destroy half the Swartland.' He put his hands on his hips, glaring at Badenhorst.

Badenhorst looked uncomfortable. 'May we have your permission to search for the man? He's a political prisoner.'

The farmer calmed down. 'You can search, but no more fires.'

'Thank you.'

Badenhorst divided the warders into four groups of two men each. The helicopter shuttled two groups across. Now covering both sides of the river, the teams headed upstream and downstream. They were convinced Themba could not have travelled far, so they triple-checked the immediate vicinity.

Badenhorst joined the pilot in the helicopter. They swept downstream, searching directly below the aircraft. Themba was almost caught in the open. He dived into the water just in time. The chopper looped and returned. Themba made it to the reeds with seconds to spare. He watched the chopper head upstream until its engine was a faint whisper. He decided to stick to the water rather than tempt fate on the river bank. He swam close to the reeds. Ahead was a large concrete bridge crossing the river, with vehicles travelling to and fro. Civilisation at last! With renewed energy he forged ahead. Once under the bridge he clambered out of the water. The teams of warders were far upstream.

He relaxed slightly, but pulled back below the level of the road when a police van sped past. Another police vehicle travelled in the opposite direction.

Themba looked at his watch. It was after half past four. He had less than thirty minutes to reach his second rendezvous. A black man came walking towards him. Themba addressed him in Xhosa. 'Hullo, brother.'

The man stopped in surprise. 'Why are you hiding under the bridge, brother?'

'The police are after me. Where is the Killarney Hotel?'

'Over there, at the next corner.'

He was so close, but he had to be careful. He didn't want to be apprehended on the last half kilometre. 'Sell me your clothes?'

The man looked from his tattered apparel to Themba's better clothes, not understanding the request. 'If I sell you my clothes, I'll be naked.'

'I'll give you ten rand for your clothes and throw mine into the bargain.'

The man smiled broadly, nodding. 'It's a deal.'

'Come under the bridge and change.'

He dressed in Themba's blue-and-white checked shirt and grey trousers, and pocketed the money. He laughed aloud when he saw Themba in his tattered shirt, torn trousers and gaping shoes. He shook his head in surprise when Themba insisted on his old crumpled hat, but Themba needed to hide his shaven convict's head. The man walked jauntily on his way with a grin from ear to ear. Themba crossed the bridge. He wanted to run, but held himself in check and sauntered along. His heart almost stopped as a police van drew level with him.

'Hey, kaffir! Where are you going?'

Themba looked up and saw a single-storey bus crossing the intersection ahead. He thought quickly. Black people travelled in single-storey buses. White people used double-decker buses. There must be a bus stop for black people ahead. 'I'm going to the bus stop, baas.'

The policeman accepted his explanation. 'Where do you come from?'

'Garden boy. I dig in the garden, *baas*.'

'Have you seen a black man in a blue-and-white checked shirt and grey trousers?'

Themba looked back over the bridge. The black man wearing his clothes was barely in sight. Themba had no qualms. It was either him or the other stranger, and the other man was not on an important mission for the ANC. He raised his arm and pointed. 'There.'

The police vehicle screeched to a halt opposite the man in Themba's clothes. Two policemen jumped out, pistols at the ready. The policemen pushed the protesting man over the hood and handcuffed his hands behind his back. The officer felt the clothes. They were damp. He smiled, they had their man.

He radioed in to base. 'We have arrested a black man in a wet blue-and-white checked shirt and grey trousers.'

'That's him, that's Memani.' Badenhorst let out a sigh of relief. 'Now my balls are safe.'

'The patrol van is taking him to Milnerton police station.'

'Okay.' Badenhorst called off the search parties.

Behind the hotel Themba saw a man with a red shirt slam down the hood of an old Opel Rekord. 'Are . . . you . . . James . . . Libode?'

The man scrutinised Themba carefully. 'Who are you?'

'Philips . . . Makeba . . . I'm . . . Philips . . . Makeba.'

'Welcome to freedom, my friend,' he said with a ready smile.

'I have important documents buried along the West-Coast road,' said Themba in concern.

'We can't go now,' answered Libode firmly. 'The area is crawling with cops. Are the documents well hidden?' Themba nodded and James continued: 'One night next week we will go and retrieve them.' Two police vans roared along Blaauwberg road. 'We must hurry,' insisted Libode. 'Lie down on the back seat.' He covered Themba with a blanket, pilling empty cardboard cartons on top of him.

Themba heard the car start. Vaguely hearing the noise of the traffic, he was overtaken by exhaustion and drifted into a peaceful sleep.

19

Eric Loots popped his head around the door. 'Knock-off time, Mr Roux. Would you like Miss Benade to take you to the guest lodge now?'

Pierre looked up angrily. 'Has Eschel Rhoodie not returned?'

Loots shook his head. 'Dr Rhoodie telephoned to say he has been delayed. He'll see you tomorrow morning at the office.'

'Rhoodie and I are headed for a blow-up.' Pierre thought of the wasted hours and the innumerable files he had been presented with. He had read the documentation carefully, but all were mundane, containing nothing secret or contentious. He looked irritably at Loots, still peering expectantly around the door. 'Please tell Miss Benade I don't require her dubious services.'

'Very well, Mr Roux.' He looked disappointed Pierre was not falling for the bait.

He was probably as jealous as all hell, thought Pierre.

'You'll have to leave now. The offices are locked up for the night. I can drop you at the guest lodge, it's not far out of my way.' Molly gave Pierre a friendly wave as they passed, but he ignored her.

They stopped at the gateway of the lodge. A gatekeeper swung open the heavy wrought-iron gates. Flanking the driveway were beautifully manicured lawns and colourful shrub borders. A Spanish-style house with arches, terracotta tiles and ornate stucco work dominated the ridge. Pierre gazed at the lavish set-up and wondered what it cost the Department of Information to maintain.

A butler greeted them and a housekeeper showed Pierre to his bedroom. It was a beautiful, large, airy room curtained from ceiling to floor. A huge double bed dominated the room with the wall above the bed a solid mirror, making the room appear even bigger than it was. The butler turned to Pierre. 'Mr Loots is waiting for you on the patio.'

Pierre strolled on to the high-walled courtyard. A sparkling pool glinted in the late-afternoon sunshine. Against a wall a gargoyle spewed water into a pond containing exotic water lilies and Japanese Koi. Loots was sitting sipping a drink under an umbrella. 'Make yourself at home, Mr Roux.'

'A drink for you, sir?' The butler looked at Pierre.

'Scotch, water and ice, please.'

'Johnny Walker Black Label, Bell's Royal Reserve or Chivas Regal twelve-year, sir?'

'I'm not fussy.' As the butler walked inside Pierre turned to Loots. 'Eschel doesn't skimp on the taxpayers' money.'

'Dr Rhoodie prides himself in associating with only the best.' Loots downed his drink. 'I must go, Mr Roux. I'll call for you tomorrow morning.'

The housekeeper presented an *à la carte* menu and Pierre ordered grilled rainbow trout with a herb-butter sauce. He carried his drink through to the bedroom. His thoughts turned to Rhoodie. The man's an enigma. He runs Information like a James Bond book – pretty girls, secret projects, subversion and a propaganda war. I wouldn't be surprised if the Department resorts to tapping telephones and bugging rooms.

The thought worried Pierre. He looked behind the pictures, under ornaments and in the bowl of flowers. He ran his hand under the edge of the bedside cabinet. His fingers felt a raised object. He looked carefully. Yes, it was a small microphone, cleverly concealed, able to pick up all conversation around and in the bed. The evidence was mounting.

'Mr Roux, your dinner is served.' Pierre ate by himself in the luxurious walnut-furnished dining room. After coffee he bade the butler and housekeeper good-night and retired to his room. He showered, got into his pyjamas and carried the files to the bed. Propped up, he studied the documents, finding no contentious issues. He did not think he would. He looked at his watch, eleven o'clock. Glancing at the pile of unread reports, he judged another hour's reading.

There was a knock on the door. He glanced up, puzzled. Surely the staff had left? Perhaps they did a last round before the guests went to sleep. 'Come in.'

'Hullo there.' He looked up quickly as Molly entered the bedroom. She locked the door and glided towards the foot of the bed, smiling down at him. She was ravishing in a long mink coat, her hair loose, framing her face.

Pierre looked at her in surprise. 'What on earth are you doing here?'

'I've come to pamper *you*, my darling.' She let the coat slip to the floor. She was naked. She rubbed her hands sensually over her body.

He stared at her spellbound, never having experienced such a blatant display of eroticism. Then he remembered the hidden bug. Every word was being listened to and probably taped. Would they use the evidence to blackmail him? Almost certainly.

'Make love to me, Pierre. I want to feel you deep inside me.' She spoke in a husky voice but seemed to be posing for the mirror.

Pierre turned around, a sick feeling in the pit of his stomach. If they made tapes, they could also make films. What if the mirror had a camera behind it, recording every action? When he demanded the secret files, he could be blackmailed into backing off.

Pierre stalked to the door, locking it from the outside. He tried the door of the room behind the mirror. It was locked. Seething with fury he kicked at the lock. The door crashed open. It took Pierre a few seconds to orientate himself. His whole bedroom was visible through the one-way glass. Molly had put on her coat and was sitting on the bed shivering. A movie camera, mounted on a tripod, was focused on the bed. Cowering in the corner was Eric Loots. In two bounds Pierre crossed the room and grabbed Loots by the neck. His fist crunched into Loots's face.

'Stop! I'm only doing my job,' he screamed in terror.

Pierre rained in punches until Loots crumpled to the floor blubbering 'Please! I'll do anything you want. Just stop.'

Pierre pulled Loots to his feet and held him up against the wall, his mind calm and calculating. 'You dirty little bastard! Where are the Department's secret project files that I'm looking for?'

'What files?'

Pierre dug three punches into his solar plexus and Loots fell forwards. Raising his knee he caught him in the face. Loots caved in. Pierre again forced him to his feet pulling back his fist. 'Where are the files?'

'I don't know.'

He hit him in the face and Loots started screaming. 'Stop! They're in the strong room at the office.'

'Do you have the keys?'

Loots nodded mutely. Pierre dragged him into the bedroom. He looked scathingly at Molly. 'Out.' She scurried from the room and he locked the door. Loots sat on the end of the bed nursing his head. Pierre quickly dressed and packed his suitcase. He frog-marched him to the front door.

'Where's your car?'

'Just inside the gate.'

Pierre forced him inside the car and ran around to the passenger side. 'Drive! And don't try anything funny.'

Loots hooted at the gateway and the sleepy gatekeeper opened for them. They drove straight to the Ad Astra Building. Once inside the offices he barked at Loots, 'Where's the strong room?' Loots pointed down the passage and Pierre forced him along. 'Open it.'

'It's a combination lock and a key. I only have the key.'

Pierre moved towards him threateningly. 'I'll kill you if I have to. Don't play games with me.'

Loots looked at him nervously. 'You don't think I enjoyed doing what I did, Mr Roux?' he whined. 'Believe me, I hated every degrading minute.'

'Making illegal films and blackmail can land you in jail,' retorted Pierre, lifting his fist.

'Sorry! Sorry!' mumbled Loots cowering against the wall. 'I'll help you if I won't be prosecuted.'

Pierre relented. 'I'll use all my influence to get you indemnity.'

'Why do you want the files?' whined Loots in a high-pitched voice.

'I'm acting on behalf of PW Botha – he wants to expose Rhoodie's squandering of secret funds.'

'That will create a scandal in the Information Department.'

'I'll see you are not implicated,' promised Pierre.

With a sigh of resignation Loots swung the dials of the combination lock. Pierre heard the tumblers click into place. He turned the key and swung open the heavy door. Inside were rows and rows of shelves. Loots knew what he was looking for, whipping files into Pierre's arms. Operation Senekal, Project Cradock, Operation Cherry, Project Annemarie, Project Chicken, 1977 British Postal Strike, Church Organisations, Film Production Companies, Book Publishing Companies, George Meary/Labour Union, Front Organisations, News and Photo Agencies, Institutes, Collaborators,

US Senate/Transkei Independence, Israel/Simon Peres, Operation Playboy.

Both Pierre and Loots were laden with files. 'I think that's about all, Mr Roux.'

'Okay, lock up again.' They placed the documents in two cardboard boxes. Pierre looked at his watch. It was almost five o'clock. 'Take me to Jan Smuts Airport, please, Eric. I want to catch the first aeroplane back to Cape Town. I'll only feel safe when these are secure in my own back yard.'

Pierre drove straight from Cape Town airport to Hermitage. The forecourt was deserted. He walked into the wine cellar. Where could he hide the files until he was ready to hand them over? He needed to study them first. The wine tanks! Pierre found a large plastic detergent drum. He cleaned it out and packed the files inside, screwing on the watertight lid. Hefting the drum he climbed up the ladder. He opened the trapdoor and carefully dropped the drum into a tank. Pierre smiled in satisfaction as the drum bobbed gently in the fermenting wine.

He glanced around carefully. No one was in sight. He climbed into his car and drove home.

'On your marks, get set, go!' The pistol cracked. The eight hundred metres final at the Colgate South African Championships in Germiston was underway. Pierre tucked into fourth spot. At the bell the pace quickened. Down the back straight Rathedi slackened slightly and Pierre passed him, his arms and legs pumping like well-oiled cylinders. Pierre caught Goosen on the second-last bend: two hundred metres to go. Pierre was breathing heavily, his lungs burning from the rarefied highveld air. McCrindle and Pierre were neck and neck as they hit the final straight. His legs felt like rubber. The crowd roared. Then he saw Lesley on the inside of the track.

'Now, Pierre! Give your final effort.'

Drawing on hidden reserves, he sprinted faster, his muscles straining as he lengthened his stride. He looked around. McCrindle was still at his shoulder. With the last three strides he put his whole being into his legs, shooting over the tape in first position.

Lesley was in his arms and they kissed, oblivious of the crowd. 'Congratulations, darling. You are the new South African champion. You did it.'

He shook his head. 'No, sunshine. We did it.'

After the medal presentation, they walked off the track, hand in hand.

'Pierre! Pierre!' He looked up. There was Eschel Rhoodie. 'I must speak to you. It's important.' He donned his most charming manner, turning to Lesley, giving her his broadest smile. 'Hullo, Lesley. We haven't met, but I know who you are. I'm Eschel Rhoodie.'

She greeted him perfunctorily. 'How can we help, Dr Rhoodie?'

'I invite you both on a holiday to a tropical island. Next week we leave for the Seychelles. Imagine idyllic days on palm-fringed beaches! A second honeymoon for you both.'

Lesley turned on him sharply. 'I also know all about you, Eschel Rhoodie. Pierre has enough evidence to sink you. I see right through your Seychelles plans. We are not the slightest bit interested in your schemes. Good day!'

Rhoodie's face turned mean as he glared scathingly at Pierre. 'You stole those files from my safe.'

'Why don't you report the matter to the police?' Pierre smiled victoriously. 'You wouldn't dare do that, would you? I've read some of the files and hidden them where BOSS will never find them. How did you think you would get away with all the deception? You paid ten million United States dollars out of a secret Swiss bank account, under a front company, Thesaurus Continental Securities Corporation, to the American John McGoff, to purchase the *Washington Star*. The deal fell flat, now you're minus the money and the newspaper. How are you going to explain that and the other frauds to the taxpayers of South Africa?'

Rhoodie's tan faded as the blood drained from his face. 'Pierre, you're one of us. You also work for the Department of Information. You took an oath when you joined.'

'That is where you're wrong. An oath is not binding when it comes to gross misappropriation of funds and deceit. I work for honour and decency.'

'The Mostert Commission cleared us of any irregularities. We are clean.' Rhoodie was desperate, clutching at straws.

'The Mostert Commission only pertained to exchange-control transgressions. You are clever, Rhoodie. You draw on unaudited secret funds, operate Swiss bank accounts and work with front organisations. You covered your trail well, but not well enough. The files will topple your toy castle.'

'Please, Pierre,' he begged.

'My wife and I are going out to celebrate my victory.'

'You think of my demise as a victory, Pierre?'

'As usual, you have the wrong end of the stick. I'm the new South African eight hundred metres champion and qualify for Springbok colours. Don't you think that's a victory to celebrate?'

They left Rhoodie gaping after them, for once in his life at a loss for words.

Themba was adamant. 'I insist on seeing Mr Tambo personally.'

'I'm sorry, sir, but he has staff meetings scheduled for the whole day. He can't possibly see you.' The receptionist opened Tambo's appointment diary. 'Friday, yes, Friday at eleven o'clock, he has an opening.'

'That's in three days' time. It's not good enough. I'll wait.'

She looked at him apologetically. Themba was immaculately dressed in a dark-blue suit. She thought he looked like someone important, but she did not recognise him and wondered why he would not divulge his name.

A man opened an inner door, talking as he left the room. 'I'll have the report on your desk within a week, Oliver.' He walked through reception, nodding to Themba.

In a flash Themba was up, walked to the door and slipped inside before the receptionist could stop him. A dapper little man with a wispy moustache and bright, intelligent eyes looked up. Themba recognised him from photographs. 'Good morning, Mr Tambo. I am Themba Memani.'

The little man nodded, looking at his watch. 'How can I help you?'

'I have come from Robben Island with a message from Nelson Mandela.'

The receptionist ran in. 'I'm sorry, Mr Tambo. This man does not have an appointment, he simply burst in here.'

Tambo saw Themba's calm, assured expression. 'All right, Sally. I have a few minutes before my next meeting. Leave us alone, please. Please sit down, Mr Memani. I have five minutes at the most. Be brief.'

Themba spoke quickly of his time on Robben Island and his escape. The buzzer flashed on Tambo's desk. Themba was

445

encouraged when he heard him say: 'Postpone my next meeting for fifteen minutes.'

'How did you reach Lusaka?'

'First with a lift to the Botswana border. I did not cross at the border post for fear of capture. I walked to the end of the electrified fence and crossed at Ramatlabama.' Tambo nodded, aware of the escape route. 'I stayed at the ANC transit camp at Mogoditshane, outside Gaborone, until it was safe. Then I flew Zambia Airlines to Lusaka. I present these documents straight from Comrade Mandela.'

Tambo accepted the file. He recognised his former legal partner's familiar handwriting. He tore open the letter from Mandela and read slowly, absorbing every word. Leaning across his desk, he pushed the intercom button. 'Sally, cancel all further meetings for today, even the one with the Soviet Ambassador. I don't want to be disturbed under any circumstances. You may bring in tea, though.' Tambo walked around the desk and embraced Themba. 'Welcome to ANC headquarters, Themba.'

'Thank you, Mr Tambo.'

The hours flew by as Tambo read Mandela's file, engrossed. He read right through the lunch-hour and it was mid-afternoon when he finally closed the file. He looked at Themba, his eyes sparkling. 'Marvellous, absolutely marvellous.'

He tapped the file. 'This is the most complete and up-to-date account of conditions on Robben Island ever to reach the outside world. Conditions are vile and the prison administration is disgusting, but Nelson's attack on the apartheid system is in a class of its own. When we release the details to the world, there will be such an explosion that even the foundations of the Nationalist government will shake.'

Themba smiled. '*Madiba* felt the same way. He made me promise to hand the file over to you personally. I have completed my assignment.' He rose to leave.

Oliver waved him down. 'Sit! Sit! You are going nowhere. You are home now. You are one of us. Nelson has asked that I take special care of you. From his letter, I gather he has a very high regard for you, Themba. He has asked that I guide you to a leadership role in the ANC. You must complete your legal studies in England or Sweden, then come back to Lusaka to join our legal team in exile.'

Themba shook his head. Tambo stopped talking to look at him questioningly. 'Study and an administrative role must wait. If I am to play a part in the leadership, I must learn the business from the bottom. I must work in every department so when I reach the top I will know everything there is to know about the ANC.'

'What did you have in mind, Themba?'

'Guerrilla training should come first. I must sweat it out in the bush like every other Umkhonto we Sizwe trainee, with no special privileges.'

Themba paced the room, his eyes blazing, his face contorted in rage. 'There is hatred, real hatred, in my heart for the apartheid system. I want to play my part in the armed struggle to pay back the regime for the suffering they have caused our people.'

Themba stopped pacing. He leant on the desk and looked Tambo straight in the eye. 'When the fire of hatred has burnt down and is out of my system, it will be rekindled with a flame of hope for the future. When that happens, then is the time to study further and accept a leadership role.'

Oliver was impressed with the intensity of the young man. He wondered how he would handle other pressures, like the Press conference he intended calling for the world's media the next day.

'Try and keep your presentation as simple and sincere as possible,' Tambo coached Themba. 'If you are convincing, you'll be a superstar.'

They walked into the media room. Portable spotlights were trained on the podium. A cluster of microphones were taped together bearing the names of world-renowned television stations. Reporters produced notepads.

Seated at the main table, Pallo Jordan introduced Themba. He paused for a minute to gather his thoughts and heighten the anticipation of his audience. Everyone in the room concentrated on Themba. He spoke without notes.

'Good afternoon, ladies and gentlemen. I am Themba Memani. I am a member of the ANC. I was arrested after the Soweto uprisings and sentenced to five years' imprisonment on Robben Island. To the best of my knowledge, I am the first prisoner to escape successfully from the island.

'My escape bid was a well-planned operation from inside the

prison, to smuggle out very important documents – the writings of Nelson Mandela. After a terrifying night at sea on a raft I reached the mainland. I slipped the South African authorities and reached Lusaka via Botswana only two days ago.'

Themba took a sip of water before continuing. 'Yesterday I presented Comrade Mandela's file to President Oliver Tambo. He will be releasing sections of these writings to you, that you may show the world the degradation of prisoners on the island.'

Alfred Nzo nudged Tambo. 'Very good! This man has class. He comes across confidently and convincingly.'

Tambo nodded. 'Let's see how good he is when he fields questions.'

The BBC presenter asked the first question. 'How is Nelson Mandela faring in prison?'

'He is fit and well, both mentally and physically. In all matters he is the leader on Robben Island.'

From a CBS interviewer: 'Does Mandela still have a role to play within the ANC even though he is in prison?'

Themba smiled warmly for the cameras. 'The whole world looks to the leadership on Robben Island to show the way. Over a thousand political prisoners there have one common goal – to end apartheid. Nelson Mandela symbolises all our hopes and aspirations, on the island, in South Africa and throughout the world. He is responsible for the winds of change sweeping our continent.'

'What is Mandela like as a person?'

'He is charismatic, a great presence in any group. He is an attentive listener and an astute summariser. For all his greatness, he is still humble. He does his fair share in the lime quarry, he cleans his cell and does any of the other tasks assigned to prisoners.'

'Mr Memani, what is your immediate future?'

'My future is inextricably linked to the ANC. I am prepared to perform any task which advances the aims and objectives of our organisation.'

As Themba stepped down to a standing ovation, Alfred Nzo nodded to Tambo. 'He passed that test all right. We should look after this young man.'

Pallo Jordan was next with his easy-going style. 'We have pre-pared news releases for each of you.' Aides handed out the folders. 'Inside you will find excerpts from Nelson Mandela's original file. We trust you will study the documentation in detail. Help us fight the racist Nationalist government by including write-ups in your newspapers, news bulletins and on prime-time television. Thank you for attending, ladies and gentlemen.'

Back in his office Tambo congratulated Themba on his performance. 'News conferences are never easy, but you handled your first one like an old hand.'

Themba coughed to hide his eagerness. 'Mr Tambo, may I ask you a personal favour?'

'Go ahead, asking is free.'

'My wife Hilda is alone at home. I will not be able to visit her for years to come. May she join me in Lusaka?'

Tambo nodded. 'It's a reasonable request. I will make the necessary arrangements.' Tambo smiled. He liked Themba more and more.

Themba was at the airport to meet her. He swept her off her feet, swung her around in delight and set her down gently, kissing her. Hilda wept tears of happiness.

As they lay quietly in each other's arms, Hilda smiled at him. 'Perhaps the seed you planted tonight will replace the baby we lost.'

Lesley shrieked as she stepped into the house. The lounge looked as if it had been hit by a tornado. The chairs were upside down, the material slit. Her yellow-wood *jonkmanskas* was lying on its face, a precious door shattered. Ornaments were scattered and broken. She ran from room to room in a daze. It was the same story. Fury built up in her as she saw her beloved possessions shattered and ruined. Lesley met Pierre at the front door, spots of rage on her cheeks. 'The bastards have been here. They've pillaged our home.'

Pierre ran inside to see for himself. 'They're after the Information files.'

'Nail them, Pierre. Make them pay.' Lesley burst out crying.

Pierre telephoned the police. They came, took statements and left. Hours later fingerprint experts arrived. They dusted their powder all over the house. 'Sorry, Mr Roux, there are no foreign fingerprints whatsoever. They were professionals.'

When Rhoodie answered the telephone Pierre blasted him. 'Enough is enough. Tomorrow I'm going straight to PW Botha. This is the beginning of the end for you, Rhoodie.' Loud music was playing in the background, Rhoodie was holding a party.

'I'm sorry about your house, Pierre. Please give me back my files. It will be in your own best interests. I'm open to negotiation. Being amenable could prove very rewarding.'

Pierre slammed the telephone down in disgust, shaking with anger.

The sun was just clearing the Klein Drakenstein Mountains as Pierre drove up Hermitage's driveway. His father and the manager were already on the stoep of the manor house, busy with their daily meeting.

Simon looked up in surprise. 'Hullo, son. What brings you to Paarl so early in the morning?'

'Morning, Dad. An emergency. May I speak to you alone?'

Pierre took his father into his confidence. He told him everything, starting with his first meeting with PW Botha and ending with the plundering of his home. Simon listened in silence, nodding every now and again. Pierre threw his hands up in exasperation. 'What must I do, Dad?'

'It smells of a power struggle to me. Politics is a dirty game, Pierre. I don't deny that the affairs of the Department of Information have unravelled into an untidy and deceitful mess, but I think the underlying motive is the ultimate prize, the premiership of South Africa.'

Pierre marvelled at his father's perception.

Simon continued. 'It's well known Vorster is tired and suffers from bouts of apathy. His possible successors are jockeying for position. Dr Connie Mulder, as Transvaal leader of the National Party, is the heir apparent, the crown prince. Since 1948 when the NP came to power, the Transvaal has always produced the Prime Minister. The other big gun in contention is the Cape leader of the party, PW Botha.'

'Who would you support, Dad?'

'I would go for Botha. He's been involved in politics since his youth as a party organiser. A total of forty-two years in politics is a long time. I served with PW in parliament. I know and trust him.'

'What about Connie Mulder?'

'From what you've told me, Mulder is influenced by Van den Bergh and Rhoodie. To stop Eschel and company turning this country into a banana republic you have to neutralise Mulder.'

'You suggest I go to PW and put my cards on the table?'

'He asked you to find out about *The Citizen*. Take that file along, but keep the rest up your sleeve for the time being. You can produce your ace when the time is right. Politics is like fishing, you play it one bite at a time.'

'Dad, you're wonderful.' Pierre hugged his father. 'I'll try and see PW today.'

Pierre locked the wine-cellar door behind him. He opened the trapdoor on top of the wine tank. He removed the watertight plastic barrel and lifted out the *Operation Annemarie* file, resealed the barrel and closed the wine tank.

PW Botha adjusted his spectacles. 'You have something for me, Pierre?'

Pierre brought him up to date on *The Citizen*. 'You've done good work, Pierre.' He stabbed his finger on his desk. 'I'll cut off Rhoodie's water. He won't get another cent from the Special Defence account. A pity it's all hearsay evidence.'

'Not so, Mr Botha.' He opened his briefcase and placed the *Operation Annemarie* file in front of him.

Botha paged through the documents, taking his time. 'I suspected subterfuge, but never on such a scale. I think you may have saved the sanity of our nation, Pierre.' Botha looked at his calendar. 'What a coincidence. Tomorrow is Mulder's Information vote, the opportune time to raise the matter in parliament.'

'What if Dr Mulder denies all knowledge?'

'Then he'll sink himself.' Botha tapped the file.

Pierre studied Botha carefully. 'Isn't it an unwritten rule that you never embarrass someone of your own party in parliament?'

'You have a point, but the issue is too serious to let it be hushed up. Mulder is responsible to the taxpayers. He must answer in parliament where his reply can be recorded in *Hansard*.'

'Can't you brief the Opposition, Mr Botha?'

'Yes, that's possible.' Botha smiled triumphantly. 'My old friend Japie Basson would help me. We served together for eleven years in the National Party. We still have respect for each other, even though he's now a member of the Progressive Federal Party. He'd do it. I'll brief him.'

Pierre rose to leave. 'I'll be in the public gallery tomorrow, following the proceedings with interest.'

451

'Pierre, it looks like once again I'm indebted to you. Thank you.'
Botha smiled in genuine appreciation.

Dr Connie Mulder was perspiring. The opposition were tearing into him. He was irritated and thirsty, but there was no respite. Damn Rhoodie! He was being forced to defend a statement made by the man which had appeared in a Sunday newspaper. He didn't agree with Rhoodie's standpoint, but he felt obliged to side with his Secretary of Information.

Harry Schwarz of the PFP quizzed him on the book, *Stepping into the Future*, and asked pointedly if it was funded by the Department. Mulder was ruffled. He was on his own, standing in a sea of upturned faces carefully scrutinising his every move. He was losing control.

Schwarz tried another angle. 'Mr Chairman, the Minister owes me a number of answers in regard to the incorrect answer he gave me previously. He promised then he would furnish the required replies. The Minister still has not given those replies and I should appreciate it if he would do so.' Schwarz sat down with a satisfied smile.

Dr Mulder shook his head in frustration. 'I shall furnish the replies at once.'

Japie Basson took up the assault. He looked at PW Botha and smiled. 'Mr Chairman, I too put a question to the Minister to which I have not yet received a reply. We specifically asked the Minister whether the rumour that the government was making secret funds available to *The Citizen* was true . . .'

Interjecting impatiently, Mulder barked out, 'Surely I have already replied to that.'

Basson was not going to let the Minister slip out of the net this time. 'The reply furnished by the Minister was that the Department of Information were not owners of newspapers. We know that. But that was not the question and I do not want it to be said again at a later stage that we are making insinuations. Therefore I again put this simple question to the Minister and we should like to have a direct answer to it.'

Connie Mulder was trapped. He committed his first mistake. 'I shall reply to it directly by saying that the Department of Information does *not* give funds to *The Citizen*. Is that clear, and does the Member accept it?'

Japie Basson drove the second nail into Mulder's coffin. He glared at the Minister. 'And the government?'

There was no escape for Connie Mulder. He had to maintain his story, compounding his mistake. 'The government does *not* give *The Citizen* funds.'

PW Botha knew that Dr Connie Mulder had just sealed his fate with two blatant lies, and he was determined that it would cost Mulder dearly in the months that lay ahead. Glancing up at the public gallery PW caught Pierre's eye and winked at him. Pierre smiled back.

The day before Themba left for military training in Angola they heard that Hilda was pregnant. She clung to him at the airport. 'I always seem to be saying goodbye to you.'

Themba looked at her gently. 'I'll miss you. I hope to be back before the baby is born.'

He flew with a group of recruits to Luanda. At the airport they were met by ANC officials and representatives of the Angolan MPLA government.

The group was housed in an ANC home in the suburb of Vienna while they waited for others to arrive. Once the whole contingent was assembled they left in camouflaged trucks supplied by the Angolan government. They drove along the coastal belt past white beaches. It was hot and humid. At Caxito the trucks stopped for the trainees to buy cold Cokes and food.

Themba smiled ruefully as he reflected on his last trip in the back of a truck, from Leeuwkop prison to Cape Town. Today was friendly and relaxed. Themba was looking forward to his training, knowing it would give him the skills to be able to hit back at the racist regime in South Africa.

The journey ended. They were parked on a large parade ground of bare red earth, surrounded on three sides by coffee groves. On the fourth side were red brick buildings and then rows of tents in a half circle.

An official in army fatigues addressed them. 'Welcome to Quibaxe. Relax for the rest of the day while you find your way around. Tomorrow your training starts. Look on the notice board outside the library to see which tents you have been allocated. You arrive here as ANC members, but leave us as MK freedom fighters.'

Themba strolled around getting acquainted with his new surroundings. The camp was an old coffee plantation. The buildings housed the officers' quarters and administration offices. He found his rectangular, four-bedded tent in the first row. He unpacked the contents of his suitcase into a metal locker.

Supper was served in the open air under African flame trees. There was meat, samp and beans, vegetables and aromatic coffee from the estate.

The next day they reported to the parade ground. Themba was allocated to 1st Company, No. 4 Platoon, under the command of the legendary Tarzan. He was of average height, but physically strong and very fit looking.

'No. 4 is known as the Iron Platoon,' whispered a recruit, 'because of Tarzan's iron discipline. He always produces the fittest and best-prepared men to finish the Infantry Platoon Commander's Course.'

They were kitted out with camouflage trousers and jackets and khaki shirts, socks and underwear. In another room they received their black boots, khaki greatcoat and knapsack.

Tarzan gave them no respite. The first week it was march and drill hour after hour. Long after the others had been dismissed for the day, Tarzan kept them on the parade ground. They perfected their style and rhythm until their flawless precision made them stand out way above the other platoons.

From the second week they began special courses. Each morning the day's schedule was posted on the library notice board. Specialised courses were run by instructors from the Soviet Union and communist East Germany. Interpreters translated into English for the recruits.

Ensconced in Hermitage's wine cellar for a week, Pierre and Lesley worked systematically through the secret files. She was determined to expose the perpetrators who had defiled her home and damaged her precious possessions. 'I'll make them pay,' she told Pierre. 'We'll find enough evidence to blow the whole dirty mess sky high.'

They built up a water-tight case against the Department, discovering mind-boggling schemes and scams involving many foreign countries. International politicians were bribed, front organisations were established, full-time collaborators appointed, film production companies purchased, institutes established abroad, motion pictures subsidised and numerous VIPs hosted on secret tours to South Africa. Huge sums of money were misappropriated and not accounted for.

Pierre flipped open *Operation Playboy*. 'Rhoodie met James Mancham, Prime Minister of the Seychelles Islands, in Paris. Rhoodie hid a miniature listening device in his top pocket and recorded the whole conversation. Two weeks later Connie Mulder accompanied Rhoodie to the same Paris hotel. Now he can't deny complicity with the Department of Information's projects. They agreed to pay Mancham twenty-five thousand rand a year to promote our interests on the islands and give us feedback on the Organisation of African Unity's deliberations.'

Lesley sat back and looked at Pierre carefully. 'We certainly have evidence of misappropriation on a grand scale. Let's draw up a report.'

They produced a fifteen-page detailed document. Pierre called in his father for his opinion.

Simon read in silence, grunting every now and again. At the end he shook his head. 'Mulder, Rhoodie and Van den Bergh are equally at fault. My advice to you is to go straight to the top this time. If you like, I'll go with you, I know John Vorster. When he's confronted by such concrete evidence he'll have to act.'

'I would appreciate your support, Dad.'

The Prime Minister looked at father and son as they walked into his office. He did not look a well man, his face pasty, his eyes tired and watery. He waved them to chairs. 'Simon, I should have followed your advice a decade ago and South Africa would not have been in the mess it's in now. To be quite frank, I'm at my wits' end.'

'Mr Vorster, what has passed is history, but what my son has to show you could ruin South Africa's whole future.'

Vorster smiled wanly, his heavy jowls hardly moving. 'Pierre, I know what you are going to tell me. I was briefed about the missing Pretoria files. Give it to me straight.'

Pierre read his report. Each revelation was like a knife thrust in Vorster's ribs. Pierre also told the Prime Minister about the wrecking of his home.

'I'm not sure whether you have brought me good news or

bad news. I don't know what to do without exposing my own flank.'

'Connie Mulder lied in parliament when he told Japie Basson that neither the Department of Information nor the government funded *The Citizen*. That lie will still catch up with him and implicate you, Prime Minister. The information is turning into a full-blown scandal. Fire them, otherwise you'll be involved.'

'I'm already implicated, though not to the full extent of all the schemes mentioned in your report.' Vorster was dejected. He saw the beginning of the end of his premiership. How could he survive against such evidence? 'I was briefed on some of the projects, but I never realised the scope and magnitude. Thank you for warning me, gentlemen.'

Prime Minister John Vorster was a sick man, working under tremendous pressure. His conscience plagued him. The stress proved too much and Vorster broke down. He was flown by military aircraft to Tygerberg hospital near Cape Town. Doctors ordered complete rest. Vorster was released from hospital two weeks later and announced his retirement.

Pierre was summoned to PW Botha's offices. 'Tell me what you've discovered, Pierre. Our country cannot afford to let Connie Mulder become Prime Minister.'

'Here's a fifteen-page report on the whole dirty Information scandal.'

Botha read in silence. 'It's an even worse scenario than I thought. Why didn't you hand me this report sooner, Pierre?'

'The time was not right. My father and I presented the original copy to Vorster urging him to do something positive. He transferred Mulder to another ministry and fired Rhoodie, but unfortunately kept the knowledge to himself.'

'I would have blown the lid off.' Botha licked his lips in determination.

'Yes, sir. But you would have done yourself irreparable political damage in the process. Mulder would have been warned and Vorster might have turned against you. This way you can honestly say you knew nothing about the matter, except for *The Citizen*. You come out clean; unscathed politically.'

Botha smiled. 'You'll make a good politician, Pierre. Very astute. I shall be standing for the premiership. Should I win,

I'll close down the Department of Information and I want you in military intelligence, where you can keep me abreast of the armed struggle.'

A solemn caucus filed into Vorster's last Cabinet meeting. The publicity following the subpoena served on Dr Mulder to appear before the Mostert Commission had done him a great deal of harm. An amount of two million rand in a secret Swiss account was rumoured. Mulder maintained his bearing, appearing his usual confident self. PW Botha waited expectantly for the day's events to unfold.

In dramatic developments John Vorster confided in his colleagues for the first time. They listened in disbelief as he outlined the full extent of the Information scandal. Revelations were greeted with incredulity. Pierre's report lay open on his table.

The election for a new Prime Minister proceeded. Pik Botha was eliminated in the first round of voting. In a straight fight between PW Botha and Connie Mulder, Botha emerged victorious.

The Angolan bush was a rolling savannah of lush grasslands, interspersed with tall, stately trees. Themba paused to rest and crawled under a river bank to avoid detection. Alone with nature, surrounded by the sounds of the bush, South Africa and the apartheid struggle seemed light-years away. They were on manoeuvres, their task was to infiltrate through mock enemy lines and reach a predetermined destination. He heard voices above him and flattened himself into a hollow.

The voices passed and Themba breathed more easily. He had enjoyed the last month, when they had put all the theory into practice in true-life situations. Platoons fought mock battles against each other in the bush. Themba had developed a sixth sense. When danger was near the hairs on the back of his neck would prickle. He became adroit at bush craft – tracking, covering his spoor, using the wind and sun as his allies.

He made his way slowly up the dry river bed. The final destination was ahead, on top of a rise. Using all his skills, he slithered from cover to cover. The 'enemy' walked within three paces of Themba's hiding place without discovering him. He saw the trip wire between the grass and back-tracked, working around to its end. With fifteen paces to go he stood up and strolled casually to the vehicle. Tarzan nodded his head grudgingly. 'Not bad, Themba.' Coming from Tarzan it was the ultimate compliment. 'You'll make a good MK cadre, but you have one shortcoming which you must learn to correct.'

Themba stared at him quizzically. 'What is that?'

'You're not a team man,' stated Tarzan categorically. 'While you excel in the individual facets of your training, you must also learn to relate to other members of a group.'

'What do you suggest?'

'Change your snobbish attitude. Be less insolent to authority and learn to treat your comrades as equals.'

'Is that how you see me?' asked Themba sharply.

'Men follow a true leader because they want to, not because they have to. Learn temperance and you will go to the top, Themba.'

'Thanks for the advice.' Themba pondered on Tarzan's counsel.

'Remember, being a loner can be a very hard way of life.' Themba smiled in acknowledgement.

The culmination of the course was a seven-day forced march over mountains and across rivers to Fazenda, close to the Angolan border with Zaire. Each platoon took a different route in a race to reach their objective first.

Tarzan chose the most difficult route for No. 4 platoon, so that when his team won, the other platoons could have no excuses. He drove them mercilessly. Two hours' jogging, ten minutes' rest, two hours' fast walk, ten minutes' rest. From before sunrise to after dark, fifteen hours a day. They were weighed down with equipment, rations, weapons and ammunition. None of the other platoons could keep up the murderous pace, but Tarzan had been physically and mentally preparing them from the first day.

They were just getting their second wind when they reached Fazenda in the record time of seventy-two hours. Tarzan had ensured it was a one-horse race. The next platoon arrived a full day later, and the rest within the next twenty-four hours. Tarzan had worked with a plan. Although he had driven his Iron Platoon hard, they had won an extra two days' rest while waiting for the stragglers to arrive. They were fresh and rested for the manoeuvres that followed.

The passing-out parade was a personal triumph for Themba,

commended for competency in Tactics, Explosives, Topography and Artillery. He was recommended as a candidate to study Military Engineering in the Soviet Union.

Colonel Chegogara offered him a permanent post as platoon commander at Quibaxe.

'Thank you for the honour,' smiled Themba, 'but no thank you. Basic training is but one spoke in my wheel of ANC knowledge. I have much to learn and must move on.'

'Pity, but good luck,' said Chegogara, shaking his hand warmly.

Themba bent forward and kissed Hilda on the forehead. She opened her eyes slowly, looking at him for a long moment. Then with a squeal of delight she was in his arms, holding him, hardly believing it was true.

'My darling, you're back.' She burst out crying. 'I've missed you so.' Hilda held him tight again. 'We have a beautiful little boy. You have a son, Themba.'

'A son!' He looked at her incredulously, joy creasing his face. 'Where is he?'

'In the nursery.' Hilda laughed at his reaction.

'I want to see him this instant.' He rushed out, meeting the sister in the passage. 'I'm Themba Memani. I've been away at Quibaxe for the last eight months. I believe I have a son. I must see him, now.'

The nurse smiled. 'As a special favour for a returning soldier, I'll bring your baby to the ward.' She placed the baby in Hilda's arms. He kissed his son on the forehead, checking his limbs, counting ten fingers and ten toes. He was so proud, beaming from ear to ear.

'My son,' he whispered in awe, listening to the sound of the words. 'Are you really my son?'

'No doubt about that.' Hilda laughed merrily. 'Look at his features, he's a definite Memani – just a smaller version of his father.'

'What are we going to name him?' Themba searched her face.

'Mothers name the daughters, fathers their sons. It's your choice, my darling.'

Themba looked perplexed. 'My mother told me my father's name was Seme. I never knew him, so his name means nothing to me. I would like to name my son Bambatha.'

'I like the name. Where does it come from?'

459

'Bambatha was one of the forefathers of the freedom struggle – a Zulu chief of the Zondi tribe. He rebelled against the introduction of poll taxes levied on black men, way back in 1905. Rather than bow to government pressure he led his followers into a forest in the Natal midlands and conducted a war of liberation against the white authorities. Colonel Mackenzie and his troops cornered them in the Mome Gorge. Orders were issued to shoot to kill and over five hundred followers died. The army beheaded Bambatha, parading his head through the countryside as a warning to other tribes to toe the line.'

'A man with the courage of his convictions.' Hilda turned to Themba. 'Our son deserves to be named after a folk legend. His name will be Bambatha.'

The letter from his grandfather arrived unexpectedly. Nomisile was desperately ill and growing weaker by the day. He urged Themba to visit his mother before it was too late.

He asked for permission to travel to Mqekezweni. Suspecting a trap from the South African security police, the ANC insisted on first checking out the authenticity of the letter. Themba waited two tortuous weeks before ANC agents confirmed it was safe to travel to the Transkei.

Using a false passport and ID book, Themba flew to Lesotho. From there he travelled slowly, in stages, wasting valuable time holing up in towns, his training making him double-check that he was not being followed. On the eighth day he reached Umtata.

He made straight for Paul Curry's house. He would have the latest news. The house was closed and looked deserted. Themba felt uneasy. He watched it for a few hours but saw no sign of life. He hurried across the road and knocked loudly on the front door. No one answered.

A masculine voice rang out. 'Can I help you?'

He saw a stranger leaning over the fence. 'I'm looking for Mr Curry.' He hedged his bets. 'I'm looking for a job.'

'Kaiser Matanzima had him locked up last week. I believe he's in police custody,' said the neighbour.

'Thank you, *baas*.' Themba spoke self-effacingly so as not to arouse the neighbour's suspicions. First things first, he decided. I'll see my mother, then worry about Paul afterwards.

His childhood memories returned when he saw the rolling green

460

hills of Mqekezweni where he had once herded cattle and sheep. A lump formed in his throat as the familiar landmarks unfolded. He got off the bus a distance from the kraal. Themba lay a long time, looking for suspicious signs. All was peaceful, the door to Nomisile's hut closed. His own hut was in need of repair. Yellow Cape weaver birds were pulling thatch grass out of the roof and taking it down to the river to build their nests over the water. The white paint was flaking off the walls.

Nomisile's door opened. Themba was instantly alert. Hilda's mother came out, walking towards her home. She was crying, wiping away her tears. Themba was alarmed; he had to take a chance and go in. He pulled his hat low over his eyes and crept closer. He covered the open ground undetected, flattening himself against the outside of the door. He heard the vague murmur of voices. In one fluid movement he slipped inside, moving away from the door while his eyes adjusted to the gloom. He kept his hand on the butt of his loaded Makarov pistol.

Recognising his grandmother he removed his hat. 'Hullo, Grandmother.'

She looked in amazement. 'Themba! Themba, is it really you?' She rushed forward, embracing him.

Themba looked past her and saw an emaciated figure lying on a reed mat in the centre of the room. 'Mother.' He fell to his knees shocked at what he saw. He remembered the vibrant, healthy woman who had visited him on Robben Island only two years previously. Now her skin was like dried parchment, her eyes big and staring in her head.

He lifted her to his breast, feeling she was as light as a feather. 'My God, Mother! What has happened to you?' Themba cried out in despair.

He laid her down gently. Themba saw her eyes were fixed on him and her lips were moving. He bent forward to hear her whisper. 'My darling Themba. I hoped you would come before I die.'

'Die! You can't die, Mother.' He was distraught. 'Please don't talk of dying.'

'It tires her to talk,' Nosakani said. 'She listens well; you talk to her.'

Fighting back the tears, he told her about Hilda and her grandson. Encouraged by her brightening eyes he spoke about his course in Angola, about Lusaka and the ANC. Nomisile held his hand, squeezing every now and then when she particularly appreciated a part of what he was telling her. Her squeeze was a feeble movement, growing weaker as her energy was tapped.

Themba could not continue, he was too overwrought. Her eyes closed and he thought she was dead. Desperately he placed his ear to her chest, hearing her shallow breathing. She was asleep.

Themba turned angrily to his grandmother. 'Why is my mother like this? What's wrong?'

'Your grandfather wrote six weeks ago, Themba.' Nosakani was distressed. 'Nomisile was weak then already. Why did you take so long to get here?'

'I had to obtain clearance before I could travel. I couldn't get here sooner. Tell me why my mother is so ill.'

'She has cancer.' His grandmother looked at Themba sadly. 'The doctor says she has a malignant tumour in her abdomen.'

'Why did you wait so long before you told me?'

'Nomisile's condition only started to deteriorate six weeks ago. Before that we thought the witch-doctor would heal her.'

'The witch-doctor?' Themba was incredulous. 'Why didn't you take her to a proper medical doctor?'

'It started a year ago. We thought it was only a stomach upset as she felt uncomfortable after meals. She started eating less and less and naturally became weaker. The witch-doctor told us not to worry; all she had were snakes and frogs in her stomach.'

Themba looked at her in horror. 'Snakes and frogs, and you believed him?'

'He is the *igqirha*. Who can doubt his powers?'

'What happened then?'

'The witch-doctor gave her potions to drink, one to expel the frogs, another for the snakes.'

He stared at her in dismay. 'And then?'

'Nomisile became better for a time, but after a while she deteriorated again.'

Themba felt so helpless, so inadequate. His voice expressed his feelings. 'I am her only son. You should have told me.'

'Your mother forbade us to do so. She received your letters, but did not want you to run the risk of being captured again. She said you were happy in Lusaka and we must leave you be.'

He shook his head in frustration.

Nosakani continued. 'Eventually she couldn't sit for long periods and could not concentrate. She stopped her sewing business and spent most of her time lying down. We packed away her machines and let her helpers go.'

'If only you had let me know,' Themba sighed in frustration.

'After she stopped taking the witch-doctor's medicines he refused to help her further. Your grandfather went to see your friend, Paul Curry.'

'What did Paul do?'

'He took her to his doctor in Umtata. He did tests and diagnosed the cancer. Paul was not satisfied. He took her through to East London to see a specialist.'

'What was his diagnosis?'

Nosakani shook her head sadly. 'He said the tumour was too enlarged, there was nothing he could do. Paul brought her back to Mqekezweni. That was six weeks ago. Your grandfather ignored Nomisile's wishes and wrote to you. Since then she seems to have given up hope, getting weaker every day. Hilda's mother and I take it in turns to watch over her.'

Themba heard footsteps approaching the door. Instinctively he fell flat on his stomach, withdrawing and cocking his pistol, training it on the doorway.

His grandmother was frantic. 'No! It's your grandfather. He comes every night.'

The door opened and Morris stepped inside. Sheepishly Themba pocketed the pistol. He embraced his grandfather, shocked at how he had aged since he had last seen him.

'I'm pleased you're here, Themba.' He looked down at Nomisile. 'I think you arrived just in time.'

Nosakani served them a simple meal of crumbly maize porridge and sour milk. Morris stoked the fire and they whiled the hours away in conversation while Nomisile slept.

'Tell me about the council, Grandfather.'

His grandfather shrugged his shoulders sadly. 'Kaiser Matanzima has ruined our centuries-old tribal system for ever. After you left, the DDP went from strength to strength and Matanzima lost support, so he retaliated by bringing charges against all the chiefs who were members of the DDP.'

'What about Paramount Chief Sabata?'

'He was also arrested. They were all acquitted of the major

charges, but Sabata was sentenced to three months' imprisonment on a minor charge.'

Themba was shocked. 'The Paramount Chief of Thembuland in jail! It's unheard of.'

'At the end of last year they released him. You know, Sabata, he continued where he had left off, attacking Matanzima at every opportunity for being a pawn of the apartheid regime.'

Themba pictured the situation. 'Matanzima is pompous, he would hate being shown up.'

'Exactly. Last week he re-arrested Sabata and some of the chiefs. Others were banned and restricted to their districts. Now, on top of all my woes, Nomisile is dying.' Morris looked old and vulnerable. 'My world is crumbling. Things will never be the same again.'

Themba placed his hand on his grandfather's shoulder. 'Where is Sabata being held?'

'In the Umtata police cells behind the police station. He's waiting for charges to be brought.'

'I heard Paul Curry is also being held?'

Morris nodded. 'Same jail but different cells.'

'Paul is a member of the ANC, grandfather.'

'I know. He's on our side.'

On the third day Nomisile was stronger and quite lucid. She talked to Themba for hours, recalling incidents from his childhood.

'Mother, please tell me about my father?'

Nomisile clammed up. She lay back, her eyes tightly closed, determined to take her secret to the grave. Themba was conscience-stricken; it seemed to be the turning point in her battle to hold on to life. She slipped into a coma and became steadily weaker.

Themba was holding her frail frame in his arms when she gave a contented whimper, shuddered and went limp. He laid her down gently and lay with his head resting on her chest, weeping bitterly. There was so much more he wanted to tell her, to experience with her. Now she was gone and only the memories remained. He covered her with a blanket, not looking at her face. He wanted to remember her as she had always been.

When Morris arrived that evening he found them in mourning. His whole body convulsed as he let his grief wash over him. 'Children should bury their parents. It's not right for parents to bury their children.'

'Grandfather, when will my mother be buried?'

'Our custom decrees she must be buried by sunset tomorrow.'

'I can't stay for the funeral. The police have informants everywhere and someone could report me.'

'We must also notify the police of her death,' stated Morris.

A plan was almost complete in Themba's mind. 'I'll do that. Once the police know I'm here they will look for me in the funeral procession. Grandfather, I want you to do something for me.' Themba searched his grandfather's face. 'I ask you to prolong the burial ceremony until sunset. I will free Sabata and Paul while the police are at the funeral.'

His grandfather nodded in agreement.

'I must go, it's getting dark.' Themba folded down the blanket and kissed his mother tenderly on the forehead. 'I love you. Goodbye, Mother.'

Reluctantly he stood up. Themba embraced his grandparents – they looked so frail and vulnerable. He greeted Hilda's mother. Without a backward glance he was gone.

Themba walked quickly to the trading store; he had heard that the owner was a police informer. The trader squinted at him through the half-open door, recognising him immediately. 'Themba Memani, I haven't seen you for a long time. I hear your mother is very ill.'

'My mother died this afternoon. We will bury her at two o'clock tomorrow afternoon. Will you please telephone the police and advise them?'

His eyes glinted at the news. 'I will let them know, Themba. Will you be at the funeral?'

'Naturally, Mr Sparks. I'm the only son, I *must* be there.'

The telephone rang at the Umtata police station. An agitated voice asked to speak to the station commander. He was put through.

'Who's speaking?'

'It's John Sparks from the trading store near Mqekezweni. I've important information for you. Themba Memani is here for his mother's funeral.'

'Hang on.' He checked the name against the black list published quarterly by security police headquarters. His finger stopped on MEMANI – Themba. 'He's definitely on the wanted list. Where's he now?'

465

'I don't know, but the time to nab him is at the funeral tomorrow afternoon at Mqekezweni.'

'Thank you, Mr Sparks, you've done the government a great service. If we catch him, you'll get your reward money.'

Themba jogged to Umtata, keeping up a steady, kilometre-devouring pace. When he arrived, the town was fast asleep. He went straight to Paul's house, watching from across the road before making a move. He slipped across the street and stopped to check again. He picked the garage lock. Paul's Datsun pick-up was inside. He searched through the garage, finding what he was looking for. On the back of the pick-up he loaded a folding ladder, spanners, screwdrivers, hose-pipe and a large jerrycan, covering them all with a tarpaulin.

Opening the front door was even easier. Themba went directly to Paul's study. He found the car keys on the desk. In the pantry he packed all the tinned goods, biscuits and dried fruit he could find into cardboard boxes. He carried the boxes as well as blankets and pillows out to the garage, hiding them under the tarpaulin.

Starting the engine, he was careful not to rev loudly. He reversed out, locked the garage doors and drove to the centre of town. He filled the tank and the jerrycan at a petrol station and parked the pick-up in front of the hotel. The vehicle was safe and inconspicuous amongst the other cars.

Keeping to the shadows, Themba walked to the police station. A blue light was shining outside the building and he could see occupants through the lighted window. He slipped around to the rear and found the cell block facing on to the back street. Alongside the pavement was a low diamond-mesh fence. He vaulted the fence and slunk across the lawn. A shrub border was planted against the wall of the cell block. Hiding behind the shrubs he counted the windows high up in the wall.

Straining his ears he could vaguely hear the night sounds of prisoners in jail. He knew them only too well. A cough, someone talking in his sleep and intermittent snoring. He longed to call out to make sure Paul and Sabata were inside, but he could not risk alerting a guard. Using a dry branch he carefully obliterated his footmarks.

There was nothing more he could do that night. He returned to Paul's home, let himself in and had a good night's sleep in the guest room.

Themba rose at sunrise. In the bathroom cabinet he found a roll of cotton wool. Using Nugget shoe polish and a solution of hot water, he dyed the cotton wool a brownish-black. Using glue, Themba fashioned a moustache and beard. With dark glasses, Paul's old fishing hat and a greatcoat over his jacket, his disguise was complete. He roared with laughter when he saw his face in the mirror.

He packed changes of clothing into a suitcase for Paul and Sabata. Tidying the house and wiping down the surfaces he left no trace of his visit. The town was waking up as he reached the hotel. Themba locked the suitcase into the cab.

Near the police station he developed a deliberate limp, shuffling around to the cells at the back. To his delight family and friends were packed along the fence shouting messages to prisoners inside. The replies filtered through the barred windows.

He turned to a woman. 'Don't the police mind?'

'They allow us an hour a day only. At eight o'clock a guard chases us away.'

Themba looked at his watch, he had fifteen minutes. Making his voice gruff he shouted in Xhosa. 'Where are you, great Chief of Thembuland?' The noise died down out of respect for their leader. Themba was afraid he had given the game away, but was overjoyed when he recognised Sabata's voice.

'I'm in the middle cell.'

'Show me.' An object thrown up to the ceiling flashed past the window.

He tried his luck again. 'Where is our crippled white brother?'

Hushed conversation came from inside the cells. A shoe flashed past the window in the end cell. 'Be ready at sunset my king and my little white mentor.'

A policeman walked around the back of the building. 'Off with you. I want complete silence from now onwards.'

Themba limped away. Once around the corner he hurried to purchase two torch batteries and twenty metres of double electrical flex. In the park opposite the police station, well hidden by bushy shrubs, he split the flex, giving him four lengths of ten metres each. Unpicking the lining of his jacket, he removed a flattened block of Plastic 4 explosive and out of the jacket's hem he lifted two miniature detonators. Themba had left Lusaka prepared for any eventuality. He was ready.

467

Impatient, Themba kept an eye on the police station. Was his plan working? Two police vans arrived, then another two. A car with East London registration plates parked under a tree. Three tall, well-built men in plain clothes climbed out of the car. Were they security police? They certainly looked so, with their hard faces. Themba *had* to know. He limped across the road holding out his hand.

'Money for a loaf of bread, boss.'

'Bugger off.'

'Please, boss, please, I'm hungry.'

'Go and find work,' barked the man, looking at him disdainfully.

'Come on, Willem,' said one of the others in Afrikaans. 'Leave the old kaffir, let's get inside and find out about Memani.'

As they disappeared into the police station Themba shuffled off, smiling to himself. Now his grandfather must play his part.

The convoy assembled – six police vans and two cars packed with policemen. The fleet of vehicles roared off. Themba limped into the police station.

'What do you want, kaffir?'

'I want to visit my brother in the cells.'

'Come back tomorrow. I'm all alone this afternoon and can't leave the front desk.' The telephone rang stridently. 'I have to answer the bloody phone too, and do everything here.'

Themba was tempted to dispose of the policeman and go in through the front, but his training taught him to stick to a well-thought-out plan. He recalled Walter Sisulu's words: *Know your enemy, know your strength.* Now he knew the cells were unguarded and only one constable was on duty.

The afternoon dragged on and still the police convoy did not return. The sun was setting; Morris was playing his part to the full. It was time. Themba fetched the Datsun, parking it down the road from the cells. He threw the ladder over the fence. Behind the bushes he unfolded and propped it against the wall. He climbed up and looked through the window of the middle cell.

Themba gave a low whistle and whispered urgently, 'Paramount Chief Sabata. I'm Themba Memani, come to free you.'

Dalindyebo's anxious face looked up at him. 'Something's happening at Mqekezweni.'

'I know. Listen carefully. I want everyone to flatten themselves against the outer wall. Cover yourselves with mats and blankets.

468

I'm going to blow out the bars. Pass the message down to Paul's cell.'

Themba twisted the pliable explosive around the steel shafts. He attached two wires to the detonator, letting the ends fall to the ground. He pushed the detonator into the Plastic 4. The procedure was repeated at the end cell. Backed up against the outer wall half-way between the two windows, he used the greatcoat to protect himself from the blast. Holding a torch battery in each hand, he pushed a wire from each window under a battery. Holding the second wires between his thumbs and forefingers he pushed the ends on top of the batteries.

Twin flashes of light rent the deepening twilight as the Plastic 4 exploded. Debris showered down on Themba. He threw off the greatcoat and scrambled up the ladder. Inside the cell a thick pall of dust hung in the air. Themba peered in at the prisoners' shocked faces.

'Lift Sabata on to your shoulders.' He grabbed Sabata's hand, pulled him through and lowered him gently to the ground. 'This is your chance to escape,' he shouted down. 'Help each other up.' A mass break-out would create a diversion. Themba grabbed the ladder and rushed to Paul's cell. He lifted Paul out and helped him down the ladder. Holding Sabata's and Paul's arms, he hurried them to the pick-up. There would be time for formal greetings later. He made them lie in the back and covered them with the tarpaulin. The policeman from the charge office rushed around the corner. Themba jumped in, fired the engine and took off with the back wheels spinning. He heard the popping sounds of gunfire. A bullet tore into the roof of the pick-up, flew over his head and lodged in the door pillar. They turned the corner.

He drove sedately through Umtata, not wanting to draw attention to himself. The convoy of police vehicles passed him, heading back to the police station. Once out of town he accelerated to full speed, heading south down the N1, then turned off on to a dirt road towards the sea. Only then did he stop. He ripped off his false beard and moustache, and pulled away the tarpaulin. The friends embraced warmly. He opened the suitcase. They stripped off their prison garb and changed into the clothes.

'Where are we headed?' Paul asked.

Themba smiled expansively. 'esiKhaleni.'

Paul was flabbergasted. 'Why Hole-in-the-Wall? Surely we should head north for the Lesotho border?'

'The first thing the police will do is radio the surrounding towns to set up road-blocks and patrol all roads to Lesotho. Transkei's borders will be sealed off with no chance of escape.'

'So you propose we head in the opposite direction?'

'Exactly.' Themba smiled. 'Who will ever think of looking for us in our isolated glen at esiKhaleni?'

Sabata was impressed. 'Good thinking, Themba. Let's get going.'

All three crowded into the cab and they drove towards the sea. They had the road to themselves, even the kraals they passed were in darkness.

In the secluded glen they parked the pick-up deep under the trees, covering it with the tarpaulin and branches. They headed up the grassy slope, holing up in a thicket with a good view of the coast.

Munching on tinned bullybeef they talked for hours, catching up on each other's news. They were exhilarated from the successful escape and chatted the night away.

'Only two tins of meat. We must ration ourselves.' Themba packed the rest away. 'I'll take the first watch. We rotate every three hours.'

The police concentrated on the area between Umtata and the Lesotho border, setting up road-blocks and combing the area. They called in reinforcements but no sign of the fugitives was found. SADF helicopters scoured the mountains and valleys to no avail. After two days of fruitless searching the Umtata station commander decided they had never left the town. House-to-house searches proved his theory wrong. Once a helicopter made a pass all the way up the coast, but they were well hidden in the thicket and the Datsun was invisible from the air. Except for occasional cattle, they had esiKhaleni to themselves.

'We must leave tonight. It's been four days and the police have probably called off the search. They usually allow three days.' Themba looked at his friends. 'I assume you are both coming with me?'

Paul nodded. 'There's nothing left for me in South Africa until there's a change of government.'

Sabata was undecided. 'My people need me. I must stay to lead them against Matanzima.'

'You can do no good if you're in jail.' Themba was adamant. 'Matanzima will hound you and keep you locked up on trumped-up charges. Come with us to Lusaka. Fight the system in exile. You'll achieve more being free.'

'I suppose you're right, but I would like to see my family first.'

Themba shook his head. 'I guarantee Mqekezweni is being watched day and night. We can't take that risk.'

Staying on the gravel roads east of Umtata they crossed into Natal at an unmanned border post near Bizana. This route enabled them to approach Lesotho from the east. With the extra petrol in the jerrycan there was no need to stop at any town. They skirted Himeville on the way to the Sani Pass border post.

Sabata and Paul climbed out a kilometre from the border and crossed on foot. When the border post opened the next morning, Themba was first in the queue. The South African officials were on the look-out for the fugitives. Themba watched them search through their lists, and smiled to himself, knowing his false passport would not be listed on their records. Eventually they stamped his papers and he was through.

In Maseru Chris Hani welcomed them at the ANC office. He arranged accommodation for them in the Holiday Inn. Paul was so impressed with having a good bath and excellent food, he donated his trusty Datsun to the ANC. Temporary passports were issued to Sabata and Paul. Three days later they landed in Lusaka.

Themba's daring escapade fired the people's imagination. The newspapers gave the story saturation coverage.

Oliver Tambo arranged a special cocktail party for Sabata, Themba and Paul. Foreign dignitaries and ambassadorial staff all attended. Sabata Dalindyebo, the spiritual head of the Xhosa nation, was welcomed to Zambia. Themba was honoured for his bravery. Paul was congratulated on joining the ANC in exile.

Paramount Chief Sabata joined the ANC staff, heading a new Transkei desk to promote the DDP in exile, working towards toppling the illegitimate government of Kaiser Matanzima.

Paul Curry was appointed headmaster of the new Solomon Mahlangu Freedom College at Mazimbu in Tanzania.

20

Simon Roux opened his secret post box at Simondium. He slipped the letter into his pocket and took it out in the privacy of his car. It was not a letter from Nomisile, but his own letter returned to him. Across the face of the envelope was written: DECEASED – RETURN TO SENDER. With a shaking hand he turned the letter over. His address on the back flap had been circled in red.

Nomisile dead? Impossible! She would have let him know if she was ill. An accident? His mind whirled, thinking of all the possibilities, but each time returning to the dreaded word: deceased.

How can I find out? Go there yourself, he decided. He drove home and walked straight to the bedroom. He threw a few changes of clothing into a suitcase. As he did so he heard the squeaking of Helena's wheelchair.

'Why are you packing, darling?' Helena looked concerned.

'I'm going to the Transkei to sort out next season's contract labour.'

'Why can't the manager go?'

'This time I'm going myself.' He spoke with finality.

He stopped off at the bank to draw cash and set off. He reached Umtata on the second evening and booked into the Royal Hotel.

After dinner he sat alone in the private bar sipping a brandy. He wondered how he was going to find out about Nomisile. He didn't want to arouse suspicions by inquiring at the police station. Of course, the barman! 'Wally, can I buy you a drink?'

'Sure thing.' He poured himself a double whisky and knocked it back in one gulp. 'Thank you, Mr Roux.'

'Another one?'

'I wouldn't say no.'

Simon tossed a ten-rand bill on the counter. 'Help yourself, Wally.'

After each had flattened two more doubles, he treated Simon like a long-lost friend.

'Wally, I had a very faithful Xhosa servant who died a month or so ago. I'd like to trace the family to convey my condolences.'

'Where did this servant live, Mr Roux?'

'A place called Mqekezweni.'

'I know the place. It's the royal kraal of the Thembu people.'

Simon was relieved. 'That's the place.'

'It's not too far out of town, about half an hour's drive.' Wally told Simon how to travel. 'Near Mqekezweni is a trading store run by one of my buddies. John Sparks knows everyone for miles around. He's the postmaster, storekeeper, doctor, trader, bank manager – all rolled into one.'

'Thanks, Wally, I'll see him tomorrow morning.' Simon placed another bill on the counter. 'For your night-cap.'

'By the way, Mr Roux, Sparks is a very lonely fellow. He craves a white face, 'cause all he sees every day are kaffirs. Have a few drinks with John and he'll help you.'

'I have a couple of bottles of KWV ten-year-old brandy in the car. I'm sure he'll like that.'

Wally's eyes grew wide. 'He'd sell his mother for a bottle of KWV.'

Simon thought he had taken the wrong turning, but then a village of round white houses showed over the next hill. To one side stood a red brick building with a signboard over the door: MQEKEZWENI TRADING STORE.

A florid man stood behind the counter. He watched Simon suspiciously as he walked in. White strangers were rare at Mqekezweni. 'Can I help you, Mister?'

His eyes lit up when Simon placed the bottle of brandy on the counter. 'A friend of yours, Wally the barman from the Royal, suggested I have a drink with you.'

'What a pleasure.' Sparks shooed all the black people out of the shop and locked the front door. 'They have nothing to do and all day to do it in.' He saw Simon's quizzical expression. 'It's okay. They'll wait on the front porch until I'm ready. The next shop is thirty kilometres away.'

474

He held out his hand. 'Any buddy of Wally's is a friend of mine. I'm John Sparks.'

'Pleased to meet you, I'm Simon Roux from Paarl.'

Sparks fetched two fly-spattered glasses from the back room and placed them on the counter. Simon cracked the seal on the bottle and poured a shot in each glass. Sparks took a sip, tasting the quality on his tongue, then downed the brandy in one mouthful. 'Liquid gold. I've never tasted such smooth brandy.'

'Help yourself,' invited Simon, leaving his glass untouched.

Filling the glass to the brim, Sparks gulped it down noisily. He raised an eyebrow at Simon, who nodded. Sparks needed no second invitation and refilled the glass.

'What are you doing in this neck of the woods, Mr Roux? You don't look like a tourist.'

'I'm here to find out about an old servant of mine who died recently.'

'What was her name?'

'She was Nomisile Memani.'

Sparks looked at Simon slowly. 'I knew Nomisile. She was a good customer of mine. Bought buttons, cotton and material.'

'When did she die?'

John Sparks needed another drink to jog his memory. This time he didn't ask permission. He counted on his fingers. 'She died in February.'

'How did she die?'

'Cancer, stomach cancer. They say she had a tumour as big as a rugby ball in her guts.'

Simon was saddened. 'Where is she buried?'

Sparks pointed below the village. He thought it suspicious for a white man to be concerned enough with a black woman to come all the way from Paarl to find out about her death. He put out a feeler. 'Her son was here at the funeral. The police are after him. He's an ANC terrorist.' He smiled with satisfaction as he saw Simon start. He had touched a nerve.

'Did you know Themba?' asked Simon.

'Sure, he grew up before me. He was a good youngster until he became involved in politics.'

Simon reflected jealously on the irony of the situation. As Themba's father he had enjoyed nothing of his son's boyhood. Yet this man had seen every stage of his son's development.

'What was Themba like?'

Sparks was starting to slur his words. 'Mr Roux, when you see black people all day, every day, one kaffir looks much the same as the next.'

Simon's immediate reaction was to lean over the counter and grab the man, but he held himself in check. 'Did Nomisile have family here?'

'Her father and mother are still alive. Morris and Nosakani Memani live about three kilometres from here. Do you want to see them?' Simon nodded. Sparks gave Simon directions to Qunu.

'Thank you, Mr Sparks. I must get going.'

'What about the rest of the bottle?'

'You keep it.'

As soon as Simon drove away Sparks walked to the telephone. He cranked the handle. The operator in Umtata answered. 'Put me through to the police station.' The station commander came on the line. 'Lieutenant, are you still looking for Themba Memani?'

He sat bolt upright. 'Yes, of course. Is he back at Mqekezweni?'

'No, but something strange has just happened. A Mr Roux from Paarl was here wanting to know about him and his deceased mother.'

'What make of car is he driving?'

'A brand new Mercedes-Benz. Light green with a CJ registration.'

'Thank you, Sparks. We'll look out for him when he comes back to town.'

Simon stopped at the small village of Qunu. Curious black children surrounded his car, looking in awe at the tall white man. Their faces creased into smiles when he took the change out of his pocket and handed it to them. 'Where can I find Morris Memani?'

'*Andiyazi*,' they shrugged. The word meant, I don't know.

A woman came forward who could speak English. 'Can I help you?'

He repeated his request. She pointed to one of the huts. Simon knocked on the door. An old man came out, followed by an old woman. From the combination of their features Simon recognised definite traces of Nomisile's countenance. He felt an affinity with them, some invisible hand through Nomisile which bound them inextricably together.

'Hullo, are you Nomisile's parents?'

They stared at him, not understanding a word. The woman who spoke English interpreted.

A smile creased Morris's face. '*Yebo*. I am her father.'

Simon smiled back. 'I heard Nomisile died. I wanted to find out about her death and visit her grave.'

The old man looked puzzled. 'Are you from the government or police?'

Shaking his head vigorously, Simon explained. 'I was a good friend of your daughter when she lived in Paarl.' He wanted to shout aloud that he loved Nomisile and Themba was his son, but he had promised her and his word was his bond.

Morris invited Simon inside. He sat on the floor, looking around the hut which was devoid of furniture. Who was he to think he was better because he lived a sophisticated lifestyle? These simple people were the salt of the earth, with customs and traditions going back centuries. Simon sat enthralled, listening to Morris's melodious voice talking to the translator. If only he could understand Xhosa. Simon thought about the anomaly. Afrikaners and Englishmen expected blacks to learn their languages, but only a few were prepared to reciprocate.

For over an hour Morris talked, with Nosakani adding details to complete the picture. Simon felt the love of two parents devoted to their daughter. He would have been proud to have welcomed them as his in-laws. Why had he not had the courage of his convictions all those years ago? He should have married Nomisile and led a complete life of joy and fulfilment.

Her parents wept when Morris described her illness. Simon cried too. She had suffered without him. His place should have been with her. Now she was dead and it was too late. He could not turn back the clock of life. He had made his choice, now he must reap what he had sown.

'Do you want to hear about Themba?'

'Please! I want to know all about him.'

Simon followed his son's life from birth to manhood. There had been regular letters over the years, but these had been like telegrams, sketchy details in the life of the boy. Morris put muscle, skin and hair on the skeleton. Simon pictured Themba's moments of triumph – over the snake, at school, as an initiate into manhood, at university, as an elder and his role in the ANC. There was a lump in his throat when Morris told him of how Themba had been present at Nomisile's death, but because of the political situation he could not attend her funeral.

'Will you eat lunch with us?' Nosakani turned to Simon.

'Of course, I would be privileged.'

Nosakani served crumbly mealie-meal in an enamel bowl. In the Transkei all ate with their fingers out of the same dish. After a moment of hesitancy he threw off his inhibitions and joined in the meal. Simon was pleased he had come, at last able to picture how Nomisile had lived her life.

'Now we go to Nomisile's grave.' Out of habit Morris set off on a well-worn sandy path cut into the grass by generations of footsteps.

'You are welcome to travel in my car.'

Filled with awe Morris clambered into the front seat when Simon held open the door for him. He touched the controls with his finger, amazement in his eyes. Simon held open the back door, urging Nosakani and the translator to climb in.

They drove to Mqekezweni and stopped at the edge of the village. Morris pointed. 'Nomisile's hut, Themba's house. I have fixed the roofs and painted the walls.' He led them to the open veld and sat cross-legged next to a mound of earth. Simon followed suit.

He looked at the grave. Already grass was spreading over it. The grave was bare. No flowers, no headstone, no markers, nothing to say it was the last resting place of Nomisile. Simon closed his eyes. He placed one hand on the mound, the other over his heart. He felt Nomisile's presence, saw her smiling face with her expressive eyes looking at him with love.

Grief welled up inside him as the finality of her death struck him. His body shook with sobs and tears streamed down his face. When Simon finally made his peace he opened his eyes. Morris and Nosakani stood on either side of him, each of their hands resting on his shoulders.

They knew instinctively there had been more than friendship between their daughter and this man, a deep and lasting bond of love. They had often seen the sadness in Nomisile's eyes and knew how she had rejected suitors. Now they knew why.

Themba's father had remained a mystery. Nomisile had never spoken, not even to her parents. Now they understood that also.

Simon placed his hands over theirs. He, Morris and Nosakani

turned towards each other, intuitively embracing. They looked at each other's grief-torn faces and cried unashamedly. Each one understood the full implication of their actions. Black and white were united as one, by a common love. They broke apart and walked towards the car. Simon gave one last, longing stare at Nomisile's grave.

On the spur of the moment he turned to Morris. 'I want to step inside Nomisile's house.'

Morris understood and led him to the hut. The door was unlocked. There was no burglary in this little village, each person respected the other's possessions. Inside the air was cool with a lingering smell of wood ashes. Against one wall her sewing machines were stacked. Simon opened one of the machine's little drawers. He recognised the post office savings book he had opened for her many years before in Paarl.

Flicking through the pages crammed with deposits and withdrawals, he remembered the incidents. Money for cattle, for the house in the township, for Themba's education, for university fees. The balance was a mere ten rand. He slipped it into his pocket, thinking he would place it in his diary at his private spot against Paarl Mountain.

Simon walked to a steel trunk and opened the lid. Inside were Nomisile's few clothes. He smelt her aroma again, that wonderful bouquet unique to herself. His heart contracted in longing, remembering their intimate times together. Simon picked up a beautifully embroidered shawl, with 'Nomisile' produced in intricate needlework stitches. He looked at her parents. 'May I take the shawl, as a reminder?'

'*Yebo.*' Nosakani smiled, seeing the sentimental value Simon placed on the garment.

Simon stood a long time gazing at the three-legged pots standing at the hearth. He visualised how Nomisile had cooked food and heated water every day. Her presence was strong in the hut. Tearing his gaze away he strode into the sunlight. He entered Themba's hut. Except for two rolled-up reed mats and a few blankets, the house was bare. He tried to obtain the same feeling of his son's existence, but it eluded him.

He said farewell to Morris and Nosakani warmly. 'Thank you. I am pleased I came.'

'You can come any time you like.'

* * *

Simon noticed the police van at the side of the road, but paid no attention until a constable flagged him down. 'You must follow us to the police station.'

'Why?'

'The station commander wants to question you. He would like to know what connection you have to Themba Memani.'

How did they know he was connected to Themba? Who knew he had been visiting Nomisile's parents? Wally at the hotel? No, he had told him he was going to Mqekezweni, but he had not mentioned names to Wally. Then it struck him – John Sparks. He had asked the storekeeper about Nomisile and had discussed Themba. Damn man, he was a police informer.

The day had upset Simon enough without him also having to explain his actions to the police. 'And if I refuse to see the station commander?'

'We'll have to arrest you and take you to the station anyway.'

His patience snapped. 'You police are so used to doing what you like, when you like and how you like that you think you can dictate to everyone.' He remembered Nomisile's fear of the police and he sympathised. 'You can only arrest me if I've committed a crime.'

'We can arrest you on suspicion of a crime. Mister, either you come quietly or else we use force.'

Simon felt the hopelessness of the situation. He was a white man in a white society. Imagine if he were black. He would simply have been bundled into the back of the van. No wonder the black man hated the police with passion. 'Lead the way. I'll follow you.'

The constable shook his head. 'My colleague will drive with you.'

All the way to town Simon seethed with anger. He strode into the police station. 'Are you the station commander?'

'I am.' He looked surprised. 'Mr Simon Roux?'

Simon nodded vigorously. 'I've had a very emotional day and I want to know why you need to question me?'

'Themba Memani is on our black list. We believe you went to Mqekezweni to find out about him and his mother?'

'So what? Nomisile was a good friend of mine from the time she worked for me in Paarl. I helped put her son through school and university.'

'Won't you please sit down, Mr Roux?'

'I don't intend staying that long. Unless you charge me, you can't hold me.'

'We can hold you for ninety days under the General Law Amendment Act on suspicion of being involved in political activities.'

'Political activities? The only politics I've been involved in are as a National Party member of parliament for Paarl. Have you run a check on me?' The policeman shook his head. 'I intend to spend the night at the Royal. I suggest you check with the security police and then report back to me.' Before he could answer, Simon stormed out.

Simon went straight to his room to avoid the talkative Wally. An hour later the telephone rang.

'Mr Roux, this is the station commander. I would like to apologise for any inconvenience we may have caused you. You're free to leave.'

Simon was tired when he walked into the manor house. He needed a drink.

'Darling, is that you?' Helena called excitedly.

'*Ja.*'

Helena rolled into the entrance hall. 'You've missed all the excitement! I have wonderful news, darling. We're grandparents!'

'Has Lesley had her baby?'

'A healthy girl – she's called Blaise.'

'Let's go and see them.' Simon's drink was forgotten. 'I can't wait to see Pierre's face.'

Themba was summoned to a meeting with the ANC president at Lusaka headquarters. Oliver Tambo smiled broadly. 'I have two pieces of exciting news for you today, Themba. The first is that Nelson Mandela, Walter Sisulu and three other Rivonia trialists have been transferred from Robben Island to the mainland. They are in Pollsmoor prison, near Cape Town.'

'Do you think this move is a prelude to their release by the Botha government?'

'I hope so for all our sakes.' Tambo's face creased with concern.

'The second item concerns you. We are moving Chris Hani back to Lusaka from Maseru. We are becoming increasingly worried about his safety. Our latest intelligence is that the SADF is out to eliminate him. Maseru is so close to the Lesotho border with South Africa, they could easily flit in, kill Chris and be out again before anyone knew it. So we are recalling him. He has been appointed Army Political Commissioner.

'He will also fill the post of Deputy Commander of Umkhonto we Sizwe. One of his tasks will be to visit ANC camps all over Africa to catalogue complaints on acts of brutality.' Tambo's face was stern. 'We cannot allow cruelty in our ranks. Our fight is against apartheid, we should not commit inhuman acts among ourselves.

'That is where you fit in, Themba. We would like you to take over from Chris Hani as ANC Chief Representative for Lesotho.'

'I'm flattered to be placed in charge of a mission.' Themba was excited at the first big test of his administrative ability. 'When do you want me to start?'

'As soon as possible. Chris will stay on for a week or so to show you the ropes, then he must travel to Lusaka. His family will follow later.'

'What do you expect of me?'

'Lesotho is an important link in the total freedom struggle. They are our allies. They house over eleven thousand refugees from South Africa. Lesotho is a springboard for many raids into South Africa and a vital transit point.'

Themba nodded, thinking of the time he had made use of the Lesotho connection.

'You'll gain valuable practical experience there. It will stand you in good stead for your future role in the ANC. You'll be at the forefront of the freedom struggle.'

'Thank you for your confidence in me, I won't disappoint you.'

'I know you won't, Themba. Good luck.'

Chris Hani met Themba at Maseru airport. They drove into Maseru and headed for Moscow House, a large, sprawling dwelling in the suburbs which was the ANC headquarters in Lesotho. The staff filed into the general office to meet their new boss.

'Themba, this is your number two, Assistant-Chief Representative Zola Nqini.' The two men took an immediate liking to each other. 'Themba, meet your secretary, Phyllis Naidoo. She's very efficient, she always smiles.' Themba noted her strength from her firm handshake. He met the clerks and administrative personnel.

Themba looked at them warmly. 'We will be working closely together. I want you to know that I will always be available when you need me. I have a hard act to follow in Chris Hani. I'm not yet in the same league, but I'll try my best.'

Themba unpacked his suitcases in the bedroom at the end of the passage. It was convenient to have his accommodation so close to the office. He joined Hani.

'I would like you to have supper at my home tonight so I can introduce you to my family.'

'Thank you, that would be nice. Tambo told me your wife will join you later in Zambia.'

Hani smiled. 'Limpho was born and bred in Lesotho. She'll find it hard to settle down in Lusaka. The kids must finish the school year before she will consider moving.'

During the afternoon they worked through all the structures of command. Hani updated Themba on outstanding issues. Moscow House was a hive of activity with a continuous stream of visitors. Its functions included interviewing new arrivals, organising accommodation in the ANC quarters, issuing new identity documents and booking flights in and out of Lesotho for MK cadres.

After the office closed for the day, Hani took Themba on a guided tour of the ANC houses in Maseru. As a safety precaution they were scattered throughout the city. To identify them for administrative purposes each house was differently named — Cuba House, Trinity House, Leningrad House, Berlin House, Warsaw House and Budapest House. Most were sparsely furnished. All rooms, except the kitchens and bathrooms, were used as dormitories. This allowed maximum accommodation for the floating population of refugees and cadres passing through Lesotho.

They drove to Hani's home in the suburb of Florida. It was an unpretentious house, but newly painted and spotless, with a neat garden. Themba met Limpho's and Hani's three daughters, nine-year-old Neo, three-year-old Nomakhwezi and the baby, Lindiwe. He was impressed with the friendly atmosphere and the love which pervaded the household.

Chris was a fun-loving, committed family man. Themba thought of the legend called Chris Hani. He had often heard MK cadres speak of him with awe, as a tough MK commander in the field of battle. The South African government branded him Public Enemy

No. 1 in their fight against communism. They don't know the real Chris Hani, thought Themba.

He turned to Hani. 'When one gets to know you, one realises you are a deep, caring person.'

'Sure I care.' Chris became serious. 'I care about so many things. Will I see a truly representative government in place in South Africa during my lifetime?' He shrugged sadly. 'I care about all our brave MK comrades killed in the line of duty. I care about the widows and fatherless children left behind.' He kept quiet for a minute, thinking, then quoted Thomas Gray:

> 'For them no more the blazing hearth shall burn,
> Or busy housewife ply her evening care;
> No children run to lisp their sire's return,
> Or climb his knees the envied kiss to share.'

Themba looked at him in surprise; the tough commander spouting poetry! 'I recognise those words. They are from "Elegy written in a Country Churchyard", are they not?'

Hani nodded. 'I love poetry. Percy Shelley and John Keats are my favourites, but my preferred reading will always be Shakespeare.'

Two days later a special ops team arrived straight from the Soviet Union. Their instructions were to report directly to Hani. Something important was in the air.

Themba looked up in surprise as three men filed into the office. He knew one of the men – they had served together on the Sasol raid, when Umkhonto we Sizwe had blown up six huge petrol storage tanks at the Sasol oil refinery. 'Chico, what are you doing here?' He embraced his comrade.

Chico smiled broadly. 'We're on the ultimate mission against the apartheid regime.'

'Bigger than Sasol?'

'Much bigger,' laughed Chico.

The other two members of the team were both strangers to Themba. Clifford Brown was a tough coloured man originally from Cape Town. The other, a powerful black man with a craggy face, was Tsepo Matroos.

Hani closed and locked the office door. Once everyone was seated he turned to the new arrivals. 'Things have changed since

484

the mission was conceived. I'm going back to Lusaka. Themba is the new Chief Representative. He'll be your liaison for the mission from now onwards. Chico, will you bring us all up to date, please.'

'We've spent the last six months at Odessa in the Ukraine with the Russian Navy's Underwater Special Unit. They trained us in all aspects of underwater attack. We learnt to operate diving bells, spent time in compression chambers, mastered underwater attack procedures on land and sea targets. Wetsuits and frogman outfits became second nature to us. We trained with oxygen cylinders and all types of explosives.'

'Underwater training?' Themba frowned. 'How will that help the freedom struggle?'

Chico sat forward. 'Our target is Koeberg, the nuclear power station being built by the Electricity Supply Commission at Melkbosstrand, north of Cape Town.'

'Koeberg?' Themba was astounded at the ambitious plan. 'I know that area. I landed near there when I escaped from Robben Island five years ago.'

'If our Sasol mission rattled the South African government, then the Koeberg raid will give them the cold shivers.' Chico smiled expansively.

'But why a nuclear power station?' Themba frowned. 'Won't you release enough radiation to kill millions of people in the Western Cape?'

'That's just the point.' Hani stabbed his finger in the air. 'It is ANC policy to limit the death of innocent citizens in guerrilla attacks. Koeberg must be destroyed before switch-on. The reactors are due to be loaded in mid-January 1983. Our raid is planned for December 1982.'

'Which surveillance team is doing the reconnaissance? Security will be tight at Koeberg.'

'It's an inside job.' Hani looked at Themba. 'MK has infiltrated one or two men into the building teams, but our main sources are an eminent nuclear professor and a French technician working for the contractor Fremetone, which is in charge of the nuclear installation.'

'What's the plan?'

'Blowing away concrete will achieve nothing, it's replaceable. Our aim is to destroy the intricate inner workings. There are kilometres of piping and the reactor is solid iron-cast from a

485

French steel foundry. They work to tolerances of hundredths of a millimetre. If we can explode these out of alignment, they'll have to be scrapped. The whole casting procedure must then start from scratch, which will cause a delay in the power station's turn-on for at least a year. The French will show us where to place our bombs.'

'Why would the French help?'

'There's tremendous anti-South African government sentiment in France. As you know, the trade unions are dominated by the Communist Party.'

'Who's our contact?'

Hani turned to Themba. 'A French female technician sympathetic to our cause. She contacts me here at Moscow House by telephone. She has smuggled out working plans to me.'

'How will I know who she is?'

'Her code name is Odile. I spoke to her last week and told her about my transfer. All future dealings will be with you.'

'Why don't you continue to control the mission from Lusaka?'

'Two reasons.' Hani sat back in his chair. 'First, I'll be on the move visiting ANC camps and far from telephones, deep in the bush. I wouldn't be available to make quick decisions.' Themba saw the soundness in the reasoning. 'Secondly, the political structure for the ANC in the Cape is operated from Lesotho. Our whole chain of command is in place. The Koeberg mission, needing Cape back-up, is better off if it's controlled from Maseru.'

Themba was impressed. 'May we see the plans?'

Unlocking the safe, Hani removed a large manila envelope. 'There are duplicate sets of plans, one copy for the office and one for the special-ops team.' Chris folded out the drawings and the five men pored over them. The first was a basic site plan showing the plant in relation to the surrounding area.

The main features were the buildings and the twin breakwaters pointing out to sea, the northern one long and straight, the southern breakwater curved inward forming a natural harbour with a narrow entrance.

Against the land was a built-up quay containing the sea-water pump-house to be used for pumping vast quantities of sea water into the condensers to cool the high-pressure turbines. A short distance inland was the main conglomerate of buildings with the twin-domed reactor buildings, twin fuel buildings, the nuclear auxiliary building and the huge turbine hall. The two-storey administration block was a hundred metres further inland.

The second plan showed the security systems in operation. A security fence started at the tip of the northern breakwater, continued inland to encircle the buildings and ended at the tip of the southern breakwater in a huge U. All the latest technology was incorporated outside the security fence – electric fences, heat sensor alarms, rolled barbed wire and halogen lights facing outwards at regular intervals.

Themba picked up the glaring flaw in an instant, stabbing his finger on the harbour mouth. 'There's no security between the ends of the breakwaters. One can slip in and out without detection.'

Chico smiled. 'That's why we trained in underwater combat procedures. We'll attack from the sea.'

His mind full of questions, Themba waited while Chris placed the third plan on the table. It was a detailed layout of the heart of the power station. Each domed reactor building was fifty-six metres high, with double reinforced 1.8 metre concrete walls and a huge nuclear reactor in the middle.

Enriched uranium dioxide pellets would be loaded into fuel rods in the reactor at switch-on. This would create nuclear fission when exposed to water, producing controlled steam which in turn would spin the huge turbines, generating electric current to augment ESCOM's electricity grid in the Western Cape.

On the highest level of the nuclear auxiliary building was the nerve centre of the whole plant, the twin control rooms, one for each reactor.

'Looks very complicated to me.' Themba studied the chart. 'How will you know where to place your explosives? The blast sites aren't marked.'

'Odile and her friends will be there to meet the MK party and show them the bomb sites.' Hani nodded to Chico. 'We must set the time and date so she can complete her planning.'

They reached consensus. As with Sasol, the raid would be timed at the end of a weekend or holiday period.

Themba pointed to a wall calendar and placed his finger on 16 December.

'Heroes' Day for us and Day of the Vow for the whites. The big Afrikaner celebration of their victory in 1838 when they defeated

487

Chief Dingane and killed three thousand Zulus. We can avenge those deaths if we attack that night.'

Chico nodded. 'The construction teams at Koeberg will be off site because of the public holiday. Even supporting services such as fire fighters, army, navy and air force will be laid-back and slack.'

Themba again pulled out the second plan of the security layout. 'I accept that there's no security at the harbour entrance, but how do you get in without looking suspicious?'

With a mischievous grin Chico explained. 'The Russian fishing fleet operates off the West Coast. They take us as far as possible, then we slip in on inflatable rubber ducks.'

Themba shook his head. 'They're driven by outboard engines. From what I remember, boat outboards make an awful noise. You'll alert Koeberg security.'

'Not these little beauties.' Clifford sat forward excitedly. 'These are one-man rubber ducks driven by battery-powered electric motors. No sound. They're so low in the water, not even radar will pick them up.'

Themba was flabbergasted. 'Where did you get them?'

'Russian Navy special issue.' Chico laughed. 'Six complete units were crated and sent to Angola by the Russian Navy. They're in a Luanda harbour warehouse at present.'

'Very good, but certain aspects are still not clear to me.' Themba frowned. 'I understand about the rubber ducks and the fishing trawler, but how do you travel from Luanda to Cape Town with all the equipment?'

'All arrangements are under control.' Hani entered the discussion. 'The special-ops team is leaving for Luanda tomorrow. Once there, they will practise for a few weeks in African waters. We have friends in the merchant fleets of the communist countries. They will travel by ship from Luanda to Dassen Island, forty-five kilometres north of Melkbosstrand. After dark a Russian fishing trawler will pick them up and transport them two kilometres off Koeberg. They'll go in with the inflatables, set their charges and get the hell out back to the trawler.'

'Once the charges blow, won't the authorities intercept the fishing boat?'

'The fishing trawler will head for international waters when the men are back on board. Once they reach twelve nautical miles from the coast they're out of South African territorial waters.

The authorities can do nothing without creating an international incident.'

'Everything sounds feasible.' Themba looked at the men. 'Why are there six rubber ducks at Luanda, when there are only three cadres?'

'Spares. Each one of us has a back-up in case something goes wrong with our original. The rubber ducks can be rolled up into small packages and can be pumped up with a car wheel-pump. The batteries are charged with a 12-volt converter from normal electricity.'

'If the sea is rough won't you get swamped?'

Chico laughed out load. 'Themba, as usual you think of everything. No,' he shook his head, 'the inflatables are very buoyant and we have hand holds to grasp and safety belts to hold us in. We're dressed in wetsuits and breathe with oxygen tanks. Waves can wash over us, but we still move forward and we can still breathe. We learnt to operate them under all conditions in Odessa.'

'Okay, gentlemen, I'll keep you up to date once I've finalised everything with Odile.' Themba looked sad. 'Do you know how jealous I am? The Koeberg mission has captured my imagination. I'd give anything to be part of it.'

Chico smiled knowingly. 'I can imagine. But your days of MK missions are behind you, Themba. You're a big shot now.'

'Damn!' Themba cursed jokingly. 'Will you be staying at the ANC house at Vienna in Luanda?' Chico nodded. 'I know the telephone number. I'll contact you there.'

Chris Hani left for Lusaka the next week, leaving Limpho and the children behind in Maseru. 'Good luck, Themba. Keep an eye on my family for me.'

Themba worked long hours; there were many matters needing the attention of the Chief Representative. He started at least an hour before the office opened and continued late into the night.

The Lesotho government assisted the freedom struggle by turning a blind eye to the comings and goings of ANC members. As Chief Representative of the ANC, Themba met Dr Leabua Jonathan when he presented his credentials at the Prime Minister's official residence.

Themba managed to fit in his first long weekend to Lusaka to be with Hilda and Bambatha. The little boy was growing so quickly,

Themba felt guilty at missing so much of his development. Hilda looked radiant, her stomach starting to show with their newest baby. The three days sped past and before he knew it Themba was back in Maseru.

The Dakota bucked and rattled in the turbulence as the aeroplane skirted around a typical highveld summer storm of massive banks of cumulus cloud forming huge thunderheads.

'Sorry about that, mate,' apologised the pilot as he adjusted the flaps. 'We'll be landing at Waterkloof air force base in twenty minutes.'

Pierre gazed abstractly at the cars on the ground. They looked like Dinky toys as they scurried along the highway. He drifted into deep thought, reflecting on the past few days. As Cape head of military intelligence, he had been called in to a debriefing session at the castle on an Umkhonto we Sizwe cadre who had chosen to turn his back on the ANC.

The man, fresh from Maseru, had said: 'The ANC, from its Lesotho base, is planning an escalation of terrorist raids into South Africa, and especially the Western Cape, during the Christmas period.'

Pierre had merely nodded in acknowledgement until the MK man added a rider: 'This year you can expect a full-blown terrorist campaign. Themba Memani has planned everything down to the last detail.'

Pierre had shot forward at the mention of Memani's name.

'Is Memani in Lesotho?' he barked.

'He's the new Chief Representative in Chris Hani's place.'

'I want Memani,' breathed Pierre as he rose quickly and telephoned the Chief of the South African Defence Force. A meeting had been hastily arranged and now Pierre was winging his way to the appointment.

'You may go through now,' said the general's aide, opening the office door.

'Good morning, General Viljoen,' smiled Pierre, extending his hand to the sprightly army officer with the silvery-grey hair and the piercing blue eyes. He knew Constand Viljoen's reputation as a fearless leader who had distinguished himself in the Angolan campaign. Viljoen was small of stature but big of heart, a man

490

who had risen to the top post as chief of South Africa's combined forces – army, navy and air force.

'Welcome, Pierre!' He waved his guest to a chair, fully aware that he was a close confidant of Prime Minister PW Botha on military matters. 'What brings you to Pretoria?'

Pierre briefed Viljoen on the Christmas onslaught planned from Maseru.

Viljoen smiled astutely. 'You want a pre-emptive strike? Let the SADF hit them before they hit us?'

'Correct, General.'

'There must be more to bring you all the way to Pretoria?' Viljoen's eyes bored into Pierre. 'I'm aware of the bad blood that exists between yourself and Memani. Do I detect a personal motive, Pierre?'

Pierre blushed slightly, but held the general's gaze. 'I want Memani behind bars, where he belongs, more than anything else I've ever wanted.'

'Why? I thought you saved his life in Soweto?'

'I did.' Pierre coughed, his voice rasping. 'Then he betrayed my trust by escaping. I can't forgive him for that.'

'But you did arrest him at Crossroads.'

'Only for him to escape from Robben Island and join the ANC in exile.'

Viljoen returned to the main task. 'We have a crack army Anti-Insurgency Unit in Natal who could do the job.'

'Send them in, General. While they're doing their work, I'll hunt down Memani.'

'All right, but don't hamper operations.'

'I won't get in the way.'

The general nodded and asked his aide to telephone Durban.

The telephone rang at No. 1 Reconnaissance Commando. The call was routed through to Colonel Smit, the commanding officer.

'Colonel Smit, intelligence has reported increased activity in Lesotho since Themba Memani took over as ANC Chief Representative. The time to strike is at hand.'

'Just give the word, General. My men are well prepared. We can obliterate the ANC in Lesotho. Where's Hani?'

'Unfortunately he is in Zambia now, but his wife and children are still in Maseru.'

'What did you have in mind, General?'

'Speak to Pierre Roux from military intelligence.' Viljoen handed the telephone to Pierre.

'We must wipe out the ANC presence in Lesotho before Christmas.' Pierre glanced at the calendar. 'I thought we could hit them early in the morning of ninth December, Human Rights Day. Everyone will be sleeping peacefully with the prospect of a public holiday. The ANC always hit us when we're relaxed, let's reverse the roles for a change.'

'That gives me a week to prepare. I must move my troops and equipment into place, but it can be done,' answered Smit.

'We have a map of Maseru with all the targets marked. The ANC themselves have a number of houses and there are houses of known terrorists or people who harbour terrorists; forty houses in all. I'll send you a map per courier bag, Colonel.'

'What sort of resistance can we expect?'

'Very little.' Pierre answered. 'Most of the ANC people are unarmed. As for the Lesotho police, I suspect they'll clear out, claiming it to be a quarrel between the SADF and the ANC. Their army is a joke, really. They're basically only a paramilitary force; I believe they will stay well ensconced in their barracks.'

'We'll start mobilising straight away. Anything else?'

'Just do the job right, first time. We won't have a second chance. By the way, I will be accompanying you.'

'Excellent.' Smit replaced the receiver, a shiver of anticipation coursing through his body. Action at last!

Phyllis Naidoo knocked urgently on Themba's office door, her face excited. 'I have Odile on the line for you.' Phyllis didn't know about the Koeberg mission, but she had been with the ANC long enough to know when something important was pending.

Themba nodded. 'Close my door and put her through.' He opened the safe and removed the file on the Koeberg codes. 'Good morning, Odile.'

Odile spoke with a heavy French accent but her mastery of English was very good. 'Hullo, *monsieur*, you have news for me?'

Using the codes, Themba told her the date and time for the planned attack – Thursday, 16 December at twenty-three hundred hours, the method of entry and contingency plans for the getaway.

She replied with the previously determined anagrams, advising Themba she would meet the team at the slipway inside the southern breakwater.

The plan was coming together beautifully. 'Odile, we appreciate your actions.'

She gave a throaty chuckle. 'Thank you, *monsieur*. I am very much a committed communist. I like it if a fascist regime it is toppled. Me and my friends, we work in hardship here because we know we contravene United Nations sanctions against *Afrique du Sud*.'

'Thank you, Odile. We're very grateful to you and your friends. I would like to see the Prime Minister's face when we knock out his prestigious, sanctions-busting masterpiece.'

'So would I, monsieur.' From her naughty chuckle Themba pictured her as young and vivacious.

Themba called the Soviet Embassy in Lesotho. He confirmed the dates with the military attaché, who returned the call an hour later. A Yugoslavian-registered cargo ship, the *Spalato*, was leaving Luanda harbour on 12 December. Arrangements had been made to carry the special-ops team and their equipment. The ship would off-load them off Dassen Island three days later. A Russian fishing trawler would pick them up at nightfall on the night of the attack. Themba heaved a sigh of relief. The mission was firmly in place.

Phyllis routed a call through to the ANC house in Luanda. Chico, Clifford and Matroos were out. She asked them to call back.

Late the same afternoon Chico came on the line. 'Sorry we were out, but we practise with our toys each day. We have mastered the craft in all weather conditions.'

Themba recognised Chico's voice but he had to make sure. 'Tell me which tanks you blew at Sasol?'

Chico laughed merrily. 'Same old cautious Themba. No problem with that question. It was the second, fifth and sixth. Satisfied?'

Themba spoke in an urgent whisper. 'Chico, memorise these details.' He outlined the schedule. 'Odile will be waiting for you at the slipway inside the harbour.'

'I've got it.'

There was envy in Themba's voice. 'Good luck, Chico. I wish I was there with you guys.'

* * *

493

The day before a public holiday was always hectic, with people trying to fit two days' work into one. The eighth of December was a busy day at Moscow House with a stream of visitors calling on the Chief Representative.

At four Themba called his staff together. 'Tomorrow is an official holiday, you may close up the office early and go home. Remember the significance of tomorrow, when we must think of all our comrades fighting for human rights in South Africa.'

Themba was still at his desk when Phyllis came to greet. 'Have a good rest, Phyllis. You need it, you work too hard.'

'You do, too, Themba. Why don't you take off the night for once?'

'I am.' Themba smiled at her concern. 'Tonight I'm going to dinner with Limpho Hani and her three daughters. Some home cooking will make a change from eating out of tins!'

The office was quiet once everyone had left. Themba worked for an hour, then took a shower, changed into fresh clothes and walked leisurely to the Hani home.

At the time Themba was strolling through the suburbs of Maseru, Colonel Smit had just finished his preparations for the raid. Smit allowed himself a cigarette, inhaling deeply as he looked around the army camp outside Ladybrand in the Free State. Everything was in place and he was well satisfied with himself. He took another draw, glancing eastwards over the Caledon River into Lesotho. The Maluti Mountains were magnificent in the setting sun, turning to shades of purple and indigo. He could make out Maseru across the river, buildings shining white in the last rays.

He glanced up as Pierre Roux joined him. 'The planning has gone like clockwork,' he told Pierre proudly. 'One hundred and forty of my crack troops have been moved from Durban to Ladybrand by troop carrier. They're resting in their tents.'

He pointed towards the huge portable searchlights with three-metre adjustable heads. 'They arrived from Voortrekkerhoogte this afternoon. They're powered by their own diesel generators. They can light up the night sky for miles.'

Five helicopters from the Tempe base near Bloemfontein sat in a hollow, like huge dragonflies. Twelve 4x4 army Land-Rovers had arrived that afternoon from the army base at Heidelberg. He had ample weaponry to complete the operation. Smit took a last draw, then threw away the butt, crushing it with his boot.

'That's how we intend to demolish the ANC,' laughed Smit heartily. He nudged Pierre. 'Are you going in with my men?'

Pierre shook his head. 'I want to operate behind your task force. Give me a Land-Rover and I'll do my own thing.'

'Can't I send some of my boys with you?'

'No, thanks.' His was a personal score and he did not want to be accountable to Colonel Smit. 'Military intelligence always acts independently from the SADF – you have a task to perform, I have information to procure.'

'Suit yourself.'

An hour before midnight the troops met in a large tent for the final briefing. Colonel Smit addressed them: 'Men, tonight you have the privilege of doing something positive for your country. All your training will now be turned into action against our enemy, the ANC in Lesotho. We're going to hit them hard tonight by destroying their property and their collaborators, stopping the insurgency into South Africa.'

Colonel Smit pinned up enlarged aerial photographs taken of the various suburbs in Maseru. Forty target houses were marked with large black crosses. 'Each platoon has four houses to destroy plus the inhabitants.' The balance of the troops he deployed with the searchlights and the helicopters as back-ups.

'We have the element of surprise, but the first half-hour is the most important if we want to catch them in their beds.'

He opened a crate of black Nugget boot polish. 'Paint your hands and faces black. This will increase the general confusion. Moreover, the enemy will be hesitant to fire at you, thinking you're black men.'

At thirty after midnight the convoy of ten Land-Rovers moved into position on the South African side of the Caledon River, facing the bridge. The six searchlights were evenly deployed on the high ground.

At exactly one o'clock the blacked-out helicopters flew in low over the river. This was the signal to the troops in the Land-Rovers. They roared over the bridge. The lead Land-Rover rammed the boom-gate barrier and the bewildered Lesotho customs officials scattered as the convoy bore down on them.

*   *   *

495

Themba walked slowly back to Moscow House. It was a marvellous, still summer's evening. Crickets and other insects competed with each other in a strident symphony of sound. Themba rubbed his stomach with satisfaction. He had not eaten such a good meal since the last time he was in Lusaka.

He unlocked the front door and glanced at his watch: one o'clock. I'll sleep late tomorrow morning, he promised himself as he walked down the passage. He had just removed his jacket when he heard the familiar chop-chop-chop-chop of rotor blades as a helicopter flew over the house. He was not alarmed until he heard the second one, then the third, fourth and fifth. His gut feeling and his intensive training warned him there was danger unfolding.

Running to the wardrobe he slipped his Makarov pistol out from under his shirts. He removed his combat camouflage jacket from the hanger and pulled it on. Into the big side pockets he slipped boxes of ammunition.

Once over the bridge the Land-Rovers split up, each heading for its target zone. A few minutes later a lone Land-Rover crossed the bridge. The powerful searchlights came to life as the operators started the diesel engines, training the powerful beams on Maseru, making it almost as bright as day.

With efficient precision the commandos surrounded their targets. One minute it was a peaceful summer's night, the next all hell broke loose as automatic machine-gun fire rattled throughout the town.

The soldiers fired in short, sharp bursts, the bullets pock-marking walls, shattering windows and splintering doors. Residents woke with a start, all in confusion. Some screamed in fear, some rolled off their beds to the floor, and some cleared out of the houses to be mown down outside.

After the initial burst of gunfire the soldiers ran across to the houses. Flattening themselves against the walls, they pulled the pins out of hand grenades and tossed them in a loop over their shoulders through demolished windows and shattered doorways. The grenades exploded, belching waves of flame and smoke through the openings. Inside, people wailed in terror as they were burnt, wounded or killed. Bedrooms turned into blazing infernos as mattresses and curtains caught alight. The flickering flames spread, roaring into full-blown fires.

The helicopters hovered over the Maseru slum area – a twisting patchwork of complicated passages and narrow streets. With precision timing they went in one by one. Ropes fell from the open hatches and the soldiers descended quickly to the ground. They sealed off the edges of the area, making escape impossible for the terrified inhabitants.

A man rushed out of his house to investigate. Five bullets smashed him to the ground. He crawled on his knees, pleading for mercy. A commando stood over him. From point-blank range he emptied his magazine. Twenty-five more shots riddled his body tossing him about like a broken rag doll. In life Sydney Mavimbela had been a gentle man, never displaying hatred or anger.

In the suburb of Florida, the Assistant-Chief Representative rushed to the doorway of his house. He was responsible for the ANC supporters in Lesotho. What was going on? Zola Nqini's eyes grew large with horror as he saw four weapons aimed at his midriff. His scream caught in his throat as he was scythed in half, his guts spattered against the inside walls of his front room. Soldiers jumped over the body combing the house. His friend sat up in bed with fright. Bullets smashed into his torso and he fell back on to the pillows, his dream of political asylum draining away as his life-blood ebbed out of his body. He died less than twenty-four hours after reaching Lesotho to start a new life.

The soldiers warmed to their task, basking in the power of the gun over frail human bodies. As piranha fish go on a voracious feeding frenzy at the taste of blood, so the commandos fed their rapacious delirium by turning flame throwers on to the fleeing people. They grimaced as the human torches burnt to death, their skins scorched to dry parchment, their clothes to smouldering ashes.

Still the awful carnage continued. At Cuba House eight young men were murdered. All were innocent teenagers in transit to further their studies at Solomon Mahlangu Freedom College. Only two of the group of ten escaped the holocaust.

In the suburb of Thamae a house was razed to the ground. The firing soldiers kept the inhabitants trapped inside. They had two options of dying – to be roasted to death or shot to death. All chose the burning hell, the stench of burning human flesh filled the air with a sickly odour.

Themba heard the screeching of tyres as a vehicle slammed to a stop outside Moscow House. He listened to footfalls crossing the concrete pavement. The next second a rain of bullets smashed into the front of the building, shattering the front windows. An exploding grenade sent shock waves rushing down the passage, blasting open the door to his suite.

The sounds of shouting voices coming around the side of the house galvanised Themba into action. He slipped through the patio door, sliding it shut behind him. Grabbing the beam he pulled himself on to the pergola, lying on the strong network of wistaria branches. He forced a round into the breech and aimed his pistol through a gap in the creeper.

He heard footsteps echoing down the passage as the assailants approached, firing an automatic burst into each room on the way. A soldier burst into his room, pressing his finger on the trigger, his weapon on full automatic, spewing a stream of destruction as he turned slowly in a circle. The bed was wrecked as stuffing and springs popped out of the mattress. His clothes were shredded as the wardrobe was bombarded. Chunks of plaster were ripped out of the wall. Bullets hit the sliding door, blowing shards of plate glass into the patio.

Themba heard gunfire behind the house: he was surrounded. He prepared for death; images of Hilda and his son flashed through his mind.

The soldier ran out on to the enclosed patio and stood under the pergola. Less than a metre away Themba's pistol was trained at his head. Holding his breath, Themba grimaced. Maybe I'll die, but I'm taking you with me, soldier, he thought.

'There's nobody here!' The soldier shouted to another platoon member in the bedroom. 'Look under the bed!'

Themba watched the man bend down and straighten up again. 'Let's move.'

The two soldiers ran out of the room. Themba exhaled a suspended breath, feeling sweat break out on his brow.

From the pavement the platoon leader shouted instructions. 'Move! Move! The next house is up the street!'

Lowering himself on the garden side of the patio wall, Themba crouched in the shadows, searching for movement. His trained eyes flitted from bush to bush. When he was convinced no soldiers had been left behind, he cautiously moved to the street. The unit was further up the road in all-out attack on Warsaw House. Themba could hear the screams of dread greeting the bullets.

I must check on Limpho and the children. Chris would do the same if our roles were reversed. Themba made his way through the suburbs. Most houses remained untouched, frightened families cringing in their beds with bated breath. It seemed only ANC houses were targeted. Trinity House was burning in the distance. He looked towards Budapest House and saw an explosion blow off the roof sheets. The eerie brightness from the searchlights lit the whole scene.

He reached the street where Hani's house was situated. A Land-Rover stood in the middle of the road, opposite the house. Commandos were letting rip into the building. A grenade thrown through the lounge window exploded in an orange ball and the house started burning.

Keeping to the shadows, Themba crept up the street. He had to divert the task force. Seeing a driver sitting in the Land–Rover, he fired a shot. His 9mm parabellum bullet punched a hole in the safety glass, hitting the driver in the shoulder.

'We're under attack!' He dived out of the vehicle. His companions fell back, surrounding the Land-Rover, lying flat on their stomachs, facing outwards. The circle of guns barked, their muzzle flashes creating sparks like a giant Catherine wheel.

Bullets filled Themba's world, plucking at the air around him. A slug snatched at his jacket. He breathed a sigh of relief as no stinging pain followed. Ducking over the low wall of the house next door, he ran towards the back of the yard. He dived head first over the fence of Hani's house, rolled to his feet and sprinted for the back door. The door was locked. Themba kicked it in. Flames engulfed the front of the house. Billowing smoke poured down the passage. There was no time to lose. The children's rooms were already on fire; Themba could not get close. He tried the main bedroom door. It was locked. He shouldered it open, bursting into the room.

Limpho screamed in terror. 'No! No! No! Please, God, no!' Themba turned towards the bed. Limpho lay there, shielding her face with her hand, covering her children with the blankets. The flames were lapping at the bedroom door, casting grotesque flickering shadows across the room.

Themba grabbed her by the shoulders. 'Limpho, it's me, Themba. We must get out of here.'

'God has answered my prayers!' Limpho clung to him.

He picked up baby Lindiwe, who shrieked in terror at being

separated from her mother. Limpho clutched little Nomakhwezi to her breast and pulled Neo along by her arm. Themba shepherded them into the kitchen. Suddenly an armed soldier filled the back doorway.

Pierre stopped the Land-Rover two hundred metres before Moscow House and approached cautiously on foot. He ducked into the shadows near the front gate and watched the house intently. He saw the shattered windows and pock-marked walls. He sprinted across the open ground and listened again at the front door. Everything was quiet. Pierre entered the house, snapping his flashlight on and off. The reception office was a mess, as was an adjacent office. Next he investigated the kitchen, then the rooms along the passage. Nothing. Cautiously he approached the door at the end. In one bound he was inside, playing the beam around the room. It was wrecked, but deserted. Pierre sighed in exasperation – he had hoped to find Memani here. Where was he, then? He walked on to the enclosed patio and back into the room.

With less caution he searched the room. He found letters from Hilda addressed to Themba in the wardrobe. He riffled through Themba's clothes carefully but could find nothing important. If this is his bedroom, thought Pierre, then Moscow House is his home. He'll return sooner or later. Pierre made himself comfortable in a chair in the reception office. He faced the door with his pistol at the ready.

Themba froze as the soldier turned his machine-gun towards them. He had never killed before. Now hatred welled up inside him as he pulled the trigger of his Makarov. The soldier was struck in the chest, his eyes turning glassy, and he crumpled to the floor.

He jumped over the body and took the back steps two at a time. He landed on the lawn in a combat position. A series of bullets flew over his head. Themba took aim and fired. A soldier cartwheeled over slowly, falling dead to the ground. Themba felt a burning pain in his left arm as a slug smashed into him. He turned, diverting the Makarov, firing three shots in quick succession. He heard the breath escape from another soldier's lungs as his cry stuck in his throat.

'Quick! Quick!' Themba pushed Limpho ahead of him. She stumbled and fell but terror drove her to her feet again. They reached the hedge at the back of the garden by forcing their way through the privet branches. 'Over the fence!' Themba helped Limpho over with his right arm, his left hanging at his side. The baby started screaming again – a high-pitched sound of dread.

'Take the baby.' Themba passed Lindiwe over and Limpho held her tight. 'Next one.' Themba's voice was urgent. He helped Neo up, she was big enough to assist by pulling herself to the top of the fence. 'Last one, here she comes!' Desperation gave Themba strength and he lifted three-year-old Nomakhwezi right over the fence in one movement. He heard footsteps approaching. 'Run into the next street, Limpho!'

Themba turned. Three soldiers were running towards hedge. He forced himself to stay calm and took a steadying breath. Three times the Makarov barked and each time a soldier was sent writhing to the ground.

Themba grasped the top of the fence with his good hand. With his feet scrabbling in the links of the diamond mesh, he reached the top, his stomach resting on the top strand of wire. He allowed himself to tip forwards and fell heavily into the adjoining yard. He was winded, but stumbled to his feet, reaching the street. Limpho and the children were huddled in a little group under a large syringa tree.

Themba looked around fearfully. The street was deserted. They ran for the park, almost floundering straight into an ambush. Five Alouette helicopters stood in the open space, glinting meanly in the suffused light. Themba forced his charges down just in time. He crept ahead to investigate. The pilots sat in the choppers talking on the radios. They were surrounded by troops, weapons at the ready. Themba was outnumbered twenty to one. He retreated and they skirted around the park.

'Where can we go to get away from the danger?' Limpho was close to hysteria.

Themba patted her arm. 'The safest place at the moment is probably the police station.'

At a fast walk they set off, Themba carrying Nomakhwezi on his good arm. In every direction there were blazing houses. The SADF continued their destruction, the rattle and whine of bullets still pervaded the night. Stopping before the police station, they double-checked for a few minutes. The SADF had left the place well alone.

He led his party into the charge office. 'I'd like to see the chief of police.'

The constable recognised Themba. 'You're lucky, Mr Memani. He came in a few minutes ago. Last office on the left.'

Themba stormed down the passage. The chief and his senior officers were packed into the room.

'There's a full-scale offensive on Maseru and you huddle in an office?' Themba's blazing eyes swept the room. 'Why are you not fighting back?'

'SADF is not attacking our people. Lesotho citizens are not in danger.' The chief of police stood up, glaring at Themba. 'It's your fight, Mr Chief Representative – an action between the ANC and the South African government.' He banged his fist on his desk. 'It's not our war. We won't become involved.'

Themba looked at the chief of police. 'Is the Lesotho army mounting a counter offensive?'

Shaking his head the chief sat down abruptly. 'They're confined to barracks and will take no part in the action.' He shrugged helplessly. 'We cannot afford to engage the SADF. It's like a mouse taking on an elephant. If they decide on reprisals, our government could topple.'

Themba's arm was throbbing. Blood dripped off his fingers on to the floor. Removing his jacket he tore away the shirt-sleeve, revealing a flesh wound in his upper arm. It was bleeding profusely.

The chief of police pointed to one of his officers. 'Take Mr Memani to hospital so they can attend to his wound.'

'Limpho Hani and her three children are in the front office. What about them?'

'They're welcome to stay here. It's safe in the police station. The SADF will withdraw before daylight. They can go home later.' Themba nodded.

At Queen Elizabeth II hospital the doctor stitched the laceration. 'Only a muscle wound that will heal quickly. No arteries were severed or bones shattered.' He dressed the injury and gave Themba an anti-tetanus injection as a safety precaution.

From the fifth floor of the hospital Themba had a bird's-eye view over Maseru. Fires lit the night sky all over the town. He tried to pin-point the houses belonging to the ANC or where employees or sympathisers lived. The powerful searchlights cast weird patterns as they criss-crossed, creating tunnels of light in the darkness.

The casualty ward was chaos. Wounded and dead were laid out

in rows on blankets along the walls. The fetid stench of burning flesh made Themba feel bilious. People moaned in agony, while the doctors and nurses rushed around, treating the most serious cases first. There was nothing Themba could do and he walked outside.

At exactly four o'clock, three hours after the action had begun, an eerie calm returned to the town as the guns fell silent. The garrulous clatter of helicopters broke the short-lived peace as they rose from the park, ferrying troops to the muster point on a hill behind the Hilton Hotel.

Themba smiled grimly as he saw bodies in tarpaulin bags lowered from the choppers. 'Good, the raid was not totally one-sided.'

Abruptly the searchlights dimmed and were extinguished as the operators cut the engines. The gathering dawn was already lighting up the eastern sky.

When the SADF were satisfied all their commandos were accounted for they withdrew from Maseru.

Birds started twittering, heralding a new day, unaware of the holocaust of the night before. With a sense of foreboding and deep anger, Themba started walking home. He needed the exercise and the time to think.

Pierre blinked as the light grew stronger. Memani was not coming back, he concluded sadly. He cocked his head at the sound of helicopters flying overhead. The SADF were pulling out, he would have to make a move otherwise he would be isolated behind enemy lines.

For the first time he saw the remains of a name plate on the office door: THEMBA MEMANI – CHIEF REPRESENTATIVE. Pierre smiled in satisfaction.

The soldiers had devastated Memani's office. Bullets had ploughed across the top of the desk, cutting deep grooves against the grain of the wood. A vase had shattered, strewing flowers across the floor. Chairs were riddled with holes, lying on their sides. Pierre rummaged through the desk's drawers. Stationery, pens, private letters – nothing of importance. He searched a cupboard, again nothing. Pierre kicked at a chair in frustration and saw the safe. It was a Chubb, and he'd had intensive training on cracking these safes. It was doubly secured with a combination and key lock. The lock was no problem, he routinely carried a pick with him. With his ear to the cold metal he listened to the tumblers clicking as he slowly twirled the combination. Four times to the left – click, click, click, then the number clunked home. Pierre nodded contentedly – it was a standard combination. He dialled three times to the right and the number fell into place. Two turns to the left and the last tumbler clicked home. Slowly Pierre turned right to '0' and the dial stopped, unlocking the combination. He picked at the lock and felt the levers turn over. Eagerly he grabbed the handle, twisted and the door swung slowly open.

The safe was loaded with papers. Desperately he pulled them out one by one, his eyes bulging as a large manila envelope fell to the floor marked: KOEBERG.

Pierre withdrew the plans. He folded them out on the floor, gasping as he saw how complete they were. They showed every detail of the Koeberg nuclear power station's layout. He returned them to the envelope and searched further.

Suddenly Pierre heard the squealing of brakes as a car stopped in front of the house. Who could that be? Memani? Pierre pushed the papers back into the safe and twirled the dial. Then he sprinted to the front door. A woman came up the path, walking quickly, her face stark. Pierre allowed her to enter the doorway and pounced from behind, holding her neck in an armlock and jamming his knee into her back.

'Where is Memani?' hissed Pierre.

'I don't know.'

'Rubbish, tell me,' demanded Pierre, strengthening his grip.

Her voice was strangulated and high-pitched. 'At this very moment he's coming here with the Lesotho police.'

Cursing under his breath, for he wanted Memani, but could not face a confrontation with the police, Pierre pulled his arm tighter and the woman blacked out. He pulled her away from the door and laid her down gently.

The light was stronger. Across the street he saw people coming out of their houses. It was too dangerous to wait any longer. Pierre sprinted to the front gate and looked up and down the street. It was deserted. He dashed over the road, into the Land-Rover and headed back towards the border.

Themba gulped as he saw the tattered reception office. Then he noticed Phyllis Naidoo lying on her back on the floor. In panic he fell to his knees, feeling her pulse. Her heartbeat was regular.

Themba slapped her gently on the cheek. Phyllis moaned and her eyelids fluttered. From the kitchen Themba fetched a glass of water and dabbed it on her face.

Phyllis opened her eyes. 'Themba, it's you. Thank God,' she croaked.

He lifted her, holding the glass to her lips and Phyllis drank thirstily. She sat bolt upright, looking around the office, her eyes widening with fear.

'Where are they?' she whispered.

'Who? There is nobody here.'

Phyllis told him of the attack on her.

'Was it only one man?' demanded Themba.

'I think so. He spoke in a cultured voice, with a slight Afrikaans accent.'

'Did you see his face?'

'No.' She shuddered at the thought.

'Probably military intelligence,' said Themba. 'They usually work alone and come in after the soldiers have wrecked a place.'

'What could they find?' asked Phyllis.

Suddenly it struck him – the Koeberg papers in the safe. Themba rushed into his office and opened the safe with trembling hands. He fell to his knees and scrabbled through the files, relieved when he found the large manila envelope. He shoved it into his desk drawer and sat down abruptly. He tried the telephone but it was dead.

'We can do nothing here,' said Phyllis. 'Come, I have a car outside. Let's go and see where we can help.'

They drove around the suburbs, taking them one by one. Themba was sickened by the destruction and the utter disregard for human life. Everywhere they saw wounded victims, or corpses. Hatred built up inside him. He had to do something to avenge the atrocities or he would go mad.

They drove out on the Mafeteng road and stopped when they saw Alfred Marwanqana's pulverised house. The home of his dreams, built to share with his family, was ravaged and teetering. Blackened walls testified to the grenade that had exploded outside the door. They found his wife Nellie and her daughter in the bathroom. Cradled in her arms were the bodies of two of her children and her husband. She was rocking them back and forth muttering incoherently. She screamed at Themba when he tried to help her up.

'Go away! Leave me alone! I've waited seventeen years to have my family reunited. You can't take them away now that we're together at last.'

The grief on her face was too much for him. He had seen tragedy in his life, but none so soul-destroying as Nellie and her shattered dreams.

Themba stumbled from the house into the middle of the road. Clenching his fists he bellowed, 'I will avenge every one of you. Before God, I promise.'

Phyllis tried to comfort him. 'Calm down, Themba. I know how you feel, but what can you do?'

His eyes were as hard as steel as the solution came to him. 'I'm going to Luanda to join the Koeberg team. We're going to knock the hell out of the South African government.'

He counted the days on his fingers. 'Today is the ninth, they leave on the *Spalato* on the twelfth.' His mind was made up. 'I have three days.' He turned to Phyllis. 'Is the telephone at your home working?'

She nodded.

'Let's go. I must telephone Oliver Tambo in Lusaka.'

When Tambo's secretary heard the urgency in his voice she put Themba straight through. Themba broke the news of the SADF raid.

'I want you to relieve me of my duty as Chief Representative – there is little left to represent. I'm asking your permission to proceed to Luanda immediately to be part of the MK raid. It's something I have to do after this butchery.'

'We can't leave Lesotho rudderless.' Tambo understood Themba. He recognised the resolve in his voice. He also knew he had to give him his head, to allow him to work the bitterness out of his system. 'Let your assistant take over.'

'Zola is dead.'

'Is there anyone whom we can appoint as a temporary measure?'

'Phyllis Naidoo. She's worked for the ANC in Maseru for six years. She knows the business inside out and she's a very capable woman.'

'Good, appoint her as temporary Chief Representative. Don't forget to sympathise with the Lesotho Prime Minister for the loss of life among his citizens. Another thing, Themba, I want all our brave comrades to have a proper burial.'

506

'It will all be done.'

'Good luck, Themba. Use your mission to salute our fallen heroes in Lesotho. Tell Phyllis to let me know details of the funeral, so that I can attend.'

By lunch-time the full cost of the SADF raid was known. It was glaringly apparent to Themba that the SADF intelligence had been outdated and erroneous. The private homes of twelve innocent Lesotho citizens who were in no way connected to the ANC had been attacked.

The police gave Themba the casualty list. A total of forty-two people dead, the hospital crowded with well over one hundred wounded.

He drove to the airport. The first flight to Luanda was in four days' time, too late to join the Koeberg mission. The next morning there was a Zambian Airlines flight to Gaborone in Botswana, but no connecting flight to Luanda. In desperation he purchased a ticket to Gaborone. At least he would be six hundred kilometres closer and could make a plan once he got there.

Themba arrived in Gaborone during mid-morning. He pestered the booking office. He simply had to reach Luanda in time.

There was no train to Luanda. By car he would be forced to travel over South African government administered Namibia. Anyway, it was too far.

Dust devils gyrated in the parched earth alongside the runway and a hot, dry wind scorched his skin. He watched as a single-engined Piper 180 landed and taxied to the terminal building. While a petrol tanker filled up the light aircraft, a couple entered the building.

'Hi there. Do you have cold Cokes?' The man mopped his brow. 'Wow, man, it sure is hot here.'

Themba recognised their American accents.

The woman flopped down in a chair. 'Only another two hours and we'll be in Maun.'

Themba pricked up his ears. Maun was almost in a straight line between Gaborone and Luanda. 'Excuse me, madam, where are you flying to after Maun?'

She looked at him in surprise. 'We're staying over at Moremi for a week.'

'And your pilot?'

'I dunno.' She shrugged her shoulders. 'He'll fetch us in a week's time.'

Themba cornered the pilot while he was checking on the fuel intake. 'Where are you going to after you've dropped the Americans in Maun?'

'Back to my base in Windhoek. I fly charter for Namibian Safaris. Why?'

'Would you take me to Luanda? I must be there before tonight.'

'It will cost fifteen hundred rand.' He looked at Themba doubtfully.

'That's okay, I can pay.'

'Show me the colour of your money.'

'Here.' He stuffed it into the pilot's hand.

'It's a deal.' He shoved the money into his back pocket, knowing this was something irregular but who was he to query it? Money was money. 'We leave in fifteen minutes.'

They touched down in Luanda just before sunset. Themba hired a taxi to take him to the ANC house in the suburb of Vienna. Chico, Clifford and Matroos were sitting down to supper when Themba walked into the kitchen.

'Themba! What are you doing here?' They all jumped to their feet in surprise.

He told them about the SADF raid on Maseru. 'I'm going on the Koeberg mission,' he said with determination.

Chico looked at Themba critically. 'I know how you feel but you would hinder our mission, not help us. Don't forget we've been in training for almost eight months now. There's no way you can catch up with all that experience.'

'I have a day and a half to learn, the whole of Saturday and Sunday morning.'

Clifford laughed. 'That's a drop in the ocean.'

Themba was adamant. 'I'm going. You can say and do what you want, but I'll be there. I know you have six sets of equipment. You need only three. I can use the fourth and there'll still be two to spare.'

'But Themba, one and a half days . . .' began Matroos.

'Don't but me!' Themba banged on the table. 'Have you forgotten that I was trained at Quibaxe? And I completed a Military Engineering course at Simferopol in the Ukraine.' Themba's voice dropped

508

to a whisper. 'You men didn't see the carnage of Maseru. Oliver Tambo gave me permission to go on this mission. I want to avenge our comrades.'

Chico came to the rescue. 'Let's give Themba a try. We'll train him for one and a half days. If he passes the test, he goes; if he fails, he stays.'

'Come on, comrades.' Themba looked imploringly at Clifford and Matroos. 'Let me try.'

'If you are proficient in inflatables, wetsuits and oxygen masks before the *Spalato* sails, I'll give you the nod.' Clifford smiled broadly. 'You'll have to be a damn quick learner, Themba.'

'I'm not so sure.' Matroos shook his head.

'You're outvoted, Matroos,' Themba cried. 'The vote is three to one.'

'Since when do you have a vote?'

'All comrades-in-arms on a mission have a vote.'

'You're a clever one, Themba Memani,' Matroos laughed, giving Themba his chance.

21

Don Landmark, project manager of Koeberg nuclear power station, made his weekly telephonic report to Ian Matchett, chief executive of Escom at Megawatt Park in Johannesburg. They chatted for a few minutes on the building progress. 'The plant closes down today for the builders' holiday. I'm worried that our security is inadequate, Ian.'

'Relax Don, our security is fine. No one will attack Koeberg. What is there to damage except concrete and metal? Besides, the place is so isolated, nobody will bother.'

'This is the dangerous time, before we load the reactors.'

'Calm down, Don. You're seeing ghosts where there are none.'

Don was insistent. 'Some of the French Fremetone staff have been behaving very strangely lately. I need tighter security.'

'Our budget is already over-extended.' Matchett was getting irritated. 'What could possibly be damaged at this stage?'

'Imagine if bombs were planted destroying cable trays and the network of piping, let alone cracking the reactor or the steam generators. It could set us back almost a year.'

'We already have the most advanced security system available.'

'On the land side.' Don felt despair. 'We're open from the sea. Our security is lacking on our western flank.'

'Maritime Command at Silvermine has the whole sea area covered, Don.' The chief executive was exasperated. 'I'll be able to justify greater security expenditure once we near switch-on stage or when there is the prospect of nuclear fall-out.'

'You're going through to Mr Landmark now,' bubbled the telephonist.

'Landmark.'

'Good afternoon, Don. This is Pierre Roux.'

'Pierre! Good to hear your voice again.' Don's tone was warm and friendly. 'How is the family?'

'Fine thanks, but I have a problem.' Pierre came straight to the point. 'Military intelligence has uncovered information that the ANC possesses a full set of working drawings of the Koeberg layout.'

'Virtually impossible!' exclaimed Don, his mind racing to the various possibilities.

'It's happened, Don. I need to know the source of the leak.'

'The possibilities are numerous,' said Don cautiously. 'We have so many contractors and sub-contractors on site – our own ESCOM staff, nuclear technicians, civil contractors, building teams, breakwater builders. It's a long list.'

'Are the staff not security screened?'

'Ours are, and all the contractors' South African staff are. But we have no way of checking on foreign staff employed by overseas contractors. We're forced to accept their word on the matter.'

'I insist that security is stepped up immediately, Don.' Pierre's tone was adamant.

Don sighed in aggravation. 'I discussed this very point with my chief executive today.'

'Did he agree?'

'No,' answered Don dully. 'Until switch-on they regard Koeberg as an industrial site. It becomes high security only once the reactors are loaded.'

'Can you step up the patrols?'

'I can justify an extra team.'

'Please do so. Another thing – I'd appreciate you instructing your head of security to get hold of me, day or night, at the merest whiff of trouble.'

'I'll arrange that. Anything else, Pierre?'

'This Koeberg thing is gnawing at me, Don. Perhaps we should get together and talk about it?'

'Thursday is a public holiday. Why don't you and your family come over for the evening? Come about seven.'

Themba spent all of Saturday training. He spent hours in the water getting used to a wetsuit and goggles. He learnt to breathe with an oxygen cylinder. Chico, Clifford and Matroos took it in turns to instruct him.

In the afternoon they launched the inflatables. Themba was impressed with the craft and their twin steering mechanisms. In the harbour Themba could sit up and steer with a hand-held bar. In the choppy waters of the open sea it was better to lie down on one's stomach and steer with the pedals by altering the pressure on each foot and changing the angle of the propeller. There were built-in hand grips and a safety belt to hold the operator in position. A double paddle was fastened to the inside floor. In each side wall was a watertight compartment. The left side held a rechargeable battery for running the propeller. The right receptacle was for holding explosives and weapons.

'Well, comrades, what do you say? Do I qualify?' Themba stripped off his wetsuit.

'You were much better than I thought you'd be,' Chico conceded, but then Themba knew he had an ally in him. They had operated together before and respected each other.

'We'll decide tomorrow morning.' Clifford refused to commit himself.

Matroos only grunted. Themba knew he was the one to convince if he was to make the mission.

Before sunrise Themba woke his companions. 'Come cadres, today is D-Day.' He chivvied them up and an hour later they were in the harbour warehouse.

'You must go solo today to see how you cope by yourself,' Matroos growled.

'If that will convince you.' Themba smiled. 'What must I do?'

'Three kilos out into the ocean and back.'

They watched Themba leave the harbour and hit the choppy swells of the high seas.

Chico looked closely at Matroos. 'What are you up to?'

'Themba's inflatable is the one with the battery that won't hold its charge. Once he's about three kilometres out the battery will give in. That will test his survival capacity.'

'You mean dog.' Chico looked at him scathingly. 'What if he drowns?'

'If he's as good as you say, he'll be all right.'

They ran to the end of the breakwater and watched Themba disappear out to sea. Later, when he was hardly more than a speck in the distance, they saw the flash of wet paddles in the sunlight.

513

Chico turned triumphantly to Matroos. 'I told you he'd be all right.'

He came closer and closer until they could see him clearly. Themba was paddling with strong strokes.

He skimmed across the harbour. 'Well, do I qualify?' He looked pointedly at Matroos, a smile of triumph on his lips.

Grudgingly Matroos nodded.

'Then I can go?' The three men smiled. Themba let out a yell of elation.

Chico looked at his watch. 'We must hurry, we still have to pack our gear and move the explosives to the *Spalato*. Themba, you're the speech-maker. Why don't you go over and make the final arrangements with the captain? We'll bring everything across by truck.'

Themba and the Yugoslav captain settled the details.

During the three and a half days they were at sea they pumped up the inflatables, charged the batteries and filled their oxygen tanks. Themba spent time with the oxygen pipe in his mouth and the goggles on, perfecting his breathing routine.

As the ship closed on Dassen Island, the four comrades donned their wetsuits. Into the watertight compartment of each craft went a limpet mine wrapped around with oilskins, blocks of explosive, a timing detonator and tinned food.

The inflatables were lowered over the side. The Yugoslavian crew lined the rail, watching in fascination as the craft pulled away. To avoid detection from the mainland and the lighthouse they headed for a sandy bay on the seaward side of the island. Cutting the engines, they surfed on to the beach on the back of a wave.

They carried the four inflatables well above the high-water mark into the lee of a large rock. They covered the craft with plastic camouflage sheets to protect them from discovery. Millions of penguins, gannets, cormorants and other sea birds vied for every square centimetre of land. With a never-ending pecking, squawking and flapping of wings they jostled for position in a continuous cacophony of sound. Undaunted by the presence of the men, the birds continued sitting on their ground nests, and they had to skirt their way around the colonies to reach the deserted house at the end of the island.

The house was furnished with only the essentials – a table, six chairs and beds with mattresses. Every few years it was used by guano collectors when the concession holders came to harvest the rich bird deposits. Themba checked the asbestos rainwater tank; luckily it still held fresh water.

They got a fire going with dry bird dung and were able to make themselves tea and warm their tinned food. They sat outside till evening and went inside when it became dark. It was risky lighting candles, the light would travel far in the clear night and they did not wish to draw attention to their presence on the island.

The next day they cleaned the hut, obliterating any signs of their stay. On the beach they chased the birds off the plastic tarpaulins. In the twenty-four hours they had been on the island, birds had roosted on top of the plastic and even laid eggs. Each one checked his own craft – battery, explosives, wiring, steering mechanisms and pressure of the inflatable side walls. They dressed in their scuba gear and checked the oxygen cylinders and flow valves. Then they waited.

The captain of the Russian fishing trawler anchored the *Kaliningrad* in international waters, twelve nautical miles off the coast. The ship rose and fell on the swells, the diesel engine idling at a steady beat. Once the dusk settled he revved the motor, charting a course eastwards towards Dassen Island. As he entered South African territorial waters he extinguished all lights, navigating by the ship's instruments.

Opposite the sandy bay he cut the engines to idle. He flashed the forecastle light: two short and three long bursts.

'It's the signal.' Chico answered with an identical signal on his flashlight. 'Let's go, men.'

'Koeberg, here we come!'

They launched their inflatables into the mild surf of the bay and headed for the trawler. They travelled four abreast through the calm sea. Every now and again Chico flashed twice and the trawler answered, keeping them on course. Soon they were bobbing next to the ship. Themba climbed a rope ladder up the steel side while Clifford held on to his inflatable.

'So, you are the freedom fighter. I am the captain, my name is Yuri.'

'I'm Themba, Themba Memani.' He extended his hand to Yuri.

The captain shouted orders to lift the rubber ducks on board. A framework covered in fish netting was dropped over the side and the craft were raised one by one. Themba introduced his three comrades. The captain greeted each one respectfully, speaking in broken English. 'We admire your courage greatly. It is good for us to help.'

Themba felt the deck vibrate as the engines roared to full power and the ship surged ahead, heading out to sea. Once they reached international waters the *Kaliningrad* turned due south. The ship was a large steel trawler, catching fish with seine nets in the Cape waters. Once the holds were full they rendezvoused with their mother ship and transferred their catch to her vast refrigerated holds, then returned to trawl again and again.

The odour of fish clung to Themba's nostrils until he became accustomed to it. In the seamen's mess the four cadres enjoyed a hot meal and a warm mug of coffee, while the batteries of the inflatables charged. They were in high spirits; so far, everything was working exactly to plan.

They stood at the rail looking towards the coast of Africa. The land looked dark and forbidding in the light of a half moon, a smudge on the eastern horizon. Each was occupied with his own thoughts. Themba thought of Hilda and Bambatha, and the new child she was carrying. She thought he was still in Maseru and would be concerned for his safety if she knew where he was now. He prayed for strength to complete the mission and protection to escape unharmed. The fear of the unknown gnawed at their nerves.

Yuri joined them at the rail. 'Weather forecast bad. South-westerly squall coming up. Reach us just after midnight.'

'We should be on our way back to the trawler by then.' Chico looked at the captain, a worried expression on his face. 'I hope the storm holds off until we're on board again.'

'For you, I hope so.' Yuri spoke seriously. 'These inflatable things, they look to us like toys.'

'Off Odessa we practised in all weather conditions,' said Clifford. 'We'll manage, even in a storm. The craft are more versatile than they look.'

'My ship must get back to international waters soon. I will wait until midnight, then I must leave.'

Themba hid the look of concern on his face. A storm could be catastrophic. It would take at least thirty minutes to get inside

Koeberg, plant the explosives and get out. That was if there were no unforeseen hitches. It allowed only half an hour to return to the ship and a storm could drive the inflatables off course. Furthermore, he had practised only in the relatively calm waters of Luanda, and the trip to Dassen Island and back had been on a flat sea.

Explaining the schedule to the captain, Themba asked: 'Please Yuri, give us another thirty minutes.'

'I give you ten more minutes, to twelve ten. That is final. I have responsibility for my ship and my men.'

It was no use arguing; he was adamant. Opposite Melkbosstrand, Yuri swung the trawler towards the coast, approaching from the south-west. They saw the yellow and white lights of the town come closer. To the north were the lights of Duinefontein, the village built to house the technical staff. Still further to the north were the concentrated lights of Koeberg nuclear power station.

Crowded on the bridge, they watched the radar. Blips of light on the screen showed the coastline.

'Look, harbour.' Yuri pointed out the images of the two break-waters jutting out to sea. 'We stop now. You go.'

'Can't you take us in closer?' Themba asked. 'The nearer you take us the less the distance we have to travel on the rubber dinghies. With a storm brewing it will save us time.'

Yuri smiled at Themba. 'I like you. You look a man straight in the eye when you talk. I will take chance for you and go little bit closer.'

The heart of the South African navy's Maritime Command surveillance network, Silvermine, was set into the mountain high above Simonstown naval base. A rabbit warren of passages and bunkers, it was cut into the solid rock of the mountain and was safe from an air, sea or land attack. Silvermine employed all the newest technology in surveillance equipment needed to monitor the shipping movements off the South African coastline. On top of the mountain a forest of aerials, linked to Fisantekraal and other radio stations at naval bases and port controls along the coast, continually received and despatched information.

A state-of-the-art radar scanner on the mountain revolved at exactly twenty-six revolutions a minute. Its huge concave scanner swept the sky, coast and sea with its powerful beam reaching out eighty kilometres.

The rating on duty watching the radar screen saw the point of light from the *Kaliningrad*. He called his superior officer. 'Sir, there's a blip on the screen. Looks like a ship entering our waters off the west coast.'

The lieutenant stretched. His skin ached from too much sun. He had reported for duty after a day on the beach with his family, and he was tired and wished his shift were over so he could go to bed. He turned to the rating. 'Don't worry, it's probably a fishing boat.'

'The fishing boats are usually in a pack, this one's alone.' The rating was insistent. 'The storm warning has been relayed to all shipping, sir. Most are heading back to their harbours.'

'Get the ship on the radio.' The lieutenant turned to the radio operator. 'Tell them to get out of there as the south-wester could push them towards the coast.'

Five minutes later he reported back. 'No reply, and I've tried every channel, sir.'

'Damn.' The lieutenant looked at the radar screen. His practised eye saw the blip. 'It's bigger than a wooden fishing boat. Looks more like a large trawler or a small ship. About five hundred tonnes.'

'It's moving dangerously close to the coast, sir.'

'Mmmm. It's just north of Melkbosstrand.'

'Should I contact Southern Air Command and ask them to investigate, sir?'

The lieutenant looked undecided. 'It's a public holiday. The men will be the hell in if we send them on a wild-goose chase while they're relaxing in bed with their mommies!'

'Looks like the ship has stopped. It's less than a kilometre off the coast, sir. The blips are stable.'

'There seems no danger of her going aground. Probably battening down hatches.' He made a decision. 'Don't contact Air Command yet. Let the Shackleton crew make their babies!'

Aromatic smoke billowed from the barbecue as the chops spluttered above the wood coals. Don Landmark shared his anxiety over Koeberg security with Pierre. 'I'm not happy about some of the French technicians working for Fremetone.'

'What are you doing about it?' Pierre asked.

'What *can* I do?' Don threw up his hands in exasperation. 'My bosses don't share my misgivings.' Unease gnawed at him and he

518

dialled the security office at Koeberg. 'Landmark here. What's your security update, Heyns?'

'All quiet, Mr Landmark. All systems are functioning normally and two patrols continue to cover the inside of the fences.'

'And the western side, towards the sea?'

'We've doubled the patrols along the wharf. I was there half an hour ago. Everything is dead quiet.'

'Nothing out to sea?'

'No lights, nothing. A gale warning has been issued for later tonight. I doubt we have to worry.'

'What about the contractors' staff.'

'Koeberg Civil Contractors and Alsthom-Atlantique are totally off site. Not one of their staff is here.'

'Fremetone?'

'There are five of them in the reactor building.'

'What are they doing there? I thought Fremetone had given their staff time off?'

'I don't know, probably technical work.' Heyns sighed in exasperation.

Doubts nagged at Don's mind. 'What security do you have inside the buildings?'

'We have an armed guard at the airlock door leading to the reactor building.'

'Heyns, if anything out of the ordinary happens, it doesn't matter how insignificant, I want you to telephone me immediately. Do you understand?'

'I go no further. We less than one kilometre from shore.' Yuri looked stubbornly at the cadres. 'I already take chance for you.' He cut the engine and cast anchor.

'All right, comrades. Let's do it.'

Slipping on their goggles and oxygen cylinders, each one was lowered into the sea and floated clear. Themba turned on the switch and the whirring propeller took him away from the ship. Koeberg had made it easy for them; a red and a green flashing light marked the ends of the breakwater.

The four inflatables skimmed across the surface. Themba glanced across his right shoulder. Masses of dark cloud were billowing in from the direction of Cape Town. Every now and again a puff of wind, a forerunner to the storm, blew strongly, breaking the sea against the side wall and spraying into the craft. The forward motion of the inflatable drained the water through the back scuppers. Themba strapped himself in and used the oxygen.

The four entered the calm of the harbour. Themba could see the two domes of the reactor halls ahead. He was behind the others and almost collided with the rubber duck in front as they reduced speed suddenly.

Two uniformed guards with a German shepherd dog on a lead walked to the top of the slipway, exactly where they had to dock.

Would their plans be thwarted? The three comrades in front of Themba reduced their propeller revolutions to idle, waiting, bobbing low in the water. With the bright lights behind them the guards were looking into the dark, but not the dog. It started barking furiously, straining at the leash, pulling the guard down the slipway.

At that moment Themba saw a blonde woman run from the direction of the buildings, her arms waving vigorously. The guard pulled the dog backwards and both guards ran towards the gesticulating figure. She was pointing excitedly towards the south. Her body language, even at that distance, showed urgency. The guards ran in the direction she pointed, dragging the snarling dog behind them.

The woman ran down the slipway to the water's edge and flashed a torch. As the noses of the inflatables grounded each man jumped out, cutting the motors and dragging the craft a way up the slipway.

'Why four? I expect only three?' The woman spoke tersely.

Themba saved the situation. 'Odile, I'm Themba Memani from Lesotho. I joined the team at the last minute.'

Odile smiled and tossed her hair – she was a very beautiful woman. 'We only identify three blast places, *monsieur*.'

'Think up a fourth one quickly, one that will do a lot of damage.' Themba spoke urgently.

'The reactor head,' she breathed excitedly. 'Only yesterday they lowered it from its place on the reactor vessel to the lower level. Now it easy to get at. It is good to explode.'

'That's mine,' smiled Themba grimly.

She watched, fascinated, as they opened the watertight compartments, removed the explosives and clamped down the hatches again.

'Lead the way, Odile.'

At the top of the slipway she peered over the flat expanse of the quay. The four cadres crouched behind her. The quay was deserted. Odile ran ahead. The stairwell was in a building abutting the reactor housing, with entry points at the various levels. They entered and ran silently up the steps until Odile stopped them.

'Main airlock door to half-way level in reactor building in front. Guard there.' She opened a fire door and pushed them into a locker room. 'You wait here. I seduce guard and bring him here. You find rope in locker No. 23. You tie him up.'

Before they could answer she was gone.

The two guards on quay duty and the dog ran towards the southern boundary. Halogen lights lit up the area. They peered through the security fence but could see no movement.

'What now?'

'We report to security at the main gate.'

Through the plate-glass windows Heyns saw them coming. He opened the door as they arrived out of breath. 'What's wrong?'

'A woman, a French technician, stopped us on the quay.'

'What was she doing there? Fremetone employees are not allowed out of the reactor building.'

The guard shook his head. 'I don't know, but she insisted she saw someone outside the fence to the south of the plant.'

'Tell me what you did.'

'We ran to the fence but could see no one in the cleared strip around the perimeter, so we came to the office.'

Heyns was puzzled. 'Funny, the heat sensors showed nothing on my alarm panels. They should have picked up a body temperature up to a hundred metres from the fence.'

'What must we do?'

'Go through the main gate and scour the area to the south. I'll radio the other two teams to join you.'

Within five minutes all three teams were outside the southern fence. Using their flashlights they combed the cleared area and then concentrated on the outlying bush. The security guards moved along the eastern fence. Finding nothing, the guards radioed in.

'Seeing you're out there, try the north fence as well.' I'd better telephone Mr Landmark, just in case, thought Heyns.

Pierre was bending to pick up a sleeping Blaise, when the telephone rang. Don glanced at him in alarm and rushed off.

'Sorry to disturb you, Mr Landmark. This is Heyns from Koeberg.'

'Yes, Heyns, what is it?'

'You told me to contact you even if something insignificant happened.'

'Get on with it, Heyns,' Don barked irritably.

'Well, a female Fremetone technician was on the quay. She stopped a patrol and told them she had seen someone outside the fence. I sent all the patrols outside to investigate, but they found nothing.'

Don cursed. 'You fool, they've come in from the sea.'

'Who has come in from the sea, Mr Landmark?'

'I don't know. Possibly saboteurs. Sound the Red Alert. Recall your teams and send one team down to the quay.'

'Red Alert? I've never used the red alarm before, Mr Landmark.' Heyns was distraught. 'All hell will break loose here. You're not serious, Mr Landmark?'

'I'm deadly serious. Push that button now so I can hear the sirens.'

'Yes, Mr Landmark.' Heyns unlocked the bullet-proof glass case with a series of code numbers. He swung the door open and held his finger on the button, afraid of the consequences.

'Push the damn button, Heyns.'

He depressed the button and the Red Alert clicked into action. Sirens wailed, searchlights flooded the whole terrain like daylight and numbers dialled automatically – ambulance, police, navy, air force, army, hospitals and fire departments.

'Come, Pierre, let's go,' shouted Don. 'There's trouble at Koeberg.'

Odile walked calmly up to the guard at the airlock door. He fancied her and had often playfully teased her. She had always brushed him off disdainfully. Tonight she moved towards him provocatively. She rubbed against him. '*Mon cher*, I want you tonight.'

He could not believe his luck. He pulled her to him, kissing her roughly. She responded by squeezing him through the front of his trousers. He breathed heavily, totally aroused.

Odile broke away. 'Come, we go to locker room. We make beautiful love.'

He followed her through the fire door. As he entered, four pairs of hands grabbed him, pinning him to the wall. Themba removed his pistol, placing it in the wetsuit's watertight pocket. They trussed the guard up, his hands behind his back, his bent legs tied to his hands. Stuffing a sock into his mouth they used insulation tape to keep it in place. Odile removed the bunch of keys from a clip around his waist and led the four MK cadres to the airlock door. She unlocked it and they entered the reactor building.

Four French Fremetone technicians waited inside. Odile took control. 'Which one got limpet?'

Chico stepped forward. 'You go with Henri.' The two disappeared along the steel walkways between the double concrete walls which formed the outer shell of the reactor building.

'Another limpet?' Matroos nodded. 'You go with Maurice.' They quickly left for the turbine hall.

'The *monsieur* with the Plastic 4?'

'That's me,' Clifford smiled. 'Make mine a worthwhile target.'

'Sure! Sure! You go with Phillipe. He take you to control room on very top level.'

'*Monsieur* Themba, I take you personally to lowest level.' She looked at the remaining technician. 'Pauli, you wait here, *cheri*, in case there problem.'

Chico and Henri dropped down to ground level. They reached a spot where a mass of electrical cables came together in a steel casing, packed tightly like the bristles of a brush.

Henri explained. 'This is a cable tray carrying the cables from the main control room to the reactor pumps. Put your limpet here.' He tapped the metal surround.

Chico clicked off the safety lever. He held the flat face of the limpet parallel to the metal and felt the magnet start to pull. He thrust the mine forward. With a solid clunk it attached itself to the cable tray. The steel blade started cutting through the lead plate. It would explode in forty-five minutes. He looked at his watch. The blast would be five minutes after midnight.

Maurice led Matroos to the turbine hall. Two forty-metre-long turbines dominated the cavernous interior of the huge building. Matroos pointed to the solid casing of the turbine. 'There?'

'No! No!' Maurice was excitable. 'You do no damage there. Come with me.' He led him along a walkway where twisted steel pipes curled over and under each other, looking like a gigantic bowl of cooked spaghetti. 'These pipes feed steam from the generators to the high- and low-pressure turbines. Place limpet here.' He indicated a spot. 'We knock steam generator out of alignment and all pipes will have to be replaced.'

Matroos pictured the twisted and tangled mess the limpet would create. He smiled grimly as he released the safety lever. 'I've finished.'

'Okay then, let's get back.'

Clifford and Phillipe were breathing heavily when they reached the control room on the top level. From here the whole power station would be monitored. A concave wall was packed with light panels that showed every part of the entire plant. In front of the wall was a flat surface containing dials and instruments. On the side were two television screens with closed-circuit television cameras monitoring the area around the reactor.

Kneading the two bars of Plastic 4 together, Clifford and Phillipe made a twelve-metre-long sausage which they placed along the length of the control panels. Clifford set the timing device to blow after three hours. The clock clicked steadily, sounding loud in the confines of the room. Clifford jammed the twin points into the middle of the Plastic-4 sausage. He nodded to Phillipe. 'All set.' He wished to savour the moment and again looked around the room. In the very centre was the operator's console. Clifford walked across and sat in it.

Themba and Odile ran along the circular passages in the shell of the reactor containment building and down a series of flights of steps.

'Where are we going?'

'You say you want reactor head, *monsieur*. Crane has lifted off head and let down to lowest level. We go there.' They passed the ground level and continued down. At the lowest level they entered the reactor building proper.

Odile pointed. 'There is reactor head.'

On the concrete floor lay a huge piece of solid metal, four metres in diameter with stud holes all the way around its perimeter. A solid mass of weld-fabricated low-carbon steel, the reactor head weighed fifty-five tonnes. Sticking out on top like the stiff quills of a porcupine were the shiny silver control rods bedded into the drive mechanism.

'Is there uranium present?' Themba wanted reassurance. He was not prepared to sacrifice innocent lives.

She shook her head. 'Only when pelleted uranium packed into rods, and they lowered into reactor,' she explained. 'You get fission under pressure with the water. No uranium here – still in fuel building.'

Themba took her word and searched the reactor head for the best spot to attach the limpet. He explained to Odile, 'A limpet mine is designed for use underwater. The water pressure from the one side of the mine helps to blow a hole through a ship's metal hull on its other side. If we can push a heavy object against the back of the limpet, it will concentrate the full force of the explosion on the reactor head.'

'We have the heavy lead shields on wheels in next cubicle. You help me push.'

Themba attached the mine to the sloping side of the reactor head, just below the control-rod drive mechanism. Odile and Themba wheeled the heavy lead screen closer and let it fall. It landed on top of the limpet mine, pushing it hard against the reactor head.

'*Monsieur*, let us go.' They started back to the half-way level.

Clifford, in the chair at the operator's console, stared fascinated at the glowing wall of instruments. Suddenly lights started flashing all over the panels. The red telephone on the console rang stridently. 'What the hell?' Clifford sprang up. 'What's wrong?'

'Red Alert!' Phillipe's face was ashen. 'The Red Alert has sounded. We must get out of here!'

The other technicians and cadres heard the wailing sirens. They met at the rendezvous point at the half-way level. Clifford and Phillipe arrived last.

'Security has been alerted.' Odile gesticulated. 'We go now.'

They all sprinted through the airlock door, down the levels of the building and through the outer doors. They were in the shadows when two guards and a dog rushed past them towards the sea.

She pointed. 'You must hurry.'

'Thanks,' waved Themba gratefully.

The French ran around the corner of the turbine hall and tumbled into their car. They drove off towards the main gates.

Heyns stopped them. 'Where are you going in such a hurry?'

Odile had a ready answer. 'The Red Alert went off so we cleared out of the building.'

'It's nothing to worry about.' Heyns relaxed. 'Mr Landmark made me sound the alarm when I told him I had turned off the security system.'

'Where are the guards?'

'Landmark told me to send them to the quay.' Heyns smiled broadly. 'He was ranting about saboteurs coming in from the sea.' He laughed heartily. 'Have you ever heard such nonsense?'

'We're going home, we're tired.' Odile flashed Heyns a dazzling smile.

'Can we go now?'

He opened the gate for them. They passed Don Landmark's car half a kilometre down the road.

'Sir! Sir! Come quickly.' There was urgency in the rating's voice. 'Red Alert from Koeberg nuclear power station.'

'Oh shit!' The lieutenant at Silvermine knocked over his chair in his urgency. 'Get hold of Southern Air Command. Tell them to have a Shackleton aircraft on standby.' He turned to the radio operator. 'The frigate *Paul Kruger* is moored in Table Bay. Alert her captain.'

The radar operator summoned him. 'Lieutenant, the blip is still eight hundred metres off the coast near Koeberg. Is it perhaps a coincidence?'

'Get hold of Koeberg first. Find out if their emergency is genuine and what the problem is. It could be a false alarm. Let's get full details before we wake the Admiral.'

The four comrades hurried over the open ground. The wind had grown in strength while they had been inside. Now it came in strong gusts, blowing straight into their faces as they made for the southern corner of the harbour. Their wetsuits hampered their speed. Finally they reached the slipway. As quickly as they could they turned their inflatables around and pulled them into the water.

Out of the corner of his eye Themba saw movement. The guards were running along the quay towards the slipway. They released the German shepherd and it bounded ahead.

Chico and Clifford launched and headed for the harbour mouth at full power. Themba and Matroos were launching when the dog reached them. It took a flying leap at Matroos. It clamped its powerful jaws over his upper arm and they tumbled into the shallow water in a tangled heap. Its teeth bit through the wetsuit and Matroos bellowed in pain.

Themba pulled out his pistol and tried to get a clear shot. He danced around the thrashing bodies, waiting for an opening. The dog moved position slightly and Themba fired. With a sharp bellow of pain it let go of Matroos's arm and ran yelping up the slipway. Themba put his shoulder under his friend's arm and helped him to his feet.

Don Landmark slammed to a stop outside the entrance. Heyns activated a switch and the gates swung open.

'What's going on, Heyns?'

'The Red Alert has sounded and I sent the guards to the sea front as you instructed.'

Gunning the motor, Don roared around the building complex and stopped at the quay. Pierre was out of the car before it halted, running towards the slipway.

A shot exploded and Pierre stopped, as a yowling German shepherd bounded in his direction, blood spraying from a wound. Then he saw the two men in wetsuits at the bottom of the slipway, the one helping the other towards an inflatable craft.

'Stop, or I'll shoot,' screamed Pierre.

Two dismayed faces turned towards him. The hood of Themba's wetsuit was pushed off his face and Pierre recognised him immediately. 'Memani,' he shouted in glee, 'I've got you at last.'

'Roux,' muttered Themba as he squeezed off a shot. Pierre fell flat and wriggled behind a barrel, took aim and fired. Matroos shrieked shrilly and tumbled into his rubber duck. Themba dived into his craft, flicked the starter switches of both inflatables, and they pulled away together. Over his shoulder Themba pressed off two more shots. They were ten metres into the harbour. Themba clung desperately to a handhold on Matroos's craft as they sped away alongside each other.

Pierre ran to the bottom of the slipway. The black inflatables were hard to see in the dark. He sprinted along the southern breakwater, keeping his eyes peeled. Seeing a flash of white water, he stopped. The lights of Koeberg were glistening off the harbour's water. Pierre grunted in satisfaction as a shiny side wall reflected the light. Holding his pistol with both hands, he fired.

Sss . . . sss . . . sss . . . the air escaped out of the side wall. Slowly the craft deflated. Sss . . . sss . . . sss . . . Themba's inflatable started slewing in the water, slowing their speed. He pulled up his hood and slipped on the goggles. As the craft began to crumple, he rolled across to the other rubber duck. He straightened out the unconscious Matroos, put on his goggles, attached the oxygen pipe to his mouth and strapped him in. The double weight of both men forced the craft deeper into the water and Themba could hear the motor straining as they hit the open sea.

The abandoned craft bobbed on the water and Pierre fired off another three shots. He looked around urgently and saw a wooden dinghy moored to a jetty alongside the quay. He ran along the wharf, down the ladder and into the boat, nodding in satisfaction when he saw the forty-horsepower Mercury outboard. The red petrol tank was full. The engine spluttered, then fired, its propeller bubbling up water. Pierre cast off, turned on full power and raced into the harbour.

'Pierre are you crazy?' Don shouted. 'Come back.'

Landmark turned as he heard footsteps. Two guards ran along the breakwater and stopped in front of him. For once in his life Don looked ruffled. 'Will you please tell me what is going on here?'

'There were four men in wetsuits,' declared one. Both babbled excitedly at the same time.

Don had to patch the story together. 'They were professionals. That can only mean one thing, they've set bombs in the power station. Jump in, we must get to the main gate and stop the Frenchmen leaving.'

At the front gate Don confronted Heyns. 'Arrest the French technicians who are on duty.'

'I can't do that, Mr Landmark. They drove out of here a few minutes before you arrived.'

Don remembered the car that had passed him. 'You mean the plant is deserted?'

'Except for the permanent guard at the airlock doors.'

'I'm going in to see if I can defuse the bombs.'

'You can't do that, Mr Landmark.' Heyns looked at him aghast. 'It's too dangerous.'

'That's my affair!' Don eyed Heyns sternly. 'Get hold of Ysterplaat – ask them to send a helicopter post haste to our heli-pad. You understand, Heyns?'

'Yes.' Sirens blared as police and army vehicles converged on Koeberg. 'What must I tell them, Mr Landmark?'

'That the ANC has planted bombs in the power station and the saboteurs have escaped out to sea. Get them to search the coast and sea for them.'

Don drove to the southern entrance of the nuclear building. Taking two steps at a time he reached the half-way level. To his horror the airlock door was standing wide open and there was no sign of the guard. He slammed and secured the door.

It was five past midnight when Chico's limpet detonated at the ground level in a flash of crimson. The explosion sent a huge force into the cable tray. A metre to each side of the impact, cables disintegrated as the electric current caused a shower of sparks to cascade over the area.

Don felt the reactor building shudder on its aseismic ball bearings, but the reinforced circular outer walls remained intact.

He jumped back as the airlock door absorbed the shock. His face was pale and strained. Don heard a tapping from down the passage. Puzzled, he walked towards the sound and turned the corner, listening. He heard it again, coming from the locker room. He opened the fire door and saw the guard in the corner, tied and gagged. The fire door closed behind him.

Matroos's limpet exploded among the maze of pipes in the turbine hall. Huge sections were flung in all directions. The immediate blast knocked a six-metre hole in the labyrinth of piping. The debris and shrapnel caused a secondary eruption, destroying a further ten metres of convolutions. The strength of the explosion shuddered back along the pipes, rocking the three giant steam generators in the reactor building, fracturing the delicate U-tubes. A blast of air was driven down the passages, knocking over safety gear, emergency gas masks attached to the walls, so hot it blistered off the paint. The searing heat passed the fire-proof door to the locker room, slammed against the impenetrable airlock door and bounced back down the passage, charring everything in its path.

Don pulled the insulation tape off the guard's mouth. 'How did you get here? You're supposed to be guarding the airlock door.'

'They overpowered me, Mr Landmark.' Don untied his bonds and he stood up on wobbly legs.

At that moment Themba's limpet went off on the lowest level. This level contained one of the thickest and strongest pre-stressed concrete floors – the reason why the huge reactor containment head was stored on this floor. The mine exploded against the side of the head. Shock waves bounced against the heavy lead screen and hit the metal a second, third and fourth time until the screen shattered into thousands of pieces.

The steel of the control-rod drive mechanism was not as strong as the solid cast of the reactor head and it buckled. The control rods, mangled and malformed, turned from sparkling silver to a messy black. The blast heated the reactor head and red patches glowed in the metal. The uneven expansion and contraction coursed towards the edges where it came into contact with the cold concrete floor. The stressed metal had to give somewhere and the weakest point was between the stud holes on the perimeter. Hairline cracks appeared.

Don grew cold as he heard the sound of this explosion – solid and deep, from the very depths of the nuclear building, the clunk of thick metal being struck. The reactor head? His mind raced. The guards had told him there were four saboteurs. How many bombs had each set? Where were they? When would they explode? It would be folly to try to disarm the explosives.

I'm an engineer, not a bomb disposal expert, he thought as he dejectedly left the nuclear building. Koeberg, his project, his life, was being torn out by the guts and he was powerless to do anything about it. I told Matchett it would happen and he wouldn't listen.

At Silvermine the radio operator's face paled as he listened to the message. He turned to his duty officer. 'Lieutenant, the army is on the line. There have been explosions at Koeberg.'

The lieutenant grabbed the receiver. 'What do you want me to do?'

'It's a navy problem.' The army officer spoke curtly. 'Four suspected terrorists escaped out to sea. On land we would sort them out, now it's your can of worms, buddy.'

He had no option but to advise the chief of the navy. A sleepy voice answered, 'Admiral Putter.'

'Sir, there have been explosions at Koeberg nuclear power station. They suspect sabotage.'

'Have you notified the army?'

'They say it's our job, the saboteurs escaped out to sea. We have a ship eight hundred metres off Koeberg on our radar scanners.'

'What have you done, Lieutenant?'

'The SAS *Paul Kruger* is on stand-by off Cape Town harbour, plus a Shackleton at Ysterplaat air force base.'

Taking control, Admiral Putter made his decisions. 'Instruct the captain of the *Paul Kruger* to put to sea immediately. Get the Shackleton up and let her strafe the ship with her searchlights and report back to me. Meanwhile contact the air force base at Langebaan Road and ask them to scramble a squadron of Impala jets, armed with rockets.'

'Anything else, Admiral?'

'I'll wait at the telephone. Keep me posted of all developments, Lieutenant.'

As Themba and Matroos left the protection of the harbour, the full force of the south-west squall hit them. The sea was a huge expanse of white horses as wave upon wave careered over the inflatable. The wind whipped at Themba as he held tightly on to the handholds. Matroos lay on the floor of the inflatable, moaning weakly.

Themba lay on top of Matroos, there was not enough space to lie side by side. The motor laboured against the strong wind. He glanced at his watch. It was past midnight. With a sinking feeling he knew they would not reach the Russian fishing trawler in time, even if the craft's battery held its charge.

His only real option was to turn around and travel with the storm towards the beach. The thought of an intensive chase by Pierre Roux, similar to the one after his escape from Robben Island, kept him doggedly heading out to sea.

Sound was snatched away by the roaring wind, but Themba was sure he heard the noise of a high revving engine. He looked around in surprise and saw the bow of a boat smashing through the waves. As its stern lifted over a swell the propeller came free of the water, screaming like a banshee. A man was swinging a flashlight in a roving arc. Any second the beam would fall on the inflatable. In the huge expanse of sea there was no place to hide.

First Clifford, and two minutes later Chico, reached the *Kaliningrad*, coming in downwind of the storm. Helping hands let down the hoist to get the craft on board. Clifford lost his inflatable in the manoeuvre to slide the framework under its belly. Without his weight the rubber duck lifted high in the water and was overturned by the blasting

wind, disappearing end over end into the darkness. A rope ladder
was flung down for Clifford as he laboured in the water.

Chico managed to attach a rope to the framework and while he
clung on, both he and the inflatable were winched aboard.

Once on deck they were struck by the full force of the blustering
wind. The trawler shuddered at each tumultuous gust, straining at
the anchor chain, the cable and hooks of the winches rattling wildly
in the wind.

Yuri welcomed them on board. 'You make successful mission?'
Chico and Clifford nodded. 'Then you come with me. I give you
good shot of vodka to warm your belly.' He took them to his cabin
and poured each a full glass. Both swallowed the strong drink in
one gulp, feeling the warmth hitting their stomachs and spreading.
The captain gave each a thick jersey, a waterproof jacket and a
sou'wester to jam on his head.

Chico was worried. 'Where are Themba and Matroos?'

'My men call me if they see your friends.' He looked at his watch.
'I only wait five minutes more, then we get hell out of here.'

'Captain! Captain!'

Yuri hurried from his cabin, followed by Clifford and Chico. As
they reached the deck, night turned into day as the Shackleton's
searchlights focused on the trawler. Frightened faces were caught
in the glare as the aeroplane circled overhead.

'Start engines.' Yuri's mind was made up. 'Weigh anchor.' The
diesel engine shook the trawler as it started. The winch began
whining and the anchor chain clattered aboard. The captain waited
only for the anchor to come clear of the ocean floor before issuing
his next command. 'Full speed ahead, due west.'

'Themba and Matroos aren't here!' Chico grabbed at Yuri's
sleeve. 'You must wait for them.'

Yuri shook his head slowly. 'Can wait no longer. No have
permission to be in South African territorial water. If they catch
me with you on board we create international incident.'

As the torchlight bounced closer, Themba made up his mind. He
was not going to be captured again, to be sent back to Robben
Island. He would rather die. He rolled off Matroos into the sea.
A second later the inflatable was lit by the flashlight.

Pierre saw the craft and veered to starboard. He cut the engine
and the boat wallowed in the swell. Pierre scrabbled to the bows

and leaned over the side, grasping the rubber duck. He pulled it alongside. A look of glee flashed over his features. I've got you Memani, he thought, as he leant far over the side, trying to pull the man aboard.

Themba dived under the surface as the beam struck the inflatable. Holding his breath he kicked out strongly. He swam under the wooden hull of the boat and surfaced on the opposite side. He grabbed the gunwale and lifted himself to peer over the lip. The man's back was turned towards him.

Waves breaking over the dinghy rocked it dangerously. Themba waited for the side to dip and quickly rolled aboard. He took the pistol from the pouch of his wetsuit and dived forward. His fingers closed over the butt of the pistol in its holster on the man's belt. Themba pulled the weapon free. He fell back into the stern and trained both pistols on the man. Pierre turned in surprise, shock etched on his face.

The two stared at each other in hatred. Themba waved a gun towards Matroos. 'Get my friend on to the boat,' he yelled to make himself heard above the gale.

'He's stuck,' answered Pierre, a look of loathing in his eyes.

'Loosen the clip of the safety belt on the right-hand side.' Themba waved the pistols menacingly.

Pierre leaned over, found the catch and lifted Matroos bodily into the boat. He lost his footing and tumbled backwards with Matroos on top of him. Themba twisted the accelerator shaft and the boat shot forward. With the lights of Koeberg astern he struck out towards the open sea.

Pierre watched Themba intently. He saw his attention was focused ahead. Slowly he crept closer, using Matroos's body to shield him. Stretching out his arm, his fingers closed over Themba's ankle and he yanked, pulling him to the floor. In a flash Pierre threw himself on top of Themba, grabbing for his neck. Their faces were centimetres apart.

'Now I've got you,' sneered Pierre triumphantly.

A huge wave smashed over them, drenching them in a cascade of water. They were flung to one side, but Pierre held on with all his strength.

Themba pushed a pistol against Pierre's temple. 'Let go or I'll shoot,' he screamed. His instinct was to pull the trigger, but deep down something inexplicable stopped him.

Pierre slowly released his hold on Themba's neck.

Themba pushed him aside roughly and Pierre landed in the bows. 'What are you doing here, Roux?' shouted Themba.

'I followed you to Koeberg. I found the plans in your safe at Maseru.'

'So it was you in my office. Why were you there?'

'Military intelligence.'

Cursing, Themba returned to his seat in the stern and viciously revved the motor. The boat shot forward.

Themba scanned the sea for the trawler, but looking for the ship in the half-light, with the bow crashing through the waves and the gale blowing streamers of water off the wave-caps, was like trying to find a needle in a haystack.

'Silvermine, this is Sierra Alpha Charlie Two.' The Shackleton reconnaissance pilot from Southern Air Command's voice came excitely over the microphone.

The lieutenant answered. 'This is Silvermine, I receive you, Sierra Alpha Charlie Two.'

'We have a ship below us caught in our searchlight. It's a Russian fishing trawler, the *Kaliningrad*, heading due west.'

'Thank you, Sierra Alpha Charlie Two. Wait one while I report to the Admiral.'

'Roger, Silvermine.'

On the second ring, Putter lifted the receiver. The lieutenant relayed the news. The radar showed him the ship was one nautical mile off the coast.

'Eleven to go before she reaches international waters. Have those Impala jets from Langebaan Road scrambled yet?'

'They're arming the cannons of the aircraft and installing rockets under the wings. They say they'll be ready for take-off any minute now.'

'What about the *Paul Kruger*?'

'Er . . . sir! It was a public holiday, Admiral.'

'So what?' Putter barked in irritation.

'They've only just cleared Duncan Dock with a skeleton crew on board.'

'Damnation!' Putter growled. 'We don't have much room to play with; twelve nautical miles is not a great deal.' He pictured the scene. 'Recall the Shackleton to base. Have the Impala jets engage the intruder by firing over its bows from starboard. That should turn her into the oncoming *Paul Kruger*. It's the best we can do.'

'If she won't deviate from her course, Admiral?'

Putter muttered over the telephone, still deciding what to do. 'I don't want to cause an international incident with the Soviet Union without knowing the true facts.' He spoke clearly. 'If the trawler won't turn, report back to me.'

'Very well, Admiral.'

Themba knew something was terribly wrong. They should have reached the *Kaliningrad* already. He gazed around desperately but saw only the waves in the pale light of a reflected moon.

He heard the steady drone of an aircraft's engines and ghostlike shadow passed overhead. Unexpectedly the Shackleton's searchlight came on, playing across the water. It latched on to the trawler. The aircraft circled, keeping the *Kaliningrad* lit up. Themba cheered – now he had a beacon to steer towards. They had overshot the mark, but the trawler was headed their way.

Chico saw the boat first. He pointed excitedly, puzzled when he recognised Themba in the stern and a white man in the bows. He pleaded with the captain. 'Slow down so we can pick them up.'

Yuri was worried about the circling aircraft, yet he knew if he didn't stop he would have them on his conscience. He gave the order and the trawler slowed and idled.

Men crowded the rail of the trawler as Chico waved the boat in. Themba brought the wooden dingy alongside and cut the engine. Clifford attached a line to a lifebuoy and threw it to him. He slipped the buoy over his shoulders, then dragged Matroos to a standing position. Themba put his arms around the injured man and was hauled upwards. Eager hands pulled them on deck.

'Who's he?' Chico demanded, pointing down to Pierre in the dinghy.

'Pierre Roux from military intelligence.'

'The enemy,' breathed Chico in hatred.

'Careful with Matroos,' instructed Themba. 'He's been shot in the back.'

'Who shot him?' Chico challenged.

'He did,' answered Themba, indicating Pierre.

'Stop! Stop!' Chico screamed in indignation, preventing the crew members from hauling Pierre up. 'Let him drown.'

A big wave dashed the dinghy against the steel plating of the trawler, splintering the wood. The next wave poured into the boat, causing it to list badly. Pierre held on for dear life. He looked pleadingly towards the crew.

'No way!' Clifford and Chico were in complete agreement. 'He's not coming aboard.'

'Definitely not,' growled Yuri, concurring. 'I no allow military man from illegal regime on my ship. He stay in boat.' Yuri waved to the first mate. 'Full speed ahead.'

The trawler shuddered as the propeller accelerated and the ship lurched forward.

'Memani, you bastard!' Pierre screamed, shaking his fist furiously. Then he was alone in the sea.

'Silvermine to Sierra Alpha Charlie Two. Come in Sierra Alpha Charlie Two.'

'I hear you loud and clear Silvermine.'

'Admiral Putter's orders – return to base.'

'Wilco. I want to report that men in a small boat have just reached the fishing trawler, two have been hauled aboard, but a third has been cast adrift.'

'Must be the suspected terrorists from Koeberg. I'll inform Admiral Putter.'

There was silence for a few moments then Putter spoke. 'Continue as planned, Lieutenant. If the pirate refuses to alter course, I order you to engage the enemy.'

'Affirmative, Admiral.'

Themba stood at the rail for a long time, staring pensively out to sea. Then he shrugged his shoulders and hurried to Matroos's cabin. A fisherman who doubled as the ship's medical orderly had cut away his wetsuit and was examining the bullet wound in his back. 'Bullet go through lung. He need hospital,' he said, shaking his head.

'Do you have a doctor aboard the mother ship?'

He nodded. 'Doctor is good.'

Themba looked at the puncture mark low on Matroos's shoulder oozing blood. There was no exit wound, the bullet was lodged inside. Matroos was breathing heavily, a coarse, rasping sound came from his chest. He was only semi-conscious.

'You're cold.' Clifford tapped Themba on the shoulder.

Only then did Themba realise his teeth were chattering. Chico led him away. The deck was in darkness. The Shackleton had disappeared. They hurried to the bridge.

'Where's the aeroplane?' Themba turned to the skipper.

'He go away. Now we head for international waters.' Yuri saw how cold Themba was and pulled out a hip flask. 'Take swallow, you feel better.' Themba coughed as the raw spirit hit his throat. 'You get out of wetsuit.'

Themba took it off and a crew member gave him a thick jersey, waterproof leggings and a jacket.

A high-pitched whining noise was heard above the howling wind. They looked at each other with puzzled expressions. A thunderous roar shook the rigging as an Impala jet passed low overhead. Altogether six jets flashed over in quick succession. Themba ran on deck just in time to see a missile explode in the sea ahead of the bows. He confronted Yuri on the bridge.

'What's happening?'

'Jets, he try to head us off. He want us to turn around.' He jabbed his finger on the radar screen which was showing a distinctive blip to port. 'Ship, he coming towards us from Cape Town harbour. I think it naval vessel.'

'What are you going to do, Yuri?'

'I have my ship, my crew and my catch to think about.'

Themba looked at him aghast. 'If they catch us in South African territorial waters they'll arrest us and take us off the trawler.'

Yuri looked at Themba closely. 'What they do to you?'

'As sure as I stand here tonight, all four of us will be hanged.' Themba spoke solemnly.

Yuri looked at him sharply. 'Maybe we all die anyway, if the jets he hit us with a missile.'

'Are they just sword rattling?' Themba studied Yuri's face. 'Will they really bomb the *Kaliningrad*?'

'Who knows.' Yuri shrugged. 'South African government, he does not like the communist Soviet Union. He could strike us.'

'How far are we from international waters?'

Looking at his charts Yuri replied slowly. 'Two nautical miles.'

'Then go for it, Yuri.' Themba urged. 'The authorities know Russia will not take kindly to one of her ships being bombed. They won't really attack, they're just trying to frighten you into changing course.'

As two more missiles struck the sea on the starboard bow, Yuri smiled. 'You talk like lawyer. I like you, Themba. I don't want you be hanged.' Yuri put his hand around his own neck and jerked upwards in a mock reference to the gallows. 'I take chance for you and heading west at full speed.'

The Impalas put up a show of bravado. Screaming in on the starboard side, they fired their twin fifty-millimetre cannons across the trawler's bows. Streamers of cannon shells struck the sea. Yuri held his course doggedly. A minute later they fired six rockets; they exploded close to the ship swamping her in a deluge of water. Yuri was quaking inwardly, but he showed no emotion as he pointed ahead and spoke to the first mate. 'Hold your course firm.'

Without warning the *Kaliningrad* buckled as a rocket hit her amidships and exploded in her depths. In a flash of light and a boom of sound, the forward hatch cover was flung into the air as tons of fish were blasted to pulp. They exploded out of the hold like an erupting volcano.

Yuri handed the bridge over to the first mate and anxiously ran to inspect the damage. He came back muttering fiercely, his face as dark as a thunder cloud. He shook his clenched fist at the sky. 'You bastards try to destroy my ship!'

'What was the damage?'

'The missile he entered above plimsoll line. We in no danger of sinking, but I have the fish paste in the forward hold!' Yuri scowled. 'My bosses he won't be pleased.'

'Keep going, Yuri, we're surely almost there.' Themba's face was filled with anxiety.

'First mate, give me our position,' demanded Yuri.

'Eleven and a half nautical miles from shore.'

As the helicopter landed Don jerked open the door and jumped inside. 'I'm Don Landmark, Koeberg's project manager,' he said to the pilot. 'Pierre Roux, my friend from military intelligence, is out on the ocean in a flimsy wooden boat. We must try and save him.'

'Sorry, Mr Landmark,' answered the pilot. 'At this very moment Impala jets are strafing a Russian trawler. It's too dangerous. We must wait.' He replaced his headphones to listen to the reports on the air force radio band. 'Hurrah!' he shouted. 'One of the jets reports a direct hit on the trawler.'

*   *   *

The jet pilot's voice crackled over the radio. 'Silver Falcon One reporting a direct hit on the intruder.'

At Silvermine the men glanced at each other, worried expressions on their faces. There was concern in the lieutenant's voice as he answered. 'Has the ship changed course, Silver Falcon One?'

'Negative, she continues due west.'

'Hold fire, let me report to Admiral Putter.'

'Roger, Silvermine.'

'Admiral, this is Silvermine. We've scored a direct hit on the Russian fishing trawler as you ordered, but she's not deviated from her course.'

'What is her position, Lieutenant?'

The officer checked the radar screen. 'Less than half a nautical mile before she leaves our territorial waters.'

'Damnation, the margin of error is too close.' Admiral Putter gave up the chase, not prepared to face a departmental board of inquiry. 'Recall the Impalas and the *Paul Kruger*.'

'Very good, Admiral.'

Huge waves crashed over the small boat as it slewed drunkenly in the water. Pierre tried to start the motor again, using up precious energy pulling and pulling the starter cord, but the engine refused to fire. Then he saw the petrol tank was under water and gave up the task. He opened a locker and found life-jackets. Thankfully he struggled into one and knotted the cords across his chest. In another locker he found a plastic bucket. He baled as fast as he could but made no headway. He stopped for a few minutes' rest, the icy wind chilling him to the bone. He no longer had the energy or the inclination to bale and sat hunched up, waiting for the inevitable.

Slowly the boat slid out under him and he floated free on the stormy sea, convinced he would die.

The howling jets banked in formation and disappeared up the west coast, heading back to base. The *Kaliningrad* was left alone in the whistling wind.

'Twelve nautical miles, we are in international waters.'

Crowding the bridge Themba, Chico and Clifford waited in apprehension for another bolt out of the blue. Nothing came.

'Fourteen nautical miles – I think we safe.' Yuri pulled out his hip flask. '*Nastarovya*.' He gulped the vodka while the three cadres cheered. Yuri passed the liquor around and they all toasted their mission.

'We rendezvous with factory ship at dawn,' said Yuri. 'Now I need a few hours' sleep.'

They visited Matroos to tell him the good news. He had regained consciousness but was still breathing painfully. Smiling wanly, he grasped Themba's hand. 'You saved my life by turning back.' His eyes glinted in appreciation. 'I had my doubts about you accompanying us, but now I'm very pleased you came along. Thank you, Themba.'

The helicopter pilot nodded at Don Landmark. 'I have authority to search for your friend.'

'Thank goodness,' breathed Don.

As the helicopter took off, it was buffeted by the wind. 'Don't pin your hopes on finding him alive,' shouted the pilot. 'Conditions out there are terrible.'

Angling the chopper against the wind, they flew over the ocean. Anxious faces peered into the murky blackness. The pilot flew back and forth, working to a set pattern. After half an hour he threw up his hands in exasperation. 'Sorry, Mr Landmark. We must return, the storm is getting worse.'

'One more time,' pleaded Don. 'He's my friend.'

'Okay, but one pass only, then back.'

'Thank you,' said Don gratefully.

Pierre floated on his back, the life-jacket keeping his head above water. He was alive, but barely, suffering from hypothermia as his body temperature dropped. His teeth chattered and he swallowed large quantities of water as the waves washed over him. His last recollection before he passed out was of Themba standing at the rail, looking disdainfully down at him.

The helicopter flashed over Pierre, its emergency light shining on the sea. One of the crew peering out of the open door saw a flash of luminous yellow. 'Captain! Captain! I saw something – make another pass.'

Turning into the teeth of the wind the pilot dropped lower. Sea spray rained against the windows.

'There! There! Lower, Captain,' shouted the crew member

excitedly. 'It's a man in a life-jacket.' Down draught from the spinning blades churned up the sea around Pierre, hurling him about like a piece of driftwood. 'I think the man's dead,' he went on. 'Look, he's not moving.'

Another crewman rolled out a rope ladder, and taking his life in his hands, lowered himself over the side, climbing down ponderously. The wind whipped at his body, swinging him from side to side like a trapeze artist. He grabbed hold of the straps of the life-jacket. The crew reeled in the ladder and willing hands pulled Pierre aboard. They felt for a pulse. 'He's alive!'

An aide applied cardio-pulmonary resuscitation. Bending over Pierre he applied five short, sharp compressions to his sternum, then pinching his nose closed blew a deep breath into Pierre's mouth. He repeated the procedure seven times before Pierre started coughing and sea water gushed out of his mouth. Twice more and he took his first ragged breath. After a few minutes Pierre's breathing became more regular, and he sat up, looking around in surprise.

'Thank goodness,' smiled Don. 'Welcome back to the world.'

The heli-pad was surrounded by personnel, vehicles and an ambulance. Pierre was strapped into a stretcher and rushed to Koeberg's sick-bay.

Don Landmark looked down from his office at the concrete apron in front of the turbine hall. The last of the three explosions had been at ten after midnight. That had been almost two and a quarter hours ago. Army bomb disposal units waited on the apron for his order to comb the building, but he refused to issue the instruction. He knew four men had entered the power station, there might well be another explosive to go off. Don was not going to risk the lives of good men.

The timer on the Plastic 4 in the control room tripped the detonator and the sausage exploded along its entire twelve-metre length. Control panels crashed down as the blast shattered everything in its path. Shards were flung across the room destroying every instrument and vestige of scientific apparatus. Wires melted and were severed and mutilated beyond recognition.

The explosion rattled the windows of the administration building. Don sat down tiredly at his desk and dialled through to Heyns. 'Okay, let the bomb disposal units enter now. How is Mr Roux?'

'Much improved. His wife has taken him home, Mr Landmark.'

Accompanied by ESCOM staff the army disposal unit searched from top to bottom. First the turbine hall, then the electrical building, moving to the nuclear building, followed by the two domed reactor buildings and even the two nuclear fuel buildings.

The army officer reported to Don. 'All clear, Mr Landmark. As far as we can ascertain there are no further explosives in the complex. Will there be anything further?'

Shaking his head, Don stood up. 'Thank you for the dangerous job of work you did. The army may withdraw now.' He sent the police observers and the ambulance crews back home. Don slowly walked through the power station. He was devastated at the vast amount of damage caused to key areas in the plant.

At the lowest level in the southern reactor building, he muttered to himself as he saw the mangled remains of the control-rod drive mechanism and the twisted control rods. Bending down he ran his fingers over the surface of the reactor head. Was that a crack? Don went down on his hands and knees looking at the surface intently. He winced when he saw the hairline cracks between the stud holes on the perimeter. 'The cracked head will never stand the pressure created by the nuclear fission,' he muttered. 'That means a brand-new reactor from France, and a twelve-month delay before switch-on.'

He walked into the control room, took one look at the absolute shambles, turned and walked out. A feeling of despondency settled over him and he quickly left the power station.

Heyns stood at the entrance. 'Everything all right, Mr Landmark?'

'Of course not! Thanks to your inefficiency Koeberg is an absolute mess. I'll be recommending your dismissal!'

Don drove home for a few hours' sleep. Come morning, the chief executive would be on his neck and the media would descend on Koeberg like a pack of wolves.

22

Themba drove straight from the hospital to the Umkhonto we Sizwe meeting. He smiled as he thought of his new baby daughter. She was a perfect little person, she had not cried once after her birth – at least, that he had heard. It was Hilda's privilege to name the girl. She had chosen Helen.

'Helen Joseph and Helen Suzman are both wonderful women and great supporters of the freedom struggle.' Themba was happy with Hilda's choice.

Umkhonto we Sizwe held a monthly meeting in Lusaka. Targets identified by the reconnaissance cells in South Africa were discussed and raids planned.

The meetings were chaired by MK Commander Joe Slovo and attended by his Deputy Chris Hani, Themba and other top-ranking MK members. They reached point 14 on the agenda: SAAF CAR BOMBING.

Slovo outlined the mission. 'We're planning a double car bombing for 20 May 1983 outside the South African Air Force headquarters in downtown Pretoria.'

'Why have you chosen that date?' Themba asked.

'It's a Friday,' Slovo replied. 'The timers will be set to explode at four-thirty, just as the government officials leave the building for their weekend.'

Themba was shocked. 'Innocent citizens, people not connected to the freedom struggle, will be killed.'

'Unfortunate,' agreed Slovo. 'As you know, up to now we have gone to extremes to ensure blameless civilians are excluded. The struggle must now enter a new phase.'

'Symbolic attacks on empty buildings such as Koeberg are not achieving the desired results,' Chris Hani added. 'It's the leadership's belief that the freedom struggle must become more effective. Tambo has stated: *Never again are our people going to be doing all the bleeding.*'

Hani looked Themba straight in the eye. 'The time has come for harsher methods. It's not only the regime we have to force away from apartheid, we must make all whites aware of the ANC and the black man's aspirations.'

Slovo turned to Themba. 'As MK's most successful saboteur we would like to appoint you Commander of the mission.' The meeting applauded.

Themba shook his head. 'Sasol and Koeberg were one thing: they were strategic targets which we sabotaged, but nobody was killed.' Themba thought of the birth of his latest child. 'If my wife and children were killed as innocent passers-by I would be devastated.' He glanced at Slovo. 'Would it be in order if you counted me out of the Pretoria mission?'

'Your feelings are respected, Themba.'

They went to the next point on the agenda: 15. VLAKPLAAS.

Hani led the discussion. 'The security police have recently bought a small farm outside Pretoria. It's called Vlakplaas. Beneath its respectable exterior, Vlakplaas is being used for sinister purposes.' He had the attention of everyone. 'They use the farm to debrief MK deserters and to house state witnesses used to testify against our cadres and identify our comrades in the townships. Vlakplaas is a viper's nest of MK traitors.'

Slovo took over. 'One of our most senior MK commanders has turned against us, bribed by the security police. With his knowledge of the ANC he's making our lives very difficult. Already he has given the security police details of our planned missions, resulting in comrades being arrested. He testifies at their trials and the police secure a conviction every time.'

'Turncoat.' Themba spat out the word.

'This traitor moves through the black townships on the Witwatersrand spotting MK comrades in the crowds and reports them to the police. Many of our reconnaissance teams are being arrested. He is hampering our effectiveness. He must be stopped.'

'Who is this bastard?' There was bitterness in Themba's voice.

'Edgar Malondo.'

'I know him,' breathed Themba. 'I trained with him at Quibaxe. He was also a member of the Iron Platoon.' Themba allowed his mind to drift back before continuing. 'He was very good, but there

544

was always something about Malondo I didn't like. I never fully trusted him. He had a shifty look in his eye.'

'After Quibaxe he trained further in the Soviet Union,' Slovo continued. 'I was the one who promoted him to Commander. I made a grave mistake. He knows too much, now he must be eliminated.'

Themba looked puzzled. 'How would you eliminate him if he's constantly surrounded by the police?'

'We've kept Vlakplaas under surveillance. Someone who would recognise him must slip in at night and do the job. You, Themba.'

'Me?'

Slovo nodded. 'We had you earmarked for either the SAAF Pretoria mission or Vlakplaas. Now you've declined Pretoria, we're sure you will accept Vlakplaas.'

Themba considered the options. He had never deliberately set out to assassinate a man before. He had killed in the line of duty, but this was different. He felt guilty at turning down the Pretoria mission; to refuse to eliminate Edgar Malondo would place him in a bad light with the MK hierarchy. Themba looked to Hani for guidance.

'It's a justified killing.' Hani felt Themba's reticence. 'Malondo jeopardises our brave freedom fighters' and other helpers' lives. Do it for us all, my friend.'

Two weeks later, with a new passport and identity documents in the name of Philips Makeba, Themba travelled by train through Zimbabwe to Botswana. He was met by an ANC contact at Gaborone station and had no trouble entering South Africa at the Koopfontein Gate border post. They travelled by car to the Atteridgeville black township outside Pretoria.

Themba was introduced to the leader of the reconnaissance team for the mission. Both men's eyes lit up in recognition when they were introduced by their MK names, Philips Makeba and Solly Baduza. Each knew the other from another time and place. At the first opportunity they strolled into the veld, away from listening ears, and renewed their acquaintance.

'Tommy Bakaco.' Themba greeted him warmly. 'I haven't seen you since our initiation in the Transkei.'

'Themba, it's good to see you again. Life has treated you well if you're now a commander in Umkhonto we Sizwe.'

He looked at Tommy. 'I still have my house at Mqekezweni.

One day when the struggle is over I'll retire to the peaceful life of Thembuland. Now tell me about Vlakplaas and Edgar Malondo.'

'We've been watching Vlakplaas around the clock for the last month. One of my team took a job on the next farm and has become friendly with Malondo. They drink together.'

Tommy drew a sketch in the dust of the layout of the buildings at Vlakplaas. There were two parallel blocks of single rooms. He marked Malondo's room. He sketched in another building away from the two blocks. 'This is the administration building. There's a flat attached to it. The white officer in charge of Vlakplaas lives there.' He stabbed the stick on the spot. 'Captain Koekemoer.'

The name hit Themba like a shock wave. He remembered Soweto in 1976, how a Koekemoer had kicked Hilda in her stomach causing her to miscarry. His words at the time came to him clearly and he mouthed them out loud. 'Koekemoer, I will remember your name and face for the rest of my life.' Again there was hatred in Themba's voice. 'If ever we meet again, I promise you I'll kill you, like you killed my unborn child.'

Tommy looked at Themba in shock. 'Could it be the same man?'

'How many Koekemoers can there be in the police force? It's an uncommon surname. Maybe it is him. He could have joined the security police; he was ruthless enough. At the time he was an adjutant-officer, but he may have progressed to lieutenant and now to captain. You've had him under surveillance; what does he look like?'

'Medium build, brown hair, moustache, bushy eyebrows and he has a mole on his face.' Tommy pointed his finger to his right cheek, just below the eye.

'That's him, that's the same Koekemoer.'

Tommy could not miss the steel in Themba's eyes. 'Will you kill him?'

It was a long time before Themba answered. He thought about his two healthy children, Bambatha and Helen. Should he not forgive and forget? Then Hilda's stricken face flashed into his mind and he knew what he would do. Koekemoer had ended the life of his first child just as surely as if he had cut its throat. There was no difference – murder was murder.

'I will kill Koekemoer, but not quickly or mercifully. He must suffer before he dies, and he must look me in the eye and know the reason why.' Themba's voice shook with emotion. 'He must die slowly, choking in his own blood to avenge the murder of my child.'

'You're serious?'

Themba nodded. 'First Koekemoer . . . then Malondo.' He remembered his main mission and glanced at Tommy. 'Tell me about Malondo.'

'A plain-clothes security policeman fetches him every morning from Monday to Friday. They drive around the townships looking for familiar MK faces of men he has met in Angola, Zambia and the Soviet Union, or on raids into South Africa. Every evening they return.'

'What does Malondo do over weekends?'

'Mainly stays at Vlakplaas. He knows his life is in danger in the townships. He drinks a lot, mostly with my man.'

'We know an important terrorism trial is starting in the Pretoria Supreme Court on Monday.' Themba spoke with passion. 'Malondo must not be allowed to testify.'

'Best time is to slip in at night.' Using his stick, Tommy drew the approach route. 'Security is not tight at Vlakplaas.'

'I like operating over weekends and public holidays. People are usually relaxed and off guard.' Themba made up his mind. 'Let's agree to Sunday night.'

'Everything will be arranged.' Tommy smiled with his gap-toothed grin. 'My friend will visit him on Sunday afternoon and make him drunk. It should make your task easier.'

'Good idea. Maybe I can catch him sleeping. What about the other men on the farm?'

'They're usually all asleep by ten at the latest. After that is the best time to strike.'

'And Koekemoer?'

'Up to now our surveillance has shown he goes home to his family at weekends.'

'You mean I'll miss him?'

'No. He returns to Vlakplaas every Sunday night at dusk.'

'Perfect.' Themba grimaced in hatred. 'So he should be asleep by eleven?'

'Usually,' Tommy nodded. 'What are your plans after the hit? Do you want to hide out in the townships until the heat is off?'

'That's not my style.' Themba pointed west. 'I want to reach the Botswana border as soon as possible. Can you organise a fast, reliable vehicle?'

'It will be done. I'll be your driver.'

On Sunday morning Themba and Tommy drove to Vlakplaas. They parked some distance away and walked the last part. Dressed in scrappy clothes, they looked like farm labourers.

From a distance they studied the layout of the farm. The two parallel buildings were converted farm sheds, with both rows of doors facing inwards towards a central thoroughfare. Tommy pointed out Malondo's room, No. 9, in the furthest block. Themba memorised the position of the administration building and Koekemoer's flat in it. After an hour they returned to Atteridgeville.

On Sunday night Tommy arrived in a spotless Toyota Hilux pick-up truck. Themba was impressed. The tyres were excellent and the vehicle had only nine thousand kilometres on the odometer. In the back was a spare jerrycan of petrol.

'Where did you get this?'

'It was stolen this afternoon.' Tommy grinned proudly. 'From a second-hand motor sales yard in Pretoria.'

Themba was alarmed. 'Won't the police be on the look-out for it.'

'Don't worry, everything's under control.' Tommy patted the pick-up. 'The watchman at the garage is an ANC sympathiser. He won't report the vehicle as stolen until tomorrow morning.' He pointed to the number plates. 'False, made by another supporter.'

'What about weapons?'

'An AK47 repeater assault rifle.' Tommy removed the weapon from behind the seat.

'Did you manage to meet my personal request?'

Tommy opened the cubby-hole. Themba took out the leather sheath and withdrew a hunting knife with a long, tapering, thick blade. Pleased, he threaded the sheath on to his belt.

They drove in silence, both thinking of the importance of the mission. If Themba failed, Edgar Malondo would appear in court the next day and condemn four good ANC cadres to the gallows. Don't think negatively, Themba admonished himself.

It was just past ten when they arrived at the entrance to Vlakplaas.

Tommy drove on a short distance, pulling off the road into a clump of trees.

A shadow detached itself and walked across. Themba heard a weapon being cocked as a man stood at the driver's window. 'Identify yourselves.'

'Solly Baduza,' Tommy whispered and the man smiled.

Walking towards the copse, Tommy introduced his comrade to Themba. They sat under a thorn tree discussing the mission.

'Where is Malondo?'

'In his room, but he's not alone.'

Tommy cursed. 'Who's with him?'

'A woman from a neighbouring farm,' the comrade explained. 'Our contact visited him this afternoon with six quarts of beer. Malondo drank four and our man two, then he left. Malondo must still have been thirsty, for he visited the shebeen and brought a bottle of brandy and the woman back with him.'

'This complicates matters but the mission continues.' Themba turned to the comrade. 'What about Captain Koekemoer?'

'He arrived soon after seven. He's in his flat. He turned his light out thirty minutes ago.'

At eleven o'clock Themba stood up. He turned to Tommy. 'Solly, once you hear shots, drive to the entrance to Vlakplaas and wait with the engine running.' He prodded the comrade. 'Lead the way, brother.' He slung the AK47 over his shoulder and jammed the spare magazine into his jacket pocket.

They crossed the veld until Themba could see the white-painted buildings ahead. A single electric light lit up the thoroughfare. They climbed through a barbed-wire fence. Ahead, a herd of cattle took off in fright, their hooves sounding loud on the hard ground. Themba waited for a few minutes, checking to make sure the cattle had disturbed no one in the compound. Breathing more easily they continued. At the last fence Themba greeted his guide. 'Thank you, comrade. I'll be fine now.'

When he reached the building that housed Koekemoer's flat, Themba crouched down and looked around slowly. All his senses were aroused, he could feel the nervous energy building up inside him. At the door to the flat he unslung the AK47 and propped it up against the wall as his back-up. He knocked on the door; three sharp taps.

'Who's there?'

Themba mumbled a reply.

'Who?'

Themba kept quiet. A light clicked on. Footsteps padded nearer.

'Who's that?' The supercilious tone of Koekemoer's voice rekindled Themba's hatred. He pictured the sneering face and the thin, cruel lips.

'*Basie* Koekemoer. It's me, Edgar Malondo, my *grootbaas*.' Themba made the tone of his voice syrupy and diffident.

'What do you want, Malondo? It's the middle of the night.'

'*Basie*, I have information.' Themba's voice sounded gruff, trying to imitate the way Malondo spoke. 'Please, my big boss.'

Koekemoer cursed loudly, but seemed convinced. The key turned in the lock. Themba slipped the knife out of its sheath and crouched low in the doorway, muscles flexed, ready to attack. Koekemoer threw the door open and stood framed in the light. He looked straight ahead, expecting to see Malondo.

For a split second he saw only the darkness. His eyes widened as he noticed a movement at his knees, but then it was too late. A streak unleashed itself from the ground like an attacking leopard. Themba sprang, aiming the point of the knife under his rib-cage. Koekemoer gasped as the steel blade entered the soft tissue under his twelfth rib, forcing upwards, rupturing his spleen. At the height of the stroke Themba twisted the blade viciously. Koekemoer screamed in pain and staggered backwards, clutching at his stomach.

With one bound Themba entered the room, closing the door behind him. Koekemoer lunged for his service pistol on the bedside table, but Themba was quicker. He knocked the policeman sprawling. Koekemoer collapsed against the wall. Themba gathered up the pistol and pointed it at Koekemoer's head.

'One move and I'll shoot you, Koekemoer.'

'Who are you?' wheezed the policeman, writhing with pain. 'How do you know my name?'

'Don't you remember me, Captain Koekemoer?' The policeman looked blankly at Themba.

'Let me refresh your memory. Soweto 1976. You were an adjutant-officer then. You raided my house.' Koekemoer looked at him with vague recognition.

'You kicked my pregnant wife twice in the stomach and caused her to abort our baby.' Now there was terror in Koekemoer's eyes as he recalled the event.

'That day I promised you I would kill you next time we met – kill you like you murdered my unborn child.' Koekemoer remembered vividly as the scene flashed before him.

He cringed away, breathing with difficulty. Blood pumping from his damaged spleen caused massive internal haemorrhaging. His speech was strained, his voice ruckling in his throat. 'I . . . was . . . only . . . doing . . . my . . . duty . . .'

'Was murder part of your duty?' Themba held the knife to his throat. His voice rang with hatred.

Koekemoer's whole face had a greyish-blue sheen. 'Have mercy on me.'

Themba laughed derisively. 'Like you had mercy on my wife and child? No Koekemoer, you're going to die.'

Pain washed over Koekemoer in waves. 'Why? Why?'

'An eye for an eye, a tooth for a tooth.' Themba's eyes blazed with hatred. 'And a life for a life.'

Themba could see death in his eyes as the policeman accepted his fate. 'Are you sorry for what you did?' Themba barked the question at him, hoping for remorse from the man.

Koekemoer's ingrained hatred refused to abate even as he stared death in the face. He slipped lower, and when he finally spoke, his voice was barely a whisper. '*Fokken . . . kaffer . . .*'

Themba checked Koekemoer's pulse. There was none. He stood up, avenged, but with a hollow feeling that left him unfulfilled. He pushed Koekemoer's death from his mind. His own vendetta had been accomplished – now his mission for Umkhonto we Sizwe must be concluded.

He wiped the knife on the bedspread and slipped it back into its sheath. He placed Koekemoer's pistol on the bedside table. Themba took a last look at Koekemoer. Was it remorse he felt? Was he cut out to be an assassin? Was his action justified? He fought down a wave of rising panic, talking to himself. 'Once more – just one more time. Edgar Malondo, then the killing must stop before it becomes second nature to me.'

Reaching the door of No. 9, in the middle of the block, he pressed his ear to the keyhole. He could hear the sound of laboured breathing. He turned the handle but the door was locked. He took two steps backwards and rushed at it. With a crash the plywood gave way.

Lying on his back on the bed, bottle in hand, was Edgar Malondo.

Themba recognised him instantly from Quibaxe. He was naked. On top of him was a fat, nude woman, perspiration running down her body as she fornicated.

Malondo was too drunk to react quickly, he merely blinked his eyes. The woman turned, saw Themba holding the weapon and opened her mouth to scream. Themba covered her mouth with his arm and stifled her shriek. He dragged her off Malondo and threw her into the corner of the room.

Themba fired a salvo of ten shots into Malondo's chest, watching hypnotically as the bullets smacked home – smashing his rib-cage, severing his femoral artery, crushing his lungs and spraying a fountain of blood into the air. Malondo never uttered a sound. He was dead in seconds.

The woman started screaming as Themba turned around and headed for the door. He hesitated momentarily, then ran the gauntlet between the two buildings. Doors crashed open as surprised men reacted. Themba fired an automatic salvo down each side. Bullets whined. Some quickly slammed their doors, others stood frozen in surprise. Themba almost made it.

As he drew level with the last doorway he saw a muzzle flash out and felt a sharp burning sensation in his side. He willed his legs to run, but they collapsed under him and he pitched sideways. Themba smashed against the building and slipped to the ground. Through the blinding pain he twisted himself around and fired blindly up the thoroughfare as men dived back into the safety of their rooms.

Bullets danced around Themba's head as gun flashes spewed out of the open doorway. With difficulty, he swung his AK47 and fired rapidly.

A figure floundered over the threshold, spiralling like a ballerina. The man screamed in a high falsetto as he twisted to the ground.

Silence returned and Themba struggled to his feet. Driven by desperation he ran sideways, crab-like, down the farm road. Twice he fell, but each time he forced himself to his feet. His guts were on fire, but by pushing his fist against the wound he eased the pain.

Where was the pick-up? The driveway seemed twice as long as it should have been. His leg was dragging. Would he make it? Had his luck finally run out? Themba was breathing heavily, his strength ebbing away. Shots started coming from the compound. He could hear the rat-ta-tat of automatic weapons. He stumbled and then crashed into the back of the waiting pick-up, tumbling over the tailgate.

'Is that you, Themba?' Tommy's voice was strained, his tone anxious.

'Yes . . . Leave . . . me . . . in . . . the . . . back . . . Drive.'

The vehicle took off at speed, twisting and turning on the gravel farm road. Themba was thrown from side to side like an empty gas cylinder. Once they reached the tarred road the ride was smoother. He was able to lie the length of the load area and take stock of his position. He felt the wound gingerly, a bullet hole just above the hip, the skin torn and scorched around the point of entry.

He could find no place where the bullet exited. With dismay he realised the slug was still inside his body, poisoning his system. The wound was bleeding profusely.

Street lights flashed overhead as they drove through the town of Brits. Themba examined the bullet hole, horrified to see slimy intestinal fluids escaping. His innards were punctured. Lying back in agony, he pushed his finger into the wound to stop the bleeding, then realised that by doing so he was trapping the fluid inside his abdomen. With a strangled cry he pulled his finger out.

Once through Brits, Tommy stopped on a side road to check on Themba. 'How are you?'

'They shot me . . . in my side . . . I'm losing lots . . . of blood.'

'Must I get you to a doctor?'

Themba shook his head. 'Drive . . . like . . . hell.'

'Do you want me to continue on the escape route we planned?' Themba nodded. 'Come and sit inside the cab.'

'I'm . . . better . . . off . . . lying . . . down.'

'All right, but bang on the back of the cab if you need help.'

Tommy continued past Beestekraal, travelling through the corridor between two sections of Bophuthatswana.

As they were leaving Thabazimbi they encountered the police road-block. Two police vans, their blue lights flashing, stood nose to nose leaving a gap wide enough for a vehicle to pass through. In the gap were three barrels, painted white, with red luminous strips. Tommy drove fast, straight for the barrels.

The police held their fire until the last minute, thinking the new pick-up might belong to a local farmer. When they saw the vehicle had no intention of slowing down, they opened

553

fire. The FN bullets shattered the front windscreen and the back window.

Sirens blared as the police turned and gave chase. The pick-up swayed dangerously as Tommy struggled to keep control. Themba was forced out of his stupor and sat up. The wind roaring through the shattered windows brought him to his senses.

The lead police van was catching up fast, its bright headlights illuminating the back of the pick-up. Themba grabbed the AK47 and fired a short burst. The bullets slammed into the front of the police vehicle, smashing the headlights. The driver lost control and the van careered across the road, crashing into the ditch.

Now the second vehicle surged forward. The policeman in the passenger seat leant far out of the window. Themba heard the sharp cracks as shots were fired, and the tearing of metal as they thumped into the pick-up's tailgate. Aiming low, Themba pulled the trigger again. With a bang a bullet exploded the right front tyre of the police van. The vehicle wobbled in the road. As the policeman braked, the vehicle spun around and around, coming to a sliding halt at the edge of the highway.

Themba turned and looked into the cab. Horrified, he saw Tommy slowly slide to the side until his head flopped on the passenger seat. 'Tommy! Tommy!' Themba screamed as the pick-up started bucking. The vehicle was still in gear and Tommy's foot had slipped off the accelerator pedal. Desperately Themba lurched through the back window frame. He grabbed the steering wheel and kept the vehicle on the road. The engine stalled and the pick-up came to a shuddering halt.

Gingerly Themba lifted himself off the back. He shook Tommy, trying to evoke a response. 'Tommy! Sit up man! Sit up!' He turned Tommy's head – his eyes were glazed. Tommy was dead.

'How many more?' Themba shouted. 'This killing must stop!'

Footfalls came towards him along the road. Frantically Themba scrabbled in the back of the pick-up for his weapon. Bullets slammed into the tailgate again, sounding like pebbles on a tin roof. Themba's groping fingers closed over the AK47 as a bullet thudded into his left knee. Screaming in agony he fell to the ground, waves of pain coursing up his leg. He threw the weapon against his shoulder and fired blindly back down the road as he dragged himself into the driver's seat. Thankfully, the engine fired first time. Using his right leg to depress the clutch, he roared away.

The journey was a nightmare. How Themba kept on the road only his guardian angel knew. His side and leg were throbbing in excruciating pain and his mind was fuzzy. He drove like an automaton. Air rushed in through the demolished windscreen making Themba's eyes water. He was forced to drive slowly and this saved him from wrecking the vehicle on many occasions.

He was not sure whether it was minutes or hours he travelled. He drove on will-power alone as he tried to blot out the agony and concentrate on the road.

In a daze, he saw the Stockpoort border post over the Limpopo River. Changing down into second gear, Themba crashed through the boom gates on either side of the border. The right headlight was smashed. Themba struggled on with only the left light burning.

Now he was heading for Gaborone. Themba alternated between waking and semi-consciousness, slewing from side to side on the tarred road. He woke with a start as the vehicle kicked up stones under the chassis. He was off the road. The noise made him sit up straight but then he fell forwards again, over the steering wheel and into unconsciousness. The pick-up hit a culvert and rolled twice, before settling on its side.

The driver of a long-haul truck driving behind Themba saw the accident and stopped. His assistant poked his head through the shattered windscreen. 'These people are dead. We must tell the police.' Then he heard Themba groan.

'The driver is still alive. Help me.' They hauled Themba out of the wreck and laid him on his back. Half an hour later they stopped in front of the hospital in Gaborone and summoned the duty doctor. The doctor certified Tommy dead and turned his attention to Themba. Nurses cut away his clothing and found his South African documents.

'Philips Makeba.' The doctor studied the passport. 'Advise the South African Consul.' As an afterthought he said, 'Also give the information to the ANC office.'

Hours later the doctor wearily removed his surgical mask. He had extracted the bullet and patched up the small intestine. Another bullet had smashed his left knee. Themba would walk with difficulty for the rest of his life. 'We've done what we can. Now it's over to God.'

Pain-killers and antibiotics were fed through the drip as a nurse watched over him in the intensive-care unit. He came round from the anaesthetic but was groggy and disorientated. Themba lapsed into a troubled sleep, mumbling, talking to his mother, his grandparents, his wife and his children. The nurse continually wiped his sweating brow, trying to keep his temperature down. For six hours Themba hovered between life and death.

In the morning he awoke. His stomach was on fire and he was as thirsty as a man stranded in the desert. He pleaded with the nurse for a drink.

She smiled, but shook her head, pointing to the electrolyte drip. 'Nil per mouth.'

The South African Consulate did not even bother to follow up the report on Philips Makeba. The Gaborone office of the ANC relayed details to Lusaka headquarters, where his name was instantly recognised. Tambo himself gave Hilda permission to travel to Botswana.

Hilda arrived on the third day, to find Themba heavily sedated. She refused to leave his side, keeping watch day and night. From the fourth day the pain-killers were reduced and Themba became lucid. He was overjoyed to see Hilda. She gave him new strength and the will to survive.

Day eight saw Themba on a bland, soft diet and he was allowed to sit up. Hilda could see he was improving when he fought with the nurse, wanting to get up. He started to talk freely, telling her details of his mission.

Hilda was terribly disturbed by the Koekemoer incident. 'Killing him didn't bring back our baby.' She started crying. 'We now have two beautiful children to take the place of the baby we lost.' She implored Themba: 'Please, my darling, stop the violence. Bearing grudges with a heart filled with hatred won't improve the situation in South Africa. Rather spend your time working for peace.'

He looked at her for a long time before nodding slowly. 'You're right. It *does* get into one's blood. I think the time has come for me to complete my legal studies.'

Themba and Hilda spent another week in Gaborone before he was strong enough to fly home. Their neighbour brought the children to Lusaka airport to meet them. On crutches, his left leg in plaster, Themba hobbled into the arrivals hall. Bambatha's little face broke into a delighted grin as he ran towards his parents on his stocky legs. Hilda grasped Helen to her breast as the baby gurgled happily.

Slovo and Hani stood respectfully to one side for the family reunion before stepping forward to welcome Themba.

'You did well. We are proud of you,' Slovo said. 'The South African authorities had to drop the charges against our MK comrades because of Malondo's death.'

'I need time to heal properly.' Themba turned to his colleagues. 'Both physically and mentally.'

'Take as much time as you need, Themba.'

With the advent of the winter the lush Zambian grasslands turned to brown and the nights had a bracing crispness. Themba was ready to resume work. He walked slowly to ANC headquarters, favouring his left leg. At first he had resented the doctor's warning that he would have a stiff knee for the rest of his life and would always walk with a limp. With time, he had accepted his injury, grateful that he had escaped with his life.

He was shown into the president's office and Tambo greeted him warmly. 'Your exploits seem to have become legend, Themba. We hear that Pierre Roux has you marked as his personal target.'

'That belongs in the past.' Themba settled himself into the chair. 'I can remember many years ago, when I first came to Lusaka, I told you that I must first work the hatred out of my system before I could think of peace. Well, I've now reached that stage.'

Tambo sat forward pulling on his wispy moustache while his intelligent eyes sparkled merrily. 'I'm glad, because the time for the next part of your training has arrived.'

Tambo took a typed letter out of a file and slid it across the desk. It was from Uppsala University in Sweden. The Swedish government, through the Swedish International Development Agency, had agreed to sponsor Themba on a six months' intensive first-language course in Swedish, followed by a Master's degree in law.

'I'm very pleased. Thank you. But why Sweden and not the Soviet Union?'

'Our top men always go to Sweden.' Tambo spread his hands on the desk. 'We want only the best for you, Themba.'

'What about my wife and children?'

Tambo was enjoying himself. 'All taken care of, by our Swedish regional office. A flat in Uppsala has been arranged for you all.' Tambo sat back in his chair. 'You don't have the make-up for an assassin, Themba. Your talents must be channelled to peacemaking for the ANC. You'll love Uppsala, it's a pretty university town fifty kilometres from Stockholm.'

Tambo walked around the desk and shook Themba's hand warmly. 'You are part of the new generation with youth on your side. One day you will live as a free man in South Africa. Enjoy your studies. Bring back your Master's degree. The legal office is waiting for you here.'

Spring in Paarl signals the start of a new season, when everyone puts the cold, wet winter behind them and looks forward to a new start. The first leaves of the vines covering the wide stoep of the Cape-Dutch manor house at Hermitage cast a dappled shade over three generations of the Roux family.

Blaise pulled Simon's ears and tickled him, but he took it all good-naturedly as she was the apple of his eye. He excused himself and walked into the house.

'Where's Grandfather going?' Blaise cried.

Helena rolled her wheelchair forward in agitation. 'Gone for a drink again, no doubt,' she muttered fiercely.

'Don't always pick on Dad.' Pierre flashed his mother an angry look.

'Your father's drinking has got out of hand.' Helena turned towards her son. Her scar turned puce when she was cross – now the twisted line showed up sharply. 'You're the only one he listens to. Go and talk some sense into his head.'

Following his father into a spare bedroom, Pierre found him with a bottle in one hand and a glass in the other. Simon coughed uncomfortably, holding out the glass. 'Would you like one?'

Shaking his head, Pierre sat, his eyes fixed on his father's face. 'Why are you drinking furtively, Dad? A quickie from a bottle hidden in the spare room is the sign of an alcoholic.'

'I've nothing to live for.' Simon sat down heavily on the bed. 'This military intelligence job takes you away so much I never see you.' Shrugging, Simon added, 'Anyway, you have your own family now.'

'I'm thinking of finishing my legal studies and settling down to a steady nine-to-five job. But that still won't help you. Dad, you must go for treatment.'

'Never!' Simon rose quickly. 'I have everything under control.'

'Please, Dad, for my sake. You used to be more like a brother to me. Now . . .'

'A brother?' Simon looked at his son – it was time to tell him about his half-brother. Tentatively he started. 'Pierre, there's a man you don't know. His name is Themba Memani . . .'

Pierre's face hardened and a wild look flashed into his eyes. 'Don't know? Of course I know Themba Memani.' Shaking with emotion, Pierre turned on his father. 'If I ever get that bastard in my sights, I'll kill him, just as he tried to kill me.'

In one gulp Simon downed his brandy, shaking like a leaf, his worst fears realised. 'Where did you meet him?'

Using short, sharp sentences Pierre told his father about Soweto, Crossroads, Maseru and Koeberg. 'Memani is a killer, Dad. He assassinated a policeman in cold blood recently at a place called Vlakplaas.' Pacing up and down, Pierre punched the air. Suddenly he stopped and stared at his father. 'How do you know Themba Memani?'

Simon's hands were shaking so badly he spilt more brandy on the floor than landed in his glass.

'Stop drinking, Dad, and answer my question.'

'Just one more, son. Last one.' Simon swallowed and shuddered. 'I don't know Memani, I've only heard of him.' His courage evaporated under Pierre's hostile stare.

'That's a lie,' shouted Pierre. 'Memani is listed only in the confidential files of military intelligence.'

'His mother worked for us before you were born. Your mother and I helped her financially to raise her son,' blurted Simon desperately. 'That's all.'

'Where does a brother come in?' Pierre stared coldly. 'That's where this conversation started.'

'I said we used to be like brothers.'

'No, Dad. I said that, then you started by telling me about Themba Memani.'

'The brandy muddles my thoughts. Perhaps you're right – I should go for treatment.'

'Tell me about Memani,' insisted Pierre.

Simon smiled apologetically, spreading his hands. 'What is there to tell? Nothing, absolutely nothing, Pierre.'

'Never mention that name to me again, Dad. Do you hear?'

'Okay! Okay!' Simon looked down, a feeling of total hopelessness overcoming him. Nomisile's secret would never be exposed. Not now, not ever. He rose unsteadily and held open his arms to his son. 'I love you Pierre – you're still the most important person in the world to me.'

Pierre's anger dissipated as he stepped forward and embraced his father. 'I love you too, Dad.'

The poignant moment was interrupted by the squeaking of rubber on the floor and they broke apart as Helena rolled into the room. 'Oh! There you are. I was becoming worried – you've been away so long.'

'Not to worry, Mom,' laughed Pierre. 'Dad and I have reached agreement on two issues. He's going to stop drinking and go for treatment and I'm planning to resign from military intelligence and become a lawyer.'

'What wonderful news on both scores.' Wheeling closer, she squeezed both their hands. 'Thank you, my two men. Now let's go outside, tea is waiting.'

Themba was surprised to find a telegram stuck on the notice board at Uppsala University. He tore open the envelope and read the message: IMPORTANT MEETING SCHEDULED ZAMBIA MIDDLE SEPTEMBER STOP WOULD LIKE YOU PRESENT STOP ORGANISE TRAVEL ARRANGEMENTS RPC STOP REGARDS OLIVER TAMBO.

During the next lecture his mind constantly travelled to Africa and his pulse quickened. Sweden had been good to him and his family, but it was not Africa – the huge, brooding continent which was in his blood. Sweden's icy winters and blankets of snow, its short summers, cool temperatures and continual rain, depressed Themba. Now he had a chance to return temporarily to Africa, poor and suffering, but with a vitality of spirit and a climate of anticipation, which drew him like a moth to a flame.

He hurried home with the news, ignoring the pain in his knee. His deep chest rose and fell evenly, with a thin film of perspiration coating his well-proportioned face.

'Daddy! Daddy!' Bambatha ran into his father's arms and Themba smiled proudly. His son was already at pre-primary school and spoke Swedish better than Xhosa. The rumpus alerted Helen who toddled in on little, fat, slightly bandy legs. Themba gathered her up, tossing her into the air and catching her, while she squealed in delight.

Hilda was surprised to hear Themba's voice in the house in mid-afternoon. Wiping her hands on her apron, she stood in the doorway of the lounge, watching Themba and the children at play. She smiled to herself, her face lighting up, accentuating her high cheek-bones and regal features. Themba glanced up and their eyes met.

She's beautiful, he thought as he slowly straightened. Despite a slight thickening around her waist she was still most attractive. Her face had stayed young and her skin glowed with good health.

'Why are you home so early, darling?' Hilda asked sweetly.

'I have something important to tell you.' Themba led the way to the bedroom, closing the door after them. He showed her the telegram and they discussed the trip to Zambia.

'We'll miss you.' There was a wistful expression on Hilda's face. 'I suppose we've been spoilt, having you at home all the time.'

Themba attended the pre-conference meeting at ANC headquarters in Lusaka. 'Welcome, gentlemen.' The ANC President glanced around the room. 'A special welcome to publicity secretary Thabo Mbeki from London and Themba Memani, who has interrupted his legal studies to be with us, just in from Stockholm.'

Oliver Tambo grinned confidently. 'I think at last we are seeing the first tangible signs of South Africa's apartheid castle starting to crumble.' He had the full attention of everyone present. 'Since PW Botha's big blunder in his Rubicon speech, top businessmen have decided to take the initiative. Ignoring opposition from the National-ist government, a delegation of prominent South African business-men is arriving tomorrow to start exploratory talks with the ANC.'

An excited buzz flashed around the room. Tambo continued, 'The leader of the delegation is Mr Gavin Relly, chairman of Anglo-American, which controls seventy per cent of the companies listed on the Johannesburg Stock Exchange.' He read the names of the full delegation.

There was a gasp from the meeting. Thabo Mbeki rose. 'This is the cream of enlightened businessmen. I look forward to meeting them.'

'Hear! Hear!'

*   *   *

The ANC members stood on the edge of the runway as the sleek white and royal-blue Gulfstream Jet from Johannesburg landed and taxied to a halt. As the white businessmen alighted from the aircraft, the ANC reception committee moved forward and greeted their guests. The mood was jovial as each became acquainted with the other group.

Themba was amazed at the openness of the discussions from the people he had regarded as the enemy of the people – the captains of capitalism in South Africa. Throughout the day he was repeatedly struck by the mutual feeling of 'South Africanism', and where they could not agree, at least they agreed to disagree.

At the end of the discussions the two groups met informally. Gavin Relly rose to thank his hosts. 'This was a get-to-know-you meeting and has succeeded admirably. Our two groups are still far apart, but the real common ground is that we are all concerned that the next generation should inherit a viable economic and political system. I believe that more talks might lead to some fruitful conclusions.'

The applause died down and Oliver Tambo stepped forward. 'I have asked Mr Themba Memani to reply on behalf of the ANC.'

Themba looked around the room, finding it useful to pause before speaking. 'The most important aspect about today is that it enabled us to hear each other's views. The ANC trusts you will return home with a picture in your mind's eye of having met decent human beings, as interested in finding a solution to common problems as yourselves.' Themba spread his hands in reconciliation. 'We admire you for ignoring the threats from the Nationalist government and coming anyway. You have today cast the foundations of a bridge over the river of apartheid.'

The splashing of the shower woke Pierre. He stretched, rubbed his eyes and sat up in bed. The warm sun streamed through the window. What a beautiful day, he thought, glad to be alive. It was Sunday. He lay back with his arms under his head. Life has been good to me, he mused. As the years had passed he had been increasingly pleased with his decision to return to law. He had completed his LL B, done his articles with a reputable firm of attorneys, and now ran his own legal practice from a Cape Town suite of offices. He had made a name for himself by scoring successes in a number of big cases. His client base had spread and he became choosy, concentrating on the high-income corporate business.

Blaise tiptoed into the room. Pierre lifted the duvet. She slipped into bed and cuddled up to her father. He stroked her hair lovingly and she looked at him with adoration.

Lesley walked out of the bathroom towelling her hair. Pierre felt desire as he watched her. If anything, her body had matured over the years into a full and voluptuous figure. She was still light on her feet, swaying her hips sensually as she walked. Her long, blonde hair reached shoulder level, framing her beautiful face.

'Morning, darling.' Lesley grinned revealing perfect white teeth. She saw Blaise's blonde hair in the crook of Pierre's arm, smiled and crept back into bed. She placed her arm over Pierre's chest. His body was still firm with not a gram of fat. She looked at her husband. His face was handsome, accentuated by his strong jaw line and aquiline nose. She touched his hair. He was starting to grey at the temples but not one hair in his black shock had fallen out. Lesley sighed in complete contentment.

Pierre smiled at his secretary as she placed a cup of coffee on his desk. He took a sip, then stretched his legs, gazing through the window at the bulk of Table Mountain dominating the western skyline.

'Mr Colin Eglin of the Progressive Federal Party to see you, Mr Roux.'

'Ask him to come through.' Pierre met Eglin at the door and shook the extended hand of the jovial, balding leader of the PFP. Eglin came straight to the point.

'The PFP would like you to stand for parliament in the next elections.' His ample face creased into a smile. 'If you accept, we would nominate you for the Gardens seat.'

'Naturally I'm flattered, Mr Eglin, but National Party blood flows through my veins. My grandfather and father were Nationalist MPs and I served in military intelligence.'

'You don't agree with the Nat's policy, Mr Roux!'

'How do you know?' retorted Pierre in surprise.

'Easy,' laughed Eglin, his stomach shaking. 'Lesley and my wife play bridge together. She is totally anti-government.'

'True,' mused Pierre. He secretly craved to enter parliament, but knew in his heart that he could not serve in the National Party while they maintained their apartheid policy – that went totally against the grain. Nor could he serve in the ANC – they were banned. The only alternative was the official opposition. Pierre sat back expansively. 'What makes you think I could help, when Frederik van Zyl Slabbert resigned as leader of the PFP, feeling he could achieve more towards meaningful change outside the constraints of parliament?'

'Slabbert's resignation came as a shock, I agree, but we must not allow the National Party to dictate terms. A strong opposition is needed to hold them in check – that is the role of the PFP.'

'Too true,' answered Pierre, his thick eyebrows knitting to emphasise his agreement. 'Although I was brought up on a strict diet of National Party politics I no longer subscribe to their doctrines – I want full representation by black people in a single parliament.'

'Nothing wrong with that – it's also the PFP's ideal.'

'I'll speak to Lesley first and come back to you,' promised Pierre. 'I must admit, working for meaningful change in our country inspires me.'

'We look forward to welcoming you to our team,' smiled Eglin, rising to leave.

Election day was cold, with an early warning of a wet Cape winter. Clouds boiled over the gap between Table Mountain and Lion's Head, sprinkling the city polling stations with regular flurries of light drizzle.

'We've done what we could,' said a tired-looking Lesley. 'It's been non-stop canvassing for months now.'

'Thank you for always being at my side.' Pierre kissed her on the cheek. 'I'm sure the results will show our hard work was worthwhile.'

They moved from one booth to the next, a ready smile and a warm handshake for the voters, encouraging them to vote for Pierre.

The polling stations closed at nine o'clock and the counting began. Hour after hour the tension built up, reaching breaking point as a re-count was announced. Both Pierre and the National Party candidate acknowledged the result would be close. Another period of waiting extended into the small hours.

The polling officer announced the result – Pierre had won by the narrowest of margins – forty-three votes. Lesley hugged him as his supporters cheered and triumphantly lifted him shoulder high.

*   *   *

Squaring his shoulders, Pierre walked confidently into his first PFP caucus meeting. He was immediately made to feel welcome.

'We're appointing you our spokesman on educational matters, Pierre,' smiled Eglin generously.

Pierre spent a lot of time studying the total scope of the education system. He was shocked to find there were four ministers responsible for education, one each for white, coloured, Indian and black; in addition each province had a separate education department for each racial group. The administration was a nightmare, the cost horrific. The quality, especially for the black pupils, suffered as a result.

On a goodwill visit to FW de Klerk, Minister of National Education for whites, he was immediately struck by De Klerk's friendly smile, his warm personality and easy-going manner. Not a tall man, De Klerk was someone whose charisma made him appear bigger than he really was.

De Klerk had a reputation for being a conservative thinker and Pierre decided to test him. 'Minister, white pupils make up only eleven per cent of the pupils in South African schools; the remainder are black, coloured and Indian.'

De Klerk watched Pierre intently, his expressive eyes anticipating the question. 'You want to know why we don't have one united education system?'

'Exactly. Also why the vast majority have a second-rate education.'

'We're getting there, just give us time.' De Klerk took a deep draw on his cigarette, blowing smoke towards the ceiling. 'It's a process of evolution – we can't right all the apartheid wrongs in one fell swoop.' He stubbed out his cigarette in the ashtray.

Pierre was surprised at the answer, having expected him to defend the system. 'Are you saying you'd be prepared to initiate meaningful change?'

'Certainly.' De Klerk shook another cigarette from the pack. 'I have a balanced view for the future of our country. I believe an enlightened approach is necessary.' Laughter lines appeared at the corners of his eyes. 'That surprised you, didn't it?'

Pierre looked intently at the open, oval face framed by a silvery monk-like hairstyle, thinking how much he liked De Klerk and his forthright manner. 'I'm very pleased to hear that, Minister.'

'Please, call me FW – all my friends do.'

'Thank you,' smiled Pierre, his eyes sparkling. 'I'd like it if you called me Pierre.'

'Do you play golf, Pierre?'

'Is it the done thing to play with the parliamentary opposition?' laughed Pierre.

'Of course! Our fathers were parliamentary friends way back in Verwoerd's time. Why not the sons? Outside parliament there's a lot of good camaraderie between members.'

'In that case I'd be delighted, FW. Thank you.'

The first round of golf turned into a weekly occurrence, and a deep friendship developed between the two men. Lesley and Marike de Klerk, both devoted supporters of their husbands' activities, also drifted into an easy-going friendship.

As Pierre was lining up a long putt on the seventh at Hermanus golf course, De Klerk passed a comment. 'You're in the wrong political party, Pierre. If you truly believe change should come from within, then you would be much more effective in the National Party, don't you think?'

Pierre missed the putt and looked at De Klerk in exasperation. 'You did that on purpose!'

'Of course.' De Klerk smiled his mischievous smile, completely relaxed, leaning on his putter. 'But answer my question.'

'The National Party under PW Botha is stuck in the apartheid groove.' Pierre putted again and sunk the ball, nodding in satisfaction. 'Unless you involve the black majority in government there's always going to be confrontation in South Africa.'

'If I told you I believed in power sharing and the normalisation of the situation, would you change your mind?'

As they walked to the next tee Pierre turned to his friend. 'Does Botha share your beliefs?'

De Klerk's caddie handed him his driver. He looked at Pierre carefully. 'Liberal elements in the Cabinet are pushing him but he's resisting.'

Pierre was sceptical. 'Do you believe in unbanning political organisations and releasing political prisoners? And what about giving everyone the vote?'

They walked down the fairway, their caddies trailing behind. De Klerk nodded. 'I believe in a negotiated settlement. For too

566

long we've prescribed to the black people, now it's time for compromise.'

'I can't believe my ears.' Pierre gave a short, cynical laugh. 'You're supposed to have strong conservative leanings. Rumour has it that you persuaded PW Botha to repudiate Pik Botha in public, when he stated it was possible for South Africa to have a black president.'

Smiling broadly, De Klerk walked towards his ball on the edge of the rough. 'When in Rome do as the Romans do! All these years I've cultivated a conservative image. In National Party politics, power is based on conservatism. Afrikaners don't trust a liberal thinker.'

'And you want me to cross over to the National Party?' Pierre shook his head. 'Where would I get with my liberal views?'

'What if I promised you change?'

'You're not State President.' Pierre spoke the words softly, not wanting to antagonise his friend.

'What if I were the next State President?'

'PW Botha is a long way from stepping down.'

De Klerk placed his arm over Pierre's shoulders. 'It could happen sooner than you think and I want you in my team.'

On their return to Lusaka the Memani family settled in a new house in the suburbs. By applying himself fully, Themba had secured his Master's degree in law. It hadn't always been easy, but then he had the advantage that he was a mature man who knew about death and suffering and the hurly-burly of the real world. By interacting with people in a foreign language, Themba had learnt co-operation and team-work; he had tempered his individualism and softened his insolent manner. Themba was thrilled to be appointed head of the ANC's legal department.

The times were changing. More and more delegations, some official, some not so, were calling on the ANC in exile. The first drops became a stream, then a flood, as South Africans made the pilgrimage north of the Zambezi.

Themba was completely removed from Umkhonto we Sizwe and the armed struggle against the South African government. Instead, he played the role of bridge builder, organising and hosting conferences and updating visitors on ANC policies.

He was amazed how little the delegates knew of the ANC and its vision for a new South Africa. It was his task to inform them, so they could return and convince their colleagues back home that the ANC was not an ogre bent on destruction, but a serious protagonist for justice and peace.

In July 1987 the most influential delegation of more than sixty Afrikaners was due to meet the ANC. Seeking a neutral venue, Themba persuaded the President of Senegal in West Africa to host the meeting in the capital city of Dakar. To maintain neutrality the conference was officially hosted by France-Liberté, a human rights organisation.

Colin Eglin banged the gavel, ordering silence in the PFP caucus room. The members hurriedly took their seats.

'Gentlemen,' began Eglin. 'Our old friend Dr Frederik van Zyl Slabbert is leading a team to Dakar in West Africa to meet with an ANC delegation. Is any member interested in joining the party?'

'Has the visit been sanctioned by the government?' asked a member.

Eglin shook his head. 'PW Botha would blow a fuse if he knew about the visit. I think it better that anyone intending to go travels as an individual.'

'To hell with PW! I'm going,' shouted Peter Gastrow. He glanced at Pierre, sitting next to him. 'Why don't you come along, Pierre?'

Eglin encouraged Pierre. 'Don't be afraid to take a step towards democracy.'

Pierre's mind raced. Lesley would encourage him, he was certain. His legal practice? They could manage for two weeks without him. His friend FW de Klerk? He must accept me as I am, he thought. He nudged Gastrow and looked Eglin in the eye. 'Count me in.'

In high spirits the South Africans gathered in Johannesburg. All were eagerly looking forward to meeting with the ANC and starting dialogue with the members of the banned organisation. A sense of adventure prevailed as they knew their actions did not carry official approval.

They stepped off the aeroplane in warm, balmy weather to a huge welcome. President Diouf had laid on a convoy from the airport, led by police outriders. At the conference centre, the Hotel Navotel Dakar, the delegates were greeted by traditional dancers. After a quick shower Pierre met the other delegates in the hotel foyer and they strolled together into the conference room to meet their hosts. The fifteen-man ANC delegation stood in line.

The cheerful smile froze on Pierre's lips as he spotted Themba Memani. Almost as if drawn by Pierre's stare of hatred, Themba turned and his mouth became a hard, straight line. They locked belligerent stares, the friendly welcome forgotten.

Hatred drove reason out of Pierre's brain. He could not stop himself as he dashed forward. Something snapped in Themba too. He limped forward and to everyone's surprise the two confronted each other between the two advancing parties.

'You left me to drown off Koeberg,' hissed Pierre.

'It was not my fault,' said Themba.

'Bullshit! You're a liar and a double-crosser.'

'Go to hell, Roux.'

Van Zyl Slabbert rushed forward. He grabbed Pierre by the arm. Barbara Masekela of the ANC scolded Themba indignantly. The two adversaries glowered at each other, then turned their backs and walked away.

'I apologise,' said Slabbert quickly. 'We came to talk peace, not to continue the struggle.'

'Don't worry,' Barbara assured him, 'that's why we're here, too.'

The two delegations proceeded with the welcome. The South Africans moved down the row of ANC members, warmly shaking their hands.

Feeling a mixture of guilt and degradation, Pierre fell in at the back of the South African line. He was seething with anger, but managed to push it into the background, greeting everyone civilly until he reached Themba.

They looked contemptuously at each other, neither proffered his hand and they turned away in disgust. Their personal vendetta was interrupted by the arrival of the Senegalese delegation.

The President and his entourage swept into the room and the delegates clapped warmly. Pierre cast a furtive glance at Themba, gleefully speculating what accident had caused him to walk with a limp.

Thabo Mbeki welcomed the delegates on behalf of the ANC. 'I view as a matter of vital importance that our white compatriots should themselves join the struggle, that they should abandon the camp of racism and become part of the democratic force of our country.'

Slabbert spoke on behalf of the South African visitors. 'There is a sadness that we have to meet so far from our common homeland. This in itself is a commentary on the history we share. Some of you have travelled far, and suffered much, in pursuing freedom for your country. Despite whatever differences there may be, we have come to talk to you because we realise your critical role in resolving the tragedy of our situation.'

The opening formalities over, the Senegalese left, to allow the two delegations to become acquainted. One by one the members of the two teams walked to the podium to state who they were and what they did. Several white and black delegates discovered they had been born in the same town, but under vastly different circumstances.

Themba drew a good chuckle from the audience with his opening words. 'I am an Afrikaner, if that is an Afrikaans term given to a person born in Africa.'

Pierre avoided looked in Themba's direction as he introduced himself. 'I am Pierre Roux, a member of parliament and a member of the Progressive Federal Party. I believe in change in South Africa, real change, where the black man can take his rightful place in society and government.'

'Liar!' Themba retorted sharply. Seeing the disapproval on the other delegates' faces, he looked away quickly.

Ignoring the interjection, Pierre pulled himself to his full height, squared his shoulders and continued: 'I will work for change within parliament and look forward to being part of the solution.' Pierre resumed his seat, casting a venomous glance in Themba's direction, but he was gazing out of the window.

President Diouf hosted a reception at his impressive white palace that evening. The delegates from both parties mingled freely, building up a feeling of solidarity, but Themba and Pierre made sure they were never in the same group.

The conference lasted two weeks. The delegates spent most of their time participating in the various workshops covering a wide spectrum of topics. Both Pierre and Themba contrived to be allocated to different workshops so that they did not have to interact with each other.

One day a large group took the ferry across Dakar Harbour to Coree Island. They visited the fortress called House of Slaves, observing the massive stone ramparts and old muzzle-loading artillery used to guard the island. They peered into the dark dungeons once used to house the black slaves on their way from West Africa to the lucrative markets of the American south.

Themba broke away from the tour party and gazed back over the ramparts at the brooding mass of the African continent.

'A penny for your thoughts,' said a delegate.

'Nothing has changed over the ages.' Themba pointed back in the direction of the dungeons. 'Black Africans have always been exploited by the white man. It happened here in Senegal, it happened throughout Africa and it is still happening today in South Africa.'

Unbeknown to them, Pierre had strolled nearer and heard Themba's words. His patience snapped. 'Typical, Memani,' he uttered scornfully. 'Selfishly thinking only of his own viewpoint. It wasn't only white men who sold the blacks into slavery. What about the Arabs and the other black men? The ANC have camps like Quatro, where you keep your own members in virtual slavery.'

Themba ignored his remark and moved pointedly away from him. Pierre walked away muttering to himself, aware that he was at fault but smarting at Themba's brush-off.

Themba and Pierre returned to the workshops the next day, but neither made any effort at reconciliation. Both made valuable contributions to their own workshops and Van Zyl Slabbert was impressed with Pierre's astuteness and powers of logic. Thabo Mbeki again was struck by the way Themba was able to step back from the discussions and set the problem in its true perspective. He had the ability to summarise clearly and allow the delegates to move forward together and reach consensus. Mbeki was singling him out as a negotiator for the future.

Pierre opened the front door of his Gardens home to FW and Marike de Klerk. 'Welcome. Come inside.' His smile was warm as he stepped aside to allow them in. 'Congratulations on your election as leader of the National Party. Does this mean you'll automatically be next State President?'

'Logically that should be the case. When it happens I want you in my team, Pierre.'

'I'll consider it seriously. I must admit to being disillusioned with opposition politics. We seem to achieve so little.'

Lesley was not going to let her liberalism be stifled. 'Until you

571

talk to the ANC, and work with them, neither of you is going to pull us out of the quagmire. You should see the ANC not as part of the problem, but as part of the solution. After all, they're seen as the symbol of the freedom struggle by the black majority.'

Pierre asked him directly, 'Would you unban the ANC if you were State President?'

'I would.' De Klerk sat back, relaxed, knowing he had the attention of everyone. 'Over the years I've undergone a political conversion. History dictates it is time for political normalisation and a sharing of power.'

'Why do you want me to join the National Party?' Pierre stared at De Klerk.

'You're a careful, intelligent man with wide experience.' De Klerk grinned enthusiastically. 'You're an Afrikaner with the right background and would immediately be accepted by the inner circle. I need young men with fresh ideas if we're to move ahead. Dialogue and negotiation will become the key words in a new dispensation. With your legal background and modern approach, you would be a valuable member of my negotiation team.' De Klerk's eyes sparkled. 'Plus, of course, you're my friend. I know we would work well together.'

'If I cross the floor it will look like a betrayal to the voters who elected me. But come the September 1989 elections, I'll make myself available as an NP candidate for Gardens.' He smiled at his friend. 'I look forward to working closely with you to achieve your goals.'

Pierre, with Lesley at his side, campaigned as never before, extolling the virtues of the National Party for real, meaningful change in South Africa. They set up a booth decorated with colourful posters and banners at Gardens Centre. They attended rallies, addressed teachers at schools and the nursing staff at Volk's hospital. The election was close, but Pierre retained his Gardens seat, this time on an NP ticket.

On 20 September 1989 FW de Klerk was sworn in as the new State President.

With Pierre at his side, De Klerk held his first meeting with coloured and black clerics in South Africa. The church leaders laid the Harare Declaration on the table. 'This is the basis on which the ANC is prepared to negotiate with the government.'

572

De Klerk nodded. 'I accept the Harare Declaration as a starting point, the time is ripe for dialogue.'

'Show your good faith by releasing the high-profile political prisoners,' urged Pierre.

Five of the Rivonia trialists were unconditionally released after a quarter of a century behind bars – Walter Sisulu, Ahmed Kathrada, Elias Motsoaledi, Andrew Mlangeni and Raymond Mhlaba.

'Now for Nelson Mandela,' pleaded Pierre.

De Klerk met Mandela in early December 1989 in Cape Town. The world held its breath, expecting his imminent release.

'Mandela refuses to accept freedom until the ANC is unbanned,' complained De Klerk.

Pierre nodded slowly. 'One must admire the man – the way he has unfalteringly stood by his principles.'

'What must I do?' De Klerk asked.

'Unban the ANC! Next year, at the opening of parliament, you are expected to give a major policy speech. That is the ideal opportunity.'

De Klerk smiled broadly, clapping his friend on the shoulder. 'You're very astute, Pierre. Let's work on it.'

'That is the final clause,' said Pierre, putting down his pen. He was exhausted but at the same time exhilarated at the progress they had made. After a week of late nights the speech was finalised. He knew it would change the face of South Africa, and once delivered, there was no turning back.

De Klerk leaned across to Pierre. 'Thank you, my friend. I'm pleased with the result.' He too was tired but managed a wry smile. 'All that remains is for the National Party caucus to accept our proposals.'

The second of February 1990 was like any other late summer's day in the Cape, hot and dry with a south-easter forming a table cloth of flat cloud over Table Mountain.

FW and Marike de Klerk arrived for the opening of parliament. Only the President's guard was in attendance. He took the national salute from the bottom step of the Houses of Parliament while the band played the national anthem. They waved to the enthusiastic crowd and entered the red brick building.

Pierre and Lesley made a striking couple as they smiled and waved at photographers. He looked up as the police turned back a group of chanting demonstrators near the end of Parliament Street. 'I wonder what their reaction will be when they hear the content of the State President's address,' he laughed.

Lesley squeezed his arm. 'I'm so pleased FW has decided to cross the Rubicon. I've waited my whole life to see meaningful change.'

'Today *will* be a red-letter day,' agreed Pierre as they took their places.

An air of anticipation prevailed. Every eye was on him as De Klerk make his way to the podium. He was neatly dressed in a dark suit, a conservative tie and his characteristic white shirt. He exuded confidence as he adjusted his papers and put on his glasses.

'The season of violence is over. The time for reconstruction and reconciliation has arrived.' The audience listened carefully, not wanting to miss a single word. Pierre felt a sense of achievement as he listened to the epoch-making address.

De Klerk announced the suspension of the death penalty and the release of all political prisoners, including Nelson Mandela. The audience gasped in surprise. He unbanned the ANC, PAC and SA Communist Party. An excited murmur swept through the great hall. The media emergency regulations were scrapped and the state of emergency terminated.

He challenged the ANC and other organisations: 'Walk through the open door and take your place at the negotiating table together with the government and other leaders.'

De Klerk walked back to his seat. Pierre winked at him, nodding his head in approval. De Klerk smiled back. Parliament's staid silence was broken as members of the National Party congratulated each other. De Klerk was surrounded by well-wishers shaking his hand and slapping him on the back.

Lesley embraced Pierre. 'FW deserves all the glory and adulation they are showering on him. Today is a wonderful day.'

Pierre kissed his wife and rose. 'FW has invited me to his office. I must shoot. See you later.'

The State President's office in Tuynhuys was filled with De Klerk's cabinet ministers. The mood was electric and the telephone rang continuously.

'It's the British Prime Minister,' gasped Pierre as he handed the telephone to De Klerk.

Foreign ministers and heads of state from all over the world telephoned to offer their congratulations.

Slowly the office emptied, until only FW and Pierre remained. 'We need to toast our victory,' said De Klerk, filling two glasses.

Pierre held up his glass. 'Congratulations on your courage.'

'Yours as well!' De Klerk looked squarely at Pierre. 'You have been the greatest influence in helping me moderate my conservative views and giving me the courage to step into the unknown.'

'I'll be there to assist in the next phase,' emphasised Pierre. 'The crucial rounds of negotiations.'

'We make a good team, you and I.' De Klerk smiled warmly. 'I may receive the accolades, but you deserve the credit.'

The news quickly reached Lusaka. Themba listened to the newscast in disbelief. What wonderful news! Not in his wildest dreams had he expected so much so soon. Oliver Tambo was in hospital recovering from a stroke, so Themba convened a meeting of the ANC executive for the next day.

An excited buzz filled the auditorium. Themba walked to the microphone. The audience grew quiet. 'This morning I received a copy of De Klerk's speech and it is true – the ANC has been unbanned.'

The audience cheered, animated expressions on every face.

'Before today's meeting I spoke to the South African Minister of Foreign Affairs and he confirmed that we will all be allowed to return.'

'Hooray!' Chris Hani stood up, waving his arms enthusiastically. 'After all these years in exile we're *really* going home.'

'Yes,' smiled Themba happily. 'A big task lies ahead of each one of us. We have no infrastructure in South Africa, so we'll need to streamline our management and set up branches in various centres. I'm sure each one will rise to the challenge.'

Thousands of people gathered outside the entrance to the Victor Verster prison outside Paarl.

In late afternoon a group of people walked towards the gate. A man with binoculars shouted, 'It's Mandela, it's Nelson Mandela!' The crowd cheered in elation.

A tall man with grey hair, impeccably dressed in a dark suit, walked down the road holding Winnie Mandela's hand.

The crowd started chanting. 'Mandela! Mandela! Madiba! Madiba!' He reached the gate and flashed the black power salute. The crowd roared back, 'Viva Mandela! Mayibuye!' People rushed forward to touch him and the spontaneous strains of '*Nkosi sikelel iAfrika*' filled the air.

Millions of television viewers all over the world shared the occasion. Throughout Britain, church bells rang in celebration.

After almost twenty-eight years of imprisonment, Nelson Mandela was a free man.

23

The Boeing rolled to a halt outside the terminal buildings at Johannesburg airport. Themba, part of the first group of returning exiles, collected his hand luggage and stood in the aircraft's aisle, impatient for the passengers ahead to disembark. They had waited so many years to return; now there was an impulsive desire to rush out of the aeroplane and feel the soil of home under their feet again. On the tarmac they formed a circle, staring at each other in wonderment.

'*Egoli*! We're back in the city of gold.' Joe Modise pointed to the mine dumps in the distance.

Thabo Mbeki's eyes grew misty. 'A whole generation has passed. What a tremendous waste of time and people. I grew up hardly knowing my father as he languished on Robben Island.'

Another smiled broadly as he pointed towards the heavens. 'Look, the sky is still there. The regime always thought it would come tumbling down if they allowed us to return.'

Themba was more serious. 'Prepare yourselves for a hard slog. There'll be no time to relax. From the beginning it will be work, work and more work.'

They walked into the arrivals hall. A huge cheer went up as thousands of ANC supporters shouted and toyi-toyied in elation. Huge banners of welcome were draped over the mezzanine railings.

Nelson Mandela and Walter Sisulu stepped forward.

'Welcome home, Themba.' Mandela embraced him. 'Thank goodness you're here, now negotiations can begin.'

'Madiba, it's wonderful to see you as a free man in South Africa.' Themba's eyes were moist. 'I know a great task rests on my shoulders. I will not fail you.'

Themba turned to Sisulu. 'Hullo, you old war-horse. Your words to me on Robben Island have always remained my personal motto – *know your enemy, know your strength*.'

'Your role in the process is already mapped out.' Sisulu smiled sadly at Themba. 'My time has passed. I'm too old to re-enter active politics. As leader of the new generation, you must stay close to Nelson and learn from his wisdom.'

Pierre's secretary came on the line. 'Mr Roux, I have a Mr Memani from the ANC wishing to speak to you.'

'Put him through, please.'

The telephone clicked and Themba spoke, his voice cutting. 'Our Groote Schuur meeting is off, Roux.'

'Why do you want to cancel our meeting?' asked Pierre sarcastically.

'We cannot afford the hotel accommodation to house our delegation. If you want to start off the negotiation process on the right foot the government must meet our costs.'

'Everything is set up for tomorrow. You're being intolerant.'

'Well, cancel the arrangements.' Themba spoke in clipped tones. 'Your government is making life difficult for the ANC. You unban our organisation and grant indemnity to our leaders, but you freeze our money coming into the country. How do you think we can finance operations without contributions from our foreign allies?'

Pierre knew De Klerk entertained high hopes for the Groote Schuur talks, the first round of negotiations between the government and the ANC. It was to be an historic moment, covered by news teams from around the world. To cancel would place De Klerk in a bad light.

'Let me speak to the State President and come back to you. What is the size of your delegation?'

'Fifty. I'm giving you one hour to come up with a positive answer, Roux.' The telephone went dead.

He telephoned the State President and explained the problem. 'Should I tell Memani to get lost?'

'No! This time we'll pay.' De Klerk's voice was strained. 'They have us over a barrel – the meeting must go on.'

Pierre reluctantly booked one whole wing at the Lord Charles Hotel near Somerset West for three days. He telephoned the ANC offices in Johannesburg.

'Memani, we've agreed to your request but under extreme duress, I may add. Does that mean the talks are still on track?'

'I'll speak to my delegation and come back to you.'

578

'You are employing delaying tactics,' said an infuriated Pierre.

'Don't forget, it's *not* the ANC who delayed discussions for five decades,' added Themba scathingly.

Mandela and De Klerk shook hands on the steps of Groote Schuur, smiling for the world to see the progress being made. Behind them the delegates crowded around. De Klerk, turning to ask Pierre a question, was surprised to see a look of abhorrence on his face. He swivelled further and observed Themba Memani, his own eyes glittering in repulsion.

'What's up with you, Pierre?' De Klerk whispered urgently as he shook Pierre's arm. 'We can't have a display of animosity today of all days!' Pierre nodded stoically. 'Please, Pierre, put your pride in your pocket and go over and shake Memani's hand.'

Pierre was about to refuse, but the urgency in De Klerk's eyes made him think twice. What was more important – his personal feud with Memani or the success of a negotiated settlement for South Africa? With a shrug of his shoulders, Pierre walked directly to his adversary.

'Hello, Memani! We meet again.' Pierre held out his hand and smiled tightly, but the smile did not reach his voice, which remained hard and cold.

Themba refused the handshake. He leaned forward and hissed into Pierre's ear, 'Listen, Roux, I know I have to work with you in the negotiation process, but that does not mean I have to make small talk.' He turned on his heel and followed the delegation into the building.

A reporter sidled up to Pierre. 'Mr Roux, it looks as if there's bad blood between yourself and Mr Themba Memani of the ANC.'

'Nonsense.' Pierre forced himself to stay calm. 'You're imagining things.'

'You seem to know each other. Were you arguing?'

'No.' Pierre turned around and walked through the door, more irritated than he cared to admit.

The ANC delegation, led by Mandela, took their seats on one side of the long table. The government members occupied the opposite side. The atmosphere was congenial until the core issues were discussed – the removal of stumbling blocks leading to true negotiations.

Three days of hard bargaining took place. Both sides had to

make concessions. At one stage the talks were on the verge of breaking down on the issue of the release of political prisoners. In dispute was the actual definition of a political offence. Following Mandela's example, the ANC delegates rose to leave.

Themba stopped them. 'Gentlemen, please, the answer is simple.' Everyone turned to him. 'Let us form a small working group of representatives from both sides. Allow this select committee to debate the matter fully and report back on their findings at the next meeting. It will remove a contentious issue from this meeting and allow us to reach consensus on other issues.'

A look of relief swept across De Klerk's face as he rose, his tone one of reconciliation. 'Excellent idea, Mr Memani. A select committee is what we need.'

De Klerk turned to Mandela. 'With your permission, may we continue?'

Mandela seemed undecided, then nodded and resumed his seat. The other ANC delegates followed suit. Themba's diplomacy had saved the talks.

Pierre cursed under his breath, jealous that Themba had outshone him.

Four thousand wildly excited people jammed the international arrivals hall at the Johannesburg airport. They were determined to accord a hero's welcome to Oliver Tambo, returning home after many years of exile.

Themba was present to welcome his friend, but there was another more personal reason: his wife and family were travelling on the same flight. He had not seen them for twelve months; now he willed the minutes to speed into seconds.

The crowd groaned when it was announced that Tambo had diverted the aeroplane to Harare to visit the Zimbabwean president. In the late afternoon the aircraft finally touched down. Themba was beside himself with agitation, but had to smile at the way the crowd toyi-toyied in excitement.

He wormed his way to the observation balcony and joined the ANC dignitaries. Tambo appeared in the aircraft's open doorway, supported by his wife Adelaide. Themba was shocked to see how he had aged and how frail he had become. Tambo wearily raised his right arm in the ANC power salute.

'*Mayibuye!*' responded the crowd.

Themba kept his eyes glued to the aeroplane's exit door. At last there they were – Hilda, with Bambatha holding one arm and Helen the other. He hurried down to the arrivals hall to meet them.

With a click the automatic doors from customs opened, and finally facing Themba were his family. He swept them into his arms, kissing and hugging them simultaneously.

Chris Hani strolled into Themba's office in Shell House, the ANC's headquarters in Johannesburg. He was older and wiser but his expressive eyes still showed the same fervour and sense of anticipation. 'Morning, Themba. We're so busy these days we hardly get time to talk.' He poured himself a cup of tea and sat down.

'You're right, old friend,' smiled Themba, looking up from a mass of paperwork piled on his desk. He sighed in frustration. 'Sometimes I wonder if the government really wants meaningful change. They say so, but are loath to make concessions to the ANC.'

A man poked his head around the door, his face happy and smiling. 'Have you guys heard the news?'

Both Themba and Chris shook their heads as Tokyo Sexwale strode purposefully into the room. 'Today De Klerk repealed the Population Registration Act and the Group Areas Act.'

'About time too!' Themba cried.

'No more racial classification,' breathed Hani in satisfaction. 'At last we are all equals.'

'Now we can purchase property in any area of our choice.' Sexwale grinned from ear to ear.

'I would like to move closer to Johannesburg,' said Themba. 'The long journey from Soweto to work and back is exhausting, with the unreliable public transport. When I get back from a trip at night I always have to use a taxi from the airport to home. It's costing me a small fortune.'

'There are excellent houses for sale at reasonable prices in Boksburg,' answered Sexwale. 'That is close to the airport and convenient for work.'

'Sounds good,' chuckled Hani, then mischievously: 'Imagine the faces of the white neighbours if we purchased houses in Boksburg, a white Afrikaner area!'

'They will have to accept us,' smiled Sexwale triumphantly. 'I've already contacted an estate agency and they are going to show me houses in Dawn Park over the weekend.'

'Can Limpho and I join you?' Hani asked excitedly.

'Us too?' inquired Themba.

During the weekend the three friends, their wives and families house-hunted.

'I'm impressed with Dawn Park.' Hilda was beside herself with eagerness. 'There are good houses and it's lovely and quiet, with lots of trees.'

By Sunday night each had signed a deed of sale.

Hilda loved her new home and immediately made friends with her amicable and helpful neighbours. Bambatha and Helen were enrolled in a local school. Themba sighed in satisfaction – at last he was seeing tangible signs of a changing South Africa, but he knew the difficulties of an equitable political solution still lay ahead.

The various delegations took their seats in the huge World Trade Centre in Kempton Park. An atmosphere of optimism prevailed, heightened when Nelson Mandela and FW de Klerk smiled at each other and shook hands warmly.

Pierre stepped forward and greeted Mandela. 'We welcome you and the ANC delegation to Codesa.' He avoided Themba Memani and walked to his seat.

Damn Memani, he cursed under his breath. It had taken all his powers of diplomacy to persuade the ANC to support the Convention for a Democratic South Africa. Memani had blocked him at every turn, squeezing more and more concessions out of him, before he had finally agreed to participate. After the ANC's initial urgency, it now seemed as if they were deliberately trying to hold up the negotiation process. Pierre wondered why.

Once the foreign dignitaries and the nineteen delegations representing the various political parties and groupings had settled down the joint chairmen, two Supreme Court judges, welcomed all present.

'Congratulations,' Pierre whispered in De Klerk's ear. 'The show of solidarity by the various leaders is going well.'

'I'm looking forward to appointing the different working groups to implement the decisions taken by Codesa.'

Judge Mohamed was relaxed as he addressed the gathering. 'The leader of each delegation is permitted twenty minutes for his opening remarks. I have permitted the State President to speak last.'

Pierre, sitting at FW de Klerk's right hand as the penultimate leader concluded his speech, turned to his friend. 'Leave out the remarks on Umkhonto we Sizwe. The day has gone so well, we don't want to upset proceedings at this stage.'

De Klerk shook his head. 'I have strong feelings on the matter. To get the right-wing white parties to the negotiating table we have to appear decisive on the MK matter.'

'I think you're making a grave mistake,' answered a disappointed Pierre.

Justice Mohamed rose. 'We will now accord the government delegation the opportunity to issue their opening remarks. Thereafter we will proceed with the signing of the Declaration of Intent to complete the first day's proceedings.'

Warm applause greeted De Klerk. He was self-assured and smiling. 'I congratulate my fellow leaders on the bold step you have taken today.' He touched on a number of issues, but hesitated as he came to the section on MK. Pierre's advice flashed through his mind, but when he saw the television cameras trained on him, beaming his words into every home in the country, he decided to go with his original decision.

De Klerk squared his shoulders. 'The continuing existence of Umkhonto we Sizwe, the ANC's armed wing, places a cloud over the negotiation process. I hereby issue an ultimatum to the ANC to dismantle its armed wing or disqualify itself from entering into binding agreements within Codesa.'

Mandela's face displayed fury as he turned to Themba. 'When I spoke to De Klerk on the telephone last night he gave no indication that he would raise the MK issue in such a way.'

'He's using his privilege of speaking last to discredit the ANC.' Themba studied his leader's face. 'I don't think you should take this lying down. Demand a chance to reply so you can put the record straight.' Themba looked thoughtful. 'I believe we should try and delay the negotiation process anyway until the ANC is sufficiently organised. We must bargain from a position of strength, not submit in weakness. De Klerk's just given you the opening.'

'All right,' agreed Mandela, 'I'll attack his integrity. That should throw the National Party into disarray and signal the end of Codesa.'

'Good.' Themba breathed a sigh of relief. 'I need time to sort out our structures.'

De Klerk finished his address and the delegates applauded spontaneously.

Amid much backslapping the leaders signed the Declaration of Intent, indicating their parties' commitment to a negotiated settlement. Mandela signed in stony silence, then took the co-chairmen to one side and spoke to them urgently.

The delegates settled back in their places, congratulating themselves on a great achievement. Not Pierre. He had been watching the interaction between Themba, Mandela and the co-chairmen and knew something was amiss.

Justice Mohamed strode to the podium. He spoke sternly and the delegates looked up in surprise. 'We have granted Mr Nelson Mandela, the leader of the ANC delegation, the opportunity to raise a matter of national importance.'

Mandela marched to the microphone. It was almost seven o'clock. 'It is with deep regret that I address you in this manner, but what I have to say cannot possibly go unsaid.' Mandela turned to De Klerk and spoke with cold fury tingeing his voice. 'I find it increasingly difficult to work with President de Klerk. His moral turpitude and duplicity are real stumbling blocks to negotiations.'

Pierre looked across at the ANC table and shot a venomous glance at Themba. He sat back, smiling delightedly at Pierre's anger. De Klerk flushed, started scribbling notes, then dropped his pen.

'Even a discredited, illegitimate minority government must observe certain standards. If President de Klerk can come to a conference of this nature and play this type of politics, then I tell you, very few people would like to deal with such a man.'

Mandela continued, 'Mr de Klerk must forget that he can impose conditions on the ANC. He does not represent us. He cannot talk to us in that language. We are going to stop him.' Mandela glared belligerently at the State President. 'You speak from a position of weakness for you have failed to stop the violence. I warn you, stop trying to undermine the ANC – it is not in the best interests of the country.'

Pierre turned to De Klerk, shocked to see the pallor on his face. He was hyper-ventilating with fury. He placed his hand on his friend's arm to try and calm him. 'Don't let Mandela get to you. This is a pre-planned move to slow down the process.'

There was a bewildered look in De Klerk's eyes. 'He has virtually destroyed Codesa. Why? Why?'

'The ANC is not ready for negotiations. Listen to what Mandela is saying, he's employing delaying tactics.'

Mandela heaped more criticism on the government, but left the door open for further discussions: 'In certain ways Mr de Klerk is a reformer, but he has to realise that he must work openly with the ANC if he expects to achieve results.'

'I demand the right to reply.' De Klerk appealed to Pierre. 'Please organise it with the chairmen.'

Pierre approached the co-chairman, Justice Schabort. 'The State President is under obligation to reply to the vicious attack. You must grant him time to speak.'

Reluctantly Schabort agreed. 'I call the convention to order and announce the State President.'

The atmosphere was electric. Would De Klerk attack Mandela in the same tone? If so, he would completely destroy any chance of a negotiated settlement. The State President rose, his face severe.

Pierre whispered in his ear. 'Go slow, my friend. The future of South Africa depends on the next few minutes. Attack the issues, not the man. Play to your strength. Let your natural diplomacy shine through.'

De Klerk nodded slowly. 'I should have listened to you the first time. I won't make the same mistake again.' He walked with a measured step to the podium, stopped opposite the ANC delegation, and flashed Mandela a smile.

Still visibly flustered, De Klerk answered Mandela's accusations but refrained from a personal attack. 'It is surely a matter of principle that no party should have a private army. The problem of weapons does not bother only the government, it is bothering everybody. I am as deeply concerned about the violence in South Africa as anybody else. I have no intention of apologising for my words.'

De Klerk looked straight at Pierre, who shook his head vigorously. From his expression he realised Pierre was advocating a more conciliatory tone. De Klerk cleared his throat. 'Up until this moment, whatever has happened has been in the past. Our future relies on the present, and I extend my hand to Mr Mandela in friendship, trusting we can work together towards the solution.'

Pierre was first to stand, clapping loudly. Others followed suit.

* * *

The months flew as Themba, as head of the legal department, and other ANC executive members set up branch offices in all the major areas of South Africa. 'We are ready to resume negotiations,' Themba told Nelson Mandela.

'Good. I'll speak to de Klerk.'

'Do I have to work with Pierre Roux?' asked Themba in exasperation.

'What is it between the two of you?'

Themba told Mandela of his experiences with Pierre. Mandela paced the room, a look of concern on his face. 'I understand your anger, Themba, but for the sake of lasting peace you have to rise above your deep-seated resentment. You don't have to like the man to work with him.'

'I suppose not,' conceded Themba.

'Try, for all our sakes. You are the ANC's most skilled negotiator. I am relying on you and so is every downtrodden person in South Africa.'

There was resolve in Themba's eyes. 'I will do my best, Madiba.'

On a sunny autumn Thursday in April 1993 the Multi-Party Negotiating Forum recessed for the Easter weekend.

Themba sat back in satisfaction. Major breakthroughs had been achieved. Consensus had been reached on the terms for political amnesty. The basis for an interim constitution had been hammered out. A few more weeks of co-operation were needed, that was all. The final goal was in sight.

Pierre was deep in thought. Was he imagining it, or was Themba's hostility towards him tempering? He could not place his finger on a specific incident, but there had been signs – an action here, a word there – that made him wonder. Pierre shrugged as he packed his papers into his briefcase. At the doorway Pierre and Themba came face to face. Pierre stepped backwards, allowing Themba to go first.

'Thank you,' said Themba. 'Going home for the Easter weekend?' They walked down the passage together.

Pierre nodded. 'I'm meeting my wife and daughter in Cape Town and spending the weekend at home.'

'Have a good rest, we're in for a tough stint next week.'

'Yes,' agreed Pierre. 'Many issues are delicately poised.'

'We'll have to take the lead. Although we're working on the basis of common consensus, with many parties represented, it all boils down to agreement being reached by the ANC and the National Party.'

'That means you and me,' sighed Pierre. 'I never thought I'd see the day when we would work together.'

'Force of circumstances.' Themba looked at Pierre sharply. 'Because I work with you doesn't mean I applaud you.'

Pierre stopped, placing his hands on his hips. 'The feeling is mutual.' The old hostility threatened to surface again. Pierre forced himself to stay calm. 'See you on Tuesday.' He quickly turned and walked towards the car-park.

Easter Saturday was a relaxing day at the Memani home. Themba slept late for the first time in months, then Hilda and the children joined him in bed for a late breakfast.

'Dad, can we go to the zoo this afternoon?' Bambatha asked excitedly.

'Please! Please!' echoed Helen. 'I want to see the lions and tigers, and those animals with long necks.'

'Giraffes,' laughed Themba as he dressed leisurely. 'Sure we can go.'

'Yippee! Yippee!' chorused the children.

The telephone rang and Bambatha rushed out of the room. A minute later he was back, a worried expression on his round face. 'It's uncle Tokyo, and he sounds upset.'

Themba picked up the receiver. 'Good morning, Tokyo. What's wrong?'

'Chris Hani has been shot outside his house.'

There was silence as the full impact of the words sunk in. Themba answered in a strained voice, 'Chris? Not Chris. Please God, not Chris . . . Is he . . . dead?'

'I'm not sure.'

'I'll be there as soon as I can.' Themba threw down the telephone and rushed to his car.

Tokyo and Themba reached Hani's house simultaneously. Chris lay with the newspaper still under his arm, his car keys next to his right hand. Themba knelt down, lifting an arm, feeling for a pulse. There was none. With his hand under Hani's head, he gently lifted him. Blood poured out of a bullet wound behind his ear.

'He's dead.' Tokyo put the horror into words. 'Chris must have died instantly.'

The two comrades looked at each other with shock, extreme consternation etched on their faces. Both had seen many horrors during the armed struggle for liberation, but nothing matched the awful sight of their friend lying dead at their feet. They turned away, sick to their stomachs, as a neighbour covered the body with a sheet. Slowly Themba walked to the front door and rang the doorbell. No response. He kicked at the door in frustration. Where were Limpho and the children?

'They're out,' said the neighbour and Themba turned away with a sigh, relieved that they would not see their husband and father in such a mutilated state.

Army troops and traffic police cordoned off the entire block. The news spread like wildfire. Within an hour the regional radio's news bulletin carried the message to the whole of the Witwatersrand. Friends and colleagues poured into Dawn Park.

Hani's bodyguard burst on to the scene. He took one look at the body and threw his arms into the air in grief. In a daze he leant against a wall sobbing quietly, wiping away his tears with his T-shirt. 'It's my fault. I was not here today. If I'd been on duty Chris would not have been dead. Now I'll never see my hero again.'

People were devastated. The mood of the crowd began to change. Utter despair was replaced by a slow-burning anger. People started chanting. Certain elements threatened to go on the rampage.

'Who did this dastardly deed?' Themba shouted at a policeman. 'You had better tell us, unless you want a riot on your hands.'

A police officer stepped forward, trying to pacify the crowd. 'A man fitting a description given by the neighbours has been arrested.'

'Who is this man?' Themba demanded angrily.

'He's a white man.' A ripple of anger swept over the crowd.

'Do you know what this means?' Themba barked at the officer. 'The peace process is finished – gone – washed up. Chris Hani was trusted, admired and loved by the people. They will seek revenge, creating a backlash never seen before in South Africa. Mark my words, there is big trouble ahead.'

'I ask you all to stay calm, please.' The officer shouted to make himself heard. 'The assassin probably wanted to create confusion and hatred. Don't let some crank disrupt the vision for a new South Africa.'

'New South Africa?' Themba barked cynically. 'Nothing has changed. The whites continue to kill the black man.' There was steel in his voice. 'This time they bit off more than they can chew. We will avenge Chris Hani's death.'

The crowd cheered and the police moved closer. The arrival of the police mortuary van reversing up the driveway, split the incensed crowd. Friends cried openly as Chris's body was loaded into the back.

Tokyo Sexwale's booming voice rang out: 'Please, comrades, let's disperse peacefully and mourn without violence.'

Slowly the crowd melted away until only a dark stain on the driveway gave testimony to the deed. Themba walked slowly to his car and drove home.

Hilda saw his face as he entered the house and immediately knew something terrible had occurred. 'What's happened?'

Themba's voice was strained. 'A white man murdered Chris Hani at his house this morning.'

Hilda let out a cry of anguish. 'Oh, no! Why Chris?' She started sobbing quietly. Like a mother hen wanting to protect her chicks from danger, she called the children to her for reassurance, encircling them and clutching them to her breast.

The teenage Bambatha held himself stiffly, awkward in his mother's embrace. He looked at his father. 'How did Uncle Chris die?'

'He was shot four times.' Themba's shoulders slumped as the finality of the deed struck him. His friend was dead, gone for ever. He would never again hear him quoting Shelley, or Keats, or Shakespeare. His warm, friendly smile was erased. His dynamic personality and his dream for a righteous South Africa had perished in a hail of bullets. A sadness overwhelmed Themba.

'I want to be alone for a while.' Shoulders drooping, Themba walked into his study and closed the door. Once at his desk, he allowed his feelings to surface. Grief took hold of his body. He lay with his head on his crossed arms and wept unashamedly until the blotter was damp from his tears. Gradually the distress gave way to emptiness and then on to a blind fury as the futility of the deed struck home. Why? Why? Why? He asked himself. What would the killing of Chris Hani achieve?

The answer was slow in coming. The whites want to retain power as long as possible. Themba banged his fist on the desk. Do whites really want peace, or are they only paying lip-service to negotiations?

Throughout all the years of the armed struggle Themba had hated the government with a passion. Then he had come to accept them as a negotiating partner on the road to peace. Now his abhorrence reached new levels of revulsion. He pictured Pierre Roux in his mind. He focused his hatred on him.

'No more concessions to you, Roux. Damn you to hell!' Themba shouted.

Pierre and De Klerk watched Chris Hani's funeral on television, a feeling of futility settling over them. When the symbolic white doves of peace refused to fly away, one actually following the coffin into the grave, De Klerk turned to his friend in exasperation.

'The key to the whole negotiating process lies between you and Themba Memani.'

'The black nation will mourn the death of Chris Hani, making it almost impossible to revive the talks,' answered Pierre. He sat forward sharply as the television cameras focused on Themba in the first row. His face mirrored his extreme suffering, but his eyes displayed unbridled hate and determination. 'FW, I think you and Mandela must continue the negotiation process,' said Pierre.

'Memani wouldn't give me ice in winter now.'

De Klerk disagreed. 'Fly to Johannesburg tomorrow and call on Memani.'

'Must I go cap in hand and plead with *him*?' Pierre pointed to the television set.

'South Africa's future depends on it,' answered his friend softly. 'If not for the country, then do it for me.'

Pierre paced the room, glanced at De Klerk and thought deeply. Should he step down as government chief negotiator and leave it to another parliamentarian to continue? There were certainly other capable men. He could bow out with honour, but he would be letting down De Klerk. His friend had kept faith with him all along, aware of the rift between Memani and himself.

No, he couldn't let FW down, he decided. But what about

himself? His pride would not tolerate failure. Did he really hate Memani? Yes, yes, oh yes! he decided. But then there was a niggling doubt. Was the original blind hate turning to jealousy, or was it grudging admiration? Not admiration, he decided, as he pushed the thought away. He could never admire a man who had left him to die on a wild sea. A man who had betrayed his trust.

Was it perhaps respect, then? Respect for Themba's staying power, his negotiating prowess and his absolute determination.

De Klerk interrupted his thoughts and Pierre stopped in mid-stride to look at his friend. 'You know what the problem is, Pierre?' De Klerk answered the question himself. 'He may be black and you white, but otherwise the two of you are the same obstinate, strong-willed sort of people. Do you know the two of you even look alike?'

That was it! Pierre thought, as he flexed his arms and continued pacing. They were so similar that Themba and himself were like opposite poles of a magnet – repelling one another. If they learnt to channel their energies in the same direction, then only could they work together. Pierre stopped pacing and turned to De Klerk. 'I'll fly to Johannesburg and talk to Memani.'

'Good.' De Klerk let out a sigh of relief. 'Thank you, Pierre.'

Security guards were present in large numbers at the entrance to Shell House. They examined Pierre's identity documents and telephoned through to Themba. He refused to see Pierre.

'Please get hold of Mr Sexwale,' Pierre asked urgently. 'Ask if he will receive me.'

The guard allowed Pierre through. 'Mr Sexwale has agreed to see you.'

'Please, Mr Sexwale, it's imperative for me to speak to Themba Memani,' entreated Pierre.

'Themba is hurting. He and Chris Hani were very close friends and the assassination has affected him deeply.'

'You do know the very future of our country is at stake?'

Tokyo nodded knowingly. 'I'll speak to Themba.'

Five minutes later Pierre was called into Themba's office and Tokyo withdrew, leaving the two men scowling at each other.

'Mr Memani, we must get the negotiations back on track,' started Pierre.

'Come and see me in a month's time,' responded Themba darkly. 'We are in mourning at present.'

'I know . . .' began Pierre.

'You know nothing,' interrupted Themba. 'You whites killed Chris Hani – now you want to negotiate.'

'Clive Derby-Lewis and Janusz Walus are the lunatic fringe of the right wing . . .'

'You Afrikaners think you're a superior race. God's own people, you call yourselves! We've had as much as we can take!'

'You can't begin to compare the AWB, the White Wolves and other far-rightist organisations with the National Party. They want to delay the peace process, we want to advance talks.'

'Chris Hani is dead,' stated Themba bitterly. 'Don't you understand? Peace died with him.'

'I understand your pain, and I sympathise.'

'Ha! You haven't a grain of sympathy in your body,' growled Themba. 'I suffered torture at the hands of the security police and the humiliation of internment on Robben Island because of you.'

'You betrayed my trust in Soweto.'

'I could have shot you in the dinghy off Koeberg if I'd wanted to.'

'Why didn't you, when you had the chance?' Pierre snapped. 'One more death to a killer like you would have made no difference.'

'Get out of my office!' screamed Themba, pointing to the door.

At that moment Nelson Mandela burst in. 'What is it with the two of you now? The whole floor can hear your slanging match.' He looked at Pierre sternly, then at Themba. 'I demand that you act civilly to one another.'

'I'm sorry – I got carried away,' apologised Pierre. 'I came with an olive branch from the President. We are anxious to resume negotiations.'

'Reconciliation is needed.' Mandela's face showed the ravages of the past week, but his eyes were as determined as ever. 'Themba, don't forget, Chris lived for democracy in our country. The most fitting legacy you can leave him is to see his dream come true.'

Themba sat down heavily. 'You're right as usual, Madiba.' The aggression was gone as he waved Pierre to a chair.

*　　*　　*

With the onset of winter the Multi-Party Forum resumed at the World Trade Centre. To catch up lost time Pierre and Themba headed their teams late into the night. By co-operating they reached consensus, and slowly but surely the plan came together. Even the withdrawal of the Conservative Party and the Zulu Inkatha Party proved only a temporary setback, as the momentum of negotiations was maintained.

It was give and take, with Pierre conceding on some points, Themba on others and the forum reaching consensus on the balance. By the end of 1993 an equitable settlement had been hammered out for a transitional period of five years in a Government of National Unity.

'At last the right-wing whites have joined the democratic process,' sighed Pierre wearily as the room emptied, leaving only Themba and himself at the table, 'now that General Constand Viljoen and his Freedom Front have agreed to participate in the elections.'

'But only after we agreed to the establishment of a board to investigate their claims for a *Volkstaat* for Afrikaners,' complained Themba.

'It was the only way to get conservative Afrikaners to become part of the election process.' Pierre sat back in his chair, rubbing his eyes in the smoke-filled room.

'That leaves only the Zulu Inkatha Party to convince.' Themba was also tired, but it did not show on his face. He had been as solid as a rock throughout the negotiation process – strong and tough, able to concentrate day and night and always sharp and concise.

'If the ANC and the Zulus would come to terms with each other, and stop the senseless killings of each other's members, then maybe they would participate,' said Pierre irritably.

'The Zulus must realise that the days of separate states are finished for ever,' retorted Themba sharply. 'The ANC will never give KwaZulu-Natal more regional autonomy – they must form an integral part of South Africa.'

'Damn it all, Memani!' Pierre exploded. 'Give the Zulu king a greater say in the region and you'll get the Zulu nation behind the peace process.'

'Don't you talk to me like that,' hissed Themba indignantly. 'You forget that I co-operate with you under constraint. Once the ANC wins the elections our collaboration is at an end, Roux.'

Anger flushed Pierre's face. 'The feeling is mutual, Memani.' He rose to his feet, roughly pushing back his chair. 'You speak to Mandela and I'll talk to De Klerk and let us sort out the Zulu issue speedily. There are only a few weeks to go and without Zulu acceptance the bloodshed will continue after the elections.'

Themba nodded, his eyes signalling his aversion to the man he had been compelled to join forces with in order to secure a settlement. 'I'll speak to Nelson Mandela and contact you.'

Pierre watched Themba walk away stiffly, his left leg dragging slightly. His inner pride would never allow him to admit that he admired the man — never to Themba, nor to anyone else. Pierre packed his briefcase and hurried from the room.

High up against the slope of Paarl Mountain a female leopard crept out of her lair under the twisted roots of a Cape beech tree. She glanced back at her twin, month-old cubs, their eyes just opened, playing on a layer of dry leaves.

The female was a magnificent specimen, weighing almost forty kilograms, in the prime of her life. She had a dusky fawn coat marked with rosettes over her back and flanks, giving way to spots on her head and neck. Her maternal instinct told her it was time to move the litter to another place, to protect her cubs from discovery. She climbed on to a rock, blending perfectly with her surroundings.

Solitary animals, leopards live alone, except at mating time or when a female rears cubs. In early January the female had come into oestrus and a male had entered her territory. The female had coaxed the male to copulation by slowly circling and rubbing up against him with her tail raised. Growling incessantly, the female had crouched down in front of the male, enticing him to mount her. He had been tempted and four days of incessant mating had followed, accompanied by lots of snarling and growling. When her heat cycle had passed the male left, returning to his solitary nomadic wanderings.

Three and a half months later two cubs were born, with tightly closed little eyes. The mother foraged for food, killing duikers and steenbok to feed her offspring. The leopard's favourite delicacy, the chacma baboon, had not entered her home range since the birth of the cubs. The eastern slopes of Paarl Mountain were in her core area, her exclusive domain, scent-marked by spraying urine around the perimeter. She killed only in her territory.

From the rock she looked down with her pale, piercing amber eyes on to Paarl Valley. Moving gracefully, she headed down the slope towards the base of Paarl Rock. Stealthily she worked her way among the splintered granite chunks scattered at the foot of the giant rock until she found her previous hide, a small cave in a rocky outcrop of loose stones. She entered the den, sniffing carefully, smelling only her previous scent, satisfied that the lair was safe.

One by one she carried the mewling cubs in her mouth to the new hide, about three hundred metres from the first one but still within the boundaries of her twenty-five square kilometre territory.

Doctors' waiting rooms were morbid places to Simon at the best of times, with unsmiling patients flipping through old magazines like prisoners waiting to be called to the dock. Today was worse, and Simon found it uncomfortable to sit with his bloated stomach, his breath coming in short, rasping gasps.

At last his turn came. 'Mr Roux, doctor will see you now,' nodded a sombre-looking nursing sister.

Simon rose with difficulty, shuffling after the nurse. She placed his file on the doctor's desk and left. A few minutes later the doctor entered, drying his hands on a paper towel.

'Afternoon, Simon. How do you feel?'

'Terrible!'

'What do you expect?' berated the doctor, showing no sympathy. 'You know what your problem is, but you don't want to listen. Have you stopped drinking?'

Simon shook his head slowly. 'I can't stop now. Brandy is all that keeps me alive.'

'And it will prove your death,' added the doctor. 'You are looking more jaundiced than on your last visit.' He made Simon lie down, and he groaned as the doctor's fingers manipulated his liver. 'You're in a bad way, Simon. Carry on like this and you'll be dead within a month.'

'Give me some more pills – they help.'

The doctor filled in a prescription. 'The diuretic will help get rid of the excess fluid, but isn't a long-term solution.' He looked at Simon sadly – the once-powerful specimen of manhood was now an emaciated, pot-bellied man with a pasty, yellow colour. 'You hold your life in your hands.'

'I know,' smiled Simon wistfully, 'but alcohol is all that keeps me sane.'

*   *   *

'Dad, you're looking dreadful,' said Pierre with concern. 'What's the problem?'

'Your father's drinking himself to death.' Helena rolled her wheelchair forward in agitation, a scowl disfiguring her face. 'He has cirrhosis of the liver. I've spoken to him, the doctor has told him, but he won't listen.'

'You must pull yourself together, Dad, for all our sakes,' pleaded Pierre.

'It's too late, son,' Simon answered sadly. 'The doctor has given me a month to live.'

'A month!' Pierre cried in shock, rising and wrenching the wine glass out of his father's hand. 'I insist you cut out the alcohol.'

Simon nodded, staring at his son with a deep feeling of affection. He *had* to tell Pierre about Themba's existence. He had made Themba a substantial beneficiary in his will and the truth would come out in a month's time anyway. He didn't want Pierre to find out at the reading of the will – then his son would think him a coward, unable to face up to his responsibilities. He had to tell him before he died, and Themba too. He also had a right to know and meet his father.

'You're right, son, I'll try for you.' Simon groaned as he shifted his position. 'Please carve the lamb for us, Pierre. I'm not up to it.'

They waited for Lesley before starting dinner. She entered the dining room, her hips swaying as she walked. Pierre watched her with satisfaction, ruing the fact that during the past year he had spent more time at the World Trade Centre than at home. Her clear blue eyes settled on him, her warm smile lighting up her face. Touching him on the shoulder lovingly, she sat down, her blonde hair loose and provocatively fluffy. 'Thanks for waiting, Mom.'

They ate in silence for a while, feeling comfortable in Hermitage's large dining room with the high yellow-wood beamed ceiling and gleaming floor. Simon, sipping from a glass of water, started the political debate rolling. 'I see you and Themba Memani are working well together.'

'Oh, no, Dad!' Lesley gasped. 'Why did you have to bring *that* up at a family dinner, on the eve of the elections.'

Simon was horrified to see the steely look flash into Pierre's eyes again. Was the deep-seated hatred Pierre spoke of still there? Should he have kept quiet? No, he had to know – somehow he had to clarify the matter, so he could die at peace with himself.

Pierre pushed his plate away and sat forward, his elbows on the table and his head resting on his hands. He bristled with indignation. 'Memani and I were forced to work together, but I hate his guts!'

Pushing her wheelchair back in consternation, Helena looked from her husband to her son, and back to her husband. She grabbed Simon by the arm. 'Not very tactful, Simon.'

Simon stood up. 'I'm tired and I'm going to bed.' He shuffled from the room, a tormented expression on his face.

'Was that necessary?' Pierre looked at his mother disparagingly as he rushed after his father.

Simon sat on the bed, tears rolling down his cheeks. How was he ever going to bring the matter to culmination without denouncement from his family? He was at a complete loss for a solution. By telling Pierre in isolation he could carry his son's curse to the grave. If he informed Themba alone, he would probably laugh in his face.

He had to tell them together and hope they were both understanding. Where? It suddenly struck him – his cave! All the evidence was in the cave – his diary, the scrap book of Themba's life and the various artefacts. Also, the cave was isolated.

If he could get them there before dark they wouldn't be able to descend the fissure at night. He would have them together for at least ten hours. Would it be enough time to achieve a miracle – the acceptance by his two sons of each other's heritage? He had to try, it was his only chance, and he must succeed.

Pierre looked down with compassion at the pathetic figure of his father wrestling with his thoughts. The once-proud man was a shadow of his former self. His clothes were dirty and creased, his shock of black hair, now greying, was uncombed and standing up like bristles on a brush. He sat down next to his father, his arm about his shoulder. 'Is there something you want to tell me, Dad?'

'Yes, but the time is not right, my son. When will you and Memani be together again?'

'In parliament, after the elections, when all candidates are sworn in as members of the National Assembly.'

'Can you organise a seat for me in the public gallery?'

'Not a problem. For Mom as well?'

'No!' Simon exclaimed. 'Leave your mother out of this – it's men's business.'

'The swearing-in ceremony will be followed by a lunch at the Cape Town City Hall and the new President will address the people from the balcony. Do you wish to attend this as well?'

'Oh yes! Then I will have an opportunity to speak to Themba Memani.'

'Why do you wish to speak to him?' Pierre searched his father's face.

'I can't tell you now. Be patient, you will learn soon enough.' A smile of contentment played on his lips.

Paarl was cloudy and cool on election day, with light showers sweeping intermittently across the Paarl Valley. The weather in no way dampened the spirits of the voters who patiently queued in a long snake around the KWV car-park. Simon, Helena, Pierre and Lesley waited their turn to cast their votes. A carnival atmosphere prevailed with black, white, coloured and Indian voters all chatting to each other in the mixed line.

'How do you feel today?' Pierre asked an old black woman.

'Today is the best day of my life,' she replied with a toothless grin. 'I have waited eighty-five years for this day, and I thank the Lord that he allowed me to live to see the start of true democracy in our country.'

'Pity it took so long!' Helena retorted.

'When you are waiting for a dream to come true, what is a year or two or even a decade or two, missus?' replied the old woman prudently.

For days Pierre remained glued to the television set as the Independent Electoral Commission released the results. It took a full week before Justice Kriegler had clarified the irregularities and declared the election substantially free and fair. International monitoring teams proclaimed themselves satisfied with the result.

'Where does that leave you, son?' Simon asked.

'I've been offered the portfolio of Provincial Affairs and Constitutional Development.'

'Congratulations,' they all chorused in delight.

'And Themba Memani?' Simon asked softly.

'He's scheduled to become Minister of Public Services and Administration.'

599

'Very close to your portfolio,' observed Simon astutely. 'So the two of you will still have to work closely together?'

Pierre sighed in frustration. 'We don't seem to be able to get away from each other.'

'Your futures are inextricably linked,' Simon answered cryptically as he walked away, a knowing smile on his face.

Pierre settled his father in the public gallery, in a front-row seat overlooking the revamped Great Hall of parliament. Extra seats had been added to cater for four hundred members of the National Assembly. Parliament had been redecorated in traditional African patterns and shades.

'Good luck, my son.' There were tears in Simon's eyes as he realised this was the last time he would sit in parliament and see his two sons together in the hallowed precincts.

'Thanks, Dad. I'll fetch you later.' Pierre squeezed his arm and hurried to join his colleagues. They filed into the Great Hall and took their seats. The birth of a new nation was evident in the changed attire of the parliamentarians. Colourful African themes now predominated. An excited buzz swept across the hall as Nelson Mandela entered with his two Deputy Presidents, Thabo Mbeki and FW de Klerk. Magnanimously, Mandela held back, clapping and allowing De Klerk to walk in front.

The old traditions of the white parliament were swept aside as an *imbongi*, or praise singer, dressed in traditional Thembu gear – a jackal skin, colourful beads, a blanket and holding a knopkierie and fighting stick in his hands – entered the House. In a flurry of dancing, he extolled the virtues of Nelson Mandela loudly in the Xhosa tongue.

Chief Justice Corbett, occupying the Speaker's chair, advised the members on the swearing-in ceremony. Batches of up to ten members at a time from each party would be called up in rotation to take the oath of allegiance.

He called up ten from the ANC first, including Mandela, Mbeki, Themba and other high-ranking members. Simon watched with interest as Themba walked forward, limping slightly, but holding himself tall and regally. They stood in a row before the table.

'I now administer the oath of solemn affirmation,' said Justice Corbett. 'You swear, or solemnly affirm, to be faithful to the Republic of South Africa, and you solemnly promise to perform your functions as a member of the National Assembly to the best of your ability. Say – so help me God, or I do.'

Simon watched with bursting pride as Themba, ramrod-straight, raised his right hand. 'My son! My son!' Simon breathed.

'Please sign the declaration,' said Justice Corbett as the next ten were called – FW de Klerk and high ranking members of the National Party, including Pierre.

Pierre took his place behind Themba. With a flourish Themba signed, stood up and turned around quickly, and bumped straight into Pierre. Simon saw Pierre stumble a pace backwards and stiffen noticeably. Simon's eyes flicked to Themba's face and he saw his look of abhorrence.

A great feeling of sadness enveloped him, replacing that of pride. Sadness that in less than a month he would be dead, and that he would never again see his son Pierre's angular, handsome face, hear his voice or feel his strong body in an embrace of love. And would he have the opportunity of embracing Themba?

The woman sitting next to Simon looked on in compassion as he wept, nodding warmly as he wiped away his tears. 'Today is a happy day,' she babbled. 'I also feel like crying tears of joy!'

Fleecy clouds, like puffs of cotton wool, lightly topped the flat summit of Table Mountain, providing an awe-inspiring backdrop to the huge crowd gathered on The Parade to listen to the newly-elected State President. Pop bands entertained the masses as they patiently waited.

At the city hall Pierre helped his father up the stairs and found a seat for him against the wall from where he had a good view of the jubilant parliamentarians as they congratulated one another. Everyone was caught up in the euphoria of the moment, relieved that the proceedings had gone so smoothly and that such goodwill abounded.

Nelson Mandela, together with his Deputy Presidents, headed for the city hall balcony overlooking The Parade. A huge roar greeted the master of ceremonies, Archbishop Desmond Tutu, as he introduced Mandela. 'And now, the rainbow people of God,' he cried out, 'let us welcome our brand-new State President, straight out of the box!' A tumultuous roar greeted Mandela as he strode to the microphone.

Far below, screaming, frenzied people welcomed their hero,

toyi-toyiing in happiness. The moment so many had suffered for, and so many had died for, had arrived in a blaze of glory.

Mandela paid tribute to the role of the resistance and pointed his finger meaningfully towards Robben Island. 'Today we are entering a new era for our country and our people. The elections have been a resounding success – a victory for all the people of South Africa.'

Inside the hall they were serving a finger lunch. Pierre took a plate of food to his father and rejoined his colleagues. Simon's eyes lit up when he saw Themba move closer.

'Mr Memani!' he called.

Themba looked up, smiled and walked over to Simon and shook his hand. 'I don't believe we've met.'

'I'm Simon Roux from Paarl,' he said blandly, when it was on the tip of his tongue to say, I am your father from Paarl.

'How do you do, Mr Roux.' Themba's handshake was firm and Simon looked at him. He immediately recognised Nomisile's features in his strong, open face. The eyes, thought Simon, the same almond-shaped, widely spaced eyes with the regal, almost contemptuous, direct stare. His teeth were just as white as Nomisile's had been.

'I knew your mother, Nomisile,' blurted out Simon.

'My mother?' Themba questioned.

Simon nodded vigorously. 'She worked for us in the house when a young woman.'

'A servant girl, a maid!' Themba spat out the words as if they were offensive in his mouth. 'You are one of those Afrikaner capitalists who exploited our people!' There was indignation, tinged with loathing, on Themba's face.

Quaking inside, Simon decided to play his trump card. 'Themba, you and Pierre are . . . are . . .'

Themba interrupted, as realisation dawned in his eyes. 'You are Pierre Roux's father?'

'Yes,' Simon nodded. 'Let me tell you about yourself and Pierre. You have more than politics in common. Both of you are my . . .'

'I don't want to hear any more about Pierre Roux,' Themba said in an acid voice, bending forward and almost spitting the words into Simon's ear. 'Our time of co-operation is over – now we go back to being opponents again.'

'You don't understand,' lamented Simon.

'I understand the situation fully. A Roux is a Roux, in my book. Good day and goodbye.' And he drew himself to his full height and limped away.

Simon slumped in his seat. His time was running out – he had less than two weeks to live. What the hell, he thought as he called to a waiter. 'A double brandy and ice, please.'

'Dad, are you all right?' asked Pierre in alarm as he noticed his father's watery eyes.

'I must speak to you, Pierre.'

'Not now, Dad. I must rush home. I have to collect Lesley and get to the airport in time for our flight. We're going to Pretoria for the President's inauguration tomorrow.'

'Please, Pierre!'

'I'll see you on my return. Will you get back to Paarl on your own?'

Simon nodded tiredly, disappointment in his voice. 'Yes, son. I have my car here.'

Pierre planted a quick kiss on his father's forehead and was gone. Simon felt totally alone, his plans in disarray. He flagged down another waiter. 'Another brandy on the rocks, please.'

Simon awoke the next morning with a splitting headache and only vague recollections of reaching home, and Helena's scorn as he had flopped into bed. He swallowed his pills, washed his face and was drawn to the family room by the noise of the TV set. Helena was in her wheelchair, eyes glued to the screen.

'What are you watching?' Simon asked.

'Don't you remember?' she answered sarcastically. 'It's Nelson Mandela's inauguration as State President.'

'Oh yes.' Simon sat down heavily.

'Look! Look!' Helena pointed excitedly as the cameras zoomed in on the Cabinet delegation. 'There are Pierre and Lesley.'

Simon shuddered as he saw Themba one seat away from Pierre and the looks of animosity that flashed between his two sons.

'Your father's as arrogant as you are!' Themba leaned across Hilda, looking Pierre straight in the eye.

Pierre bristled with hostility as he gazed at Themba. 'Leave my father out of this! He's a dying man, he doesn't deserve your scorn.'

603

'Please, you two,' said Hilda, shaking their arms, 'put your personal differences aside, at least for today.'

'Thank you, Mrs Memani.' Lesley leaned across and held Hilda's hand. 'Let's savour this moment in peace.'

It was a perfect autumn day in Pretoria with a cloudless blue sky, a light breeze and pleasantly warm. The impressive sandstone Union Buildings formed a long, symmetrical line, hugging the ridge and overlooking the centre of the city. Immediately in front of the twin-domed building was a large horseshoe-shaped amphitheatre. A specially constructed podium overlooked both it and the huge lawns falling away below.

Folk singers, choirs, dancing boys and girls, drawn from all cultures and ethnic groups, entertained the VIP guests as they filled the amphitheatre, in the greatest gathering of world leaders ever assembled. Kings, sultans, princes, presidents, prime ministers, one hundred and eighty heads of state, were there to pay homage to Nelson Mandela and to celebrate the triumphant return of South Africa to the international brotherhood of nations. On the lawns a crowd in excess of fifty thousand waited in anticipation.

The new six-colour flag was unfurled and raised on the flagpole. It fluttered gently as the dual national anthems were played – first '*Die Stem*', and then '*Nkosi sikelel 'iAfrika*'.

First, Thabo Mbeki and FW de Klerk were sworn in as Deputy Presidents, then Chief Justice Corbett asked Mandela to take his oath of office.

Lifting Mbeki's and De Klerk's hands into the air the President hailed them. 'Mr De Klerk is one of the greatest reformers, one of the great sons of our soil, who turned his back on apartheid and put South Africa on the road to democracy.' The crowd cheered warmly. Turning to Thabo, he said: 'Mr Mbeki sacrificed his youth to work for liberation and today that dedication has materialised.'

Simon sat forward and stared at the screen as Mandela said: 'The time for the healing of wounds has come. The moment to bridge the chasms that divide us has come. The time to build is upon us.' Simon stood up quickly, moved to the door and heard Mandela's next wish. 'Each time one of us touches the soil of this land, we must feel a sense of personal renewal.'

He hurried out of the house, walking on the freshly tilled soil between the grape-vines. Simon picked up two handfuls of his beloved Hermitage's earth, each hand representing a son, and brought them to his lips. Mandela has inspired me, he thought feverishly – the time to bridge the chasm *has* arrived. His mind was made up – he would surmount all obstacles and bring his two sons together before he died.

After finding out Themba's home number from inquiries, Simon tried every half-hour until at last a woman answered. 'Hilda Memani.'

'Is your husband at home, Mrs Memani?'

'No, but can I help you?'

'Please. I must speak to him about his father.'

'He never knew his father,' Hilda said abruptly. 'As far as I know his father is dead.'

'Themba's father is alive and wants to meet him.'

'Alive!' Hilda gasped. 'Themba will be thrilled. Can I get him to call you back when he gets in?'

'My name is Simon Roux.' He gave her his telephone number.

'I'll give him the message, Mr Roux.'

Themba sat in his study, deep in thought. He was both excited and anxious at the prospect of eventually finding out about his father. He reached for the telephone, then another notion struck him. Was it perhaps another act of humiliation by the Roux family? Damn them, they would surely not fool with such a sensitive subject? He stretched for the receiver, started to dial, then slammed the telephone back on its cradle.

Why had his father not contacted him before? He had lived his whole life not knowing the man's identity. Did he really want to find out now? Maybe he was some down-and-out, wanting to sponge on his election to parliament. 'My father is alive!' Themba savoured the words. Could my father make a difference? Yes! Yes! The children? They had a right to know their grandfather. Themba dialled the number, his hand trembling.

The call was answered on the second ring. 'Simon Roux.'

Hiding his eagerness, Themba spoke coolly. 'My wife told me you had telephoned with news about my father.'

'Would you like to meet him?' Simon asked anxiously.

'My father was Seme, a Pondo man, whom my mother met in Paarl.'

605

'He wasn't your father – not your blood father.'

Themba was silent for a few minutes, his mind racing. True, he had always doubted the story about Seme. His mother had always been evasive on the issue. Who was his real father? Did Simon Roux really know? His heart beat wildly in anticipation. Yes! He truly wanted to find the missing link with his past. Themba cleared his throat. 'Who is my father?'

Simon evaded the question. 'Come to Paarl and meet him.'

'How do I know it's not a hoax?'

'I have documentary proof – letters, photographs.'

'Post them to me. I'll examine them first, then decide if I want to meet the man.'

'No. You must come personally and meet your father at the place of your origin.'

'Tell me about the documents,' Themba insisted.

'Your mother was Nomisile Memani and you were born on 20 October 1955 at Qunu in the Transkei.'

'So what?' Themba laughed sceptically. 'You said you knew my mother. She could have told you that.'

'Who else knows you were bitten in the leg by a puff-adder while you were herding cattle. You almost died and the witch-doctor saved your life.'

Themba's mind whirled. 'How do you know about that?'

'It's all here in black and white. Come to Paarl and I'll show you.'

'If you know who my father is, then tell me.' For the first time Themba was unsure of himself.

Simon was adamant. 'You'll only meet him in Paarl.'

'Is he a good man?' Themba spoke softly for the first time.

'He loves you very much, Themba.' The tremor in Simon's voice convinced him.

'I believe you, Mr Roux.'

'When will you come?'

'On Thursday.' Themba looked at the calendar. 'I'll fly to Cape Town on Thursday.'

Simon let our a sigh of relief. 'Let me know your flight number and I'll meet you at the airport.'

Pierre parked in the shade of the stately oaks and walked towards the manor house. He took a deep breath of clean farm air, so different from the claustrophobic rooms where he seemed to spend his days. Clouds were coming in over Paarl Mountain, the forerunners of a cold front. He hurried into the house, calling his parents.

'I'm in the sewing room, Pierre,' answered his mother. 'Come through.' She was busy embroidering a table cloth, with intricate, colourful patterns.

'Hullo, Mom.' Pierre bent down and kissed her on the mouth. She smiled up at him. 'Where's Dad? He said there was something urgent he needed to discuss with me. He was very insistent.'

'Your father is at the airport,' Helena answered. 'I overheard him making the arrangements on the telephone.'

'Then why did he tell me to be here?'

'He's bringing a guest to meet you.'

'Who?' asked Pierre sharply.

Helena agonised for a long time before she answered. 'He's bringing Themba Memani.'

'Memani!' Pierre spat out the word, his features stiffening in disgust. 'Why would Dad bring Memani to Hermitage?'

'Your father is dying, Pierre. He won't stop his drinking and his liver is packing up . . .'

'I know that,' interrupted Pierre, 'but what has Memani got to do with the matter?'

'He wants to bring the two of you together before he dies.'

'I already know Memani,' snapped Pierre.

'What do you think of him?' asked Helena, searching her son's face.

'I despise the man.'

'How does he feel about you?'

'The feeling is mutual, I'm sure.'

'Then you are in for a tough time this afternoon.'

Pierre looked at his mother intently. 'You seem to know something that I don't know. Would you care to explain what is going on, Mom?'

She covered her face with her hands, trying to blot out a lifetime of living a lie. She knew about Themba. She had found in Simon's pockets some of Nomisile's letters which had confirmed incontrovertibly what she had guessed all along. Helena shuddered when she thought of the way Simon had conversed with Nomisile in his drunken stupors. Always, without fail, she had kept quiet, bottling up the matter inside her, accepting the

607

humiliation to hold on to the security that marriage to Simon gave her.

Should she tell Pierre? He would hear soon enough from his father. She had a great need to share her grief. With Simon, that was impossible, but perhaps her son would understand her decades of suffering. The indignation of years of suppressed anguish bubbled up inside her, and like a champagne cork popping the words frothed out. 'Themba Memani is your half-brother, Pierre.'

'What!' shouted Pierre as he flopped into a chair, his unbelieving eyes riveted on his mother's face. 'Don't play games with me, Mom.'

'I'm deadly serious.' Starting with the pregnancies, she told Pierre all she knew. It was a great source of relief to Helena to make a clean breast of the whole matter, bringing almost forty years of misery into the open at last.

Pierre stared at her transfixed, his mind numb, each word like a knife thrust into his body. He could not dispute his mother's evidence, it was so logical and concrete.

Helena finished the story and stopped, her face softening in her new-found solace, but all she had done was transfer the affliction from herself to her son.

Pushing back his chair, Pierre stumbled to his feet, his mind in torment.

'Don't go, Pierre. Come to me.' Helena held out her arms, a beseeching expression on her face.

Pierre fell to his knees, snuggling into his mother's embrace for the first time since he was a boy. 'I should have known! I should have known!' repeated Pierre. 'Dad has alluded to Memani for a while now. I wondered why he was so interested in the man; now I realise why.'

Kissing Pierre on the top of his head, squeezing him and patting him gently, Helena felt needed and wanted for the first time in many years. She had so much suppressed love to give, and now she showered it on her son.

Eventually Pierre looked up. He no longer noticed her disfigured face. Instead he responded to the warmth in her eyes. Helena used her beautiful table cloth to wipe his brow. She held his head in her hands and kissed him. 'I love you, Pierre.'

He looked into her eyes, ashamed that he had allowed himself to drift apart from this wonderful, caring person, and kissed her back.

'I love you too, Mom. With all my heart.' Helena cried tears of pure joy and the years rolled back as they rediscovered each other.

'I've watched you and Themba on television and I've noticed the hatred,' said Helena. 'But under that layer is a deep-seated respect and understanding for each other.'

'You don't understand, Mom. Memani shattered my trust.'

'The Bible says you must turn the other cheek,' said Helena softly.

'He left me to drown in the sea off Koeberg.'

'Are you not guilty of the same?'

'Yes, I suppose so,' answered Pierre hesitantly. 'I had him arrested at Crossroads and he spent years in jail and on Robben Island.'

'You were in military intelligence, Pierre. What are the conditions like in South African prisons?'

'Themba must have suffered and I was responsible.'

'How would you have felt if the roles had been reversed?'

'Resentful, angry, unforgiving,' answered Pierre from the heart.

'We have a new nation now. Isn't it time to bury the past and look to the future?'

'You're right, Mom.'

'How do you feel about having a brother?'

Pierre smiled. 'I've always wanted a brother. It was sometimes lonely being an only child.'

'Does it worry you that you have a black man as your brother?'

'No, I'm not bigoted,' answered Pierre sincerely.

'Will you accept Themba as your brother?'

'Yes,' replied Pierre after a long pause. 'I think we always clashed because we were so alike. We can overcome that.' Then a thought struck Pierre and he looked at his mother carefully. 'How did you feel about Dad being unfaithful to you?'

Helena smiled. 'I must be completely honest with you, Pierre. I was not able to satisfy your father as a wife should. I drove him into Nomisile's arms.'

'Didn't it disgust you that it was a black woman?'

She shook her head. 'I never was a racist and Nomisile Memani was a fine person – a Thembu princess. I liked her very much.'

'Why did Dad give her up?'

'It happened in the 1950s. They were caught under the Immorality Act and Nomisile fled back to the Transkei.'

'What happened to Dad?'

'He bribed the police to drop the charges,' answered Helena truthfully.

'And you never discussed this with him?' Pierre asked his mother incredulously.

Helena answered in a whisper. 'No.'

'So Dad doesn't realise you know?'

'I kept quiet to keep our marriage intact.' She stroked Pierre's face. 'You've always idolised your father – I hope this won't affect your relationship.'

'Who am I to sit in judgement?'

'Are you upset that I told you?' asked Helena anxiously.

Pierre shook his head. 'Thank you for telling me, Mom. It'll make it easier to face Dad and Themba.'

Helena squeezed Pierre. 'You are a wonderful son.'

'And you are a marvellous mother.' He kissed her on her scar. 'I promise we'll spend more time together to make up for our lost years.'

The tears rolled out of Helena's eyes.

'Hullo, Themba.' Simon stepped forward, smiling, his hand extended.

'Where's my father?' Themba demanded, glancing around the airport arrivals hall.

'I told you you would meet him in Paarl.'

'Lead the way, Mr Roux.'

When Simon and Themba arrived at Hermitage, Pierre's car was in the driveway. Simon led Themba to the garage. 'Wait in the pick-up please,' instructed Simon. 'I'll be back soon.' He hurried into the house, stopping in the sewing-room doorway when he found Helena with Pierre on his knees and the two of them hugging each other. With a pang of envy he saw the softness in Helena's eyes and the tears that flowed. He stood for a moment watching the tender spectacle of shared love and then coughed gently. They looked up at him and both smiled warmly. Encouraged, he entered the room.

'Come and join us, my darling,' said Helena lifting one arm.

Simon was hesitant, then, with emotion choking in his throat, he fell to his knees and the three of them embraced.

Helena kissed Simon on the mouth, her lips quivering.

'Oh, sweetie, my sweetie,' Simon cried as he held Helena's head in his huge hands and kissed her all over her face. He turned to Pierre and hugged him and he smiled back happily.

'Mom and I know about Themba,' Pierre whispered.

'You know,' he said disbelievingly, jerking away in alarm.

Helena pulled him back. 'I've known since the very beginning.'

Simon searched her face frantically. 'And you don't despise me?'

'I love you, my darling. I forgave you your indiscretions many years ago.'

'Why didn't you tell me?' breathed Simon, kissing her.

'I was scared it would drive us apart.'

'You mean we both lived in dread of the other finding out?' Simon asked incredulously.

She nodded sadly. 'Take Pierre and Themba and tell them what you have to, then come back to me – I'll be waiting for you, my darling.'

'Come, Dad,' said Pierre, tugging his father's sleeve. 'Let's go and tell Themba the good news,' suddenly relishing the encounter.

Simon stood up, placed a last lingering kiss on Helena's lips and followed Pierre. In the study Simon collected a rucksack and his double-barrelled Webly and Scott. Together father and son walked towards the garage.

'What trick is this?' shouted Themba, jumping out of the pick-up as he saw Pierre.

'Trust me!' Simon implored as he dumped the canvas bag and shotgun in the back of the pick-up and got into the driver's seat. 'Both of you get in. Please!'

Still protesting, Themba joined them in the cab. Simon smiled in satisfaction as he drove up the farm road between the vineyards, past the farm dam and as far towards Paarl Rock as the vehicle could go.

The two men followed Simon. He started breathing heavily and Pierre supported his father. Fleecy clouds were now billowing in, darkening the sky and blotting out the sunset. At the base of Paarl Rock they halted. Pierre and Themba looked up in awe at the massive face of granite merging with the sullen sky.

'Are we going up there?' Pierre cried in alarm.

'Yes!'

'There's no way up,' announced Themba after examining the sheer face.

'Of course there is,' insisted Simon, and he led them to the fissure. He pointed out the ledge. 'There's a cave at the back.'

'Are you telling me my father is a caveman?' Themba turned away in fury and retraced his steps. 'You're wasting my time,' he flung over his shoulder, bitterness in his voice.

Pierre ran after Themba. 'Please come back, Themba.'

'Your father said he was going to introduce me to my father. I don't know what is going on here.'

'My father knows what he's doing. Give him credit, Themba.'

Themba had not always agreed with Pierre but he respected his judgement. Now, as he saw the entreaty in Pierre's eyes, he made a decision. 'All right.' He retraced his steps reluctantly.

Simon flashed Pierre a grateful glance, then showed Themba how to wedge himself into the crevice and shimmy his way up. 'You'll find a rope on the ledge,' Simon called to Themba. 'Lower it down for me.' Breathing hard, with Themba pulling from above and Pierre pushing from below Simon struggled up the fissure and flopped on to the ledge, moving to one side to allow Pierre to scramble over the lip.

The first droplets of rain spattered against the rock as Pierre and Themba reconnoitred every section of the ledge in wonder. Simon crawled into the cave, lit two paraffin lamps and placed his rucksack and gun in a corner. Simon looked past the two men as they entered, satisfied to see it was dark and raining outside – now he had them captive until first light the next day.

Themba looked in awe at the bushman painting, kneeling to see it better. Pierre allowed his father to set the pace.

Sitting down, Themba looked expectantly at Simon. 'You promised I'd meet my father. Where is he?'

'I'm your father,' answered Simon softly.

'You?' Themba cried, aghast. 'I don't believe you.'

Simon undid the knot on the plastic bag and prised open the old coffee tin. He took out Nomisile's white shawl and handed it to Themba. He saw his mother's name embroidered in a corner. Tears sprang into his eyes as he held it to his face and smelled her scent again, and saw her in his mind in their hut in Mqekezweni.

Themba closed his eyes tightly. The wind blew across the ledge, whistling eerily in the mouth of the cave. Where had he heard that sound before? He was transported back in time to his initiation ceremony. He saw a huge sandstone boulder jutting out from the hillside. Again he perceived the outline of a big man, his head a smaller rock, balancing on the boulder.

Simon and Pierre watched intently as Themba swayed from side to side, in a world of his own. Suddenly he shouted: 'I hear your words, Father. Are you a man called Seme, who my mother says is my father?'

Sighing in satisfaction, Themba heard the reply wafting over time and space. 'No, my name is Simon.'

'Simon!' he shouted, opening his eyes. Themba's mouth dropped open as he saw the man before him. 'Simon Roux,' he whispered, 'are you really my father?'

'Yes, my son. I am.'

'No! It can't be,' Themba muttered. 'I asked my mother once and she denied you were a white man.'

'Your mother and I had a secret pact,' explained Simon, 'to ensure that you never discovered my identity.'

'Why?' Themba frowned unhappily. 'Were you ashamed to admit the fact?'

Simon shook his head. 'I wanted to acknowledge you as my son, but your mother wanted you to grow up hating apartheid. Things were different then – Afrikaner nationalism was riding the crest of the wave and a boy of mixed blood would have been ostracised by both whites and blacks.'

'True,' agreed Themba slowly, then remembered Simon's promise. 'You said you had irrefutable proof you are my father. Where is it?'

'Will you listen if I talk?' Simon looked from Themba to Pierre. 'There is so much I have to tell you both before I die.'

They nodded.

Simon removed the hard-cover scrap book, marked: PERSONAL DIARY OF SIMON ROUX. He opened the book and started to read. They were transported back to 1945 when Simon was a fourteen-year-old boy. They learnt about his childhood experiences and his dreams. Helena entered the narrative, then Nomisile. Themba's eyes misted over when he heard about Nomisile's and Simon's passionate affair, their deep love for each other and then the humiliation of being trapped in the cottage bedroom by the policeman.

Lifting up the diary Simon showed his sons the series of question

613

marks he had scribbled across the page and then the words, 'May God grant compassion to my loved ones and me.'

At this juncture Themba started accepting the irrefutability of the situation, but a lifetime of not knowing the identity of his father made him cautious. 'Read on,' he instructed Simon.

Themba sat forward, listening intently as Simon described his visit to the Minister of Justice. A missing piece of the jigsaw of his life fell into place. So it was Simon Roux who had arranged for his mother and Hilda to visit him on Robben Island!

All right, so Simon Roux might be his father, but that did not mean he had to acknowledge him, thought Themba angrily.

Simon finished reading the book and handed it to Pierre. 'The book is yours to keep, my son.'

Pierre smiled in acceptance, holding the diary to his chest.

'Why must he get it?' Themba lunged for the book. He grabbed one side and pulled, while Pierre held on tightly.

'Stop!' Simon cried, coming between the two men.

Themba let go, staring sullenly at Pierre with renewed hate.

Dipping into the coffee tin, Simon removed the scrap book. 'This one is for you, Themba. It contains every letter and photograph your mother sent me.'

Grudgingly Themba accepted the book. He opened it and his hands began to shake as he recognised the first photograph from his youth. His mother had always displayed a copy in her hut, forever telling him it was the first photograph taken of him. It had curled at the edges and yellowed with time, until eventually even the faces had faded. This copy was crisp and clear.

Themba recognised his mother's handwriting and read her first letter to Simon: '*My dearest Simon . . . our baby Themba was born on 20 October 1955 . . . I have decided my son shall grow up as a Xhosa . . . it is my wish that he must never discover a white man was his father . . . please respect that desire.*' Themba's mind was in a turmoil, the letter evoked so many different emotions.

He turned to Simon abruptly. 'Why did my mother want you kept a secret? Was she ashamed of you?'

'We loved each other,' answered Simon. 'Read on, my son, and you will see.'

Turning the page he read the next letter, and the next, reliving his life from his mother's hand. He shared in the joy Nomisile had had with Simon. His heart sang. He had been born out of a deep love, a love strictly forbidden in the apartheid-tainted era, otherwise his father would have married his mother. His life was complete – he was a whole man at last.

The love in Simon's eyes was unwavering and real. Themba's heart went out to him. He knew that Simon was not only undeniably his true father, but that he whole-heartedly delighted in the acceptance.

'Fa . . . ther!' mumbled Themba hesitantly.

Simon opened his arms. 'Come to me, Themba, my son.'

In a flash Themba was up and they embraced, hugging desperately, trying to make up for the lost years. 'Father! Father!' Themba cried in triumph, his dreams fulfilled many times over.

Pierre watched the remarkable pageant, but he did not interfere or allow the enchantment to be broken. His own feelings towards the two men had also changed greatly in the last few hours.

After a long time Simon remembered Pierre. He looked up and put out an arm, inviting Pierre to join them. Moving closer, Pierre placed an arm on each man's shoulder.

'Welcome to the family,' smiled Pierre.

Themba lurched away as reality sunk in. '*You* are my half-brother?'

'Yes,' Pierre nodded.

'I accept and respect *you* as my father,' said Themba, looking at Simon. 'But I don't have to tolerate *him*.' His finger pointed straight at Pierre's throat and his voice was gravelly with pent-up emotion.

God, I need a drink, thought Simon desperately, but he forced the craving from his mind. Tonight he *had* to remain sober. His two sons accepted him, but Themba refused to acknowledge Pierre. Should he have left the *status quo* unchanged, with Pierre contented and Themba ignorant? He realised with a sinking feeling that it was too late for that. He had to try another approach to make Themba accept Pierre.

Simon opened the rucksack in the strained silence. He poured mugs of steaming coffee and handed out sandwiches. Each was pensive as new thoughts and feelings coursed through him.

'Themba, my son,' began Simon, 'you would allow me to die a happy man if you would accept Pierre as your brother.'

'There is too much bad blood between us for me ever to forgive and forget,' replied Themba.

His look of scorn caused Pierre to move away despondently. It was snug and warm inside the cave and Pierre closed his eyes. The dripping of the rain outside soon lulled him to sleep.

Simon and Themba continued through the scrap book, laughing together at each new revelation, revelling in their new-found closeness. They talked for hours until Themba saw that his father was dog-tired. He laid him down gently, hugging him. Simon fell asleep with a contented smile on his face.

Still the rain came down in torrents, but Themba's mind was overactive and he could not sleep. He started reading the scrap book from the beginning again, every now and then casting a loving look at his father and stroking his head. Themba searched in the coffee tin and discovered his mother's post office book, noting that the deposits tallied accurately with the duplicate slips pasted into the scrap book.

So my father never deserted me, he realised – it was he who paid for my extra tuition with Paul, my dual university degrees, my defence at the Johannesburg trial. You are a wonderful man, he thought with affection. It's only a pity it has taken so long for us to find each other. He bent down and kissed Simon on the lips, lying down next to him. Themba closed his eyes, remembering. He drifted into a restful slumber.

Simon woke with a start. The storm had blown itself out, the first rays of the rising sun shone over the peaks of the Klein Drakenstein Mountains and streamed into the cave. He sat up stiffly and reached for the Thermos flask. It fell over and clattered on the rock, waking Themba and Pierre.

Memories of the previous night filled their minds, and they looked at each other inquiringly.

'Hullo, brother,' smiled Pierre.

'I am *not* your brother,' said Themba scathingly.

'Themba,' cried Simon in anguish. 'I thought you would be considerate and accept Pierre as your brother.'

'Never! Not now, or ever!' Themba answered in disgust. 'You don't know the suffering he caused me.' Themba shook a balled fist in Pierre's face. 'After I saved his damned life at Crossroads he had me arrested and thrown in jail.' His voice grew pained as he remembered. 'At The Grays they tortured me until I passed out. They gave me electric shocks. I almost died thanks to you, Pierre Roux.'

'I'm sorry,' mumbled Pierre.

'I don't accept your apology.' Themba turned to Simon. 'I'm going back to the house now. I'll wait for you there, then we can talk.' He pointed to Pierre. 'But see that *he* is not there.'

With a heavy heart Simon crept out of the cave, watching sadly as Themba disappeared down the slope. He called to Pierre. 'Bring my rucksack and gun out of the cave.' Simon washed his face at the pool, drank some of the icy water and approached the top of the fissure. 'Help me down please, Pierre.'

Pierre supported his father and they reached the ground.

'You go down to your mother,' said Simon. 'Leave me here. I need to be alone for a while.'

'Will you be all right, Dad?'

Simon nodded tiredly. 'I'll take it slowly on the way down. Leave me the pick-up.' He glanced at Pierre. 'Go now.'

Pierre stuffed his father's diary into his shirt-front and followed after Themba. Simon sat down, his head in his hands, crying. His whole scheme to bring his sons together had failed.

He looked up and saw a movement in the yellow-wood copse. He stared intently. Baboons! There was a troop of chacma baboons digging in the composted carpet of fallen leaves. Damn baboons, he thought angrily, forever stealing my grapes. He needed something on which to vent his suppressed anger. Working quietly he jammed a cartridge into each chamber and snapped the shotgun closed. Simon crept carefully towards the copse.

Abruptly the wind changed and the scent of the baboons wafted towards the leopard's hide. She was instantly alert at the prospect of her favourite food. She crept out of her lair, her sharp ears pricked up, eyes fixed on the copse. She growled softly as she spotted her prey. Keeping to the base of Paarl Rock, she made her way stealthily towards the trees, keeping downwind of the troop of baboons.

Simon moved closer. Out of the corner of his eye he caught a movement to his left. He made out a flattened, spotted shape creeping towards the copse. He blinked a few times to make sure. Yes, it definitely was a leopard. He threw the shotgun to his shoulder and aimed at the leopard's heart.

His movement was instantly detected by the alert animal. Curling back her lips in a snarl, the female hurtled forward like a released spring. Simon pulled the trigger and the left barrel exploded. The leopard took the full blast of the shot in her stomach. She grunted in pain as half her gut was blown out and bounded back among the rocks with Simon after her.

A male sentinel baboon barked a warning and the troop retreated in the opposite direction.

The leopard disappeared between the rocks. Ahead was a wild white pear tree. She climbed it and lay on a branch overhanging the path, biting at her gaping wound, watching warily as the man approached. She was perfectly camouflaged, but she had left her tail hanging down.

He hurried up the path, moving cautiously as he saw the long spotted tail dangling down from the limb. He moved around to secure a better shot. At that moment their eyes met. Hatred flowed in the leopard's pale eyes and she launched herself at Simon's face, shooting through the air in a yellow streak.

Baring the long nails in her front paws, she scratched at his eyes. Sharp as blades, they cut through the soft tissue, lacerating his cheeks. The leopard clamped her powerful jaws around the base of Simon's neck. Screaming in pain, Simon toppled over backwards with the leopard on top. Her teeth ripped into his neck trying to sever his main artery, while at the same time she tried to claw out his eyes.

Using all his strength, Simon brought the shotgun up and pulled the trigger, blowing her chest away. The leopard relaxed its grip and slowly collapsed on top of him.

Simon crawled out from under the body. He was bleeding profusely from the neck – blood spraying in a mist from the puncture marks in his artery. His face was a shredded mess of torn flesh. Instinctively he stumbled towards Paarl Rock and the fissure leading to his private ledge.

Themba walked quickly for ten minutes, then his pace slowed as nagging doubts took over. Eventually he sat down on a rock to reflect. He looked over the valley, thinking. He heard footsteps approaching and saw Pierre.

Pierre stopped opposite him. 'You're a hard-arsed one, Themba! Why can't you accept me as a brother? At first when I was confronted with the facts, I also rebelled. Now I've accepted the situation. I'm very proud you're my brother.'

'We've been through this last night,' said Themba sharply.

'It was my mother who persuaded me. Perhaps if your mother had still been alive she would have talked sense into that hard head of yours.'

'Don't bring my mother into this,' snapped Themba.

'Let's try, please, Themba.'

Themba was about to retort when a shot rang out, echoing against Paarl Rock and booming in waves down the mountain. Pierre looked questioningly at Themba. 'Our father is up there with a shotgun.'

The two brothers hurried back up the slope, Pierre easily outdistancing the hobbling Themba.

'Pierre, wait for me.'

'Hurry.' Pierre held out his hand to help Themba, using his strength to pull him along faster.

A second shot rang out, more muted. 'Something weird is happening,' shouted Pierre. 'Come on!'

Together they ran around a splintered boulder and came across the dead leopard. Pierre's practised eye took in the situation at a glance. 'The first shot blew away its guts and the second its chest. At least Dad is safe.'

'No,' said Themba pointing, his tracker's eyes alert. 'There's a blood spoor. Father is injured.'

They followed the spoor and came across Simon at the bottom of the fissure. Rolling him on his back, both were horrified at the extent of his injuries. Simultaneously they fell to their knees.

'He's alive,' breathed Pierre in relief.

'Let's use our shirts to try and stop the bleeding,' urged Themba.

Both men stripped off their shirts, Themba winding his tightly around Simon's neck and Pierre's around his head. Simon followed their movements.

'We must get him to the pick-up and then to hospital,' insisted Pierre.

Themba looked down the steep mountain slope and shuddered. 'How do we do that?'

Simon's breath wheezed in his chest. 'Work together, my sons.'

They helped Simon to a sitting position and slipped their arms under his knees, grasping each other's wrists firmly. They linked behind his back and gently lifted him up. Half walking, half running, they struggled down the slope. It was hard work and the sweat glistened on their bare torsos.

They laboured as one, not because they had to but because now they wanted to. Their sweat mingled and then mixed with their father's blood. The blood bond had been forged.

The two sons looked at their father and then at each other, and for the first time they saw genuine understanding in each other's eyes.

Bibliography

Bernstein, Hilda: *The World that was Ours*. SA Writers, London, 1989.

Cameron, Trewella and Spies, SB: *A New Illustrated History of South Africa*. Southern Book Publishers, Johannesburg, 1991.

Conolly, Denis: *The Tourist in South Africa*. Travel-Guide (Pty) Ltd, Durban, Sixth Edition.

Davenport, TRH: South *Africa – A Modern History*. Macmillan, London, Fourth Edition, 1991.

De Klerk Willem: *FW de Klerk: The Man in his Time*. Jonathan Ball Publishers, Johannesburg, 1991.

Dingake, Michael: *My Fight Against Apartheid*. Kliptown Books, London, 1987.

Fitzsimons FW: *The Snakes of South Africa*. Maskew Miller, Cape Town, 1913.

Hinde, Gerald: *Leopard*. HarperCollins Publishers, London, 1992.

International Defence and Aid Fund: Fact Paper: *Massacre at Maseru*. IDAF Publications, London, 1985.

Johns, Sheridan and Davis, R Hunt, Jr: *Mandela, Tambo and the African National Congress*. Oxford University Press, New York, 1991.

Kamsteeg, Aad and van Dijk, Evert: *FW de Klerk: Man of the Moment*. Vlaeberg Publishers, Cape Town, 1990.

Mandela, Nelson: *The Struggle is my Life*. IDAF Publications, London, 1978.

Pottinger, Brian: *The Imperial Presidency*. Southern Book Publishers, Johannesburg, 1988.

Rhoodie, Eschel: *PW Botha: The Last Betrayal*. SA Politics, Johannesburg, 1989.

Riley, Eileen: *Major Political Events in South Africa: 1948–1990*. Facts on File Limited, Oxford, 1991.

Sacks, Albie and Naidoo, Indres: *Island in Chains: Ten years on Robben Island by Prisoner 885/63*. Penguin Books Ltd, Harmondsworth, 1982.

Spink, Kathryn: *Black Sash – The Beginning of a Bridge in South Africa*. Methuen, London, 1991.

Strydom, Lauritz: *Rivonia Unmasked*. Voortrekker Press, Johannesburg, 1964.

Van Dijk, Evert: *Mandela – The First Year of Freedom*. Vlaeberg Publishers, Cape Town, 1991.

NICHOLAS LUARD

SANCTUARY

Violet Somerset is the daughter of rich and aristocratic diplomats.

Billy Ramsden is an illegitimate orphan, the son of an Indian army bugler.

In 1944 an old Masai tracker takes the children to an ancient and magical Kenyan valley, where they watch elephants drinking from a hidden river.

Billy's life leads him from the slums of Brixton into organised crime, and then into the French Foreign Legion. Violet's life spirals down through three marriages into drug and alcohol addiction.

Finally they meet again in Africa at the place where they saw the elephants first.

The valley is almost certainly the site of the Garden of Eden, and Billy and Violet are faced with a stark choice. To excavate the gorge will mean the certain death of the elephant herd. But to conserve the elephants will mean passing up the opportunity to investigate the very origins of man.

HODDER AND STOUGHTON PAPERBACKS